65
Great Tales
of
Horror

65
Great Tales
of
Horror

Edited by
Mary Danby

Sundial

This edition first published in Great Britain in 1981 by
Octopus Books Limited
59 Grosvenor Street
London W1
in collaboration with
William Heinemann Limited
10 Upper Grosvenor Street
London W1
and
Martin Secker & Warburg Limited
54 Poland Street
London W1

Second impression 1982

ISBN 0 86273 024 4

Printed in the
United States of America

Contents

Contents   7

The Salvationists

Villiers de L'Isle Adam

Many years ago, as evening was closing in, the venerable Pedro Arbuez d'Espila, sixth prior of the Dominicans of Segovia, and third Grand Inquisitor of Spain, followed by a *fra redemptor*, and preceded by two familiars of the Holy Office, the latter carrying lanterns, made their way to a subterranean dungeon. The bolt of a massive door creaked, and they entered a mephitic *in pace*, where the dim light revealed between rings fastened to the wall a bloodstained rack, a brazier and a jug. On a pile of straw, loaded with fetters and his neck encircled by an iron carcan, sat a haggard man, of uncertain age, clothed in rags.

This prisoner was no other than Rabbi Aser Abarbanel, a Jew of Aragon, who – accused of usury and pitiless scorn for the poor had been badly subjected to torture for more than a year. Yet his blindness was as dense as his hide, and he had refused to abjure his faith.

Proud of a filiation dating back thousands of years, proud of his ancestors, he descended Talmudically from Othoniel and consequently from Ipsiboa, the wife of the last judge of Israel, a circumstance which had sustained his courage amid incessant torture. With tears in his eyes at the thought of this resolute soul rejecting salvation, the venerable Pedro Arbuez d'Espila, approaching the shuddering rabbi, addressed him as follows:

'My son, rejoice: your trials here below are about to end. If in the presence of such obstinacy I was forced to permit, with deep regret, the use of great severity, my task of fraternal correction has its limits. You are the fig tree which, having failed so many times to bear fruit, at last withered, but God alone can judge your soul. Perhaps Infinite Mercy will shine upon you at the last moment! We must hope so. There are examples. So sleep in peace tonight. Tomorrow you will be included in the *auto da fe:* that is, you will be exposed to the *quemadero*, the symbolical flames of the Everlasting Fire: it burns, as you know, only at a distance, my son; and Death is at least two hours (often three) in coming, on account of the wet, iced bandages with which we protect the heads and hearts of the condemned. There will be forty-three of you. Placed in the last row, you will have time to invoke God and offer to Him this baptism of fire, which is of the Holy Spirit. Hope in the Light, and rest.'

With these words, having signed to his companions to unchain the prisoner, the prior tenderly embraced him. Then came the turn of the *fra redemptor*, who, in a low tone, entreated the Jew's forgiveness for what he had made him suffer for the purpose of redeeming him; then the two familiars silently kissed him. This ceremony over, the captive was left, solitary and bewildered in the darkness.

Rabbi Aser Abarbanel, with parched lips and face worn by suffering, at first, gazed at the closed door with vacant eyes. Closed? The word unconsciously roused a vague fancy in his mind, the fancy that he had seen for an instant the light of the lanterns through a chink between the door and the wall. A morbid idea of hope, due to the weakness of his brain, stirred his whole being. He dragged himself towards the strange *appearance*. Then very gently and cautiously slipping one finger into the crevice, he drew the door towards him. Marvellous! By an extraordinary accident the familiar who closed it had turned the huge key an instant before it struck the stone casing, so that the rusty bolt not having entered the hole, the door again rolled on its hinges.

The rabbi ventured to glance outside. By the aid of a sort of luminous dusk he distinguished at first a semi-circle of walls indented by winding stairs; and opposite to him, at the top of five or six stone steps, a sort of black portal, opening into an immense corridor, whose first arches only were visible from below.

Stretching himself flat he crept to the threshold. Yes, it was really a corridor, but endless in length. A wan light illuminated it: lamps suspended from the vaulted ceiling lightened at intervals the dull hue of the atmosphere – the distance was veiled in shadow. Not a single door appeared in the whole extent! Only on one side, the left, heavily grated loopholes, sunk in the walls, admitted a light which must be that of evening, for crimson bars at intervals rested on the flags of the pavement. What a terrible silence! Yet, yonder, at the far end of that passage there might be a doorway of escape! The Jew's vacillating hope was tenacious, for it was the last.

Without hesitating, he ventured on the flags, keeping close under the loopholes trying to make himself part of the blackness of the long walls. He advanced slowly, dragging himself along on his breast, forcing back the cry of pain when some raw wound sent a keen pang through his whole body.

Suddenly the sound of a sandalled foot approaching reached his ears. He trembled violently, fear stifled him, his sight grew dim. Well, it was over, no doubt. He pressed himself into a niche and, half lifeless with terror, waited.

It was a familiar hurrying along. He passed swiftly by, holding in his clenched hand an instrument of torture and vanished. The suspense which the rabbi had endured seemed to have suspended the functions of life, and he lay nearly an hour unable to move. Fearing an increase of tortures if he were captured, he thought of returning to his dungeon. But the old hope whispered in his soul, that divine *perhaps*. A miracle had happened. He could doubt no longer. He began to crawl towards the chance of escape. Exhausted by suffering and hunger, trembling with pain, he pressed onward. The sepulchral corridor seemed to lengthen mysteriously, while he, still advancing, gazed into the gloom where there *must* be some avenue of escape.

Oh! oh! He again heard footsteps, but this time they were slower, more heavy. The white and black forms of two inquisitors appeared, emerging from the obscurity beyond. They were conversing in low tones, and seemed to be discussing some important subject, for they were gesticulating vehemently.

At this spectacle Rabbi Aser Abarbanel closed his eyes: his heart beat so violently that it almost suffocated him; his rags were damp with the cold sweat of agony; he lay motionless by the wall, his mouth wide open, under the rays of a lamp praying to the God of David.

Just opposite to him the two inquisitors paused under the light of the lamp – doubtless owing to some accident due to the course of their argument. One, while listening to his companion, gazed at the rabbi! And, beneath the look – whose absence of expression the hapless man did not at first notice – he fancied he again felt the burning pincers on his flesh. Fainting, breathless, with fluttering eyelids, he shivered at the touch of the monk's floating robe. But – strange yet natural fact – the inquisitors' gaze was evidently that of a man deeply absorbed in his intended reply, engrossed by what he was hearing; his eyes were fixed – and seemed to look at the Jew without seeing him.

In fact, after the lapse of a few minutes, the two gloomy figures slowly pursued their way, still conversing in low tones, towards the place whence the prisoner had come; *he had not been seen!* Amid the horrible confusion of the rabbi's thoughts, the idea darted through his brain: 'Can I be already dead that they did not see me?' A hideous impression roused him from his lethargy: in looking at the wall against which his face was pressed, he imagined he beheld two fierce eyes watching him. He flung his head back in a sudden frenzy of fright, his hair fairly bristling. Yet, no! No. His hand groped over the stones: it was the *reflection* of the inquisitor's eyes, still retained in his own, which had been refracted from two spots on the wall.

Forward! He must hasten towards that goal which he fancied (absurdly, no doubt), to be his deliverance, towards the darkness from which he was now barely thirty paces distant. He pressed forward faster on his knees, his hands, at full length, dragging himself painfully along, and soon entered the dark portion of this terrible corridor.

Suddenly the poor wretch felt a gust of cold air on the hands resting upon the flags; it came from under the little door to which the two walls led.

Oh, Heaven, if that door should open outward. Every nerve in the fugitive's body thrilled with hope. He examined it from top to bottom, though scarcely able to distinguish its outlines in the surrounding darkness. He passed his hand over it: no bolt, no lock. A latch! He started up, the latch yielded to the pressure of his thumb; the door silently swung open before him.

'Halleluia!' murmured the rabbi in a transport of gratitude as, standing on the threshold, he beheld the scene before him.

The door had opened into the gardens, above which arched a starlit sky, into spring, liberty, life! It revealed the neighbouring fields, stretching towards the sierras, whose sinuous blue lines were relieved against the horizon. Yonder lay freedom! Oh, to escape! He would journey all night through the lemon groves whose fragrance reached him. Once in the mountains and he was safe! He inhaled the delicious air; the breeze revived him, his lungs expanded. And to thank once more the God who had bestowed this mercy upon him, he extended his arms, raising his eyes towards Heaven.

Then he fancied he saw the shadow of his arms approach him – fancied that he felt these shadowy arms enclose, embrace him – and that he was pressed tenderly to someone's breast. A tall figure actually did stand directly before him. He lowered his eyes – and remained motionless, gasping for breath, dazed, with fixed eyes, fairly drivelling with terror.

Horror! He was in the clasp of the Grand Inquisitor himself, the venerable Pedro Arbuez d'Espila, who gazed at him with tearful eyes, like a good shepherd who had found his stray lamb.

The dark-robed priest pressed the hapless Jew to his heart with so fervent an outburst of love, that the edges of the monachal hair-cloth rubbed the Dominican's breast. And while Aser Abarbanel with protruding eyes gasped in agony in the ascetic's embrace, vaguely comprehending that *all the phrases of this fatal evening were only a prearranged torture, that of* Hope, the Grand Inquisitor with an accent of touching reproach and a look of consternation murmured in his ear, his breath parched and burning from long fasting:

'What, my son! On the eve, perchance, of salvation – you wished to leave us?'

The Mysterious Mansion

Honoré de Balzac

About a hundred yards from the town of Vendôme, on the borders of the Loire, there is an old grey house, surmounted by very high gables, and so completely isolated that neither tanyard nor shabby hostelry, such as you may find at the entrance to all small towns, exists in its immediate neighbourhood.

In front of this building, overlooking the river, is a garden, where the once well-trimmed box borders that used to define the walks now grow wild as they list. Several willows that spring from the Loire have grown as rapidly as the hedge that encloses it, and half conceal the house. The rich vegetation of those weeds that we call foul adorns the sloping shore. Fruit trees, neglected for the last ten years, no longer yield their harvest, and their shoots form coppices. The wall-fruit grows like hedges against the walls. Paths once gravelled are overgrown with moss, but, to tell the truth, there is no trace of a path. From the height of the hill, to which cling the ruins of the old castle of the Dukes of Vendôme, the only spot whence the eye can plunge into this enclosure, it strikes you that, at a time not easy to determine, this plot of land was the delight of a country gentleman, who cultivated roses and tulips and horticulture in general, and who was besides a lover of fine fruit. An arbour is still visible, or rather the debris of an arbour, where there is a table that time has not quite destroyed. The aspect of this garden of bygone days suggests the negative joys of peaceful provincial life, as one might reconstruct the life of a worthy tradesman by reading the epitaph on his tombstone. As if to complete the sweetness and sadness of the ideas that possess one's soul, one of the walls displays a sun-dial decorated with the following commonplace Christian inscription: 'Ultimam cogita!' The roof of this house is horribly dilapidated, the shutters are always closed, the balconies are covered with swallows' nests, the doors are perpetually shut, weeds have drawn green lines in the cracks of the flights of steps, the locks and bolts are rusty. Sun, moon, winter, summer, and snow have worn the panelling, warped the boards, gnawed the paint. The lugubrious silence which reigns there is only broken by birds, cats, martins, rats and mice, free to course to and fro, to fight and to eat each other. Everywhere an invisible hand has graven the word *mystery*.

Should your curiosity lead you to glance at this house from the side that points to the road, you would perceive a great door which the children of the place have riddled with holes. I afterward heard that this door had been closed for the last ten years. Through the holes broken by the boys you would have observed the perfect harmony that existed between the façades of both garden and courtyard. In both the same disorder prevails. Tufts of weed encircle the paving-stones. Enormous cracks furrow the walls, round whose blackened crests twine the thousand garlands of the pellitory. The steps are out of joint, the wire of the bell is rusted, the spouts are cracked. What fire from heaven has fallen here? What tribunal has decreed that salt should be strewn on this dwelling? Has God been blasphemed, has France been here betrayed? These are the questions we ask ourselves, but get no answer from the crawling things that haunt the place. The empty and deserted house is a gigantic enigma, of which the key is lost. In bygone times it was a small fief, and bears the name of the Grande Bretêche.

I inferred that I was not the only person to whom my good landlady had communicated the secret of which I was to be the sole recipient, and I prepared to listen.

'Sir,' she said, 'when the Emperor sent the Spanish prisoners of war and others here, the Government quartered on me a young Spaniard who had been sent to Vendôme on parole. Parole notwithstanding he went out every day to show himself to the sous-préfet. He was a Spanish grandee! Nothing less! His name ended in os and dia, something like Burgos de Férédia. I have his name on my books; you can read it if you like. Oh! but he was a handsome young man for a Spaniard; they are all said to be ugly. He was only five feet and a few inches high, but he was well grown; he had small hands that he took such care of; ah! you should have seen! He had as many brushes for his hands as a woman for her whole dressing apparatus! He had thick black hair, a fiery eye, his skin was rather bronzed, but I liked the look of it. He wore the finest linen I have ever seen on anyone, although I have had princesses staying here, and, among others, General Bertrand, the Duke and Duchess d'Abrantès, Monsieur Decazes, and the King of Spain. He didn't eat much; but his manners were so polite, so amiable, that one could not owe him a grudge. Oh! I was very fond of him, although he didn't open his lips four times in the day, and it was impossible to keep up a conversation with him. For if you spoke to him, he did not answer. It was a fad, a mania with them all, I heard say. He read his breviary like a priest, he went to Mass and to all the services regularly. Where did he sit? Two steps from the chapel of Madame de Merret. As he took his place there the first time he went to church, nobody suspected him of any intention in so doing. Besides, he never raised his eyes from his prayer-book, poor young man! After that, sir, in the evening he would walk on the mountains, among the castle ruins. It was the poor man's only amusement, it reminded him of his country. They say that Spain is all mountains! From the commencement of his imprisonment he stayed out late. I was anxious when I found that he did not come home before midnight; but we got accustomed to this fancy of his. He took the key of the door, and we left off sitting up for him. He lodged in a house of ours in the Rue des Casernes. After that, one of our stable-men told us that in the evening when he led the horses to the water, he thought he had seen the Spanish grandee swimming far down the river like a live fish. When he returned, I told him to take care of the rushes; he appeared vexed to have been seen in the water. At last, one day, or rather one morning, we did not find him in his room; he had not returned. After searching everywhere, I found some writing in the drawer of a table, where there were fifty gold pieces of Spain that are called doubloons and were worth about five thousand francs; and ten thousand francs' worth of diamonds in a small sealed box. The writing said, that in case he did not return, he left us the money and the diamonds, on condition of paying for Masses to thank God for his escape, and for his salvation. In those days my husband had not been taken from me; he hastened to seek him everywhere.

'And now for the strange part of the story. He brought home the Spaniard's clothes, that he had discovered under a big stone, in a sort of pilework by the river-side near the castle, nearly opposite to the Grande Bretêche. My husband had gone there so early that no one had seen him. After reading the letter, he burned the clothes, and according to Count Férédia's desire we declared that he had escaped. The sous-préfet sent all the gendarmerie in pursuit of him; but brust! they never caught him. Lepas believed that the Spaniard had drowned himself. I, sir, don't think so; I am more inclined to beleive that he had something to do with the affair of Madame de Merret, seeing that Rosalie told me that the crucifix that her mistress thought so much of, that she had it buried with her, was of ebony and silver. Now in the beginning of his stay here, Monsieur de Férédia had one in ebony and silver, that I never saw him with later. Now, sir, don't you consider that I need have no scruples about the Spaniard's fifteen thousand francs, and that I have a right to them?'

'Certainly; but you haven't tried to question Rosalie?' I said.

'Oh, yes, indeed, sir; but to no purpose! the girl's like a wall. She knows something, but it is impossible to get her to talk.'

After exchanging a few more words with me, my landlady left me a prey to vague and gloomy thoughts, to a romantic curiosity, and a religious terror not unlike the profound impression produced on us when by night, on entering a dark church, we perceive a faint light under high arches; a vague figure glides by – the rustle of a robe or cassock is heard, and we shudder.

Suddenly the Grande Bretêche and its tall weeds, its barred windows, its rusty ironwork, its closed doors, its deserted apartments, appeared like a fantastic apparition before me. I essayed to penetrate the mysterious dwelling, and to find the knot of its dark story – the drama that had killed three persons. In my eyes Rosalie became the most interesting person in Vendôme. As I studied her, I discovered the traces of secret care, despite the radiant health that shone in her plump countenance. There was in her the germ of remorse or hope; her attitude revealed a secret, like the attitude of a bigot who prays to excess, or of the infanticide who ever hears the last cry of her child. Yet her manners were rough and ingenuous – her silly smile was not that of a criminal, and could you have seen the great kerchief that encompassed her portly bust, framed and laced in by a lilac and blue cotton gown, you would have dubbed her innocent. No, I thought, I will not leave Vendôme without learning the history of the Grande Bretêche. To gain my ends I will strike up a friendship with Rosalie, if needs be.

'Rosalie,' said I, one evening.

'Sir?'

'You are not married?'

She started slightly.

'Oh, I can find plenty of men, when the fancy takes me to be made miserable,' she said, laughing.

She soon recovered from the effects of her emotion, for all women, from the great lady to the maid of the inn, possess a composure that is peculiar to them.

'You are too good-looking and well favoured to be short of lovers. But tell me, Rosalie, why did you take service in an inn after leaving Madame de Merret? Did she leave you nothing to live on?'

'Oh, yes! But, sir, my place is the best in all Vendôme.'

The reply was one of those that judges and lawyers would call evasive. Rosalie appeared to me to be situated in this romantic history like the square in the midst of a chessboard. She was at the heart of the truth and chief interest; she seemed to me to be bound in the very knot of it. The conquest of Rosalie was no longer to be an ordinary siege – in this girl was centred the last chapter of a novel, therefore from this moment Rosalie became the object of my preference.

One morning I said to Rosalie: 'Tell me all you know about Madame de Merret.'

'Oh!' she replied in terror, 'do not ask that of me, Monsieur Horace.'

Her pretty face fell – her clear, bright colour faded – and her eyes lost their innocent brightness.

'Well, then,' she said, 'if you must have it so, I will tell you about it; but promise to keep my secret!'

'Done! my dear girl, I must keep your secret with the honour of a thief, which is the most loyal in the world.'

Were I to transcribe Rosalie's diffuse eloquence faithfully, an entire volume would scarcely contain it; so I shall abridge.

The room occupied by Madame de Merret at the Bretêche was on the ground-floor. A little closet about four feet deep, built in the thickness of the wall, served as her wardrobe. Three months before the eventful evening of which I am about to speak, Madame de Merret had been so seriously indisposed that her husband had left her to herself in her own apartment, while he occupied another on the first floor. By one of those chances that it is impossible to foresee, he returned home from the club (where he was accustomed to read the papers and discuss politics with the inhabitants of the place) two hours later than usual. His wife supposed him to be at home, in bed and asleep. But the invasion of France had been the subject of a most animated discussion; the billiard-match had been exciting, he had lost forty francs, an enormous sum for Vendôme, where every one hoards, and where manners are restricted within the limits of praiseworthy modesty, which perhaps is the source of the true happiness that no Parisian covets. For some time past Monsieur de Merret had been satisfied to ask Rosalie if his wife had gone to bed; and on her reply, which was always in the affirmative, had immediately gained his own room with the good temper engendered by habit and confidence. On entering his house, he took it into his head to go and tell his wife of his misadventure, perhaps by way of consolation. At dinner he found Madame de Merret most coquettishly attired. On his way to the club it had occurred to him that his wife was restored to health, and that her convalescence had added to her beauty. He was, as husbands are wont to be, somewhat slow in making this discovery. Instead of calling Rosalie, who was occupied just then in watching the cook and coachman play a difficult hand at brisque, Monsieur de Merret went to his wife's room by the light of a lantern that he deposited on the first step of the staircase. His unmistakable step resounded under the vaulted corridor. At the moment that the Count turned the handle of his wife's door, he fancied he could hear the door of the closet I spoke of close; but when he entered Madame de Merret was alone before the fire-place. The husband thought ingenuously that Rosalie was in the closet, yet a suspicion that jangled in his ear put him on his guard. He looked at his wife and saw in her eyes I know not what wild and hunted expression.

'You are very late,' she said. Her habitually pure, sweet voice seemed changed to him.

Monsieur de Merret did not reply, for at that moment Rosalie entered. It was a thunderbolt for him. He strode about the room, passing from one window to the other, with mechanical motion and folded arms.

'Have you heard bad news, or are you unwell?' inquired his wife timidly, while Rosalie undressed her.

He kept silent.

'You can leave me,' said Madame de Merret to her maid; 'I will put my hair in curl papers myself.'

From the expression of her husband's face she foresaw trouble, and wished to be alone with him. When Rosalie had gone, or was supposed to have gone (for she stayed in the corridor for a few minutes), Monsieur de Merret came and stood in front of his wife, and said coldly to her:

'Madáme, there is someone in your closet!' She looked calmly at her husband, and replied simply:

'No, sir.'

This answer was heartrending to Monsieur de Merret; he did not believe in it. Yet his wife had never appeared to him purer or more saintly than at that moment. He rose to open the closet door; Madame de Merret took his hand, looked at him with an expression of melancholy, and said in a voice that betrayed singular emotion:

'If you find no one there, remember this, all will be over between us!' The extraordinary dignity of his wife's manner restored the Count's profound esteem for her, and inspired him with one of those resolutions that only lack a vaster stage to become immortal.

'No,' said he, 'Josephine, I will not go there. In either case it would separate us for ever. Hear me, I know how pure you are at heart, and that your life is a holy one. You would not commit a mortal sin to save your life.'

At these words Madame de Merret turned a haggard gaze upon her husband.

'Here, take your crucifix,' he added. 'Swear to me before God that there is no one in there; I will believe you, I will never open that door.'

Madame de Merret took the crucifix and said:

'I swear.'

'Louder,' said the husband, 'and repeat "I swear before God that there is no one in that closet."'

She repeated the sentence calmly.

'That will do,' said Monsieur de Merret, coldly.

After a moment of silence:

'I never saw this pretty toy before,' he said, examining the ebony crucifix inlaid with silver, and most artistically chiselled.

'I found it at Duvivier's, who bought it off a Spanish monk when the prisoners passed through Vendôme last year.'

'Ah!' said Monsieur de Merret, as he replaced the crucifix on the nail,

and he rang. Rosalie did not keep him waiting. Monsieur de Merret
went quickly to meet her, led her to the bay window that opened on to
the garden and whispered to her:

'Listen! I know that Gorenflot wishes to marry you, poverty is the only
drawback, and you told him that you would be his wife if he found the
means to establish himself as a master mason. Well! go and fetch him,
tell him to come here with his trowel and tools. Manage not to awaken
anyone in his house but himself; his fortune will be more than your
desires. Above all, leave this room without babbling, otherwise——' He
frowned. Rosalie went away, he recalled her.

'Here, take my latchkey,' he said. 'Jean!' then cried Monsieur de
Merret, in tone of thunder in the corridor. Jean, who was at the same
time his coachman and his confidential servant, left his game of cards
and came.

'Go to bed, all of you,' said his master, signing to him to approach;
and the Count added, under his breath: 'When they are all asleep –
asleep, d'ye hear? – you will come down and tell me.' Monsieur de
Merret, who had not lost sight of his wife all the time he was giving his
orders, returned quietly to her at the fireside and began to tell her of
the game of billiards and the talk of the club. When Rosalie returned
she found Monsieur and Madame de Merret conversing very amicably.

The Count had lately had all the ceilings of his reception rooms on
the ground floor repaired. Plaster of Paris is difficult to obtain in
Vendôme; the carriage raises its price. The Count had therefore bought
a good deal, being well aware that he could find plenty of purchasers
for whatever might remain over. This circumstance inspired him with
the design he was about to execute.

'Sir, Gorenflot has arrived,' said Rosalie in low tones.

'Show him in,' replied the Count in loud tones.

Madame de Merret turned rather pale when she saw the mason.

'Gorenflot,' said her husband, 'go and fetch bricks from the coach-
house, and bring sufficient to wall up the door of this closet; you will
use the plaster I have over to coat the wall with.' Then calling Rosalie
and the workman aside:

'Listen, Gorenflot,' he said in an undertone, 'you will sleep here
tonight. But tomorrow you will have a passport to a foreign country,
to a town to which I will direct you. I shall give you six thousand francs
for your journey. You will stay ten years in that town; if you do not like
it, you may establish yourself in another, provided it be in the same
country. You will pass through Paris, where you will await me. There
I will insure you an additional six thousand francs by contract, which
will be paid to you on your return, provided you have fulfilled the
conditions of our bargain. This is the price for your absolute silence as
to what you are about to do tonight. As to you, Rosalie, I will give you

ten thousand francs on the day of your wedding, on condition of your marrying Gorenflot; but if you wish to marry, you must hold your tongues; or – no dowry.'

'Rosalie,' said Madame de Merret, 'do my hair.'

The husband walked calmly up and down, watching the door, the mason, and his wife, but without betraying any insulting doubts. Madame de Merret chose a moment when the workman was unloading bricks and her husband was at the other end of the room to say to Rosalie: 'A thousand francs a year for you, my child, if you can tell Gorenflot to leave a chink at the bottom.' Then out loud, she added coolly:

'Go and help him!'

Monsieur and Madame de Merret were silent all the time that Gorenflot took to brick up the door. This silence, on the part of the husband, who did not choose to furnish his wife with a pretext for saying things of a double meaning, had its purpose; on the part of Madame de Merret it was either pride or prudence. When the wall was about half-way up, the sly workman took advantage of a moment when the Count's back was turned, to strike a blow with his trowel in one of the glass panes of the closet-door. This act informed Madame de Merret that Rosalie had spoken to Gorenflot.

All three then saw a man's face; it was dark and gloomy with black hair and eyes of flame. Before her husband turned, the poor woman had time to make a sign to the stranger that signified: Hope!

At four o'clock, towards dawn, for it was the month of September, the construction was finished. The mason was handed over to the care of Jean, and Monsieur de Merret went to bed in his wife's room.

On rising the following morning, he said carelessly:

'The deuce! I must go to the Mairie for the passport.' He put his hat on his head, advanced three steps towards the door, altered his mind and took the crucifix.

His wife trembled for joy. 'He is going to Duvivier,' she thought. As soon as the Count had left, Madame de Merret rang for Rosalie; then in a terrible voice:

'The trowel, the trowel!' she cried, 'and quick to work! I say how Gorenflot did it; we shall have time to make a hole and to mend it again.'

In the twinkling of an eye, Rosalie brought a sort of mattock to her mistress, who with unparalleled ardour set about demolishing the wall. She had already knocked out several bricks and was preparing to strike a more decisive blow when she perceived Monsieur de Merret behind her. She fainted.

'Lay Madame on her bed,' said the Count coldly. He had foreseen what would happen in his absence and had set a trap for his wife; he had simply written to the mayor, and had sent for Duvivier. The jeweller arrived just as the room had been put in order.

'Duvivier,' inquired the Count, 'did you buy crucifixes of the Spaniards who passed through here?'

'No, sir.'

'That will do, thank you,' he said, looking at his wife like a tiger. 'Jean,' he added, 'you will see that my meals are served in the Countess's room; she is ill, and I shall not leave her until she has recovered.'

The cruel gentleman stayed with his wife for twenty days. In the beginning, when there were sounds in the walled closet, and Josephine attempted to implore his pity for the dying stranger, he replied, without permitting her to say a word:

'You have sworn on the cross that there is no one there.'

Negotium Perambulans ...

E. F. Benson

The casual tourist in West Cornwall may just possibly have noticed, as he bowled along over the bare high plateau between Penzance and Land's End, a dilapidated signpost pointing down a steep lane and bearing on its battered finger the faded inscription 'Polearn 2 miles', but probably very few have had the curiosity to traverse those two miles in order to see a place to which their guide-books award so cursory a notice. It is described there, in a couple of unattractive lines, as a small fishing village with a church of no particular interest except for certain carved and painted wooden panels (originally belonging to an earlier edifice) which form an altar-rail. But the church at St Creed (the tourist is reminded) has a similar decoration far superior in point of preservation and interest, and thus even the ecclesiastically disposed are not lured to Polearn. So meagre a bait is scarce worth swallowing, and a glance at the very steep lane which in dry weather presents a carpet of sharp-pointed stones, and after a rain a muddy watercourse, will almost certainly decide him not to expose his motor or his bicycle to risks like these in so sparsely populated a district. Hardly a house has met his eye since he left Penzance, and the possible trundling of a punctured bicycle for half a dozen weary miles seems a high price to pay for the sight of a few painted panels.

Polearn, therefore, even in the high noon of the tourist season, is little liable to invasion, and for the rest of the year I do not suppose that a couple of folk a day traverse those two miles (long ones at that) of steep and stony gradient. I am not forgetting the postman in this exiguous estimate, for the days are few when, leaving his pony and cart at the top of the hill, he goes as far as the village, since but a few hundred yards down the lane there stands a large white box, like a sea-trunk, by the side of the road, with a slit for letters and a locked door. Should he have in his wallet a registered letter or be the bearer of a parcel too large for insertion in the square lips of the sea-trunk, he must needs trudge down the hill and deliver the troublesome missive, leaving it in person on the owner, and receiving some small reward of coin or refreshment for his kindness. But such occasions are rare, and his general routine is to take out of the box such letters as may have been deposited there, and insert in their place such letters as he has brought. These will be called for, perhaps that day or perhaps the next, by an emissary from the Polearn post-office. As for the fishermen of the place, who, in their export trade, constitute the chief link of movement between Polearn and the outside world, they would not dream of taking their catch up the steep lane and so, with six miles farther of travel, to the market at Penzance. The sea route is shorter and easier, and they deliver their wares to the pier-head. Thus, though the sole industry of Polearn is sea-fishing, you will get no fish there unless you have bespoken your requirements to one of the fishermen. Back come the trawlers as empty as a haunted house, while their spoils are in the fish-train that is speeding to London.

Such isolation of a little community, continued, as it has been, for centuries, produces isolation in the individual as well, and nowhere will you find greater independence of character than among the people of Polearn. But they are linked together, so it has always seemed to me, by some mysterious comprehension: it is as if they had all been initiated into some ancient rite, inspired and framed by forces visible and invisible. The winter storms that batter the coast, the vernal spell of the spring, the hot, still summers, the season of rains and autumnal decay, have made a spell which, line by line, has been communicated to them, concerning the powers, evil and good, that rule the world, and manifest themselves in ways benignant or terrible...

I came to Polearn first at the age of ten, a small boy, weak and sickly, and threatened with pulmonary trouble. My father's business kept him in London, while for me abundance of fresh air and a mild climate were considered essential conditions if I was to grow to manhood. His sister had married the vicar of Polearn, Richard Bolitho, himself native to the place, and so it came about that I spent three years, as a paying guest, with my relations. Richard Bolitho owned a fine house in the place, which he inhabited in preference to the vicarage, which he let to a young artist, John Evans, on whom the spell of Polearn had fallen, for from year's beginning to year's end he never left it. There was a solid roofed shelter, open on one side to the air, built for me in the garden, and here I lived and slept, passing scarcely one hour out of the twenty-four behind walls and windows. I was out on the bay with the fisher-folk, or wandering along the gorse-clad cliffs that climbed steeply to right and left of the deep combe where the village lay, or pottering about on the pier-head, or birds' nesting in the bushes with the boys of the village. Except on Sunday and for the few daily hours of my lessons, I might do what I pleased so long as I remained in the open air. About the lessons, there was nothing formidable; my uncle conducted me through flowering bypaths among the thickets of arithmetic, and made pleasant excursions into the elements of Latin grammar, and above all, he made me daily give him an account, in clear and grammatical sentences, of what had been occupying my mind or my movements. Should I select to tell him about a walk along the cliffs, my speech must be orderly, not vague, slip-shod notes of what I had observed. In this way, too, he trained my observation, for he would bid me tell him what flowers were in bloom, and what birds hovered fishing over the sea or were building in the bushes. For that I owe him a perennial gratitude, for to observe and to express my thoughts in the clear spoken word became my life's profession.

But far more formidable than my weekday tasks was the prescribed routine for Sunday. Some dark embers compounded of Calvinism and mysticism smouldered in my uncle's soul, and made it a day of terror. His sermon in the morning scorched us with a foretaste of the eternal fires reserved for unrepentant sinners, and he was hardly less terrifying at the children's service in the afternoon. Well do I remember his exposition of the doctrine of guardian. angels. A child, he said, might think himself secure in such angelic care, but let him beware of committing any of those numerous offences which would cause his guardian to turn his face from him, for as sure as there were angels to protect us, there were also evil and awful presences which were ready to pounce; and on them he dwelt with peculiar gusto. Well, too, do I remember in the morning sermon his commentary on the carved panels of the altar-rails to which I have already alluded. There was the angel of Annunciation there, and the angel of Resurrection, but not less was there the witch of Endor, and, on the fourth panel, a scene that concerned me most of all. This fourth panel (he came down from his pulpit to trace its time-worn features) represented the lych-gate of the church-yard at Polearn itself, and indeed the resemblance when thus pointed out was remarkable. In the entry stood the figure of a robed priest holding up a Cross, with which he faced a terrible creature like a gigantic slug, that reared itself up in front of him. That, so ran my uncle's interpretation, was some evil agency, such as he had spoken about to us children, of almost infinite malignity and power, which could alone be combated by firm faith and a pure heart. Below ran the legend. 'Negotium perambulans in tenebris' from the ninety-first Psalm. We should find it translated there, 'the pestilence that walketh in darkness,' which but feebly rendered the Latin. It was more deadly to the soul than any pestilence that can only kill the body: it was the Thing, the Creature, the Business that trafficked in the outer Darkness, a minister of God's wrath on the unrighteous...

I could see, as he spoke, the looks which the congregation exchanged with each other, and knew that his words were evoking a surmise, a remembrance. Nods and whispers passed between them, they understood to what he alluded, and with the inquisitiveness of boyhood I could not rest till I had wormed the story out of my friends among the fisher-boys, as, next morning, we sat basking and naked in the sun after our bathe. One knew one bit of it, one another, but it pieced together into a truly alarming legend. In bald outline it was as follows:

A church far more ancient than that in which my uncle terrified us every Sunday had once stood not three hundred yards away, on the shelf of level ground below the quarry from which its stones were hewn. The owner of the land had pulled this down, and erected for himself a house on the same site out of these materials, keeping, in a very ecstasy of wickedness, the altar, and on this he dined and played dice afterwards. But as he grew old some black melancholy seized him, and he would have lights burning there all night, for he had deadly fear of the darkness. On one winter evening there sprang up a gale as was never before known, which broke in the windows of the room where he had supped, and extinguished the lamps. Yells of terror brought in his servants, who found him lying on the floor with the blood streaming from his throat. As they entered some huge black shadow seemed to move away from him, crawled across the floor and up the wall and out of the broken window.

'There he lay a-dying,' said the last of my informants, 'and him that had been a great burly man was withered to a bag o' skin, for the critter had drained all the blood from him. His last breath was a scream, and he hollered out the same words as parson read off the screen.'

'*Negotium perambulans in tenebris,*' I suggested eagerly.

'Thereabouts. Latin anyhow.'

'And after that?' I asked.

'Nobody would go near the place, and the old house rotted and fell in ruins till three years ago, when along come Mr Dooliss from Penzance, and built the half of it up again. But he don't care much about such critters, nor about Latin, neither. He takes his bottle of whisky a day and gets drunk's a lord in the evening. Eh, I'm gwine home to my dinner.'

Whatever the authenticity of the legend, I had certainly heard the truth about Mr Dooliss from Penzance, who from that day became an object of keen curiosity on my part, the more so because the quarry-house adjoined my uncle's garden. The Thing that walked in the dark failed to stir my imagination, and already I was so used to sleeping alone in my shelter that the night had no terrors for me. But it would be intensely exciting to wake at some timeless hour and hear Mr Dooliss yelling, and conjecture that the Thing had got him.

But by degrees the whole story faded from my mind, overscored by the more vivid interests of the day, and, for the last two years of my out-door life in the vicarage gardens, I seldom thought about Mr Dooliss and the possible fate that might await him for this temerity in living in the place where that Thing of darkness had done business. Occasionally I saw him over the garden fence, a great yellow lump of a man, with slow and staggering gait, but never did I set eyes on him outside his gate, either in the village street or down on the beach. He interfered with none, and no one interfered with him. If he wanted to run the risk of being the prey of the legendary nocturnal monster, or quietly drink himself to death, it was his affair. My uncle, so I gathered, had made several attempts to see him when first he came to live at Polearn, but Mr Dooliss appeared to have no use for parsons, but said he was not at home and never returned the call.

After three years of sun, wind, and rain, I had completely outgrown my early symptoms and had become a tough, strapping youngster of thirteen. I was sent to Eton and Cambridge, and in due course ate my dinners and became a barrister. In twenty years from that time I was earning a yearly income of five figures, and had already laid by in sound securities a sum that brought me dividends which would, for one of my simple tastes and frugal habits, supply me with all the material comforts I needed on this side of the grave. The great prizes of my profession were already within my reach, but I had no ambition beckoning me on, nor did I want a wife and children, being, I must suppose, a natural celibate. In fact there was only one ambition which through these busy years had held the lure of blue and far-off hills to me, and that was to get back to Polearn, and live once more isolated from the world with the sea and the gorse-clad hills for play-fellows, and the secrets that lurked there for exploration. The spell of it had been woven about my heart, and I can truly say that there had hardly passed a day in all those years in which the thought of it and the desire for it had been wholly absent from my mind. Though I had been in frequent communication with my uncle there during his lifetime, and, after his death, with his widow who still lived there, I had never been back to it since I embarked on my profession, for I knew that if I went there, it would be a wrench beyond my power to tear myself away again. But I had made up my mind that when once I had provided for my own independence, I would go back there not to leave it again. And yet I did leave it again, and now nothing in the world would induce me to turn down the lane from the road that leads from Penzance to Land's End, and see the sides of the combe rise steep above the roofs of the village and hear the gulls chiding as they fish in the bay. One of the things invisible, of the dark powers, leaped into light, and I saw it with my eyes.

The house where I had spent those three years of boyhood had been left for life to my aunt, and when I made known to her my intention of coming back to Polearn, she suggested that, till I found a suitable house or found her proposal unsuitable, I should come to live with her.

'The house is too big for a lone old woman,' she wrote, 'and I have often thought of quitting and taking a little cottage sufficient for me and my requirements. But come and share it, my dear, and if you find me troublesome, you or I can go. You may want solitude – most people in Polearn do – and will leave me. Or else I will leave you: one of the main reasons of my stopping here all these years was a feeling that I must not let the old house starve. Houses starve, you know, if they are not lived in. They die a lingering death; the spirit of them grows weaker and weaker, and at last fades out of them. Isn't this nonsense to your London notions? . . .'

Naturally I accepted with warmth this tenative arrangement, and on an evening in June found myself at the head of the lane leading down to Polearn, and once more I descended into the steep valley between the hills. Time had stood still apparently for the combe, the dilapidated signpost (or its successor) pointed a rickety finger down the lane, and a few hundred yards farther on was the white box for the exchange of letters. Point after remembered point met my eye, and what I saw was not shrunk, as is often the case with the revisited scenes of childhood, into a smaller scale. There stood the post-office, and there the church and close beside it the vicarage, and beyond, the tall shrubberies which separated the house for which I was bound from the road, and beyond that again the grey roofs of the quarry-house damp and shining with the moist evening wind from the sea. All was exactly as I remembered it, and, above all, that sense of seclusion and isolation. Somewhere above the tree-tops climbed the lane which joined the main road to Penzance, but all that had become immeasurably distant. The years that had passed since last I turned in at the well-known gate faded like a frosty breath, and vanished in this warm, soft air. There were law-courts somewhere in memory's dull book which, if I cared to turn the pages, would tell me that I had made a name and a great income there. But the book was closed now, for I was back in Polearn, and the spell was woven around me.

And if Polearn was unchanged, so too was Aunt Hester, who met me at the door. Dainty and china-white she had always been, and the years had not aged but only refined her. As she sat and talked after dinner she spoke of all that had happened in Polearn in that score of years, and yet somehow the changes of which she spoke seemed but to confirm the immutability of it all. As the recollection of names came back to me, I asked her about the quarry-house and Mr Dooliss, and her face gloomed a little as with a shadow of a cloud on a spring day.

'Yes, Mr Dooliss,' she said, 'poor Mr Dooliss, how well I remember him, though it must be ten years and more since he died. I never wrote to you about it, for it was all very dreadful, my dear, and I did not want to darken your memories of Polearn. Your uncle always thought that something of the sort might happen if he went on in his wicked, drunken ways, and worse than that, and though nobody knew exactly what took place, it was the sort of thing that might have been anticipated.'

'But what more or less happened, Aunt Hester?' I asked.

'Well, of course I can't tell you everything, for no one knew it. But he was a very sinful man, and the scandal about him at Newlyn was shocking. And then he lived, too, in the quarry-house ... I wonder if by any chance you remember a sermon of your uncle's when he got out of the pulpit and explained that panel in the altar-rail, the one, I mean, with the horrible creature rearing itself up outside the lych-gate?'

'Yes, I remember perfectly,' said I.

'Ah. It made an impression on you, I suppose, and so it did on all who heard him, and that impression got stamped and branded on us all when the catastrophe occurred. Somehow Mr Dooliss got to hear about your uncle's sermon, and in some drunken fit he broke into the church and smashed the panel to atoms. He seems to have thought that there was some magic in it, and that if he destroyed that he would get rid of the terrible fate that was threatening him. For I must tell you that before he committed that dreadful sacrilege he had been a haunted man: he hated and feared darkness, for he thought that the creature on the panel was on his track, but that as long as he kept lights burning it could not touch him. But the panel, to his disordered mind, was the root of his terror, and so, as I said, he broke into the church and attempted – you will see why I said "attempted" – to destroy it. It certainly was found in splinters next morning, when your uncle went into church for matins, and knowing Mr Dooliss's fear of the panel, he went across to the quarry-house afterwards and taxed him with its destruction. The man never denied it; he boasted of what he had done. There he sat, though it was early morning, drinking his whisky.

'"I've settled your Thing for you," he said, "and your sermon too. A fig for such superstitions."

'Your uncle left him without answering his blasphemy, meaning to go straight into Penzance and give information to the police about this outrage to the church, but on his way back from the quarry-house he went into the church again, in order to be able to give details about the damage, and there in the screen was the panel, untouched and uninjured. And yet he had himself seen it smashed, and Mr Dooliss had confessed that the destruction of it was his work. But there it was, and whether the power of God had mended it or some other power, who knows?'

This was Polearn indeed, and it was the spirit of Polearn that made me accept all Aunt Hester was telling me as attested fact. It had happened like that. She went on in her quiet voice.

'Your uncle recognized that some power beyond police was at work, and he did not go to Penzance or give information about the outrage, for the evidence of it had vanished.'

A sudden spate of scepticism swept over me.

'There must have been some mistake,' I said. 'It hadn't been broken...'

She smiled.

'Yes, my dear, but you have been in London so long,' she said. 'Let me, anyhow, tell you the rest of my story. That night, for some reason, I could not sleep. It was very hot and airless; I dare say you will think that the sultry conditions accounted for my wakefulness. Once and again, as I went to the window to see if I could admit more air, I could see from it the quarry-house, and I noticed the first time that I left my bed that it was blazing with lights. But the second time I saw that it was all in darkness, and as I wondered at that, I heard a terrible scream, and the moment afterwards the steps of someone coming at full speed down the road outside the gate. He yelled as he ran; "Light, light!" he called out. "Give me light, or it will catch me!" It was very terrible to hear that, and I went to rouse my husband, who was sleeping in the dressing-room across the passage. He wasted no time, but by now the whole village was aroused by the screams, and when he got down to the pier he found that all was over. The tide was low, and on the rocks at its foot was lying the body of Mr Dooliss. He must have cut some artery when he fell on those sharp edges of stone, for he had bled to death, they thought, and though he was a big burly man, his corpse was but skin and bones. Yet there was no pool of blood round him, such as you would have expected. Just skin and bones as if every drop of blood in his body had been sucked out of him!'

She leaned forward.

'You and I, my dear, know what happened,' she said, 'or at least can guess. God has His instruments of vengeance on those who bring wickedness into places that have been holy. Dark and mysterious are His ways.'

Now what I should have thought of such a story if it had been told me in London I can easily imagine. There was such an obvious explanation: the man in question had been a drunkard what wonder if the demons of delirium pursued him? But here in Polearn it was different.

'And who is in the quarry-house now?' I asked. 'Years ago the fisherboys told me the story of the man who first built it and of his horrible end. And now again it has happened. Surely no one has ventured to inhabit it once more?'

I saw in her face, even before I asked that question, that somebody had done so.

'Yes, it is lived in again,' she said, 'For there is no end to the blindness

... I don't know if you remember him. He was the tenant of the vicarage many years ago.'

'John Evans,' said I.

'Yes. Such a nice fellow he was too. Your uncle was pleased to get so good a tenant. And now——'

She rose.

'Aunt Hester, you shouldn't leave your sentences unfinished,' I said. She shook her head.

'My dear, that sentence will finish itself,' she said. 'But what a time of night! I must go to bed, and you too or they will think we have to keep lights burning here through the dark hours.'

Before getting into bed I drew my curtains wide and opened all the windows to the warm tide of the sea air that flowed softly in. Looking out into the garden I could see in the moonlight the roof of the shelter, in which for three years I had lived, gleaming with dew. That, as much as anything, brought back the old days to which I had now returned, and they seemed of one piece with the present, as if no gap of more than twenty years sundered them. The two flowed into one like globules of mercury uniting into a softly shining globe, of mysterious lights and reflections. Then, raising my eyes a little, I saw against the black hillside the windows of the quarry-house still alight.

Morning, as is so often the case, brought no shattering of my illusion. As I began to regain consciousness, I fancied that I was a boy again waking up in the shelter in the garden, and though, as I grew more widely awake, I smiled at the impression, that on which it was based I found to be indeed true. It was sufficient now as then to be here, to wander again on the cliffs, and hear the popping of the ripened seed-pods on the gorse-bushes; to stray along the shore to the bathing-cove, to float and drift and swim in the warm tide, and bask on the sand, and watch the gulls fishing, to lounge on the pier-head with the fisher-folk, to see in their eyes and hear in their quiet speech the evidence of secret things not so much known to them as part of their instincts and their very being. There were powers and presences about me; the white poplars that stood by the stream that babbled down the valley knew of them, and showed a glimpse of their knowledge sometimes, like the gleam of their white underleaves; the very cobbles that paved the street were soaked in it ... All that I wanted was to lie there and grow soaked in it too; unconsciously, as a boy, I had done that but now the process must be conscious. I must know what stir of forces, fruitful and mysterious, seethed along the hill-side at noon, and sparkled at night on the sea. They could be known, they could even be controlled by those who were masters of the spell, but never could they be spoken of, for they were dwellers in the innermost, grafted into the eternal life of the world. There were dark secrets as well as these clear, kindly powers, and to these no doubt belonged the *negotium perambulans in tenebris* which, though of deadly malignity, might be regarded not only as evil, but as the avenger of sacrilegious and impious deeds ... All this was part of the spell of Polearn, of which the seeds had long lain dormant in me. But now they were sprouting, and who knew what strange flower would unfold on their stems?

It was not long before I came across John Evans. One morning, as I lay on the beach, there came shambling across the sand a man stout and middle-aged with the face of Silenus. He paused as he drew near and regarded me from narrow eyes.

'Why, you're the little chap that used to live in the parson's garden,' he said. 'Don't you recognize me?'

I saw who it was when he spoke: his voice, I think instructed me, and recognizing it, I could see the features of the strong, alert young man in this gross caricature.

'Yes, you're John Evans,' I said. 'You used to be very kind to me: you used to draw pictures for me.'

'So I did, and I'll draw you some more. Been bathing? That's a risky performance. You never know what lives in the sea, nor what lives on the land for that matter. Not that I heed them. I stick to work and whisky. God! I've learned to paint since I saw you, and drink too for that matter. I live in the quarry-house, you know, and it's a powerful thirsty place. Come and have a look at my things if you're passing. Staying with your aunt, are you? I could do a wonderful portrait of her. Interesting face; she knows a lot. People who live at Polearn get to know a lot, though I don't take much stock in that sort of knowledge myself.'

I do not know when I have been at once so repelled and interested. Behind the mere grossness of his face there lurked something which, while it appalled, yet fascinated me. His thick lisping speech had the same quality. And his paintings, what would they be like? ...

'I was just going home,' I said. 'I'll gladly come in, if you'll allow me.'

He took me through the untended and overgrown garden into the house which I had never yet entered. A great grey cat was sunning itself in the window, and an old woman was laying lunch in a corner of the cool hall into which the door opened. It was built of stone, and the carved mouldings let into the walls, the fragments of gargoyles and sculptured images, bore testimony to the truth of its having been built out of the demolished church. In one corner was an oblong and carved wooden table littered with a painter's apparatus and stacks of canvases leaned against the walls.

He jerked his thumb towards a head of an angel that was built into the mantelpiece and giggled.

'Quite a sanctified air,' he said, 'so we tone it down for the purposes of ordinary life by a different sort of art. Have a drink? No? Well, turn over some of my pictures while I put myself to rights.'

He was justified in his own estimate of his skill: he could paint (and apparently he could paint anything), but never have I seen pictures so inexplicably hellish. There were exquisite studies of trees, and you knew that something lurked in the flickering shadows. There was a drawing of his cat sunning itself in the window, even as I had just now seen it, and yet it was no cat but some beast of awful malignity. There was a boy stretched naked on the sands, not human, but some evil thing which had come out of the sea. Above all, there were pictures of his garden overgrown and jungle-like, and you knew that in the bushes were presences ready to spring out on you...

'Well, do you like my style?' he said as he came up, glass in hand. (The tumbler of spirits that he held had not been diluted.) 'I try to paint the essence of what I see, not the mere husk and skin of it, but its nature, where it comes from and what gives it birth. There's much in common between a cat and a fuchsia-bush if you look at them closely enough. Everything came out of the slime of the pit, and it's all going back there. I should like to do a picture of you some day. I'd hold the mirror up to Nature, as that old lunatic said.'

After this first meeting I saw him occasionally throughout the months of that wonderful summer. Often he kept to his house and to his painting for days together, and then perhaps some evening I would find him lounging on the pier, always alone, and every time we met thus the repulsion and interest grew, for every time he seemed to have gone farther along a path of secret knowledge towards some evil shrine where complete initiation awaited him ... And then suddenly the end came.

I had met him thus one evening on the cliffs while the October sunset still burned in the sky, but over it with amazing rapidity there spread from the west a great blackness of cloud such as I have never seen for denseness. The light was sucked from the sky, the dusk fell in ever thicker layers. He suddenly became conscious of this.

'I must get back as quick as I can,' he said. 'It will be dark in a few minutes, and my servant is out. The lamps will not be lit.'

He stepped out with extraordinary briskness for one who shambled and could scarcely lift his feet, and soon broke out into a stumbling run. In the gathering darkness I could see that his face was moist with the dew of some unspoken terror.

'You must come with me,' he panted, 'for so we shall get the lights burning the sooner. I cannot do without light.'

I had to exert myself to the full to keep up with him, for terror winged him, and even so I fell behind, so that when I came to the garden gate, he was already halfway up the path to the house. I saw him enter, leaving the door wide, and found him fumbling with matches. But his hand so trembled that he could not transfer the light to the wick of the lamp.

'But what's the hurry about?' I asked.

Suddenly his eyes focused themselves on the open behind me, and he jumped from his seat beside the table which had once been the altar of God, with a gasp and scream.

'No, no!' he cried. 'Keep it off!...'

I turned and saw what he had seen. The Thing had entered and now was swiftly gliding across the floor towards him, like some gigantic caterpillar. A stale phosphorescent light came from it, for though the dusk had grown to darkness outside, I could see it quite distinctly in the awful light of its own presence. From it too there came an odour of corruption and decay, as from slime that has long lain below water. It seemed to have no head, but on the front of it was an orifice of puckered skin which opened and shut and slavered at the edges. It was hairless, and slug-like in shape and in texture. As it advanced its fore-part reared itself from the ground, like a snake about to strike, and it fastened on him...

At that sight, and with the yells of his agony in my ears, the panic which had struck me relaxed into a hopeless courage, and with palsied impotent hands I tried to lay hold of the Thing. But I could not: though something material was there, it was impossible to grasp it; my hands sunk in it as in thick mud. It was like wrestling with a nightmare.

I think that but a few seconds elapsed before all was over. The screams of the wretched man sank to moans and mutterings as the Thing fell on him: he panted once or twice and was still. For a moment longer there came gurglings and sucking noises, and then it slid out even as it had entered. I lit the lamp which he had fumbled with, and there on the floor he lay, no more than a rind of skin in loose folds over projecting bones.

Text for Today

Charles Birkin

(*St Paul to the Corinthians, Chapter 14, Verse 21.*)

The Reverend Herbert Wessel and his wife, May, had lived on Namavava for three years. It was a beautiful island, a near earthly paradise, and lay less than a day's sail from Misima but, for all the contact which they had with the other and larger land masses of the group, they might just as well have been posted to Pitcairn.

Not that they minded. So long as May had Herbert, and so long as Herbert had his work among the natives, doing God's will, they were both of them perfectly content.

Herbert was the first resident missionary to have been sent to live on Namavava. Formerly it had been treated as an outpost of the D'Entrecasteaux Group, and had been visited on rare occasions by their predecessor, Cecil Oliver, who had been based on Misima, but upon his retirement there had been a reallocation of territory, and the Church of England had increased the numbers of its representatives in order to combat the growing menace of the Church of Rome, which was sending out more and more of their militant priests, although Namavava had so far escaped their attentions.

Herbert and May Wessel were of the same age. They had been married for twenty-five years, and had seen much of the world, generally in the more remote and unattractive corners of Africa and China, before this Melanesian appointment had been given to them, and a very pleasant one it had turned out to be. The climate was, for the greater part of the year, ideal, the inhabitants were cheerful and easy going, and there were no poisonous snakes or insects. True there was a species of large cockroach of which May had an unreasoning horror, and against which her carefully hoarded supply of Keating's Powder seemed to have very little effect. Nevertheless they referred to Namavava as their Garden of Eden.

Herbert sometimes thought that his career had been an undistinguished one and that now he could never expect to rise to any great heights. When this feeling of failure came upon him May would become as impatient with him as it was possible for her to be. It was not, she said quite forcibly, necessarily the Bishops and the high dignitaries of the Church who undertook the most important work, although she could not but agree that they were all of them fine and upright men. It was someone like Herbert who really counted in the eyes of God, a man who was selfless, and who asked for nothing for himself, one who had dedicated the whole of his life to the spiritual and physical well-being of the backward communities among whom he had been sent, and whose sole desire had been to serve. 'And no one,' she would say, 'no one is more self denying than you, and no one has a greater gift for making converts enjoy their religion. Under your guidance Christianity is for them a case of Te Deum rather than, as is so often the case I am afraid, one of tedium.' She used to smile brightly when she made this little joke.

They were the only white people on the island. When Queen Victoria had died during the previous year it had taken the news six months to reach them. Although they had not visited England for a decade they felt the loss as keenly as if it had been a personal bereavement, and Herbert had made the deceased monarch, with her many admirable virtues the subject of his next address in the rickety corrugated iron church that he had caused to be built on the outskirts of the main centre on Namavava, which was merely a straggle of extremely primitive dwellings that housed some six hundred souls.

Herbert's thick fair hair was already greying, while May's had been for a long time a mixture of pepper and salt in which the latter predominated. In appearance they were strangely alike, both being on the heavy side, both constantly smiling with a sincere and determined benignity, both viewing the world through thick spectacles. Despite the tropical sun there was scarcely a line on their faces, which resembled ripe and downy apricots.

Their own house had been erected on a narrow plateau about a hundred yards from, and fifty feet above, the winding village. It was perched on a forest of squat bamboo stilts and encircled by a shaded veranda to which access was given by half a dozen steps. The walls were of woven bamboo and the roof had been thatched with palm. In addition to the veranda, where the majority of their scant free time was spent, there was a bedroom, a living-room and, built on to the back, a more spacious annexe which served as May's workroom and dispensary, where she did her best with inadequate equipment to attend to the health of any who might be ailing.

A short distance from this were the cookhouse and the lean-to where their two 'boys' slept. May had to laugh when Herbert referred to them as 'the boys'. It always seemed to her so comical for in fact they were

handsome young men in their twenties, brothers, and as broad
shouldered and impressively muscled as gladiators.

The one who did the cooking was married. Herbert had conducted
the ceremony a few weeks after they had moved in, and had at the same
time taken the opportunity of baptizing the three children, when he had
baptized their parents. Their father had chosen the name of Zebedee,
and after some argument Herbert had given in to this wish. He would
himself have preferred to bestow upon him the name of one of the
disciples or apostles but had unwillingly allowed that Zebedee was
perhaps near enough.

Zebedee's brother, not to be outdone, had requested Boanerges, and
this demand, although their relationship was scripturally wrong, had
also been granted. Zebedee's wife had been content to become Mary.
Their Melanesian names had been quite unpronounceable, and so this
solution had been simpler for all.

May was uneasy that Zebedee insisted on sleeping in the lean-to
rather than in his own hut on the shore of the lagoon. Marriage was
sacred, and surely his proper place was at his wife's side? She had
resolved many times to speak to him about it, and had tried once to get
Herbert to do so but he had been embarrassed by the idea. Zebedee
would want to know why, and they neither of them had any desire to
embark upon so delicate a topic.

It had been a matter of nagging distress to May and Herbert that they
were such very poor linguists. Maybe, Herbert thought, if he had
possessed a better ear for languages he might have advanced further in
his vocation. It had been a tremendous handicap and one that probably
had held him back. May, however, in an attempt to remedy this
weakness had trained herself to become an excellent, if unorthodox,
teacher of English. She was blessed with patience and humour and had
a talent for pantomime which had stood them in good stead. Nor had
their frequent transfers been helpful. Sierra Leone, Uganda, Kweichow,
Kansu and finally Namavava had made it difficult for them to become
completely identified with their surroundings, since they had never had
the opportunity of putting down roots, not strong tap roots, which were
so essential in their life.

They hoped that they would be permitted to stay on Namavava for
many years. After all, May told herself, it was Herbert who had started
the mission. It was his creation, and she considered and also prayed, that
they would be allowed to remain there until the time should come for
their retirement. The islanders were so charming and lovable, as naive
as children, of course, but friendly and biddable children, and from a
total of the two thousand scattered population they could already lay
claim to at least a quarter of that number as converts.

Wisely, Herbert had not, upon their arrival, insisted on the destruction or disfigurement of the idols which they had found. Rather had he sought to wean away their worshippers by treating the images as interesting antiquities whose interest could be compared to those on Easter Island. He had taken immense pains to put over this viewpoint.

They had encountered no trouble. There had been no unpleasant incidents, that is to say, there had been none until a month before. Then, unhappily, there had been a murder, a crime which was unheard of on the island.

When they had been informed of it they had hoped, at the beginning, that it could have been treated as a case of assault but, as a result of the injuries which had been inflicted, the victim had later died. It was, or so Herbert had been told, the sole case of its kind to have happened on Namavava within living memory.

Mahele, who was one of the innumerable nephews of the Chief, had enticed a girl into a cave which was in the Bay of Shells, and there he had raped her. She had been betrothed to Ke-Kulah, who was related to Zebedee. Through the ages rape on Namavava had been taboo, especially where a betrothed girl had been involved. The girl had immediately confessed to her father what had occurred and Ke-Kulah with the assistance of her brother Manè had waylaid Mahele, and after beating him almost senseless had clumsily castrated him and had then left him for dead in the cave where his offence had been committed. It was fortunate, May thought, that none of those concerned was as yet a Christian.

Mahele had been found on the following morning and carried back by members of his family to the missionary's house and May had done her utmost to save his life. It had been the day that the schooner from Misima had been due for its monthly call with the Wessels' mail and supplies.

Herbert had not made an official report to the schooner's Captain, and in failing to do so he might have been wrong, but he had hoped that Mahele would recover and had wanted to postpone any action for as long as it could be arranged, and to avoid, if it were possible, the necessity of the men having to face a capital charge. But soon after the schooner had sailed, when the victim had died, Herbert had had a case of murder or, at the best, of manslaughter, on his hands.

Accordingly, since there would be no communication with the outside world for a further four weeks, and as the island possessed neither a gaol nor a police force, Herbert had put Mahele's assailants under arrest in a hut which he had ordered to be converted into a makeshift prison, and had appointed a roster of guards to ensure that they did not escape. Both May and himself made a routine visit twice daily to the prisoners in order to satisfy themselves that they were being well treated until the date when they could be sent to Misima to stand their trial.

He was most upset by this outbreak of violence, and his anguish was made the more acute as he was unable, to any appreciable extent, to communicate with or to comfort the accused men, and their bewilderment at having been apprehended for doing only what they had conceived as being their duty was another cross for him to bear, since he could not explain to them the error of their thinking.

Herbert's depression was in no way shared by the islanders, to whom the affair was fraught with drama and excitement. As capital punishment at the hands of white men had been hitherto unknown, the prisoners came to be regarded as sacrificial animals who would be called upon to expiate their misdeeds for the sake of the community, and once they had been enclosed behind bars they enjoyed that odd veneration accorded to the doomed, being regarded, to all intents and purposes, as already convicted and waiting for the hangman's noose.

This aspect of the situation Zebedee and Boanerges endeavoured to put forward to Herbert, and they were at a loss to comprehend why he should continue to be so cast down and to worry himself about their fate. It had been an exciting event, a welcome break in the monotony of their uneventful lives. The target of their criticism had been shifted from Mahele to Manè and Ke-Kulah for their bungling in not having finished off the culprit cleanly and throwing his body to the sharks, a course which would have avoided all the fuss and interference from outside authorities as well as obeying their ancient and unwritten laws.

The two houseboys, in common with Herbert's regular congregation, were devoted to their employers and were proud of the cachet which their positions in God's House endowed them, for the missionary's home ranked equally in their minds with the precincts of the church. So far as it lay in their power they were determined to help him in his tilling of the Lord's vineyard, and none were more active in canvassing and gaining new proselytes although, it must be admitted, conversion was looked upon more in the nature of being allowed into a select Club than of embracing an uplifting creed.

They had done their best to increase and widen the Wessels' grasp of their dialect and so improve their potentialities for free expression, but it had been uphill and unrewarding work and they had begun to despair of success.

The day before that of the schooner's expected return fell on a Friday, and Herbert was seated on the cooler side of the veranda wrestling with the weekly problem of Sunday's sermon, which had to be elementary, basic, and intelligible. He had given them The Ten Commandments repeatedly and in varying homely guises, and was planning to discourse once more on Thou Shalt Do No Murder, both to point Manè's and Ke-Kulah's crime and to try to make his listeners understand the justice of retribution. He gazed thoughtfully at a lizard plastered motionless on

a newel post near to his elbow. The task which he was setting himself
was a sad and a difficult one.

By reason of their mutually limited vocabularies his flock's perception
was confined to bare essentials, and the stirring events in the Old and
New Testaments had to be recounted as one would tell them to infants
in a kindergarten. The Flood, The Tower of Babel, The Fall of Jericho
and above all the life of Jesus Christ had come to sound in his own ears
like far away fairy stories, while confusion was apt to take place over
such differing injunctions in the Holy Book as demanding an eye for an
eye and, alternatively, meekly turning the other cheek.

Herbert put down his pencil and decided that he would go and see
Ke-Kulah and Manè once more after he had revised his sermon, and
that Zebedee should go with him to act as his interpreter. It would be
in the nature of a farewell for he might not be seeing them alone again.
The men seemed to have no idea of their predicament or of the prolonged proceedings which were awaiting them, and their families had
cast them off in new found horror when they had realized that Captain
Marriott's schooner and the important island of Misima were to be
involved. It would be a public scandal and would bring shame upon
them all.

Herbert's visit was not a success, and despite the blood bond between
Zebedee and one of the accused, it rapidly deteriorated into a slanging
match, for the houseboy resented bitterly the discredit which had been
brought down on them all and which had reflected not only upon
Namavava but on The Reverence as well.

The evening was sultry and suffocating and the sky was obscured by
a mass of leaden clouds. The rainy season was due to start, but Herbert
thought there would be several days of this breathless and unbearable
heat before the weather finally broke.

He was writing in his diary when May emerged from her dispensary
to summon him to the evening meal. Each night he confided to the pages
in his neat hand exactly where he considered that he had failed in his
calling, often when he had been needed most. Tonight he had written
that he should have been more resolute in the guidance of his people
by setting them a more combative example in the Christian cause. If he
had done so, the murder of Mahele, and even the rape of the girl, might
never have occurred. He blamed himself for having been too lax.

There was no breath of wind to stir the oppressive humid air, but the
table had been laid as usual on the eastern side of the veranda. Apart
from her modest store of tinned foods, which May doled out herself with
strict economy, she left the housekeeping to Zebedee. Their menu was
supplied from such bounty as the island could provide, eggs, scrawny
chickens, goat meat, and fish and fruit in abundance.

Tonight Zebedee had given them a clam soup followed by a stew of tongue with which he had served sweet potatoes. A basket of multi-coloured fruit, arranged by an artist's hand, stood upon the little wicker side table.

Herbert did not say a great deal during dinner, and May told him of her own afternoon's activities. Three more of the women had come to her and had asked if they could have cotton dresses, which was a minor triumph, for they preferred to leave their breasts bare. She had lanced the festering finger of a small boy. She had written a long letter to her sister Hilda in Essex, where she was married to a farmer and was the mother of four sons. May would have liked to live near her when they returned to England. She often discussed this possibility with Herbert. She wondered why the Lord had denied issue to themselves. No doubt He had His own reasons for having done so but it had been a great disappointment. May said that she hoped that Captain Marriott would bring sorely wanted medical supplies. There was hardly a drop of iodine left and her stock of aspirin and bandages was dangerously low. Besides which, they were nearly out of tea.

At the end of the meal Herbert returned to his task of recording the day's doings and to smoke the second of the ration of three pipes which he allowed himself. Before he went to bed he would try again to communicate with Ke-Kulah and Manè and this time he would ask his wife to accompany him.

May left him to his labours and went over to the cookhouse. Really Zebedee and Boanerges had excelled themselves. The soup had been delicious and the tongue had been more like that of a calf than of a goat. He must have simmered it for hours to make it so tender. He was a born cook and one to whom she had at once admitted that she could teach nothing. She gave grateful thanks to her Maker for having allowed them such a luxury.

'The boys' were together, talking in low voices and squatting upon their heels on the ground. Boanerges had stripped off the loose coat which he had worn while serving them and they were both of them clad only in abbreviated loincloths, one of scarlet the other of patterned green and blue, that left their magnificent torsos and well developed limbs exposed. They leapt to their feet at May's approach.

They were delighted by her appreciation, towering over her and grinning with pleasure. 'It was good, Missah?' said Zebedee eagerly. 'Good, eh? But no goat, Missah. No goat.' He clapped his brother on the back. 'See, Boanerges, the Missah liked! The Reverence too? Now we shall see, Missah! Now The Reverence happy he will speak Namavan like native man. They will all see. Is not that so, Boanerges?' He swung round to his brother for confirmation. 'Now everyone will understand what he is trying to tell us.'

'Yes, Missah,' Boanerges said. 'As The Reverence gentleman told us in the church in the words of the Mighty Saint Paul,' he frowned in an effort of memory. ' "With other men's tongues and through my lips will I speak unto this peoples".' He quoted the text with great pride. 'My peoples, they shall all hear,' he said. 'On Sunday they shall all hear.'

May was puzzled. Surely it was Corinthians 13. 'Tongues of men and of angels.' No, that was not right. Boanerges had been correct. What had the text actually been? 'With men *of* other tongues and *other* lips will I speak unto this people.' Still, Boanerges had made a gallant effort and she beamed her approval at him.

'God will speak to you in His own way,' she said.

'Yes, Missah,' replied Boanerges. 'God will now be able to speak to us. It will be made easy for The Reverence.'

Zebedee was smiling, showing his magnificent teeth. They had held a meeting last night down in the village and they had all been in agreement. 'Those no good men down there won't need them no more, Missah,' he assured her. 'And they can now take their part in the spreading of the Gospel to the whole of our peoples. Even to those savages from Bwago and Zagu.' These were two remote villages on the island's northern tip. 'Even they will understand,' he said scornfully. 'Will they not, Boanerges?'

'Praise the Lord they will,' said his brother, 'now that The Reverence has had the gift of tongues!'

An icy fear struck at May. 'What do you mean, Zebedee,' she said. 'What do you mean? What is it that you have done?'

The young giant grinned down at her. 'We ain't done nothing wrong, Missah. Just turned those lazy wicked-bad murderers into good Christians. They going to die by execution when they go Misima, so why should they not help The Reverence and Missah before they are taken away?' He spoke reasonably as if May were being rather dense.

She stared up at them unable to speak, her mind battling against the implication of what she had heard. Then she turned away and holding up her long white skirt hurried past the house and down the rough path in the direction of the stockade where the two men had been imprisoned. Her plump erect little figure in its unyielding blouse and wide starched belt with the square silver buckle stood out against the background of palm trees whose leaves hung limply under the threatening sky which had drained all colour from the sea. As she stumbled through the brief tropical twilight strands of hair escaped from their confining net and caressed her skin.

She would have to discover for herself what it was that had taken place before she sought out Herbert. She remembered his fears that he spoke above the heads of his congregation. Whatever the misunderstanding that might have arisen it was not his fault. He had felt it incumbent upon him that he should explain about the Holy Ghost, for

was not that the corner-stone of their faith? He had had to try to share
with them that glory of the Spirit which was God's most important gift
to His followers. What could they do to Herbert, should something
ghastly have happened? Could that saintly man be pilloried? Would he
be dishonoured and disgraced? Pray God that it would not be so.

At the entrance to the stockade which surrounded the hut three men
lounged on guard. They were not regular attendants at the services and
she saw that she scarcely knew them. They stiffened at her approach and
drew closer together, for it was their obvious intention to bar her way.

'Let me pass,' she called out. May did not slacken her pace until she
had drawn level with them. She held out her hand for the key.

The oldest of the men gave it to her, but reluctantly. 'No go in there,
Missah,' he said. 'No go in there.'

'Rubbish!' she said. She motioned authoritatively for them to stand
aside and they looked at one another in some confusion.

One of the guards put a hand on her arm as if he would restrain her.
'Sick,' he said, nodding towards the opening of the hut. 'Bad men's very
sick. No go in there, Missah.'

She brushed away his hand and unlocked the gate. A sound of
moaning came from the interior of the hut. She took the few steps to the
entrance and peered into the gloom inside, Ke-Kulah and Manè were
hunched on the beaten earth of the floor, their backs resting against the
wall of packed mud. Their expressions were vacant as they turned their
heads to look at her with the frightening and blank vacuity of idiots.

Blood still trickled from their mouths, ebbing over that which had
congealed in ridges on their chins and prior flow ebbed down upon their
naked chests. Their lips sagged slackly, torn and bruised when their
tongues had been hacked out. Already the flies were clustering greedily
upon their bodies.

Sickened by what she saw May Wessel swayed, and steadied herself
by an effort. From behind her, outside the stench of the hut, came the
rumble of thunder, and lightning forked down, violating the mass of
darkening clouds.

'With other tongues ... will I speak unto this people.'

Return to the Sabbath

Robert Bloch

It's not the kind of story that the columnists like to print; it's not the yarn press-agents love to tell. When I was still in the Public Relations Department at the studio, they wouldn't let me break it. I knew better than to try, for no paper would print such a tale.

We publicity men must present Hollywood as a gay place; a world of glamour and stardust. We capture only the light, but underneath the light there must always be shadows. I've always known that – it's been my job to gloss over those shadows for years – but the events of which I speak form a disturbing pattern too strange to be withheld. The shadow of these incidents is not *human*.

It's been the cursed weight of the whole affair that has proved my own mental undoing. That's why I resigned from the studio post, I guess. I wanted to forget, if I could. And now I know that the only way to relieve my mind is to tell the story. I must break the yarn, come what may. Then perhaps I can forget Karl Jorla's eyes . . .

The affair dates back to one September evening almost three years ago. Les Kincaid and I were slumming down on Main Street in Los Angeles that night. Les is an assistant producer up at the studio, and there was some purpose in his visit; he was looking for authentic types to fill minor roles in a gangster film he was doing. Les was peculiar that way; he preferred the real article, rather than the Casting Bureau's ready-made imitations.

We'd been wandering around for some time, as I recall, past the great stone Chows that guard the narrow alleys of Chinatown, over through the tourist-trap that is Olvera Street, and back along the flophouses of lower Main. We walked by the cheap burlesque houses, eyeing the insolent Filipinos that sauntered past, and jostling our way through the usual Saturday night slumming parties.

We were both rather weary of it all. That's why, I suppose, the dingy little theatre appealed to us.

'Let's go in and sit down for a while,' Les suggested. 'I'm tired.'

Even a Main Street burlesque show has seats in it, and I felt ready for a nap. The callipygy of the stage-attraction did not appeal to me, but I acceded to the suggestion and purchased our tickets.

We entered, sat down, suffered through two strip-tease dances, an incredibly ancient black-out sketch, and a 'Grand Finale'. Then, as is the custom in such places, the stage darkened and the screen flickered into life.

We got ready for our doze, then. The pictures shown in these houses are usually ancient specimens of the 'quickie' variety; fillers provided to clear the house. As the first blaring notes of the sound-track heralded the title of the opus, I closed my eyes, slouched lower in my seat, and mentally beckoned to Morpheus.

I was jerked back to reality by a sharp dig in the ribs. Les was nudging me and whispering.

'Look at this,' he murmured, prodding my reluctant body into wakefulness. 'Ever see anything like it?'

I glanced up at the screen. What I expected to find I do not know, but I saw – *horror*.

There was a country graveyard, shadowed by ancient trees through which flickered rays of mildewed moonlight. It was an old graveyard with rotting headstones set in grotesque angles as they leered up at the midnight sky.

The camera cut down on one grave, a fresh one. The music on the sound-track grew louder, in cursed climax. But I forgot camera and film as I watched. That grave was reality – hideous reality.

The grave was *moving*!

The earth beside the headstone was heaving and churning, as though it were being dug out. Not from above, but from *below*. It quaked upward ever so slowly; terribly. Little clods fell. The sod pulsed out in a steady stream and little rills of earth kept falling in the moonlight as though there were something clawing the dirt away ... something clawing from beneath.

That something – it would soon appear. And I began to be afraid. I – I didn't want to see what it was. The clawing from below was not natural; it held a purpose not altogether *human*.

Yet I had to look. I had to see him – it – emerge. The sod cascaded in a mound, and then I was staring at the edge of the grave, looking down at the black hole that gaped like a corpse-mouth in the moonlight. Something was coming out.

Something slithered through that fissure, fumbled at the side of the opening. It clutched the ground above the grave, and in the baleful beams of that demon's moon I knew it to be a human hand. A thin, white human hand that held but half its flesh. The hand of a lich, a skeleton claw ...

A second talon gripped the other side of the excavation top.

And now, slowly, insidiously, arms emerged. Naked, fleshless arms.

They crawled across the earth-sides like leprous white serpents. The arms of a cadaver, a rising cadaver. It was pulling itself up. And as *it* emerged, a cloud fell across the moonpath. The light faded to shadows as the bulky head and shoulders came into view. One could see nothing, and I was thankful.

But the cloud was falling away from the moon now. In a second the face would be revealed. The face of the thing from the grave, the resurrected visage of that which should be rotted in death – what would it be?

The shadows fell back. A figure rose out of the grave, and the face turned towards me. I looked and saw——

Well, you've been to 'horror pictures'. You know what one usually sees. The 'ape-man', or the 'maniac', or the 'death's-head'. The papier-mâché grotesquerie of the make-up artist. The 'skull' of the dead.

I saw none of that. Instead, there was *horror*. It was the face of a child, I thought, at first; no, not a child, but a man with a child's soul. The face of a poet, perhaps, unwrinkled and calm. Long hair framed a high forehead; crescent eyebrows tilted over closed lids. The nose and mouth were thin and finely chiselled. Over the entire countenance was written an unearthly peace. It was as though the man were in a sleep of somnambulism or catalepsy. And then the face grew larger, the moon-light brighter, and I saw – more.

The sharper light disclosed tiny touches of evil. The thin lips were fretted, maggot-kissed. The nose had *crumbled* at the nostrils. The fore-head was flaked with putrefaction, and the dark hair was dead, encrusted with slime. There were shadows in the bony ridges beneath the closed eyes. Even now, the skeletal arms were up, and bony fingers brushed at those dead pits as the rotted lids fluttered apart. The eyes opened.

They were wide, staring, flaming – and in them was the grave. They were eyes that had closed in death and opened in the coffin under earth. They were eyes that had seen the body rot and the soul depart to mingle in worn-ravened darkness below. They were eyes that held an alien life, a life so dreadful as to animate the cadaver's body and force it to claw its way back to outer earth. They were *hungry* eyes – triumphant, now, as they gazed in graveyard moonlight on a world they had never known before. They hungered for the world as only Death can hunger for Life. And they blazed out of the corpse-pallid face in icy joy.

Then the cadaver began to walk. It lurched between the graves, lumbered before ancient tombs. It shambled through the forest night until it reached a road. Then it turned up that road slowly ... slowly.

And the hunger in those eyes flamed again as the lights of a city flared below. Death was preparing to mingle with men.

II

I sat through all this entranced. Only a few minutes had elapsed, but I felt as though uncounted ages had passed unheeded. The film went on. Les and I didn't exchange a word, but we watched.

The plot was rather routine after that. The dead man was a scientist whose wife had been stolen from him by a young doctor. The doctor had tended him in his last illness and unwittingly administered a powerful narcotic with cataleptic effects.

The dialogue was foreign and I could not place it. All of the actors were unfamiliar to me, and the setting and photography was quite unusual, unorthodox treatment as in *The Cabinet of Dr Caligari* and other psychological films.

There was one scene where the living-dead man became enthroned as arch-priest at a Black Mass ceremonial, and there was a little child ... His eyes as he plunged the knife ...

He kept *decaying* throughout the film ... the Black Mass worshippers knew him as an emissary of Satan, and they kidnapped the wife as sacrifice for his own resurrection ... the scene with the hysterical woman when she saw and recognized her husband for the first time, and the deep, evil whispering voice in which he revealed his secret to her ... the final pursuit of the devil-worshippers to the great altar-stone in the mountains ... the death of the resurrected one.

Almost a skeleton in fact now, riddled by bullets and shot from the weapons of the doctor and his neighbours, the dead one crumbled and fell from his seat on the altar-stone. And as those eyes glazed in second death the deep voice boomed out in a prayer to Sathanas. The lich crawled across the ground to the ritual fire, drew painfully erect, and tottered into the flames. And as it stood weaving for a moment in the blaze the lips moved again in infernal prayer, and the eyes implored not the skies, but the earth. The ground opened in a final flash of fire, and the charred corpse fell through. The Master claimed his own ...

It was grotesque, almost a fairy-tale in its triteness. When the film had flickered off and the orchestra blared the opening for the next 'flesh-show' we rose in our seats, conscious once more of our surroundings. The rest of the mongrel audience seemed to be in a stupor almost equal to our own. Wide-eyed Japanese sat staring in the darkness; Filipinos muttered covertly to one another; even the drunken labourers seemed incapable of greeting the 'Grand Opening' with their usual ribald hoots.

Trite and grotesque the plot of the film may have been, but the actor who played the lead had instilled it with ghastly reality. He *had* been dead; his eyes *knew*. And the voice was the voice of Lazarus awakened.

Les and I had no need to exchange words. We both felt it. I followed him silently as he went up the stairs to the manager's office.

Edward Relch was glowering over the desk. He showed no pleasure at seeing us barge in. When Les asked him where he had procured the film for this evening and what its name was, he opened his mouth and emitted a cascade of curses.

We learned that *Return to the Sabbath* had been sent over by a cheap agency from out Inglewood way, that a Western had been expected, and the 'damned foreign junk' substituted by mistake. A hell of a picture this was, for a girl-show! Gave the audience the lousy creeps, and it wasn't even in English! Stinking imported films!

It was some time before we managed to extract the name of the agency from the manager's profane lips. But five minutes after that, Les Kincaid was on the phone speaking to the head of the agency; an hour later we were out at the office. The next morning Kincaid went in to see the big boss, and the following day I was told to announce for publication that Karl Jorla, the Austrian horror-star, had been signed by cable to our studio; and he was leaving at once for the United States.

III

I printed these items, gave all the build-up I could. But after the initial announcements I was stopped dead. Everything had happened too swiftly; we knew nothing about this man Jorla, really. Subsequently cables to Austrian and German studios failed to disclose any information about the fellow's private life. He had evidently never played in any film prior to *Return to the Sabbath*. He was utterly unknown. The film had never been shown widely abroad, and it was only by mistake that the Inglewood agency had obtained a copy and run it here in the United States. Audience reaction could not be learned, and the film was not scheduled for general release unless English titles could be dubbed in.

I was up a stump. Here we had the 'find' of the year, and I couldn't get enough material out to make it known!

We expected Karl Jorla to arrive in two weeks however. I was told to get to work on him as soon as he got in, then flood the news agencies with stories. Three of our best writers were working on a special production for him already; the Big Boss meant to handle it himself. It would be similar to the foreign film, for that 'return from the dead' sequence must be included.

Jorla arrived on October 7th. He put up at a hotel; the studio sent down its usual welcoming committee, took him out to the lot for formal testing, then turned him over to me.

I met the man for the first time in the little dressing-room they had assigned him. I'll never forget that afternoon of our first meeting, or my first sight of him as I entered the door.

What I expected to see I don't know. But what I did see amazed me. For Karl Jorla was the dead-alive man of the screen in *life*.

The features were not fretted, of course. But he was tall, and almost as cadaverously thin as in his role; his face was pallid, and his eyes blue-circled. And the eyes were the dead eyes of the movie; the deep, *knowing* eyes!

The booming voice greeted me in hesitant English. Jorla smiled with his lips at my obvious discomfiture, but the expression of the eyes never varied in their alien strangeness.

Somewhat hesitantly I explained my office and my errand. 'No pub-leecity,' Jorla intoned. 'I do not weesh to make known what is affairs of mine own doeeng.'

I gave him the usual arguments. How much he understood I cannot say, but he was adamant. I learned only a little; that he had been born in Prague, lived in wealth until the upheavals of the European depression, and entered film work only to please a director friend of his. This director had made the picture in which Jorla played, for private showings only. By mischance a print had been released and copied for general circulation. It had all been a mistake. However, the American film offer had come opportunely, since Jorla wanted to leave Austria at once.

'After the feelm app-ear, I am in bad lights weeth my – friends,' he explained slowly. 'They do not weesh it to be shown, that cere-monee.'

'The Black Mass?' I asked. 'Your *friends*?'

'Yes. The wor-ship of Lucifer. It was real, you know.'

Was he joking? No – I couldn't doubt the man's sincerity. There was no room for mirth in those alien eyes. And then I knew what he meant, what he so casually revealed. He had been a devil-worshipper himself – he and that director. They had made the film and meant it for private display in their own occult circles. No wonder he sought escape abroad!

It was incredible, save that I knew Europe, and the dark Northern mind. The worship of Evil continues today in Budapest, Prague, Berlin. And he, Karl Jorla the horror-actor, admitted to being one of them!

'What a story!' I thought. And then I realized that it could, of course, never be printed. A horror-star admitting belief in the parts he played? Absurd!

All the features about Boris Karloff played up the fact that he was a gentle man who found true peace in raising a small garden. Lugosi was pictured as a sensitive neurotic, tortured by the roles he played in the films. Atwill was a socialite and a stage star. And Peter Lorre was always written up as being gentle as a lamb, a quiet student whose ambition was to play comedy parts.

No, it would never do to break the story of Jorla's devil-worship. And he was so damnably reticent about his private affairs!

I sought out Kincaid after the termination of our unsatisfactory interview. I told him what I had encountered and asked for advice. He gave it.

'The old line,' he counselled. 'Mystery man. We say nothing about him until the picture is released. After that I have a hunch things will work out for themselves. The fellow is a marvel. So don't bother about stories until the film is canned.'

Consequently I abandoned publicity efforts in Karl Jorla's direction. Now I am very glad I did so, for there is no one to remember his name, or suspect the horror that was soon to follow.

IV

The script was finished. The front office approved. Stage Four was under construction; the casting director got busy. Jorla was at the studio every day; Kincaid himself was teaching him English. The part was one in which very few words were needed, and Jorla proved a brilliant pupil, according to Les.

But Les was not as pleased as he should have been about it all. He came to me one day about a week before production and unburdened himself. He strove to speak lightly about the affair, but I could tell that he felt worried.

The gist of his story was very simple. Jorla was behaving strangely. He had had trouble with the front office; he refused to give the studio his living address, and it was known that he had checked out from his hotel several days after first arriving in Hollywood.

Nor was that all. He wouldn't talk about his part, or volunteer any information about interpretation. He seemed to be quite uninterested – admitting frankly to Kincaid that his only reason for signing a contract was to leave Europe.

He told Kincaid what he had told me – about the devil-worshippers. And he hinted at more. He spoke of being followed, muttered about 'avengers' and 'hunters who waited'. He seemed to feel that the witch-cult was angry at him for the violation of secrets, and held him responsible for the release of *Return to the Sabbath*. That, he explained, was why he would not give his address, nor speak of his past life for publication. That is why he must use very heavy make-up in his film debut here. He felt at times as though he were being watched, or followed. There were many foreigners here ... too many.

'What the devil can I do with a man like that?' Kincaid exploded, after he had explained this to me. 'He's insane, or a fool. And I confess that he's too much like his screen character to please me. The damned casual way in which he professes to have dabbled in devil-worship and sorcery! He believes all this, and – well, I'll tell you the truth I came here today because of the last thing he spoke of to me this morning.

'He came down to the office, and at first when he walked in I didn't know him. The dark glasses and muffler helped, of course, but he himself had changed. He was trembling, and walked with a stoop. And when he spoke his voice was like a groan. He showed me – this.'

Kincaid handed me the clipping. It was from the London *Times*, through European press dispatches. A short paragraph, giving an account of the death of Fritz Ohmmen, the Austrian film director. He had been found strangled in a Paris garret, and his body had been frightfully mutilated; it mentioned an inverted cross branded on his stomach above the ripped entrails. Police were seeking the murderer ...

I handed the clipping back in silence. 'So what?' I asked. But I had already guessed his answer.

'Fritz Ohmmen,' Kincaid said, slowly, 'was the director of the picture in which Karl Jorla played, the director, who with Jorla, knew the devil-worshippers. Jorla says that he fled to Paris, and that *they* sought him out.'

I was silent.

'Mess,' grunted Kincaid. 'I've offered Jorla police protection, and he's refused. I can't coerce him under the terms of our contract. As long as he plays the part, he's secure with us. But he has the jitters. And I'm getting them.'

He stormed on. I couldn't help him. I sat thinking of Karl Jorla, who believed in devil-gods, worshipped, and betrayed them. And I could have smiled at the absurdity of it all if I hadn't seen the man on the screen and watched his evil eyes. He *knew*! It was then that I began to feel thankful we had not given Jorla any publicity. I had a hunch.

During the next few days I saw Jorla but seldom. The rumours, however, began to trickle in. There had been an influx of foreign 'sightseers' at the studio gates. Someone had attempted to crash through the barriers in a racing-car. An extra in a mob scene over on Lot Six had been found carrying an automatic beneath his vest; when apprehended he had been lurking under the executive office windows. They had taken him down to headquarters, and so far the man had refused to talk. He was a German ...

Jorla came to the studios every day in a shuttered car. He was bundled up to the eyes. He trembled constantly. His English lessons went badly. He spoke to no one. He had hired two men to ride with him in his car. They were armed.

A few days later news came that the German extra had talked. He was evidently a pathological case ... he babbled wildly of a 'Black Cult of Lucifer' known to some of the foreigners around town. It was a secret society purporting to worship the Devil, with vague connections in the mother countries. He had been 'chosen' to avenge a wrong. More than that he dared not say, but he did give an address where the police might find cult headquarters. The place, a dingy house in Glendale, was quite deserted, of course. It was a queer old house with a secret cellar beneath the basement, but everything seemed to have been abandoned. The man was being held for examination by an alienist.

I heard this report with deep misgivings. I knew something of Los Angeles and Hollywood's heterogeneous foreign population! God knows. Southern California has attracted mystics and occultists from all over the world. I've even heard rumours about stars being mixed up in unsavoury secret societies, things one would never dare to admit in print. And Jorla was afraid.

That afternoon I tried to trail his black car as it left the studio for his mysterious home, but I lost the track in the winding reaches of Topanga Canyon. It had disappeared into the secret twilight of the purple hills, and I knew then that there was nothing I could do. Jorla had his own defences, and if they failed, we at the studio could not help.

That was the evening he disappeared. At least he did not show up the next morning at the studio, and production was to start in two days. We heard about it. The boss and Kincaid were frantic. The police were called in, and I did my best to hush things up. When Jorla did not appear the following morning I went to Kincaid and told him about my following the car to Topanga Canyon. The police went to work. Next morning was production.

We spent a sleepless night of fruitless vigil. There was no word. Morning came, and there was unspoken dread in Kincaid's eyes as he faced me across the office table. Eight o'clock. We got up and walked silently across the lot to the studio cafeteria. Black coffee was badly needed, we hadn't had a police report for hours. We passed Stage Four, where the Jorla crew was at work. The noise of hammers was mockery. Jorla, we felt, would never face a camera today, if ever.

Bleskind, the director of the untitled horror opus, came out of the Stage office as we passed.

His paunchy body quivered as he grasped Kincaid's lapels and piped, 'Any news?'

Kincaid shook his head slowly. Bleskind thrust a cigar into his tense mouth.

'We're shooting ahead,' he snapped. 'We'll shoot around Jorla. If he doesn't show up when we finish the scenes in which he won't appear, we'll get another actor. But we can't wait.' The squat director bustled back to the Stage.

Moved by a sudden impulse, Kincaid grasped my arm and propelled me after Bleskind's waddling form.

'Let's see the opening shots,' he suggested. 'I want to see what kind of story they've given him.'

We entered Stage Four.

A Gothic Castle, the ancestral home of Baron Ulmo. A dark, gloomy stone crypt of spidery horror. Cobwebbed, dust-shrouded, deserted by men and given over to the rats by day and the unearthly horrors that crept by night. An altar stood by the crypt, an altar of evil, the great black stone on which the ancient Baron Ulmo and his devil-cult had held their sacrifices. Now, in the pit beneath the altar, the Baron lay buried. Such was the legend.

According to the first shot scheduled, Sylvia Channing, the heroine, was exploring the castle. She had inherited the place and taken it over with her young husband. In this scene she was to see the altar for the first time, read the inscription on its base. This inscription was to prove an unwitting invocation, opening up the crypt beneath the altar and awakening Jorla, as Baron Ulmo, from the dead. He was to rise from the crypt then, and walk. It was at this point that the scene would terminate, due to Jorla's strange absence.

The setting was magnificently handled. Kincaid and I took our places beside Director Bleskind as the shot opened. Sylvia Channing walked out on the set; the signals were given, lights flashed and the action began.

It was pantomimic. Sylvia walked across the cob-webbed floor, noticed the altar, examined it. She stooped to read the inscription, then whispered it aloud. There was a drone, as the opening of the altar-crypt was mechanically begun. The altar swung aside, and the black gaping pit was revealed. The upper cameras swung to Sylvia's face. She was to stare at the crypt in horror, and she did it most magnificently. In the picture she would be watching Jorla emerge.

Bleskind prepared to give the signal to cut action. Then——

Something emerged from the crypt!

It was dead, that thing – that horror with a mask of faceless flesh. Its lean body was clothed in rotting rags, and on its chest was a bloody crucifix, inverted – carved out of dead flesh. The eyes blazed loathsomely. It was Baron Ulmo, rising from the dead. *And it was Karl Jorla!*

The make-up was perfect. His eyes were dead, just as in the other film. The lips seemed shredded again, the mouth even more ghastly in its slitted blackness. And the touch of the bloody crucifix was immense.

Bleskind nearly swallowed his cigar when Jorla appeared. Quickly, he controlled himself, silently signalled the men to proceed with the shooting. We strained forward, watching every move, but Les Kincaid's eyes held a wonder akin to my own.

Jorla was acting as never before. He moved slowly, as a corpse must move. As he raised himself from the crypt, each tiny effort seemed to cause him utter agony. The scene was soundless; Sylvia had fainted. But Jorla's lips moved, and we heard a faint whispering murmur which heightened the horror. Now the grisly cadaver was almost half out of the crypt. It strained upward, still murmuring. The bloody crucifix of flesh gleamed redly on the chest ... I thought of the one found on the body of the murdered foreign director, Fritz Ohmmen, and realized where Jorla had gotten the idea.

The corpse strained up ... it was to rise now ... up ... and then, with a sudden rictus, the body stiffened and slid back into the crypt.

Who screamed first I do not know. But the screaming continued after the prop-boys had rushed to the crypt and looked down at what lay within.

When I reached the brink of the pit I screamed, too.

For it was utterly empty.

V

I wish there were nothing more to tell. The papers never knew. The police hushed things up. The studio is silent, and the production was dropped immediately. But matters did not stop there. There was a sequel to that horror on Stage Four.

Kincaid and I cornered Bleskind. There was no need of any explanation, how could what we had just seen be explained in any sane way?

Jorla had disappeared; no one had let him into the studio; no make-up man had given him his attention. Nobody had seen him enter the crypt. He had appeared in the scene, then disappeared. The crypt was empty.

These were the facts. Kincaid told Bleskind what to do. The film was developed immediately, though two of the technicians fainted. We three sat in the projection booth and watched the morning's rushes flicker across the screen. The sound-track was specially dubbed in.

That scene – Sylvia walking and reading the incantation – the pit opening – and God, when *nothing* emerged!

Nothing but that great red scar suspended in midair – that great inverted crucifix cut in bleeding flesh; no Jorla visible at all! That bleeding cross in the air, and then the mumbling...

Jorla – the thing – whatever it was – had mumbled a few syllables on emerging from the crypt. The sound-track had picked them up. And we couldn't see anything but that scar; yet we heard Jorla's voice now coming from nothingness. We heard what he kept repeating, as he fell back into the Crypt.

It was an address in Topanga Canyon.

The lights flickered on, and it was good to see them. Kincaid phoned the police and directed them to the address given on the sound-track.

We waited, the three of us, in Kincaid's office, waited for the police call. We drank, but did not speak. Each of us was thinking of Karl Jorla the devil-worshipper who had betrayed his faith; of his fear of vengeance. We thought of the director's death, and the bloody crucifix on his chest; remembered Jorla's disappearance. And then that ghastly ghost-thing on the screen, the bloody thing that hung in mid-air as Jorla's voice groaned the address...

The phone rang.

I picked it up. It was the police department. They gave their report. I fainted.

It was several minutes before I came to. It was several more minutes before I opened my mouth and spoke.

'They've found Karl Jorla's body at the address given on the screen,' I whispered. 'He was lying dead in an old shack up in the hills. He had been – murdered. There was a bloody cross, inverted on his chest. They think it was the work of some fanatics, because the place was filled with books on sorcery and Black Magic. They say——'

I paused. Kincaid's eyes commanded. 'Go on.'

'They say,' I murmured, 'that Jorla had been dead for at least three days.'

Hothouse

Sydney J. Bounds

For eleven miles after leaving Bredan village, the tarmac road wound between hedgerows that screened distant cows and lonely trees. Farther on, Howard Parker glimpsed a pair of open wrought-iron gates and slowed his car. Approaching them, he read a name-plate: *The Plantation*, and swung between the gates, following the drive up to the house. He switched off the motor and climbed stiffly from behind the wheel.

The house was big and old, in need of repair. Parker climbed stone steps and hammered twice with a rusty iron knocker, then waited, looking about him. The grounds were wooded, extensive, and in need of care. It was so quiet that he became aware of his own breathing; and, self-conscious, he adjusted his knitted-wool tie and buttoned the cord jacket.

A tall, lugubrious-faced man wearing an apron came round a corner of the house from the direction of the gardens. 'Yes, sir? Can I help you?'

Parker offered a pasteboard card which the man scrutinized.

' "Organic Fertilizers ..." The Colonel told me to expect you. This way, sir.'

Parker followed the man round the outside of the house, along a flagstoned veranda with cobwebs between the pillars, towards a large domed building. Weak sunlight glinted off hundreds of glass panes; the interior lay hidden behind a dense panoply of broad green leaves. The woodwork had been newly painted.

Heat leaked out as the door opened. Beyond was a kind of air-lock and another door. When this opened, heat struck like the blast from a furnace.

Parker's mouth gaped involuntarily to suck in a lungful of damp, scent-laden air. He stepped into a green gloom of steamed-over windows, moved between giant sprays of fern and hanging vines and bamboo stems. Exotic flowers blazed magenta and yellow-on-white and violet-blue, hiding an array of metal pipes.

In a central clearing was a wicker chair in which an old man reclined; with faded hair and limp moustache he appeared Dresden-fragile, dehydrated. Palm leaves sheltered and almost obscured him. The sharply-pointed spines of woody canes threatened his translucent flesh like a battery of hypodermic needles.

'This is Mr Parker, Colonel. Representing Organic Fertilizers.'

Colonel West stared with intense, brooding eyes, gestured with a bony finger. 'Sit down, Mr Parker. A drink for our guest, Johns. You will take port, sir?'

Parker collapsed into a wicker seat, mopping sweat, his clothes sticking to him. 'A long one, please – plenty of lemonade.'

The door opened with a swirl of humid air, closed again.

'You are looking at my life's work,' Colonel West said. 'I've hunted plants all over the tropics, learnt a few things, too. Now I've retired, it pleases me to sit among the things I enjoy. There's more to plants than you might think, Mr Parker.'

Johns returned bearing a tall glass on a silver tray. Parker, wilting, took it and sipped gratefully.

'Borneo,' the Colonel continued reminiscently. 'I remember the Monkeycups there – a pitcher plant. The pitcher leaves fill with rain water in which insects drown. The plant absorbs the insects. Ingenious really.

'You can have no grasp of the prolificity of plants unless you've been in a rain forest. A path will be grown over as fast as you clear it. Stand still for only a few minutes and you can see them grow. Plenty of sun, plenty of rain . . . and, of course, natural fertilizers. Organic. Plants need that. Animals drop where they die, the ground absorbs their juices, plants grow.'

Colonel West relaxed, the intenseness faded from his eyes.

'It is discourteous to keep you here so long, Mr Parker. Excuse an old man's rambling. I need manure and I've no faith in chemicals. You can supply a range of organic fertilizers?'

Parker loosened his tie desperately, gasping, 'Made up to your requirements.'

'I want blood – can't beat blood for healthy plants. How do you sell it?'

'By the hundredweight. Balanced compounds, unless otherwise specified.'

'What kind of blood?'

'Bullocks, calves, sheep or pigs.'

'I'll take five hundredweight initially. Compound. Bullocks' blood, thirty per cent.'

Parker drained his glass, scribbled a notation with sweaty fingers. 'Thirty per cent blood . . . thank you, sir.' He rose, dodging vines.

'I'll arrange delivery for next week.'

He jerked open the door and stumbled into fresh air, gasping with relief.

Three months passed before Parker called again at *The Plantation*, in answer to a fresh inquiry from the Colonel. The grounds appeared even more neglected, the house even more run down. As he used the iron knocker, flakes of rust fell away.

Worry deepened the lines on Johns's lugubrious face.

'I'm glad to see you, sir. The Colonel doesn't leave the hothouse at all these days – you're the first visitor in over a month. 'Perhaps –' Johns hesitated. 'You'll notice a difference. I'm afraid he's not long to go.'

They moved along the flagstoned path, weeds growing between cracks. The domed greenhouse sparkled in sunlight, a cherished island in a sea of neglect.

Although Parker anticipated the heat as the inner door opened, it still hit him. He stepped into the aquarium-gloom, confronting a barrage of giant fronds studded with blood-red and yellow and violet. He couldn't see the Colonel at first, so buried was he under foliage, shrouded by a curtain of vines. The cloying scent of blooms in that damp heat made Parker gag.

He fumbled his way to a seat opposite the Colonel, a frail figure with waxen skin.

'My plants are doing well, young man. A good mixture your people made up. I'm pleased with it – pleased with you.'

Johns returned with port and lemon and Parker drank thirstily. He watched fascinated as spiked stems drooped and hovered above the Colonel, settled on his bare skin like insects coming to rest.

Colonel West seemed not to notice. 'The orchids are doing especially well. Heat. Water. Fertilizer. The reason I asked you to call – I want another five hundredweight delivered as soon as you can. Stick to bullocks' blood, but double the amount this time. Sixty per cent blood. You can do that?'

'Of course, sir.' Parker made a note. 'I suggest not too near the stems.'

The brooding eyes flashed. 'Don't tell me how to feed plants!' He sank back, exhausted.

Parker said, mildly alarmed, 'I'm sorry, sir. Of course you know best ... Perhaps I'm tiring you?'

The Colonel barked a laugh. 'Johns been worrying you, has he? He's a bit of an old maid. Take no notice – I don't intend to die!'

Parker gulped the rest of his drink. 'Delivery in three to four days, sir – and thank you.'

He hurried to escape, feeling uncomfortable in a way that had nothing to do with the temperature.

Parker forgot about Colonel West until the laboratory asked him to look in to check the result of the new mixture. Passing close to Bredan he decided, reluctantly, that he'd best get it over with. He followed the tarmac road to *The Plantation*, drove between the still-open gates and stopped in front of the house.

A gloomy silence hung over the grounds. He climbed the steps and used the knocker; no one came. Finally he tried the door and it swung open at his touch.

'Mr Johns?'

His voice echoed emptily in the hall. Unmarked dust lay on the floor. The air smelt musty, as though the house had been deserted for some time.

Parker waited, uncertain, then walked round the side of the house towards the greenhouse. He saw immediately some broken panes, a tangle of creepers thrusting out. A solid wall of green leaves prevented him from seeing inside.

The outer door opened easily; the heat was no more than a gentle warmth. He had to exert force on the inner door and, when it gave, the stink hit him. He peered through a jungle of leaves and creepers, bamboo stems and exotic blossoms.

'Colonel? Colonel West?'

It seemed idiotic to call out. No one could be in there now. Johns would never have left without a powerful motive.

But some inner unease prompted Parker to push forward, force a passage through the wild and tangled growth. He brushed aside ferns and palm leaves and advanced towards the centre of the forest of plants.

He saw the wicker chair and, in it, a figure reclining motionless, smothered beneath a network of lianas.

'Colonel West!'

The still figure made no reply. Parker pushed closer, frowning. The body of the Colonel was bloated, the flesh tinged with green. Long, sharp spines pierced his skin, reaching to the veins. Parker detected a faint pulse.

The eyes moved, watching him. The lips parted in a smug smile.

The October Game

Ray Bradbury

He put the gun back into the bureau drawer and shut the drawer.

No, not that way. Louise wouldn't suffer that way. She would be dead and it would be over and she wouldn't suffer. It was very important that this thing have, above all, duration. Duration through imagination. How to prolong the suffering? How, first of all, to bring it about? Well.

The man standing before the bedroom mirror carefully fitted his cuff-links together. He paused long enough to hear the children run by swiftly on the street below, outside this warm two-storey house; like so many grey mice the children, like so many leaves.

By the sound of the children you knew the calendar day. By their screams you knew what evening it was. You knew it was very late in the year. October. The last days of October, with white bone masks and cut pumpkins and the smell of dropped candle fat.

No. Things hadn't been right for some time. October didn't help any. If anything it made things worse. He adjusted his black bow-tie. If this were spring, he nodded slowly, quietly, emotionlessly, at his image in the mirror, then there might be a chance. But tonight all the world was burning down into ruin. There was no green of spring, none of the freshness, none of the promise.

There was a soft running in the hall. 'That's Marion,' he told himself. 'My little one. All eight quiet years of her. Never a word. Just her luminous grey eyes and her wondering little mouth.' His daughter had been in and out all evening, trying on various masks, asking him which was most terrifying, most horrible. They had both finally decided on the skeleton mask. It was 'just awful!' It would 'scare the beans' from people!

Again he caught the long look of thought and deliberation he gave himself in the mirror. He had never liked October. Ever since he first lay in the autumn leaves before his grandmother's house many years ago and heard the wind and saw the empty trees. It had made him cry, without a reason. And a little of that sadness returned each year to him. It always went away with spring.

But, it was different tonight. There was a feeling of autumn coming to last a million years.

There would be no spring.

He had been crying quietly all evening. It did not show, not a vestige of it, on his face. It was all somewhere hidden, but it wouldn't stop.

A rich syrupy smell of candy filled the bustling house. Louise had laid out apples in new skins of caramel, there were vast bowls of punch fresh mixed, stringed apples in each door, scooped, vented pumpkins, peering triangularly from each cold window. There was a waiting water tub in the centre of the living-room, waiting, with a sack of apples nearby, for bobbling to begin. All that was needed was the catalyst, the inpouring of children, to start the apples bobbling, the string apples to penduluming in the crowded doors, the candy to vanish, the halls to echo with fright or delight, it was all the same.

Now, the house was silent with preparation. And just a little more than that.

Louise had managed to be in every room save the room he was in today. It was her very fine way of intimating, Oh look, Mich, see how busy I am! So busy that when you walk into a room *I'm* in there's always something I need to do in *another* room! Just see how I dash about!

For a while he had played a little game with her, a nasty childish game. When she was in the kitchen then he came to the kitchen, saying, 'I need a glass of water.' After a moment, him standing, drinking water, she like a crystal witch over the caramel brew bubbling like a prehistoric mudpot on the stove, she said, 'Oh, I must light the window pumpkins!' and she rushed to the living-room to make the pumpkins smile with light. He came after her, smiling, 'I must get my pipe.' 'Oh, the cider!' she had cried, running to the dining-room. 'I'll check the cider,' he had said. But when he tried following she ran to the bathroom and locked the door.

He stood outside the bath door, laughing strangely and senselessly, his pipe gone cold in his mouth, and then, tired of the game, but stubborn, he waited another five minutes. There was not a sound from the bath. And lest she enjoy in any way knowing that he waited outside, irritated, he suddenly jerked about and walked upstairs, whistling merrily.

At the top of the stairs he had waited. Finally he had heard the bath door unlatch and she had come out and life below-stairs had resumed, as life in a jungle must resume once a terror has passed on away and the antelope return to their spring.

Now, as he finished his bow-tie and put on his dark coat there was a mouse-rustle in the hall. Marion appeared in the door, all skeletonous in her disguise.

'How do I look, Papa?'

'Fine!'

From under the mask, blonde hair showed. From the skull sockets small blue eyes smiled. He sighed. Marion and Louise, the two silent denouncers of his virility, his dark power. What alchemy had there been in Louise that took the dark of a dark man and bleached and bleached the dark brown eyes and black black hair and washed and bleached the ingrown baby all during the period before birth until the child was born, Marion, blonde, blue-eyed, ruddy-cheeked? Sometimes he suspected that Louise had conceived the child as an idea, completely asexual, an immaculate conception of contemptuous mind and cell. As a firm rebuke to him she had produced a child in her *own* image, and, to top it, she had somehow *fixed* the doctor so he shook his head and said, 'Sorry, Mr Wilder, your wife will never have another child. This is the *last* one.'

'And I wanted a boy,' Mich had said, eight years ago.

He almost bent to take hold of Marion now, in her skull mask. He felt an inexplicable rush of pity for her, because she had never had a father's love, only the crushing, holding love of a loveless mother. But most of all he pitied himself, that somehow he had not made the most of a bad birth, enjoyed his daughter for herself, regardless of her not being dark and a son and like himself. Somewhere he had missed out. Other things being equal, he would have loved the child. But Louise hadn't wanted a child, anyway, in the first place. She had been frightened of the idea of birth. He had forced the child on her, and from that night, all through the year until the agony of birth itself, Louise had lived in another part of the house. She had expected to die with the forced child. It had been very easy for Louise to hate this husband who so wanted a son that he gave his only wife over to the mortuary.

But – Louise had lived. And in triumph! Her eyes, the day he came to the hospital, were cold. I'm alive, they said. And I have a *blonde* daughter! Just look! And when he had put out a hand to touch, the mother had turned away to conspire with her new pink daughter-child – away from that dark forcing murderer. It had all been so beautifully ironic. His selfishness deserved it.

But now it was October again. There had been other Octobers and when he thought of the long winter he had been filled with horror year after year to think of the endless months mortared into the house by an insane fall of snow, trapped with a woman and child, neither of whom loved him, for months on end. During the eight years there had been respites. In spring and summer you got out, walked, picnicked; these were desperate solutions to the desperate problem of a hated man.

But, in winter, the hikes and picnics and escapes fell away with the leaves. Life, like a tree, stood empty, the fruit picked, the sap run to earth. Yes, you invited people in, but people were hard to get in winter with blizzards and all. Once he had been clever enough to save for a Florida trip. They had gone south. He had walked in the open.

But now, the eighth winter coming, he knew things were finally at an end. He simply could not wear this one through. There was an acid walled off in him that slowly had eaten through tissue and tissue over the years, and now, tonight, it would reach the wild explosive in him and all would be over.

There was a mad ringing of the bell below. In the hall, Louise went to see. Marion, without a word, ran down to greet the first arrivals. There were shouts and hilarity.

He walked to the top of the stairs.

Louise was below, taking wraps. She was tall and slender and blonde to the point of whiteness, laughing down upon the new children.

He hesitated. What was all this? The years? The boredom of living? Where had it gone wrong? Certainly not with the birth of the child alone. But it had been a symbol of all their tensions, he imagined. His jealousies and his business failures and all the rotten rest of it. Why didn't he just turn, pack a suitcase, and leave? No. Not without hurting Louise as much as she had hurt him. It was simple as that. Divorce wouldn't hurt her at all. It would simply be an end to numb indecision. If he thought divorce would give her pleasure in any way he would stay married the rest of his life to her, for damned spite. No, he must hurt her. Figure some way, perhaps to take Marion away from her, legally. Yes. That was it. That would hurt most of all. To take Marion away.

'Hello down there!' He descended the stairs, beaming.

Louise didn't look up.

'Hi, Mr Wilder!'

The children shouted, waved, as he came down.

By ten o'clock the doorbell had stopped ringing, the apples were bitten from stringed doors, the pink child faces were wiped dry from the apple bobbing, napkins were smeared with caramel and punch, and he, the husband, with pleasant efficiency had taken over. He took the party right out of Louise's hands. He ran about talking to the twenty children and the twelve parents who had come and were happy with the special spiked cider he had fixed them. He supervised PIN THE TAIL ON THE DONKEY, SPIN THE BOTTLE, MUSICAL CHAIRS, and all the rest, midst fits of shouting laughter. Then, in the triangular-eyed pumpkin shine, all house lights out, he cried, 'Hush! Follow me!' he said, tiptoeing towards the cellar.

The parents on the outer periphery of the costumed riot, commented to each other, nodding at the clever husband, speaking to the lucky wife. How *well* he got on with children, they said.

The children crowded after the husband, squealing.

'The cellar!' he cried. 'The tomb of the witch!'

More squealing. He made a mock shiver. 'Abandon hope all ye who enter here!'

The parents chuckled.

One by one the children slid down a slide which Mich had fixed up from lengths of table-section, into the dark cellar. He hissed and shouted ghastly utterances after them. A wonderful wailing filled the dark pumpkin-lighted house. Everybody talked at once. Everybody but Marion. She had gone through all the party with a minimum of sound or talk; it was all inside her, all the excitement and joy. What a little troll, he thought. With a shut mouth and shiny eyes she had watched her own party, like so many serpentines, thrown before her.

Now, the parents. With laughing reluctance they slid down the short incline, uproarious, while little Marion stood by, always wanting to see it all, to be last. Louise went down without his help. He moved to aid her, but she was gone even before he bent.

The upper house was empty and silent in the candleshine.

Marion stood by the slide. 'Here we go,' he said, and picked her up.

They sat in a vast circle in the cellar. Warmth came from the distant bulk of the furnace. The chairs stood on a long line down each wall, twenty squealing children, twelve rustling relatives, alternately spaced, with Louise down at the far end, Mich up at this end, near the stairs. He peered but saw nothing. They had all groped to their chairs, catch-as-you-can in the blackness. The entire programme from here on was to be enacted in the dark, he as Mr Interlocutor. There was a child scampering, a smell of damp cement, and the sound of the wind out in the October stars.

'Now!' cried the husband in the dark cellar. 'Quiet!'

Everybody settled.

The room was black black. Not a light, not a shine, not a glint of an eye.

A scraping of crockery, a metal rattle.

'The witch is dead,' intoned the husband.

'Eeeeeeeeeeeee,' said the children.

'The witch is dead, she has been killed, and here is the knife she was killed with.'

He handed over the knife. It was passed from hand to hand, down and around the circle, with chuckles and little odd cries and comments from the adults.

'The witch is dead, and this is her head,' whispered the husband, and handed an item to the nearest person.

'Oh, I know how this game is played,' some children cried, happily, in the dark. 'He gets some old chicken innards from the icebox and hands them around and says, "These are her innards!" And he makes a clay head and passes it for her head, and passes a soup-bone for her arm. And he takes a marble and says, "This is her eye!" And he takes some corn and says, "This is her teeth!" And he takes a sack of plum pudding and gives that and says, "This is her stomach!" I know how *this* is played!'

'Hush, you'll spoil everything,' some girl said.

'The witch came to her, and this is her arm,' said Mich.

'Eeeee!'

The items were passed and passed, like hot potatoes, around the circle. Some children screamed, wouldn't touch them. Some ran from their chairs to stand in the centre of the cellar until the grisly items had passed.

'Aw, it's only chicken insides,' scoffed a boy. 'Come back, Helen!'

Shot from hand to hand, with small scream after scream, the items went down the line, down, down, to be followed by another and another.

'The witch cut apart, and this is her heart,' said the husband.

Six or seven items moving at once through the laughing, trembling dark.

Louise spoke up. 'Marion, don't be afraid; it's only play.'

Marion didn't say anything.

'Marion?' asked Louise. 'Are you afraid?'

Marion didn't speak.

'She's all right,' said the husband. 'She's not afraid.'

On and on the passing, the screams, the hilarity.

The autumn wind sighed about the house. And he, the husband, stood at the head of the dark cellar, intoning the words handing out the items.

'Marion?' asked Louise again, from far across the cellar.

Everybody was talking.

'Marion?' called Louise.

Everybody quieted.

'Marion, answer me, are you afraid?'

Marion didn't answer.

The husband stood there, at the bottom of the cellar steps.

Louise called, 'Marion, are you there?'

No answer. The room was silent.

'Where's Marion?' called Louise.

'She was here,' said a boy.

'Maybe she's upstairs.'

'Marion!'

No answer. It was quiet.

Louise cried out, 'Marion, Marion!'

'Turn on the lights,' said one of the adults.

The items stopped passing. The children and adults sat with the witch's items in their hands.

'No.' Louise gasped. There was a scraping of her chair, wildly, in the dark. 'No. Don't turn on the lights, don't turn on the lights, oh God, God, God, don't turn them on, please, please *don't* turn on the lights, *don't*!' Louise was shrieking now. The entire cellar froze with the scream.

Nobody moved.

Everybody sat in the dark cellar, suspended in the suddenly frozen task of this October game; the wind blew outside, banging the house, the smell of pumpkins and apples filled the room with the smell of the objects in their fingers while one boy cried, 'I'll go upstairs and look!' and he ran upstairs hopefully and out around the house, four times around the house, calling 'Marion, Marion, Marion!' over and over and at last coming slowly down the stairs into the waiting, breathless cellar and saying to the darkness, 'I can't find her.'

Then ... some idiot turned on the lights.

The Horror at Chilton Castle

Joseph Payne Brennan

I had decided to spend a leisurely summer in Europe, concentrating, if at all, on genealogical research. I went first to Ireland, journeying to Kilkenny, where I unearthed a mine of legend and authentic lore concerning my remote Irish ancestors, the O'Braonains, chiefs of Ui Duach in the ancient kingdom of Ossory. The Brennans (as the name was later spelled) lost their estates in the British confiscation under Thomas Wentworth, Earl of Strafford. The thieving Earl, I am happy to report, was subsequently beheaded in the Tower.

From Kilkenny I travelled to London and then to Chesterfield in search of maternal ancestors: the Holborns, Wilkersons, Searles, etc. Incomplete and fragmentary records left many great gaps, but my efforts were moderately successful and at length I decided to go farther north and visit the vicinity of Chilton Castle, seat of Robert Chilton-Payne, the twelfth Earl of Chilton. My relationship to the Chilton-Paynes was a most distant one, and yet there existed a tenuous thread of past connection and I thought it would amuse me to glimpse the castle.

Arriving in Wexwold, the tiny village near the castle, late in the afternoon, I engaged a room at the Inn of the Red Goose – the only one there was – unpacked and went down for a simple meal consisting of a small loaf, cheese and ale.

By the time I finished this stark and yet satisfying repast, darkness had set in, and with it came wind and rain.

I resigned myself to an evening at the inn. There was ale enough and I was in no hurry to go anywhere.

After writing a few letters, I went down and ordered a pint of ale. The taproom was almost deserted; the bartender, a stout gentleman who seemed forever on the point of falling asleep, was pleasant but taciturn, and at length I fell to musing on the strange and frightening legend of Chilton Castle.

There were variations of the legend, and without doubt the original tale had been embroidered down through the centuries but the essential outline of the story concerned a secret room somewhere in the castle. It was said that this room contained a terrifying spectacle which the Chilton-Paynes were obliged to keep hidden from the world.

Only three persons were ever permitted to enter the room: the presiding Earl of Chilton, the Earl's male heir and one other person designated by the Earl. Ordinarily this person was the Factor of Chilton Castle. The room was entered only once in a generation; within three days after the male heir came of age, he was conducted to the secret room by the Earl and the Factor. The room was then sealed and never opened again until the heir conducted his own son to the grisly chamber.

According to the legend, the heir was never the same person again after entering the room. Invariably he would become sombre and withdrawn; his countenance would acquire a brooding, apprehensive expression which nothing could long dispel. One of the earlier earls of Chilton had gone completely mad and hurled himself from the turrets of the castle.

Speculation about the contents of the secret room had continued for centuries. One version of the tale described the panic-stricken flight of the Gowers, with armed enemies hot on their flagging heels. Although there had been bad blood between the Chilton-Paynes and the Gowers, in their desperation the Gowers begged for refuge at Chilton Castle. The Earl gave them entry, conducted them to a hidden room and left with a promise that they would be shielded from their pursuers. The Earl kept his promise; the Gowers' enemies were turned away from the Castle, their murderous plans unconsummated. The Earl, however, simply left the Gowers in the locked room to starve to death. The chamber was not opened until thirty years later, when the Earl's son finally broke the seal. A fearful sight met his eyes. The Gowers had starved to death slowly, and at the last, judging by the appearance of the mingled skeletons, had turned to cannibalism.

Another version of the legend indicated that the secret room had been used by medieval earls as a torture chamber. It was said that the ingenious instruments of pain were yet in the room and that these lethal apparatuses still clutched the pitiful remains of their final victims, twisted fearfully in their last agonies.

A third version mentioned one of the female ancestors of the Chilton-Paynes, Lady Susan Glanville, who had reputedly made a pact with the Devil. She had been condemned as a witch but had somehow managed to escape the stake. The date and even the manner of her death were unknown, but in some vague way the secret room was supposed to be connected with it.

As I speculated on these different versions of the gruesome legend, the storm increased in intensity. Rain drummed steadily against the leaded windows of the inn and now I could occasionally hear the distant mutter of thunder.

Glancing at the rain-streaked panes, I shrugged and ordered another pint of ale.

I had the fresh tankard halfway to my lips when the taproom door burst open, letting in a blast of wind and rain. The door was shut and a tall figure, muffled to the ears in a dripping greatcoat, moved to the bar. Removing his cap, he ordered brandy.

Having nothing better to do, I observed him closely. He looked about seventy, grizzled and weather-worn, but wiry, with an appearance of toughness and determination. He was frowning, as if absorbed in thinking through some unpleasant problem, yet his cold blue eyes inspected me keenly for a brief but deliberate interval.

I could not place him in a tidy niche. He might be a local farmer, and yet I did not think that he was. He had a vague aura of authority, and though his clothes were certainly plain, they were, I thought, somewhat better in cut and quality than those of the local countrymen I had observed.

A trivial incident opened a conversation between us. An unusually sharp crack of thunder made him turn towards the window. As he did so, he accidentally brushed his wet cap on to the floor. I retrieved it for him; he thanked me; and then we exchanged commonplace remarks about the weather.

I had an intuitive feeling that although he was normally a reticent individual, he was presently wrestling with some severe problem which made him want to hear a human voice. Realizing there was always the possibility that my intuition might, for once, have failed me, I nevertheless babbled on about my trip, about my genealogical researches in Kilkenny, London and Chesterfield, and finally about my distant relationship to the Chilton-Paynes and my desire to get a good look at Chilton Castle.

Suddenly I found that he was gazing at me with an expression which, if not fierce, was disturbingly intense. An awkward silence ensued. I coughed, wondering uneasily what I had said to make those cold blue eyes stare at me so fixedly.

At length he became aware of my growing embarrassment. 'You must excuse me for staring,' he apologized, 'but something you said ...' He hesitated. 'Could we perhaps take that table?' He nodded towards a small table which sat half in shadow in the far corner of the room.

I agreed, mystified but curious, and we took our drinks to the secluded table.

He sat frowning for a minute, as if uncertain how to begin. Finally he introduced himself as William Cowath. I gave him my name and still he hesitated. At length he took a swallow of brandy and then looked straight at me. 'I am,' he stated, 'the Factor at Chilton Castle.'

I surveyed him with surprise and renewed interest. 'What an agreeable coincidence!' I exclaimed. 'Then perhaps tomorrow you could arrange for me to have a look at the castle?'

He seemed scarcely to hear me. 'Yes, yes, of course,' he replied absently.

Puzzled and a bit irritated by his air of detachment, I remained silent.

He took a deep breath and then spoke rapidly, running some of his words together. 'Robert Chilton-Payne, the Twelfth Earl of Chilton, was buried in the family vaults one week ago. Frederick, the young heir and now Thirteenth Earl, came of age just three days ago. Tonight it is imperative that he be conducted to the secret chamber!'

I gaped at him in incredulous amazement. For a moment I had an idea that he had somehow heard of my interest in Chilton Castle and was merely 'pulling my leg' for amusement in the belief that I was the greenest of gullible tourists.

But there could be no mistaking his deadly seriousness. There was not the faintest suspicion of humour in his eyes.

I groped for words. 'It seems so strange – so unbelievable! Just before you arrived, I had been thinking about the various legends connected with the secret room.'

His cold eyes held my own. 'It is not legend that confronts us; it is fact.'

A thrill of fear and excitement ran through me. 'You are going there – tonight?'

He nodded. 'Tonight. Myself, the young Earl – and one other.'

I stared at him.

'Ordinarily,' he continued, 'the Earl himself would accompany us. That is the custom. But he is dead. Shortly before he passed away, he instructed me to select someone to go with the young Earl and myself. That person must be male – and preferably of the blood.'

I took a deep drink of ale and said not a word.

He continued. 'Besides the young Earl, there is no one at the Castle save his elderly mother, Lady Beatrice Chilton, and an ailing aunt.'

'Who could the Earl have had in mind?' I enquired cautiously.

The Factor frowned. 'There are some distant male cousins residing in the country. I have an idea he thought at least one of them might appear for the obsequies. But not one of them did.'

'That was most unfortunate!' I observed.

'Extremely unfortunate. And I am therefore asking you, as one of the blood, to accompany the young Earl and myself to the secret room tonight!'

I gulped like a bumpkin. Lightning flashed against the windows and

I could hear rain swishing along the stones outside. When feathers of
ice stopped fluttering in my stomach, I managed a reply.

'But I ... that is ... my relationship is so very remote! I am "of the
blood" by courtesy only, you might say. The strain in me is so very
diluted.'

He shrugged. 'You bear the name. And you possess at least a few
drops of the Payne blood. Under the present urgent circumstances, no
more is necessary. I am sure that the old Earl would agree with me,
could he still speak. You will come?'

There was no escaping the intensity, the pressure, of those cold blue
eyes. They seemed to follow my mind about as it groped for further
excuses.

Finally, inevitably it seemed, I agreed. A feeling grew in me that the
meeting had been preordained, that somehow I had always been
destined to visit the secret chamber in Chilton Castle.

We finished our drinks and I went up to my room for rainwear. When
I descended, suitably attired for the storm, the obese bartender was
snoring on his stool, in spite of savage crashes of thunder which had now
become almost incessant. I envied him as I left the cosy room with
William Cowath.

Once outside, my guide informed me that we would have to go on
foot to the castle. He had purposely walked down to the inn, he
explained, in order that he might have time and solitude to straighten
out in his own mind the things which he would have to do.

The sheets of heavy rain, the strong wind and the roar of thunder
made conversation difficult. I walked Indian-fashion behind the Factor,
who took enormous strides and appeared to know every inch of the way
in spite of the darkness.

We walked only a short distance down the village street and then
struck into a side road, which very soon dwindled to a footpath made
slippery and treacherous by the driving rain.

Abruptly the path began to ascend; the footing became more
precarious. It was at once necessary to concentrate all one's attention
on one's feet. Fortunately, the flashes of lightning were frequent.

It seemed to me that we had been walking for an hour – actually, I
suppose, it was only a few minutes – when the Factor finally stopped.

I found myself standing beside him on a flat, rocky plateau. He
pointed up an incline which rose before us. 'Chilton Castle,' he said.

For a moment I saw nothing in the unrelieved darkness. Then the
lightning flashed.

Beyond high battlemented walls, fissured with age, I glimpsed a great
square Norman castle with four rectangular corner towers pierced by
narrow window apertures which looked like evil slitted eyes. The huge,
weathered pile was half-covered by a mantle of ivy which appeared

more black than green.

'It looks incredibly old!' I commented.

William Cowath nodded. 'It was begun in 1122 by Henry de Montargis.' Without another word he started up the incline.

As we approached the castle wall, the storm grew worse. The slanting rain and powerful wind now made speech all but impossible. We bent our heads and staggered upwards.

When the wall finally loomed in front of us, I was amazed at its height and thickness. It had been constructed, obviously, to withstand the best siege guns and battering rams which its early enemies could bring to bear on it.

As we crossed a massive, timbered drawbridge, I peered down into the black ditch of a moat but I could not be sure whether there was water in it. A low, arched gateway gave access through the wall to an inner, cobblestoned courtyard. This courtyard was entirely empty, save for rivulets of rushing water.

Crossing the cobblestones with swift strides, the Factor led me to another arched gateway in yet another wall. Inside was a second, smaller yard and beyond spread the ivy-clutched base of the ancient keep itself.

Traversing a darkened, stone-flagged passage, we found ourselves facing a ponderous door, age-blackened oak reinforced with pitted bands of iron. The Factor flung open this door and there before us was the great hall of the castle.

Four long, hand-hewn tables with their accompanying benches stretched almost the entire length of the hall. Metal torch brackets, stained with age, were affixed to sculptured stone columns which supported the roof. Ranged around the walls were suits of armour, heraldic shields, halberds, pikes and banners – the accumulated trophies and prizes of bloody centuries when each castle was almost a kingdom unto itself. In flickering candlelight, which appeared to be the only illumination, the grim array was eerily impressive.

William Cowath waved a hand. 'The holders of Chilton lived by the sword for many centuries.'

Walking the length of the great hall, he entered another dim passageway. I followed silently.

As we strode along, he spoke in a subdued voice. 'Frederick, the young heir, does not enjoy robust health. The shock of his father's death was severe – and he dreads tonight's ordeal, which he knows must come.'

Stopping before a wooden door embellished with carved fleurs-de-lis and metal scrollwork, he gave me a shadowed, enigmatic glance and then knocked.

Someone enquired who was there and he identified himself. Presently a heavy bolt was lifted and the door opened.

If the Chilton-Paynes had been stubborn fighters in their day, the warrior blood appeared to have become considerably diluted in the veins of Frederick, the young heir and now Thirteenth Earl. I saw before me a thin, pale-complexioned young man whose dark sunken eyes looked haunted and fearful. His dress was both theatrical and anachronistic: a dark green velvet coat and trousers, a green satin waist-band, flounces of white lace at neck and wrists.

He beckoned us in as if with reluctance and closed the door. The walls of the small room were entirely covered with tapestries depicting the hunt or medieval battle scenes. A draught of air from a window or other aperture made them undulate constantly; they seemed to have a disturbing life of their own. In one corner of the room there was an antique canopy bed; in another a large writing-table with an agate lamp.

After a brief introduction which included an explanation of how I came to be accompanying them, the Factor enquired if his Lordship was ready to visit the chamber.

Although he was wan in any case, Frederick's face now lost every last trace of colour. He nodded, however, and preceded us into the passage.

William Cowath led the way; the young Earl followed him, and I brought up the rear.

At the far end of the passage, the Factor opened the door of a cobwebbed supply room. Here he secured candles, chisels, a pick and a sledgehammer. After packing these into a leather bag which he slung over one shoulder, he picked up a faggot torch which lay on one of the shelves in the room. He lit this, then waited while it flared into a steady flame. Satisfied with this illumination, he closed the room and beckoned for us to continue after him.

Nearby was a descending spiral of stone steps. Lifting his torch, the factor started down. We trailed after him wordlessly.

There must have been fifty steps in that long, downward spiral. As we descended, the stones became wet and cold; the air, too, grew colder, but the cold was not of the type that refreshes. It was too laden with the smell of mould and dampness.

At the bottom of the steps we faced a tunnel, pitch-black and silent.

The Factor raised his torch. 'Chilton Castle is Norman, but is said to have been reared over a Saxon ruin. It is believed that the passageways in these depths were constructed by the Saxons.' He peered, frowning, into the tunnel. 'Or by some still earlier folk.'

He hesitated briefly, and I thought he was listening. Then, glancing round at us, he proceeded down the passage.

I walked after the Earl, shivering. The dead, icy air seemed to pierce to the pith of my bones. The stones underfoot grew slippery with a film of slime. I longed for more light, but there was none save that cast by the flickering, bobbing torch of the Factor.

Partway down the passage he paused, and again I sensed that he was listening. The silence seemed absolute, however, and we went on.

The end of the passage brought us to more descending steps. We went down some fifteen and entered another tunnel which appeared to have been cut out of the solid rock on which the castle had been reared. White-crusted nitre clung to the walls. The reek of mould was intense. The icy air was fetid with some other odour which I found peculiarly repellent, though I could not name it.

At last the Factor stopped, lifted his torch and slid the leather bag from his shoulder.

I saw that we stood before a wall made of some kind of building stone. Though damp and stained with nitre, it was obviously of much more recent construction than anything we had previously encountered.

Glancing round at us, William Cowath handed me the torch. 'Keep a good hold on it, if you please. I have candles, but ...'

Leaving the sentence unfinished, he drew the pick from his sling bag and began an assault on the wall. The barrier was solid enough but after he had worked a hole in it, he took up the sledgehammer and quicker progress was made. Once I offered to take up the hammer while he held the torch, but he only shook his head and went on with his work of demolition.

All this time the young Earl had not spoken a word. As I looked at his tense white face, I felt sorry for him, in spite of my own mounting trepidation.

Abruptly there was silence as the Factor lowered the sledge-hammer. I saw that a good two feet of the lower wall remained.

William Cowath bent to inspect it. 'Strong enough,' he commented cryptically. 'I will leave that to build on. We can step over it.'

For a full minute he stood looking silently into the blackness beyond. Finally, shouldering his bag, he took the torch from my hand and stepped over the ragged base of the wall. We followed suit.

As I entered that chamber, the fetid odour which I had noticed in the passage seemed to overwhelm us. It washed around us in a nauseating wave and we all gasped for breath.

The Factor spoke between coughs. 'It will subside in a minute or two. Stand near the aperture.'

Although the reek remained repellently strong, we could at length breathe more freely.

William Cowath lifted his torch and peered into the black depths of the chamber. Fearfully, I gazed around his shoulder.

There was no sound and at first I could see nothing but nitre-encrusted walls and wet stone floor. Presently, however, in a far corner, just beyond the flickering halo of the faggot torch, I saw two tiny, fiery spots of red. I tried to convince myself that they were two red jewels, two rubies, shining in the torchlight.

But I knew at once – I *felt* at once – what they were. They were two red eyes and they were watching us with a fierce, unwavering stare.

The Factor spoke softly. 'Wait here.'

He crossed towards the corner, stopped halfway and held out his torch at arm's length. For a moment he was silent. Finally he emitted a long, shuddering sigh.

When he spoke again, his voice had changed. It was only a sepulchral whisper. 'Come forward,' he told us in that strange, hollow voice.

I followed Frederick until we stood at either side of the Factor.

When I saw what crouched on a stone bench in that far corner, I felt sure that I would faint. My heart literally stopped beating for perceptible seconds. The blood left my extremities; I reeled with dizziness. I might have cried out, but my throat would not open.

The entity which rested on that stone bench was like something that had crawled up out of hell. Piercing, malignant red eyes proclaimed that it had a terrible life, and yet that life sustained itself in a black, shrunken, half-mummified body which resembled a disinterred corpse. A few mouldy rags clung to the cadaver-like frame. Wisps of white hair sprouted out of its ghastly grey-white skull. A red smear or blotch of some sort covered the wizened slit which served it as a mouth.

It surveyed us with a malignancy which was beyond anything merely human. It was impossible to stare back into those monstrous red eyes. They were so inexpressibly evil, one felt that one's soul would be consumed in the fires of their malevolence.

Glancing aside, I saw that the Factor was now supporting Frederick. The young heir had sagged against him, staring fixedly at the fearful apparition with terror-glazed eyes. In spite of my own sense of horror, I pitied him.

The Factor sighed again and then he spoke once more in that low, sepulchral voice.

'You see before you,' he told us, 'Lady Susan Glanville. She was carried into this chamber and fettered to the wall in 1473.'

A thrill of horror coursed through me; I felt that we were in the presence of malign forces from the Pit itself.

To me the hideous thing had appeared sexless, but at the sound of its name, the ghastly mockery of a grin contorted the puckered, red-smeared mouth.

I noticed now for the first time that the monster actually was secured to the wall. The great double shackles were so blackened with age, I had not noticed them before.

The Factor went on, as if he spoke by rote. 'Lady Glanville was a maternal ancestor of the Chilton-Paynes. She had commerce with the

Devil. She was condemned as a witch but escaped the stake. Finally her own people forcibly overcame her. She was brought in here, fettered and left to die.'

He was silent a moment and then continued. 'It was too late. She had already made a pact with the Powers of Darkness. It was an unspeakably evil thing and it has condemned her issue to a life of torment and nightmare, a lifetime of terror and dread.'

He swung his torch towards the blackened, red-eyed thing. 'She was a beauty once. She hated death. She feared death. And so she finally bartered her own immortal soul – and the bodies of her issue – for eternal earthly life.'

I heard his voice as in a nightmare; it seemed to be coming from an infinite distance.

He went on. 'The consequences of breaking the pact are too terrible to describe. No descendant of hers has ever dared to do so, once the forfeit is known. And so she has bided here for these nearly five hundred years.'

I had thought he was finished, but he resumed. Glancing upwards, he lifted his torch towards the roof of that accursed chamber. 'This room,' he said, 'lies directly underneath the family vaults. Upon the death of the Earl, the body is ostensibly left in the vaults. When the mourners have gone, however, the false bottom of the vault is thrust aside and the body of the Earl is lowered into this room.'

Looking up, I saw the square rectangle of a trap-door above.

The Factor's voice now became barely audible. 'Once every generation Lady Glanville feeds – on the corpse of the deceased Earl. It is a provision of that unspeakable pact which cannot be broken.'

I knew now – with a sense of horror utterly beyond description – whence came that red smear on the repulsive mouth of the creature before us.

As if to confirm his words, the Factor lowered his torch until its flame illuminated the floor at the foot of the stone bench where the vampiric monster was fettered.

Strewn about the floor were the scattered bones and skull of an adult male, red with fresh blood. And at some distance were other human bones, brown and crumbling with age.

At this point, Frederick began to scream. His shrill, hysterical cries filled the chamber. Although the Factor shook him roughly, his terrible shrieks continued, terror-filled, nerve-shaking.

For moments the corpse-like thing on the bench watched him with its frightful red eyes. It uttered sound finally, a kind of animal squeal which might have been intended as laughter.

Abruptly then, and without any warning, it slid from the bench and lunged towards the young Earl. The blackened shackles which fettered it to the wall permitted it to advance only a yard or two. It was pulled back sharply; yet it lunged again and again, squealing with a kind of hellish glee which stirred the hair on my head.

William Cowath thrust his torch towards the monster, but it continued to lunge at the end of its fetters. The nightmare room resounded with the Earl's screams and the creature's horrible squeals of bestial laughter. I felt that my own mind would give way unless I escaped from that anteroom of hell.

For the first time during an ordeal which would have sent any lesser man fleeing for his life and sanity, the iron control of the Factor appeared to be shaken. He looked beyond the wild lunging thing towards the wall where the fetters were fastened.

I sensed what was in his mind. Would those fastenings hold, after all these centuries of rust and dampness?

On a sudden resolve he reached into an inner pocket and drew out something which glittered in the torchlight. It was a silver crucifix. Striding forward, he thrust it almost into the twisted face of the leaping monstrosity which had once been the ravishing Lady Susan Glanville.

The creature reeled back with an agonized scream which drowned out the cries of the Earl. It cowered on the bench, abruptly silent and motionless, only the pulsating of its wizened mouth and the fires of hatred in its red eyes giving evidence that it still lived.

William Cowath addressed it grimly. 'Creature of hell! If ye leave that bench 'ere we quit this room and seal it once again, I swear that I shall hold this cross against ye!'

The thing's red eyes watched the Factor with an expression of abysmal hatred which no combination of mere letters could convey. They actually appeared to glow with fire. And yet I read in them something else – fear.

I suddenly became aware that silence had descended on that room of the damned. It lasted only a few moments. The Earl had finally stopped screaming, but now came something worse. He began to laugh.

It was only a low chuckle, but it was somehow worse than all his screams. It went on and on, softly, mindlessly.

The Factor turned, beckoning me towards the partially demolished wall. Crossing the room, I climbed out. Behind me the Factor led the young Earl, who shuffled like an old man, chuckling to himself.

There was then what seemed an interminable interval, during which the factor carried back a sack of mortar and a keg of water which he had previously left somewhere in the tunnel. Working by torchlight, he prepared the cement and proceeded to seal up the chamber, using the same stones which he had displaced.

While the Factor laboured, the young Earl sat motionless in the tunnel, chuckling softly.

There was silence from within. Once, only, I heard the thing's fetters clank against the stone.

At last the Factor finished and led us back through those nitre-stained passageways and up the icy stairs. The Earl could scarcely ascend; with difficulty the Factor supported him from step to step.

Back in his tapestry-panelled chamber, Frederick sat on his canopy bed and stared at the floor, laughing quietly. With horror I noticed that his black hair had actually turned grey. After persuading him to drink a glass of liquid which I had no doubt contained a heavy dose of sedative, the Factor managed to get him stretched out on the bed.

William Cowath then led me to a nearby bedchamber. My impulse was to rush from that hellish pile without delay, but the storm still raged and I was by no means sure I could find my way back to the village without a guide.

The Factor shook his head sadly. 'I fear his Lordship is doomed to an early death. He was never strong and tonight's events may have deranged his mind ... may have weakened him beyond hope of recovery.'

I expressed my sympathy and horror. The Factor's cold blue eyes held my own 'It may be,' he said, 'that in the event of the young Earl's death, you yourself might be considered ...' He hesitated. 'Might be considered,' he finally concluded, 'as one somewhat in line of succession.'

I wanted to hear no more. I gave him a curt goodnight, bolted the door after him and tried – quite unsuccessfully – to salvage a few minutes' sleep.

But sleep would not come. I had feverish visions of that red-eyed thing in the sealed chamber escaping its fetters, breaking through the wall and crawling up those icy, slime-covered stairs ...

Even before dawn I softly unbolted my door and, like a marauding thief, crept shivering through the cold passageways and the great deserted hall of the castle. Crossing the cobbled courtyards and the black moat, I scrambled down the incline towards the village.

Long before noon I was well on my way to London. Luck was with me; the next day I was on a boat bound for the Atlantic run.

I shall never return to England. I intend always to keep Chilton Castle and its permanent occupant at least an ocean away.

An American Organ

Anthony Burgess

There was no room for a piano in our new (and very small) house, but my fingers itched for a keyboard of some kind. 'Why,' suggested my wife, 'don't you get a piece of wood and plane it smooth and then paint it with black and white keys? You could practise on that.' Practise, yes, but practise for what? Practise for the time when we should have a piano again? There wasn't room, you see: it was a very small house, stiflingly small but all that we could get. And afford. There might have been room, of course, if we weren't so cluttered up with all my wife's mother's furniture and knick-knacks. When I walked through the house it rang with jolting china dogs. 'Throw some of these things away,' I advised. 'Sell them. Then we could have money enough for a second-hand piano. Also, indeed, space.' But I had uttered blasphemy. Sell the precious things which had belonged to her dear, dead mother: How could I be so heartless?

But one day, when my wife was out at work (I wasn't allowed to work, you see, because I was considered unstable. There was something wrong, said the doctors, but they couldn't say what.) As I say, when my wife was out at work, I took a big bag and in it placed several china dogs, some china pigs at a china trough, an ebony elephant or so and some genuine genuine Sèvres, then caught the bus to Chipping Wellwater. There was a filthy antique shop there, filthy, one that no self-respecting American tourist (and all American tourists are self-respecting) would dream of entering. For that matter, I never saw anyone go in. But, this grey filthy day, I went in and encountered a strong dusty smell of antiquity. There was, I could see at once, nothing of either value or beauty in the outer room of the shop – gilt-framed Holman Hunts, a huge anonymous engraving of a highwayman in the stocks and a pretty serving-wench stealing keys to free him from a snoring bellied beadle, a tray or two, hideous Victorian vases, copies of *An Illustrated History of England*, a broken bellows, a tarnished brass fire-screen, unknown decaying filthy wrack of the nineteenth-century sea hiding behind the above, and other just presentable things.

   The shop's owner came out from a sort of den, shambling like a den-living animal. He was chewing bread and wore a dirty waistcoat, was unwashed and so myopic that he had to come straight up to me, as though we were television actors about to start a long scene together. 'These,' I said, opening the bag. He grumbled, handling them myopically, bringing them up to his face as though he were testing their usefulness as disguises. He belched at the china pigs, a sweet strong tea belch. He said:

   'Can't give you no money because I've got no money. Not one penny in till or pocket I haven't got. Not that any of these is worth all that much.'

   'Oh, come,' I said. 'The Sèvres, for instance ...'

   He held a dinner plate to his face as though draining gravy from it. 'You can take your choice of the shop. Whatever takes your fancy to the value, no more. I know what these is worth.' I went into the inner room of the shop. There I saw an American organ. I treadled the pedals, feeding it wind, as I lifted the lid. Yellow keys. Hungrily I fingered them. I played the Pilgrims' Chorus from *Tannhauser*. The shopman came in, suspicious. 'You can play that all right,' he said grudgingly.

   'Could I have it, do you think?' I said. 'That Sèvres is worth far, far more.'

   'Nice bit of stuff, that is,' he said, as if it were a girl. 'Had many an offer for that, I have.'

   'I don't believe it,' I said. 'Who would want an American organ nowadays?'

   'Religious people,' said the man. 'You,' he added, coming close and examining my face as if for a particular minute scar he'd been told about, 'don't look religious to me.' That seemed, somehow, to decide matters for him. 'You can have it,' he said. 'Take it away.'

   This man had a nephew who ran a small coal business. This nephew expressed himself willing, when I crossed the road to see him, to take both me and the organ back to our little house. He had, he said, to deliver a ton or so beyond my village. He would do the job for five bob. He did it for five bob. There were we, the organ and I, sitting on the coal-sacks under the drizzle, bumping home proudly. I even played a bumping tune – to the astonishment of odd cyclists and pedestrians – as we went: the big tune from the Prelude to Act III of *Lohengrin*, the bridal tune.

   The coalman helped me hump the organ into the house. We scratched the walls a bit and sent a china dog flying (there were still plenty of china dogs). The organ wouldn't go anywhere, that was the trouble. We tried the little dining-room, but it looked silly sitting in the middle of the carpet. Besides, *she* wouldn't have it, I knew she wouldn't. The sitting-room, bunged up with her mother's massive lounge suite, that wouldn't do either. The coalman had a cleft palate. 'Ghe ghlanghin,' he suggested, several times. 'The what?' I said. 'Ghe ghlanghin.' That seemed the only place, the landing. So we heaved the organ up the stairs, scratching and tearing the wallpaper. We got it up, though, yes we did. Panting, we stood and surveyed it, standing on the landing outside the tiny bathroom. Passing it to get into the bathroom was difficult, and the spare room was blocked for ever. As for a stool to sit on to play the organ, that was simple: my wife's dressing-table stool did fine. 'Ghray uh homehing,' snorted the coalman. I played him something. I played the melody from the slow movement of Beethoven's *Pathétique*. He called for more, a most musical coalman, but I wanted to clean the organ up and provide a little surprise for my wife when she came home. So I sent him away with half-a-crown for his help in humping the thing.

My wife was home at five. 'A surprise,' I said. 'Come upstairs and see the little surprise.'

'You're filthy,' said my wife. 'What on earth have you been doing?' With her sharp woman's eyes she saw that the wallpaper of the little hallway had been torn in places. Suspicious, she looked farther, but could find only further tears and scratches. The house was so full of china, especially china dogs, that it would be many days, perhaps weeks, before she would find that anything was missing. Still, she railed at me for a time, but did not go on too long, for she knew I was not well. She just went into the kitchen for a while for a little cry. 'Come on up,' I invited. 'Come and see what I've got.' Then I thought that it would be an even bigger surprise if she just heard the music, strange music coming from the upper part of the house, before she actually saw the source of the music. Up I went, then, sat on her dressing-table stool, and, in the autumn twilight, began to play. I played the Andante Cantabile horn tune from Tchaikovsky's Fifth Symphony. Diddidy DA daaaaaa, diddidy DOO daaaaaa ... It sounded well. It drew my wife running upstairs.

'What?' she said. 'OH.' She knew I was happy, something for my fingers to do. She was perhaps not pleased, but she knew I was happy. 'Very hard,' she said, 'to get in and out of the bathroom.'

'You can squeeze past,' I said. 'You better than me. You're very slim.' She had, indeed, a lovely slim figure.

'Now,' she said. 'Just listen to me. Wouldn't it be far nicer if you could sit and play that organ *clean*? Clean and tidy, ummm? You're covered with coal and fluff and dust and things.'

'It was the coalman,' I said. Diddidy DA daaaaaa ...

'Stoke up the boiler,' she said. 'Have a nice hot bath. Put on some clean clothes. Then you can give me a lovely organ recital, clean.'

'Yes,' I said. Full of love and gratitude, I rose from the stool and embraced her, filthy as I was.

'Oh,' she said, 'don't. Oh, you're covered with dust. It's all over me now.'

I went down to the kitchen stove and filled it full of coke. I opened and shut things and soon had a great draught lashing the flames. The water began to sing and bubble. 'When you've finished,' she said, 'I'll have a bath too. There's going to be plenty of hot water.'

'You have it first,' I said.

'No, you first. Then you can play the organ to me while I'm having mine.'

I had a good hot bath, then I changed my clothes. I found a clean shirt with a stiff collar. Downstairs my wife was putting something in the oven for our evening meal. She was a good wife and there would never be another like her. I dressed myself very formally, in a dark suit with black shoes. I was to give an organ recital. 'Come up now,' I called down to my wife. 'I've cleaned the bath and there's still plenty of lovely hot water.'

After a few minutes she came upstairs. Meanwhile I sat at the organ, still in my stiff clothes. I tried to imagine that a forest of pipes proliferated above the keyboard, rising like trees into the high air, invisible at the crown. My wife went into the bedroom and took off her clothes. She came out naked, ready for her bath. There had never been any shame between us, no nonsense about dressing-gowns. She edged past me, finding it, for all her slimness, a difficult squeeze. 'Whoops,' she said. Then she was in the bathroom, drawing water. 'What shall I play?' I asked. 'What?' she shouted. The noise of the two taps was very loud. I waited till she had turned them off, then I asked, 'What shall I play?' She was in the bath now, splashing. 'Oh,' she said, 'anything.' I remembered my triumphal journey of that morning, playing Wagner to the drizzly country sky, jolting on top of the coal-lorry. I smiled and then laughed aloud. Then I started the *Lohengrin* Act III Prelude, bridal music. She splashed away happily. Myself, I had not felt so happy for a long time. Bridal music. I stopped playing and went into the bathroom, squeezing past my lovely new organ with difficulty. I kissed the hot wet nape of her neck. 'A bride in the bath,' I said. 'Who was that man?'

'Oh, that? Smith, I think.' Like most women, she liked to read of murders.

I sat on the lavatory seat, smiling. She smiled back, glad to see me so happy, so much better, having got something I'd wanted. 'He played the organ while she was dying,' I said. 'What was the tune?'

'*Nearer, my God, to Thee*,' said my wife, sponging herself soapy.

I got up off the lavatory seat. 'How did he do it?' I asked.

'He hit her head on the bath and made her unconscious. Then he lowered her into the water and left her to drown.'

'Why did he do that?'

'The usual reason,' said my wife. 'Money. Pass me the towel. I've got soap in my eyes.'

I picked up the towel from the rail but I didn't pass it to her. Instead I took her head in both my hands. She was surprised and said, 'Don't play about. I can't see. Give me that towel.' Then, holding it firm, I cracked her head quite hard against the head of the bath. This wasn't enough, so I cracked it again. Then I let her slide into the water so that her head was covered. She was not a very tall woman and, even in that small bath, there was plenty of room. While she was bubbling away I quickly edged round my organ, sat down on the stool, treadled air into the organ's lungs, and then started to play *Nearer, my God, to Thee.* But, damn it, I couldn't think of the tune. I tried humming, I one-fingered something I thought was it, but knew it wasn't right. And, of course, no other tune would do. It had to be that, or else the whole thing was wasted. I could have cried with vexation, not knowing the tune. I went back into the bathroom, but it was obviously all too late. Everything had been wasted. I didn't know any hymns at all. That shopman had been right, saying, 'You don't look religious to me.' Anyway, what was done couldn't be undone, so I started to play, with great expression, that piece of Tchaikovsky, then some Beethoven, then various odds and ends of more modern composers. I played till the bathwater was quite cold and the food in the oven was burnt.

The Bird

Thomas Burke

It is a tale that they tell softly in Pennyfields, when the curtains are drawn and the shapes of the night are shut out ...

Those who held that Captain Chudder, S.S. *Peacock*, owners, Peter Dubbin & Co., had a devil in him, were justified. But they were nearer the truth who held that his devil was not within him, but at his side, perching at his elbow, dropping sardonic utterance in his ear; moving with him day and night and prompting him – so it was held – to frightful excesses. His devil wore the shape of a white parrot, a bird of lusty wings and the cruellest of beaks. There were those who whispered that the old man had not always been the man that his crew knew him to be: that he had been a normal, kindly fellow until he acquired his strange companion from a native dealer in the malevolent Solomons. Certainly his maniac moods dated from its purchase; and there was truth in the dark hints of his men that there was something wrong with that damned bird ... a kind of ... something you sort of felt when it looked at you or answered you back. For one thing, it had a diabolical knack of mimicry, and many a chap would cry: 'Yes, George!' or 'Right, sir!' in answer to a commanding voice which chuckled with glee as he came smartly to order. They invariably referred to it as 'that bloody bird', though actually it had done nothing to merit such opprobrium. When they thought it over calmly, they could think of no harm that it had done to them: nothing to arouse such loathing as every man on the boat felt towards it. It was not spiteful; it was not bad-tempered. Mostly it was in cheery mood and would chuckle deep in the throat, like the Captain, and echo or answer, quite pleasantly, such remarks, usually rude, as were addressed to it.

And yet ... Somehow ...

There it was. It was always there – everywhere; and in its speech they seemed to find a sinister tone which left them guessing at the meaning of its words. On one occasion, the cook, in the seclusion of the fo'c'sle, had remarked that he would like to wring its neck if he could get hold of it; but old grizzled Snorter had replied that the bird couldn't be killed.

There was something about that bird that ... well, he betted no one
wouldn't touch that bird without trouble. And a moment of panic
stabbed the crowd as a voice leapt from the sombre shadows of the
corner.

'That's the style, me old brown son. Don't try to come it with me –
what?' and ceased in a spasmodic flutter of wicked white wings.

That night, as the cook was ascending the companion, he was caught
by a huge sea, which swept across the boat from nowhere and dashed
him, head-on, below. For a week he was sick with a broken head, and
throughout that week the bird would thrust its beak to the berth where
he lay, and chortle to him:

'Yep, me old brown son. Wring his bleeding neck – what? Waltz me
around again, Willie, round and round and round!'

That is the seamen's story and, as the air of Limehouse is thick with
seamen's stories, it is not always good to believe them. But it is a widely
known fact that on the last voyage the Captain did have a devil with
him, the foulest of all devils that possess mortal men, not the devil of
slaughter, but the devil of cruelty. They were from Swatow to London,
and it was noted that he was drinking heavily ashore, and he continued
the game throughout the voyage. He came aboard from Swatow, drunk,
bringing with him a Chinese boy called Sung Dee, also drunk. The
greaser, being a big man, kicked him below, otherwise, the boat in his
charge would have gone there, and so he sat or sprawled in his cabin,
with a rum-bottle before him and, on the corner of his chair, the white
parrot, which conversed with him and sometimes fluttered on deck to
shout orders in the frightful voice of his master and chuckle to see them
momentarily obeyed.

'Yes,' repeated old man Snorter, sententiously, 'I'd run a hundred
miles 'fore I'd try to monkey with the old man or his bloody bird. There's
something about that bird ... I said so before. I 'eard a story once about
a bird. Out in T'ai-ping I 'eard it. It'll make yeh sick if I tell it ...'

Now while the Captain remained drunk in his cabin, he kept with him
for company the miserable, half-starved Chinese boy whom he had
brought aboard. And it would make others sick if the full dark tale were
told here of what the master of the *Peacock* did to that boy. You may read
of monstrosities in police reports of cruelty cases, you may read old
records of the Middle Ages, but the bestialities of Captain Chudder
could not be told in words.

His orgy of drink and delicious torture lasted till they were berthed
in the Thames, and the details remain sharp and clear in the memories
of those who witnessed it. At all the ceremonial horrors which were
wrought in that wretched cabin, the parrot was present. It jabbered to
the old man, the old man jabbered back, and gave it an occasional sip
of rum from his glass, and the parrot would mimic the boy's entreaties,

and wag a grave claw at him as he writhed under the ritual of
punishment, and when that day's ceremony was finished it would
flutter from bow to stern of the boat, its cadaverous figure stinging
the shadows with shapes of fear for all aboard, perching here,
perching there, simpering and whining in tune with Sung Dee's placid
moaning.

Placid; yes, outwardly. But the old man's wickedness had lighted a
flame beneath that yellow skin which nothing could quench, nothing
but the floods of vengeance. Had the old man been a little more
cute and a little less drunk, he might have remembered that a Chinaman
does not forget. He would have read danger in the face that was
so submissive under his devilries. Perhaps he did see it, but, because of
the rum that was in him, felt himself secure from the hate of any outcast
Chinese; knew that his victim would never once get the chance to repay
him, Captain Chudder, master of the *Peacock*, and one of the very
smartest. Sung Dee was alone and weaponless, and dare not come
aft without orders. He was master of the boat, he had a crew to help
him, and knives and guns, and he had his faithful white bird to warn
him. Too, as soon as they docked at Limehouse, he would sling him off
or arrange quick transfer to an outward boat, since he had no further
use for him.

But it happened that he made no attempt to transfer. He had
forgotten that idea. He just sat below, finished his last two bottles, paid
off his men, and then, after a sleep, went ashore to report. Having
done that, he forgot all trivial affairs, such as business, and set
himself seriously to search for amusement. He climbed St George's,
planning a real good booze-up, and the prospect that spread itself
before his mind was so compelling that he did not notice a lurking yellow
phantom that hung on his shadow. He visited the Baltic on the chance
of finding an old pal or so, and, meeting none, he called at a shipping
office in Fenchurch Street, where he picked up an acquaintance, and
they two returned eastward to Poplar, and the Phantom feet *sup-supped*
after them. Through the maze and glamour of the London streets and
traffic the shadow slid; it dodged and danced about the Captain's little
cottage in Gill Street, and when he, and others, came out and strolled
to a bar, and, later, to a music-hall, it flitted, moth-like, around
them.

Surely since there is no step in the world that has just the obvious
stealth of the Chinaman's, he must have heard those whispering feet?
Surely his path was darkened by that shadow? But no. After the music-
hall he drifted to a water-side wine-shop and then, with a bunch of
others, went wandering.

It was late. Eleven notes straggled across the waters from many grey
towers. Sirens were screeching their derisive song, and names of various

Scotch whiskies spelt themselves in letters of yellow flame along the night. Far in the darkness a voice was giving the chanty:

'What shall we do with a drunken sailor?'

The Captain braced himself up and promised himself a real glittering night of good-fellowship, and from gin-warmed bar to gin-warmed bar he roved, meeting the lurid girls of the places and taking one of them upstairs. At the last bar his friends, too, went upstairs with their ladies, and, it being then one o'clock in the morning, he brought a pleasant evening to a close at a certain house in Poplar High Street, where he took an hour's amusement by flinging half-crowns over the fan-tan table.

But always the yellow moth was near, and when, at half-past two, he came, with uncertain steps, into the sad street, now darkened and loud only with the drunken, who found unfamiliar turnings in familiar streets, and old landmarks many yards away from their rightful places, the moth buzzed closer and closer.

The Captain talked as he went. He talked of the night he had had, and the girls his hands had touched. His hard face was cracked to a meaningless smile, and he spat words at obstructive lamp posts and kerbstones, and swears dropped like toads from his lips. But at last he found his haven in Gill Street, and his hefty brother, with whom he lived when ashore, shoved him upstairs to his bedroom. He fell across the bed, and the sleep of the swinish held him fast.

The grey towers were tolling three o'clock, and the thick darkness of the water-side covered the night like a blanket. The lamps were pale and few. The waters sucked miserably at the staples of the wharves. One heard the measured beat of a constable's boot, sometimes the rattle of chains and blocks, mournful hooters, shudders of noise as engines butted lines of trucks at the shunting station.

Captain Chudder slept, breathing stertorously, mouth open, limbs heavy and nerveless. His room was deeply dark, and so little light shone on the back reaches of the Gill Street cottages that the soft raising of the window made no visible aperture. Into this blank space something rose from below, and soon it took the shape of a flat, yellow face which hung motionless, peering into the room. Then a yellow hand came through, the aperture was widened, and swiftly and silently a lithe, yellow body hauled itself up and slipped over the sill.

It glided, with outstretched hand, from the window and, the moment it touched the bed, its feeling fingers went here and there, and it stood still, gazing upon the sleep of drunkenness. Calmly and methodically a yellow hand moved to its waist and withdrew a kreese. The same hand raised the kreese and held it poised. It was long, keen, and beautifully curved, but not a ray of light was in the room to fall upon it, and the yellow hand had to feel its bright blade to find whether the curve ran from or towards it.

Then, with terrific force and speed, it came down, one – two – three. The last breath rushed from the open lips. Captain Chudder was out.

The strong yellow hand withdrew the kreese for the last time, wiped it on the coverlet of the bed, and replaced it in its home. The figure turned, like a wraith, for the window, turned for the window and found, in a moment of panic, that it knew not which way to turn. It hesitated for a moment. It thought it heard a sound at the bed. It touched the coverlet and the boots of the Captain; all was still. Stretching a hand to the wall, Sung Dee began to creep and to feel his way along. Dark as the room was, he had found his way in, without matches or illuminant. Why could he not find his way out? Why was he afraid of something?

Blank wall was all he found at first. Then his hand touched what seemed to be a picture frame. It swung and clicked and the noise seemed to echo through the still house. He moved farther, and a sharp rattle told him that he had struck the loose handle of the door. But that was of little help. He could not use the door, he knew not what perils lay behind it. It was the window he wanted – the window.

Again he heard that sound from the bed. He stepped boldly and judged that he was standing in the middle of the room. Momentarily a sharp shock surged over him. He prayed for matches, and something in his throat was almost crying, 'The window! The window!' He seemed like an island in a sea of darkness, one man surrounded by legions of immortal intangible enemies. His cold Chinese heart went hot with fear.

The middle of the room he judged, and took another step forward, a step which landed his chin sharply against the jutting edge of the mantelshelf over the fireplace. He jumped like a cat and his limbs shook, for now he had lost the door and the bed, as well as the window, and had made terrible noises which might bring disaster. All sense of direction was gone. He knew not whether to go forward or backward, to right or left. He heard the tinkle of the shunting trains, and he heard a rich voice crying something in his own tongue. But he was lapped around by darkness and terror, and a cruel fancy came to him that he was imprisoned here for ever and for ever, and that he would never escape from this enveloping, suffocating room. He began to think that——

And then a hot iron of agony rushed down his back as, sharp and clear at his elbow, came the Captain's voice:

'Get forrard, you damn lousy Chink – get forrard. Lively there! Get out of my room!'

He sprang madly aside from the voice that had been the terror of his life for so many weeks, and collided with the door; realized that he had made further fearful noises; dashed away from it and crashed into the bed; fell across it and across the warm, wet body that lay there. Every nerve in every limb of him was seared with horror at the contact, and he leapt off, kicking, biting, writhing. He leapt off, and fell against a table, which tottered, and at last fell with a stupendous crash into the fender.

'Lively, you damn Chink!' said the Captain. 'Lively, I tell yeh. Dance, d'yeh hear? I'll have yeh for this. I'll learn you something. I'll give you something with a sharp knife and a bit of hot iron, my cocky. I'll make yer yellow skin crackle, yeh damn lousy chopstick. I'll have yeh in a minute. And when I get yeh, orf with yeh clothes. I'll cut yeh to pieces I will.'

Sung Dee shrieked. He ran round and round, beating the wall with his hands, laughing, crying, jumping, while all manner of shapes arose in his path, lit by the grey light of fear. He realized that it was all up now. He cared not how much noise he made. He hadn't killed the old man; only wounded him. And now all he desired was to find the door and any human creatures who might save him from the Captain. He met the bed again, suddenly, and the tormentor who lay there. He met the upturned table and fell upon it, and he met the fireplace and the blank wall; but never, never the window or the door. They had vanished. There was no way out. He was caught in that dark room, and the Captain would do as he liked with him ... He heard footsteps in the passage and sounds of menace and alarm below. But to him they were friendly sounds, and he screamed loudly towards them.

He cried to the Captain, in his pidgin, for mercy.

'Oh, Captain – no burn me today, Captain. Sung Dee be heap good sailor, heap good servant, all same slave. Sung Dee heap plenty solly hurt Captain. Sung Dee be good boy. No do feller bad lings no feller more. O Captain. Let Sung Dee go lis time. Let Sung Dee go. O Captain!'

But 'Oh, my Gawd!' answered the Captain. 'Bless your yellow heart. Wait till I get you trussed up. Wait till I get you below. I'll learn yeh.'

And now those below came upstairs, and they listened in the passage, and for the space of a minute they were hesitant. For they heard all manner of terrible noises, and by the noises there might have been half a dozen fellows in the Captain's room. But very soon the screaming and the pattering feet were still, and they heard nothing but low moans; and at last the bravest of them, the Captain's brother, swung the door open and flashed a large lantern.

And those who were with him fell back in dumb horror, while the brother cried harshly: 'Oh! ... my ... God!' For the lantern shone on a Chinaman seated on the edge of the bed. Across his knees lay the dead body of the Captain, and the Chinaman was fondling his damp, dead face, talking baby talk to him, dancing him on his knee, and now and then making idiot moans. But what sent the crowd back in horror was that a great death-white Thing was flapping about the yellow face of the Chinaman, cackling: 'I'll learn yeh! I'll learn yeh!' and dragging strips of flesh away with every movement of the beak.

Heartburn

Hortense Calisher

The light, gritty wind of a spring morning blew in on the doctor's shining, cleared desk, and on the tall buttonhook of a man who leaned agitatedly towards him.

'I have some kind of small animal lodged in my chest,' said the man. He coughed, a slight, hollow apologia to his ailment, and sank back in his chair.

'Animal?' said the doctor, after a pause which had the unfortunate quality of comment. His voice, however, was practised, deft, coloured only with the careful suspension of judgment.

'Probably a form of newt or toad,' answered the man, speaking with clipped distaste, as if he would disassociate himself from the idea as far as possible. His face quirked with sad foreknowledge. 'Of course, you don't believe me.'

The doctor looked at him noncommittally. Paraphrased, an old refrain of the poker table leapt erratically in his mind. 'Nits' – no – 'newts and gnats and one-eyed jacks,' he thought. But already the anecdote was shaping itself, trim and perfect, for display at the clinic luncheon table. 'Go on,' he said.

'Why won't any of you come right out and say what you think!' the man said angrily. Then he flushed, not hectically, the doctor noted, but with the well-bred embarrassment of the normally reserved. 'Sorry. I didn't mean to be rude.'

'You've already had an examination?' The doctor was a neurologist, and most of his patients were referrals.

'My family doctor. I live up in Boston.'

'Did you tell him – er . . .?' The doctor sought gingerly for a phrase.

One corner of the man's mouth lifted, as if he had watched others in the same dilemma. 'I went through the routine first. Fluoroscope, metabolism, cardiograph. Even gastroscopy.' He spoke, the doctor noted, with the regrettable glibness of the patient who has shopped

'And – the findings?' said the doctor, already sure of the answer.

The man leaned forward, holding the doctor's glance with his own. A faint smile riffled his mouth. 'Positive.'

'Positive!'

'Well,' said the man, 'machines have to be interpreted after all, don't they?' He attempted a shrug, but the quick eye of the doctor saw that the movement masked a slight contortion within his tweed suit, as if the man writhed away from himself but concealed it quickly, as one masks a hiccup with a cough. 'A curious flutter in the cardiograph, a strange variation in the metabolism, an alien shadow under the fluoroscope.' He coughed again and put a genteel hand over his mouth, but this time the doctor saw it clearly – the slight, cringing motion.

'You see,' added the man, his eyes helpless and apologetic above the polite covering hand, 'it's alive. It *travels*.'

'Yes. Yes, of course,' said the doctor, soothingly now. In his mind hung the word, ovoid and perfect as a drop of water about to fall. Obsession. A beautiful case. He thought again of the luncheon table.

'What did your doctor recommend?' he said.

'A place with more resources, like the Mayo Clinic. It was then that I told him I knew what it was, as I've told you. And how I acquired it.' The visitor paused. 'Then, of course, he was forced to pretend he believed me.'

'Forced?' said the doctor.

'Well,' said the visitor, 'actually, I think he did believe me. People tend to believe anything these days. All this mass media information gives them the habit. It takes a strong individual to disbelieve evidence.'

The doctor was confused and annoyed. 'Well, what then?' he said peremptorily, ready to rise from his desk in dismissal.

Again came the fleeting bodily grimace and the quick cough. 'He – er . . . he gave me a prescription.'

The doctor raised his eyebrows, in a gesture he was swift to retract as unprofessional.

'For heartburn, I think it was,' added his visitor demurely.

Tipping back in his chair, the doctor tapped a pencil on the edge of the desk. 'Did he suggest you seek help – on another level?'

'Many have suggested it,' said the man.

'But I'm not a psychiatrist!' said the doctor irritably.

'Oh, I know that. You see, I came to you because I had the luck to hear one of your lectures at the Academy. The one on "Overemphasis on the Non-somatic Causes of Nervous Disorders." It takes a strong man to go against the tide like that. A disbeliever. And that's what I sorely need.' The visitor shuddered, this time letting the *frisson* pass uncontrolled. 'You see,' he added, thrusting his clasped hands forward on the desk, and looking ruefully at the doctor, as if he would cushion him against his next remark, 'you see – I am a psychiatrist.'

The doctor sat still in his chair.

'Ah, I can't help knowing what you are thinking,' said the man. 'I would think the same. A streamlined version of the Napoleonic delusion.' He reached into his breast pocket, drew out a wallet, and fanned papers from it on the desk.

'Never mind. I believe you!' said the doctor hastily.

'Already?' said the man sadly.

Reddening, the doctor hastily looked over the collection of letters, cards of membership in professional societies, licences, and so on – very much the same sort of thing he himself would have had to amass, had he been under the same necessity of proving his identity. Sanity, of course, was another matter. The documents were all issued to Dr Curtis Retz at a Boston address. Stolen, possibly, but something in the man's manner, in fact everything in it except his unfortunate hallucination, made the doctor think otherwise. Poor guy, he thought. Occupational fatigue, perhaps. But what a form! The Boston variant, possibly. 'Suppose you start from the beginning,' he said benevolently.

'If you can spare the time ...'

'I have no more appointments until lunch.' And what a lunch that'll be, the doctor thought, already cherishing the pop-eyed scene – Travis the clinic's director (that plethoric Nestor), and young Gruenberg (all of whose cases were unique), his hairy nostrils dilated for once in a *mise-en-scène* which he did not dominate.

Holding his hands pressed formally against his chest, almost in the attitude of one of the minor placatory figures in a *Pietà*, the visitor went on. 'I have the usual private practice,' he said, 'and clinic affiliations. As a favour to an old friend of mine, headmaster of a boys' school nearby, I've acted as guidance consultant there for some years. The school caters for boys of above average intelligence and is run along progressive lines. Nothing's ever cropped up except run-of-the-mill adolescent problems, coloured a little, perhaps, by the type of parents who tend to send their children to a school like that – people who are – well – one might say, almost tediously aware of their commitments as parents.'

The doctor grunted. He was that kind of parent himself.

'Shortly after the second term began, the head asked me to come down. He was worried over a sharp drop of morale which seemed to extend over the whole school – general inattention in classes, excited note-passing, nightly disturbances in the dorms – all pointing, he had thought at first, to the existence of some fancier than usual form of hazing, or to one of those secret societies, sometimes laughable, sometimes with overtones of the corrupt, with which all schools are familiar. Except for one thing. One after the other, a long list of boys had been sent to the infirmary by the various teachers who presided in the dining-room. Each of the boys had shown a marked debility, and what the resident doctor called "All the stigmata of pure fright. Complete unwillingness to confide." Each of the boys pleaded stubbornly for his own release, and a few broke out of their own accord. The interesting thing was that each child did recover shortly after his own release, and it was only after this that another boy was seen to fall ill. No two were afflicted at the same time.'

'Check the food?' said the doctor.

'All done before I got there. According to my friend, all the trouble seemed to have started with the advent of one boy, John Hallowell, a kid of about fifteen, who had come to the school late in the term with a history of having run away from four other schools. Records at these classed him as very bright, but made oblique references to "personality difficulties" which were not defined. My friend's school, ordinarily pretty independent, had taken the boy at the insistence of old Simon Hallowell, the boy's uncle, who is a trustee. His brother, the boy's father, is well known for his martial exploits which have nourished the tabloids for years. The mother lives mostly in France and South America. One of these perennial dryads, apparently, with a youthfulness maintained by money and a yearly immersion in the fountains of American plastic surgery. Only time she sees the boy ... Well, you can imagine. What the feature articles call a Broken Home.'

The doctor shifted in his chair and lit a cigarette.

'I won't keep you much longer,' said the visitor. 'I saw the boy.' A violent fit of coughing interrupted him. This time his curious writhing motion went frankly unconcealed. He got up from his chair and stood at the window, gripping the sill and breathing heavily until he had regained control, and went on, one hand pulling unconsciously at his collar. 'Or, at least, I think I saw him. On my way to visit him in his room I bumped into a tall red-headed boy in a football sweater, hurrying down the hall with a windbreaker and a poncho slung over his shoulder. I asked for Hallowell's room; he jerked a thumb over his shoulder at the door just behind him, and continued past me. It never occurred to me ... I was expecting some adenoidal gangler with acne ... or one of these sinister little angel faces, full of neurotic sensibility.

'The room was empty. Except for its finicky neatness, and a rather large amount of livestock, there was nothing unusual about it. The school, according to the current trend, is run like a farm, with the boys doing the chores, and pets are encouraged. There was a tank with a couple of turtles near the window, beside it another, full of newts, and in one corner a large cage of well-tended, brisk white mice. Glass cases, with carefully mounted series of lepidoptera and hymenoptera, showing the metamorphic stages, hung on the walls, and on a drawing board there was a daintily executed study of Branchippus, the "fairy shrimp".

'While I paced the room, trying to look as if I wasn't prying, a greenish little wretch, holding himself together as if he had an imaginary shawl draped around him, slunk into the half-dark room and squeaked "Hallowell?" When he saw me he started to duck, but I detained him and found that he had had an appointment with Hallowell too. When it was clear, from his description, that Hallowell must have been the redhead I'd seen leaving, the poor urchin burst into tears.

' "I'll never get rid of it now!" he wailed. From then on it wasn't hard to get the whole maudlin story. It seems that shortly after Hallowell's arrival at school he acquired a reputation for unusual proficiency with animals and for out-of-the-way lore which would impress the ingenuous. He circulated the rumour that he could swallow small animals and regurgitate them at will. No one actually saw him swallow anything, but it seems that in some mumbo-jumbo with another boy who had shown cynicism about the whole thing, it was claimed that Hallowell had, well, divested himself of something, and passed it on to the other boy, with the statement that the latter would only be able to get rid of his cargo when he in turn found a boy who would disbelieve *him*.'

The visitor paused, calmer now, and leaving the window sat down again in the chair opposite the doctor, regarding him with such fixity that the doctor shifted uneasily, with the apprehension of one who is about to be asked for a loan.

'My mind turned to the elementary sort of thing we've all done at times. You know, circle of kids in the dark, piece of cooked cauliflower passed from hand to hand with the statement that the stuff is the fresh brains of some neophyte who hadn't taken his initiation seriously. My young informer, Moulton his name was, swore however that this hysteria (and of course, that's what I thought it) was passed on singly, from boy to boy, without any such sèances. He'd been home to visit his family, who are missionaries on leave, and had been infected by his room-mate on his return to school, unaware that by this time the whole school had protectively turned believers, en masse. His own terror came, not only from his conviction that he was possessed, but from his inability to find anybody who would take his dare. And so he'd finally come to Hallowell ...

'By this time the room was getting really dark and I snapped on the light to get a better look at Moulton. Except for an occasional shudder, like a bodily tic, which I took to be the after-effects of hard crying, he looked like a healthy enough boy who'd been scared out of his wits. I remember that a neat little monograph was already forming itself in my mind, a group study on mass psychosis, perhaps, with effective anthropological references to certain savage tribes whose dances include a rite known as "eating evil".

'The kid was looking at me. "Do you believe me?" he said suddenly. "Sir?" he added, with a naïve cunning which tickled me.

' "Of course," I said, patting his shoulder absently. "In a way."

'His shoulder slumped under my hand. I felt its tremor, direct misery palpitating between my fingers.

' "I thought ... maybe for a man ... it wouldn't be ..." His voice trailed off.

' "Be the same? ... I don't know," I said slowly, for of course, I was answering, not his actual question, but the overtone of some cockcrow of meaning that evaded me.

'He raised his head and petitioned me silently with his eyes. Was it guile, or simplicity, in his look, and was it for conviction, or the lack of it, that he arraigned me? I don't know. I've gone back over what I did then, again and again, using all my own knowledge of the mechanics of decision, and I know that it wasn't just sympathy, or a pragmatic reversal of therapy, but something intimately important for me, that made me shout with all my strength – "Of course I don't believe you!"

'Moulton, his face contorted, fell forward on me so suddenly that I stumbled backwards, sending the tank of newts crashing to the floor. Supporting him with my arms, I hung on to him while he heaved, face downwards. At the same time I felt a tickling, sliding sensation in my own ear, and an inordinate desire to follow it with my finger, but both my hands were busy. It wasn't a minute till I'd gotten him on to the couch, where he drooped, a little white about the mouth, but with that chastened, purified look of the physically relieved, although he hadn't actually upchucked.

'Still watching him, I stooped to clear up the debris, but he bounded from the couch with amazing resilience.

' "I'll do it," he said.

' "Feel better?"

'He nodded, clearly abashed, and we gathered up the remains of the tank in a sort of mutual embarrassment. I can't remember that either of us said a word, and neither of us made more than a halfhearted attempt to search for the scattered pests which had apparently sought crannies in the room. At the door we parted, muttering as formal a good night as was possible between a grown man and a small boy. It wasn't until I reached my own room and sat down that I realized, not only my own extraordinary behaviour, but that Moulton, standing, as I suddenly recalled for the first time quite straight, had sent after me a look of pity and speculation.

'Out of habit, I reached into my breast pocket for my pencil, in order to take notes as fresh as possible. And then I felt it ... a skittering, sidling motion, almost beneath my hand. I opened my jacket and shook myself, thinking that I'd picked up something in the other room ... but nothing.

I sat quite still, gripping the pencil, and after an interval it came again
– an inchoate creeping, a twitter of movement almost *lackadaisical*, as of
something inching itself lazily along – but this time on my other side.
In a frenzy, I peeled off my clothes, inspected myself wildly, and
enumerating to myself a reassuring abracadabra of explanation –
skipped heartbeat, intercostal pressure of gas – I sat there naked, waiting. And after a moment, it came again, that wandering, aquatic
motion, as if something had flipped itself over just enough to make me
aware, and then settled itself, this time under the sternum, with a nudge
like that of some inconceivable foetus. I jumped up and shook myself
again, and as I did so I caught a glimpse of myself in the mirror in the
closet door. My face, my own face, was ajar with fright, and I was
standing there, hooked over, as if I were wearing an imaginary shawl.'

In the silence after his visitor's voice stopped, the doctor sat there in
the painful embarrassment of the listener who has played confessor, and
whose expected comment is a responsibility he wishes he had evaded.
The breeze from the open window fluttered the papers on the desk.
Glancing out at the clean, regular façade of the hospital wing opposite,
at whose evenly shaded windows the white shapes of orderlies and nurses
flickered in consoling routine, the doctor wished petulantly that he had
fended off the man and all his papers in the beginning. What right had
the man to arraign *him*? Surprised at his own inner vehemence, he pulled
himself together. 'How long ago?' he said at last.

'Four months.'

'And since?'

'It's never stopped.' The visitor now seemed brimming with a
tentative excitement, like a colleague discussing a mutually puzzling
case. 'Everything's been tried. Sedatives do obtain some sleep, but that's
all. Purgatives. Even emetics.' He laughed slightly, almost with pride.
'Nothing like that works,' he continued, shaking his head with the
doting fondness of a patient for some symptom which has confounded
the best of them. 'It's too cagey for that.'

With his use of the word 'it', the doctor was propelled back into that
shapely sense of reality which had gone admittedly askew during the
man's recital. To admit the category of 'it', to dip even a slightly co-
operative finger in another's fantasy, was to risk one's own equilibrium.
Better not to become involved in argument with the possessed, lest one's
own apertures of belief be found to have been left ajar.

'I am afraid,' the doctor said blandly, 'that your case is outside my
field.'

'As a doctor?' said his visitor. 'Or as a man?'

'Let's not discuss me, if you please.'

The visitor leaned intently across the desk. 'Then you admit that to
a certain extent, we *have* been——?'

'I admit nothing!' said the doctor, stiffening.

'Well,' said the man disparagingly, 'of course, that, too, is a kind of stand. The commonest, I've found.' He sighed, pressing one hand against his collarbone. 'I suppose you have a prescription too, or a recommendation. Most of them do.'

The doctor did not enjoy being judged. 'Why don't you hunt up young Hallowell?' he said, with malice.

'Disappeared. Don't you think I tried?' said his vis-à-vis ruefully. Something furtive, hope, perhaps, spread its guileful corruption over his face. 'That means you do give a certain credence——'

'Nothing of the sort!'

'Well then,' said his interrogator, turning his palms upward.

The doctor leaned forward, measuring his words with exasperation. 'Do you mean you *want* me to tell you you're crazy!'

'In my spot,' answered his visitor meekly, 'which would you prefer?'

Badgered to the point of commitment, the doctor stared back at his inconvenient Diogenes. Swollen with irritation, he was only half conscious of an uneasy, vestigial twitching of his ear muscles, which contracted now as they sometimes did when he listened to atonal music.

'O.K., O.K ... !' he shouted suddenly, slapping his hand down on the desk and thrusting his chin forward. 'Have it your own way then! I don't believe you!'

Rigid, the man looked back at him cataleptically, seeming, for a moment, all eye. Then, his mouth stretching in that medieval grimace, risorial and equivocal, whose mask appears sometimes on one side of the stage, sometimes on the other, he fell forward on the desk, with a long, mewing sigh.

Before the doctor could reach him, he had raised himself on his arms and their foreheads touched. They recoiled, staring downward. Between them on the desk, as if one of its mahogany shadows had become animate, something seemed to move – small, seal-coloured, and ambiguous. For a moment it filmed back and forth, arching in a crude, primordial inquiry; then, homing straight for the doctor, whose jaw hung down in a rictus of shock, it disappeared from view.

Sputtering, the doctor beat the air and his own person wildly with his hands, and staggered upward from his chair. The breeze blew hypnotically, and the stranger gazed back at him with such perverse calm that already he felt an assailing doubt of the lightning, untoward event. He fumbled back over his sensations of the minute before, but already piecemeal and chimerical, they eluded him now, as they might forever.

'It's unbelievable,' he said weakly.

His visitor put up a warding hand, shaking it fastidiously. '*Au contraire!*' he replied daintily, as though by the use of another language he would remove himself still further from commitment. Reaching forward, he gathered up his papers into a sheaf, and stood up, stretching himself straight with an all-over bodily yawn of physical ease that was like an affront. He looked down at the doctor, one hand fingering his wallet. 'No,' he said reflectively, 'guess not'. He tucked the papers away. 'Shall we leave it on the basis of – er – professional courtesy?' he inquired delicately.

Choking on the sludge of his rage, the doctor looked back at him, inarticulate.

Moving towards the door, the visitor paused. 'After all,' he said, 'with your connections ... try to think of it as a temporary inconvenience.' Regretfully, happily, he closed the door behind him.

The doctor sat at his desk, humped forward. His hands crept to his chest and crossed. He swallowed, experimentally. He hoped it was rage. He sat there, waiting. He was thinking of the luncheon table.

Miriam

Truman Capote

For several years, Mrs H. T. Miller had lived alone in a pleasant apartment (two rooms with kitchenette) in a remodelled brownstone near the East River. She was a widow: Mr H. T. Miller had left a reasonable amount of insurance. Her interests were narrow, she had no friends to speak of, and she rarely journeyed farther than the corner grocery. The other people in the house never seemed to notice her: her clothes were matter-of-fact, her hair iron-grey, clipped and casually waved; she did not use cosmetics, her features were plain and inconspicuous, and on her last birthday she was sixty-one. Her activities were seldom spontaneous: she kept the two rooms immaculate, smoked an occasional cigarette, prepared her own meals and tended a canary.

Then she met Miriam. It was snowing that night. Mrs Miller had finished drying the supper dishes and was thumbing through an afternoon paper when she saw an advertisement of a picture playing at a neighbourhood theatre. The title sounded good, so she struggled into her beaver coat, laced her galoshes and left the apartment, leaving one light burning in the foyer: she found nothing more disturbing than a sensation of darkness.

The snow was fine, falling gently, not yet making an impression on the pavement. The wind from the river cut only at street crossings. Mrs Miller hurried, her head bowed, oblivious as a mole burrowing a blind path. She stopped at a drugstore and bought a package of peppermints.

A long line stretched in front of the box office; she took her place at the end. There would be (a tired voice groaned) a short wait for all seats. Mrs Miller rummaged in her leather handbag till she collected exactly the correct change for admission. The line seemed to be taking its own time and, looking around for some distraction, she suddenly became conscious of a little girl standing under the edge of the marquee.

Her hair was the longest and strangest Mrs Miller had ever seen: absolutely silver-white, like an albino's. It flowed waist-length in smooth, loose lines. She was thin and fragilely constructed. There was a simple, special elegance in the way she stood with her thumbs in the pockets of a tailored plum-velvet coat.

Mrs Miller felt oddly excited, and when the little girl glanced towards her, she smiled warmly. The little girl walked over and said, 'Would you care to do me a favour?'

'I'd be glad to, if I can,' said Mrs Miller.

'Oh, it's quite easy. I merely want you to buy a ticket for me; they won't let me in otherwise. Here, I have the money.' And gracefully she handed Mrs Miller two dimes and a nickel.

They went into the theatre together. An usherette directed them to a lounge; in twenty minutes the picture would be over.

'I feel just like a genuine criminal,' said Mrs Miller gaily, as she sat down. 'I mean that sort of thing's against the law, isn't it? I do hope I haven't done the wrong thing. Your mother knows where you are, dear? I mean she does, doesn't she?'

The little girl said nothing. She unbuttoned her coat and folded it across her lap. Her dress underneath was prim and dark blue. A gold chain dangled about her neck, and her fingers, sensitive and musical-looking, toyed with it. Examining her more attentively, Mrs Miller decided the truly distinctive feature was not her hair, but her eyes; they were hazel, steady, lacking any childlike quality whatsoever and, because of their size, seemed to consume her small face.

Mrs Miller offered a peppermint. 'What's your name, dear?'

'Miriam,' she said, as though, in some curious way, it were information already familiar.

'Why, isn't that funny – my name's Miriam, too. And it's not a terribly common name either. Now, don't tell me your last name's Miller!'

'Just Miriam.'

'But isn't that funny?'

'Moderately,' said Miriam, and rolled the peppermint on her tongue.

Mrs Miller flushed and shifted uncomfortably. 'You have such a large vocabulary for such a little girl.'

'Do I?'

'Well, yes,' said Mrs Miller, hastily changing the topic to: 'Do you like the movies?'

'I really wouldn't know,' said Miriam. 'I've never been before.'

Women began filling the lounge; the rumble of the newsreel bombs exploded in the distance. Mrs Miller rose, tucking her purse under her arm. 'I guess I'd better be running now if I want to get a seat,' she said. 'It was nice to have met you.'

Miriam nodded ever so slightly.

It snowed all week. Wheels and footsteps moved soundlessly on the street, as if the business of living continued secretly behind a pale but impenetrable curtain. In the falling quiet there was no sky or earth, only snow lifting in the wind, frosting the window glass, chilling the rooms, deadening and hushing the city. At all hours it was necessary to keep a lamp lighted and Mrs Miller lost track of the days: Friday was no different from Saturday and on Sunday she went to the grocery; closed, of course.

That evening she scrambled eggs and fixed a bowl of tomato soup. Then, after putting on a flannel robe and cold-creaming her face, she propped herself up in bed with a hotwater bottle under her feet. She was reading the *Times* when the doorbell rang. At first she thought it must be a mistake and whoever it was would go away. But it rang and rang and settled to a persistent buzz. She looked at the clock; a little after eleven; it did not seem possible, she was always asleep by ten.

Climbing out of bed, she trotted barefoot across the living-room. 'I'm coming, please be patient.' The latch was caught; she turned it this way and that way and the bell never paused an instant. 'Stop it,' she cried. The bolt gave way and she opened the door an inch. 'What in heaven's name?'

'Hello,' said Miriam.

'Oh ... why, hello,' said Mrs Miller, stepping hesitantly into the hall. 'You're that little girl.'

'I thought you'd never answer, but I kept my finger on the button; I knew you were home. Aren't you glad to see me?'

Mrs Miller did not know what to say. Miriam, she saw, wore the same plum-velvet coat and now she had also a beret to match; her white hair was braided in two shining plaits and looped at the ends with enormous white ribbons.

'Since I've waited so long, you could at least let me in,' she said.

'It's awfully late ...'

Miriam regarded her blankly. 'What difference does that make? Let me in. It's cold out here and I have on a silk dress.' Then, with a gentle gesture, she urged Mrs Miller aside and passed into the apartment.

She dropped her coat and beret on a chair. She was indeed wearing a silk dress. White silk. White silk in February. The skirt was beautifully pleated and the sleeves long; it made a faint rustle as she strolled about the room. 'I like your place,' she said. 'I like the rug, blue's my favourite colour.' She touched a paper rose in a vase on the coffee table. 'Imitation,' she commented wanly. 'How sad. Aren't imitations sad?' She seated herself on the sofa, daintily spreading her skirt.

'What do you want?' asked Mrs Miller.

'Sit down,' said Miriam. 'It makes me nervous to see people stand.'

Mrs Miller sank to a hassock. 'What do you want?' she repeated.

'You know, I don't think you're glad I came.'

For a second time Mrs Miller was without an answer; her hand motioned vaguely. Miriam giggled and pressed back on a mound of chintz pillows. Mrs Miller observed that the girl was less pale than she remembered; her cheeks were flushed.

'How did you know where I lived?'

Miriam frowned. 'That's no question at all. What's your name? What's mine?'

'But I'm not listed in the phone book.'

'Oh, let's talk about something else.'

Mrs Miller said, 'Your mother must be insane to let a child like you wander around at all hours of the night – and in such ridiculous clothes. She must be out of her mind.'

Miriam got up and moved to a corner where a covered bird cage hung from a ceiling chain. She peeked beneath the cover. 'It's a canary,' she said. 'Would you mind if I woke him? I'd like to hear him sing.'

'Leave Tommy alone,' said Mrs Miller, anxiously. 'Don't you dare wake him.'

'Certainly,' said Miriam. 'But I don't see why I can't hear him sing.' And then, 'Have you anything to eat? I'm starving! Even milk and a jam sandwich would be fine.'

'Look,' said Mrs Miller, rising from the hassock, 'look – if I make some nice sandwiches will you be a good child and run along home? It's past midnight, I'm sure.'

'It's snowing,' reproached Miriam. 'And cold and dark.'

'Well, you shouldn't have come here to begin with,' said Mrs Miller, struggling to control her voice. 'I can't help the weather. If you want anything to eat you'll have to promise to leave.'

Miriam brushed a braid against her cheek. Her eyes were thoughtful, as if weighing the proposition. She turned towards the bird cage. 'Very well,' she said, 'I promise.'

How old is she? Ten? Eleven? Mrs Miller, in the kitchen, unsealed a jar of strawberry preserves and cut four slices of bread. She poured a glass of milk and paused to light a cigarette. *And why has she come?* Her hand shook as she held the match, fascinated, till it burned her finger. The canary was singing; singing as he did in the morning and at no other time. 'Miriam,' she called, 'Miriam, I told you not to disturb Tommy.' There was no answer. She called again; all she heard was the canary. She inhaled the cigarette and discovered she had lighted the cork-tip end and – oh, really, she mustn't lose her temper.

She carried the food in on a tray and set it on the coffee table. She saw first that the bird cage still wore its night cover. And Tommy was singing. It gave her a queer sensation. And no one was in the room. Mrs Miller went through an alcove leading to her bedroom; at the door she caught her breath.

'What are you doing?' she asked.

Miriam glanced up and in her eyes there was a look that was not ordinary. She was standing by the bureau, a jewel case opened before her. For a minute she studied Mrs Miller, forcing their eyes to meet, and she smiled. 'There's nothing good here,' she said. 'But I like this.' Her hand held a cameo brooch. 'It's charming.'

'Suppose – perhaps you'd better put it back,' said Mrs Miller, feeling suddenly the need of some support. She leaned against the door frame; her head was unbearably heavy; a pressure weighted the rhythm of her heartbeat. The light seemed to flutter defectively. 'Please, child – a gift from my husband . . .'

'But it's beautiful and I want it,' said Miriam. *'Give it to me.'*

As she stood, striving to shape a sentence which would somehow save the brooch, it came to Mrs Miller there was no one to whom she might turn; she was alone; a fact that had not been among her thoughts for a long time. Its sheer emphasis was stunning. But here in her own room in the hushed snow-city were evidences she could not ignore or, she knew with startling clarity, resist.

Miriam ate ravenously, and when the sandwiches and milk were gone, her fingers made cobweb movements over the plate, gathering crumbs. The cameo gleamed on her blouse, the blonde profile like a trick reflection of its wearer. 'That was very nice,' she sighed, 'though now an almond cake or a cherry would be ideal. Sweets are lovely, don't you think?'

Mrs Miller was perched precariously on the hassock, smoking a cigarette. Her hair net had slipped lopsided and loose strands straggled down her face. Her eyes were stupidly concentrated on nothing and her cheeks were mottled in red patches, as though a fierce slap had left permanent marks.

'Is there a candy – a cake?'

Mrs Miller tapped ash on the rug. Her head swayed slightly as she tried to focus her eyes. 'You promised to leave if I made the sandwiches,' she said.

'Dear me, did I?'

'It was a promise and I'm tired and I don't feel well at all.'

'Mustn't fret,' said Miriam. 'I'm only teasing.'

She picked up her coat, slung it over her arm, and arranged her beret in front of a mirror. Presently she bent close to Mrs Miller and whispered, 'Kiss me good night.'

'Please – I'd rather not,' said Mrs Miller.

Miriam lifted a shoulder, arched an eyebrow. 'As you like,' she said, and went directly to the coffee table, seized the vase containing the paper roses, carried it to where the hard surface of the floor lay bare, and hurled it downwards. Glass sprayed in all directions and she stamped her foot on the bouquet.

Then slowly she walked to the door, but before closing it she looked back at Mrs Miller with a slyly innocent curiosity.

Mrs Miller spent the next day in bed, rising once to feed the canary and drink a cup of tea; she took her temperature and had none, yet her dreams were feverishly agitated; their unbalanced mood lingered even as she lay staring wide-eyed at the ceiling. One dream threaded through the others like an elusively mysterious theme in a complicated symphony, and the scenes it depicted were sharply outlined, as though sketched by a hand of gifted intensity: a small girl, wearing a bridal gown and a wreath of leaves, led a grey procession down a mountain path, and among them there was unusual silence till a woman at the rear asked, 'Where is she taking us?' 'No one knows,' said an old man marching in front. 'But isn't she pretty?' volunteered a third voice. 'Isn't she like a frost flower . . . so shining and white?'

Tuesday morning she woke up feeling better; harsh slats of sunlight, slanting through Venetian blinds, shed a disrupting light on her unwholesome fancies. She opened the window to discover a thawed, mild-as-spring day; a sweep of clean new clouds crumpled against a vastly blue, out-of-season sky; and across the low line of roof-tops she could see the river and smoke curving from tug-boat stacks in a warm wind. A great silver truck ploughed the snow-banked street, its machine sound humming in the air.

After straightening the apartment, she went to the grocer's, cashed a cheque and continued to Schrafft's where she ate breakfast and chatted happily with the waitress. Oh, it was a wonderful day – more like a holiday – and it would be so foolish to go home.

She boarded a Lexington Avenue bus and rode up to Eighty-sixth Street; it was here that she had decided to do a little shopping.

She had no idea what she wanted or needed, but she idled along, intent only upon the passers-by, brisk and preoccupied, who gave her a disturbing sense of separateness.

It was while waiting at the corner of Third Avenue that she saw the man: an old man, bow-legged and stooped under an armload of bulging packages; he wore a shabby brown coat and a checkered cap. Suddenly she realized they were exchanging a smile: there was nothing friendly about this smile, it was merely two cold flickers of recognition. But she was certain she had never seen him before.

He was standing next to an El pillar, and as she crossed the street he turned and followed. He kept quite close; from the corner of her eye she watched his reflection wavering on the shop windows.

Then in the middle of the block she stopped and faced him. He stopped also and cocked his head, grinning. But what could she say? Do? Here, in broad daylight, on Eighty-sixth Street? It was useless and, despising her own helplessness, she quickened her steps.

Now Second Avenue is a dismal street, made from scraps and ends; part cobblestone, part asphalt, part cement; and its atmosphere of desertion is permanent. Mrs Miller walked five blocks without meeting anyone, and all the while the steady crunch of his footfalls in the snow stayed near. And when she came to a florist's shop, the sound was still with her. She hurried inside and watched through the glass door as the old man passed; he kept his eyes straight ahead and didn't slow his pace, but he did one strange, telling thing: he tipped his cap.

'Six white ones, did you say?' asked the florist. 'Yes,' she told him, 'white roses.' From there she went to a glassware store and selected a vase, presumably a replacement for the one Miriam had broken, though the price was intolerable and the vase itself (she thought) grotesquely vulgar. But a series of unaccountable purchases had begun, as if by prearranged plan: a plan of which she had not the least knowledge or control.

She bought a bag of glazed cherries, and at a place called the Knickerbocker Bakery she paid forty cents for six almond cakes.

Within the last hour the weather had turned cold again; like blurred lenses, winter clouds cast a shade over the sun, and the skeleton of an early dusk coloured the sky; a damp mist mixed with the wind and the voices of a few children who romped high on mountains of gutter snow seemed lonely and cheerless. Soon the first flake fell, and when Mrs Miller reached the brownstone house, snow was falling in a swift screen and foot tracks vanished as they were printed.

The white roses were arranged decoratively in the vase. The glazed cherries shone on a ceramic plate. The almond cakes, dusted with sugar, awaited a hand. The canary fluttered on its swing and picked at a bar of seed.

At precisely five the doorbell rang. Mrs Miller *knew* who it was. The hem of her housecoat trailed as she crossed the floor. 'Is that you?' she called.

'Naturally,' said Miriam, the word resounding shrilly from the hall. 'Open this door.'

'Go away,' said Mrs Miller.

'Please hurry ... I have a heavy package.'

'Go away,' said Mrs Miller. She returned to the living-room, lighted a cigarette, sat down and calmly listened to the buzzer; on and on and on. 'You might as well leave. I have no intention of letting you in.'

Shortly the bell stopped. For possibly ten minutes Mrs Miller did not move. Then, hearing no sound, she concluded Miriam had gone. She tiptoed to the door and opened it a sliver; Miriam was half-reclining atop a cardboard box with a beautiful French doll cradled in her arms.

'Really, I thought you were never coming,' she said peevishly. 'Here, help me get this in, it's awfully heavy.'

It was not spell-like compulsion that Mrs Miller felt, but rather a curious passivity; she brought in the box, Miriam the doll. Miriam curled up on the sofa, not troubling to remove her coat or beret, and watched disinterestedly as Mrs Miller dropped the box and stood trembling, trying to catch her breath.

'Thank you,' she said. In the daylight she looked pinched and drawn, her hair less luminous. The French doll she was loving wore an exquisite powdered wig and its idiot glass eyes sought solace in Miriam's. 'I have a surprise,' she continued. 'Look into my box.'

Kneeling, Mrs Miller parted the flaps and lifted out another doll; then a blue linen dress which she recalled as the one Miriam had worn that first night at the theatre; and of the remainder she said, 'It's all clothes. Why?'

'Because I've come to live with you,' said Miriam, twisting a cherry stem. 'Wasn't it nice of you to buy me the cherries ... ?'

'But you can't! For God's sake go away – go away and leave me alone!'

'... and the roses and the almond cakes? How really wonderfully generous. You know, these cherries are delicious. The last place I lived was with an old man; he was terribly poor and we never had good things to eat. But I think I'll be happy here.' She paused to snuggle her doll closer. 'Now, if you'll just show me where to put my things ...'

Mrs Miller's face dissolved into a mask of ugly red lines; she began to cry, and it was an unnatural, tearless sort of weeping, as though, not having wept for a long time, she had forgotten how. Carefully she edged backward till she touched the door.

She fumbled through the hall and down the stairs to a landing below. She pounded frantically on the door of the first apartment she came to; a short, red-headed man answered and she pushed past him. 'Say, what the hell is this?' he said. 'Anything wrong, lover?' asked a young woman who appeared from the kitchen, drying her hands. And it was to her that Mrs Miller turned.

'Listen,' she cried, 'I'm ashamed behaving this way but – well, I'm Mrs H. T. Miller and I live upstairs and ...' She pressed her hands over her face. 'It sounds so absurd ...'

The woman guided her to a chair, while the man excitedly rattled pocket change. 'Yeah?'

'I live upstairs and there's a little girl visiting me, and I suppose

that I'm afraid of her. She won't leave and I can't make her and – she's
going to do something terrible. She's already stolen my cameo, but she's
about to do something worse – something terrible!'

The man asked, 'Is she a relative, huh?'

Mrs Miller shook her head. 'I don't know who she is. Her name's
Miriam, but I don't know for certain who she is.'

'You gotta calm down, honey,' said the woman, stroking Mrs Miller's
arm. 'Harry here'll tend to this kid. Go on, lover.' And Mrs Miller said,
'The door's open – 5A.'

After the man left, the woman brought a towel and bathed Mrs
Miller's face. 'You're very kind,' Mrs Miller said. 'I'm sorry to act like
such a fool, only this wicked child ...'

'Sure, honey,' consoled the woman. 'Now, you better take it easy.'

Mrs Miller rested her head in the crook of her arm; she was quiet
enough to be asleep. The woman turned a radio dial; a piano and a
husky voice filled the silence and the woman, tapping her foot, kept
excellent time. 'Maybe we oughta go up too,' she said.

'I don't want to see her again. I don't want to be anywhere near
her.'

'Uh huh, but what you shoulda done, you shoulda called a cop.'

Presently they heard the man on the stairs. He strode into the room
frowning and scratching the back of his neck. 'Nobody there,' he said,
honestly embarrassed. 'She musta beat it.'

'Harry, you're a jerk,' announced the woman. 'We been sitting here
the whole time and we woulda seen ...' she stopped abruptly, for the
man's glance was sharp.

'I looked all over,' he said, 'and there just ain't nobody there. Nobody,
understand?'

'Tell me,' said Mrs Miller, rising, 'tell me, did you see a large box?
Or a doll?'

'No, ma'am, I didn't.'

And the woman, as if delivering a verdict, said, 'Well, for cryin' out
loud ...'

Mrs Miller entered her apartment softly; she walked to the centre of the
room and stood quite still. No, in a sense it had not changed: the roses,
the cakes, and the cherries were in place. But this was an empty room,
emptier than if the furnishings and familiars were not present, lifeless
and petrified as a funeral parlour. The sofa loomed before her with a
new strangeness: its vacancy had a meaning that would have been less
penetrating and terrible had Miriam been curled on it. She gazed
fixedly at the space where she remembered setting the box and, for a
moment, the hassock spun desperately. And she looked through the
window; surely the river was real, surely snow was falling – but then,

one could not be certain witness to anything: Miriam, so vividly *there* – and yet, where was she? Where, where?

As though moving in a dream, she sank to a chair. The room was losing shape; it was dark and getting darker and there was nothing to be done about it; she could not lift her hand to light a lamp.

Suddenly, closing her eyes, she felt an upward surge, like a diver emerging from some deeper, greener depth. In times of terror or immense distress, there are moments when the wind waits, as though for a revelation, while a skein of calm is woven over thought; it is like a sleep, or a supernatural trance; and during this lull one is aware of a force of quiet reasoning: well, what if she had never really known a girl named Miriam? that she had been foolishly frightened on the street? In the end, like everything else, it was of no importance. For the only thing she had lost to Miriam was her identity, but now she knew she had found again the person who lived in this room, who cooked her own meals, who owned a canary, who was someone she could trust and believe in: Mrs H. T. Miller.

Listening in contentment, she became aware of a double sound: a bureau drawer opening and closing; she seemed to hear it long after completion – opening and closing. Then gradually, the harshness of it was replaced by the murmur of a silk dress and this, delicately faint, was moving nearer and swelling in intensity till the walls trembled with the vibration and the room was caving under a wave of whispers. Mrs Miller stiffened and opened her eyes to a dull, direct stare.

'Hello,' said Miriam.

The Monster

R. Chetwynd-Hayes

They were kind to her in their own, cold way, but she was young and would ask questions, and Aunt Mabs sighed heavily, knowing the truth must be unveiled sooner or later.

'Aunt, why can't I leave the house?'

'You aren't well, child. Don't keep bothering me.'

'But I feel fine.'

'Well, you aren't fine, so be quiet.'

A little later.

'Aunt, I see children pass the house twice a day. Where are they going?'

'School.'

'What's school?'

The woman shook her head in exasperation, then quickly left the room.

That evening Uncle Carl came to her room, the lines on his lean face set into a determined expression. He put her dinner tray down on the all-purpose table, then sat down on the edge of the bed and watched her eat.

'Caroline, you've been asking questions again.'

She was frightened when he spoke this way – and for good reason; she paused and looked at his stern face with wide open, fear-glazed eyes, and the man shuddered.

'I only wanted to know.'

'If you ask such questions again, I shall beat you. Be grateful that there are two people who are willing to feed and keep you in comfort. Give praise to Almighty Jehovah that He has in His great mercy, spared you the terror of His wrath. Seek not knowledge, revel in ignorance, for that is Jehovah's gift to sinful man.'

'All praise to Jehovah,' she muttered the conventional phrase. 'I promise to sin no more.'

' 'Tis well.' He rose slowly, a man worn and tired by a lifetime of fear. 'I do not wish to hear of questions again.' He walked to the door, then looked back, his hand on the doorknob. 'Do not make us regret what we have done.'

'No, Uncle,' she answered, grateful that he was leaving, her mind now a vast, trembling question.

Next day they moved her into a new room, well back from the street, and the window was veiled by a thick gauze curtain which was tacked to the window frame on all sides so she could not pull it aside. But Satan Atomo entered her heart and whispered that a small hole could be made in the centre; not large enough for the Aunt to detect, for she was somewhat shortsighted, but sufficient for one young eye to peep out – to see the small garden, and what lay beyond the far wall.

There was a house on the left, and a fairly large garden that ran obliquely to Uncle Carl's; complete with a dark green lawn and bordered by white flower beds. Caroline liked this view better than the old one, for the street was only a mud-churned track, with the crop fields on the other side, and the ever-smoking bad lands in the far distance. A range of tall hills shut off whatever lay beyond on this side, and the scene was restful, at the same time exciting, for one could hope for something new to come over the hills, and Caroline lived on hope.

She had been in the new room three days when the young man appeared in the far garden. He was not the first young man she had seen, for many had passed along the street, but he was the first she had been able to study for any length of time. He erected a garden chair, then seated himself and stretched out his long legs, clearly determined to absorb as much of the sunlight as he could before moon rising. He was, she decided, a most handsome young man, and there was an unaccountable quickening of her heart when he stripped off his tunic and bared his torso. A man minus his clothes was a phenomenon she had never considered; in fact any human being undressed had been, to that moment, an impossibility. Aunt Mabs always made her bath in the dark, maintaining it was sinful to see even one's own naked flesh, and Caroline jerked back from the window like a frightened bird, and took refuge on her bed.

It stood to reason that Jehovah must have noted this sinful act, and was without doubt preparing to bring down His wrath upon the not-to-be-thought-of young man, not to mention the equally evil girl who now trembled on her bed. She waited for the thunder clap, the bellow of divine rage, and was strangely disappointed when it did not come. The hours passed, then Aunt Mabs brought in her supper, glancing at the girl with her usual worried expression that deepened when she saw the white face and troubled eye.

'What have you been up to?'

Caroline knew she should confess and risk a beating, but logic suggested that if Almighty Jehovah had withheld His hand, it would be blasphemous for Uncle Carl to wield his belt. So she said:

'Nothing, Gracious Aunt, only I feel a little unwell.'

The woman grunted and there was a glimmer of hope in her eyes.

'Then you must get to bed so soon as moonrising prayers are over. Pray for forgiveness, and thank Almighty Jehovah that he has spared you from his wrath.'

As Caroline muttered 'Amen', she wondered for one panic-stricken moment if Aunt Mabs knew, but on reflection decided she was only referring to the perpetual wrath that the Almighty only just restrained Himself from pouring down upon her own sinful person.

Aunt Mabs left the room to prepare herself for the nightly moonrising prayers, and Caroline quickly ate her yeast cutlet and nut roast, before moving fearfully towards the window, for it was necessary that everyone witness the moonrising so as to remember the sins of the forefathers.

The young man was still there, but now, thankfully, fully clothed, and with him were two older people, a man and woman, clearly his Uncle and Aunt. They were kneeling on small, dark red cushions, gazing intently at the distant hills, from behind which the moon would soon rise. Uncle Carl and Aunt Mabs came out into their small garden and knelt on identical cushions, and Caroline knelt on her chair, her eye sinfully glued to the hole in her curtain.

The familiar rumble began, and the earth trembled; the three people in the far garden prostrated themselves, for this was Almighty Jehovah's voice, growling out his rage, bidding them all to remember – to remember; renewing His covenant made to man after the great sin, that He would punish and destroy, unless all tremble as the earth trembled, for He was a jealous God, a terrible God, an everlastingly angry God.

The moon slid up from behind the hills; its face was grey, speckled with bright pimples of light where the sun was reflected on its mountain peaks, and it was vast. It reared up with fearsome speed, filling the entire western sky, and the earth shook with fear, the house quivered, the sacred ornaments on Caroline's mantelpiece danced a reel of terror, and Almighty Jehovah blew, and a great wind tore across the fields, over the roof tops, tearing, ripping, alive with the god's lust to destroy. The moon was now high up in the heavens, and Caroline, try as she might, could not lower her head; she saw the vast craters, the towering mountains that seemed to be reaching down in an attempt to tear open the sinful flesh of the earth. This was the crisis, the one moment when the angry God might decide to make an end; to surrender completely to His all-consuming rage and let the moon fall down upon the world. The moon was now covering the entire sky, the earth was cloaked in darkness, broken only by a halo of light that ran round the satellite's rim. Then came the rebirth of hope, a faint glimmer of light in the western sky, that grew larger by the second, became a crescent of cold blue, and presently developed into a patch of unclouded sky. The moon was passing away; it would race out into the heavens, become a speck of light, until drawn back by Almighty the following night. For twenty-four hours man was safe.

II

The sin in Caroline's heart became a canker, and Satan Atomo, no doubt gloating over his conquest, made sure temptation was always before her. The young man seemed to live in the garden. He hoed the black earth that glowered beneath the linen-white flowers, he trimmed the dark green grass with a scythe, and all the time his naked brown back screamed its untranslatable message to Caroline, so that her mind became a hothouse of searing, forbidden thoughts. She kept away from the window for as long as she could, walked round and round the room, and prayed silently to Almighty Jehovah for forgiveness, but always, whenever her attention flagged, she came back to that fatal hole in the curtain.

It was inevitable that her guilty secret would be discovered.

'What are you doing?' Aunt Mabs was standing behind her, and Caroline spun around, her eyes dilated with terror. Aunt Mabs pushed her roughly to one side, then peeped through the gaping hole herself. When she turned round her face was unexpectedly sad.

'How long has this been going on?' she asked.

'For a long time,' Caroline answered, for to lie was to bring down Jehovah's certain wrath.

'I see,' the woman nodded slowly. 'Why do you watch him?'

Caroline thought carefully, then answered:

'Because he is beautiful.'

Aunt Mabs nodded again, then said: 'Beautiful' before leaving the room.

Caroline waited – waited for hours. She would be beaten, of that there was no doubt, but why had Jehovah not chastised her Himself long since. Could it be Uncle Carl was to be His instrument, because the God's time was fully occupied in punishing the world?

Uncle Carl brought up her supper tray as usual, and under his arm he carried a large book. Caroline recognized it as the Book, written by the holy Elijah Ebenezer Brown, as dictated to him by Almighty Jehovah Himself in the year One. The Uncle did not speak, but made a gesture denoting she was to eat her supper, and sat silently staring at the carpet, only looking up when she pushed the plate to one side.

'You can read your letters?'

'Yes, Uncle, the gracious Aunt taught me to read.'

'That is well.' He handed her the Book. 'Open it – to the first page.'

Caroline turned the hard cover, it was old and possibly had once encased another book.

'Read,' commanded the Uncle.

'THE WORD OF JEHOVAH AS WRITTEN BY THE HOLY ELIJAH EBENEZER BROWN WHILST IN THE SPIRIT.'

'And!' Uncle Carl's voice was low.

'JEHOVAH CREATED HE MAN IN HIS OWN IMAGE.'

'Close the book and give it to me.'

Caroline obeyed, knowing this was not going to be something simple like a thrashing; this would be worse, much worse.

'Jehovah created He man in His own image,' Uncle Carl repeated the text, and Caroline remembered seeing the blazing letters printed on a banner, carried by the children on their way to Sabbath school, 'and because Almighty Jehovah is beautiful Himself, then all men must be beautiful also.' His cold eyes switched their gaze from the bedside rug, and stared straight at the girl.

'You thought the young man beautiful?'

'Yes, gracious Uncle, and I sinned ...'

The Uncle raised his hand.

'You did not sin in that, for it is good that one gaze upon the beauty that Jehovah has created. Your sin is a far greater one.'

Caroline trembled and waited for the enormity of her transgressions to be revealed.

'Your sin is that of ugliness. Listen to me, and I will read the holy word.'

Uncle Carl opened the good book, and began to read slowly, raising his voice in the traditional style, so his words were full and sonorous.

'In the beginning Almighty Jehovah gave the world to man as his playground. The entire earth was his, and the fruits thereof, the sea, and that which lived therein; the air above in which he might besport himself, and next to the Almighty, man was the lord of creation.

'So great was Jehovah's love he gave gifts beyond price; the ability to speak over large distances, chariots that raced faster than the wind, magic wings that took man above the earth, and the power to hunt under the sea. And the children of man dwelt in fine houses, were clad in soft linen; white bread lay daily upon their tables, and Jehovah spoke to them every seventh day. And he spake thus: ' "All that is upon the earth is yours, but all that is in the heavens is mine."

'Now it came to pass that Satan Atomo walked the earth in those days, and he whispered into the ears of men: "Why should you not go out into the heavens? The moon is bright, the stars are diamonds beyond price; go forth, and I will protect you." '

'And men made strange chariots and they went forth into the

heavens, and Jehovah struck out in his anger. He blazed fire and
brimstone upon the earth, and He ate up the great houses, the chariots,
the magic wings, and many men died, even unto three parts of men
died.

'Then the daughters of men, in their fear, took unto themselves the
sons of Satan Atomo, and they did bring forth monsters.

'And Jehovah brought down the moon, and it hovered over the earth,
and His voice spoke from a thunder cloud. "Ye shall destroy all that is
not born in my image."'

'And all those that still followed in the ways of the Godly obeyed this
commandment. They took the ugly, the monster-born, and burnt them
on the altar, and behold the smoke of the burning was good unto the
Almighty, and He did withhold His hand, and the moon fell not on to
the earth, and some men lived.'

Uncle Carl slammed the book closed with such force, Caroline
jumped, then he spoke in the same awesome tone.

'A thousand summers have passed, and rarely are monsters born, but
when they are, the people take them into the temple and burn them
upon the altar.'

Caroline at first did not understand, then the man's cold, expressionless stare relayed its message, and she whimpered:

'I'm not a monster.'

'Child, can you not see?' The Uncle snapped out the question. 'Put
out your hand. Now I will lay mine alongside. Look. Mine is shaped
by the Almighty, yours ... Do not force me to describe what your eyes
must see. Look at my face, then feel your own, the skin – the monstrous
growth that covers your head. Can't you understand that I feel sick in
your presence, and I have gazed upon you for nigh on sixteen years.
Think how that young man would react were he to see you as you are.
He would hand you over to the temple elders for burning, as indeed I
should have long since.'

Caroline looked at the horror that was her hands with new eyes; the
difference she had always known, and accepted. Now truth had been
savagely thrust through the doors of her consciousness, and her body
screamed with repulsion. She was more than ugly, more than hideous
– she was the monster-born. A blot that should be wiped away, a
loathsome fragment fit only for burning.

'Why,' she sobbed, 'why did you not hand me over at birth?'

'Our sin was great,' the Uncle nodded, and a tear ran down his
otherwise expressionless face, 'but my sister was young, and much loved.
She hid you until it was too late. If I had given you up, they would have
taken her also, and my foolish, soft love overcame my sacred duty. We
have lived in fear all these years, your Aunt and I. We felt that as
Almighty Jehovah had withheld His hand, perhaps He understood, but

who can calculate His mysterious ways? He struck down your mother, He burnt your father with a thunderflash, and we – and you, He has spared. But I dread lest you be seen.'

'Forgive me,' Caroline sat with lowered head, 'my sin is great,' but the tired man shook his head.

'No, child, the sin is mine. I should have handed you over for burning, and you would not be suffering now.'

He took up the book, and left without uttering a further word.

III

Caroline opened her door and crept out on to the landing. The house slept; the world – Jehovah slept, for the silence was absolute. She trod softly down the stairs, tip-toed along the hall and opened the front door.

Outside the sky was a dark blue roof, pinpointed with stars, and she was afraid, for there was so much emptiness, no comforting walls, and the night breeze was an evil thing that tore at her robe. Only the great urge stopped her from rushing back into the house, for she must go out into the wild lands; to die perhaps, but it would be a clean death, and no harm would come to the Uncle and Aunt.

The rough road was cruel to her bare feet, and the starlit gloom was alive with gibbering shadows that mocked and tried vainly with voiceless mouths to shout her presence aloud. She passed houses, all built of wood and painted black, so that Jehovah might not see them, but of course He did; one had been shaken down. Only the temple was built of stone. Jehovah's statue stood a little way to the right; thirty feet tall, the work of three generations. His stern face looked upwards, gazing with sightless eyes at the stars; in His right hand He held a seven-thonged flail, and in His left a forked thunderflash. On the base was etched the familiar words:

JEHOVAH CREATED HE MAN IN HIS OWN IMAGE.

Caroline fled from the temple, fled from the presence of dread Jehovah, and ran past the last few houses, until she came within sight of the open wild lands that stretched out great arms to greet her. She did not know about the night watch, the two men who prowled the village limits, ever alert lest some raiding party from afar should suddenly strike. They came out of the shadows and shouted:

'Who are you? Stop.'

Caroline turned on her tracks and ran, and the hard pounding of booted feet came after her. She darted between two houses, stumbled across a cultivated back garden, tore her gown clambering through a low hedge. But now doors were opening, people were pouring out; she ran into a man when turning a corner, and he saw her face.

'Monster – a monster!'

He clutched her gown and it ripped as she broke away, and the cry was relayed from mouth to mouth, until the earth – the very heavens – were screaming the dreadful word:

'Monster – monster!'

She had never run before in her life, never before walked on bare earth, and her strength was soon exhausted. Somehow, she had come back into the main street, and there was Jehovah, standing before His temple, staring up at the stars, and judging the world. She collapsed at His feet, and looked up at His stone face.

'Mercy, Almighty, mercy on me – a monster.'

But the face was pitiless, the great flail was poised above her, and the pursuers, many with lighted torches, were closing in, and there was no hope anywhere, either on the earth, in the badlands, or in the stars.

They pulled her roughly to her feet, ripped the tattered gown from her body, and their faces became twisted with disgust when the malformed shape was revealed.

'Where did you come from?' a watchman struck her across the face, 'who's been hiding you?'

That was a question that must not be answered, and she tried not to scream when they punched her stomach, kicked her and flung her to the ground.

The temple Elders were gaunt from much fasting, and one had a large pin driven through his cheeks, and the crowd drew back, for he was very holy. His voice was muffled, as the pin stopped his tongue from functioning naturally, and his face was like Jehovah's, as though it, too, were hewn from stone.

'Cease. No one in the village would dare harbour her. If they had, we would have been smitten long since.'

Caroline marvelled, and looked up again at the stone God.

'She has come in from the badlands, a gift from Jehovah, so that we might sacrifice. Bring her into the temple, and let us give praise.'

She was dragged in through the doorway, across the paved floor, speckled with colour where the red kneeling cushions were laid out in neat rows; up on to the raised altar, and tied to the stone cross. Her back was pressed against the centre pillar, each wrist was lashed to a crosspiece, and her ankles tied firmly to the base.

Torches were lit and placed in wall sconces, a mirror of polished bronze was placed before her so that the entire congregation should be able to see the vileness of the Satan-born. They piled faggots at her feet, and the priests began to chant, and the people responded.

'Jehovah, created He man.'

'In His own image,' the voices behind her shouted.

'With one head.'

'And two arms.'

'Two legs, only two legs.'

One priest with a particularly sonorous voice carried on in solo.

'And at the bottom of the legs, shall be two feet.'

'Yea, there shall be two feet.'

'And at the end of the two arms shall be two hands.'

'Yea, there shall be two hands.'

The priest raised his voice to a near scream.

'And what shall there be on the head?'

'There shall be two ears.'

'And how shall the ears be shaped?'

'They will be large, and black, and shall hang down, even to the shoulders.'

'And what shall be on the face?'

'There shall be two eyes, one large, one small, and two noses, and twin tusks will grow forth from the cheeks, and the lips shall be black and spread wide, and the teeth shall never be covered. Thus saith the Almighty Jehovah.'

'And what shall be on the hands?'

'Two fingers, and they shall have talons, even as the feet hath two toes, and a small tail, not more than twelve inches long, shall hang from the spine, even as Jehovah has decreed.'

Caroline was crying now, not because they had lighted the faggots, but because she could see her reflection in the bronze mirror. She was ugly – it was good that all this ugliness was about to be burnt. She had no lovely brown wrinkled skin; hers was obscenely white and smooth; her head, instead of being nobly domed and ridged, was covered with a grotesque mop of corn-coloured growth, which covered her horrible small ears; she only had one nose, and her eyes were both the same size, but, and this was worst of all, not delicately addled, but blue, surrounded with white, and fringed by the same hideous growth that marred her head. Each hand had four long fingers and a shorter one that stuck out at an angle, and there were five toes to each foot. Her lips were red, not black, and covered her teeth, which should have been irregular, one behind the other; hers were disgustingly white and even.

'And the skin shall be wrinkled, and the face pitted, even as the face of Father Moon, and there shall be no furry growth, either on the head or other parts, for this is an abomination in Jehovah's sight, as it has been, and will be, for evermore.'

'Cursed by the Satan-Born,' the priest chanted.

'May they be cursed for ever.'

Caroline heard Jehovah laugh as the flames licked upwards, and He laughed with a million voices, over a million years, and before merciful oblivion came, she laughed too. In that last revealing moment she understood.

The Last Séance

Agatha Christie

Raoul Daubreuil crossed the Seine humming a little tune to himself. He was a good-looking young Frenchman of about thirty-two, with a fresh-coloured face and a little black moustache. By profession he was an engineer. In due course he reached the Cardonet and turned in at the door of No. 17. The concierge looked out from her lair and gave him a grudging 'Good morning', to which he replied cheerfully. Then he mounted the stairs to the apartment on the third floor. As he stood there waiting for his ring at the bell to be answered he hummed once more his little tune. Raoul Daubreuil was feeling particularly cheerful this morning. The door was opened by an elderly Frenchwoman whose wrinkled face broke into smiles when she saw who the visitor was.

'Good morning, Monsieur.'

'Good morning, Elise,' said Raoul.

He passed into the vestibule, pulling off his gloves as he did so.

'Madame expects me, does she not?' he asked over his shoulder.

'Ah, yes, indeed, Monsieur.'

Elise shut the front door and turned towards him.

'If Monsieur will pass into the little *salon* Madame will be with him in a few minutes. At the moment she reposes herself.'

Raoul looked up sharply.

'Is she not well?'

'*Well!*'

Elise gave a snort. She passed in front of Raoul and opened the door of the little *salon* for him. He went in and she followed him.

'*Well!*' she continued. 'How should she be well, poor lamb? *Séances*, *séances*, and always *séances*! It is not right – not natural, not what the good God intended for us. For me, I say straight out, it is trafficking with the devil.'

Raoul patted her on the shoulder reassuringly.

'There, there, Elise,' he said soothingly, 'do not excite yourself, and do not be too ready to see the devil in everything you do not understand.'

Elise shook her head doubtingly.

'Ah, well,' she grumbled under her breath, 'Monsieur may say what he pleases, I don't like it. Look at Madame, every day she gets whiter and thinner, and the headaches!'

She held up her hands.

'Ah, no, it is not good, all this spirit business. Spirits indeed! All the good spirits are in Paradise, and the others are in Purgatory.'

'Your view of the life after death is refreshingly simple, Elise,' said Raoul as he dropped into a chair.

The old woman drew herself up.

'I am a good Catholic, Monsieur.'

She crossed herself, went towards the door, then paused, her hand on the handle.

'Afterwards when you are married, Monsieur,' she said pleadingly, 'it will not continue – all this?'

Raoul smiled at her affectionately.

'You are a good faithful creature, Elise,' he said, 'and devoted to your mistress. Have no fear, once she is my wife, all this "spirit business" as you call it, will cease. For Madame Daubreuil there will be no more *séances*.'

Elise's face broke into smiles.

'Is it true what you say?' she asked eagerly.

The other nodded gravely.

'Yes,' he said, speaking almost more to himself than to her. 'Yes, all this must end. Simone has a wonderful gift and she has used it freely, but now she has done her part. As you have justly observed, Elise, day by day she gets whiter and thinner. The life of a medium is a particularly trying and arduous one, involving a terrible nervous strain. All the same, Elise, your mistress is the most wonderful medium in Paris – more, in France. People from all over the world come to her because they know that with her there is no trickery, no deceit.'

Elise gave a snort of contempt.

'Deceit! Ah, no, indeed. Madame could not deceive a new-born babe if she tried.'

'She is an angel,' said the young Frenchman with fervour. 'And I – I shall do everything a man can to make her happy. You believe that?'

Elise drew herself up, and spoke with a certain simple dignity.

'I have served Madame for many years, Monsieur. With all respect I may say that I love her. If I did not believe that you adored her as she deserves to be adored – *eh bien*, Monsieur! I should be willing to tear you limb from limb.'

Raoul laughed.

'Bravo, Elise! You are a faithful friend, and you must approve of me now that I have told you Madame is going to give up the spirits.'

He expected the old woman to receive this pleasantry with a laugh, but somewhat to his surprise she remained grave.

'Supposing, Monsieur,' she said hesitatingly, 'the spirits will not give *her* up?'

Raoul stared at her.

'Eh! What do you mean?'

'I said,' repeated Elise, 'supposing the spirits will not give *her* up?'

'I thought you didn't believe in the spirits, Elise?'

'No more I do,' said Elise stubbornly. 'It is foolish to believe in them. All the same——'

'Well?'

'It is difficult for me to explain, Monsieur. You see, me, I always thought that these mediums, as they call themselves, were just clever cheats who imposed on the poor souls who had lost their dear ones. But Madame is not like that. Madame is good. Madame is honest and——'

She lowered her voice and spoke in a tone of awe.

'*Things happen.* It is not trickery, things happen, and that is why I am afraid. For I am sure of this, Monsieur, it is not right. It is against nature and le bon Dieu, and *somebody will have to pay.*'

Raoul got up from his chair and came and patted her on the shoulder.

'Calm yourself, my good Elise,' he said, smiling. 'See, I will give you some good news. Today is the last of these *séances*; after today there will be no more.'

'There *is* one today then?' asked the old woman suspiciously

'The last, Elise, the last.'

Elise shook her head disconsolately.

'Madame is not fit——' she began.

But her words were interrupted, the door opened and a tall, fair woman came in. She was slender and graceful, with the face of a Botticelli Madonna. Raoul's face lighted up, and Elise withdrew quickly and discreetly.

'Simone!'

He took both her long, white hands in his and kissed each in turn. She murmured his name very softly.

'Raoul, my dear one.'

Again he kissed her hands and then looked intently into her face.

'Simone, how pale you are! Elise told me you were resting; you are not ill, my well-beloved?'

'No, not ill——' she hesitated.

He led her over to the sofa and sat down on it beside her.

'But tell me then.'

The medium smiled faintly.

'You will think me foolish,' she murmured.

'I? Think you foolish? Never.'

Simone withdrew her hand from his grasp. She sat perfectly still for
a moment or two gazing down at the carpet. Then she spoke in a low,
hurried voice.

'I am afraid, Raoul.'

He waited for a minute or two expecting her to go on, but as she did
not he said encouragingly:

'Yes, afraid of what?'

'Just afraid – that is all.'

'But——'

He looked at her in perplexity, and she answered the look quickly.

'Yes, it is absurd, isn't it, and yet I feel just that. Afraid, nothing more.
I don't know what of, or why, but all the time I am possessed with the
idea that something terrible – terrible, is going to happen to me ...'

She stared out in front of her. Raoul put an arm gently round her.
'My dearest,' he said, 'come, you must not give way. I know what it is,
the strain, Simone, the strain of a medium's life. All you need is rest –
rest and quiet.'

She looked at him gratefully.

'Yes, Raoul, you are right. That is what I need, rest and quiet.'

She closed her eyes and leant back a little against his arm.

'And happiness,' murmured Raoul in her ear.

His arm drew her closer. Simone, her eyes still closed, drew a deep
breath.

'Yes,' she murmured, 'yes. When your arms are round me I feel safe.
I forget my life – the terrible life – of a medium. You know much, Raoul,
but even you do not know all it means.'

He felt her body grow rigid in his embrace. Her eyes opened again,
staring in front of her.

'One sits in the cabinet in the darkness, waiting, and the darkness
is terrible, Raoul, for it is the darkness of emptiness, of nothingness. Deliberately one gives oneself up to be lost in it. After that
one knows nothing, one feels nothing, but at last there comes the
slow, painful return, the awakening out of sleep, but so tired – so
terribly tired.'

'I know,' murmured Raoul, 'I know.'

'So tired,' murmured Simone again.

Her whole body seemed to droop as she repeated the words.

'But you are wonderful, Simone.'

He took her hands in his, trying to rouse her to share his enthusiasm.

'You are unique – the greatest medium the world has ever known.'

She shook her head, smiling a little at that.

'Yes, yes,' Raoul insisted.

He drew two letters from his pocket.

'See here, from Professor Roche of the *Salpêtrière*, and this one from

Dr Genir at Nancy, both imploring that you will continue to sit for them occasionally.'

'Ah, no!'

Simone sprang suddenly to her feet.

'I will not, I will not. It is to be all finished – all done with. You promised me, Raoul.'

Raoul stared at her in astonishment as she stood wavering, facing him almost like a creature at bay. He got up and took her hand.

'Yes, yes,' he said. 'Certainly it is finished, that is understood. But I am so proud of you, Simone, that is why I mentioned those letters.'

She threw him a swift sideways glance of suspicion.

'It is not that you will ever want me to sit again?'

'No, no,' said Raoul, 'unless perhaps you yourself would care to, just occasionally for these old friends——'

But she interrupted him, speaking excitedly.

'No, no, never again. There is a danger. I tell you. I can feel it, great danger.'

She clasped her hands on her forehead a minute, then walked across to the window.

'Promise me never again,' she said in a quieter voice over her shoulder.

Raoul followed her and put his arms round her shoulders.

'My dear one,' he said tenderly, 'I promise you after today you shall never sit again.'

He felt the sudden start she gave.

'Today,' she murmured. 'Ah, yes – I had forgotten Madame Exe.'

Raoul looked at his watch.

'She is due any minute now; but perhaps, Simone, if you do not feel well——'

Simone hardly seemed to be listening to him; she was following out her own train of thought.

'She is – a strange woman, Raoul, a very strange woman. Do you know I – I have almost a horror of her.'

'Simone!'

There was, reproach in his voice, and she was quick to feel it.

'Yes, yes, I know, you are like all Frenchmen, Raoul. To you a mother is sacred and it is unkind of me to feel like that about her when she grieves so for her lost child. But – I cannot explain it, she is so big and black, and her hands – have you ever noticed her hands, Raoul? Great big strong hands, as strong as a man's. Ah!'

She gave a little shiver and closed her eyes. Raoul withdrew his arm and spoke almost coldly.

'I really cannot understand you, Simone. Surely you, a woman, should have nothing but sympathy for another woman, a mother bereft of her only child.'

Simone made a gesture of impatience.

'Ah, it is you who do not understand, my friend! One cannot help these things. The first moment I saw her I felt——'

She flung her hands out.

'*Fear!* You remember, it was a long time before I would consent to sit for her? I felt sure in some way she would bring me misfortune.'

Raoul shrugged his shoulders.

'Whereas, in actual fact, she brought you the exact opposite,' he said drily. 'All the sittings have been attended with marked success. The spirit of the little Amelie was able to control you at once, and the materializations have really been striking. Professor Roche ought really to have been present at the last one.'

'Materializations,' said Simone in a low voice. 'Tell me, Raoul (you know that I know nothing of what takes place while I am in the trance), are the materializations really so wonderful?'

He nodded enthusiastically.

'At the first few sittings the figure of the child was visible in a kind of nebulous haze,' he explained, 'but at the last *séance*——'

'Yes?'

He spoke very softly.

'Simone, the child that stood there was an actual living child of flesh and blood. I even touched her – but seeing that the touch was acutely painful to you, I would not permit Madame Exe to do the same. I was afraid that her self-control might break down, and that some harm to you might result.'

Simone turned away again towards the window.

'I was terribly exhausted when I woke,' she murmured. 'Raoul, are you sure – are you really sure that all this is *right*? You know what dear old Elise thinks, that I am trafficking with the devil?'

She laughed rather uncertainly.

'You know what I believe,' said Raoul gravely. 'In the handling of the unknown there must always be danger, but the cause is a noble one, for it is the cause of Science. All over the world there have been martyrs to Science, pioneers who have paid the price so that others may follow safely in their footsteps. For ten years now you have worked for Science at the cost of a terrific nervous strain. Now your part is done, from today onward you are free to be happy.'

She smiled at him affectionately, her calm restored. Then she glanced quickly up at the clock.

'Madame Exe is late,' she murmured. 'She may not come.'

'I think she will,' said Raoul. 'Your clock is a little fast, Simone.'

Simone moved about the room, rearranging an ornament here and there.

'I wonder who she is, this Madame Exe?' she observed. 'Where she comes from, who her people are? It is strange that we know nothing about her.'

Raoul shrugged his shoulders.

'Most people remain incognito if possible when they come to a medium,' he observed. 'It is an elementary precaution.'

'I suppose so,' agreed Simone listlessly.

A little china vase she was holding slipped from her fingers and broke to pieces on the tiles of the fireplace. She turned sharply on Raoul.

'You see,' she murmured, 'I am not myself. Raoul, would you think me very – very cowardly if I told Madame Exe I could not sit today?'

His look of pained astonishment made her redden.

'You promised, Simone——' he began gently.

She backed against the wall.

'I won't do it, Raoul. I won't do it.'

And again that glance of his, tenderly reproachful, made her wince.

'It is not of the money I am thinking, Simone, though you must realize that the money this woman has offered you for a last sitting is enormous – simply enormous.'

She interrupted him defiantly.

'There are things that matter more than money.'

'Certainly there are,' he agreed warmly. 'That is just what I am saying. Consider – this woman is a mother, a mother who has lost her only child. If you are not really ill, if it is only a whim on your part – you can deny a rich woman a caprice, can you deny a mother one last sight of her child?'

The medium flung her hands out despairingly in front of her.

'Oh, you torture me,' she murmured. 'All the same you are right I will do as you wish, but I know now what I am afraid of – it is the word "mother".'

'Simone!'

'There are certain primitive elementary forces, Raoul. Most of them have been destroyed by civilization, but motherhood stands where it stood at the beginning. Animals – human beings, they are all the same. A mother's love for her child is like nothing else in the world. It knows no law, no pity, it dares all things and crushes down remorselessly all that stands in its path.'

She stopped, panting a little, then turned to him with a quick, disarming smile.

'I am foolish today, Raoul. I know it.'

He took her hand in his.

'Lie down for a minute or two,' he urged. 'Rest till she comes.'

'Very well.' She smiled at him and left the room.

Raoul remained for a minute or two lost in thought, then he strode to the door, opened it, and crossed the little hall. He went into a room the other side of it, a sitting-room very much like the one he had left, but at one end was an alcove with a big armchair set in it. Heavy black velvet curtains were arranged so as to pull across the alcove. Elise was busy arranging the room. Close to the alcove she had set two chairs and a small round table. On the table was a tambourine, a horn, and some paper and pencils.

'The last time,' murmured Elise with grim satisfaction. 'Ah, Monsieur, I wish it were over and done with.'

The sharp ting of an electric bell sounded.

'There she is, the great gendarme of a woman,' continued the old servant. 'Why can't she go and pray decently for her little one's soul in a church, and burn a candle to Our Blessed Lady? Does not the good God know what is best for us?'

'Answer the bell, Elise,' said Raoul peremptorily.

She threw him a look, but obeyed. In a minute or two she returned ushering in the visitor.

'I will tell my mistress you are here, Madame.'

Raoul came forward to shake hands with Madame Exe. Simone's words floated back to his memory.

'So big and so black.'

She *was* a big woman, and the heavy black of French mourning seemed almost exaggerated in her case. Her voice when she spoke was very deep.

'I fear I am a little late, Monsieur.'

'A few moments only,' said Raoul, smiling. 'Madame Simone is lying down. I am sorry to say she is far from well, very nervous and overwrought.'

Her hand, which she was just withdrawing, closed on his suddenly like a vice.

'But she will sit?' she demanded sharply.

'Oh, yes, Madame.'

Madame Exe gave a sigh of relief, and sank into a chair, loosening one of the heavy black veils that floated round her.

'Ah, Monsieur!' she murmured, 'you cannot imagine, you cannot conceive the wonder and the joy of these *séances* to me! My little one! My Amelie! To see her, to hear her, even – perhaps – yes, perhaps to be even able to – stretch out my hand and touch her.'

Raoul spoke quickly and peremptorily.

'Madame Exe – how can I explain? – on no account must you do anything except under my express directions, otherwise there is the gravest danger.'

'Danger to me?'

'No, Madame,' said Raoul, 'to the medium. You must understand that the phenomena that occur are explained by Science in a certain way. I will put the matter very simply, using no technical terms. A spirit, to manifest itself, has to use the actual physical substance of the medium. You have seen the vapour of fluid issuing from the lips of the medium. This finally condenses and is built up into the physical semblance of the spirit's dead body. But this ectoplasm we believe to be the actual substance of the medium. We hope to prove this some day by careful weighing and testing – but the great difficulty is the danger and pain which attends the medium on any handling of the phenomena. Were anyone to seize hold of the materialization roughly the death of the medium might result.'

Madame Exe had listened to him with close attention.

'That is very interesting, Monsieur. Tell me, shall not a time come when the materializations shall advance so far that it shall be capable of detachment from its parent, the medium?'

'That is a fantastic speculation, Madame.'

She persisted.

'But, on the facts, not impossible?'

'Quite impossible today.'

'But perhaps in the future?'

He was saved from answering, for at that moment Simone entered. She looked languid and pale, but had evidently regained entire control of herself. She came forward and shook hands with Madame Exe, though Raoul noticed the faint shiver that passed through her as she did so.

'I regret, Madame, to hear that you are indisposed,' said Madame Exe.

'It is nothing,' said Simone rather brusquely. 'Shall we begin?'

She went to the alcove and sat down in the arm-chair. Suddenly Raoul in his turn felt a wave of fear pass over him.

'You are not strong enough,' he exclaimed. 'We had better cancel the *séance*. Madame Exe will understand.'

'Monsieur!'

Madame Exe rose indignantly.

'Yes, yes, it is better not, I am sure of it.'

'Madame Simone promised me one last sitting.'

'That is so,' agreed Simone quietly, 'and I am prepared to carry out my promise.'

'I hold you to it, Madame,' said the other woman.

'I do not break my word,' said Simone coldly. 'Do not fear, Raoul,' she added gently, 'after all, it is for the last time – the last time, thank God.'

At a sign from her Raoul drew the heavy black curtains across the alcove. He also pulled the curtains of the window so that the room was in semi-obscurity. He indicated one of the chairs to Madame Exe and prepared himself to take the other. Madame Exe, however, hesitated.

'You will pardon me, Monsieur, but – you understand I believe absolutely in your integrity and in that of Madame Simone. All the same, so that my testimony may be the more valuable, I took the liberty of bringing this with me.'

From her handbag she drew a length of fine cord.

'Madame!' cried Raoul. 'This is an insult!'

'A precaution.'

'I repeat it is an insult.'

'I don't understand your objection, Monsieur,' said Madame Exe coldly. 'If there is no trickery you have nothing to fear.'

Raoul laughed scornfully.

'I can assure you that I have nothing to fear, Madame. Bind me hand and foot if you will.'

His speech did not produce the effect he hoped, for Madame Exe merely murmured unemotionally:

'Thank you, Monsieur,' and advanced upon him with her roll of cord.

Suddenly Simone from behind the curtain gave a cry.

'No, no, Raoul, don't let her do it.'

Madame Exe laughed derisively.

'Madame is afraid,' she observed sarcastically.

'Yes, I am afraid.'

'Remember what you are saying, Simone,' cried Raoul. 'Madame Exe is apparently under the impression that we are charlatans.'

'I must make sure,' said Madame Exe grimly.

She went methodically about her task, binding Raoul securely to his chair.

'I must congratulate you on your knots, Madame,' he observed ironically when she had finished. 'Are you satisfied now?'

Madame Exe did not reply. She walked round the room examining the panelling of the walls closely. Then she locked the door leading into the hall, and, removing the key, returned to her chair.

'Now,' she said in an indescribable voice, 'I am ready.'

The minutes passed. From behind the curtain the sound of Simone's breathing became heavier and more stertorous. Then it died away altogether, to be succeeded by a series of moans. Then again there was silence for a little while, broken by the sudden clattering of the tambourine. The horn was caught up from the table and dashed to the ground. Ironic laughter was heard. The curtains of the alcove seemed to have been pulled back a little, the medium's figure was just visible through the opening, her head fallen forward on her breast. Suddenly Madame Exe drew in her breath sharply. A ribbon-like stream of mist was issuing from the medium's mouth. It condensed and began gradually to assume a shape, the shape of a little child.

'Amelie! My little Amelie!'

The hoarse whisper came from Madame Exe. The hazy figure condensed still further. Raoul stared almost incredulously. Never had there been a more successful materialization. Now, surely it was a real child, a real flesh and blood child standing there.

'*Maman!*'

The soft childish voice spoke.

'My child!' cried Madame Exe. 'My child!'

She half rose from her seat.

'Be careful, Madame,' cried Raoul warningly.

The materialization came hesitatingly through the curtains. It was a child. She stood there, her arms held out.

'*Maman!*'

'Ah!' cried Madame Exe.

Again she half rose from her seat.

'Madame,' cried Raoul, alarmed, 'the medium——'

'I must touch her,' cried Madame Exe hoarsely.

She moved a step forward.

'For God's sake, Madame, control yourself,' cried Raoul.

He was really alarmed now.

'Sit down at once.'

'My little one, I must touch her.'

'Madame, I command you, sit down!'

He was writhing desperately with his bonds, but Madame Exe had done her work well; he was helpless. A terrible sense of impeding disaster swept over him.

'In the name of God, Madame, sit down!' he shouted. 'Remember the medium.'

Madame Exe paid no attention to him. She was like a woman transformed. Ecstasy and delight showed plainly in her face. Her outstretched hand touched the little figure that stood in the opening of the curtains. A terrible moan came from the medium.

'My God!' cried Raoul. 'My God! This is terrible. The medium——'

Madame Exe turned on him with a harsh laugh.

'What do I care for your medium?' she cried. 'I want my child.'

'You are mad!'

'My child, I tell you. Mine! My own! My own flesh and blood! My little one come back to me from the dead, alive and breathing.'

Raoul opened his lips, but no words would come. She was terrible, this woman! Remorseless, savage, absorbed by her own passion. The baby lips parted, and for the third time the same word echoed:

'*Maman!*'

'Come then, my little one,' cried Madame Exe.

With a sharp gesture she caught up the child in her arms. From behind the curtains came a long-drawn scream of utter anguish.

'Simone!' cried Raoul. 'Simone!'

He was aware vaguely of Madame Exe rushing past him, of the unlocking of the door, of retreating footsteps down the stairs.

From behind the curtain there still sounded the terrible high long-drawn scream – such a scream as Raoul had never heard. It died away in a horrible kind of gurgle. Then there came the thud of a body falling . . .

Raoul was working like a maniac to free himself from his bonds. In his frenzy he accomplished the impossible, snapping the rope by sheer strength. As he struggled to his feet, Elise rushed in crying, 'Madame!'

'Simone!' cried Raoul.

Together they rushed forward and pulled the curtain.

Raoul staggered back.

'My God!' he murmured. 'Red – all red . . .'

Elise's voice came beside him harsh and shaking.

'So Madame is dead. It is ended. But tell me, Monsieur, what has happened. *Why is Madame all shrunken away – why is she half her usual size? What has been happening here?*'

'I do not know,' said Raoul.

His voice rose to a scream.

'I do not know. I do not know. But I think – I am going mad . . . Simone! Simone!'

De Mortuis

John Collier

Dr Rankin was a large and rawboned man on whom the newest suit at once appeared outdated, like a suit in a photograph of twenty years ago. This was due to the squareness and flatness of his torso, which might have been put together by a manufacturer of packing cases. His face also had a wooden and a roughly constructed look; his hair was wiglike and resentful of the comb. He had those huge and clumsy hands which can be an asset to a doctor in a small upstate town where people still retain a rural relish for paradox, thinking that the more apelike the paw, the more precise it can be in the delicate business of a tonsillectomy.

This conclusion was perfectly justified in the case of Dr Rankin. For example, on this particular fine morning, though his task was nothing more ticklish than the cementing over of a large patch on his cellar floor, he managed those large and clumsy hands with all the unflurried certainty of one who would never leave a sponge within or create an unsightly scar without.

The doctor surveyed his handiwork from all angles. He added a touch here and a touch there till he had achieved a smoothness altogether professional. He swept up a few last crumbs of soil and dropped them into the furnace. He paused before putting away the pick and shovel he had been using, and found occasion for yet another sweep of his trowel, which made the new surface precisely flush with the surrounding floor. At this moment of supreme concentration the porch door slammed with the report of a minor piece of artillery, which, appropriately enough, caused Dr Rankin to jump as if he had been shot.

The doctor lifted a frowning face and an attentive ear. He heard two pairs of heavy feet clump across the resonant floor of the porch. He heard the house door opened and the visitors enter the hall, with which his cellar communicated by a short flight of steps. He heard whistling and then the voices of Buck and Bud crying, 'Doc! Hi, Doc! They're biting!'

Whether the doctor was not inclined for fishing that day, or whether, like others of his large and heavy type, he experienced an especially sharp, unsociable reaction on being suddenly startled, or whether he was merely anxious to finish undisturbed the job in hand and proceed to more important duties, he did not respond immediately to the inviting outcry of his friends. Instead, he listened while it ran its natural course, dying down at last into a puzzled and fretful dialogue.

'I guess he's out.'

'I'll write a note – say we're at the creek, to come on down.'

'We could tell Irene.'

'But she's not here, either. You'd think *she'd* be around.'

'Ought to be, by the look of the place.'

'You said it, Bud. Just look at this table. You could write your name———'

'Sh-h-h! Look!'

Evidently the last speaker had noticed that the cellar door was ajar and that a light was shining below. Next moment the door was pushed wide open and Bud and Buck looked down.

'Why, Doc! There you are!'

'Didn't you hear us yelling?'

The doctor, not too pleased at what he had overheard, nevertheless smiled his rather wooden smile as his two friends made their way down the steps. 'I thought I heard someone,' he said.

'We were bawling our heads off,' Buck said. 'Thought nobody was home. Where's Irene?'

'Visiting,' said the doctor. 'She's gone visiting.'

'Hey, what goes on?' said Bud. 'What are you doing? Burying one of your patients, or what?'

'Oh, there's been water seeping up through the floor,' said the doctor. 'I figured it might be some spring opened up or something.'

'You don't say!' said Bud, assuming instantly the high ethical standpoint of the realtor. 'Gee, Doc, I sold you this property. Don't say I fixed you up with a dump where there's an underground spring.'

'There was water,' said the doctor.

'Yes, but, Doc, you can look on that geological map the Kiwanis Club got up. There's not a better section of subsoil in the town.'

'Looks like he sold you a pup,' said Buck, grinning.

'No,' said Bud. 'Look. When the Doc came here he was green. You'll admit he was green. The things he didn't know!'

'He bought Ted Webber's jalopy,' said Buck.

'He'd have bought the Jessop place if I'd let him,' said Bud. 'But I wouldn't give him a bum steer.'

'Not the poor, simple city slicker from Poughkeepsie,' said Buck.

'Some people would have taken him,' said Bud. 'Maybe some people did. Not me. I recommended this property. He and Irene moved straight in as soon as they were married. I wouldn't have put the Doc on to a dump where there'd be a spring under the foundations.'

'Oh, forget it,' said the doctor, embarrassed by this conscientiousness. 'I guess it was just the heavy rains.'

'By gosh!' Buck said, glancing at the besmeared point of the pickaxe. 'You certainly went deep enough. Right down into the clay, huh?'

'That's four feet down, the clay,' Bud said.

'Eighteen inches,' said the doctor.

'Four feet,' said Bud. 'I can show you the map.'

'Come on. No arguments,' said Buck. 'How's about it, Doc? An hour or two at the creek, eh? They're biting.'

'Can't do it, boys,' said the doctor. 'I've got to see a patient or two.'

'Aw, live and let live, Doc,' Bud said. 'Give 'em a chance to get better. Are you going to depopulate the whole darn town?'

The doctor looked down, smiled, and muttered, as he always did when this particular jest was trotted out. 'Sorry, boys,' he said. 'I can't make it.'

'Well,' said Bud, disappointed, 'I suppose we'd better get along. How's Irene?'

'Irene?' said the doctor. 'Never better. She's gone visiting. Albany. Got the eleven-o'clock train.'

'Eleven o'clock?' said Buck. 'For Albany?'

'Did I say Albany?' said the doctor. 'Watertown, I meant.'

'Friends in Watertown?' Buck asked.

'Mrs Slater,' said the doctor. 'Mr and Mrs Slater. Lived next door to 'em when she was a kid, Irene said, over on Sycamore Street.'

'Slater?' said Bud. 'Next door to Irene? Not in *this* town.'

'Oh, yes,' said the doctor. 'She was telling me all about them last night. She got a letter. Seems this Mrs Slater looked after her when her mother was in the hospital one time.'

'No,' said Bud.

'That's what she told me,' said the doctor. 'Of course, it was a good many years ago.'

'Look, Doc,' said Buck. 'Bud and I were raised in this town. We've known Irene's folks all our lives. We were in and out of their house all the time. There was never anybody next door called Slater.'

'Perhaps,' said the doctor, 'she married again, this woman. Perhaps it was a different name.'

Bud shook his head.

'What time did Irene go to the station?' Buck asked.

'Oh, about a quarter of an hour ago,' said the doctor.

'You didn't drive her?' said Buck.

'She walked,' said the doctor.

'We came down Main Street,' Buck said. 'We didn't meet her.'

'Maybe she walked across the pasture,' said the doctor.

'That's a tough walk with a suitcase,' said Buck.

'She just had a couple of things in a little bag,' said the doctor.

Bud was still shaking his head.

Buck looked at Bud and then at the pick, at the new, damp cement on the floor. 'Jesus Christ!' he said.

'Oh, God, Doc!' Bud said. 'A guy like you!'

'What in the name of heaven are you two bloody fools thinking?' asked the doctor. 'What are you trying to say?'

'A spring!' said Bud. 'I ought to have known right away it wasn't any spring.'

The doctor looked at his cement-work, at the pick, at the large worried faces of his two friends. His own face turned livid. 'Am I crazy?' he said. 'Or are you? You suggest that I've – that Irene – my wife – oh, go on! Get out! Yes, go and get the sherriff. Tell him to come here and start digging. You – get out!'

Bud and Buck looked at each other, shifted their feet, and stood still again.

'Go on,' said the doctor.

'I don't know,' said Bud.

'It's not as if he didn't have the provocation,' Buck said.

'God knows,' Bud said.

'God knows,' Buck said. 'You know. I know. The whole town knows. But try telling it to a jury.'

The doctor put his hand to his head. 'What's that?' he said. 'What is it? Now what are you saying? What do you mean?'

'If this ain't being on the spot!' said Buck. 'Doc, you can see how it is. It takes some thinking. We've been friends right from the start. Damn good friends.'

'But we've got to think,' said Bud. 'It's serious. Provocation or not, there's a law in the land. There's such a thing as being an accomplice.'

'You were talking provocation,' said the doctor.

'You're right,' said Buck. 'And you're our friend. And if ever it could be called justified——'

'We've got to fix this somehow,' said Bud.

'Justified?' said the doctor.

'You were bound to get wised up sooner or later,' said Buck.

'We could have told you,' said Bud. 'Only – what the hell?'

'We could,' said Buck. 'And we nearly did. Five years ago. Before ever you married her. You hadn't been here six months, but we sort of cottoned to you. Thought of giving you a hint. Spoke about it. Remember, Bud?'

Bud nodded. 'Funny,' he said. 'I came right out in the open about that Jessop property. I wouldn't let you buy that, Doc. But getting married, that's something else again. We could have told you.'

'We're that much responsible,' Buck said.

'I'm fifty,' said the doctor. 'I suppose it's pretty old for Irene.'

'If you was Johnny Weissmuller at the age of twenty-one, it wouldn't make any difference,' said Buck.

'I know a lot of people think she's not exactly a perfect wife,' said the doctor. 'Maybe she's not. She's young. She's full of life.'

'Oh, skip it!' said Buck sharply, looking at the raw cement. 'Skip it, Doc, for God's sake.'

The doctor brushed his hand across his face. 'Not everybody wants the same thing,' he said. 'I'm a sort of dry fellow. I don't open up very easily. Irene – you'd call her gay.'

'You said it,' said Buck.

'She's no housekeeper,' said the doctor. 'I know it. But that's not the only thing a man wants. She's enjoyed herself.'

'Yeah,' said Buck. 'She did.'

'That's what I love,' said the doctor. 'Because I'm not that way myself. She's not very deep, mentally. All right. Say she's stupid. I don't care. Lazy. No system. Well, I've got plenty of system. She's enjoyed herself. It's beautiful. It's innocent. Like a child.'

'Yes. If that was all,' Buck said.

'But,' said the doctor, turning his eyes full on him, 'you seem to know there was more.'

'Everybody knows it,' said Buck.

'A decent, straightforward guy comes to a place like this and marries the town floozy,' Bud said bitterly. 'And nobody'll tell him. Everybody just watches.'

'And laughs,' said Buck. 'You and me, Bud, as well as the rest.'

'We told her to watch her step,' said Bud. 'We warned her.'

'Everybody warned her,' said Buck. 'But people get fed up. When it got to truck-drivers——'

'It was never us, Doc,' said Bud, earnestly. 'Not after you came along, anyway.'

'The town'll be on your side,' said Buck.

'That won't mean much when the case comes to trial in the county seat,' said Bud.

'Oh!' cried the doctor, suddenly. 'What shall I do? What shall I do?'

'It's up to you, Bud,' said Buck. 'I can't turn him in.'

'Take it easy, Doc,' said Bud. 'Calm down. Look, Buck. When we came in here the street was empty, wasn't it?'

'I guess so,' said Buck. 'Anyway, nobody saw us come down cellar.'

'And we haven't been down,' Bud said, addressing himself forcefully to the doctor. 'Get that, Doc? We shouted upstairs, hung around a minute or two, and cleared out. But we never came down into this cellar.'

'I wish you hadn't,' the doctor said heavily.

'All you have to do is say Irene went out for a walk and never came back,' said Buck.'Bud and I can swear we saw her headed out of town with a fellow in a – well, say in a Buick sedan. Everybody'll believe that, all right. We'll fix it. But later. Now we'd better scram.'

'And remember, now. Stick to it. We never came down here and we haven't seen you today,' said Bud. 'So long!'

Buck and Bud ascended the steps, moving with a rather absurd degree of caution. 'You'd better get that ... that thing covered up,' Buck said over his shoulder.

Left alone, the doctor sat down on an empty box, holding his head with both hands. He was still sitting like this when the porch door slammed again. This time he did not start. He listened. The house door opened and closed. A voice cried, 'Yoo-hoo! Yoo-hoo! I'm back.'

The doctor rose slowly to his feet. 'I'm down here, Irene!' he called.

The cellar door opened. A young woman stood at the head of the steps. 'Can you beat it?' she said. 'I missed the damn train.'

'Oh!' said the doctor. 'Did you come back across the field?'

'Yes, like a fool,' she said. 'I could have hitched a ride and caught the train up the line. Only I didn't think. If you'd run me over to the junction, I could still make it.'

'Maybe,' said the doctor. 'Did you meet anyone coming back?'

'Not a soul,' she said. 'Aren't you finished with that old job yet?'

'I'm afraid I'll have to take it all up again,' said the doctor. 'Come down here, my dear, and I'll show you.'

A Terribly Strange Bed

William Wilkie Collins

Shortly after my education at college was finished, I happened to be staying at Paris with an English friend. We were both young men then, and lived, I am afraid, rather a wild life, in the delightful city of our sojourn. One night we were idling about the neighbourhood of the Palais Royal, doubtful to what amusement we should next betake ourselves. My friend proposed a visit to Frascati's; but his suggestion was not to my taste. I knew Frascati's, as the French saying is, by heart; had lost and won plenty of five-franc pieces there, merely for amusement's sake, until it was amusement no longer, and was thoroughly tired, in fact, of all the ghastly respectabilities of such a social anomaly as a respectable gambling-house. 'For heaven's sake,' said I to my friend, 'let us go somewhere where we can see a little genuine, blackguard, poverty-stricken gaming, with no false gingerbread glitter thrown over it at all. Let us get away from fashionable Frascati's, to a house where they don't mind letting in a man with a ragged coat, or a man with no coat, ragged or otherwise.' – 'Very well,' said my friend, 'we needn't go out of the Palais Royal to find the sort of company you want. Here's the place just before us; as blackguard a place, by all report, as you could possibly wish to see.' In another minute we arrived at the door, and entered the house, the back of which you have drawn in your sketch.

When we got upstairs, and left our hats and sticks with the door-keeper, we were admitted into the chief gambling-room. We did not find many people assembled there. But, few as the men were who looked up at us on our entrance, they were all types – lamentably true types – of their respective classes.

We had come to see blackguards; but these men were something worse. There is a comic side, more or less appreciable, in all black-guardism – here there was nothing but tragedy – mute, weird tragedy. The quiet in the room was horrible. The thin, haggard, long-haired young man, whose sunken eyes fiercely watched the turning up of the cards, never spoke; the flabby, fat-faced, pimply player, who pricked his piece of pasteboard perseveringly, to register how often black won, and how often red – never spoke; the dirty, wrinkled old man, with the vulture eyes and the darned greatcoat, who had lost his last *sou*, and still looked on desperately, after he could play no longer – never spoke. Even the voice of the croupier sounded as if it were strangely dulled and thickened in the atmosphere of the room. I had entered the place to laugh, but the spectacle before me was something to weep over. I soon found it necessary to take refuge in excitement from the depression of spirits which was fast stealing on me. Unfortunately I sought the nearest excitement, by going to the table, and beginning to play. Still more unfortunately, as the event will show, I won – won prodigiously; won incredibly; won at such a rate, that the regular players at the table crowded round me, and, staring at my stakes with hungry, superstitious eyes, whispered to one another that the English stranger was going to break the bank.

The game was *Rouge et Noir*. I had played at it in every city in Europe, without, however, the care or the wish to study the Theory of Chances – that philosopher's stone of all gamblers! And a gambler, in the strict sense of the word, I had never been. I was heart-whole from the corroding passion for play. My gaming was a mere idle amusement. I never resorted to it by necessity, because I never knew what it was to want money. I never practised it so incessantly as to lose more than I could afford, or to gain more than I could coolly pocket without being thrown off my balance by my good luck. In short, I had hitherto frequented gambling-tables – just as I frequented ball-rooms and opera-houses – because they amused me, and because I had nothing better to do with my leisure hours.

But on this occasion it was very different – now, for the first time in my life, I felt what the passion for play really was. My success first bewildered, and then, in the most literal meaning of the word, in-toxicated me. Incredible as it may appear, it is nevertheless true, that I only lost when I attempted to estimate chances, and played according to previous calculation. If I left everything to luck, and staked without any care or consideration, I was sure to win – to win in the face of every recognized probability in favour of the bank. At first, some of the men present ventured their money safely enough on my colour; but I speedily increased my stakes to sums which they dared not risk. One after another they left off playing, and breathlessly looked on at my game.

Still, time after time, I staked higher and higher, and still won. The excitement in the room rose to fever pitch. The silence was interrupted by a deep-muttered chorus of oaths and exclamations in different languages every time the gold was shovelled across to my side of the table – even the imperturbable croupier dashed his rake to the floor in a (French) fury of astonishment at my success. But one man present preserved his self-possession; and that man was my friend. He came to my side and, whispering in English, begged me to leave the place, satisfied with what I had already gained. I must do him the justice to say that he repeated his warnings and entreaties several times, and only left me and went away, after I had rejected his advice (I was to all intents and purposes gambling-drunk) in terms which rendered it impossible for him to address me again that night.

Shortly after he had gone, a hoarse voice behind me cried: 'Permit me, my dear sir! – permit me to restore to their proper place two Napoleons which you have dropped. Wonderful luck, sir! I pledge you my word of honour, as an old soldier, in the course of my long experience in this sort of thing, I never saw such luck as yours! – never! Go on, sir – *sacré mille bombes!* Go on boldly, and break the bank!'

I turned round and saw, nodding and smiling at me with inveterate civility, a tall man, dressed in a frogged and braided surtout.

If I had been in my senses, I should have considered him, personally, as being rather a suspicious specimen of an old soldier. He had goggling blood-shot eyes, mangy mustachios, and a broken nose. His voice betrayed a barrack-room intonation of the worst order, and he had the dirtiest pair of hands I ever saw – even in France. These little personal peculiarities exercised, however, no repelling influence on me. In the mad excitement, the reckless triumph of that moment, I was ready to 'fraternize' with anybody who encouraged me in my game. I accepted the old soldier's offered pinch of snuff; clapped him on the back, and swore he was the honestest fellow in the world – the most glorious relic of the Grand Army that I had ever met with. 'Go on!' cried my military friend, snapping his fingers in ecstasy – 'Go on, and win! Break the bank – *mille tonnerres!* my gallant English comrade, break the bank!'

And I *did* go on – went on at such a rate that in another quarter of an hour the croupier called out: 'Gentlemen! the bank has discontinued for tonight.' All the notes, and all the gold in that 'bank', now lay in a heap under my hands; the whole floating capital of the gambling-house was waiting to pour into my pockets!

'Tie up the money in your pocket-handkerchief, my worthy sir,' said the old soldier, as I wildly plunged my hands into my heap of gold. 'Tie it up, as we used to tie up a bit of dinner in the Grand Army; your winnings are too heavy for any breeches pockets that ever were sewed. There! that's it! – shovel them in, notes and all! *Credié!* what luck! – Stop! another Napoleon on the floor! *Ah! sacré petit polisson de Napoléon!* have I found thee at last? Now then, sir – two tight double knots each way with your honourable permission, and the money's safe. Feel it! feel it, fortunate sir! hard and round as a cannon ball – *ah, bah!* if they had only fired such cannon balls at us at Austerlitz – *nom d'une pipe!* if only they had! And now, as an ancient grenadier, as an ex-brave of the French Army, what remains for me to do? I ask what? Simply this: to entreat my valued English friend to drink a bottle of champagne with me, and toast the goddess Fortune in foaming goblets before we part!'

Excellent ex-brave! Convivial ancient grenadier! Champagne by all means! An English cheer for an old soldier! Hurrah! hurrah! Another English cheer for the goddess Fortune! Hurrah! hurrah! hurrah!

'Bravo! the Englishman; the amiable, gracious Englishman, in whose veins circulates the vivacious blood of France! Another glass? *Ah, bah!* – the bottle is empty! Never mind! *Vive le vin!* I, the old soldier, order another bottle, and half a pound of *bonbons* with it!'

'No, no, ex-brave; never – ancient grenadier! *Your* bottle last time; *my* bottle this. Behold it! Toast away! The French Army! – the great Napoleon! – the present company! the croupier! the honest croupier's wife and daughters – if he has any! the Ladies generally! Everybody in the world!'

By the time the second bottle of champagne was emptied, I felt as if I had been drinking liquid fire – my brain seemed all a-flame. No excess in wine ever had this effect on me before in my life. Was it the result of a stimulant acting upon my system when I was in a highly excited state? Was my stomach in a particularly disordered condition? Or was the champagne amazingly strong?

'Ex-brave of the French Army!' cried I, in a mad state of exhilaration, '*I am on fire! how are you?* You have set me on fire! Do you hear, my hero of Austerlitz? Let us have a third bottle of champagne to put the flame out!'

The old soldier wagged his head, rolled his goggle eyes, until I expected to see them slip out of their sockets; placed his dirty forefinger by the side of his broken nose; solemnly ejaculated 'Coffee!' and immediately ran off into an inner room.

The word pronounced by the eccentric veteran seemed to have a magical effect on the rest of the company present. With one accord they all rose to depart. Probably they had expected to profit by my intoxication; but finding that my new friend was benevolently bent on preventing me from getting dead drunk, had now abandoned all hope of thriving pleasantly on my winnings. Whatever their motive might be, at any rate they went away in a body. When the old soldier returned, and sat down again opposite to me at the table, we had the room to ourselves. I could see the croupier, in a sort of vestibule which opened out of it, eating his supper in solitude. The silence was now deeper than ever.

A sudden change, too, had come over the 'ex-brave'. He assumed a portentously solemn look! and when he spoke to me again, his speech was ornamented by no oaths, enforced by no finger-snapping, enlivened by no apostrophes or exclamations.

'Listen, my dear sir,' said he, in mysteriously confidential tones –

'listen to an old soldier's advice. I have been to the mistress of the house (a very charming woman, with a genius for cookery!) to impress on her the necessity of making us some particularly strong and good coffee. You must drain this coffee in order to get rid of your little amiable exaltation of spirits before you think of going home – you *must*, my good and gracious friend! With all that money to take home tonight, it is a sacred duty to yourself to have your wits about you. You are known to be a winner to an enormous extent by several gentlemen present tonight, who, in a certain point of view, are very worthy and excellent fellows, but they are mortal men, my dear sir, and they have their amiable weaknesses! Need I say more? Ah, no, no! you understand me! Now, this is what you must do – send for a cabriolet when you feel quite well again – draw up all the windows when you get into it – and tell the driver to take you home only through the large and well-lighted thoroughfares. Do this; and you and your money will be safe. Do this; and tomorrow you will thank an old soldier for giving you a word of honest advice.'

Just as the ex-brave ended his oration in very lachrymose tones, the coffee came in, ready poured out into two cups. My attentive friend handed me one of the cups with a bow. I was parched with thirst, and drank it off at a draught. Almost instantly afterwards, I was seized with a fit of giddiness, and felt more completely intoxicated than ever. The room whirled round and round furiously; the old soldier seemed to be regularly bobbing up and down before me like the piston of a steam-engine. I was half deafened by a violent singing in my ears; a feeling of utter bewilderment, helplessness, idiocy, overcame me. I rose from my chair, holding on by the table to keep my balance, and stammered out that I felt dreadfully unwell – so unwell that I did not know how I was to get home.

'My dear friend,' answered the old soldier – and even his voice seemed to be bobbing up and down as he spoke – 'my dear friend, it would be madness to go home in *your* state; you would be sure to lose your money; you might be robbed and murdered with the greatest ease. *I* am going to sleep here: do *you* sleep here, too – they make up capital beds in this house – take one; sleep off the effects of the wine, and go home safely with your winnings tomorrow – tomorrow, in broad daylight.'

I had but two ideas left: – one, that I must never let go hold of my handkerchief full of money; the other, that I must lie down somewhere immediately, and fall off into a comfortable sleep. So I agreed to the proposal about the bed, and took the offered arm of the old soldier, carrying my money with my disengaged hand. Preceded by the croupier, we passed along some passages and up a flight of stairs into the bedroom which I was to occupy. The ex-brave shook me warmly by the hand, proposed that we should breakfast together, and then, followed by the croupier, left me for the night.

I ran to the wash-hand stand; drank some of the water in my jug; poured the rest out, and plunged my face into it; then sat down in a chair and tried to compose myself. I soon felt better. The change for my lungs, from the fetid atmosphere of the gambling-room to the cool air of the apartment I now occupied; the almost equally refreshing change for my eyes, from the glaring gas-lights of the 'salon' to the dim, quiet flicker of one bedroom candle, aided wonderfully the restorative effects of cold water. The giddiness left me, and I began to feel a little like a reasonable being again. My first thought was of the risk of sleeping all night in a gambling-house; my second, of the still greater risk of trying to get out after the house was closed, and of going home alone at night, through the streets of Paris, with a large sum of money about me. I had slept in worse places than this on my travels; so I determined to lock, bolt, and barricade my door, and take my chance till the next morning.

Accordingly, I secured myself against all intrusion; looked under the bed, and into the cupboard; tried the fastening of the window; and then, satisfied that I had taken every proper precaution, pulled off my upper clothing, put my light, which was a dim one, on the hearth among a feathery litter of wood ashes, and got into bed, with the handkerchief full of money under my pillow.

I soon felt not only that I could not go to sleep, but that I could not even close my eyes. I was wide awake, and in a high fever. Every nerve in my body trembled – every one of my senses seemed to be preternaturally sharpened. I tossed and rolled, and tried every kind of position, and perseveringly sought out the cold corners of the bed, and all to no purpose. Now, I thrust my arms over the clothes; now, I poked them under the clothes; now, I violently shot my legs straight out down to the bottom of the bed; now, I convulsively coiled them up as near my chin as they would go; now, I shook out my crumpled pillow, changed it to the cool side, patted it flat, and lay down quietly on my back; now, I fiercely doubled it in two, set it up on end, thrust it against the board of the bed, and tried a sitting posture. Every effort was in vain; I groaned with vexation, as I felt that I was in for a sleepless night.

What could I do? I had no book to read. And yet, unless I found out some method of diverting my mind, I felt certain that I was in the condition to imagine all sorts of horrors; to rack my brain with forebodings of every possible and impossible danger; in short, to pass the night in suffering all conceivable varieties of nervous terror.

I raised myself on my elbow, and looked about the room – which was brightened by a lovely moonlight pouring straight through the window – to see if it contained any pictures or ornaments that I could at all clearly distinguish. While my eyes wandered from wall to wall, a remembrance of Le Maistre's delightful little book, *Voyage autour de ma Chambre*, occurred to me. I resolved to imitate the French author, and find occupation and amusement enough to relieve the tedium of my wakefulness, by making a mental inventory of every article of furniture I could see, and by following up to their sources the multitude of associations which even a chair, a table, or a wash-hand stand may be made to call forth.

In the nervous unsettled state of my mind at that moment, I found it much easier to make my inventory than to make my reflections, and thereupon soon gave up all hope of thinking in Le Maistre's fanciful track – or, indeed, of thinking at all. I looked about the room at the different articles of furniture, and did nothing more.

There was, first, the bed I was lying in; a four-post bed, of all things in the world to meet with in Paris! – yes, a thoroughly clumsy British four-poster, with the regular top lined with chintz – the regular fringed valance all around – the regular stifling unwholesome curtains, which I remembered having mechanically drawn back against the posts without particularly noticing the bed when I first got into the room. Then there was the marble-topped wash-hand stand, from which the water I had spilt, in my hurry to pour it out, was still dripping, slowly and more slowly, on to the brick floor. Then two small chairs, with my coat, waistcoat, and trousers flung on them. Then a large elbow-chair covered with dirty-white dimity, with my cravat and shirt-collar thrown over the back. Then a chest of drawers with two of the brass handles off, and a tawdry, broken china inkstand placed on it by way of ornament for the top. Then the dressing-table, adorned by a very small looking-glass, and a very large pincushion. Then the window – an unusually large window. Then a dark old picture, which the feeble candle dimly showed me. It was the picture of a fellow in a high Spanish hat, crowned with a plume of towering feathers. A swarthy sinister ruffian, looking upward, shading his eyes with his hand, and looking intently upward – it might be at some tall gallows at which he was going to be hanged. At any rate, he had the appearance of thoroughly deserving it.

This picture put a kind of constraint upon me to look upward too – at the top of the bed. It was a gloomy and not an interesting object, and I looked back at the picture. I counted the feathers in the man's hat – they stood out in relief – three white, two green. I observed the crown of his hat, which was of a conical shape, according to the fashion supposed to have been favoured by Guido Fawkes. I wondered what he was looking up at. It couldn't be at the stars; such a desperado was neither astrologer nor astronomer. It must be at the high gallows, and he was going to be hanged presently. Would the executioner come into possession of his conical-crowned hat and plume of feathers? I counted the feathers again – three white, two green.

While I still lingered over this very improving intellectual employment, my thoughts insensibly began to wander. The moonlight shining into the room reminded me of a certain moonlight night in England – the night after a picnic party in a Welsh valley. Every incident of the drive homeward, through lovely scenery, which the moonlight made lovelier than ever, came back to my remembrance, though I had never given the picnic a thought for years; though, if I had *tried* to recollect it, I could certainly have recalled little or nothing of that scene long past. Of all the wonderful faculties that help to tell us we are immortal, which speaks the sublime truth more eloquently than memory? Here was I, in a strange house of the most suspicious character, in a situation of uncertainty, and even of peril, which might seem to make the cool exercise of my recollection almost out of the question; nevertheless, remembering, quite involuntarily, places, people, conversations, minute circumstances of every kind, which I had thought forgotten for ever; which I could not possibly have recalled at will, even under the most favourable auspices. And what cause had produced in a moment the whole of this strange, complicated, mysterious effect? Nothing but some rays of moonlight shining in at my bedroom window.

I was still thinking of the picnic – of our merriment on the drive home – of the sentimental young lady who *would* quote *Childe Harold* because it was moonlight. I was absorbed by these past scenes and past amusements, when, in an instant, the thread on which my memories hung snapped asunder; my attention immediately came back to present things more vividly than ever, and I found myself, I neither knew why nor wherefore, looking hard at the picture again.

Looking for what?

Good God! the man had pulled his hat down on his brows! – No! the hat itself was gone! Where was the conical crown? Where the feathers – three white, two green? Not there! In place of the hat and feathers, what dusky object was it that now hid his forehead, his eyes, his shading hand?

Was the bed moving?

I turned on my back and looked up. Was I mad? drunk? dreaming? giddy again? or was the top of the bed really moving down – sinking slowly, regularly, silently, horribly, right down throughout the whole of its length and breadth – right down upon me, as I lay underneath?

My blood seemed to stand still. A deadly paralysing coldness stole all over me, as I turned my head round on the pillow, and determined to test whether the bed-top was really moving or not by keeping my eye on the man in the picture.

The next look in that direction was enough. The dull, black, frowsy outline of the valance above me was within an inch of being parallel with his waist. I still looked breathlessly. And steadily, and slowly – very slowly – I saw the figure, and the line of frame below the figure, vanish, as the valance moved down before it.

I am, constitutionally, anything but timid. I have been on more than one occasion in peril of my life, and have not lost my self-possession for an instant; but when the conviction first settled on my mind that the bed-top was really moving, was steadily and continuously sinking down upon me, I looked up shuddering, helpless, panic-stricken, beneath the hideous machinery for murder, which was advancing closer and closer to suffocate me where I lay.

I looked up, motionless, speechless, breathless. The candle, fully spent, went out; but the moonlight still brightened the room. Down and down, without pausing and without sounding, came the bed-top, and still my panic-terror seemed to bind me faster and faster to the mattress on which I lay – down and down it sank, till the dusty odour from the lining of the canopy came stealing into my nostrils.

At that final moment, the instinct of self-preservation startled me out of my trance, and I moved at last. There was just room for me to roll myself sideways off the bed. As I dropped noiselessly to the floor, the edge of the murderous canopy touched me on the shoulder.

Without stopping to draw my breath, without wiping the cold sweat from my face, I rose instantly on my knees to watch the bed-top. I was literally spellbound by it. If I had heard footsteps behind me, I could not have turned round; if a means of escape had been miraculously provided for me, I could not have moved to take advantage of it. The whole life in me was, at that moment, concentrated in my eyes.

It descended – the whole canopy, with the fringe round it, came down – down – close down; so close that there was not room now to squeeze my finger between the bed-top and the bed. I felt at the sides, and discovered that what had appeared to me from beneath to be the ordinary light canopy of a four-post bed, was in reality a thick, broad mattress, the substance of which was concealed by the valance and its fringe. I looked up and saw the four posts rising, hideously bare. In the middle of the bed-top was a huge wooden screw that had evidently worked it down through a hole in the ceiling, just as ordinary presses are worked down on the substance selected for compression. The frightful apparatus moved without making the faintest noise. There had been no creaking as it came down; there was now not the faintest sound from the room above. Amid a dead and awful silence I beheld before me – in the nineteenth century, and in the civilized capital of France – such a machine for secret murder by suffocation as might have existed in the worst days of the Inquisition, in the lonely inns among the Hartz Mountains, in the mysterious tribunals of Westphalia! Still, as I looked on it, I could not move, I could hardly breathe, but I began to recover the power of thinking, and in a moment I discovered the murderous conspiracy framed against me in all its horror.

My cup of coffee had been drugged, and drugged too strongly. I had been saved from being smothered by having taken an overdose of some narcotic. How I had chafed and fretted at the fever-fit which had preserved my life by keeping me awake! How recklessly I had confided myself to the two wretches who had led me into this room, determined, for the sake of my winnings, to kill me in my sleep by the surest and most horrible contrivance for secretly accomplishing my destruction! How many men, winners like me, had slept, as I had proposed to sleep, in that bed, and had never been seen or heard of more! I shuddered at the bare idea of it.

But, ere long, all thought was again suspended by the sight of the murderous canopy moving once more. After it had remained on the bed – as nearly as I could guess – about ten minutes, it began to move up again. The villains who worked it from above evidently believed that their purpose was now accomplished. Slowly and silently, as it had descended, that horrible bed-top rose towards its former place. When it reached the upper extremities of the four posts, it reached the ceiling too. Neither hole nor screw could be seen; the bed became in appearance an ordinary bed again – the canopy an ordinary canopy – even to the most suspicious eyes.

Now, for the first time, I was able to move – to rise from my knees – to dress myself in my upper clothing – and to consider of how I should escape. If I betrayed, by the smallest noise, that the attempt to suffocate me had failed, I was certain to be murdered. Had I made any noise already? I listened intently, looking towards the door.

No! no footsteps in the passage outside – no sound of a tread, light or heavy, in the room above – absolute silence everywhere. Besides locking and bolting the door, I had moved an old wooden chest against it, which I had found under the bed. To remove this chest (my blood ran cold as I thought of what its contents *might* be!) without making some disturbance was impossible; and, moreover, to think of escaping through the house, now barred up for the night, was sheer insanity. Only one chance was left me – the window. I stole to it on tiptoe.

My bedroom was on the first floor, above an *entresol*, and looked into the back street, which you have sketched in your view. I raised my hand to open the window, knowing that on that action hung, by the merest hair's-breadth, my chance of safety. They keep vigilant watch in a House of Murder. If any part of the frame cracked, if the hinge creaked, I was a lost man! It must have occupied me at least five minutes, reckoning by time – five *hours*, reckoning by suspense – to open that window. I succeeded in doing it silently – in doing it with all the dexterity of a housebreaker – and then looked down into the street. To leap the distance beneath me would be almost certain destruction! Next, I looked round at the sides of the house. Down the left side ran the thick water-pipe which you have drawn – it passed close by the outer edge of the window. The moment I saw the pipe, I knew I was saved. My breath came and went freely for the first time since I had seen the canopy of the bed moving down upon me!

To some men the means of escape which I had discovered might have seemed difficult and dangerous enough – to *me* the prospect of slipping down the pipe into the street did not suggest even a thought of peril. I had always been accustomed, by the practice of gymnastics, to keep up my schoolboy powers as a daring and expert climber; and knew that my head, hands, and feet would serve me faithfully in any hazards of ascent or descent. I had already got one leg over the window-sill, when I remembered the handkerchief filled with money under my pillow. I could well have afforded to leave it behind me, but I was revengefully determined that the miscreants of the gambling-house should miss their plunder as well as their victim. So I went back to the bed and tied the heavy handkerchief at my back by my cravat.

Just as I had made it tight and fixed it in a comfortable place, I thought I heard a sound of breathing outside the door. The chill feeling of horror ran through me again as I listened. No! dead silence still in the passage – I had only heard the night air blowing softly into the room. The next moment I was on the window-sill – and the next I had a firm grip on the water-pipe with my hands and knees.

I slid down into the street easily and quietly, as I thought I should, and immediately set off at the top of my speed to a branch 'Prefecture' of Police, which I knew was situated in the immediate neighbourhood. A 'Sub-prefect', and several picked men among his subordinates, happened to be up, maturing, I believe, some scheme for discovering the perpetrator of a mysterious murder which all Paris was talking of just then. When I began my story, in a breathless hurry and in very bad French, I could see that the Sub-prefect suspected me of being a drunken Englishman who had robbed somebody; but he soon altered his opinion as I went on, and before I had anything like concluded, he shoved all the papers before him into a drawer, put on his hat, supplied me with another (for I was bare-headed), ordered a file of soldiers, desired his expert followers to get ready all sorts of tools for breaking open doors and ripping up brick-flooring, and took my arm, in the most friendly and familiar manner possible, to lead me with him out of the house. I will venture to say, that when the Sub-prefect was a little boy, and was taken for the first time to the play, he was not half as much pleased as he was now at the job in prospect for him at the gambling-house!

Away we went through the streets, the Sub-prefect cross-examining and congratulating me in the same breath as we marched at the head of our formidable *posse comitatus*. Sentinels were placed at the back and front of the house the moment we got to it; a tremendous battery of knocks was directed against the door; a light appeared at a window; I was told to conceal myself behind the police – then came more knocks, and a cry of 'Open in the name of the law!' At that terrible summons bolts and locks gave way before an invisible hand, and the moment after the Sub-prefect was in the passage, confronting a waiter half-dressed and ghastly pale. This was the short dialogue which immediately took place:

'We want to see the Englishman who is sleeping in this house.'

'He went away hours ago.'

'He did no such thing. His friend went away; *he* remained. Show us to his bedroom!'

'I swear to you, Monsieur le Sous-prefect, he is not here! he——'

'I swear to you, Monsieur le Garçon, he is. He slept here – he didn't find your bed comfortable – he came to us to complain of it – here he is among my men – and here am I ready to look for a flea or two in his bedstead. Renaudin!' (calling to one of the subordinates, and pointing to the waiter) 'collar that man, and tie his hands behind him. Now, then, gentlemen, let us walk upstairs!'

Every man and woman in the house was secured – the 'Old Soldier' the first. Then I identified the bed in which I had slept, and then we went into the room above.

No object that was at all extraordinary appeared in any part of it. The Sub-prefect looked round the place, commanded everybody to be silent, stamped twice on the floor, called for a candle, looked attentively at the spot he had stamped on, and ordered the flooring there to be carefully taken up. This was done in no time. Lights were produced, and we saw a deep raftered cavity between the floor of this room and the ceiling of the room beneath. Through this cavity there ran perpendicularly a sort of case of iron thickly greased; and inside the case appeared the screw, which communicated with the bed-top below. Extra lengths of screw, freshly oiled; levers covered with felt; all the complete upper works of a heavy press – constructed with infernal ingenuity so as to join the fixtures below, and when taken to pieces again to go into the smallest possible compass – were next discovered and pulled out on the floor. After some little difficulty, the Sub-prefect succeeded in putting the machinery together, and, leaving his men to work it, descended with me to the bedroom. The smothering canopy was then lowered, but not so noiselessly as I had seen it lowered. When I mentioned this to the Sub-prefect, his answer, simple as it was, had a terrible significance. 'My men,' said he, 'are working down the bed-top for the first time – the men whose money you won were in better practice.'

We left the house in the sole possession of two police agents – every one of the inmates being removed to prison on the spot. The Sub-prefect, after taking down my *procès-verbal* in his office, returned with me to my hotel to get my passport. 'Do you think,' I asked, as I gave it to him, 'that any men have really been smothered in that bed, as they tried to smother *me*?'

'I have seen dozens of drowned men laid out at the Morgue,' answered the Sub-prefect, 'in whose pocketbooks were found letters, stating that they had committed suicide in the Seine, because they had lost everything at the gaming-table. Do I know how many of those men entered the same gambling-house that *you* entered? won as *you* won? took that bed as *you* took it? slept in it? were smothered in it? and were privately thrown into the river, with a letter of explanation written by the murderers and placed in their pocket-books? No man can say how many or how few have suffered the fate from which you have escaped. The people of the gambling-house kept their bedstead machinery a secret from *us* – even from the police! The dead kept the rest of the secret for them. Good night, or rather good morning, Monsieur Faulkner! Be at my office again at nine o'clock – in the meantime, *au revoir!*'

The rest of my story is soon told. I was examined and re-examined; the gambling-house was strictly searched all through from top to bottom; the prisoners were separately interrogated; and two of the less guilty among them made a confession. *I* discovered that the old soldier was the master of the gambling-house – *justice* discovered that he had been drummed out of the army as a vagabond years ago; that he had been guilty of all sorts of villainies since; that he was in possession of stolen property, which the owners identified; and that he, the croupier, another accomplice, and the woman who had made my cup of coffee, were all in the secret of the bedstead. There appeared some reason to doubt whether the inferior persons attached to the house knew anything of the suffocating machinery; and they received the benefit of that doubt, by being treated simply as thieves and vagabonds. As for the old soldier and his two head-myrmidons, they went to the galleys; the woman who had drugged my coffee was imprisoned for I forget how many years; the regular attendants at the gambling-house were considered 'suspicious', and placed under 'surveillance'; and I became, for one whole week (which is a long time), the head 'lion' in Parisian society. My adventure was dramatized by three illustrious playmakers, but never saw theatrical daylight; for the censorship forbade the introduction on the stage of a correct copy of the gambling-house bedstead.

One good result was produced by my adventure, which any censorship must have approved: – it cured me of ever again trying *Rouge et Noir* as an amusement. The sight of a green cloth, with packs of cards and heaps of money on it, will henceforth be for ever associated in my mind with the sight of a bed-canopy descending to suffocate me in the silence and darkness of the night.

Green Fingers

R. C. Cook

Widow Bowen was getting old. She was seventy-five, perhaps, or eighty. No one in Breth Common really knew. But then, it didn't really matter. She looked the same trim little person that she had always been, even while her husband, Ernest, had been alive, and he had died ten years ago.

The little grey stone cottage on the hill lane up to the common was half hidden by damson trees from the road, and wrapped snugly, as if in a woollen comforter, by the flowering creeper which grew up beside the door. The round hawthorn hedge at the bottom of the garden by the road was neatly trimmed and looked like a long green sponge roll.

At times, the villagers expressed surprise and a little pride in the old lady when they saw how well kept the garden still was. It was a lot of work for an old woman, and a house-proud woman at that. Widow Bowen would just smile when the baker remarked on how strong and green her shallots were growing, or when Nurse Foley called up from the road, with her laughing red face, to say that the broad beans looked a picture. Widow Bowen would say, and her blue eyes would twinkle, 'I think I must have green fingers. Everything grows well here.' And she thought she was being rather modest at that, for she could not remember anything that had not grown for her when she planted it.

She would say the same thing to Mrs Beddoe at the farm when, in summer, she took down a basketful of long runner beans to help pay for the milk she fetched. 'I must have green fingers,' she would say and smile into Mrs Beddoe's sceptical face. Mrs Beddoe didn't quite know what to think. She didn't really want the vegetables that Widow Bowen brought in her basket, and yet, neither did she want to show the old lady how mercenary she was by asking for money instead, so she just looked down at the white bobbed hair and placed the jug of milk carefully into the thin hands.

Often when Widow Bowen knelt polishing the red-tiled step at her front door she would pause and smile to herself because the brass edge on the step and the kettle on the hob in the kitchen gleamed so brightly. There could not have been a brighter house on the common than hers, for Ernest and she had never had children, and she was a spotless housekeeper.

But most of all she was pleased with the garden behind her. Not a weed showing itself, and everything so very green and growing. 'Really, I must be very clever,' she thought. She was not superstitious, and wasn't sure at times that there was in fact a God in the sky – often she would look up when it was blue and couldn't see even a trace of him – but she felt that, in some way, she must have a gift. She would trot on her small feet around into the shade at the back of the house and plant another cutting from the rose tree near the lavatory, which had a seat scrubbed white as snow.

'I think I could make just anything grow,' she said to herself once, and to prove it she broke a twig off the old apple tree and stuck it into the ground. It was February, and the buds were still hard. Sure enough, in a week, the buds began to show green. She examined the twig each morning, and soon there were slender green shoots bursting out with a flare of leaf at their tips.

She felt it was all so very simple. Indeed, they were only ordinary things that she planted, such as anyone on the common might grow. It wasn't enough for a person with really green fingers. So, when the gardener from the big house in the valley walked by, up the hill, one Sunday afternoon, she stopped him at her gate and asked him in a quiet little voice if he would do her the kindness of bringing her a few bits of the tropical plants from the hothouses. He smiled at her, thinking she couldn't possibly have anywhere to plant them, but promised.

'It'd be a pleasure, Mrs Bowen,' he said, touching his cap. 'I'll find something for you.' And on the following Sunday he brought a chip basket to her door filled with queer little bits of dark shiny leaves and pieces of cactus.

'Won't you come in and have a cup of tea?' she asked, smiling up at him, and though he was anxious to be off to his sister's house at the corner of the coppice, he took off his cap and bowed his head to go in under the low doorway. He blushed and mumbled, 'Thank you, kindly,' when she brought him sweet milky tea in a china cup with blackberries painted on it. He wet his finger on his tongue and dabbed up all the crumbs of the piece of faintly scented cake she placed by his arm.

'I can make those plants grow,' she said, smoothing her hands on her black apron.

'Are you going to have them in pots indoors, then?' he asked.

'Oh, no,' she laughed, carelessly. 'In the garden. They'll grow all right.'

'I think you'll find it's too cold for 'em out there,' he said. 'I could've brought you some proper outdoor plants if you'd said anything, only . . .'

'No. These are just what I want. I want to try something really difficult for a change.'

He was puzzled a little, and when he had gone down the path and the gate had clicked behind him she fetched her broom and tidied up the dust his boots had brought in.

'How are they growing?' he asked with a secret sort of smile when he came up on the following Sunday. 'I've brought you a few more.'

'Very nicely,' she said, with a rather straight face, because she could see that he didn't quite believe her. 'That grey woolly one is in flower,' she added, looking up at him from under her eyebrows. She watched his eyes upon just a little wider. 'Come and see,' she said, and took him along to the corner of the house.

There they were against the wall: dark, shiny blue-green leaves, coloured fancy-patterned leaves, and on the grey woolly plant a deep wine-coloured flower. He lifted his cap and scratched his head thoughtfully, trying to work out how he had made a mistake, but he left his new lot of cuttings and took away his old basket and determined to find something she wouldn't be able to grow for next week.

Widow Bowen chuckled to herself as he went through the gate, and knelt down on the path to sort out the plants. 'They shall grow!' she said with her mouth held rather tight, and she puddled them into the soil with a little pot of rainwater. When she looked at them next morning they had already begun to perk up and look settled. Fern fronds and spiky leaves reached out towards the wall of the house, and the narrow border had begun to look like a section of tropical jungle. 'I'll show that gardener what he knows about growing things,' she muttered as she scrubbed the lavatory seat, and it was with a little high-pitched laugh of triumph that she met him at the gate at the weekend.

When he had gone, Widow Bowen wondered if she could have offended him because he made no promise to bring anything more. She did not press him. She thought perhaps it was as well that she had finished with him. His plants grew so very easily. She even had a sense of having wasted time, and she pressed the roots of the delicate trailing creeper he had brought into the ground with an offhand dig of her thin fingers. She said to Mrs Beddoe the next morning when she went to fetch her jug of milk, 'You know, I really believe I could make a stick of firewood grow.'

The woman looked at her with uncertain eyes and felt that perhaps Widow Bowen was going a little dotty in her old age. It was not altogether surprising after losing her husband and living on her own all the time. The old lady understood the look, but she did not care very deeply. Mrs Beddoe's thoughts did not worry her, and as she sat knitting by her fire in the evening she said, 'Well, and why not? A stick of firewood had to grow at one time or another.' And she decided to try it. No harm could come of it, after all. 'If it doesn't grow, perhaps it will stop me being a conceited old woman for a bit.' But in spite of this she laughed in her throat as she thought of the gardener and his tropical plants. 'Oh! the look on his face!' She laughed until a tear fell on her knitting.

She had been buying bundles of chopped firewood from the shop up the hill for more than a month. Her tree prunings had all been used up, and she was too nervous of the dark coppice to fetch sticks from there, so it was a piece of the shop firewood that she took out into the garden the following morning. She shook her head over it as she carried it round to the back of the house.

'I really am stupid,' she thought. 'It looks as dead as a doornail.' She couldn't decide what sort of wood it was, either. The grain was very straight and soft – nothing like apple or damson wood. As she bent down to press it into the ground she looked around carefully for fear someone might be watching her. 'Then they would think I'm mad!' she said loudly to make herself feel better. She stood back and looked at the stick in the ground, holding her soiled hands away from her sides. It stuck up out of the earth like a long thin bar of yellow soap cut off smartly at the top. For a moment she seriously considered the possibility that she might be going mad, and then she hurried away to put the potatoes on for dinner.

The delicate creeper grew just as if she had planted it with the utmost care, just as though it were in its native climate, and she stopped bothering about her tropical plants. When no one was passing up the lane and she thought she was unobserved she would hurry around to the back of the house, up past the rainwater butt, to look at her piece of firewood. Each time she went she felt more and more silly.

After three days had gone by and she couldn't see any change, she was tempted to pull it up and have done with the whole business. But then it rained hard for three or four days so that she was hardly able to go out of the house at all. She sat at her window and watched the mist of the rain sweeping up the valley. When she got tired of that she would put on the headphones of Ernest's crystal set and sit listening to the radio programme. And she cleaned and polished the house from top to bottom until she could see her wrinkled little face in the shine on the floor tiles.

Only when the rain had stopped and she was able to go out into the garden again did she realize how long she had been cooped up. Little specks of chickweed and groundsel were dotting the spaces between her rows of peas and onions. She put on her leather-topped clogs and went to work with the rake. The piece of firewood was completely forgotten.

It was only when she took a steaming hot bucket of water and a scrubbing brush up the steps outside the back door to scour the lavatory seat that it came to mind. When she saw it she set down her bucket with a clank. Flaky brown bark had covered up the yellow wood, and the chopped-off top was now a beautifully pointed spear, a shoot, reaching nearly a foot high, with a small arrow-head of pale-green pine needles at its top. Then she said, 'Well, of course, I knew it would,' and picked up her bucket and went into the lavatory to scrub the seat. But when she had finished and dried the woodwork off with a steaming cloth, she examined her new plant carefully. It was a little thick around the base, perhaps, but a very pretty little tree for all that. She looked around to see if anyone was watching, but the house was a perfect screen from the road, and the damson trees in the top corner of the orchard hid her effectively from all the cottages higher up the hill. A sudden feeling of elation filled her so that she picked up her bucket and almost danced down the steps into her small kitchen. Over and over again she sang, 'I've got green fingers,' to a tune that came into her head, and she got out a small pot of honey for tea.

Next morning while she was washing in the kitchen she studied her face in the mirror. 'Your hair wants cutting!' she said, suddenly noticing some stray pieces that had become rather long. Before she coiled her hair into its bob and pinned it she fetched her best scissors from her sewing basket in the window and cut the wisps of her hair carefully. 'Really, you still look quite pretty,' she said to the glass and twisted the corners of her mouth into a mocking little smile. For a few seconds she stood daydreaming with the puffs of white hair in her hand. Then, coming to with a start, she went out to the dark little patch of earth at the back and pressed the hair together in a little tuft in the ground.

The tree was growing fast. It was many inches higher, and shoots had begun to press out all round the sides of it. Suddenly she was worried in case it should become a large tree because the small kitchen window needed all the light it could get. 'If it grows too big,' she said firmly, 'I shall have to chop it down.' And with that she went back into the house and put on the kettle for her morning cup of tea.

She began to say less and less to Mrs Beddoe when she went down for her milk. She took money now and refrained from offering the woman vegetables. She knew that if she mentioned her garden now she wouldn't be believed. The tuft of hair was growing tall and bushy, and new sprouts of golden brown were coming up from the bottom. She couldn't possibly tell Mrs Beddoe that.

By the middle of summer she was becoming a little uneasy. The tropical creeper was growing all up the end wall of the house and was beginning to push back her own wisteria. She had tried to cut it back, but it only seemed to shoot out more strongly. The bush of hair needed trimming every few days or it hung over the path in great curling locks. And the piece of firewood was now a strong tree over seven feet tall. She was worried, too, by the little accidents she had been having. They depressed her. The first had happened when she clipped back the climbing plant. Being a tiny woman, she was unable to reach the higher tentacles it shot out, and she fetched a chair to stand on. As she reached high to cut the last spray the chair tipped sideways, and she fell, twisting her ankle, so that for a few days it was swollen and painful. While she was hobbling about with this she tried to twist off one of the branches of the young tree because it was reaching out in front of the lavatory door. A tuft of pine needles caught her in the eye so that she believed for a few painful moments that it had blinded her. She had hardly recovered from these injuries when she scratched her leg deeply with the point of the shears while she was clipping the bush of hair. As she said to the baker when he called, 'I've been knocking myself about lately.'

But pushing things into the ground had become a habit with her. Any little pieces of wood or vegetable peelings she had she pressed into the ground behind the house. In time, they all began to grow, and the small hidden patch of earth was becoming a flourishing little garden of mixed odds and ends. She wondered at times whether the lack of sun behind the house might not prevent some of her experiments from doing well, but the various growths seemed to prefer the shade.

Thinking of the hair that had grown, she pushed into the soil one day a piece of broken fingernail that she had cut off. It grew up like a long slender leaf, milky white and swaying in the wind. At times, when she stood and watched it, there seemed to be something mocking and truculent about it. She had the feeling that it, and the other things too, were returning a challenge that she had thrown down by sticking them into the soil. It increased her uneasiness, but she couldn't stop herself doing it. She swung between moods of triumphant success and timid disgust.

It was about the time when her leg had finally healed that she noticed something sticking out of her little plot of earth that had not been there a few days before. She racked her brains to remember what she could possibly have planted, but she could think of nothing, and she couldn't quite see what it was that was growing. It wasn't green, certainly. It seemed to be a small brown knob covered with a thin greyish slime. 'Oh, a toadstool, I expect,' she said and went off up the road to the shop. But on the way back with her groceries and firewood, a thought suddenly struck her. The gamekeeper from the big house had brought her a rabbit the week before, and rather than suffer the smell of burning the bones, she had buried them.

'But I never meant those to be planted!' she said aloud as she hurried down the lane. 'Not to *grow*!' Without stopping to put her shopping basket indoors, she hastened round to the back of the house and peered closely again at the new thing. At last she decided that it was in fact one of the rabbit bones, but rather high out of the ground, and looking very sticky and wet. It was ugly, too, and she drew her hand back quickly when she realized that she had just been about to touch it.

The next day she refused to look at it as she went past. Indeed, for a few days she managed to half convince herself that if she ceased to show any more interest in her experiments, they would stop growing. 'After all,' she said, 'It's *me* that has the green fingers – not them!' But at last she could not curb her curiosity, and she went to examine the thing. There was more of it out of the ground by this time. The slimy covering had dried a little, and there were thin red lines running criss-cross all over it. Right down near the ground a fine grey mould had begun to form.

Gradually she accommodated herself to the idea. There were soon three more shoots near the first, all beginning to reach up to the same height. The grey mould had become thick and fluffy, growing nearly to the tops of the stems, which were beginning to spread out so much in the manner of tall toadstools that she began to think her first idea had been the right explanation. And yet their centres remained pink and milky, unlike any toadstool she had ever seen.

When her damsons were ripe, Widow Bowen spent all her time picking and packing them off to market. She refused all the offers of the menfolk of the village to help with the ladder work. And so, for a few weeks, her secret garden was forgotten. By the beginning of October many of her plants had died off, and the leaves on the various young trees had turned yellow. Even the bush of hair had begun to slow in its growth, and she was able to gather up handfuls of the trailing fronds and lay them back from the path on to the garden. The four grey plants had spread right out at the top until they met, and they were growing one thick bulbous blob on top of them all.

'There's no doubt about it,' she said quietly as she stood looking at it. 'It's them rabbit bones. What would that smarty gardener say if I showed him this?' She couldn't imagine. It was the last thing in the world she would have dreamed of mentioning to anyone. By the time winter came, all signs of pink in the peculiar animal plant had been covered up by the grey fur, and the rough form of the animal had become apparent. Widow Bowen was not always sure in the full light of the late afternoons whether she imagined it or whether the form did actually twitch, as it appeared to do.

At last, in early January, the snow came and hung in sheets on the branches of the pine tree. The whole of her cottage was lit up with the whiteness of the snow outside. Only the top of the rabbit plant was visible, but short ears had begun to sprout, and now, definitely, she noticed that there was some movement in the snow. It was this that disturbed her far more than the growth itself, though she did not know why. For nearly a fortnight she woke each morning to find it had snowed in the night, and she would stand at her bedroom window and look out across the valley with its fields, trees, everything covered in white. Then she would look down sadly at her paths and know that she must put on stockings over her shoes and go out with tingling fingers to sweep.

One morning the snow was marked with little black dots leading down to the hedge. She knew at once what they were, and because she knew she was shocked. She hurried out to the back of the house with a fearful choking in her throat. It was gone. There was a black hole in the snow and four imprints in the damp earth beneath. She stood a long time too dazed to think. When at last she was able to think, her thoughts frightened her so much that she ran back into the house and did not venture out again all day. She sat huddled in her chair by the empty fireplace, too frightened to move, and did not think of eating. She slept there that night.

Next morning the sun shone fiercely and the snow began to melt. Widow Bowen stirred herself and laid the fire. The sunlight shone into her room and everything seemed cheerful once more. She thought carefully about her fears, and the more she thought, the more silly they appeared. 'It's gone. I'm well rid of it.' With that she began to clean up the house and sweep the slushy snow away from her door. By afternoon nearly all the snow had gone. 'I've been worried more than enough by all these growing things,' she said firmly. 'I'm going to lay my axe at the butt of that tree. It's darkened my window long enough.'

The axe was heavy and sharp. Milk-white chips of wood jumped out on to the earth as she chopped at the small V-shaped cut she had made in the trunk, and after a few minutes she was very hot and tired. She stood up with the branches all about her head, looking at her little cottage. For the first time in many years she wished that Ernest were still alive. Chopping this small tree down would have been nothing to him. It was less than four inches across the bottom, but she had made very little progress.

At her second attempt she steadied herself by resting her left hand low down on the trunk, and swung the axe slowly with one hand, letting the weight of the head do the work. The chips were smaller now, and the neat V had become a ragged notch in the white wood. She felt that she was going to expend all her energy without cutting more than halfway through it, and with a burst of determination she began to hack fiercely at it, so that the blood came to her bowed head, making her feel a little dizzy. The end of the haft caught her bent knee as she swung the axe. With a sickening pain the blade swung up into her hand on the trunk.

She fell down in a faint, with the blood spurting from the stump of her forefinger. When her vision cleared she knew what had happened. She felt weak and knew that the bleeding must be stopped. There was no pain now, only a dull numbness all up her arm. She crawled shakily to her feet and tottered uncertainly down the steps into her kitchen. She found a piece of white cloth and wrapped it around her bleeding hand. She felt old, very old, and wanted to die.

Soon the blood was soaking through the cloth, and she realized that she needed a doctor or she would indeed die very soon. She stirred herself and went down to the front gate, holding her bandaged hand up in front of her like a dog with a lame paw. Her neighbour's little boy was circling in the lane on his bicycle, and she called weakly to him to ride down the hill and ask the nurse to come quickly in her little car.

When the nurse came, Widow Bowen was leaning on the gate for support, with the blood dripping from her bandage. Nurse Foley took one look at the hand and carried the old lady into the back of her car. Then she set off for the town hospital.

It was only when they were driving back in the dark that Widow Bowen truly woke up to what had happened to her. A huge white pad of bandage held her mutilated hand firmly bound.

'You must take things easy for a week or so,' said Nurse Foley, half-turning her red face to the back seat. 'You've lost a lot of blood, you know. I asked them if they could keep you in for a few days, but they just haven't got a bed to spare.' Widow Bowen smiled weakly and said she felt very well, considering. But there was something troubling her at the back of her mind. 'Shall I ask Mrs Jones to come in and help you get your tea?' the nurse asked when she had taken the old lady in and lit the lamp for her.

'I think I can manage well enough one-handed,' said Widow Bowen, and her blue eyes twinkled a little again now that she was back home. To prove it she made a cup of tea for herself and the nurse and sat gazing at the big round-faced woman in her sitting-room. The tea made her feel a lot better, and she brought out some scones and put a light to the laid fire in the grate. She felt quite safe with the house round her.

At last the nurse went, promising to call in the morning, and the old woman sat thinking in her chair. Her fingers, her precious green fingers, were irrevocably damaged. Slowly she got up and walked, carrying the lamp, out through the kitchen to the back of the house. Little splashes of blood had dried in a trail across the kitchen floor. She stood in the wavering light of the lamp, looking at the hacked

tree with the chips of white wood lying all round it, and felt very sorry
that she had tried to cut it down. She could sympathize now that the
axe had cut her too. The axe lay at the foot of the tree with a little stain
of blood on the blade.

Suddenly, in the chippings, she saw a finger, bent and white. Her
stomach lurched, and she felt a bit dizzy again. Wondering, she
stooped and set her lamp down and picked up the finger and looked at
it. It looked so old and wrinkled and white. Many times she had pressed
holes into the earth with it for seedlings, and now it was cut off. She held
it against her breast, crying a little. It looked so forlorn. 'And you'll
never plant another thing!' she sobbed sadly to it, as though it were a
dead child. The frustrated maternal instincts of years welled up in her
small bent body, and she nursed this small part of her close in the
warmth of her dress.

After standing there a long while, with the lamp at her feet throwing
up the shadows all around her, she said with sudden determination.
'You shan't die! I'll put you in the ground and you shall *grow*.' In spite
of her resolve her heart was beating rapidly as she stepped on to the
garden and crouched down in the darkness behind the rose bush
at the side of the lavatory. With tears pooling in her eyes she made
a hole in the ground and placed her finger in it. For minutes she
crouched brooding over this strange child of her body until her legs
ached with cramp, and then she went into the house and up to bed.

Many times in the night she woke crying with the pain in her hand,
and when the morning came she was pale and worn out. Nurse Foley
suggested that a woman should come in and look after her for a few days,
but the old woman refused fiercely. The nurse sighed and said,
'Very well.' She tucked the stray ends of her grey hair into her cap and
left. Widow Bowen went round to the back of the house to look at her
finger. The dew of the night had taken all the limpness out of it. It
pointed straight up at the sky and had a tinge of colour again around
the knuckles. A wave of defiant will flowed through her, and then left
her feeling weary and apathetic.

She was no longer surprised. It was difficult for her even to think
clearly about it. The thing was growing. She only felt that at all
costs she must prevent anyone from ever seeing it. In a few days there
were the tips of other fingers showing. The old lady nodded her white
head tiredly when she saw them. She felt it was out of her control now.

In a fortnight a full hand had appeared. Fear began to fill the old
widow. She wandered about her cottage in a vague dream. The brass
door knob began to discolour and the kettle grew tarnished and
blackened. Crumbs of food lay on the floors, and a fine film of dust
was thickening on her sideboard. Out in the garden the unplanted earth
had a thin carpet of weeds, and the hedge at the roadside grew

woolly. Often she forgot to go for her milk, and cried peevishly one morning when Mrs Beddoe brought it up to her. For many days at a time she was too frightened to go and look at the growing thing in the shadows behind her house, but eventually she would have to go, and would stand staring at it with a glaze over her blue eyes. A wrist and an arm had appeared, with the skin wrinkled slightly, like her own, and by the time the cherries blossomed, the crest of a white head had begun to appear, like the top of a large horse mushroom.

She would spend hours staring at it, with a terrible fascination. The fear that anyone should see it became an obsession with her. She began to meet the baker at the gate to prevent him from walking up to the house, and she covered the naked head and shoulder over with brown potato sacks. The eyes of the figure were closed, but on the face and the bare shoulders were the wrinkles and freckles that resembled her own in the minutest detail. Night after night she lay tossing in a half stupor of sleep while horrible dreams flashed through her frightened mind.

By the time the damsons were ripe, the white body was out of the ground to its knees, bent slightly forward, as she herself stood. Widow Bowen let her damsons rot on the trees. Birds settled in screaming crowds, pecking at the decaying fruit, and as the season passed over, shrivelled brown drops remained to hang like tiny bats from all the branches. The cottage was now thick in dirt, and the forest of weeds in the garden had already begun to die down. The hawthorn hedge had sprung up unchecked, hiding the house from the view of the villagers, and, but for her occasional dishevelled appearance at the gate to wait for the baker, they would have believed her to be dead. At first they had inquired whether they might lend a hand in the house or garden, but she answered them with such hysterical outbursts that they stopped asking, and hurried past her gate with heads down whenever she happened to be standing there.

As December passed, the snow came again, bearing down the tall raggedness of the hedge, and settling like a mantle on the sack-covered shoulders of the growing figure behind the house. Mornings would come, and the old lady would wake from her fitful sleep to find the room flooded with white light from the blanket of snow outside. She dreaded it. Each morning she expected to see a dark trail leading across the garden from the back of the house, as she had done the year before. But each morning the snow stretched, untouched, down to the hedge, startlingly white. Every day she would take a quick frightened look behind the rambling rose tree beside the lavatory, to be sure the figure still stood there. At times it would sway a little, and Widow Bowen would stand, rigid with horror, until it was still again.

The lavatory seat was no longer white. Cobwebs and dusty bits of newspaper littered its once-scrubbed surface. Widow Bowen was almost too frightened to go in there, for fear of the figure outside.

The snow still covered the ground in a hard frozen layer when she came out of the lavatory late one afternoon and took her usual hurried look behind the rose bush. Her heart stopped beating for a second, and the breath choked in her throat. Two black patches of soil were all that remained to show where it had been. She looked wildly about her. With a terrified scream she stumbled down the steps into her kitchen and slammed the door behind her. She bolted it at top and bottom with dithering fingers and scurried into the sitting-room to lock the front door.

There in her chair sat the figure, staring at her. She stood with her back against the door, unable to move. The other did not move either. It was her exact double, from the white hair to the twinkling blue eyes, but clothed, almost demurely, in sacks. The old lady stared at the white thin hands spread out on the arms of the chair. The fingers were complete, whole. Widow Bowen looked up into the eyes again, they looked into hers with a faint mocking smile, as though they could see into the deepest corners of her mind. She was rigid with terror. The blood began to leave her head. A gradual blackness clouded out her sight, and she sank to the floor unconscious.

Nurse Foley came down the hill in her car next morning. The snow had almost melted in the night, and the sun was shining. Catching sight of the old lady, she stopped and put her head out. 'I'm glad to see you trimming your hedge,' she said. 'It had begun to look untidy.'

The old lady smiled, holding the shears in front of her. 'Yes,' she said, 'the whole place is in a terrible mess. I've been dying to get started on it, but the snow held me up, you know.' Her blue eyes twinkled brightly.

'I suppose you've heard the news,' said the nurse, pushing her head farther out of the window.

'No, I haven't. What's that, then?'

'Oh, my dear! I've been up there for hours. They found a body in the coppice, you know. Little Chris Bradley found it first – at least, a piece of it. Horrible it is – all chopped to pieces with an axe or something. The police are there now. They think it's probably an old woman, but it's so wickedly smashed about that they can't recognize anything.'

'What a nasty thing!'

'Oh, terrible! Yes. Still, you don't want to bother your head about that. You've had enough trouble. How is your hand going on?' She looked from one hand to the other, confused between left and right, but there was no missing finger.

'Oh, beautifully,' said the old lady, smiling and nodding her head. 'Everything grows well here. I think I must have green fingers.'

The Landlady

Roald Dahl

Billy Weaver had travelled down from London on the slow afternoon train, with a change at Swindon on the way, and by the time he got to Bath it was about nine o'clock in the evening and the moon was coming up out of a clear starry sky over the houses opposite the station entrance. But the air was deadly cold and the wind was like a flat blade of ice on his cheeks.

'Excuse me,' he said, 'but is there a fairly cheap hotel not too far away from here?'

'Try The Bell and Dragon,' the porter answered, pointing down the road. 'They might take you in. It's about a quarter of a mile along on the other side.'

Billy thanked him and picked up his suitcase and set out to walk the quarter-mile to The Bell and Dragon. He had never been to Bath before. He didn't know anyone who lived there. But Mr Greenslade at the Head Office in London had told him it was a splendid city. 'Find your own lodgings,' he had said, 'and then go along and report to the Branch Manager as soon as you've got yourself settled.'

Billy was seventeen years old. He was wearing a new navy-blue overcoat, a new brown trilby hat, and a new brown suit, and he was feeling fine. He walked briskly down the street. He was trying to do everything briskly these days. Briskness, he had decided, was *the* one common characteristic of all successful businessmen. The big shots up at Head Office were absolutely fantastically brisk all the time. They were amazing.

There were no shops on this wide street that he was walking along, only a line of tall houses on each side, all of them identical. They had porches and pillars and four or five steps going up to their front doors, and it was obvious that once upon a time they had been very swanky residences. But now, even in the darkness, he could see that the paint was peeling from the woodwork on their doors and windows, and that the handsome white façades were cracked and blotchy from neglect.

Suddenly, in a downstairs window that was brilliantly illuminated by a street-lamp not six yards away, Billy caught sight of a printed notice propped up against the glass in one of the upper panes. It said BED AND BREAKFAST. There was a vase of pussy-willows, tall and beautiful, standing just underneath the notice.

He stopped walking. He moved a bit closer. Green curtains (some sort of velvety material) were hanging down on either side of the window. The pussy-willows looked wonderful beside them. He went right up and peered through the glass into the room, and the first thing he saw was a bright fire burning in the hearth. On the carpet in front of the fire, a pretty little dachshund was curled up asleep with its nose tucked into its belly. The room itself, so far as he could see in the half-darkness, was filled with pleasant furniture. There was a baby-grand piano and a big sofa and several plump armchairs; and in one corner he spotted a large parrot in a cage. Animals were usually a good sign in a place like this, Billy told himself; and all in all, it looked to him as though it would be a pretty decent house to stay in. Certainly it would be more comfortable than The Bell and Dragon.

On the other hand, a pub would be more congenial than a boarding-house. There would be beer and darts in the evenings, and lots of people to talk to, and it would probably be a good bit cheaper, too. He had stayed a couple of nights in a pub once before and he had liked it. He had never stayed in any boarding-houses, and, to be perfectly honest, he was a tiny bit frightened of them. The name itself conjured up images of watery cabbage, rapacious landladies, and a powerful smell of kippers in the living-room.

After dithering about like this in the cold for two or three minutes, Billy decided that he would walk on and take a look at The Bell and Dragon before making up his mind. He turned to go.

And now a queer thing happened to him. He was in the act of stepping back and turning away from the window when all at once his eye was caught and held in the most peculiar manner by the small notice that was there. BED AND BREAKFAST, it said. BED AND BREAKFAST, BED AND BREAKFAST, BED AND BREAKFAST. Each word was like a large black eye staring at him through the glass, holding him, compelling him, forcing him to stay where he was and not to walk away from that house, and the next thing he knew, he was actually moving across from the window to the front door of the house, climbing the steps that led up to it, and reaching for the bell.

He pressed the bell. Far away in a back room he heard it ringing, and then at once – it must have been at once because he hadn't even had time to take his finger from the bell-button – the door swung open and a woman was standing there.

Normally you ring the bell and you have at least a half-minute's wait before the door opens. But this dame was like a jack-in-the-box. He pressed the bell – and out she popped! It made him jump.

She was about forty-five or fifty years old, and the moment she saw him, she gave him a warm welcoming smile.

'*Please* come in,' she said pleasantly. She stepped aside, holding the door wide open, and Billy found himself automatically starting forward into the house. The compulsion or, more accurately, the desire to follow after her into that house was extraordinarily strong.

'I saw the notice in the window,' he said, holding himself back.

'Yes, I know.'

'I was wondering about a room.'

'It's *all* ready for you, my dear,' she said. She had a round pink face and very gentle blue eyes.

'I was on my way to The Bell and Dragon,' Billy told her. 'But the notice in your window just happened to catch my eye.'

'My dear boy,' she said, 'why don't you come in out of the cold?'

'How much do you charge?'

'Five and sixpence a night, including breakfast.'

It was fantastically cheap. It was less than half of what he had been willing to pay.

'If that is too much,' she added, 'then perhaps I can reduce it just a tiny bit. Do you desire an egg for breakfast? Eggs are expensive at the moment. It would be sixpence less without the egg.'

'Five and sixpence is fine,' he answered. 'I should like very much to stay here.'

'I knew you would. Do come in.'

She seemed terribly nice. She looked exactly like the mother of one's best school-friend welcoming one into the house to stay for the Christmas holidays. Billy took off his hat, and stepped over the threshold.

'Just hang it there,' she said, 'and let me help you with your coat.'

There were no other hats or coats in the hall. There were no umbrellas, no walking sticks – nothing.

'We have it *all* to ourselves,' she said, smiling at him over her shoulder as she led the way upstairs. 'You see, it isn't very often I have the pleasure of taking a visitor into my little nest.'

The old girl is slightly dotty, Billy told himself. But at five and sixpence a night, who gives a damn about that? 'I should've thought you'd be simply swamped with applicants,' he said politely.

'Oh, I am, my dear, I am, of course I am. But the trouble is that I'm inclined to be just a teeny weeny bit choosy and particular – if you see what I mean.'

'Ah, yes.'

'But I'm always ready. Everything is always ready day and night in this house just on the off-chance that an acceptable young gentleman will come along. And it is such a pleasure, my dear, such a very great pleasure when now and again I open the door and I see someone standing there who is just *exactly* right.' She was halfway up the stairs, and she paused with one hand on the stair-rail, turning her head and smiling down at him with pale lips. 'Like you,' she added, and her blue eyes travelled slowly all the way down the length of Billy's body, to his feet, and then up again.

On the first-floor landing she said to him, 'This floor is mine.'

They climbed up a second flight. 'And this one is *all* yours,' she said. 'Here's your room. I do hope you'll like it.' She took him into a small charming front bedroom, switching on the light as she went in.

'The morning sun comes right in the window, Mr Perkins. It *is* Mr Perkins, isn't it?'

'No,' he said. 'It's Weaver.'

'Mr Weaver. How nice. I've put a water-bottle between the sheets to air them out, Mr Weaver. It's such a comfort to have a hot water-bottle in a strange bed with clean sheets, don't you agree? And you may light the gas fire at any time you feel chilly.'

'Thank you,' Billy said. 'Thank you ever so much.' He noticed that the bedspread had been taken off the bed, and that the bedclothes had been neatly turned back on one side, all ready for someone to get in.

'I'm so glad you appeared,' she said, looking earnestly into his face. 'I was beginning to get worried.'

'That's all right,' Billy answered brightly, 'You mustn't worry about me.' He put his suitcase on the chair and started to open it.

'And what about supper, my dear? Did you manage to get anything to eat before you came here?'

'I'm not a bit hungry, thank you,' he said. 'I think I'll just go to bed as soon as possible because tomorrow I've got to get up rather early and report to the office.'

'Very well, then. I'll leave you now so that you can unpack. But before you go to bed, would you be kind enough to pop into the sitting-room on the ground floor and sign the book? Everyone has to do that because it's the law of the land, and we don't want to go breaking any laws at *this* stage in the proceedings, do we?' She gave him a little wave of the hand and went quickly out of the room and closed the door.

Now, the fact that this landlady appeared to be slightly off her rocker didn't worry Billy in the least. After all, she was not only harmless – there was no question about that – but she was also quite obviously a kind and generous soul. He guessed that she had probably lost a son in the war, or something like that, and had never got over it.

So a few minutes later, after unpacking his suitcase and washing his hands, he trotted downstairs to the ground floor and entered the living-room. His landlady wasn't there, but the fire was glowing in the hearth, and the little dachshund was still sleeping in front of it. The room was wonderfully warm and cosy. I'm a lucky fellow, he thought, rubbing his hands. This is a bit of all right.

He found the guest-book lying open on the piano, so he took out his pen and wrote down his name and address. There were only two other entries above his on the page, and, as one always does with guest-books, he started to read them. One was a Christopher Mulholland from Cardiff. The other was Gregory W. Temple from Bristol.

'That's funny, he thought suddenly. Christopher Mulholland. It rings a bell.

Now where on earth had he heard that rather unusual name before? Was he a boy at school? No. Was it one of his sister's numerous young men, perhaps, or a friend of his father's? No, no, it wasn't any of those. He glanced down again at the book.

Christopher Mulholland   *231 Cathedral Road, Cardiff*
Gregory W. Temple   *27 Sycamore Drive, Bristol*

As a matter of fact, now he came to think of it, he wasn't at all sure that the second name didn't have almost as much of a familiar ring about it as the first.

'Gregory Temple?' he said aloud, searching his memory. 'Christopher Mulholland? . . .'

'Such charming boys,' a voice behind him answered, and he turned and saw his landlady sailing into the room with a large silver tea-tray in her hands. She was holding it well out in front of her, and rather high up, as though the tray were a pair of reins on a frisky horse.

'They sound somehow familiar,' he said.

'They do? How interesting.'

'I'm almost positive I've heard those names before somewhere. Isn't that queer? Maybe it was in the newspapers. They weren't famous in any way, were they? I mean famous cricketers or footballers or something like that?'

'Famous,' she said, setting the tea-tray down on the low table in front of the sofa. 'Oh no, I don't think they were famous. But they were extraordinarily handsome, both of them, I can promise you that. They were tall and young and handsome, my dear, just exactly like you.'

Once more, Billy glanced down at the book. 'Look here,' he said, noticing the dates. 'This last entry is over two years old.'

'It is?'

'Yes, indeed. And Christopher Mulholland's is nearly a year before that – more than *three years ago*.'

'Dear me,' she said, shaking her head and heaving a dainty little sigh. 'I would never have thought it. How time does fly away from us all, doesn't it, Mr Wilkins?'.

'It's Weaver,' Billy said. 'W-e-a-v-e-r.'

'Oh, of course it is!' she cried, sitting down on the sofa. 'How silly of me. I do apologize. In one ear and out the other, that's me, Mr Weaver.'

'You know something?' Billy said. 'Something that's really quite extraordinary about all this?'

'No, dear, I don't.'

'Well, you see – both of these names, Mulholland and Temple, I not only seem to remember each one of them separately, so to speak, but somehow or other, in some peculiar way, they both appear to be sort of connected together as well. As though they were both famous for the same sort of thing, if you see what I mean – like . . . well . . . like Dempsey and Tunney, for example, or Churchill and Roosevelt.'

'How amusing,' she said. 'But come over here now, dear, and sit down beside me on the sofa and I'll give you a nice cup of tea and a ginger biscuit before you go to bed.'

'You really shouldn't bother,' Billy said. 'I didn't mean you to do anything like that.' He stood by the piano, watching her as she fussed about with the cups and saucers. He noticed that she had small, white, quickly moving hands, and red fingernails.

'I'm almost positive it was in the newspapers I saw them,' Billy said. 'I'll think of it in a second. I'm sure I will.'

There is nothing more tantalizing than a thing like this which lingers just outside the borders of one's memory. He hated to give up.

'Now wait a minute,' he said. 'Wait just a minute. Mulholland . . . Christopher Mulholland . . . wasn't *that* the name of the Eton schoolboy who was on a walking-tour through the West Country, and then all of a sudden . . .'

'Milk?' she said. 'And sugar?'

'Yes, please. And then all of a sudden . . .'

'Eton schoolboy?' she said. 'Oh no, my dear, that can't possibly be right because *my* Mr Mulholland was certainly not an Eton schoolboy when he came to me. He was a Cambridge undergraduate. Come over here now and sit next to me and warm yourself in front of this lovely fire. Come on. Your tea's all ready for you.' She patted the empty place beside her on the sofa, and she sat there smiling at Billy and waiting for him to come over.

He crossed the room slowly, and sat down on the edge of the sofa. She placed his teacup on the table in front of him.

'*There* we are,' she said. 'How nice and cosy this is, isn't it?'

Billy started sipping his tea. She did the same. For half a minute or so, neither of them spoke. But Billy knew that she was looking at him. Her body was half turned towards him, and he could feel her eyes resting on his face, watching him over the rim of her teacup. Now and again, he caught a whiff of a peculiar smell that seemed to emanate directly

from her person. It was not in the least unpleasant, and it reminded him
– well, he wasn't quite sure what it reminded him of. Pickled walnuts?
New leather? Or was it the corridors of a hospital?

'Mr Mulholland was a great one for his tea,' she said at length. 'Never
in my life have I seen anyone drink as much tea as dear, sweet Mr
Mulholland.'

'I suppose he left fairly recently,' Billy said. He was still puzzling his
head about the two names. He was positive now that he had seen them
in the newspapers – in the headlines.

'Left?' she said, arching her brows. 'But my dear boy, he never left.
He's still here. Mr Temple is also here. They're on the third floor, both
of them together.'

Billy set down his cup slowly on the table, and stared at his landlady.
She smiled back at him, and then she put out one of her white hands
and patted him comfortingly on the knee. 'How old are you, my dear?'
she asked.

'Seventeen.'

'Seventeen!' she cried. 'Oh, it's the perfect age! Mr Mulholland was
also seventeen. But I think he was a trifle shorter than you are, in fact
I'm sure he was, and his teeth weren't *quite* so white. You have the most
beautiful teeth, Mr Weaver, did you know that?'

'They're not as good as they look,' Billy said. 'They've got simply
masses of fillings in them at the back.'

'Mr Temple, of course, was a little older,' she said, ignoring his
remark. 'He was actually twenty-eight. And yet I never would have
guessed it if he hadn't told me, never in my whole life. There wasn't a
blemish on his body.'

'A what?' Billy said.

'His skin was *just* like a baby's.'

There was a pause. Billy picked up his teacup and took another sip
of tea, then he set it down again gently in its saucer. He waited for her
to say something else, but she seemed to have lapsed into another of her
silences. He sat there staring straight ahead of him into the far corner
of the room, biting his lower lip.

'That parrot,' he said at last. 'You know something? It had me
completely fooled when I first saw it through the window from the street.
I could have sworn it was alive.'

'Alas, no longer.'

'It's most terribly clever the way it's been done,' he said. 'It doesn't
look in the least bit dead. Who did it?'

'I did.'

'*You* did?'

'Of course,' she said. 'And have you met my little Basil as well?' She
nodded towards the dachshund curled up so comfortably in front of the

fire. Billy looked at it. And suddenly, he realized that this animal had all the time been just as silent and motionless as the parrot. He put out a hand and touched it gently on the top of its back. The back was hard and cold, and when he pushed the hair to one side with his fingers, he could see the skin underneath, greyish-black and dry and perfectly preserved.

'Good gracious me,' he said. 'How absolutely fascinating.' He turned away from the dog and stared with deep admiration at the little woman beside him on the sofa. 'It must be most awfully difficult to do a thing like that.'

'Not in the least,' she said 'I stuff *all* my little pets myself when they pass away. Will you have another cup of tea?'

'No, thank you,' Billy said. The tea tasted faintly of bitter almonds, and he didn't much care for it.

'You did sign the book, didn't you?'

'Oh, yes.'

'That's good. Because later on, if I happen to forget what you were called, then I can always come down here and look it up. I still do that almost every day with Mr Mulholland and Mr ... Mr ...'

'Temple,' Billy said. 'Gregory Temple. Excuse my asking, but haven't there been *any* other guests here except them in the last two or three years?'

Holding her teacup high in one hand, inclining her head slightly to the left, she looked up at him out of the corners of her eyes and gave him another gentle little smile.

'No, my dear,' she said. 'Only you.'

Nursery Tea

Mary Danby

'It won't be the same without them,' said Olivia, sealing a Christmas card in its envelope.

Her brother Hugh rose from his chair and took a tin of tobacco from the mantelpiece. He filled his pipe, then thrust his hands deep into the sack-like pockets of his knitted cardigan. 'Matches ... matches ...' he muttered to himself. 'Ah!' as he finally located them on the bamboo coffee table. 'Mother loved Christmas,' he said.

'And Father,' added Olivia. She adjusted a lock of greying, mud-brown hair that had slipped from the bun high on her head. At forty-four, she was what is known as a fine-looking woman – not pretty, but she had good bones, like a well-bred horse. She had never done anything to improve or enhance her appearance, feeling that others should be content with what God had given her. She took the same attitude to her character, never attempting to control the less pleasant aspects of her nature. And the fact that her brittle, domineering self had never appealed enough to any man to make him want to marry her, seemed not to bother her.

Hugh, on the other hand, was a shy, nervous person. He had a job in banking, because his father had told him he had to be in something, but he would perhaps have been happier as a clergyman, or a market gardener. The reason he had never married was that, even if he had ever formed a close relationship with a woman, he would never have dared to propose. She might have said 'no', and that would have been so crushing. But never mind, he had Olivia.

'Will it be just us two,' he asked, puffing at his pipe, 'for Christmas dinner?'

'Did you want to ask someone else?' Olivia raised an eyebrow.

'No,' said Hugh.

There was silence for a while. Hugh settled back in his chair and made a half-hearted attempt at the *Observer* crossword. Olivia finished writing her Christmas cards and went to draw the curtains. Outside, the yew tree at the end of the garden merged darkly into the winter sky. Beyond it was the church ... and the little churchyard where her mother and father lay beneath pots of yellow chrysanthemums. Olivia suddenly had a picture of them all, young and vital, having tea on the lawn under the yew: Pa, in his panama hat, Hugh, in short cotton trousers buttoned on to his shirt, Mother, in a low-waisted dress, setting out cups on a wrought-iron table, and Nanny, come to take them in at bedtime. Always Nanny.

'At least we don't have to have Nanny,' she said.

'*Don't* we?' said Hugh, putting down his paper. 'But she's *always* come for tea on Boxing Day. For – gosh – thirty years, I suppose.'

'Which is thirty years too many,' said Olivia.

But then, Nanny was an institution. Every year, at about this time, their mother, slipping a cheque into Nanny's Christmas card, used to say: 'Dear old Nanny. She was so good to you children.'

But she wasn't. That was the ridiculousness of the whole business. She *wasn't*. They had been conned into thinking of her as the treasure of their youth, but Hugh sometimes remembered the reality, and the memory hurt with a pain that made him almost tremble. Far from being a treasure, their nanny had been specious and crawling, keeping her smiles and sympathy for the grown-ups and turning her dark side to the nursery. Behind that heavy closed door, cruelties were perpetrated in the name of discipline, and tortures were performed on little minds, whose scars were less tangible than those of the body. They had been terrified of her, but 'Nonsense, darling,' and 'Nanny knows best,' was their mother's reaction to their tales of oppression. And, inexperienced as they were, they had accepted their fate, believing it to be a natural and inescapable side of childhood. It was only as they had grown older, and Nanny had moved on, that they realized how unnecessarily they had suffered.

'Did I ever tell you,' said Hugh, 'that when I was five she made me stand on one leg for half an hour because I'd wet my bed?'

'She said I was so ugly I'd never get a man. She said I had a face like a gargoyle. I believed her,' said Olivia.

'She was a swine,' said Hugh fervently.

'And she still won't let up, will she,' went on Olivia. 'Even now, she says "Sit still", as if I were a dog, and tells me to mind my "P"s and "Q"s. I think she gets worse every year.'

Hugh nodded. 'And every year she says: "I know someone not a million miles from here who was sick all over his Teddy." Mother used to think it was hilarious. But it wasn't funny – ever. I was sick because she forced me to eat all her left-over cabbage stalks.'

Olivia moved away from the window. 'Hugh ...?' she said.

'Yes?'

As she passed behind his chair, she gently touched the top of his head.

'I think we *should* have Nanny to tea,' she said slowly. 'After all, it's what Mother would have wanted.'

'You said . . .' began Hugh.

But Olivia just smiled and stroked his hair.

Everyone said Nanny Pritchard was wonderful for her age. 'Isn't she amazing?' they said in front of her, as if she were a performing doll. (Privately, most people thought her a tiresome old crab, but it didn't do to say so. Expressing one's dislike of a ninety-year-old was the next worst thing to speaking ill of the dead.)

While other residents of the By-and-By Old People's Home were visited by their children and grandchildren, Nanny Pritchard had nobody. She had spent her life caring for Hugh, and Olivia, and the two little Barrett girls, and Nicholas Dycehart, and Nicholas Dycehart's children, and all the others. Their families were her family. She had lived for her children, and now there were only memories. In her room, she kept a scrapbook for each of them, cutting engagement notices from *The Times* to follow on from the chubby-cheeked photographs and first attempts at painting. 'To Nanny, love from Olivia': a square, two-dimensional house, with smoke coming from the chimney. 'The big fat man next door, by Hugh.' Ah, the little monkey.

She kept her scrapbooks hidden, so the cleaning lady wouldn't see them and try to dust them. People didn't understand. Not like in the old days . . .

Very sad about Hugh and Olivia's parents, going so suddenly, one after the other. She had always got on well with them. 'Nanny, you're a marvel,' they used to say to her. And now Hugh and Olivia had sweetly asked her to tea on Boxing Day, just as if nothing had happened. Hugh would be here in a moment to fetch her.

She fastened her grey tweed coat and, leaning heavily on her stick, made her way to the front hall. She heard tyres on the gravel, and the next moment Hugh, his sports jacket flapping about him, was ushering her into his car. 'You naughty boy!' she said, poking a knobbly finger at his midriff. 'You'll catch your death!'

She sat in the front seat for the half-hour drive, keeping a tight hold on her stick and thumping with it on the floor every time she thought Hugh was exceeding a speed limit. Hugh, braking meekly, smiled to himself as he thought of the surprise that awaited Nanny at the end of her journey.

'Ah, Nanny dear.' Olivia, girlish in pale blue chiffon, opened the door. 'How well you're looking.'

'Unlike some,' retorted Nanny. She peered at Hugh. 'Peaky, if you ask me.'

'Perhaps I haven't been eating my greens, Nanny,' said Hugh.

Nanny shot him a look of stone.

'Yes, well,' said Olivia. 'Happy Christmas, Nanny.' She kissed the leathery cheek. It was, paradoxically, as soft as milk.

In the hall, Hugh took Nanny's coat, then Olivia moved towards the staircase.

'Not in the drawing-room?' queried Nanny. 'Your mother always served tea in the drawing-room.'

'Up the wooden hill . . .' quoted Hugh, with a little smirk.

They helped Nanny climb the two flights, then waited while she stood, panting, trying to get her breath. Where once she had towered over them, shepherding them upstairs after their good-night kisses, now, in her shrunken old age, she was dwarfed.

'This way,' said Olivia gaily, enjoying her view of Nanny's bald patch.

At the end of the landing, they came to the room that had once been their day nursery. A fire burned in the grate, and in its gentle light the toys spread around the room looked less dilapidated than they actually were.

'Good gracious me!' exclaimed Nanny.

'Yes,' said Olivia. 'Nursery tea, just as it used to be.'

Nanny moved around the room, shaking her head. 'Well,' she mumbled, 'I don't know, I'm sure. That was never there,' she declared, pointing to the old wooden rocking-horse. 'We always had it over by the window.' She picked up a motheaten doll. 'Isn't this Pamela? Oh, you loved your Pamela.'

'*You* didn't. You held her upside-down in a basin of water. You said that's what would happen to me if I didn't wash my face properly,' Olivia remarked conversationally.

Nanny thumped on the ground with her stick. 'Stuff and nonsense! I won't have such fibs in my nursery.'

'Oh, really, Nanny,' said Olivia, taking the doll and putting it back on its chair.

'Now, now,' said Nanny, 'don't snatch.'

Hugh was standing with his back to the fire, looking anxious. 'Come and sit down, Nanny,' he suggested.

Nanny lowered herself into the armchair by the fire and smoothed her beige wool dress over her knees. 'You always were a polite boy, Hugh,' she said, nodding. 'Nanny's little pumpkin pie, I used to call you.'

Olivia, behind her chair, smothered a giggle.

Nanny pursed her lips.

'Now, Nanny,' said Hugh, leaning against the big brass fireguard, 'how is everything with you?'

Nanny grunted, then launched herself on her annual list of

complaints: the Matron at the home, the food, the old man in the next room, the television, the radio, the *Sunday Telegraph* and the Communists. 'And I'll tell you,' she concluded darkly, 'Mrs Augustus, who came last week, has a grandson who plays in one of those pop groups!'

'Is that so terrible, Nanny?' asked Olivia, laying the table for tea.

Nanny stiffened. 'Of course it is. You've only to look at the papers. If it's not drugs, it's the other – all over the place.'

'The other?' said Olivia. 'Oh, sex, you mean.'

'We'll have no dirty talk here, miss,' said Nanny.

Olivia groaned while Nanny went on: 'And I know someone not a million miles from here who could have found herself a nice young man if she'd learnt a little self-discipline.'

'Hah!' Olivia exploded. 'That's rich! It used to be my face that put 'em off – now it's my personality, is it? From someone who was never even glanced at by anything in trousers, male or female, that's rich!'

Nanny struggled to her feet, red in the face. 'I will not have this naughtiness, Olivia!' she snapped, her breath coming in gasps. 'If you're not careful, I'll be taking you to meet——'

'Mr Slipper-Slapper?' asked Olivia. 'Remember, Hugh? Remember Mr Slipper-Slapper?' She produced from the window-seat a worn old slipper. 'I found him in the boxroom. Such a *dear* old friend, wasn't he, Hugh?' She took a step towards Nanny, who fell back in her chair. 'Remember, Nanny ...?' she said, smacking the slipper against the palm of her hand, softly at first, then harder. 'Mmm ...?'

Nanny's jaw dropped open, but she remained silent.

'I say, Olivia ...' began Hugh, looking worried.

'Oh, it's all right,' said Olivia. 'Nanny and I are just having a little joke. It's only a game.'

'A very silly one, if you ask me,' said Nanny.

Olivia wagged a finger. 'Now don't be such a crosspatch, Nanny.'

'Can't we have tea?' said Hugh. 'I'm sure Nanny must be hungry.' He led the way over to the table, which was covered by a gingham cloth. 'Here, Nanny,' he said, pulling out a chair.

Nanny, fixing them both with an eagle gaze, sat down. Olivia poured out a glass of milk and placed it in front of her. 'Drink up, now, Nanny,' she said with a smile.

'What's this?' asked Nanny.

'Milk, of course. Now drink it up.'

'Are you not going to make any tea?'

'Tea isn't good for you,' said Hugh, enjoying the joke.

Nanny sighed. 'I think you're both being very silly. But since this is all there is ...' She raised the glass and sipped at the milk.

Hugh and Olivia watched her.

'Biscuit, Nanny?' asked Hugh, offering a plate.

Olivia pushed his hand away. 'Bread and butter first, Hugh,' she said. 'You know we always have bread and butter first.'

'No, thank you,' said Nanny.

Olivia tutted. 'Now come along. There's many a poor child would be glad of it. Pass your plate.'

After the bread and butter came plain biscuits, then the *pièce de résistance* – a bowl of cold sago pudding.

'Oh no, really,' said Nanny. 'This is going too far.'

'Eat it up, now,' urged Olivia. 'Think of all the starving children in India. Let me see a nice clean plate.'

'I can't,' said Nanny, for the first time a note of desperation in her voice.

'Can't?' said Hugh, leaning across the table at her, his eyes bright. '*Can't?* There's no such word as can't.'

'Her eyes were bigger than her stomach,' crowed Olivia.

'A dose, a dose!' chanted Hugh, growing pink with excitement. 'Have you got the Milk of Mags?'

'Oh, damn ... No, I haven't,' said Olivia.

'Wash your mouth out with soap!' ordered Nanny automatically. She tried to get up from the table, but dropped her stick.

Olivia picked it up.

'Give it back,' said Nanny, dropping back on to her chair. 'Give it back at once!'

'Say "please",' demanded Olivia.

'Please.'

'No,' said Olivia.

'She can't move without it,' said Hugh.

'Good,' said Olivia, 'because I want to tell her a story, and I want her to listen. You are listening, aren't you, Nanny? Now, once upon a time, there was a little girl who liked to suck her thumb. She wasn't any different from any other little girl, you know, except that she had a nanny who got cross about it. This nanny used to keep on and on about the great, long, red-legged Scissor-man, who would cut off her thumbs – snip, snap!' Olivia snapped her fingers under Nanny's nose. 'And then, you see, there was this picture – a boy crying, and blood coming from where his thumbs once were. I thought the Scissor-man would come for me, too – I really did. The first thing I did when I woke up each morning was to look and see if my thumbs were still there.'

'You were a very silly little girl,' said Nanny. 'Always play-acting and making a fuss. Now give me back my stick.'

'No,' said Olivia, pouting.

The old woman held out a crooked hand. 'Give it to Nanny, now ...'

'Shan't.'

'D-d-do you know,' said Hugh, 'she stole my clockwork clown.'

Nanny looked at him. 'What a wicked thing to say.'

'It's true,' said Hugh. 'You said only good children could have such lovely toys. You said you knew a little boy who was much nicer than me, and that he should have it.'

'I did not.'

'You did, you did.'

'Don't answer back.'

Olivia, who had been gazing out of the window, spun round suddenly. 'Hugh,' she said, 'I think Nanny needs a spell in the Bad Room, don't you?'

'Now Olivia,' warned Nanny. 'This will all end in tears, if you're not careful. You've had your joke, and it was all very funny, wasn't it. Now if Hugh wouldn't mind just running me home . . .'

Hugh giggled. 'There are monsters in the Bad Room, aren't there, Nanny. Bogeymen, and great big spiders, and things with huge teeth, you said.'

Off the nursery was a tiny boxroom, with a high, sealed window. It was empty except for a wooden stool and a broken ironing-board.

'In here, Nanny,' commanded Olivia. 'Perhaps in the Bad Room you'll learn to behave yourself.'

Nanny reached for her stick, but Olivia lifted it above her head. 'Help her, Hugh,' she said.

Hugh held out an arm, and Nanny, taking it, raised herself from the chair. 'If you think I'm going in there . . .' she said.

'You *are*,' said Olivia.

'In that case,' declared Nanny, 'you'll soon find yourself in *real* trouble. When I tell the police how you've been carrying on, they'll lock you away somewhere. You're not fit to be living here on your own. What your dear parents would have thought – well!'

'Sorry there's no light in there,' said Olivia. 'I took the bulb out.'

Nanny struggled briefly with Hugh, then allowed herself to be led, muttering, furiously, into the boxroom. 'You won't get away with this,' she warned.

Hugh turned to Olivia. 'Nanny's having a little tantrum,' he said gleefully.

'Shut the door,' Olivia said coldly. 'Lock it, and give me the key.'

Hugh did as he was told. 'It's only for a little while, isn't it?' he whispered anxiously. 'Part of the game . . .'

Olivia nodded, listening at the boxroom door. She could hear nothing. 'What do you want to do now?' she asked Hugh.

He gazed around the room, then gave a little excited jump and hurried towards the old rocking-horse. 'Bags I first!' he shouted and swung a leg over the saddle. He rocked back and forth for a while, a dreamy expression on his face, while his sister arranged a row of skittles along the edge of the hearthrug.

They soon tired of their games and found it more entertaining to stand outside the boxroom, baiting Nanny.

'Cinderella's gone to town, with her knickers hanging down,' sang Olivia.

'Bum,' said Hugh.

'Every little Master, every little Miss, there behind the greenhouse, having a lovely – yoo-hoo, Nanny!'

'Titties,' said Hugh.

Olivia listened again. There was still no sound.

'Do you think we ought to let her out?' asked Hugh.

Olivia shrugged. 'Let's just *look* at her.' She moved around the room, searching for the key. 'Where the hell did I put it?'

It was Hugh who found it on the mantelpiece and who, in his excitement, knocked it off, so that it bounced against his chest and fell into the fire. He turned to Olivia, stricken. 'I didn't mean to, honestly, I ...'

'Really, Hugh, you're such a butterfingers!' she said exasperatedly. 'Ah well, we'll have to break the door down, I suppose.'

Hugh was leaning over the fireguard. 'Perhaps I can fish it out ...'

'No, no ...' Olivia pushed him away. 'Let me.' She began to unhook the fireguard.

'Ohh!' said Hugh, hand to mouth. He glanced towards the boxroom. 'You're not *allowed*.'

'Tell-tale-tit,' sneered Olivia. 'What's the matter? Afraid of what Nanny will say? You're really still afraid of her? An old woman of ninety, locked up in a cupboard? Oh, *Hugh*! And I thought today would stop all that. I thought we could wipe out the past, get our own back. I thought I could begin to make a man of you at last. But you're just as weak as you always were.'

Hugh cringed.

Olivia by now removed the fireguard and was bending low over the fire with a pair of short-handled tongs. As she turned to berate Hugh still further, her wrist touched the scorching hot hood above the grate. 'Ow!' she cried, jumping back.

If she had tidied away the skittles, as she would have had to in Nanny's day ('We always tidy up one thing before we go on to the next'), she might have suffered nothing more than a burnt wrist, but she had left them lying untidily on the hearthrug, so that when she jumped back she landed on them, lost her balance, and toppled right into the fire.

Hugh, his face a mask of helplessness, watched, trembling, as her dress flared up. She shrieked and put out a hand for him to pull her out, but he could only stand there, gaping.

By the time she had dragged herself clear, she was a stumbling, screeching torch. Her screams were so pitiful that Hugh had to put his hands over his ears. Then she stopped screaming and stood still for a moment, eyes wide with horror, before collapsing in a bubbling, writhing mass on the floor.

Hugh, retreating, terror-stricken, from the flames, heard beneath her moans heavy thumping on the boxroom door. Then there were no more moans and, after a while, no more thumps. Just crackling, as the fire edged towards him over the faded Peter Pan carpet.

Hugh squatted on his haunches, watching it. He put his thumb in his mouth and sucked hard. He didn't like the smoke. It was making him cough. When he could feel the heat of the flames on his skin he screwed up his face and howled. 'Nanneee!' he sobbed. 'Nanneee!'

But though he called and called, Nanny never came.

Activity Time

Monica Dickens

There it was again. Thump! on the end of the trailer, followed by a giggle and another thump right by the head of his bed. That crude young couple in Number 23 South coming home from the bar and trying to scare him as he lay hoping for sleep in Number 21.

Neighbours. When he sold the house after his wife died, and moved upstate into a rented trailer in Canalside Mobilehome Park, Dick had thought that he was finished with the aggravation of them. No lawn for their dogs to run over; no hedge for their children to trample down, taking a short cut to school; no windows to be splattered with eggs or marked with soap on Hallowe'en night.

Canalside Park, which nestled by one of the huge stone abutments under the soaring span of the bridge, should be more secure. He had spoken to his landlord about the crude couple, and the landlord, who laughed at everything, had laughed and said, 'Open the window and pour boiling water on them.' But all the trailer windows were fastened shut for the winter.

Since the angina attack, Dick had hardly been out in this terrible winter when snow had fallen for three days and now lay about the trailer park in dirty lumps. He had sold his car when his eyes got bad, and he could not ride his bicycle. His doctor had arranged, just for this winter – he was no deadbeat Welfare customer – for him to have Meals on Wheels. Every weekday, a dirty white Volkswagen crunched on the icy cinders, and Dick quickly let down the curtain, so Rosemary would not know he had been watching for her.

Rosemary was a Scottish girl with bright cheeks and raspberry lipstick, and a way of laying the containers of food on the flap table in his tiny kitchen as if she were setting out a banquet.

'What have you brought me today?' He knew what it was, because she brought him a menu at the beginning of the month. The fish was dreadful. The chicken had often seen better days. She would wait while he turned back the cover of the foil dish, so that he could say, 'Swiss steak! I thought that kind of stuff only went into dog food.'

'Hoo, come on now, Dick,' she would say in her soft Scottish voice. 'Why do they always think old people want to eat carrots?'

'Hoo, come on, Dick. I'll pop it in the wee toaster oven, so it'll be ready when you want it.'

'While you're here, will you look at my ankle?' He tried to make Rosemary stay, and although she had a dozen customers to visit in the dirty little car, she would refasten his elastic bandage, or turn the mattress, or sew on a button before she hurried away with, 'See you tomorrow.'

She was usually the only person he did see. He showed her the knick-knacks he and Alice had collected on vacations, and could not resist giving her a little mug from Aberdeen, South Dakota, to remind her of her homeland.

Rosemary was going to have a baby, but not yet. She would last him out the winter. One Friday, however, when she brought him his sliced beef and noodles, with the salad and jelly in styrofoam bowls and a piece of cornbread so neatly wrapped, she said, 'I won't be coming any more. The doctor says no more driving.'

'The baby? But surely——'

'It's twins.' She pulled a funny face. 'I've to be careful they're not born too soon.'

'Who will bring the meals to me?' As he said it, he heard the selfishness of not first asking, 'Are you all right?', but it was too late, because she was answering, 'There's a nice new volunteer, and not in any danger of having a baby, ha ha.'

She bent to stroke the old white cat, pulled her hand away when she saw the sores it had scratched on itself, and patted Dick on the shoulder. 'I'll bring the twins to see you,' she said as she went out with her raspberry coloured smile, and he said, 'You do that, dear,' although he knew she never would.

She had brought him an extra can of stew and an orange, which his stiff fingers could not peel. At weekends, Annette from 16 West brought in his few groceries, and came across the snow and mud with a plate of Sunday dinner and a piece of pie. Her food was not good – even worse than Meals on Wheels – but it pleased her to do this, so he put up with it.

'Another poor creature gone off the bridge,' she told him this Sunday when she brought the pot roast.

'That's three jumpers since October.' Dick kept a tally of the feckless, cowardly people who launched themselves into eternity from the arching span of the canal bridge, high above him. 'As long as they don't fall on my roof.'

The new volunteer was never quite on time. Rosemary was like a clock, but now Dick waited longer at the window for Florence's wide old blue car with the rust patches.

When he complained, she said, 'There's folks worse off than you that need my time.'

Florence was wide, like her car, a comfortably shaped woman smelling of cheap lavender, her short black hair turning white in patches. Alice's thick hair had been snow white, like the cat. The thing she minded most about the brain tumour operation was having a large chunk of hair shaved. If she had known she was going to die on the table, she need not have fussed.

Florence had been a nurse. 'I know how to make an old gentleman comfortable.' If he was not well enough to get up, she would go at him with her strong rounded arms, and plump up his pillows, and from his bed in the space across the end of the trailer, he could see her fluffing up the settee cushions and dusting things off with a wad of paper towel.

He wanted to show her Alice's picture, but the little photograph in the silver frame was not in its place on the bureau.

'More years you gain, more things you lose,' Florence said. But there began to be other things missing – a carved salt spoon from Vermont, the spotted china dog from Gettysburg. Dick did not feel well. His appetite had gone off, and he began to think there was something wrong with the food. He gave most of it to the old cat.

On Monday, instead of giving Florence the seventy-five cents in an envelope, as he had with Rosemary, he mumbled that he could not manage it this week.

'Think nothing of it,' she said, but he had nothing to do but think, and the thoughts grew more confused.

He stayed long in bed, and went in and out of dreams. One afternoon, with a lowering sun gilding the stone bridgework, he awoke in fright and pain and vomited. So. She was not only a thief, but a poisoner as well.

When he had collected enough breath, he rolled out of the low bed, staggered into the kitchen and picked up the cat's dish. Thank God It had not eaten any of this morning's meat loaf. Elder Services still had not put in his phone, so he put a sweater and overcoat over his pyjama jacket, and boots over the trousers, and shambled through the fading light to the pay phone in the laundry.

There were a couple of women in there. There were always women in there, eternally feeding or emptying the rotating drums. They looked at him without recognition and went on with their talking and folding.

When a woman answered at Elder Services, he told her right away, no beating about the bush: 'Complaint against the new Wheels on Meals woman … Things missing in my home. I strongly suspect … And the food's gone off. I'm scared.' He heard his voice grow shrill. 'She'll steal the money, you know. It's not right to put elderly people——'

'Excuse me.' The woman cut into his rising voice. 'I think you have the wrong number. This is Bayside Auto Parts.'

'Oh, damn.' He was looking in his pocket for another dime to try and dial the right number, but he heard the women giggling and whispering, so he let it go.

He was in the kitchen next morning when Florence stumped up the steps, put her basket on the table, thrust her fists into the pockets of the tomato red coat which flared over her wide hips and said, 'It's turkey with all the fixings. Now complain about *that!*'

But he had not complained. Or had he? He never got through. Or did he? She was not only a thief and a poisoner, but a mind-bedeviller as well.

When she left, the cat was by the door, and she shooed it out into the icy rain.

'No, don't.' Dick was letting the old cat use a litter box.

'Nonsense,' Florence said briskly. 'Good for him to run.'

By nightfall, the cat had not come back. Dick had managed to fall asleep when – thump! He started awake, got himself out of bed and somehow through the trailer, hanging on to furniture, dragged open the door and shouted into the night, 'God damn you!'

A faraway laugh. The woman's voice. Slam of a metal trailer door. Very faint, the woman's voice again. Or was it a cat mewing?

'Kippy! Kippy!' He stood on the top step in the rain. Nothing. The trailers slept in rows. The bridge stood sentinel.

When the car stopped outside next morning, he was upright on the settee, fully dressed in jacket and trousers, alert, though his heart was twanging.

As the door opened, he began, 'Now look here——'

A tall young man in a yellow oilskin stepped in, filling the trailer with his loose-jointed presence. 'Sorry I'm late. It took me a while to——'

'Where's Florence?'

'Who?'

'Brought me my meals.'

'Rosemary? Well . . .' He sketched a mound in front of him.

'No, no.' The boy was daft. 'The woman since her.'

'Dunno. I took over Rosemary's route. Gotta go.'

He dumped down the foil dish and bowls. Clumsy in the small kitchen, he stumbled on his way to the door. 'Oops – sorry.' He bent to pick up something. 'Clean break. I'll bring glue tomorrow.' Dick was left staring at the two halves of the missing china dog from Gettysburg.

A long while later, he was able to stand up. After some difficulty with the sleeves, he put on his coat and went out. Amid all the confusion and lies and wavery thoughts he could not pin down, one fact came clear to the front of his mind. He had heard the cat mewing last night.

The rain had lashed itself into a full-blown storm. Walking about between the trailers, he strained to hear the mewing again, but the wind made too much noise in the trees. Soaking wet, his thin hair plastered against his chilled face, he walked out to the road where the cars swished past, expecting to see a flattened body, its insides already washed away. Distraught, he wandered to the bank of the canal, where small ice floes bumped about in the tide that swirled out under the bridge to the open bay – carrying the cat's body with it? High above him on the lighted bridge, a tiny figure walked by the rail. *Go on then, damn you – jump!*

Wet through, shivering, he somehow got himself back to the laundry room, and found the number of the local vet.

'. . . to ask if anyone reported a dead or injured cat. What? Yes. Pure white.'

'A white cat.' The vet's voice was young and confident. 'Someone did bring in an old one yesterday to be put down. None too soon.'

'Who? Who brought it?'

'The owner, I suppose.'

'What she——' Dick's voice was a hoarse whisper. 'What she look——'

'I don't remember. Woman in a red coat.'

Whether he hung up the phone or let it drop, he never afterwards knew. Whether he ever made the call to the vet, he was not sure. He was not sure of anything. Times were out of joint. Things that hadn't yet happened had already happened. While he was in the Intensive Care Unit, wired up fore and aft, he need not struggle to make sense of the confusion. When Annette from 16 West came with a harried face, she brought him Alice's photograph.

'I thought she stole it.'

'Who? I found it behind the bureau when I was cleaning up a bit. Give me a fright, you taking a heart attack.'

'It was the cat. When the cat died——'

'What do you mean, cat died?' Thinking she spoke too loud, Annette glanced round the unit, where wired and tubed bodies lay sacrificially on high beds, and the nurses moved like silent priestesses in the central glass booth where they received the messages of the bodies. 'He's hale and hearty. I found him outside your door, and I'm in to feed him every day and clean his litter box.'

Dick struggled to sit up, eyes staring, breath rasping. One of the priestesses put a hand on his chest, and he fell back through the pillows into a wide black hole which welcomed him as the black waters of the canal welcomed the jumpers.

The hospital was a limbo, not needing organized thought, which was becoming difficult. They kept congratulating him on doing well enough to be discharged.

'I'd rather——'

But the social worker had it all arranged. Jokey, considerate ambulance men, extensions of the reassuring hospital staff, took him across the bridge to Fairview Nursing Home and wheeled him into a small room with a fair view of a high slatted fence with dead Christmas wreaths hanging on its pointed tops like severed heads.

The private room was expensive, but it was only a few weeks, and he had money in the bank from the sale of the house. Across the corridor, an old man shrieked and hooted, and another old man cursed him with a foul tongue. The cusser was called John, and when their doors were left open at night Dick could see him struggling in his sleep, as if in continual conflict with some nightmare opponent.

The food was even worse than in the hospital. When Annette came, he asked her to bring him a Sunday dinner. She brought tough chicken and buttered corn, which he spilled on his lap rug, and the Administrator marched in with the dictum: Against State Law to bring in food.

'Get me out of here.' Dick tried his feet on the floor, found they would not take weight, and returned them to the foot rests before Annette noticed.

'I don't know.' She wore her harried face. 'They stopped me on the way in and told me to try to explain to you what the doctor said. Remember the letter to the lawyer I helped you to sign, dear? He's cancelling the trailer rental, as you agreed.'

'Who agreed? They forged my signature. You did it. I must go back. What about the cat?'

'Remember, dear, I told you. I had to have him put to sleep, his sores were so bad, and that nice young vet said, "None too soon."'

'Murderess.' He spat at her.

'That's it.' Annette stood up. 'I've tried to help, but I'll not come here to be insulted.'

'Don't.' Dick was so angry that he almost managed to stand up. He pushed against the arms of the wheelchair; it shot backwards, and when he collapsed he would have fallen, if Annette had not caught him in her treacherous arms. Hanging limply, he stared at the arm across his chest in the cranberry red coat sleeve.

Spring came, and summer, and in the fall, when the brown leaves blew in drifts against the fence where the wreaths still hung, the Administrator told him that since his money had run out and he was now on a lower fee as a Medicaid patient, he would go into a threesome room as soon as a bed was available.

'I won't.'

'Come along, old feller. Activity time.' A new nurse wheeled him to the dining room, where the bodies were ranged around the walls. Had she heard him? Speaking was getting more difficult all the time. Trying to say, 'I won't,' he twisted round and smelled lavender, and saw that the new nurse was Meals on Wheels Florence, with a straining white uniform and magpie hair.

After she settled him by the wall and tied him to the chair with the soft straitjacket, he grabbed her plump hand. 'I know you.'

'This is my first day.'

'Florence.'

'Mrs Macky.'

She was different. Not so mean and crafty. He was getting things mixed up again. It was not really Florence, but he put Alice's photograph and his bits and pieces into his bedside drawer, with the candy the night staff would steal if you left it out.

State Law insisted on Activities every day. Each morning Mrs Activities, a wiry, manic woman with bolting eyes, read bits out of the newspaper, while the heads nodded all around her and bodies flopped against restrainers. When Mrs Activities did flower arranging, you knew someone had died. The wreaths were sent to Fairview after the funeral. Once when Dick was in his chair near the entrance, waiting for Annette who never came, the trolley of flowers was trundled in from the car park, and the woman in the next chair remarked, 'Anyone seen Mabel lately?'

Dick was losing his grip. He hung on desperately, but his mind was slipping away, like his body. Maybe he should be in the funny farm. Maybe he already was. For the Hallowe'en party, the bodies wore masks. Some of them looked better than usual. Mrs Macky wore a witch's costume. At least that made sense.

'You want me dead, don't you?' he asked her when she put him back to bed.

'Hup she goes.' None of the nurses answered you. They said sayings, or just laughed, or scolded. Dick had tried to write a list of complaints, a letter to Annette, to Elder Services who sold auto parts, but the pad and pencil fell to the floor.

'Everything all right?' The Administrator came into the room dressed as a ghost, watching him through holes in the sheet.

Dick shook his head. It kept on shaking.

'He likes to complain,' Mrs Macky said comfortably, a witch in a pointed hat.

'You're lucky to be here,' the Administrator said. 'We've a long waiting list.'

Of private paying patients. 'You want my bed.' He could not be sure if he had said that, or, 'You want me dead', or if he had spoken at all.

He saw them exchange a look, the holes in the sheet, the eyes under the witch's hat. So that was it. All was lost.

Even if Mrs Macky was not actively trying to kill him, she was not
trying to keep him alive. She lied, pretending he had had a bath, or not
had pills, to overdose him. She lied about the time of day, the day of
the week, to confuse him. She put his meal on the tray table, and if he
could not feed himself she came in hours later with, 'Not hungry?' and
took away the cold food. He wore diapers and rubber pants, and wept
to think what Alice would say. His bell was on a string, but the string
had been disconnected. It led nowhere. When Mrs Macky came in red
and flustered after he had lain soaking for hours, she said, 'On a day
like this, wet diapers is pretty low on my list of priorities.' The hooter
hooted like an owl. Why didn't old John cuss him out?

That night he dreamt of jumping from the bridge, falling, falling ...
His heart dropped, and he awoke in a sweat and sat up to see through
the open door a naked, bony corpse on the bed across the corridor where
cussing John slept. But was it a corpse? Suddenly, the eyes popped open
and stared at him, round and bulging, like balls of pale pink bubble gum.

He raised an arm in limp salute, but John could no longer see him.
A nurse had placed two fingers on his eyelids and was holding them
down. Dick wanted to shout, *Stop it! Leave him alone!* but his mouth was
too dry. Another nurse, blonde, with hair cut square to match her figure,
had arranged John's arms straight down by his sides, so that he lay at
attention, and turned away to wring out a cloth in a bowl of water. One
of John's arms flopped off the edge of the bed and swung to and fro. Dick
saw it as a sign of life, a call for help, but he was powerless, as useless
as a cabbage. The nurse with the cloth turned round, casually replaced
the arm and began to wash John's narrow, hairless chest, whistling
tunelessly through her teeth as she casually wiped and rinsed. The skin
looked clammy, shiny, reptilian.

The other nurse was doing something to the old man's slack mouth,
stretching the lips with her fingers while she savagely rammed in his false
teeth. He looked worse, now. She had propped him up against his
pillows, and his head was lolling on one side while his jaw gaped in
toothy imbecility. Deftly, she wound a bandage around his head and
under his jaw, giving his face a firm expression that wasn't the dribbling
old man Dick knew.

He looked like a corpse now, like pictures in old books of ghosts in
their grave-clothes. But he wasn't dead. Dick knew that, because his
eyes had popped open again and were staring across at him in a kind
of blank despair, as if he were resigned to his fate. One of the nurses
tutted in disgust and playfully slapped John's side. 'Come on now, you
stubborn old bag o' bones,' she said, sighing and holding his eyelids
down again.

Something dreadful was happening further down. The blonde nurse
seemed to be pressing on John's stomach – where his bladder must be.

Dick turned his head away. It wasn't right to watch such indignities. Oh, why couldn't they leave him to die in peace?

They were plugging him now, rolling him over on to his face, rolling him back, throwing remarks to each other across his defenceless body. 'Seen that crummy movie at the Bridge cinema?' 'Nah, Gary's doing nights up the gas station this week.' They filled his nostrils with little pellets of cotton, so that he couldn't breathe. It was murder, but who could Dick tell? The eyes stayed closed now, and the nurses pushed John's arms into the sleeves of a paper shroud and tied tapes in bows down his back. They took away the pillows and rocked the body to and fro like a rolling pin as they inserted a clean sheet underneath it. One of them tied a label to John's big toe, and the other taped a card to his chest, then they wrapped him up in the sheet like a Christmas parcel and left the room. Dick heard them chatting and laughing as the rubber soles of their white lace-up shoes squeaked away down the corridor.

In the morning light, they would not say that John was dead, but the bed was empty, made up clean like a mortuary slab. The hooter hooted last trumps for him, and a new man was wheeled in. *Watch out*, Dick wanted to say to him. *All is lost.* Later that day – next day, next week?– the new man was wheeled out. 'Come along, old feller. Activity time. We're going to do flower arranging.'

They want me dead. If I don't die soon, they won't wait, they'll lay me out while I'm still alive, still breathing. They had done it before, they would do it again, given half a chance. This was not something he had imagined, or remembered all wrong. This nightmare was real. This was murder. For the first time, he understood the cowards who jumped off the canal bridge. Was it horror like this they were so desperate to escape?

Dick tried to speak to the room cleaners, but State Law forbade them to talk to patients. He tried to call for help to anyone who passed the door – the hurrying young nurses, glum visitors, the man who came to restock the Coca-Cola machine – but his voice was a croak and his blotched, stranger's claw could only pluck at the sheets.

He remembered the safety of the hospital. Had he been there yet, or was he going? A heart attack. He'd make one, and the ambulance men would come with jokes and take him away to intensive care. Next time the cramping pains came in his chest, instead of pulling on the broken bell string, he forced himself somehow to move his racked body forward. Inch by inch, he got a leg over the edge, then another, feet dangling, sore bottom on the edge of the bed, shoulders on the mattress. He had a leg over the rail in the teeth of the wind, straining in an agony that almost burst his heart. Mrs Macky tried to pull him back, but he pitched over the rail and was a long time falling without breath before he hit the black waters of the shining linoleum, and the trolley of lavender flowers trundled past.

The Brazilian Cat

Arthur Conan Doyle

It is hard luck on a young fellow to have expensive tastes, great expectations, aristocratic connections, but no actual money in his pocket, and no profession by which he may earn any. The fact was that my father, a good, sanguine, easy-going man, had such confidence in the wealth and benevolence of his bachelor elder brother Lord Southerton, that he took it for granted that I, his only son, would never be called upon to earn a living for myself. He imagined that if there were not a vacancy for me on the great Southerton Estates, at least there would be found some post in that diplomatic service which still remains the special preserve of our privileged classes. He died too early to realize how false his calculations had been. Neither my uncle nor the State took the slightest notice of me, or showed any interest in my career. An occasional brace of pheasants, or basket of hares, was all that ever reached me to remind me that I was heir to Otwell House and one of the richest estates in the country. In the meantime, I found myself a bachelor and man about town, living in a suite of apartments in Grosvenor Mansions, with no occupation save that of pigeon-shooting and polo-playing at Hurlingham. Month by month I realized that it was more and more difficult to get the brokers to renew my bills, or to cash any further post-obits upon an unentailed property. Ruin lay right across my path, and every day I saw it clearer, nearer, and more absolutely unavoidable.

What made me feel my own poverty the more was that, apart from the great wealth of Lord Southerton, all my other relations were fairly well-to-do. The nearest of these was Everard King, my father's nephew and my own first cousin, who had spent an adventurous life in Brazil, and had now returned to this country to settle down on his fortune. We never knew how he made his money, but he appeared to have plenty of it, for he bought the estate of Greylands, near Clipton-on-the-Marsh, in Suffolk. For the first year of his residence in England he took no more notice of me than my miserly uncle; but at last one summer morning, to my very great relief and joy, I received a letter asking me to come down that very day and spend a short visit at Greylands Court. I was expecting a rather long visit to Bankruptcy Court at the time, and this interruption seemed almost providential. If I could only get on terms with this unknown relative of mine, I might pull through yet. For the family credit he could not let me go entirely to the wall. I ordered my valet to pack my valise, and I set off the same evening for Clipton-on-the-Marsh.

After changing at Ipswich, a little local train deposited me at a small, deserted station lying amidst a rolling grassy country, with a sluggish and winding river curving in and out amidst the valleys, between high, silted banks, which showed that we were within reach of the tide. No carriage was awaiting me (I found afterwards that my telegram had been delayed), so I hired a dog-cart at the local inn. The driver, an excellent fellow, was full of my relative's praises, and I learned from him that Mr Everard King was already a name to conjure with in that part of the country. He had entertained the school-children, he had thrown his grounds open to visitors, he had subscribed to charities – in short, his benevolence had been so universal that my driver could only account for it on the supposition that he had Parliamentary ambitions.

My attention was drawn away from my driver's panegyric by the appearance of a very beautiful bird which settled on a telegraph-post beside the road. At first I thought that it was a jay, but it was larger, with a brighter plumage. The driver accounted for its presence at once by saying that it belonged to the very man whom we were about to visit. It seems that the acclimatization of foreign creatures was one of his hobbies, and that he had brought with him from Brazil a number of birds and beasts which he was endeavouring to rear in England. When once we had passed the gates of Greylands Park we had ample evidence of this taste of his. Some small spotted deer, a curious wild pig known, I believe, as a peccary, a gorgeously feathered oriole, some sort of armadillo, and a singular lumbering intocd beast like a very fat badger, were among the creatures which I observed as we drove along the winding avenue.

Mr Everard King, my unknown cousin, was standing in person upon the steps of his house, for he had seen us in the distance, and guessed that it was I. His appearance was very homely and benevolent, short and stout, forty-five years old, perhaps, with a round, good-humoured face, burned brown with the tropical sun, and shot with a thousand wrinkles. He wore white linen clothes, in true planter style, with a cigar between his lips, and a large Panama hat upon the back of his head. It was such a figure as one associates with a verandahed bungalow, and it looked curiously out of place in front of this broad, stone, English mansion, with its solid wings and its Palladio pillars before the doorway.

'My dear!' he cried, glancing over his shoulder; 'my dear, here is our guest! Welcome, welcome to Greylands! I am delighted to make your aquaintance, Cousin Marshall, and I take it as a great compliment that you should honour this sleepy little country place with your presence.'

Nothing could be more hearty than his manner, and he set me at my ease in an instant. But it needed all his cordiality to atone for the frigidity and even rudeness of his wife, a tall, haggard woman, who came forward at his summons. She was, I believe, of Brazilian extraction, though she spoke excellent English, and I excused her manners on the score of her ignorance of our customs. She did not attempt to conceal, however, either then or afterwards, that I was no very welcome visitor at Greylands Court. Her actual words were, as a rule, courteous, but she was the possessor of a pair of particularly expressive dark eyes, and I read in them very clearly from the first that she heartily wished me back in London once more.

However, my debts were too pressing and my designs upon my wealthy relative were too vital for me to allow them to be upset by the ill-temper of his wife, so I disregarded her coldness and reciprocated the extreme cordiality of his welcome. No pains had been spared by him to make me comfortable. My room was a charming one. He implored me to tell him anything which could add to my happiness. It was on the tip of my tongue to inform him that a blank cheque would materially help towards that end, but I felt that it might be premature in the present state of our acquaintance. The dinner was excellent, and as we sat together afterwards over his Havanas and coffee, which latter he told me was specially prepared upon his own plantation, it seemed to me that all my driver's eulogies were justified, and that I had never met a more large-hearted and hospitable man.

But, in spite of his cheery good nature, he was a man with a strong will and a fiery temper of his own. Of this I had an example upon the following morning. The curious aversion which Mrs Everard King had conceived towards me was so strong, that her manner at breakfast was almost offensive. But her meaning became unmistakable when her husband had quitted the room.

'The best train in the day is at twelve-fifteen,' said she.

'But I was not thinking of going today,' I answered, frankly – perhaps even defiantly, for I was determined not to be driven out by this woman.

'Oh, if it rests with you——' said she, and stopped with a most insolent expression in her eyes.

'I am sure,' I answered, 'that Mr Everard King would tell me if I were outstaying my welcome.'

'What's this? What's this?' said a voice, and there he was in the room. He had overheard my last words, and a glance at our faces had told him the rest. In an instant his chubby, cheery face set into an expression of absolute ferocity.

'Might I trouble you to walk outside, Marshall?' said he. (I may mention that my own name is Marshall King.)

He closed the door behind me, and then, for an instant, I heard him talking in a low voice of concentrated passion to his wife. This gross breach of hospitality had evidently hit upon his tenderest point. I am no eavesdropper, so I walked out on to the lawn. Presently I heard a hurried step behind me, and there was the lady, her face pale with excitement, and her eyes red with tears.

'My husband has asked me to apologize to you, Mr Marshall King,' said she, standing with downcast eyes before me.

'Please do not say another word, Mrs King.'

Her dark eyes suddenly blazed out at me.

'You fool!' she hissed, with frantic vehemence, and turning on her heel swept back to the house.

The insult was so outrageous, so insufferable, that I could only stand staring after her in bewilderment. I was still there when my host joined me. He was his cheery, chubby self once more.

'I hope that my wife has apologized for her foolish remarks,' said he.

'Oh, yes – yes, certainly!'

He put his hand through my arm and walked with me up and down the lawn.

'You must not take it seriously,' said he. 'It would grieve me inexpressibly if you curtailed your visit by one hour. The fact is – there is no reason why there should be any concealment between relatives – that my poor dear wife is incredibly jealous. She hates that anyone – male or female – should for an instant come between us. Her ideal is a desert island and an eternal *tête-à-tête*. That gives you the clue to her actions, which are, I confess, upon this particular point, not very far removed from mania. Tell me that you will think no more of it.'

'No, no; certainly not.'

'Then light this cigar and come round with me and see my little menagerie.'

The whole afternoon was occupied by this inspection, which included all the birds, beasts, and even reptiles which he had imported. Some were free, some in cages, a few actually in the house. He spoke with enthusiasm of his successes and his failures, his births and his deaths, and he would cry out in his delight, like a schoolboy, when, as we walked, some gaudy bird would flutter up from the grass, or some curious beast slink into the cover. Finally he led me down a corridor which extended from one wing of the house. At the end of this there was a heavy door with a sliding shutter in it, and beside it there projected from the wall an iron handle attached to a wheel and a drum. A line of stout bars extended across the passage.

'I am about to show you the jewel of my collection,' said he. 'There is only one other specimen in Europe, now that the Rotterdam cub is dead. It is a Brazilian cat.'

'But how does that differ from any other cat?'

'You will soon see that,' said he, laughing. 'Will you kindly draw that shutter and look through?'

I did so, and found that I was gazing into a large, empty room, with stone flags, and small, barred windows upon the farther wall. In the centre of this room, lying in the middle of a golden patch of sunlight, there was stretched a huge creature, as large as a tiger, but as black and sleek as ebony. It was simply a very enormous and very well-kept black cat, and it cuddled up and basked in that yellow pool of light exactly as a cat would do. It was so graceful, so sinewy, and so gently and smoothly diabolical, that I could not take my eyes from the opening.

'Isn't he splendid?' said my host, enthusiastically.

'Glorious! I never saw such a noble creature.'

'Some people call it a black puma, but really it is not a puma at all. That fellow is nearly eleven feet from tail to tip. Four years ago he was a little ball of black fluff, with two yellow eyes staring out of it. He was sold me as a new-born cub up in the wild country at the head-waters of the Rio Negro. They speared his mother to death after she had killed a dozen of them.'

'They are ferocious, then?'

'The most absolutely treacherous and bloodthirsty creatures upon earth. You talk about a Brazilian cat to an up-country Indian, and see him get the jumps. They prefer humans to game. This fellow has never tasted living blood yet, but when he does he will be a terror. At present he won't stand anyone but me in his den. Even Baldwin, the groom, dare not go near him. As to me, I am his mother and father in one.'

As he spoke he suddenly, to my astonishment, opened the door and slipped in, closing it instantly behind him. At the sound of his voice the huge, lithe creature rose, yawned and rubbed its round, black head affectionately against his side, while he patted and fondled it.

'Now, Tommy, into your cage!' said he.

The monstrous cat walked over to one side of the room and coiled itself up under a grating. Everard King came out, and, taking the iron handle which I have mentioned, he began to turn it. As he did so the line of bars in the corridor began to pass through a slot in the wall and closed up the front of this grating, so as to make an effective cage. When it was in position he opened the door once more and invited me into the room, which was heavy with the pungent, musty smell peculiar to the great carnivora.

'That's how we work it,' said he. 'We give him the run of the room for exercise, and then at night we put him in his cage. You can let him out by turning the handle from the passage, or you can, as you have seen, coop him up in the same way. No, no, you should not do that!'

I had put my hand between the bars to pat the glossy, heaving flank. He pulled it back, with a serious face.

'I assure you that he is not safe. Don't imagine that because I can take liberties with him anyone else can. He is very exclusive in his friends – aren't you, Tommy? Ah, he hears his lunch coming to him! Don't you, boy?'

A step sounded in the stone-flagged passage, and the creature had sprung to his feet and was pacing up and down the narrow cage, his yellow eyes gleaming, and his scarlet tongue rippling and quivering over the white line of his jagged teeth. A groom entered with a coarse joint upon a tray, and thrust it through the bars to him. He pounced lightly upon it, carried it off to the corner, and there, holding it between his paws, tore and wrenched at it, raising his bloody muzzle every now and then to look at us. It was a malignant and yet fascinating sight.

'You can't wonder that I am fond of him, can you?' said my host, as we left the room, 'especially when you consider that I have had the rearing of him. It was no joke bringing him over from the centre of South America; but here he is safe and sound – and, as I have said, far the most perfect specimen in Europe. The people at the Zoo are dying to have him, but I really can't part with him. Now, I think that I have inflicted my hobby upon you long enough, so we cannot do much better than follow Tommy's example, and go to our lunch.'

My South American relative was so engrossed by his grounds and their curious occupants, that I hardly gave him credit at first for having any interests outside them. That he had some, and pressing ones, was soon borne in upon me by the number of telegrams which he received. They arrived at all hours, and were always opened by him with the utmost eagerness and anxiety upon his face. Sometimes I imagined that it must be the Turf, and sometimes the Stock Exchange, but certainly he had some very urgent business going forwards which was not trans- acted upon the Downs of Suffolk. During the six days of my visit he had never fewer than three or four telegrams a day, and sometimes as many as seven or eight.

I had occupied these six days so well, that by the end of them I had succeeded in getting upon the most cordial terms with my cousin. Every night we had sat up late in the billiard-room, he telling me the most extraordinary stories of his adventures in America – stories so desperate and reckless that I could hardly associate them with the brown little, chubby man before me. In return, I ventured upon some of my own reminiscences of London life, which interested him so much that he vowed he would come up to Grosvenor Mansions and stay with me. He was anxious to see the faster side of city life, and certainly, though I say it, he could not have chosen a more competent guide. It was not until the last day of my visit that I ventured to approach that which was on my mind. I told him frankly about my pecuniary difficulties and my impending ruin, and I asked his advice – though I hoped for something more solid. He listened attentively, puffing hard at his cigar.

'But surely,' said he, 'you are the heir of our relative, Lord Southerton?'

'I have every reason to believe so, but he would never make me any allowance.'

'No, no, I have heard of his miserly ways. My poor Marshall, your position has been a very hard one. By the way, have you heard any news of Lord Southerton's health lately?'

'He has always been in a critical condition ever since my childhood.'

'Exactly – a creaking hinge, if ever there was one. Your inheritance may be a long way off. Dear me, how awkwardly situated you are!'

'I had some hopes, sir, that you, knowing all the facts, might be inclined to advance——'

'Don't say another word, my dear boy,' he cried, with the utmost cordiality; 'we shall talk it over tonight, and I give you my word that whatever is in my power shall be done.'

I was not sorry that my visit was drawing to a close, for it is unpleasant to feel that there is one person in the house who eagerly desires your departure. Mrs King's sallow face and forbidding eyes had become more and more hateful to me. She was no longer actively rude – her fear of her husband prevented her – but she pushed her insane jealousy to the extent of ignoring me, never addressing me, and in every way making my stay at Greylands as uncomfortable as she could. So offensive was her manner during that last day that I should certainly have left had it not been for that interview with my host in the evening which would, I hoped, retrieve my broken fortunes.

It was very late when it occurred, for my relative, who had been receiving even more telegrams than usual during the day, went off to his study after dinner, and only emerged when the household had retired to bed. I heard him go round locking the doors, as his custom was of a night, and finally he joined me in the billiard-room. His stout figure was wrapped in a dressing-gown, and he wore a pair of red Turkish slippers without any heels. Settling down into an arm-chair, he brewed himself a glass of grog, in which I could not help noticing that the whisky considerably predominated over the water.

'My word!' said he, 'what a night!'

It was indeed. The wind was howling and screaming round the house, and the latticed windows rattled and shook as if they were coming in. The glow of the yellow lamps and the flavour of our cigars seemed the brighter and more fragrant for the contrast.

'Now, my boy,' said my host, 'we have the house and the night to ourselves. Let me have an idea of how your affairs stand, and I will see what can be done to set them in order. I wish to hear every detail.'

Thus encouraged, I entered into a long exposition, in which all my tradesmen and creditors from my landlord to my valet figured in turn. I had notes in my pocketbook, and I marshalled my facts, and gave, I flatter myself, a very business-like statement of my own unbusiness-like ways and lamentable position. I was depressed, however, to notice that my companion's eyes were vacant and his attention elsewhere. When he did occasionally throw out a remark it was so entirely perfunctory and pointless that I was sure he had not in the least followed my remarks. Every now and then he roused himself and put on some show of interest, asking me to repeat or to explain more fully, but it was always to sink once more into the same brown study. At last he rose and threw the end of his cigar into the grate.

'I'll tell you what, my boy,' said he. 'I never had a head for figures, so you will excuse me. You must jot it all down upon paper, and let me have a note of the amount. I'll understand it when I see it in black and white.'

The proposal was encouraging. I promised to do so.

'And now it's time we were in bed. By Jove, there's one o'clock striking in the hall.'

The tingling of the chiming clock broke through the deep roar of the gale. The wind was sweeping past with the rush of a great river.

'I must see my cat before I go to bed,' said my host. 'A high wind excites him. Will you come?'

'Certainly,' said I.

'Then tread softly and don't speak, for everyone is asleep.'

We passed quietly down the lamp-lit Persian-rugged hall, and through the door at the farther end. All was dark in the stone corridor, but a stable lantern hung on a hook, and my host took it down and lit it. There was no grating visible in the passage, so I knew that the beast was in its cage.

'Come in!' said my relative, and opened the door.

A deep growling as we entered showed that the storm had really excited the creature. In the flickering light of the lantern we saw it, a huge black mass coiled in the corner of its den and throwing a squat, uncouth shadow upon the whitewashed wall. Its tail switched angrily among the straw.

'Poor Tommy is not in the best of tempers,' said Everard King, holding up the lantern and looking in at him. 'What a black devil he looks, doesn't he? I must give him a little supper to put him in a better humour. Would you mind holding the lantern for a moment?'

I took it from his hand and he stepped to the door.

'His larder is just outside here,' said he. 'You will excuse me for an instant, won't you?' He passed out, and the door shut with a sharp metallic click behind him.

That hard crisp sound made my heart stand still. A sudden wave of terror passed over me. A vague perception of some monstrous treachery turned me cold. I sprang to the door, but there was no handle upon the inner side.

'Here!' I cried. 'Let me out!'

'All right! Don't make a row!' said my host from the passage. 'You've got the light all right.'

'Yes, but I don't care about being locked in alone like this.'

'Don't you?' I heard his hearty, chuckling laugh. 'You won't be alone long.'

'Let me out, sir!' I repeated angrily. 'I tell you I don't allow practical jokes of this sort.'

'Practical is the word,' said he, with another hateful chuckle. And then suddenly I heard, amidst the roar of the storm, the creak and whine of the winch-handle turning, and the rattle of the grating as it passed through the slot. Great God, he was letting loose the Brazilian cat!

In the light of the lantern I saw the bars sliding slowly before me. Already there was an opening a foot wide at the farther end. With a scream I seized the last bar with my hands and pulled with the strength of a madman. I *was* a madman with rage and horror. For a minute or more I held the thing motionless. I knew that he was straining with all his force upon the handle, and that the leverage was sure to overcome me. I gave inch by inch, my feet sliding along the stones, and all the time I begged and prayed this inhuman monster to save me from this horrible death. I conjured him by his kinship. I reminded him that I was his guest; I begged to know what harm I had ever done him. His only answers were the tugs and jerks upon the handle, each of which, in spite of all my struggles, pulled another bar through the opening. Clinging and clutching, I was dragged across the whole front of the cage, until at last, with aching wrists and lacerated fingers, I gave up the hopeless struggle. The grating clanged back as I released it, and an instant later I heard the shuffle of the Turkish slippers in the passage, and the slam of the distant door. Then everything was silent.

The creature had never moved during this time. He lay still in the corner, and his tail had ceased switching. This apparition of a man adhering to his bars and dragged screaming across him had apparently filled him with amazement. I saw his great eyes staring steadily at me. I had dropped the lantern when I seized the bars, but it still burned upon the floor, and I made a movement to grasp it, with some idea that its light might protect me. But the instant I moved, the beast gave a deep and menacing growl. I stopped and stood still, quivering with fear in every limb. The cat (if one may call so fearful a creature by so homely

a name) was not more than ten feet from me. The eyes glimmered like
two discs of phosphorus in the darkness. They appalled and yet fascinated me. I could not take my own eyes from them. Nature plays strange
tricks with us at such moments of intensity, and those glimmering lights
waxed and waned with a steady rise and fall. Sometimes they seemed
to be tiny points of extreme brilliancy – little electric sparks in the black
obscurity – then they would widen until all that corner of the room was
filled with their shifting and sinister light. And then suddenly they went
out all together.

The beast had closed its eyes. I do not know whether there may be
any truth in the old idea of the dominance of the human gaze, or
whether the huge cat was simply drowsy, but the fact remains that, far
from showing any symptom of attacking me, it simply rested its sleek,
black head upon its huge forepaws and seemed to sleep. I stood, fearing
to move lest I should rouse it into malignant life once more. But at least
I was able to think clearly now that the baleful eyes were off me. Here
I was shut up for the night with the ferocious beast. My own instincts,
to say nothing of the words of the plausible villain who laid this trap for
me, warned me that the animal was as savage as its master. How could
I stave it off until morning? The door was hopeless, and so were the
narrow, barred windows. There was no shelter anywhere in the bare,
stone-flagged room. To cry for assistance was absurd. I knew that this
den was an outhouse, and that the corridor which connected it with the
house was at least a hundred feet long. Besides, with that gale thundering outside, my cries were not likely to be heard. I had only my own
courage and my own wits to trust to.

And then, with a fresh wave of horror, my eyes fell upon the lantern.
The candle had burned low, and was already beginning to gutter. In
ten minutes it would be out. I had only ten minutes then in which to
do something, for I felt that if I were once left in the dark with that
fearful beast I should be incapable of action. The very thought of it
paralysed me. I cast my despairing eyes round this chamber of death,
and they rested upon one spot which seemed to promise I will not say
safety, but less immediate and imminent danger than the open floor.

I have said that the cage had a top as well as a front, and this top
was left standing when the front was wound through the slot in the wall.
It consisted of bars at a few inches' interval, with stout wire-netting
between, and it rested upon a strong stanchion at each end. It stood now
as a great barred canopy over the crouching figure in the corner. The
space between the iron shelf and the roof may have been from two to
three feet. If I could only get up there, squeezed in between bars and
ceiling, I should have only one vulnerable side. I should be safe from
below, from behind, and from each side. Only on the open face of it
could I be attacked. There, it is true, I had no protection whatever; but,

at least, I should be out of the brute's path when he began to pace about his den. He would have to come out of his way to reach me. It was now or never, for if once the light were out it would be impossible. With a gulp in my throat I sprang up, seized the iron edge of the top, and swung myself panting on to it. I writhed in face downwards, and found myself looking straight into the terrible eyes and yawning jaws of the cat. Its fetid breath came up into my face like the steam from some foul pot.

It appeared, however, to be rather curious than angry. With a sleek ripple of its long, black nose it rose, stretched itself, and then, rearing itself on its hind legs, with one forepaw against the wall, it raised the other and drew its claws across the wire meshes beneath me. One sharp, white hook tore through my trousers – for I may mention that I was still in evening dress – and dug a furrow in my knee. It was not meant as an attack, but rather as an experiment, for upon my giving a sharp cry of pain he dropped down again, and springing lightly into the room, he began walking swiftly round it, looking up every now and again in my direction. For my part I shuffled backwards until I lay with my back against the wall, screwing myself into the smallest space possible. The farther I got the more difficult it was for him to attack me.

He seemed more excited now that he had begun to move about, and he ran swiftly and noiselessly round and round the den, passing continually underneath the iron couch upon which I lay. It was wonderful to see so great a bulk passing like a shadow, with hardly the softest thudding of velvety pads. The candle was burning low – so low that I could hardly see the creature. And then, with a last flare and splutter, it went out altogether. I was alone with the cat in the dark!

It helps one to face a danger when one knows that one has done all that possibly can be done. There is nothing for it then but to quietly await the result. In this case, there was no chance of safety anywhere except the precise spot where I was. I stretched myself out, therefore, and lay silently, almost breathlessly, hoping that the beast might forget my presence if I did nothing to remind him. I reckoned that it must already be two o'clock. At four it would be full dawn. I had not more than two hours to wait for daylight.

Outside, the storm was still raging, and the rain lashed continually against the little windows. Inside, the poisonous and fetid air was overpowering. I could neither hear nor see the cat. I tried to think about other things – but only one had power enough to draw my mind from my terrible position. That was the contemplation of my cousin's villainy, his unparalleled hypocrisy, his malignant hatred of me. Beneath that cheerful face there lurked the spirit of a medieval assassin. And as I thought of it I saw more clearly how cunningly the thing had been arranged. He had apparently gone to bed with the others. No doubt he had his witness to prove it. Then, unknown to them, he had slipped

down, had lured me into this den and abandoned me. His story would
be so simple. He had left me to finish my cigar in the billiard-room. I
had gone down on my own account to have a last look at the cat. I had
entered the room without observing that the cage was opened, and I had
been caught. How could such a crime be brought home to him?
Suspicion, perhaps – but proof, never!

How slowly those dreadful two hours went by! Once I heard a low,
rasping sound, which I took to be the creature licking its own fur.
Several times those greenish eyes gleamed at me through the darkness,
but never in a fixed stare, and my hopes grew stronger that my presence
had been forgotten or ignored. At last the least faint glimmer of light
came through the windows – I first dimly saw them as two grey squares
upon the black wall, then grey turned to white, and I could see my
terrible companion once more. And he, alas, could see me!

It was evident to me at once that he was in a much more dangerous
and aggressive mood than when I had seen him last. The cold of the
morning had irritated him, and he was hungry as well. With a continual
growl he paced swiftly up and down the side of the room which was
farthest from my refuge, his whiskers bristling angrily, and his tail
switching and lashing. As he turned at the corners his savage eyes always
looked upwards at me with a dreadful menace. I knew then that he
meant to kill me. Yet I found myself even at that moment admiring the
sinuous grace of the devilish thing, its long, undulating, rippling movements, the gloss of its beautiful flanks, the vivid, palpitating scarlet of
the glistening tongue which hung from the jet-black muzzle. And all the
time that deep, threatening growl was rising and rising in an unbroken
crescendo. I knew that the crisis was at hand.

It was a miserable hour to meet such a death so cold, so comfortless,
shivering in my light dress clothes upon this gridiron of torment upon
which I was stretched. I tried to brace myself to it, to raise my soul above
it, and at the same time, with the lucidity which comes to a perfectly
desperate man, I cast round for some possible means of escape. One
thing was clear to me. If that front of the cage was only back in its
position once more, I could find a sure refuge behind it. Could I possibly
pull it back? I hardly dared to move for fear of bringing the creature
upon me. Slowly, very slowly, I put my hand forward until it grasped
the edge of the front, the final bar which protruded through the wall.
To my surprise it came quite easily to my jerk. Of course the difficulty
of drawing it out arose from the fact that I was clinging to it. I pulled
again, and three inches of it came through. It ran apparently on wheels.
I pulled again ... and then the cat sprang!

It was so quick, so sudden, that I never saw it happen. I simply heard
the savage snarl, and in an instant afterwards the blazing yellow eyes,
the flattened black head with its red tongue and flashing teeth, were

within reach of me. The impact of the creature shook the bars upon which I lay, until I thought (as far as I could think of anything at such a moment) that they were coming down. The cat swayed there for an instant, the head and front paws quite close to me, the hind paws clawing to find a grip upon the edge of the grating. I heard the claws rasping as they clung to the wire-netting, and the breath of the beast made me sick. But its bound had been miscalculated. It could not retain its position. Slowly, grinning with rage and scratching madly at the bars, it swung backwards and dropped heavily upon the floor. With a growl it instantly faced round to me and crouched for another spring.

I knew that the next few moments would decide my fate. The creature had learned by experience. It would not miscalculate again. I must act promptly, fearlessly, if I were to have a chance for life. In an instant I had formed my plan. Pulling off my dress-coat, I threw it down over the head of the beast. At the same moment I dropped over the edge, seized the end of the front grating, and pulled it frantically out of the wall.

It came more easily than I could have expected. I rushed across the room, bearing it with me; but, as I rushed, the accident of my position put me upon the outer side. Had it been the other way, I might have come off scathless. As it was, there was a moment's pause as I stopped it and tried to pass in through the opening which I had left. That moment was enough to give time to the creature to toss off the coat with which I had blinded him and to spring upon me. I hurled myself through the gap and pulled the rails to behind me, but he seized my leg before I could entirely withdraw it. One stroke of that huge paw tore off my calf as a shaving of wood curls off before a plane. The next moment, bleeding and fainting, I was lying among the foul straw with a line of friendly bars between me and the creature which ramped so frantically against them.

Too wounded to move, and too faint to be conscious of fear, I could only lie, more dead than alive, and watch it. It pressed its broad, black chest against the bars and angled for me with its crooked paws as I have seen a kitten do before a mouse-trap. It ripped my clothes, but, stretch as it would, it could not quite reach me. I have heard of the curious numbing effect produced by wounds from the great carnivora, and now I was destined to experience it, for I had lost all sense of personality, and was as interested in the cat's failure or success as if it were some game which I was watching. And then gradually my mind drifted away into strange vague dreams, always with that black face and red tongue coming back into them, and so I lost myself in the nirvana of delirium, the blessed relief of those who are too sorely tried.

Tracing the course of events afterwards, I conclude that I must have been insensible for about two hours. What roused me to consciousness once more was that sharp metallic click which had been the precursor of my terrible experience. It was the shooting back of the spring lock. Then, before my senses were clear enough to entirely apprehend what they saw, I was aware of the round, benevolent face of my cousin peering in through the open door. What he saw evidently amazed him. There was the cat crouching on the floor. I was stretched upon my back in my shirt-sleeves within the cage, my trousers torn to ribbons and a great pool of blood all round me. I can see his amazed face now, with the morning sunlight upon it. He peered at me, and peered again. Then he closed the door behind him, and advanced to the cage to see if I were really dead.

I cannot undertake to say what happened. I was not in a fit state to witness or to chronicle such events. I can only say that I was suddenly conscious that his face was away from me – that he was looking towards the animal.

'Good old Tommy!' he cried. 'Good old Tommy!'

Then he came near the bars, with his back still towards me.

'Down, you stupid beast!' he roared. 'Down, sir! Don't you know your master?'

Suddenly even in my bemuddled brain a remembrance came of those words of his when he had said that the taste of blood would turn the cat into a fiend. My blood had done it, but he was to pay the price.

'Get away!' he screamed. 'Get away, you devil! Baldwin! Baldwin! Oh, my God!'

And then I heard him fall, and rise, and fall again, with a sound like the ripping of sacking. His screams grew fainter until they were lost in the worrying snarl. And then, after I thought that he was dead, I saw, as in a nightmare, a blinded, tattered, blood-soaked figure running wildly round the room – and that was the last glimpse which I had of him before I fainted once again.

I was many months in my recovery – in fact, I cannot say that I have ever recovered, for to the end of my days I shall carry a stick as a sign of my night with the Brazilian cat. Baldwin, the groom, and the other servants could not tell what had occurred, when, drawn by the death-cries of their master, they found me behind the bars, and his remains – or what they afterwards discovered to be his remains – in the clutch of the creature which he had reared. They stalled him off with hot irons, and afterwards shot him through the loophole of the door before they could finally extricate me. I was carried to my bedroom, and there, under the roof of my would-be murderer, I remained between life and death for several weeks. They had sent for a surgeon from Clipton and a nurse from London, and in a month I was able to be carried to the station, and so conveyed back once more to Grosvenor Mansions.

I have one remembrance of that illness, which might have been part of the ever-changing panorama conjured up by a delirious brain were it not so definitely fixed in my memory. One night, when the nurse was absent, the door of my chamber opened, and a tall woman in blackest mourning slipped into the room. She came across to me, and as she bent her sallow face I saw by the faint gleam of the night-light that it was the Brazilian woman whom my cousin had married. She stared intently into my face, and her expression was more kindly than I had ever seen it.

'Are you conscious?' she asked.

I feebly nodded – for I was still very weak.

'Well, then, I only wished to say to you that you have yourself to blame. Did I not do all I could for you? From the beginning I tried to drive you from the house. By every means, short of betraying my husband, I tried to save you from him. I knew that he had a reason for bringing you here. I knew that he would never let you get away again. No one knew him as I knew him, who had suffered from him so often. I did not dare to tell you all this. He would have killed me. But I did my best for you. As things have turned out, you have been the best friend that I have ever had. You have set me free, and I fancied that nothing but death would do that. I am sorry if you are hurt, but I cannot reproach myself. I told you that you were a fool – and a fool you have been.' She crept out of the room, the bitter, singular woman, and I was never destined to see her again. With what remained from her husband's property she went back to her native land, and I have heard that she afterwards took the veil at Pernambuco.

It was not until I had been back in London for some time that the doctors pronounced me to be well enough to do business. It was not a very welcome permission to me, for I feared that it would be the signal for an inrush of creditors; but it was Summers, my lawyer, who first took advantage of it.

'I am very glad to see that your lordship is so much better,' said he. 'I have been waiting a long time to offer my congratulations.'

'What do you mean, Summers? This is no time for joking.'

'I mean what I say,' he answered. 'You have been Lord Southerton for the last six weeks, but we feared that it would retard your recovery if you were to learn it.'

Lord Southerton! One of the richest peers in England! I could not believe my ears. And then suddenly I thought of the time which had elapsed, and how it coincided with my injuries.

'Then Lord Southerton must have died about the same time that I was hurt?'

'His death occurred that very day.' Summers looked hard at me as I spoke, and I am convinced – for he was a very shrewd fellow – that he had guessed the true state of the case. He paused for a moment as if awaiting a confidence from me, but I could not see what was to be gained by exposing such a family scandal.

'Yes, a very curious coincidence,' he continued, with the same knowing look. 'Of course, you are aware that your cousin Everard King was the next heir to the estates. Now, if it had been you instead of him who had been torn to pieces by this tiger, or whatever it was, then of course he would have been Lord Southerton at the present moment.'

'No doubt,' said I.

'And he took such an interest in it,' said Summers. 'I happen to know that the late Lord Southerton's valet was in his pay, and that he used to have telegrams from him every few hours to tell him how he was getting on. That would be about the time when you were down there. Was it not strange that he should wish to be so well informed, since he knew that he was not the direct heir?'

'Very strange,' said I. 'And now, Summers, if you will bring me my bills and a new cheque-book, we will begin to get things into order.'

The Specialty of the House

Stanley Ellin

'And this,' said Laffler, 'is Sbirro's.' Costain saw a square brownstone façade identical with the others that extended from either side into the clammy darkness of the deserted street. From the barred windows of the basement at his feet a glimmer of light showed behind heavy curtains.

'Lord,' he observed, 'it's a dismal hole, isn't it?'

'I beg you to understand,' said Laffler stiffly, 'that Sbirro's is the restaurant without pretensions. Besieged by these ghastly, neurotic times, it has refused to compromise. It is perhaps the last important establishment in this city lit by gas jets. Here you will find the same honest furnishing, the same magnificent Sheffield service, and possibly, in a far corner, the very same spider webs that were remarked by the patrons of a half-century ago!'

'A doubtful recommendation,' said Costain, 'and hardly sanitary.'

'When you enter,' Laffler continued, 'you leave the insanity of this year, this day, and this hour, and you find yourself for a brief span restored in spirit, not by opulence, but by dignity, which is the lost quality of our time.'

Costain laughed uncomfortably. 'You make it sound more like a cathedral than a restaurant,' he said.

In the pale reflection of the street lamp overhead, Laffler peered at his companion's face. 'I wonder,' he said abruptly, 'whether I have not made a mistake in extending this invitation to you.'

Costain was hurt. Despite an impressive title and large salary, he was no more than clerk to this pompous little man, but he was impelled to make some display of his feelings. 'If you wish,' he said coldly, 'I can make other plans for my evening with no trouble.'

With his large, cowlike eyes turned up to Costain, the mist drifting into the ruddy, full moon of his face, Laffler seemed strangely ill at ease. Then 'No, no,' he said at last, 'absolutely not. It's important that you dine at Sbirro's with me.' He grasped Costain's arm firmly and led the

way to the wrought-iron gate of the basement. 'You see, you're the sole
person in my office who seems to know anything at all about good food.
And on my part, knowing about Sbirro's but not having some appreciative friend to share it, is like having a unique piece of art locked in a room
where no one else can enjoy it.'

Costain was considerably mollified by this. 'I understand there are
a great many people who relish that situation.'

'I'm not one of that kind!' Laffler said sharply. 'And having the secret
of Sbirro's locked in myself for years has finally become unendurable.'
He fumbled at the side of the gate and from within could be heard the
small, discordant jangle of an ancient pull-bell. An interior door opened
with a groan, and Costain found himself peering into a dark face whose
only discernible feature was a row of gleaming teeth.

'Sair?' said the face.

'Mr Laffler and a guest.'

'Sair,' the face said again, this time in what was clearly an invitation.
It moved aside and Costain stumbled down a single step behind his host.
The door and gate creaked behind him, and he stood blinking in a small
foyer. It took him a moment to realize that the figure he now stared at
was his own reflection in a gigantic pier glass that extended from floor
to ceiling. 'Atmosphere,' he said under his breath and chuckled as he
followed his guide to a seat.

He faced Laffler across a small table for two and peered curiously
around the dining-room. It was no size at all, but the half-dozen
guttering gas jets which provided the only illumination threw such a
deceptive light that the walls flickered and faded into uncertain
distance.

There were no more than eight or ten tables about, arranged to ensure
the maximum privacy. All were occupied, and the few waiters serving
them moved with quiet efficiency. In the air was a soft clash and scrape
of cutlery and a soothing murmur of talk. Costain nodded appreciatively.

Laffler breathed an audible sigh of gratification. 'I knew you would
share my enthusiasm,' he said. 'Have you noticed, by the way, that there
are no women present?'

Costain raised inquiring eyebrows.

'Sbirro,' said Laffler, 'does not encourage members of the fair sex to
enter the premises. And, I can tell you, his method is deridedly effective.
I had the experience of seeing a woman get a taste of it not long ago.
She sat at a table for not less than an hour waiting for service which was
never forthcoming.'

'Didn't she make a scene?'

'She did.' Laffler smiled at the recollection. 'She succeeded in
annoying the customers, embarrassing her partner, and nothing more.'

'And what about Mr Sbirro?'

'He did not make an appearance. Whether he directed affairs from behind the scenes, or was not even present during the episode, I don't know. Whichever it was he won a complete victory. The woman never reappeared nor, for that matter, did the witless gentleman who by bringing her was really the cause of the entire contretemps.

'A fair warning to all present,' laughed Costain.

A waiter now appeared at the table. The chocolate-dark skin, the thin, beautifully moulded nose and lips, the large liquid eyes, heavily lashed, and the silver white hair so heavy and silken that it lay on the skull like a cap, all marked him definitely as an East Indian. The man arranged the stiff table linen, filled two tumblers from a huge, cut glass pitcher, and set them in their proper places.

'Tell me,' Laffler said eagerly, 'is the special being served this evening?'

The waiter smiled regretfully and showed teeth as spectacular as those of the majordomo. 'I am so sorry, sair. There is no special this evening.'

Laffler's face fell into lines of heavy disappointment. 'After waiting so long. It's been a month already, and I hoped to show my friend here ...'

'You understand the difficulties, sair.'

'Of course, of course.' Laffler looked at Costain sadly and shrugged. 'You see, I had in mind to introduce you to the greatest treat that Sbirro's offers, but unfortunately it isn't on the menu this evening.'

The waiter said: 'Do you wish to be served now, sair?' and Laffler nodded. To Costain's surprise the waiter made his way off without waiting for any instructions.

'Have you ordered in advance?' he asked.

'Ah,' said Laffler, 'I really should have explained. Sbirro's offers no choice whatsoever. You will eat the same meal as everyone else in this room. To-morrow evening you would eat an entirely different meal, but again without designating a single preference.'

'Very unusual,' said Costain, 'and certainly unsatisfactory at times. What if one doesn't have a taste for the particular dish set before him?'

'On that score,' said Laffler solemnly, 'you need have no fears. I give you my word that, no matter how exacting your tastes, you will relish every mouthful you eat in Sbirro's.'

Costain looked doubtful, and Laffler smiled. 'And consider the subtle advantages of the system,' he said. 'When you pick up the menu of a popular restaurant, you find yourself confronted with innumerable choices. You are forced to weigh, to evaluate, to make uneasy decisions which you may instantly regret. The effect of all this is a tension which, however slight, must make for discomfort.

'And consider the mechanics of the process. Instead of a hurly-burly of sweating cooks rushing about a kitchen in a frenzy to prepare a hundred varying items, we have a chef who stands serenely alone, bringing all his talents to bear on one task, with all the assurance of a complete triumph!'

'Then you have seen the kichen?'

'Unfortunately, no,' said Laffler sadly. 'The picture I offer is hypothetical, made of conversational fragments I have pieced together over the years. I must admit, though, that my desire to see the functioning of the kitchen here comes very close to being my sole obsession nowadays.'

'But have you mentioned this to Sbirro?'

'A dozen times. He shrugs the suggestion away.'

'Isn't that a rather curious foible on his part?'

'No, no,' Laffler said hastily, 'a master artist is never under the compulsion of petty courtesies. Still,' he sighed, 'I have never given up hope.'

The waiter now reappeared bearing two soup bowls which he set in place with mathematical exactitude, and a small tureen from which he slowly ladled a measure of clear, thin broth. Costain dipped his spoon into the broth and tasted it with some curiosity. It was delicately flavoured, bland almost to the verge of tastelessness. Costain frowned, tentatively reached for the salt and pepper cellars, and discovered there were none on the table. He looked up, saw Laffler's eyes on him, and although unwilling to compromise with his own tastes, he hesitated to act as a damper on Laffler's enthusiasm. Therefore he smiled and indicated the broth.

'Excellent,' he said.

Laffler returned his smile. 'You do not find it excellent at all,' he said coolly. 'You find it flat and badly in need of condiments. I know this,' he continued as Costain's eyebrows shot upward, 'because it was my own reaction many years ago, and because like yourself I found myself reaching for salt and pepper after the first mouthful. I also learned with surprise that condiments are not available in Sbirro's.'

Costain was shocked. 'Not even salt!' he exclaimed.

'Not even salt. The very fact that you require it for your soup stands as evidence that your taste is unduly jaded. I am confident that you will now make the same discovery that I did: by the time you have nearly finished your soup your desire for salt will be non-existent.'

Laffler was right; before Costain had reached the bottom of his plate he was relishing the nuances of the broth with steadily increasing delight. Laffler thrust aside his own empty bowl and rested his elbows on the table. 'Do you agree with me now?'

'To my surprise,' said Costain, 'I do.'

As the waiter busied himself clearing the table, Laffler lowered his voice significantly. 'You will find,' he said, 'that the absence of condiments is but one of several noteworthy characteristics which mark

Sbirro's. I may as well prepare you for these. For example, no alcoholic beverages of any sort are served here, nor for that matter any beverage except clear, cold water, the first and only drink necessary for a human being.'

'Outside of mother's milk,' suggested Costain dryly.

'I can answer that in like vein by pointing out that the average patron of Sbirro's has passed that primal stage of his development.'

Costain laughed. 'Granted,' he said.

'Very well. There is also a ban on the use of tobacco in any form.'

'But, good heavens,' said Costain, 'doesn't that make Sbirro's more a teetotaller's retreat than a gourmet's sanctuary?'

'I fear,' said Laffler solemnly, 'that you confuse the words, *gourmet* and *gourmand*. The gourmand, through glutting himself, requires a wider and wider latitude of experience to stir his surfeited senses, but the very nature of the gourmet is simplicity. The ancient Greek in his coarse chiton savouring the ripe olive; the Japanese in his bare room contemplating the curve of a single flower stem – these are the true gourmets.'

'But an occasional drop of brandy, or pipeful of tobacco,' said Costain dubiously, 'are hardly over-indulgences.'

'By alternating stimulant and narcotic,' said Laffler, 'you seesaw the delicate balance of your taste so violently that it loses its most precious quality: the appreciation of fine food. During my years as a patron of Sbirro's I have proved this to my satisfaction.'

'May I ask,' said Costain, 'why you regard the ban on these things as having such deep aesthetic motives? What about such mundane reasons as the high cost of a liquor licence, or the possibility that patrons would object to the smell of tobacco in such confined quarters?'

Laffler shook his head violently. 'If and when you meet Sbirro,' he said, 'you will understand at once that he is not the man to make decisions on a mundane basis. As a matter of fact, it was Sbirro himself who first made me cognisant of what you call "aesthetic" motives.'

'An amazing man,' said Costain, as the waiter prepared to serve the entrée.

Laffler's next words were not spoken until he had savoured and swallowed a large portion of meat. 'I hesitate to use superlatives,' he said, 'but to my way of thinking Sbirro represents man at the apex of his civilization!'

Costain cocked an eyebrow and applied himself to his roast which rested in a pool of stiff gravy ungarnished by green or vegetable. The thin steam rising from it carried to his nostrils a subtle, tantalizing odour which made his mouth water. He chewed a piece as slowly and thoughtfully as if he were analysing the intricacies of a Mozart symphony. The range of taste he discovered was really extraordinary, from the pungent nip of the crisp outer edge to the peculiarly flat yet soul-satisfying ooze of blood which the pressure of his jaws forced from the half-raw interior.

Upon swallowing, he found himself ferociously hungry for another piece, and then another, and it was only with an effort that he prevented himself from wolfing down all his share of the meat and gravy without waiting to get the full voluptuous satisfaction from each mouthful. When he had scraped his platter clean, he realized that both he and Laffler had completed the entire course without exchanging a single word. He commented on this, and Laffler said: 'Can you see any need for words in the presence of such food?'

Costain looked round at the shabby, dimly lit room, the quiet diners, with a new perception. 'No,' he said humbly, 'I cannot. For any doubts I had I apologize unreservedly. In all your praise of Sbirro's there was not a single word of exaggeration.'

'Ah,' said Laffler delightedly. 'And that is only part of the story. You heard me mention the special which unfortunately was not on the menu tonight. What you have just eaten is nothing when compared to the absolute delights of that special!'

'Good lord!' cried Costain; 'What is it? Nightingales' tongues? Fillet of unicorn?'

'Neither,' said Laffler. 'It is lamb.'

'Lamb?'

Laffler remained lost in thought for a minute. 'If,' he said at last, 'I were to give you in my own unstinted words my opinion of this dish you would judge me completely insane. That is how deeply the mere thought of it affects me. It is neither the fatty chop, nor the too solid leg; it is, indeed, a select portion of the rarest sheep in existence and is named after the species – lamb Amirstan.'

Costain knit his brows 'Amirstan?'

'A fragment of desolation almost lost on the border which separates Afghanistan and Russia. From chance remarks dropped by Sbirro, I gather it is no more than a plateau which grazes the pitiful renmants of a flock of superb sheep. Sbirro, through some means or other, obtained rights to the traffic in this flock and is, therefore, the sole restaurateur ever to have lamb Amirstan on his bill of fare. I can tell you that the appearance of this dish is a rare occurrence indeed, and luck is the only guide in determining for the clientele the exact date when it will be served.'

'But surely,' said Costain, 'Sbirro could provide some advance knowledge of this event.'

'The objection to that is simply stated,' said Laffler. 'There exists in this city a large number of professional gluttons. Should advance information slip out, it is quite likely that they will, out of curiosity, become familiar with the dish and thenceforth supplant the regular patrons at these tables.'

'But you don't mean to say,' objected Costain, 'that these few people present are the only ones in the entire city, or for that matter, in the whole wide world, who know of the existence of Sbirro's!'

'Very nearly. There may be one or two regular patrons who, for some reason, are not present at the moment.'

'That's incredible.'

'It is done,' said Laffler, the slightest shade of menace in his voice, 'by every patron making it his solemn obligation to keep the secret. By accepting my invitation this evening, you automatically assume that obligation. I hope you can be trusted with it.'

Costain flushed. 'My position in your employ should vouch for me. I only question the wisdom of a policy which keeps such magnificent food away from so many who would enjoy it.'

'Do you know the inevitable result of the policy *you* favour?' asked Laffler bitterly. 'An influx of idiots who would nightly complain that they are never served roast duck with chocolate sauce. Is that picture tolerable to you?'

'No,' admitted Costain, 'I am forced to agree with you.'

Laffler leaned back in his chair wearily and passed his hand over his eyes in an uncertain gesture. 'I am a solitary man,' he said quietly, 'and not by choice alone. It may sound strange to you, it may border on eccentricity, but I feel to my depths that this restaurant, this warm haven in a coldly insane world, is both family and friend to me.'

And Costain, who to this moment had never viewed his companion as other than tyrannical employer or officious host, now felt an overwhelming pity twist inside his comfortably expanded stomach.

By the end of two weeks the invitations to join Laffler at Sbirro's had become something of a ritual. Every day, at a few minutes after five, Costain would step out into the office corridor and lock his cubicle behind him; he would drape his overcoat neatly over his left arm, and peer into the glass of the door to make sure his Homburg was set at the proper angle. At one time he would have followed this by lighting a cigarette, but under Laffler's prodding he had decided to give abstinence a fair trial. Then he would start down the corridor, and Laffler would fall in step at his elbow, clearing his throat. 'Ah, Costain. No plans for this evening, I hope.'

'No,' Costain would say, 'I'm foot-loose and fancy-free,' or 'At your service,' or something equally inane. He wondered at times whether it would not be more tactful to vary the ritual with an occasional refusal, but the glow with which Laffler received his answer, and the rough friendliness of Laffler's grip on his arm, forestalled him.

Among the treacherous crags of the business world, reflected Costain, what better way to secure your footing than friendship with one's employer. Already, a secretary close to the workings of the inner office had commented publicly on Laffler's highly favourable opinion of Costain. That was all to the good.

And the food! The incomparable food at Sbirro's! For the first time in his life, Costain, ordinarily a lean and bony man, noted with gratification that he was certainly gaining weight; within two weeks his bones had disappeared under a layer of sleek firm flesh, and here and there were even signs of incipient plumpness. It struck Costain one night, while surveying himself in his bath, that the rotund Laffler himself might have been a spare and bony man before discovering Sbirro's.

So there was obviously everything to be gained and nothing to be lost by accepting Laffler's invitations. Perhaps after testing the heralded wonders of lamb Amirstan and meeting Sbirro, who thus far had not made an appearance, a refusal or two might be in order. But certainly not until then.

That evening, two weeks to a day after his first visit to Sbirro's, Costain had both desires fulfilled: he dined on lamb Amirstan, and he met Sbirro. Both exceeded all his expectations.

When the waiter leaned over their table immediately after seating them and gravely announced: 'Tonight is special, sair,' Costain was shocked to find his head pounding with expectation. On the table before him he saw Laffler's hands trembling violently. 'But it isn't natural,' he thought suddenly: 'Two full-grown men, presumably intelligent and in the full possession of their senses, as jumpy as a pair of cats waiting to have their meat flung at them!'

'This is it!' Laffler's voice startled him so that he almost leaped from his seat. 'The culinary triumph of all times! And faced by it you are embarrassed by the very emotions it distils.'

'How did you know that?' Costain asked faintly.

'How? Because a decade ago I underwent your embarrassment. Add to that your air of revulsion and it's easy to see how affronted you are by the knowledge that man has not yet forgotten how to slaver over his meat.'

'And these others,' whispered Costain, 'do they all feel the same thing?'

'Judge for yourself.'

Costain looked furtively around at the nearby tables. 'You are right,' he finally said. 'At any rate, there's comfort in numbers.'

Laffler inclined his head slightly to the side. 'One of the numbers,' he remarked, 'appears to be in for a disappointment.'

Costain followed the gesture. At the table indicated a grey-haired man sat conspicuously alone, and Costain frowned at the empty chair opposite him.

'Why, yes,' he recalled, 'that very stout, bald man, isn't it? I believe it's the first dinner he's missed here in two weeks.'

'The entire decade more likely,' said Laffler sympathetically. 'Rain or shine, crisis or calamity, I don't think he's missed an evening at Sbirro's since the first time I dined here. Imagine his expression when he's told that on his very first defection lamb Amirstan was the *plat du jour*.'

Costain looked at the empty chair again with a dim discomfort. 'His very first?' he murmured.

'Mr Laffler! And friend! I am so pleased. So very, very pleased. No, do not stand; I will have a place made.' Miraculously a seat appeared under the figure standing there at the table. 'The lamb Amirstan will be an unqualified success, hurr? I myself have been stewing in the miserable kitchen all the day, prodding the foolish chef to do everything just so. The just so is the important part, hurr? But I see your friend does not know me. An introduction, perhaps?'

The words ran in a smooth, fluid eddy. They rippled, they purred, they hypnotized Costain so that he could do no more than stare. The mouth that uncoiled this sinuous monologue was alarmingly wide, with thin mobile lips that curled and twisted with every syllable. There was a flat nose with a straggling line of hair under it; wide-set eyes, almost oriental in appearance, that glittered in the unsteady flare of gaslight; and long sleek hair that swept back from high on the unwrinkled forehead – hair so pale that it might have been bleached of all colour. An amazing face surely, and the sight of it tortured Costain with the conviction that it was somehow familiar. His brain twitched and prodded but could not stir up any solid recollection.

Laffler's voice jerked Costain out of his study. 'Mr Sbirro. Mr Costain, a good friend and associate.' Costain rose and shook the proffered hand. It was warm and dry, flint hard against his palm.

'I am so very pleased, Mr Costain. So very, very pleased,' purred the voice. 'You like my little establishment, hurr? You have a great treat in store, I assure you.'

Laffler chuckled. 'Oh, Costain's been dining here regularly for two weeks,' he said. 'He's by way of becoming a great admirer of yours, Sbirro.'

The eyes were turned on Costain. 'A very great compliment. You compliment me with your presence and I return same with my food, hurr? But the lamb Amirstan is far superior to anything of your past experience, I assure you. All the trouble of obtaining it, all the difficulty of preparation, is truly merited.'

Costain strove to put aside the exasperating problem of that face. 'I have wondered,' he said, 'why with all these difficulties you mention, you even bother to present lamb Amirstan to the public. Surely your dishes are excellent enough to uphold your reputation.'

Sbirro smiled so broadly that his face became perfectly round. 'Perhaps it is a matter of the psychology, hurr? Someone discovers a wonder and must share it with others. He must fill his cup to the brim, perhaps, by observing the so evident of pleasure of those who explore it with him. 'Or,' he shrugged, 'perhaps it is just a matter of good business.'

'Then in the light of all this,' Costain persisted, 'and considering all the conventions you have imposed on your customers, why do you open the restaurant to the public instead of operating it as a private club?'

The eyes abruptly glinted into Costain's, then turned away. 'So perspicacious, hurr? Then I will tell you. Because there is more privacy in a public eating place than in the most exclusive club in existence! Here no one inquires of your affairs; no one desires to know the intimacies of your life. Here the business is eating. We are not curious about names and addresses or the reasons for the coming and going of our guests. We welcome you when you are here; we have no regrets when you are here no longer. That is the answer, hurr?'

Costain was startled by his vehemence. 'I had no intention of prying,' he stammered.

Sbirro ran the tip of his tongue over his thin lips. 'No, no,' he reassured, 'you are not prying. Do not let me give you that impression. On the contrary, I invite your questions.'

'Oh, come, Costain,' said Laffler. 'Don't let Sbirro intimidate you. I've known him for years and I guarantee that his bark is worse than his bite. Before you know it, he'll be showing you all the privileges of the house – outside of inviting you to visit his precious kitchen, of course.'

'Ah,' smiled Sbirro, 'for that, Mr Costain may have to wait a little while. For everything else I am at his beck and call.'

Laffler slapped his hand jovially on the table. 'What did I tell you!' he said. 'Now let's have the truth, Sbirro. Has anyone, outside of your staff, ever stepped into the sanctum sanctorum?'

Sbirro looked up. 'You see on the wall above you,' he said earnestly, 'the portrait of one to whom I did the honour. A very dear friend and a patron of most long standing, he is evidence that my kitchen is not inviolate.'

Costain studied the picture and started with recognition. 'Why,' he said excitedly, 'That's the famous writer – you know the one, Laffler – he used to do such wonderful short stories and cynical bits and then suddenly took himself off and disappeared in Mexico!'

'Of course!' cried Laffler, 'and to think I've been sitting under this portrait for years without even realizing it!' He turned to Sbirro. 'A dear friend, you say? His disappearance must have been a blow to you.'

Sbirro's face lengthened. 'It was, it was, I assure you. But think of it this way, gentlemen: he was probably greater in his death than in his

life, hurr? A most tragic man, he often told me that his only happy hours
were spent here at this very table. Pathetic, is it not? And to think the
only favour I could ever show him was to let him witness the mysteries
of my kitchen, which is, when all is said and done, no more than a plain,
ordinary kitchen.'

'You seem very certain of his death,' commented Costain. 'After all,
no evidence has ever turned up to substantiate it.'

Sbirro contemplated the picture. 'None at all,' he said softly. 'Remarkable, hurr?'

With the arrival of the entrée Sbirro leaped to his feet and set about
serving them himself. With his eyes alight he lifted the casserole from
the tray and sniffed at the fragrance from within with sensual relish.
Then, taking great care not to lose a single drop of gravy, he filled two
platters with chunks of dripping meat. As if exhausted by this task, he
sat back in his chair, breathing heavily. 'Gentlemen,' he said, 'to your
good appetite.'

Costain chewed his first mouthful with great deliberation and
swallowed it. Then he looked at the empty tines of his fork with glazed
eyes.

'Good God!' he breathed.

'It is good, hurr? Better than you had imagined?'

Costain shook his head dazedly. 'It is as impossible,' he said slowly,
'for the uninitiated to conceive the delights of lamb Amirstan as for
mortal man to look into his own soul.'

'Perhaps,' Sbirro thrust his head so close that Costain could feel the
warm, fetid breath tickle his nostrils, 'perhaps you have just had a
glimpse into your soul, hurr?'

Costain tried to draw back slightly without giving offence. 'Perhaps,'
he laughed, 'and a gratifying picture it made: all fang and claw. But
without intending any disrespect, I should hardly like to build my
church on *lamb en casserole*.'

Sbirro rose and laid a hand gently on his shoulder. 'So perspicacious,'
he said. 'Sometimes when you have nothing to do, nothing, perhaps, but
sit for a very little while in a dark room and think of this world – what
it is and what it is going to be – then you must turn your thoughts a
little to the significance of the Lamb in religion. It will be so interesting.
And now,' he bowed deeply to both men, 'I have held you long enough
from your dinner. I was most happy' – he nodded to Costain – 'and I
am sure we will meet again.' The teeth gleamed, the eyes glittered, and
Sbirro was gone down the aisle of tables.

Costain twisted around to stare after the retreating figure. 'Have I
offended him in some way?' he asked.

Laffler looked up from his plate. 'Offended him? He loves that kind
of talk. Lamb Amirstan is a ritual with him; get him started and he'll

be back at you a dozen times worse than a priest making a conversion.'

Costain turned to his meal with the face still hovering before him. 'Interesting man,' he reflected. 'Very.'

It took him a month to discover the tantalizing familiarity of that face, and when he did, he laughed aloud in his bed. Why, of course! Sbirro might have sat as the model for the Cheshire cat in *Alice*!

He passed this thought on to Laffler the very next evening as they pushed their way down the street to the restaurant against a chill, blustering wind. Laffler only looked blank.

'You may be right,' he said, 'but I'm not a fit judge. It's a far cry back to the days when I read the book. A far cry, indeed.'

As if taking up his words, a piercing howl came ringing down the street and stopped both men short in their tracks. 'Someone's in trouble there,' said Laffler. 'Look!'

Not far from the entrance to Sbirro's two figures could be seen struggling in the near darkness. They swayed back and forth and suddenly tumbled into a writhing heap on the sidewalk. The piteous howl went up again, and Laffler, despite his girth, ran towards it at a fair speed with Costain tagging cautiously behind.

Stretched out full length on the pavement was a slender figure with the dusky complexion and white hair of one of Sbirro's servitors. His fingers were futilely plucking at the huge hands which encircled his throat, and his knees pushed weakly up at the gigantic bulk of a man who brutally bore down with his full weight.

Laffler came up panting. 'Stop this!' he shouted. 'What's going on here?'

The pleading eyes almost bulging from their sockets turned towards Laffler. 'Help, sair. This man – drunk——'

'Drunk am I, ya dirty——' Costain saw now that the man was a sailor in a badly soiled uniform. The air around him reeked with the stench of liquor. 'Pick me pocket and then call me a drunk, will ya!' He dug his fingers in harder, and his victim groaned.

Laffler seized the sailor's shoulder. 'Let go of him, do you hear! Let go of him at once!' he cried, and the next instant was sent careering into Costain, who staggered back under the force of the blow.

The attack on his own person sent Laffler into immediate and berserk action. Without a sound he leaped at the sailor, striking and kicking furiously at the unprotected face and flanks. Stunned at first, the man came to his feet with a rush and turned on Laffler. For a moment they stood locked together, and then as Costain joined the attack, all three went sprawling to the ground. Slowly Laffler and Costain got to their feet and looked down at the body before them.

'He's either out cold from liquor,' said Costain, 'or he struck his head going down. In any case, it's a job for the police.'

'No, no, sair!' The waiter crawled weakly to his feet, and stood swaying, 'No police, sair. Mr Sbirro do not want such. You understand, sair.' He caught hold of Costain with a pleading hand, and Costain looked at Laffler.

'Of course not,' said Laffler. 'We won't have to bother with the police. They'll pick him up soon enough, the murderous sot. But what in the world started all this?'

'That man, sair. He make most erratic way while walking, and with no meaning I push against him. Then he attack me, accusing me to rob him.'

'As I thought.' Laffler pushed the waiter gently along. 'Now go on in and get yourself attended to.'

The man seemed ready to burst into tears. 'To you, sair, I owe my life. If there is anything I can do——'

Laffler turned into the areaway that led to Sbirro's door. 'No, no, it was nothing. You go along, and if Sbirro has any questions send him to me. I'll straighten it out.'

'My life, sair,' were the last words they heard as the inner door closed behind them.

'There you are, Costain,' said Laffler, as a few minutes later he drew his chair under the table: 'civilized man in all his glory. Reeking with alcohol, strangling to death some miserable innocent who came too close.'

Costain made an effort to gloss over the nerve-shattering memory of the episode. 'It's the neurotic cat that takes to alcohol,' he said. 'Surely there's a reason for that sailor's condition.'

'Reason? Of course there is. Plain atavistic savagery!' Laffler swept his arm in an all-embracing gesture. 'Why do we all sit here at our meat? Not only to appease physical demands, but because our atavistic selves cry for release. Think back, Costain. Do you remember that I once described Sbirro as the epitome of civilization? Can you now see why? A brilliant man, he fully understands the nature of human beings. But unlike lesser men he bends all his efforts to the satisfaction of our innate natures without resultant harm to some innocent bystander.'

'When I think back on the wonder of lamb Amirstan,' said Costain, 'I quite understand what you're driving at. And, by the way, isn't it nearly due to appear on the bill of fare? It must have been over a month ago that it was last served.'

The waiter, filling the tumblers, hesitated. 'I am so sorry, sair. No special this evening.'

'There's your answer,' Laffler grunted, 'and probably just my luck to miss out on it altogether the next time.'

Costain stared at him. 'Oh, come, that's impossible.'

'No, blast it.' Laffler drank off half his water at a gulp and the waiter immediately refilled the glass. 'I'm off to South America for a surprise tour of inspection. One month, two months, Lord knows how long.'

'Are things that bad down there?'

'They could be better.' Laffler suddenly grinned. 'Mustn't forget it takes very mundane dollars and cents to pay the tariff at Sbirro's.'

'I haven't heard a word of this around the office.'

'Wouldn't be a surprise tour if you had. Nobody knows about this except myself – and now you. I want to walk in on them completely unsuspected. Find out what flimflammery they're up to down there. As far as the office is concerned, I'm off on a jaunt somewhere. Maybe recuperating in some sanatorium from my hard work. Anyhow, the business will be in good hands. Yours, among them.'

'Mine?' said Costain, surprised.

'When you go in tomorrow you'll find yourself in receipt of a promotion, even if I'm not there to hand it to you personally. Mind you, it has nothing to do with our friendship either; you've done fine work, and I'm immensely grateful for it.'

Costain reddened under the praise. 'You don't expect to be in tomorrow. Then you're leaving tonight?'

Laffler nodded. 'I've been trying to wrangle some reservations. If they come through, well, this will be in the nature of a farewell celebration.'

'You know,' said Costain slowly, 'I devoutly hope that your reservations don't come through. I believe our dinners here have come to mean more to me than I ever dared imagine.'

The waiter's voice broke in. 'Do you wish to be served now, sair?' and they both started.

'Of course, of course,' said Laffler sharply, 'I didn't realize you were waiting.'

'What bothers me,' he told Costain as the waiter turned away, 'is the thought of the lamb Amirstan I'm bound to miss. To tell you the truth, I've already put off my departure a week, hoping to hit a lucky night, and now I simply can't delay any more. I do hope that when you're sitting over your share of lamb Amirstan, you'll think of me with suitable regrets.'

Costain laughed. 'I will indeed,' he said as he turned to his dinner.

Hardly had he cleared the plate when a waiter silently reached for it. It was not their usual waiter, he observed; it was none other than the victim of the assault.

'Well,' Costain said, 'how do you feel now? Still under the weather?'

The waiter paid no attention to him. Instead, with the air of a man under great strain, he turned to Laffler. 'Sair,' he whispered. 'My life. I owe it to you. I can repay you!'

Laffler looked up in amazement, then shook his head firmly. 'No,' he

said; 'I want nothing from you, understand? You have repaid me
sufficiently with your thanks. Now get on with your work and let's hear
no more about it.'

The waiter did not stir an inch, but his voice rose slightly. 'By the body
and blood of your God, sir, I will help you even if you do not want!
Do not go into the kitchen, sair. I trade you my life for yours, sair, when I
speak this. Tonight or any night of your life, do not go into the kitchen
at Sbirro's!'

Laffler sat back, completely dumbfounded. 'Not go into the kitchen?
Why shouldn't I go into the kitchen if Mr Sbirro ever took it into his
head to invite me there? What's all this about?'

A hard hand was laid on Costain's back, and another gripped the
waiter's arm. The waiter remained frozen to the spot, his lips compressed, his eyes downcast.

'What is all *what* about, gentlemen?' purred the voice. 'So opportune
an arrival. In time as ever, I see, to answer all the questions, hurr?'

Laffler breathed a sigh of relief. 'Ah, Sbirro, thank heaven you're
here. This man is saying something about my not going into your
kitchen. Do you know what he means?'

The teeth showed in a broad grin. 'But of course. This good man was
giving you advice in all amiability. It so happens that my too emotional
chef heard some rumour that I might have a guest into his precious
kitchen, and he flew into a fearful rage. Such a rage, gentlemen! He even
threatened to give notice on the spot, and you can understand what that
should mean to Sbirro's, hurr? Fortunately, I succeeded in showing him
what a signal honour it is to have an esteemed patron and true connoisseur observe him at his work first hand, and now he is quite
amenable. Quite, hurr?'

He released the waiter's arm. 'You are at the wrong table,' he said
softly. 'See that it does not happen again.'

The waiter slipped off without daring to raise his eyes and Sbirro drew
a chair to the table. He seated himself and brushed his hand lightly over
his hair. 'Now I am afraid that the cat is out of the bag, hurr? This
invitation to you, Mr Laffler, was to be a surprise; but the surprise is
gone, and all that is left is the invitation.'

Laffler mopped beads of perspiration from his forehead. 'Are you
serious?' he said huskily. 'Do you mean that we are really to witness the
preparation of your food tonight?'

Sbirro drew a sharp fingernail along the tablecloth, leaving a thin,
straight line printed in the linen. 'Ah,' he said, 'I am faced with a
dilemma of great proportions.' He studied the line soberly. 'You, Mr
Laffer, have been my guest for ten long years. But our friend here——'

Costain raised his hand in protest. 'I understand perfectly. This
invitation is solely to Mr Laffler, and naturally my presence is em-

barrassing. As it happens, I have an early engagement for this evening
and must be on my way anyhow. So you see there's no dilemma at all,
really.'

'No,' said Laffler, 'absolutely not. That wouldn't be fair at all. We've
been sharing this until now, Costain, and I won't enjoy this experience
half as much if you're not along. Surely Sbirro can make his conditions
flexible, this one occasion.'

They both looked at Sbirro, who shrugged his shoulders regretfully.

Costain rose abruptly. 'I'm not going to sit here, Laffler, and spoil
your great adventure. And then, too,' he bantered, 'think of that ferocious chef waiting to get his cleaver on you. I prefer not to be at the scene.
I'll just say goodbye,' he went on, to cover Laffler's guilty silence, 'and
leave you to Sbirro. I'm sure he'll take pains to give you a good show.'
He held out his hand and Laffler squeezed it painfully hard.

'You're being very decent, Costain,' he said, 'I hope you'll continue
to dine here until we meet again. It shouldn't be too long.'

Sbirro made way for Costain to pass. 'I will expect you,' he said. '*Au
'voir.*'

Costain stopped briefly in the dim foyer to adjust his scarf and fix his
Homburg at the proper angle. When he turned away from the mirror,
satisfied at last, he saw with a final glance that Laffler and Sbirro were
already at the kitchen door; Sbirro holding the door invitingly wide with
one hand, while the other rested, almost tenderly, on Laffler's meaty
shoulders.

If Thy Right Hand Offend Thee ...

A. E. Ellis

In view of disquieting rumours which have come to his notice, relating to certain unusual occurrences at St Chrysostom's College last Michaelmas Term, the Headmaster feels compelled to make public the following Report, which to the best of his belief is an accurate and trustworthy record of what took place. This has been done with the consent of the Medical Officer, who agrees that the good name of the school must not be prejudiced by the exaggerated and damaging fabrications at present current.

Report of the Resident Medical Officer at St Chrysostom's College to the Headmaster and Governors of the College, December 1925.

Gentlemen,

In the course of my annual Report on the state of health of the School, I had occasion to allude to a puzzling case of fever, therein stated to be 'possibly a form of recurrent malaria', but which in truth even so eminent an authority as Sir Humphrey Chambers was unable to diagnose with anything approaching confidence. I accordingly beg to lay before you the following narrative, as the extraordinary occurrences which I am about to relate, although outside the scope of medical practice, appear to have a bearing on this curious case.

The case in question first came to my notice when the telephone in my private room in college rang at about 5.30 p.m. on Sunday, October 25th, and I was urgently summoned by the Matron in charge of the sanatorium to attend to a boy who had just been brought in by his companions and who was becoming delirious.

On reaching the sanatorium, which as you are aware is situated some two hundred yards from the main College buildings, at the end of an avenue of beech trees, I found the boy, Richard Henryson, in bed, restless and feverish and unable to speak coherently. I at first thought it might be a case of pneumonia, but the boy's lungs proved to be sound and, so far as could be ascertained, he suffered from no organic disorder.

Concluding that he must have contracted a sudden chill on the liver, I prescribed appropriate treatment and left.

The following incident may appear trivial and irrelevant, but in the light of subsequent events I am inclined to attach to it some significance.

On returning down the avenue from the sanatorium, I had a quite definite feeling that someone was moving along parallel with me a few yards to the rear, hidden from sight by the trees. As this seemed unusual, I paused to allow this person to overtake me, in order to see who it was. That it was unlikely to be one of the boys I knew, for they were then at evensong in the College chapel. Whoever was there, however, did not appear, so I walked on a few paces and then abruptly faced about.

Ten yards off, standing with one hand on the bole of a beech, stood a figure, whether male or female I could not discern in the dim light, attired in what looked like a thin coat or mackintosh, with some sort of scarf or shawl enveloping the head. The coat and shawl struck me as odd, for it had been a sunny autumn day and the air was still warm. The figure made no movement, so I called out, 'Who is there?' and took a pace nearer. The person instantly dodged behind the tree and made off up the avenue at some speed, though it appeared to glide rather than to run. I started to give chase but soon found myself outdistanced. Concluding that the stranger must be some vagrant on the look-out for pickings around the College, I went back to my rooms and soon forgot about the incident.

After supper that day three boys came to see me, saying they wished to make a statement about Henryson, with whom they had spent the afternoon. The four of them had gone to Hoccourt Ring, the site of a Romano-British temple in the neighbourhood, where they had lain down to rest. Doubtless prompted by the mystical associations of the place, they had started talking about ghosts and spiritualism, and finally, as a sort of game, decided to hold a seance.

The boys sat round in a circle in the middle of the Ring and one of them, a tall, dark youth of arresting appearance, commenced to make hypnotic passes over Henryson, who is a slim, sensitive boy of a rather girlish type. At first they treated the proceedings as a jest and there was a good deal of laughter. Then Henryson seemed to grow sleepy and they thought he was pretending to fall into a hypnotic trance. Presently the boy started muttering to himself and his eyes acquired an unnaturally intent expression. This startled his companions, who told him not to look like a stuffed owl, and one of them gave him a shake. This produced no effect, and Henryson soon lost consciousness and lolled back against a tree.

At this point in his narrative, the boy who was acting as spokesman hesitated and looked somewhat embarrassed, as if there was something more which he was reluctant to mention. I urged them to relate everything that had occurred, and each boy admitted that he had felt just then as if someone else was present with them – 'somebody who ought not to have been there,' as one of them expressed it. Another boy remarked that he felt as he did once when he was smoking an illicit cigarette and suddenly became aware that his housemaster was watching him over the fence – 'only,' he added, 'it was far worse than that, very much worse.' They could see no one about, however, and as Henryson now seemed to be really ill, they carried him in scared silence across the two or three fields between Hoecourt Ring and the College sanatorium. That was all they could tell me, except that Henryson had been in perfect health and high spirits before their seance.

On Monday Henryson's condition had worsened; he had become delirious and was getting difficult to control. Accordingly I called in the eminent specialist, Sir Humphrey Chambers, who, after a thorough examination of the patient, was obliged to confess himself puzzled by the symptoms. Febrifuges were prescribed, but we both felt far from satisfied with the nature of the case. It was decided not to send the boy to hospital, so that I could maintain direct observation, and a night-nurse was engaged.

In relating the following episodes, I am fully aware that my professional reputation is imperilled, yet I do so in the conviction that these incredible events are not unrelated to the mysterious complaint of my patient.

Mr Matthews, the biology master, was accustomed to working late in the evening in his laboratory, which is situated at a little distance from the main College buildings, and is almost overshadowed by the avenue of trees leading to the sanatorium. One night – it was the last day of October – as Mr Matthews was walking across to his laboratory, he noticed somebody attired in what appeared to be a faded mackintosh standing under the trees and looking towards him. The face was in shadow, and Mr Matthews, thinking it might be a College servant, called out in his friendly manner, 'What a delightful evening!' The person took no notice, so Mr Matthews, out of curiosity to see who it might be, turned aside so as to pass nearer.

At that moment a light was switched on in one of the rooms of the College and the beam from the open window fell on the face of the figure under the trees. Mr Matthews stopped dead, for he beheld, not the features of anyone he knew, but the grinning face of a skull – yet not merely a skull, for there were some parched and blackened remnants of skin drawn over it, adding to the unutterable horror of the thing.

For some moments Mr Matthews stood petrified. Then a probable explanation occurred to him, and his terror gave place to wrath, for he remembered that this was All Hallows E'en, and concluded that some mischievous boys must have removed the mounted skeleton from the biology laboratory, dressed it up and played this ghastly trick on him. Having reached this solution, he was about to approach for a closer inspection when the thing moved, stretched out its right hand and moved towards him.

Mr Matthews turned and ran, with the grisly horror at his heels. Fortunately the door of the laboratory stood open. He dashed through and slammed it behind him with a crash and the spring lock clicked home. But something had dropped behind him inside the door as it shut. Groping for the switch he turned on the light and saw, lying just within the door, a dead and bony hand.

This was too much for Mr Matthews. Through the frosted glass of the door he could see that the Thing was still outside, fumbling at the door as though trying to open it. Mr Matthews crossed to the other side of the laboratory, opened a casement window and, with a backward glance to make sure that his pursuer was still outside the door, jumped out and raced for his rooms in the College. He dared not glance back, nor did he dare to tell anyone of his macabre encounter, as he was sure to be disbelieved and would be thought drunk or mad.

Next morning when Mr Matthews cautiously entered his laboratory, the hand had gone and there was no trace of his ghastly visitor. But perhaps it is scarcely accurate to say no trace, for caught on the fastener of the window, which he had left open in his escape the previous night, was a ragged strip of greyish cloth with an unwholesome, earthy smell. This, however, may merely have been a piece of one of the laboratory assistant's dusters.

Mr Matthews was destined to see his grim visitant again, three days after his harrowing experience on the eve of All Saints. Having somewhat recovered confidence, he had ventured across to his laboratory after dinner at about 8.30 p.m., and was occupied on a dissection for demonstration to a class next day. Presently he heard someone moving about in the next room, but was surprised not to see any light. As he was about to investigate, the door of his laboratory opened and the grisly apparition, from which he had fled a few evenings before, entered the room and came towards him.

Mr Matthews was overcome with horror and revulsion as he stood fascinated by the menacing advance of this hideous spectre. The Thing seemed to be beseeching him to do something for it. Its dead face was thrust close to Mr Matthews, and he observed that it carried its severed right hand in a fold of its cloak, which was nothing other than a winding-sheet. With its left hand the Thing pointed to Mr Matthews's right hand, in which he still held a pair of dissecting scissors, and opened its mouth as if to speak, though no sound came out of those gaping, lipless jaws.

Mr Matthews stood paralysed. Exasperated by his unresponsiveness, the Thing appeared to grow angry, and what Mr Matthews afterwards described as an oppressive sense of evil intent emanated from it. It raised its bony left hand, seized Mr Matthews by the jaw and, wrenching his mouth open grasped hold of his tongue. At this fearful moment Mr Matthews heard voices outside, which he recognized as those of two of his sixth-form pupils who were coming for private tuition. His grim assailant evidently heard them too, for it hastily left Mr Matthews, went out through an open window and vanished, just as the boys came in to find the biology master lying in a faint, his face scratched and bleeding.

I was immediately summoned, but although Mr Matthews soon recovered consciousness, his tongue was too sore and swollen to allow him to speak or to eat for some days. However, he wrote an account of this and also of his previous encounter, which he placed at my disposal. So broken down was he by these terrifying and inexplicable experiences that he was obliged to go away for a fortnight to recuperate. By the time he returned the College had ceased to be to be troubled by an unearthly visitant.

On the evening of the second day after the last visitation of Mr Matthews, I was sitting in my study in College, engaged in polishing some of my surgical instruments. The casement window stood wide open, as it was a calm night, and everything was very quiet, the boys all being in evening preparation. Hearing a slight noise behind me, I glanced round and perceived someone just inside the window, partly hidden by the curtains. I had just been reading Mr Matthews's extraordinary narrative, so I arose in some alarm and turned the reading-lamp so that its light fell on the intruder.

There it stood, the same gruesome Thing that Mr Matthews had described, and the very same, I feel certain, as the person I had seen lurking in the sanatorium avenue on the Sunday when Henryson fell ill. I shouted in alarm and backed towards the door, but as my rooms are in a lonely wing of the College, my cries were unheard. The Thing then moved rapidly between me and the door, and with a wave of its shrouded arms it drove me, shrinking with fear and horror, towards the table on which lay my surgical instruments. Pointing to one of the larger scalpels, it drew near and held its hideous mummy of a face within a few inches of mine, with its mouth open and its withered tongue protruding as though in obscene mockery. I stood bewildered and horrified, while experiencing a sensation of terror such as I have never before known.

The Thing seemed to radiate evil. I cannot hope to convey in words the feeling of deadly menace that overpowered me while confronting this loathsome corpse. All the time it seemed to be striving to get me to do something for it, and indicated my surgical instruments with impatient gestures of its left hand. Its right hand had been severed at the wrist, and I could see its claw-like fingers protruding from a fold in the cerement. I was incapable of action, however, and felt that the Thing would soon become actively malevolent and attack me, even as it had assaulted Mr Matthews. This I consider would indeed have occurred, had not the boys at that moment been released from evening preparation, and the noise of their shouting as they ran along the corridor to the dormitories disturbed my visitor. With a final gesture of threatening appeal, it turned and disappeared through the window, which I hastily closed and fastened.

After this unnerving experience, I decided that Henryson's condition would warrant my vacating my own bedroom for the night and taking up quarters in the sanatorium, ostensibly to be on hand in case the patient became worse but in reality to be within sight and call of human beings.

On my way up the avenue I caught a glimpse of a shrouded figure approaching from the direction of the wing where my rooms are situated, but breaking into a run I reached the welcome sanctuary of the sanatorium without any further encounter.

Joshua Mullins, the College gardener, was walking homewards shortly after sunset on Friday, November 6th, after working late clipping the hedge bordering his chrysanthemum beds, which are situated some thirty yards from the sanatorium avenue. While pruning the hedge he had been vaguely aware of somebody watching him from the avenue, and concluded it must be some convalescent from the sanatorium who had nothing better to occupy him. Mullins finished trimming the hedge at sundown, and was taking his shears home with him, intending to clip the hedge of his own cottage next day. His homeward path led along the north-east and south-west sides of a broad, sloping meadow, in which a dozen bullocks were placidly grazing, and he noticed that the workmen, who had been digging a drain across the field, had gone home.

As he was turning the east corner of the field, Mullins observed someone who, as he could just make out in the fading light, was wearing some sort of long cloak or overall, start off from the upper, north corner of the field and move rapidly across the meadow so as to intercept him at the lower, south corner. Mullins supposed it must be some belated workman anxious not to miss the bus home, but was surprised to see the grazing cattle throw up their heads as the runner passed them and gallop with terrified snorts to the remotest corner of the field. Arrived at the south corner of the field, the figure halted and waited under the shadow of an elm for Mullins to come along. As the gardener reached the corner, the person lurking there stepped out to meet him.

It was with the utmost difficulty that I was able, weeks later, to persuade Mullins to tell me what it was that accosted him that evening.

All he would or could say was that 'it was like someone who was dead, sir, almost a skelington, as you might say, only with something very nasty about it. And it never spoke, sir, but just came at me, and I backed against the fence. Then it reached out towards my shears, which I held in my left hand, and caught hold of my hand with its left hand and held it. Then I sort of dodged sideways and took the shears in my right hand and hurled them at it as hard as I could, so that the points stuck in its chest. Then it let go, and I set off running as hard as I could for a quarter of a mile till I got to the Packhorse Inn on the main road, where I went in and had a drop or two of something till I felt better, and then the bus came and I went home.'

On going to work next day, Mullins found his shears lying on the path at the spot where the encounter had taken place. Caught between the blades was a ragged piece of dirty cloth, which he gave me, and which Mr Matthews asserted to be of exactly the same material and sepulchral odour as the strip he had found on the laboratory window. Mullins was very careful after this adventure always to leave work while the light was still good, and showed an unwonted desire for company on his homeward walk.

The afternoon of the Sunday following the gardener's alarming-experience was unusually mild and sunny for November. Miss Johnson, matron of one of the boarding houses, as she sat sewing at the window of her sitting-room, had been watching the bees flying in and out of the hives in the housemaster's garden, eager to make full use of this unexpected recrudescence of summer. But the brief spell of sunshine was now over, the bees had returned to their hives, and Miss Johnson, after observing the flocks of starlings flying in to roost in the beeches by the sanatorium, closed the window and resumed her needlework. The last rays of the setting sun dimmed into twilight and it became too dark to sew.

Miss Johnson, still holding a pair of scissors, rose to switch on the light, when she noticed someone standing outside the window looking in at her. Whoever it was realized that he had been seen, and motioned with his left hand, apparently indicating that she should open the window, and also kept pointing at the scissors she was holding. Before approaching the window, Miss Johnson switched on the light, which shone full on the face pressed against the pane. The matron gave a scream of terror and shut herself into her bedroom, where her maid, attracted by her cry, found her in hysterics on the bed, only able to repeat. 'The dead thing, mind the dead thing! Don't let it in!'

Next morning the bees from the hives below the matron's window were found dead and dying on the alighting boards.

I now come to the final episode in this amazing case, which took place on Wednesday, November 11th. I had been to the sanatorium to see

Henryson, whose condition showed no improvement, although he had now been ill for two and a half weeks. At about 9.30 p.m. I went into the College library, in the forlorn hope of finding something to shed light upon his baffling complaint. As you are aware, the library is arranged on the plan of medieval libraries, with bookcases standing out at right-angles to the walls, forming recesses or bays, and opening off two of these bays are classrooms. As I sat turning over the pages of an encyclopaedia, I heard a casement window banging now and then in one of these classrooms, and formed the intention of fastening it before leaving the library.

Presently I heard sounds as if someone was moving about in that classroom, and concluded that it must be Mr Heppelthwaite, the senior English master, preparing some work for next day. I was sitting some distance from the classroom, with my back towards its door, and did not trouble to look round when I heard someone come out and start pottering about at a shelf in the adjoining bay. The person then came down the centre of the library in my direction, moving a chair which blocked the way, so I called out, 'Hallo, Heppel, been burning the midnight oil?' As there was no answer to my jocular greeting, I turned round in some surprise – and there the Thing was, standing beside the table at which I sat.

My former horror returned and held me helpless. Rising shakily from the chair, I stared abjectly at the Thing's dead face, with its eyeless yet seeing sockets. With a swift movement it turned from me and bent down towards my surgical case, which I had brought with me from the sanatorium and laid on the table by my side. With its left hand it deftly unfastened the catch and then with a jerk scattered the instruments over the table. Then, selecting an operating scalpel, the creature advanced upon me. Fearing an attack, I shrank back against the bookcase, but it came on until we were about two feet apart and held out the knife, handle towards me, for me to take. This I did and stood sweating with fear, for the sense of evil which I had previously experienced in the presence of this Thing was now intensified and malignant.

The shrouded death now opened its lipless mouth, as it had done before, protruding its shrivelled and speechless tongue. I sensed that it urgently wanted me to do something for it. I could feel the intense, diabolical will of the Thing being exerted at me, overcoming my reason and governing my mind. That horrid tongue, lolling in the gruesome mouth, fascinated me, and all at once, moved by an uncontrollable impulse, I thrust the knife I held between those yawning jaws, with one frenzied stroke cut through the root of the tongue, then fell back, half fainting, into a chair.

The Thing picked up its severed tongue, wrapped it together with its amputated right hand in a fold of its winding-sheet, then turned towards

me again. The change that had now come over this unearthly being was
as amazing as anything in this extraordinary affair. Although its aspect
underwent no change, yet I no longer felt that I was in the presence of
some devilishly evil thing, but that it was filled with the happiness of
some great joy, was a blessed spirit freed from some overwhelming
trouble. Yet the Thing *looked* as foul and revolting as before; this radiant
gladness was something far beyond its mutilated dead body.

The Thing then turned away and moved slowly to the end of the
library, where stood a reading-desk on which lay a massive 1613 Bible.
It stood before the lectern for some minutes with bowed head, then
opened the book and turned over the pages until it reached some passage
which appeared to rivet its attention, for it drew its finger along the lines
as though reading. It then passed out through the doorway of the library
and was never seen again.

When the transfigured being had thus departed, I went up to the
Bible, which lay open at the fifth chapter of St Matthew's Gospel. After
gazing for some time at the open pages, I noticed that the thirtieth verse
had been underlined, as if with a none-too-clean finger-nail:

> '*And if thy right hand offend thee, cut it off, and cast it from thee. For it
> is profitable for thee that one of thy members should perish, and not that thy
> whole body should be cast into hell.*'

What evil had that right hand done, that the unresting dead should thus
return to harass mortal men? And the tongue, what heinous blasphemy
had it spoken, that only by its extirpation could the lost soul be
redeemed from the everlasting fire?

Some days after the final exit of the supernatural visitant whom, for
lack of a better name, I have referred to as the Thing, the librarian
discovered in the College library an ancient manuscript volume, dating
from the sixteenth century, inscribed in barbarous Latin on vellum. The
book was wedged between some little-read volumes on the divinity
shelves, close to the door of the classroom where the Thing had effected
its entry on its last visit. The book was not listed in the catalogue, and
the librarian had never seen it before. Moreover, it was certainly not the
kind of work that would ever be put in a school library, and it was indeed
fortunate that it was inscribed in an archaic tongue and script. If any
boy had got hold of the book and succeeded in deciphering its contents,
I should be concerned for his peace of mind.

The book proved to be a treatise on sorcery and witchcraft written
by one who was not only conversant with all the most nefarious branches
of the black art, but, from the name on the title-page and the intimacy
with which he treated the subject, was a leading exponent of these
unhallowed practices. Those who have made a study of sorcery will be

able to imagine something of what that book was like. I regret that I am unable to produce the obscene volume, as it would constitute valuable confirmatory evidence of the veracity of my Report, but the Chaplain, to whom I showed it, after translating a number of pages, was not to be restrained from putting it on the fire.

On looking up the trials for sorcery in the sixteenth century, it was found that the perpetrator of this infamous work met with retribution for his misdeeds and, as far as could be ascertained, suffered death at or near Hoecourt Ring. That he was not finally laid to rest until nearly four hundred years later this record tends to suggest.

There is but one more paragraph to add to my Report: on the night when the final visitation occurred, Henryson's condition began to improve. He slept peacefully and all signs of fever left him. Convalescence was swift, and within a week he was back in school.

The Spider

Hanns Heinz Ewers
Translated by Walter F. Kohn

When Richard Bracquemont, medical student, decided to move into Room No. 7 of the little Hotel Stevens at 6 Rue Alfred Stevens, three people had already hanged themselves from the window-sash of the room on three successive Fridays.

The first was a Swiss travelling salesman. His body was not discovered until Saturday evening; but the physician established the fact that death must have come between five and six o'clock on Friday afternoon. The body hung suspended from a strong hook which had been driven into the window-sash, and which ordinarily served for hanging clothes. The window was closed, and the dead man had used the curtain cord as a rope. Since the window was rather low, his legs dragged on the ground almost to his knees. The suicide must consequently have exercised considerable will power in carrying out his intention. It was further established that he was married and the father of four children; that he unquestionably had an adequate and steady income; and that he was of a cheerful disposition, and well contented in life. Neither a will nor anything in writing that might give a clue to the cause of the suicide was found; nor had he ever intimated leanings towards suicide to any of his friends or acquaintances.

The second case was not very different. The actor Karl Krause, who was employed at the nearby Cirque Medrano as a lightning bicycle artiste, engaged Room No. 7 two days after the first suicide. When he failed to appear at the performance the following Friday evening, the manager of the theatre sent an usher to the little hotel. The usher found the actor hanged from the window-sash in the unlocked room, in identically the same circumstances that had attended the suicide of the Swiss travelling salesman. This second suicide seemed no less puzzling than the first: the actor was popular, drew a very large salary, was only twenty-five years old, and seemed to enjoy life to the utmost. Again, nothing was left in writing, nor were there any other clues that might help solve the mystery. The actor was survived only by an aged mother, to whom he used to send three hundred marks for her support promptly on the first of each month.

For Madame Dubonnet, who owned the cheap little hotel, and whose clientele was made up almost exclusively of the actors of the nearby vaudevilles of Montmartre, this second suicide had very distressing consequences. Already several of her guests had moved out, and other regular customers had failed to come back. She appealed to the Commissioner of the Ninth Ward, whom she knew well, and he promised to do everything in his power to help her. So he not only pushed his investigation of reasons for the suicides with considerable zeal, but he also placed at her disposal a police officer who took up his residence in the mysterious room.

It was the policeman Charles-Maria Chaumié who had volunteered his services in solving the mystery. An old 'Marousin' who had been a marine infantryman for eleven years, this sergeant had guarded many a lonely post in Tonkin and Annam single-handed, and had greeted many an uninvited deputation of river pirates, sneaking like cats through the jungle darkness, with a refreshing shot from his rifle. Consequently he felt himself well heeled to meet the 'ghosts' of which the Rue Stevens gossiped. He moved into the room on Sunday evening and went contentedly to sleep after doing high justice to the food and drink Madame Dubonnet set before him.

Every morning and evening Chaumié paid a brief visit to the police station to make his reports. During the first few days his reports confined themselves to the statement that he had not noticed even the slightest thing out of the ordinary. On Wednesday evening, however, he announced that he believed he had found a clue. When pressed for details he begged to be allowed to say nothing for the present: he said he was not certain that the thing he thought he had discovered necessarily had any bearing on the two suicides. And he was afraid of being ridiculed in case it should all turn out to be a mistake. On Thursday evening he seemed to be even more uncertain, although somewhat graver; but again he had nothing to report. On Friday morning he seemed quite excited: half seriously and half in jest he ventured the statement that the window of the room certainly had a remarkable power of attraction. Nevertheless he still clung to the theory that the fact had nothing whatever to do with the suicides, and that he would only be laughed at if he told more. That evening he failed to come to the police station: they found him hanged from the hook on the window-sash.

Even in this case the circumstances, down to the minutest detail, were again the same as they had been in the other cases: the legs dragged on the floor, and the curtain cord had been used as a rope. The window was closed, and the door had not been locked; death had evidently come at about six o'clock in the afternoon. The dead man's mouth was wide open and his tongue hung out.

As a consequence of this third suicide in Room No. 7, all the guests left the Hotel Stevens that same day, with the exception of the German high school teacher in Room No. 16, who took advantage of this opportunity to have his rent reduced one-third. It was small consolation for Madame Dubonnet to have Mary Garden, the famous star of the Opéra Comique, drive by in her Renault a few days later and stop to buy the red curtain cord for a price she beat down to two hundred francs. Of course she had two reasons for buying it: in the first place, it would bring luck; and in the second – well, it would get into the newspapers.

If these things had happened in summer, say in July or August, Madame Dubonnet might have got three times as much for her curtain cord; at that time of the year the newspapers would certainly have filled their columns with the case for weeks. But at an uneasy time of the year, with elections, disorders in the Balkans, a bank failure in New York, a visit of the English King and Queen – well, where could the newspapers find room for a mere murder case? The result was that the affair in the Rue Alfred Stevens got less attention than it deserved, and such notices of it as appeared in the newspapers were concise and brief, and confined themselves practically to repetitions of the police reports, without exaggerations.

These reports furnished the only basis for what little knowledge of the affair the medical student Richard Bracquemont had. He knew nothing of one other little detail that seemed so inconsequential that neither the Commissioner nor any of the other witnesses had mentioned it to the reporters. Only afterwards, after the adventure the medical student had in the room, was this detail remembered. It was this: when the police took the body of Sergeant Charles-Maria Chaumié down from the window-sash, a large black spider crawled out of the mouth of the dead man. The porter flicked it away with his finger, crying: 'Ugh! Another such ugly beast!' In the course of the subsequent autopsy – that is, the one held later for Bracquemont – the porter told that when they had taken down the corpse of the Swiss travelling salesman, a similar spider had been seen crawling on his shoulder – But of this Richard Bracquemont knew nothing.

He did not take up his lodging in the room until two weeks after the last suicide, on a Sunday. What he experienced there he entered very conscientiously in a diary.

THE DIARY OF RICHARD BRACQUEMONT,
MEDICAL STUDENT

Monday, February 28

I moved in here last night. I unpacked my two suitcases, put a few things in order, and went to bed. I slept superbly: the clock was just striking nine when a knock at the door awakened me. It was the landlady, who brought me my breakfast herself. She is evidently quite solicitous about me, judging from the eggs, the ham, and the splendid coffee she brought me. I washed and dressed, and then watched the porter make up my room. I smoked my pipe while he worked.

So here I am. I know right well that this business is dangerous, but I know too that my fortune is made if I solve the mystery. And if Paris was once worth a mass – one could hardly buy it that cheaply nowadays – it might be worth risking my little life for it. Here is my chance, and I intend to make the most of it.

At that there were plenty of others who saw this chance. No less than twenty-seven people tried, some through the police, some through the landlady, to get the room. Three of them were women. So there were enough rivals – probably all poor devils like myself.

But I got it! Why? Oh, I was probably the only one who could offer a 'solution' to the police. A neat solution! Of course it was a bluff.

These entries are of course intended for the police, too. And it amuses me considerably to tell these gentlemen right at the outset that it was all a trick on my part. If the Commissioner is sensible he will say, 'Hm! Just because I knew he was tricking us, I had all the more confidence in him!' As far as that is concerned, I don't care what he says afterward; now I'm here. And it seems to me a good omen to have begun my work by bluffing the police so thoroughly.

Of course I first made my application to Madame Dubonnet, but she sent me to the police station. I lounged about the station every day for a week, only to be told that my application 'was being given consideration' and to be asked always to come again next day. Most of my rivals had long since thrown up the sponge; they probably found some better way to spend their time than waiting for hour after hour in the musty police court. But it seems the Commissioner was by this time quite irritated by my perseverance. Finally he told me point blank that my coming back would be quite useless. He was very grateful to me as well as to all the other volunteers for our good intentions, but the police could not use the assistance of 'dilettante laymen'. Unless I had some carefully worked out plan of procedure ...

So I told him that I had exactly that kind of a plan. Of course I had no such thing and couldn't have explained a word of it. But I told him that I could tell him about my plan – which was good, although dangerous, and which might possibly come to the same conclusion as the investigation of the police-sergeant – only if he would promise me on his word of honour that he was ready to carry it out. He thanked me for it, but regretted that he had no time for such things. But I saw that I was getting the upper hand when he asked me whether I couldn't at least give him some intimation of what I planned doing.

And I gave it to him. I told him the most glorious nonsense, of which I myself hadn't had the least notion even a second beforehand. I don't know even now how I came by this unusual inspiration so opportunely. I told him that among all the hours of the week there was one that had a secret and strange significance. That was the hour in which Christ left His grave to go down to hell: the sixth hour of the afternoon of the last day of the Jewish week. And he might take into consideration, I went on, that it was exactly in this hour, between five and six o'clock on Friday afternoon, in which all three of the suicides had been committed. For the present I could not tell him more, but I might refer him to the Book of Revelations according to St John.

The Commissioner put on a wise expression, as if he had understood it all, thanked me, and asked me to come back in the evening. I came back to his office promptly at the appointed time; I saw a copy of the New Testament lying in front of him on the table. In the meantime I had done just what he had: I had read the Book of Revelations through and – had not understood a word of it. Perhaps the Commissioner was more intelligent than I was; at least he told me that he understood what I was driving at in spite of my very vague hints. And that he was ready to grant my request and to aid me in every possible way.

I must admit that he has actually been of very considerable assistance. He has made arrangements with the landlady under which I am to enjoy all the comforts and facilities of the hotel free of charge. He has given me an exceptionally fine revolver and a police pipe. The policemen on duty have orders to go through the little Rue Alfred Stevens as often as possible, and to come up to the room at a given signal. But the main thing is his installation of a desk telephone that connects directly with the police station. Since the station is only four minutes' walk from the hotel, I am thus enabled to have all the help I want immediately. With all this, I can't understand what there is to be afraid of . . .

Tuesday, March 1

Nothing has happened, neither yesterday nor today. Madame Dubonnet brought me a new curtain cord from another room – Heaven knows she has enough of them vacant. For that matter, she seems to take every possible opportunity to come to my room; every time she comes she brings me something. I have again had all the details of the suicides told me, but have discovered nothing new. As far as the causes of the suicides were concerned, she had her own opinions. As for the actor, she thought he had had an unhappy love affair; when he had been her guest the year before, he had been visited frequently by a young woman who had not come at all this year. She admittedly couldn't quite make out why the Swiss gentleman had decided to commit suicide, but of course one couldn't know everything. But there was no doubt that the police sergeant had committed suicide only to spite her.

I must confess these explanations of Madame Dubonnet's are rather inadequate. But I let her gabble on; at least she helps break up my boredom.

Thursday, March 3

Still nothing. The Commissioner rings me up several times a day and I tell him that everything is going splendidly. Evidently this information doesn't quite satisfy him. I have taken out my medical books and begun to work. In this way I am at least getting something out of my voluntary confinement.

Friday, March 4, 2 P.M.

I had an excellent luncheon. Madame Dubonnet brought a half bottle of champagne along with it. It was the kind of dinner you get before your execution. She already regards me as being three-fourths dead. Before she left me she wept and begged me to go with her. Apparently she is afraid I might also hang myself 'just to spite her'.

I have examined the new curtain cord in considerable detail. So I am to hang myself with that? Well, I can't say that I feel much like doing it. The cord is raw and hard, and it would make a good slipknot only with difficulty – one would have to be pretty powerfully determined to emulate the example of the other three suicides in order to make a success of the job. But now I'm sitting at the table, the telephone at my left, the revolver at my right. I certainly have no fear – but I am curious.

6 P.M.

Nothing happened – I almost write with regret. The crucial hour came and went, and was just like all the others. Frankly I can't deny that sometimes I felt a certain urge to go to the window – oh, yes, but for other reasons! The Commissioner called me up at least ten times between five and six. He was just as impatient as I was. But Madame Dubonnet is satisfied: someone has lived for a week in No. 7 without hanging himself. Miraculous!

Monday, March 7

I am now convinced that I shall discover nothing; and I am inclined to think that the suicides of my predecessors were a matter of pure coincidence. I have asked the Commissioner to go over all the evidence

in all three cases again, for I am convinced that eventually a solution
to the mystery will be found. But as far as I am concerned, I intend to
stay here as long as possible. I probably will not conquer Paris, but in
the meantime I'm living here free and am already gaining considerably
in health and weight. On top of it all I'm studying a great deal, and I
notice I am rushing through in great style. And of course there is another
reason that keeps me here.

Wednesday, March 9
    I've progressed another step. Clarimonde——
    Oh, but I haven't said a word about Clarimonde yet. Well, she is –
my third reason for staying here. And it would have been for her sake
that I would gladly have gone to the window in that fateful hour – but
certainly not to hang myself. Clarimonde – but why do I call her that?
I haven't the least idea as to what her name might be; but it seems to
me as if I simply *must* call her Clarimonde. And I'd like to bet that some
day I'll find out that that is really her name.
    I noticed Clarimonde during the first few days I was here. She lives
on the other side of this very narrow street, and her window is directly
opposite mine. She sits there·back of her curtains. And let me also say
that she noticed me before I was aware of her, and that she visibly
manifested an interest in me. No wonder – every one on the street
knows that I am here, and knows why, too. Madame Dubonnet saw to
that.
    I am in no way the kind of person who falls in love. My relations with
women have always been very slight. When one comes to Paris from
Verdun to study medicine and hardly has enough money to have a
decent meal once every three days, one has other things besides love to
worry about. I haven't much experience, and I probably began this
affair pretty stupidly. Anyhow, it's quite satisfactory as it stands.
    At first it never occurred to me to establish communications with my
strange neighbour. I simply decided that since I was here to make
observations, and that I probably had nothing real to investigate
anyhow, I might as well observe my neighbour while I was at it. After
all, one can't pore over one's books all day long. So I have come to the
conclusion that, judging from appearances, Clarimonde lives all alone
in her little apartment. She has three windows, but she sits only at the
one directly opposite mine. She sits there and spins, spins at a little old-
fashioned distaff. I once saw such a distaff at my grandmother's, but
even my grandmother never used it. It was merely an heirloom left her
by some great-aunt or other. I didn't know that they were still in use.
For that matter, Clarimonde's distaff is a very tiny, fine thing, white,
and apparently made of ivory. The threads she spins must be infinitely
fine. She sits behind her curtains all day long and works incessantly,

stopping only when it gets dark. Of course it gets dark very early these foggy days. In this narrow street the loveliest twilight comes about five o'clock. I have never seen a light in her room.

How does she look? – Well, I really don't know. She wears her black hair in wavy curls, and is rather pale. Her nose is small and narrow, and her nostrils quiver. Her lips are pale, too, and it seems as if her little teeth might be pointed, like those of a beast of prey. Her eyelids throw long shadows; but when she opens them her large, dark eyes are full of light. Yet I seem to sense rather than know all this. It is difficult to identify anything clearly back of those curtains.

One thing further: she always wears a black, closely-buttoned dress, with large purple dots. And she always wears long black gloves, probably to protect her hands while working. It looks strange to see her narrow black fingers quickly taking and drawing the threads, seemingly almost through each other – really almost like the wriggling of an insect's legs.

Our relations with each other? Oh, they are really quite superficial. And yet it seems as if they were truly much deeper. It began by her looking over to my window, and my looking over to hers. She noticed me, and I her. And then I evidently must have pleased her, because one day when I looked at her she smiled. And of course I did, too. That went on for several days, and we smiled at each other more and more. Then I decided almost every hour that I would greet her; I don't know exactly what it is that keeps me from carrying out my decision.

I have finally done it, this afternoon. And Clarimonde returned the greeting. Of course the greeting was ever so slight, but nevertheless I distinctly saw her nod.

Thursday, March 10

Last night I sat up late over my books. I can't truthfully say that I studied a great deal: I spent my time building air castles and dreaming about Clarimonde. I slept very lightly, but very late into the morning.

When I stepped up to the window, Clarimonde was sitting at hers. I greeted her and she nodded. She smiled, and looked at me for a long time.

I wanted to work, but couldn't seem to find the necessary peace of mind. I sat at the window and stared at her. Then I suddenly noticed that she, too, folded her hands in her lap. I pulled at the cord of the white curtain and – practically at the same instant – she did the same. We both smiled and looked at one another.

I believe we must have sat like that for an hour.

Then she began spinning again.

*

Saturday, March 12

These days pass swiftly. I eat and drink, and sit down to work. I light my pipe and bend over my books. But I don't read a word. Of course I always make the attempt, but I know beforehand that it won't do any good. Then I go to the window. I greet Clarimonde, and she returns my greeting. We smile and gaze at one another – for hours.

Yesterday afternoon at six I felt a little uneasy. Darkness settled very early, and I felt a certain nameless fear. I sat at my desk and waited. I felt an almost unconquerable urge to go to the window – certainly not to hang myself, but to look at Clarimonde. I jumped up and stood back of the curtain. It seemed as if I had never seen her so clearly, although it was already quite dark. She was spinning, but her eyes looked across at me. I felt a strange comfort and a very subtle fear.

The telephone rang. I was furious at the silly old Commissioner for interrupting my dreams with his stupid questions.

This morning he came to visit me, along with Madame Dubonnet. She seems to be satisfied enough with my activities: she takes sufficient consolation from the fact that I have managed to *live* in Room No. 7 for two whole weeks. But the Commissioner wants results besides. I confided to him that I had made some secret observations, and that I was tracking down a very strange clue. The old fool believed all I told him. In any event I can still stay here for weeks – and that's all I care about. Not on account of Madame Dubonnet's cooking and cellar – God, how soon one becomes indifferent to that when one always has enough to eat! – only because of the window, which she hates and fears, and which I love so dearly: this window that reveals Clarimonde to me.

When I light the lamp I no longer see her. I have strained my eyes trying to see whether she goes out, but I have never seen her set foot on the street. I have a comfortable easy chair and a green lampshade whose glow warmly suffuses me. The Commissioner has sent me a large package of tobacco. I have never smoked such good tobacco. And yet I cannot do any work. I read two or three pages, and when I have finished I realize that I haven't understood a word of their contents. My eyes grasp the significance of the letters, but my brain refuses to supply the connotations. Queer! Just as if my brain bore the legend: 'No Admittance.' Just as if it refused to admit any thought other than the one: Clarimonde ...

Finally I push my books aside, lean far back in my chair, and dream.

Sunday, March 13

This morning I witnessed a little tragedy. I was walking up and down in the corridor while the porter made up my room. In front of the little court window there is a spider web hanging, with a fat garden spider sitting in the middle of it. Madame Dubonnet refuses to let it be swept away: spiders bring luck, and Heaven knows she has had enough bad luck in her house. Presently I saw another much smaller male spider cautiously running around the edge of the web. Tentatively he ventured down one of the precarious threads towards the middle; but the moment the female moved, he hastily withdrew. He ran around to another end of the web and tried again to approach her. Finally the powerful female spider in the centre of the web seemed to look upon his suit with favour, and stopped moving. The male spider pulled at one of the threads of the web – first lightly, then so vigorously that the whole web quivered. But the object of his attention remained immovable. Then he approached her very quickly, but carefully. The female spider received him quietly and let him embrace her delicately while she retained the utmost passivity. Motionless the two of them hung for several minutes in the centre of the large web.

Then I saw how the male spider slowly freed himself, one leg after another. It seemed as if he wanted to retreat quietly, leaving his companion alone in her dream of love. Suddenly he let her go entirely and ran out of the web as fast as he could. But at the same instant the female seemed to awaken to a wild rush of activity, and she chased rapidly after him. The weak male spider let himself down by a thread, but the female followed immediately. Both of them fell to the window-sill; and, gathering all his energies, the male spider tried to run away. But it was too late. The female spider seized him in her powerful grip, carried him back up into the net, and set him down squarely in the middle of it. And this same place that had just been a bed for passionate desire now became the scene of something quite different. The lover kicked in vain, stretched his weak legs out again and again, and tried to disentangle himself from this wild embrace. But the female would not let him go. In a few minutes she had spun him in so completely that he could not move a single member. Then she thrust her sharp pincers into his body and sucked out the young blood of her lover in deep draughts. I even saw how she finally let go of the pitiful, unrecognizable little lump – legs, skin and threads – and threw it contemptuously out of the net.

So that's what love is like among these creatures! Well, I can be glad I'm not a young spider.

Monday, March 14

I no longer so much as glance at my books. Only at the window do I pass all my days. And I keep on sitting there even after it gets dark. Then she is no longer there; but I close my eyes and see her anyhow ...

Well, this diary has become quite different than I thought it would be. It tells about Madame Dubonnet and the Commissioner, about

spiders and about Clarimonde. But not a word about the discovery I
had hoped to make—— Well, is it my fault?

Tuesday, March 15

Clarimonde and I have discovered a strange new game, and we play
it all day long. I greet her, and immediately she returns the greeting.
Then I drum with my fingers on my windowpane. She has hardly had
time to see it before she begins drumming on hers. I wink at her, and
she winks at me. I move my lips as if I were talking to her and she follows
suit. Then I brush the hair back from my temples, and immediately her
hand is at the side of her forehead. Truly child's play. And we both laugh
at it. That is, she really doesn't laugh: it's only a quiet, passive smile she
has, just as I suppose mine must be.

For that matter all this isn't nearly as senseless as it must seem. It isn't
imitation at all: I think we would both tire of that very quickly. There
must be a certain telepathy or thought transference involved in it. For
Clarimonde repeats my motions in the smallest conceivable fraction of
a second. She hardly has time to see what I am doing before she does
the same thing. Sometimes it even seems to me that her action is
simultaneous with mine. That is what entices me: always doing something new and unpremeditated. And it's astounding to see her doing the
same thing at the same time. Sometimes I try to catch her. I make a
great many motions in quick succession, and then repeat them again;
and then I do them a third time. Finally I repeat them for the fourth
time, but change their order, introduce some new motion, or leave out
one of the old ones. It's like children playing Follow the Leader. It's
really remarkable that Clarimonde never makes a single mistake,
although I sometimes change the motions so rapidly that she hardly has
time to memorize each one.

That is how I spend my days. But I never feel for a second that I'm
squandering my time on something nonsensical. On the contrary, it
seems as if nothing I had ever done were more important.

Wednesday, March 16

Isn't it queer that I have never thought seriously about putting my
relations with Clarimonde on a more sensible basis than that of these
hour-consuming games? I thought about it last night. I could simply
take my hat and coat and go down two flights of stairs, five steps across
the street, and then up two other flights of stairs. On her door there
is a little coat-of-arms engraved with her name: 'Clarimonde ...'
Clarimonde what? I don't know what; but the name Clarimonde is
certainly there. Then I could knock, and then ...

That far I can imagine everything perfectly, down to the last move

I might make. But for the life of me I can't picture what would happen after that. The door would open – I can conceive that. But I would remain standing in front of it looking into her room, into a darkness – a darkness so utter that not a solitary thing could be distinguished in it. She would not come – nothing would come; as a matter of fact, there would be nothing there. Only the black impenetrable darkness.

Sometimes it seems as if there could be no other Clarimonde than the one I play with at my window. I can't picture what this woman would look like if she wore a hat, or even some dress other than her black one with the large purple dots; I can't even conceive her without her gloves. If I could see her on the street, or even in some restaurant, eating, drinking, talking – well, I really have to laugh: the thing seems so utterly inconceivable.

Sometimes I ask myself whether I love her. I can't answer that question entirely, because I have never been in love. But if the feeling I bear towards Clarimonde is really – well, love – then love is certainly very, very different from what I saw of it among my acquaintances or learned about it in novels.

It is becoming quite difficult to define my emotions. In fact, it is becoming difficult even to think about anything at all that has no bearing on Clarimonde – or rather, on our game. For there is truly no denying it: it's really the game that preoccupies me – nothing else. And that's the thing I understand least of all.

Clarimonde – well, yes, I feel attracted to her. But mingled with the attraction there is another feeling – almost like a sense of fear. Fear? No, it isn't fear either: it is more of a temerity, a certain inarticulate alarm or apprehension before something I cannot define. And it is just this apprehension that has some strange compulsion, something curiously passionate that keeps me at a distance from her and at the same time draws me constantly nearer to her. It is as if I were going around her in a wide circle, came a little nearer at one place, withdrew again, went on, approached her again at another point and again retreated rapidly. Until finally – of that I am absolutely certain – I *must* go to her.

Clarimonde is sitting at her window and spinning. Threads – long, thin, infinitely fine threads. She seems to be making some fabric – I don't know just what it is to be. And I can't understand how she can make the network without tangling or tearing the delicate fabric. There are wonderful patterns in her work – patterns full of fabulous monsters and curious grotesques.

For that matter – but what am I writing? The fact of the matter is that I can't even see what it is she is spinning: the threads are much too fine. And yet I can't help feeling that her work must be exactly as I see it – when I close my eyes. Exactly. A huge network peopled with many creatures – fabulous monsters, and curious grotesque ...

Thursday, March 17

I find myself in a strange state of agitation. I no longer talk to any one; I hardly even say good morning to Madame Dubonnet or the porter. I hardly take time to eat; I only want to sit at the window and play with her. It's an exacting game. Truly it is.

And I have a premonition that tomorrow something must happen.

Friday, March 18

Yes, yes. Something must happen today ... I tell myself – oh, yes, I talk aloud, just to hear my own voice – that it is just for *that* I am here. But the worst of it is that I am afraid. And this fear that what has happened to my predecessors in this room may also happen to me is curiously mingled with my other fear – the fear of Clarimonde. I can hardly keep them apart.

I am afraid. I would like to scream.

6 P.M.

Let me put down a few words quickly, and then get into my hat and coat.

By the time five o'clock came, my strength was gone. Oh, I know now for certain that it must have something to do with this sixth hour of the next to the last day of the week ... Now I can no longer laugh at the fraud with which I duped the Commissioner. I sat on my chair and stayed there only by exerting my will power to the utmost. But this thing drew me, almost pulled me to the window. I had to play with Clarimonde – and then again there rose that terrible fear of the window. I saw them hanging there – the Swiss travelling salesman, a large fellow with a thick neck and a grey stubble beard. And the lanky acrobat and the stocky, powerful police sergeant. I saw all three of them, one after another and then all three together, hanging from the same hook with open mouths and with tongues lolling far out. And then I saw myself among them.

Oh, this fear! I felt I was as much afraid of the window-sash and the terrible hook as I was of Clarimonde. May she forgive me for it, but that's the truth: in my ignominious fear I always confused her image with that of the three who hanged there, dangling their legs heavily on the floor.

But the truth is that I never felt for an instant any desire or inclination to hang myself: I wasn't even afraid I would do it. No – I was afraid only of the window itself – and of Clarimonde – and of something terrible, something uncertain and unpredictable that was now to come.

I had the pathetic irresistable longing to get up and go to the window. And I *had* to do it ...

Then the telephone rang. I grabbed the receiver and before I could hear a word I myself cried into the mouthpiece: 'Come! Come at once!'

It was just as if my unearthly yell had instantly chased all the shadows into the farthest cracks of the floor. I became composed immediately. I wiped the sweat from my forehead and drank a glass of water. Then I considered what I ought to tell the Commissioner when he came. Finally I went to the window, greeted Clarimonde, and smiled.

And Clarimonde greeted me and smiled.

Five minutes later the Commissioner was here. I told him that I had finally struck the root of the whole affair; if he would only refrain from questioning me today, I would certainly be able to make some remarkable disclosures in the very near future. The queer part of it was that while I was lying to him I was at the same time fully convinced in my own mind that I was telling the truth. And I still feel that that is the truth – against my better judgment.

He probably noticed the unusual condition of my temper, especially when I apologized for screaming into the telephone and tried to explain – and failed to find any plausible reason for my agitation. He suggested very amiably that I need not take undue consideration of him: he was always at my service – that was his duty. He would rather make a dozen useless trips over here than let me wait for him once when I really needed him. Then he invited me to go out with him tonight, suggesting that that might help distract me   it wasn't a good thing to be alone all the time. I have accepted his invitation, although I think it will be difficult to go out: I don't like to leave this room.

Saturday, March 19

We went to the Gaieté Rochechouart, to the Cigale, and to the Lune Rousse. The Commissioner was right: it was a good thing for me to go out and breathe another atmosphere. At first I felt rather uncomfortable, as if I were doing something wrong (as if I were a deserter, running away from our flag). But by and by that feeling died; we drank a good deal, laughed, and joked.

When I went to the window this morning, I seemed to read a reproach in Clarimonde's look. But perhaps I only imagined it: how could she know that I had gone out last night? For that matter, it seemed to last for only a moment; then she smiled again.

We played all day long.

Sunday, March 20

Today I can only repeat: we played all day long.

Monday, March 21
We played all day long.

Tuesday, March 22
Yes, and today we did the same. Nothing, absolutely nothing else. Sometimes I ask myself why we do it. What is it all for? Or, what do I really want, to what can it all lead? But I never answer my own question. For it's certain that I want nothing other than just this. Come what may, that which is coming is exactly what I long for.

We have been talking to one another these last few days, of course not with any spoken word. Sometimes we moved our lips, at other times we only looked at one another. But we understood each other perfectly.

I was right: Clarimonde reproached me for running away last Friday. But I begged her forgiveness and told her I realized that it had been very unwise and horrid of me. She forgave me and I promised her never again to leave the window. And we kissed each other, pressing our lips against the panes for a long, long time.

Wednesday, March 23
I know now that I love her. It must be love – I feel it tingling in every fibre of my being. It may be that with other people love is different. But is there any one among a thousand millions who has a head, an ear, a hand that is like anyone else's? Everyone is different, so it is quite conceivable that our love is very singular. But does that make it any less beautiful? I am almost happy in this love.

If only there would not be this fear! Sometimes it falls asleep. Then I forget it. But only for a few minutes. Then it wakes up again and will not let me go. It seems to me like a poor little mouse fighting against a huge and beautiful snake, trying to free itself from its overpowering embrace. Just wait, you poor foolish little fear, soon our love will devour you!

Thursday, March 24
I have made a discovery: I don't play with Clarimonde – *she plays with me.*
It happened like this.
Last night, as usual, I thought about our game. I wrote down five intricate movements with which I wanted to surprise her today. I gave every motion a number. I practised them so as to be able to execute them as quickly as possible, first in order, and then backwards. Then only the even numbers and then the odd, and then only the first and last parts of each of the five motions. It was very laborious, but it gave me great satisfaction because it brought me nearer to Clarimonde, even though I could not see her. I practised in this way for

hours, and finally they went like clockwork.

This morning I went to the window. We greeted each other, and the game began. Forward, backward – it was incredible to see how quickly she understood me, and how instantaneously she repeated all the things I did.

Then there was a knock at my door. It was the porter, bringing me my boots. I took them; but when I was going back to the window my glance fell on the sheet of paper on which I had recorded the order of the movements. *And I saw that I had not executed a single one of these movements.*

I almost reeled. I grabbed the back of the easy chair and let myself down into it. I couldn't believe it. I read the sheet again and again. But it was true: of all the motions I had made at the window, not a single one was mine.

And again I was aware of a door opening somewhere far away – her door. I was standing before it and looking in ... nothing, nothing – only an empty darkness. Then I knew that if I went out, I would be saved; and I realized that now I *could* go. Nevertheless I did not go. That was because I was distinctly aware of one feeling: that I held the secret of the mystery. Held it tightly in both hands. – Paris – I was going to conquer Paris!

For a moment Paris was stronger than Clarimonde.

Oh, I've dropped all thought of it now. Now I am aware only of my love, and in the midst of it this quiet, passionate fear.

But in that instant I felt suddenly strong. I read through the details of my first movement once more and impressed it firmly in my memory. Then I went back to the window.

And I took exact notice of what I did: *not a single motion I executed was among those I had set out to do.*

Then I decided to run my index finger along my nose. But instead I kissed the window-pane. I wanted to drum on the window-sill, but ran my hand through my hair instead. So it was true: Clarimonde did not imitate the things I did: on the contrary, I repeated the things she indicated. And I did it so quickly, with such lightning rapidity, that I followed her motions in the same second, so that even now it seems as if I were the one who exerted the will power to do these things.

So it is I – I who was so proud of the fact that I had determined her mode of thought – I was the one who was being so completely influenced. Only, her influence is so soft, so gentle that it seems as if nothing on earth could be so soothing.

I made other experiments. I put both my hands in my pockets and resolved firmly not to move them; then I looked across at her. I noticed how she lifted her hand and smiled, and gently chided me with her index finger. I refused to budge. I felt my right hand wanting to take itself out of my pocket, but I dug my fingers deep into the pocket lining. Then slowly, after several minutes, my fingers relaxed, my hand came out of the pocket, and I lifted my arm. And I chided her with my index finger and smiled. It seemed as if it were really not I who was doing all this, but some stranger whom I watched from a distance. No, no – that wasn't the way of it. I, I was the one who did it – and some stranger was watching me. It was the stranger – that other me – who was so strong, who wanted to solve this mystery with some great discovery. But that was no longer I.

I – oh, what do I care about the discovery? I am only here to do her bidding, the bidding of my Clarimonde, whom I love with such tender fear.

Friday, March 25
I have cut the telephone wire. I can no longer stand being perpetually bothered by the silly old Commissioner, least of all when the fateful hour is at hand...

God, why am I writing all this? Not a word of it is true. It seems as if someone else were guiding my pen.

But I do – I want to set down here what actually happens. It is costing me a tremendous effort. But I want to do it. If only for the last time to do – what I really want to do.

I cut the telephone wire ... oh ...

Because I had to ... There, I finally got it out! Because I had to, I had to!

We stood at the window this morning and played. Our game has changed a little since yesterday. She goes through some motions and I defend myself as long as possible. Until finally I have to surrender, powerless to do anything but her bidding. And I can scarcely tell what a wonderful sense of exaltation and joy it gives me to be conquered by her will, to make this surrender.

We played. And then suddenly she got up and went back into her room. It was so dark that I couldn't see her; she seemed to disappear into the darkness. But she came back very shortly, carrying in her hands a desk telephone just like mine. Smiling, she set it down on the window-sill, took a knife, cut the wire, and carried it back again.

I defended myself for about a quarter of an hour. My fear was greater than ever, but that made my slow surrender all the more delectable. And I finally brought my telephone to the window, cut the wire, and set it back on the table.

That is how it happened.

I am sitting at the table. I have had my tea, and the porter has just taken the dishes out. I asked him what time it was – it seems my watch isn't keeping time. It's five fifteen ... five fifteen ...

I know that if I look up now Clarimonde will be doing something or other. Doing something or other that I will have to do too.

I look up anyhow. She is standing there and smiling. Well ... if I could only tear my eyes away from her! ... now she is going to the curtain. She is taking the cord off – it is red, just like the one on my window. She is tying a knot – a slipknot. She is hanging the cord up on the hook in the window-sash.

She is sitting down and smiling.

... No, this is no longer a thing one can call fear, this thing I am experiencing. It is a maddening, choking terror – but nevertheless I wouldn't trade it for anything in the world. It is a compulsion of an unheard-of nature and power, yet so subtly sensual in its inescapable ferocity.

Of course I could rush up to the window and do exactly what she wants me to do. But I am waiting, struggling, and defending myself. I feel this uncanny thing getting stronger every minute ...

So, here I am, still sitting here. I ran quickly to the window and did the thing she wanted me to do: I took the curtain cord, tied a slipknot in it, and hung it from the hook ...

And now I am not going to look up any more. I am going to stay here and look only at this sheet of paper. For I know now what she would do if I looked up again – now in the sixth hour of the next to the last day of the week. If I see her, I shall have to do her bidding ... I shall have to ...

I shall refuse to look at her.

But I am suddenly laughing – loudly. No, I'm not laughing – it is something laughing within me. I know why, too: it's because of this 'I will not ...'

I don't want to, and yet I know certainly that I must. I must. I must look at her ... must, must do it ... and then – the rest.

I am only waiting to stretch out the torment. Yes, that is it ... For these breathless sufferings are my most rapturous transports. I am writing ... quickly, quickly, so that I can remain sitting here longer ... in order to stretch out these seconds of torture, which carry the ecstasy of love into infinity ...

More ... longer ...

Again this fear, again! I know that I shall look at her, that I shall get up, that I shall hang myself. *But it isn't that that I fear.* Oh, no – that is sweet, that is beautiful.

But there is something else ... something else associated with it – *something that will happen afterwards.* I don't know what it will be – but it is coming, it is certainly coming, certainly ... certainly. For the joy of my torments is so infinitely great – oh, I feel it is so great that something terrible must follow it.

Only I must not think ...

Let me write something, anything, no matter what. Only quickly, without thinking ...

My name – Richard Bracquemont, Richard Bracquemont, Richard – oh, I can't go any farther – Richard Bracquemont – Richard Bracquemont – now – now – I must look at her ... Richard Bracquemont – I must – no – no, more – more ... Richard ... Richard Bracque——

The Commissioner of the Ninth Ward, after failing repeatedly to get a reply to his telephone calls, came to the Hotel Stevens at five minutes after six. In Room No. 7 he found the body of the student Richard Bracquemont hanging from the window-sash, in exactly the same position as that of his three predecessors.

Only his face had a different expression; it was distorted in horrible fear, and his eyes, wide open, seemed to be pushing themselves out of their sockets. His lips were drawn apart, but his powerful teeth were firmly and desperately clenched.

And glued between them, bitten and crushed to pieces, there was a large black spider, with curious purple dots.

On the table lay the medical student's diary. The Commissioner read it and went immediately to the house across the street. There he discovered that the second apartment had been vacant and unoccupied for months and months ...

Someone in the Room

Elizabeth Fancett

She woke up suddenly, sharply, in swift transition from deep sleep to full consciousness.

It was her first night alone with her small son, Peter. That afternoon her husband, Paul, had left her, the inevitable climax of months of endless bickerings, violent rows and mutual bitterness.

They had parted in hate and terrible anger. She had not been able to sleep for hours, thinking about their final violent quarrel over their son. Paul had threatened to take Peter with him, and at one stage she'd thought he was going to take him by force. But he'd changed his mind at the last moment, storming out of the house in a blaze of hate and fury.

Sleep had been heavy when it had finally come. But now she was wide awake, and she knew *why* she had woken.

There was someone in the room!

Stay quiet! said her brain, insisting that her heart fight to still its panicked beating. The intruder must have forced an entrance through one of the downstairs windows. Yet she thought she'd securely locked everything. She'd made sure of that, especially tonight, now that she and Peter were alone. But a burglar, if he were determined, if he had the time and he was quiet enough, could gain an entry somewhere no matter how many precautions one took.

She lay perfectly still, in an ache of dread and fear. She thought of her young son sleeping in the next room. What if the intruder had entered that way – through Peter's bedroom? Had he been harmed? She prayed not. But what if he should waken, come into her room ... ?

Her body remained rigid, her eyes wide open, staring into the blackness about her. She could see nothing. The entire room was in total darkness, the heavy curtains having been pulled right over in order to shut out every chink of light. Yet she knew that a presence stood within the darkness, unmoving, silent in the blackness.

A confusion of thoughts raced through her mind. *Could* it be a burglar? This was a very lonely place, a large and lonely house – even larger and lonelier now that she and Peter were alone. And there was plenty to steal, plenty to make a break-in well worthwhile. And some of her jewellery was here in the bedroom.

Did the intruder know that Paul had gone, that there was only herself and a small defenceless boy to cope with? And surely a burglar didn't steal in total darkness – unless he knew exactly where to go and what to steal?

Another possibility entered into her mind – could the intruder be ... could it possibly be ... Paul himself? But if so – why? Had he come to steal from her? Unlikely. To punish her perhaps – by scaring her? Yes, he was mad enough, angry enough, to do just that.

Then another even more frightening possibility was suddenly in her mind. Had her husband come back to steal *Peter*? He'd threatened to take him away eventually, hadn't he? He had stormed and raved that Peter would not remain with her for long, that he would come when she least expected it and take him away, that she would never in her life see her son again.

No! She pushed away the thought. Not even Paul would do it like this just to get even with her, not this way, not this secret, frightening, terrifying way. No, it *must* be a burglar. And yet if it were, why the darkness, why not *some* light – a torch, even a brief striking of a match, just to get his bearings? Maybe the intruder was waiting, listening, for some sound or movement from her before he dared put on a light?

She closed her eyes quickly, lest at any moment a torch might suddenly break the darkness and he would *know* she was awake. But the darkness remained, and the awful silence. Not even the sound of breathing to tell her that anyone was there. But he was there! Someone was there ... waiting ... waiting ...

Wave upon wave of fear broke over her until her whole body was adrench with it. What if she were attacked – killed even! In mental anguish she visualized the shock to her son when he found her in the morning. That is – if the intruder didn't kill him, too – if he hadn't *already* killed him ... !

No. She was creating terrors that might never come to pass. She tried to rationalize her thoughts. No one had any *reason* to kill her son. Yet who *was* it? What was the intruder's intention? Why didn't he make a move? How long had she to lie here, thinking, imagining, tearing at her mind for some solution as to who it was, and why he was here?

Think, now, think! Not *who* it is – but how to deal with him, what to do! She must do *something* ... anything ... anything rather than just lie here!

Should she 'waken', switch on the light, challenge him, meet the fear, *see* the danger? Her fingers ached to move towards the lamp beside the bed. But she remained still.

There! That was a movement, surely – a footstep, a shuffling footstep!

And breathing now, soft, light breathing! Whoever it was, was moving now – and *towards* her!

Her heart was tight with terror, but her mind continued to work furiously, as though it were totally apart from her person, desperately thinking, wondering, how to deal with the menace in the room.

There was a light scraping noise, as if the intruder had knocked into something. That could be the chair – and the chair was but two feet away from her bed!

For a further moment or two there was silence, as if the intruder was waiting to see if the slight noise had woken her. She willed herself to absolute stillness. Then a slight rustling sound broke the silence.

She peered from beneath half-closed eyelids, in the direction of the chair, hoping for some glimpse of the intruder, some inclination as to what – whom – she had to deal with.

There! Just there! Her eyes, now more used to the darkness, saw a vague outline, a shadow in shadow, but a figure – someone bending over her! The figure was motionless, as though listening for her breathing, seeking assurance that she was still asleep. She closed her eyes tightly, started to breathe evenly in a reassuring rhythm. But maybe even now it was too late! Maybe he had already seen her eyes wide open, searching the darkness ...

God! What should she do? What *could* she do? Must she just lie here, waiting for the sudden light upon her face ... waiting for attack? If only she had a weapon – any kind of a weapon! But what? The nearest knife was in the kitchen. Scissors? There were only the nail scissors, and they were on the dressing-table, too far away.

Think, now, think! The book-ends on the bedside table? They were heavy enough, but not near enough. One of the bedside lamps? That was it! The one on the left table had a heavy base. It could crack a man's skull, wielded viciously enough, and fear would lend her strength. She would kill if she had to!

Slowly, soundlessly, she stretched out her left arm across the bed and towards the table, trusting that the outline of her arm was not visible to eyes maybe now accustomed as her own were to the darkness. She reached blindly, groping, inch by inch, conscious that at any moment an attack could come before the weapon was in her hands.

Careful now, don't knock it over and alert him that you're awake!

The lamp was still beyond her grasp. She dared not move her body or stretch her arm any further. The lamp on the right table – maybe that was nearer? It wasn't quite as heavy, but it would do – *anything* would do!

Not daring to move her left arm, still outstretched towards the left lamp, she reached out her right arm towards the other table. To her intense relief her fingertips touched the lamp almost instantly. She pulled it slowly and carefully towards her. Her hand slid up to the top of the stand and grasped it firmly.

In the same instant, fingers touched her left wrist. Instinctively she raised her right arm and brought the lamp down with all the force of the raging terror within her.

Even as her arm sliced an arc through the air, she heard the voice. Then the heavy weight of the lamp make its contact.

The hand on her wrist slid away. She heard a moan, heard the chair creak and scrape back, as someone who'd been standing on it – someone small, someone once softly breathing – crumpled and pitched forward on to the floor.

She screamed in the darkness, her stricken mind still hearing the softly whispering voice as the lamp came down to kill.

It had said: 'Mummy.'

A Rose for Emily

William Faulkner

When Miss Emily Grierson died, our whole town went to her funeral: the men through a sort of respectful affection for a fallen monument, the women mostly out of curiosity to see the inside of her house, which no one save an old manservant – a combined gardener and cook – had seen in at least ten years.

It was a big, squarish frame house that had once been white, decorated with cupolas and spires and scrolled balconies in the heavily lightsome style of the seventies, set on what had once been our most select street. But garages and cotton gins had encroached and obliterated even the august names of that neighbourhood; only Miss Emily's house was left, lifting its stubborn and coquettish decay above the cotton wagons and the petrol pumps – an eyesore among eyesores. And now Miss Emily had gone to join the representatives of those august names where they lay in the cedar-demused cemetery among the ranked and anonymous graves of Union and Confederate soldiers who fell at the battle of Jefferson.

Alive, Miss Emily had been a tradition, a duty, and a care; a sort of hereditary obligation upon the town, dating from that day in 1894 when Colonel Sartoris, the mayor – he who fathered the edict that no Negro woman should appear on the streets without an apron – remitted her taxes, the dispensation dating from the death of her father on into perpetuity. Not that Miss Emily would have accepted charity. Colonel Sartoris invented an involved tale to the effect that Miss Emily's father had loaned money to the town, which the town, as a matter of business, preferred this way of repaying. Only a man of Colonel Sartoris's generation and thought could have invented it, and only a woman could have believed it.

When the next generation, with its more modern ideas, became mayors and aldermen, this arrangement created some little dissatisfaction. On the first of the year they mailed her a tax notice. February came, and there was no reply. They wrote her a formal letter asking her to call at the sheriff's office at her convenience. A week later the mayor wrote her himself, offering to call or to send his car for her, and received in reply a note on paper of an archaic shape, in a thin, flowing calligraphy in faded ink, to the effect that she no longer went out at all. The tax notice was also enclosed, without comment.

They called a special meeting of the Board of Aldermen. A deputation waited upon her, knocked at the door through which no visitor had passed since she ceased giving china-painting lessons eight or ten years earlier. They were admitted by the old Negro into a dim hall from which a stairway mounted into still more shadow. It smelled of dust and disuse – a close, dank smell. The Negro led them into the parlour. It was furnished in heavy, leather-covered furniture. When the Negro opened the blinds of one window, they could see that the leather was cracked; and when they sat down, a faint dust rose sluggishly about their thighs, spinning with slow notes in the single sunray. On a tarnished gilt easel before the fireplace stood a crayon portrait of Miss Emily's father.

They rose when she entered – a small, fat woman in black, with a thin gold chain descending to her waist, and vanishing into her belt, leaning on an ebony cane with a tarnished gold head. Her skeleton was small and spare; perhaps that was why what would have been merely plumpness in another was obesity in her. She looked bloated, like a body long submerged in motionless water, and of that pallid hue. Her eyes, lost in the fatty ridges of her face, looked like two small pieces of coal pressed into a lump of dough as they moved from one face to another while the visitors stated their errand.

She did not ask them to sit. She just stood in the doorway and listened quietly until the spokesman came to a stumbling halt. Then they could hear the invisible watch ticking at the end of the gold chain.

Her voice was dry and cold. 'I have no taxes in Jefferson. Colonel Sartoris explained it to me. Perhaps one of you can gain access to the city records and satisfy yourselves.'

'But we have. We are the city authorities, Miss Emily. Didn't you get a notice from the sheriff, signed by him?'

'I received a paper, yes,' Miss Emily said. 'Perhaps he considers himself the sheriff . . . I have no taxes in Jefferson.'

'But there is nothing on the books to show that, you see. We must go by the——'

'See Colonel Sartoris. I have no taxes in Jefferson.'

'But Miss Emily——'

'See Colonel Sartoris.' (Colonel Sartoris had been dead almost ten years.) 'I have no taxes in Jefferson. Tobe!' The Negro appeared. 'Show these gentlemen out.'

II

So she vanquished them, horse and foot, just as she had vanquished their fathers thirty years before about the smell. That was two years after her father's death and a short time after her sweetheart – the one we believed would marry her – had deserted her. After her father's death she went out very little; after her sweetheart went away, people hardly saw her at all. A few of the ladies had the temerity to call, but were not received, and the only sign of life about the place was the Negro man – a young man then – going in and out with a market basket.

'Just as if a man – any man – could keep a kitchen properly,' the ladies said; so they were not surprised when the smell developed. It was another link between the gross, teeming world and the high and mighty Griersons.

A neighbour, a woman, complained to the mayor, Judge Stevens, eighty years old.

'But what will you have me to do about it, madam?' he said.

'Why, send her word to stop it,' the woman said. 'Isn't there a law?'

'I'm sure that won't be necessary,' Judge Stevens said. 'It's probably just a snake or a rat that nigger of hers killed in the yard. I'll speak to him about it.'

The next day he received two more complaints, one from a man who came in diffident deprecation. 'We really must do something about it, Judge. I'd be the last one in the world to bother Miss Emily, but we've got to do something.' That night the Board of Aldermen met – three greybeards and one younger man, a member of the rising generation.

'It's simple enough,' he said. 'Send her word to have her place cleaned up. Give her a certain time to do it in, and if she don't . . .'

'Dammit, sir,' Judge Stevens said, 'will you accuse a lady to her face of smelling bad?'

So the next night, after midnight, four men crossed Miss Emily's lawn and slunk about the house like burglars, sniffing along the base of the brickwork and at the cellar openings, while one of them performed a regular sowing motion with his hand out of a sack slung from his shoulder. They broke open the cellar door and sprinkled lime there, and in all the outbuildings. As they recrossed the lawn, a window that had been dark was lighted and Miss Emily sat in it, the light behind her, and her upright torso motionless as that of an idol. They crept quietly across the lawn and into the shadow of the locusts that lined the street. After a week or two the smell went away.

That was when people had begun to feel really sorry for her. People in our town, remembering how Old Lady Wyatt, her great-aunt, had gone completely crazy at last, believed that the Griersons held themselves a little too high for what they really were. None of the young men was quite good enough to Miss Emily and such. We had long thought of them as a tableau: Miss Emily a slender figure in white in the background, her father a spraddled silhouette in the foreground, his back to her and clutching a horsewhip, the two of them framed by the back-flung front door. So when she got to be thirty and was still single, we were not pleased exactly, but vindicated; even with insanity in the family she wouldn't have turned down all of her chances if they had really materialized.

When her father died, it got about that the house was all that was left to her; and in a way, people were glad. At last they could pity Miss Emily. Being left alone, and a pauper, she had become humanized. Now she too would know the old thrill and the old despair of a penny more or less.

The day after his death all the ladies prepared to call at the house and offer condolence and aid, as is our custom. Miss Emily met them at the door, dressed as usual and with no trace of grief on her face. She told them that her father was not dead. She did that for three days, with the ministers calling on her, and the doctors, trying to persuade her to let them dispose of the body. Just as they were about to resort to law and force, she broke down, and they buried her father quickly.

We did not say she was crazy then. We believed she had to do that. We remembered all the young men her father had driven away, and we knew that, with nothing left, she would have to cling to that which had robbed her, as people will.

III

She was sick for a long time. When we saw her again, her hair was cut short, making her look like a girl, with a vague resemblance to those angels in coloured church windows – sort of tragic and serene.

The town had just let the contracts for paving the sidewalks, and in the summer after her father's death they began the work. The construction company came with niggers and mules and machinery, and a foreman named Homer Barron, a Yankee – a big, dark, ready man, with a big voice and eyes lighter than his face. The little boys would follow in groups to hear him cuss the niggers, and the niggers singing in time to the rise and fall of picks. Pretty soon he knew everybody in town. Whenever you heard a lot of laughing anywhere about the square, Homer Barron would be in the centre of the group. Presently we began to see him and Miss Emily on Sunday afternoons driving in the yellow-wheeled buggy and the matched team of bays from the livery stable.

At first we were glad that Miss Emily would have an interest, because the ladies all said, 'Of course a Grierson would not think seriously of a Northerner, a day labourer.' But there were still others, older people, who said that even grief could not cause a real lady to forget *noblesse oblige* – without calling it *noblesse oblige*. They just said, 'Poor Emily. Her kinsfolk should come to her.' She had some kin in Alabama; but years ago her father had fallen out with them over the estate of Old Lady Wyatt, the crazy woman, and there was no communication between the two families. They had not even been represented at the funeral.

And as soon as the old people said, 'Poor Emily,' the whispering began. 'Do you suppose it's really so?' they said to one another. 'Of course it is. What else could ...' This behind their hands; rustling of craned silk and satin behind jalousies closed upon the sun of Sunday afternoon as the thin, swift clop-clop-clop of the matched team passed: 'Poor Emily.'

She carried her head high enough – even when we believed that she was fallen. It was as if she demanded more than ever the recognition of her dignity as the last Grierson; as if it had wanted that touch of earthiness to reaffirm her imperviousness. Like when she bought the rat poison, the arsenic. That was over a year after they had begun to say 'Poor Emily', and while the two female cousins were visiting her.

'I want some poison,' she said to the druggist. She was over thirty then, still a slight woman, though thinner than usual, with cold haughty black eyes in a face the flesh of which was strained across the temples and about the eye-sockets as you imagine a lighthouse-keeper's face ought to look. 'I want some poison,' she said.

'Yes, Miss Emily. What kind? For rats and such? I'd recom——'

'I want the best you have. I don't care what kind.'

The druggist named several. 'They'll kill anything up to an elephant. But what you want is——'

'Arsenic,' Miss Emily said. 'Is that a good one?'

'Is ... arsenic? Yes, ma'am. But what you want——'

'I want arsenic.'

The druggist looked down at her. She looked back at him, erect, her face like a strained flag. 'Why, of course,' the druggist said. 'If that's what you want. But the law requires you to tell what you are going to use it for.'

Miss Emily just stared at him, her head tilted back in order to look him eye for eye, until he looked away and went and got the arsenic and wrapped it up. The Negro delivery boy brought her the package; the druggist didn't come back. When she opened the package at home there was written on the box, under the skull and bones: 'For rats.'

IV

So the next day we all said, 'She will kill herself'; and we said it would be the best thing. When she had first begun to be seen with Homer Barron, we had said, 'She will marry him.' Then we said, 'She will persuade him yet,' because Homer himself had remarked – he liked men, and it was known that he drank with the younger men in the Elks' Club – that he was not a marrying man. Later we said, 'Poor Emily' behind the jalousies as they passed on Sunday afternoon in the glittering buggy, Miss Emily with her head high and Homer Barron with his hat cocked and a cigar in his teeth, reins and whip in a yellow glove.

Then some of the ladies began to say that it was a disgrace to the town and a bad example to the young people. The men did not want to interfere, but at last the ladies forced the Baptist minister – Miss Emily's people were Episcopal – to call upon her. He would never divulge what happened during that interview, but he refused to go back again. The next Sunday they again drove about the streets, and the following day the minister's wife wrote to Miss Emily's relations in Alabama.

So she had blood-kin under her roof again and we sat back to watch developments. At first nothing happened. Then we were sure that they were to be married. We learned that Miss Emily had been to the jeweller's and ordered a man's toilet set in silver, with the letters H.B. on each piece. Two days later we learned that she had bought a complete outfit of men's clothing including a night-shirt, and we said, 'They are married.' We were really glad. We were glad because the two female cousins were even more Grierson than Miss Emily had ever been.

So we were not surprised when Homer Barron – the streets had been finished some time since – was gone. We were a little disappointed that there was not a public blowing-off, but we believed that he had gone on to prepare for Miss Emily's coming, or to give her a chance to get rid of the cousins. (By that time it was a cabal, and we were all Miss Emily's allies to help circumvent the cousins.) Sure enough, after another week they departed. And, as we had expected all along, within three days Homer Barron was back in town. A neighbour saw the Negro man admit him at the kitchen door at dusk one evening.

And that was the last we saw of Homer Barron. And of Miss Emily for some time. The Negro man went in and out with the market basket, but the front door remained closed. Now and then we would see her at a window for a moment, as the men did that night when they sprinkled the lime, but for almost six months she did not appear on the streets. Then we knew that this was to be expected too; as if that quality of her father which had thwarted her woman's life so many times had been too virulent and too furious to die.

When we next saw Miss Emily, she had grown fat and her hair was turning grey. During the next few years it grew greyer and greyer until it attained an even pepper-and-salt iron-grey, when it ceased turning. Up to the day of her death at seventy-four it was still that vigorous iron-grey, like the hair of an active man.

From that time on her front door remained closed, save for a period of six or seven years, when she was about forty, during which she gave lessons in china-painting. She fitted up a studio in one of the downstairs rooms, where the daughters and grand-daughters of Colonel Sartoris's contemporaries were sent to her with the same regularity and in the same spirit that they were sent to church on Sundays with a twenty-five cent piece for the collection plate. Meanwhile her taxes had been remitted.

Then the newer generation became the backbone and the spirit of the town, and the painting pupils grew up and fell away and did not send their children to her with boxes of colour and tedious brushes and pictures cut from the ladies' magazines. The front door closed upon the last one and remained closed for good. When the town got free postal delivery, Miss Emily alone refused to let them fasten the metal numbers above her door and attach a mail-box to it. She would not listen to them.

Daily, monthly, yearly we watched the Negro grow greyer and more stooped, going in and out with the market basket. Each December we sent her a tax notice, which would be returned by the post office a week later, unclaimed. Now and then we would see her in one of the downstairs windows — she had evidently shut up the top floor of the house — like the carven torso of an idol in a niche, looking or not looking at us, we could never tell which. Thus she passed from generation to generation — dear, inescapable, impervious, tranquil, and perverse.

And so she died. Fell ill in the house filled with dust and shadows, with only a doddering Negro man to wait on her. We did not even know she was sick; we had long since given up trying to get any information from the Negro. He talked to no one, probably not even to her, for his voice had grown harsh and rusty, as if from disuse.

She died in one of the downstairs rooms, in a heavy walnut bed with a curtain, her grey head propped on a pillow yellow and mouldy with age and lack of sunlight.

V

The Negro met the first of the ladies at the front door and let them in, with their hushed, sibilant voices, and their quick curious glances, and then he disappeared. He walked right through the house and out the back and was not seen again.

The two female cousins came at once. They held the funeral on the second day, with the town coming to look at Miss Emily beneath a mass of bough flowers, with the crayon face of her father musing profoundly above the bier and the ladies sibilant and macabre; and the very old men – some in their brushed Confederate uniforms – on the porch and the lawn, talking of Miss Emily as if she had been a contemporary of theirs, believing that they had danced with her and courted her perhaps, confusing time with its mathematical progression, as the old do, to whom all the past is not a diminishing road but, instead, a huge meadow which no winter ever quite touches, divided from them now by the narrow bottle-neck of the most recent decade of the years.

Already we knew that there was one room in that region above stairs which no one had seen in forty years, and which would have to be forced. They waited until Miss Emily was decently in the ground before they opened it.

The violence of breaking down the door seemed to fill this room with pervading dust. A thin, acrid pall as of the tomb seemed to lie everywhere upon this room decked and furnished as for a bridal: upon the valance curtains of faded rose colour, upon the rose-shaded lights, upon the dressing-table, upon the delicate array of crystal and the man's toilet things backed with tarnished silver, silver so tarnished that the monogram was obscured. Among them lay a collar and tie, as if they had just been removed, which, lifted, left upon the surface a pale crescent in the dust. Upon a chair hung the suit, carefully folded; beneath it the two mute shoes and the discarded socks.

The man himself lay in the bed.

For a long while we just stood there, looking down at the profound and fleshless grin. The body had apparently once lain in the attitude of an embrace, but now the long sleep that outlasts love, that conquers even the grimace of love, had cuckolded him. What was left of him, rotted beneath what was left of the night-shirt, had become inextricable from the bed in which he lay; and upon him and upon the pillow beside him lay that even coating of the patient and biding dust.

Then we noticed that in the second pillow was the indentation of a head. One of us lifted something from it, and leaning forward, that faint and invisible dust dry and acrid in the nostrils, we saw a long strand of iron-grey hair.

The Man Who Didn't Ask Why

C. S. Forester

It was inevitable that Carpmael should ask those questions eventually. He could not restrain himself in the end from making use of his peculiar gift to seek the answers.

He had looked into the future a hundred times, always with satisfactory results.

Even his earlier excursions, timid and unskilful, had brought enormous financial profit, which was not surprising, seeing that they had revealed to him stock exchange prices and racing results a week ahead.

Now he was rich, he was successful, he was famous – or notorious – as the most successful gambler of the century, and he was happily married.

In fact, by practically any standard, and most certainly by his own, he was a very happy man.

He cannot be blamed for wanting to know how long his happiness would endure. While he was resisting the temptation to find out he did at least argue with himself regarding the desirability of knowing the time, the place and the manner of his dying.

The knowledge might not help his happiness, but on the other hand once his curiosity had been roused he could not be happy until he had gratified it. He had to know.

He made his preparations. He did those things which he believed to be black magic but which the unbeliever might consider to be a convenient ritual to induce self-hypnosis.

He made the great effort of will which carried him into the billowing grey clouds, the further effort which opened a peep-hole in them for him, and the further effort still which widened the peep-hole.

He was looking into a hospital room – nothing surprising about that; there was even reassurance to be found in knowing he would die in a hospital bed.

There was a nurse beside the bed, and as the peep-hole widened he could see that she was talking to Viola, his wife.

It was not very distinct, as yet. He had to crane round the peep-hole to see that lying on the bed was a Thing. That Thing was himself, and he looked anxiously at it, to find the answers to his questions.

The sprouting beard on the unshaven cheeks was black; the expressionless face was unlined, the hair – several inches long – was thick and dark and curly still. But the Thing was a Thing. It was not human.

He could see that it was blind. He could see that this slobbering Thing was completely and utterly helpless, horrible to look at with all the muscles of the face useless.

He made the effort to listen to what was being said – it was harder, in these excursions, to hear than to see.

'*I can't help but say that it's a merciful release,*' said Viola.

'He is feeling nothing in any case,' said the nurse. Her fingers were on the Thing's pulse.

'*Do you think he has known anything at all?*' asked Viola.

'I don't think so,' said the nurse. 'With complete paralysis like this it is hard to say, cut from all communication, but he cannot know much, blind and helpless, poor fellow.'

It was important that Carpmael should discover the date. He strained to find out.

He realized that Viola was wearing a coat and skirt that he knew well. That and the hair of The Thing told him that it could not be far off in the future.

Then he thought of the notes above the bed. They would be dated; they were a daily record. He strained and strained to get a glimpse of them.

One final convulsive effort revealed them to him. Just for a second they were before his eyes, just long enough to read the date.

The effort broke the spell – terminated the self-hypnosis, and he was back in his chair with the sweat running down him in streams, and in his mind the knowledge that he had only a year to live – 51 weeks to be exact, he worked out, as he checked on today's date.

He had 51 weeks to live, and he was going to die blind and paralysed, a dreadful, horrible Thing. And it would take many – most – of those 51 weeks for that Thing to die.

He had heard that paralysis cases died in the end of exhaustion resulting from bedsores.

And this would be in 51 weeks' time. If he were going to forestall it he did not have much time to spare. He could not doubt the accuracy of what he had seen.

He had only to look around him, at all the evidence of wealth and success, to know that he had never been wrong, that his gift had never failed him. He could be quite sure of it.

If he were going to forestall his fate he must act immediately, before the paralysis came to prevent him. The motives of suicide, like those of murder, are usually inadequate in the estimation of the onlooker.

He got out his pistol; it was only a .22 but it would do his business for him. He saw that it was loaded. He looked once more round at the evidence of wealth and success. Then he pushed the muzzle up under his chin and pulled the trigger. He went out into darkness.

He came into darkness again, not remembering. The darkness was intense, darker than any darkness he had ever known.

He tried to see – he could not even be sure if his eyes were open or not. He tried again to look through the darkness. He tried to raise his hand to his eyes, and his hand would not move.

Then he realized that he was blind and paralysed, cut off from all communication, and he still had 51 weeks to live.

It was perhaps typical that Carpmael had sought answers to the questions when and where and how. He had not asked why.

Jane

Jane Gaskell

Actually, at the time, I think they were far more interested in Jane's birth than in mine. We were born on the same day, see, me being a few hours the elder.

They must have taken some notice of me, Mum anyway, seeing I was their baby and (as far as I know, like) them not being Jane's real parents. After that, though, they left me to get on with my slow, steady, dribbling little progressions for the first months, for the first years – while they looked after Jane.

They felt their superior interest in Jane was further justified when Jane proved to be absolutely normal and I did not. When my fits became frequent they moved me from my attic bedroom into the Big Blue Room, where I could stifle my screams and sobbing in the pillow without disturbing the household.

It was much later though, that I first became afraid of Jane.

I don't know why they allowed Jane to be in my room at all, because it was late summer, late twilight and it was chilly, Jane should have been warm in bed. They allowed me to put myself to bed because I had just recovered from a fit, and they were feared to touch me. My eyes were all red rimmed, and my heart was not beating quite normal being as I had worn myself out.

Not liking ever to go to bed, I was half curled into the big wicker chair with the ashtray set into the arm. Jane was on the bed opposite me, her high little head on its funny neck bent sideways in a childlike stare.

We were both six years old, but Jane had progressed far quicker than I, except maybe in brain. Both our brains were weak, but Jane was far stronger in body. As yet we had never quarrelled, as I felt instinctively that I was the intruder in the house where Jane was the little mistress. This is also how my parents looked on the matter.

In the almost non-existent light I looked across to where Jane was regarding me. Suddenly I was horrified at the cold, merciless eyes that

glowed like tiny black, or maybe silver, beads in the dark. I was terrified
to be alone with her, for the first time in my life, and my mouth was harsh
and sticky and my tongue swollen between my teeth. Those tiny,
reptilian eyes, glossed over with some intangible glassy screen, never
blinked – never moved. Jane's head was poised menacingly – protruding
unnaturally from the great coils of her body all around. I was hypnotized and if her mind had been capable of giving me my orders, I would
say that Jane's little vicious head, backed up by those muscle-bound
coils, was like a young teddy boy of the '50s, secure in his knowledge
of the gang surrounding him.

Jane did not leave me that night so I stayed in the wicker chair, my
eyes wide in anticipation and horror, never sleeping, but of course Jane
did not attack me. Jane would never attack me, I knew that, but I was
still terrified of her in the dark.

During the day, when I was allowed out if they were certain I was
quite sane, I did not mind Jane. In the big back garden, among all the
tall nettles and big shrubbery leaves, I was never alarmed to see Jane's
evil little head peeping out – but we did not play together. When they
called Jane in for her dinner, I would scurry after, and then I could sit
at the kitchen table and swing my legs across the big stone tiles and after
Jane was served in the corner with her live mouse on regular order from
the pet shop, and while she constricted herself around it and engulfed
it with her jaws and then inched herself along the crushed pulp, I could
stir my pudding with a big wooden spoon and make mountains and
valleys in my rice.

In the winter there would be a fire in the enormous kitchen fireplace
but Jane would usually curl in front of this and leave me only a little
space to curl beside her. What used to amaze me was how Jane could
stay curled for hours upon hours, expecially after her fortnightly feed,
and she never stretched, except her head. When I had the fire to myself
I would stretch right out and purr like a cat and pull my jumper over
my head so as my face would not be burned red. My parents took no
notice of my behaviour, as other parents would have done, for they
expected me to be quite abnormal, not only during one of my fits, but
all the time. If I had preferred pretending to be a reptile instead of a
kitten, I think they might have grown to be fond of me.

I notice that thinking back, I call them Mum and Dad.

But then I never addressed them and always referred to them as the
mother and the father. It was a kind of title. I was well trained by them.
In spite of our mutual lack of affection, I regarded them with respect,
and being ashamed of my fits, I would retire hurriedly to my Big Room
as soon as I felt one coming on.

It is a funny feeling to suddenly know you are going to have a short
attack of violent insanity.

First, my hair would prickle all over my scalp, then my heart would beat wildly in both my ears, my fingers would be taut, and suddenly I would wish to be very sick. My head reeling and my stomach upheaving strangely I would gallop madly up the stairs, crash headlong into my big dark room and roll myself over on to the bed. Then I would remember no more until the next morning when I would awake calm, like from a long sleep, to find myself so stiff, my eyes red and sore, my pillow damp and rumpled and stained, the furniture disarranged, the light wicker chairs perhaps tipped over. My creased clothes were usually around my neck. I never dared to wear jewellery in case it strangled or pierced me. When I was very young my mother would come in much later and tidy up. After, though, I was left to do that myself. Then I would pull the curtains and look out. If it was sunny I would be happy again and call to my parents to unlock the big door and let me out to play. If it was grey I would drift into a dream and not move for hours, indeed until I was quite weak from hunger. There was never a fire in my room and the fireplace was large and draughty and very cold even in the summer.

My parents were cousins.

They always lived in West Kensington and I cannot tell how they came to have this love for snakes. But in other ways they were both quite normal.

I believe they were both very tall and rather thin – even allowing for the fact I was always a small child, they seemed very *high* people. Mother's hair all pulled back from her face. It was tied with a long blue ribbon into a very long, skimpy, twisted sort of ponytail. Dad had ever such thick glasses, and very, very wide trouser legs with such thin ankles coming out of them.

It took them a long time to catch on that West Ken. wasn't at all such a good-class place as it used to be; but still we never rented most of our big house out, like the people on either side did. We never got any magazines, only newsletters from Uncle Pecilyn in Brazil, who had given Jane to us. Jane had not been born out of an egg, which had worried Mother and Father at first, until they found a book and read all about boa-constrictors.

I first learned the facts of life from Jeremy.

He was a tenant next door, and was ten years old when he first managed to climb over the high garden wall.

It was easy to climb down on my side seeing as of all the creepers and convolvulus.

We and Jane used to sit down the bottom of our garden and discuss life in general. Jeremy was two years older than me, and very different. He was highly intelligent and told me all about streets and buses and people and he took me quite in hand and brought me up to date. He brought me magazines and books and I read them to him as I was a much better reader.

My governess was called Miss Tock. She was fat and kind but she and my parents did not get on. I think she would argue with them about not letting me go out, and always locking me in the garden with Jane when they went out.

Jeremy said I should go to school.

Jeremy never met my parents. They found out first about him when I started talking different. They could not imagine where I had picked up such 'slovenly interpretation of the English language'. Then my mother died.

It was funny, her beloved Jane never blinked an eyelid but I cried buckets and it brought on an early fit. Father started beating me then, and I hardly had anything to eat except what I stole from the kitchen and what Miss Tock and Jeremy brought me.

Up until now, when actually I was eleven years old, I had always worn plain blue or pink dresses and a navy or red jumper, brown sandals and white or grey ankle socks. For cold weather I had a red felt jacket. I never wore my long wincey nightdress.

Then Miss Tock, in secret, one summer, the summer when I was eleven, made me a beautiful green and blue striped dress with a stiff built-in petticoat. And a beautiful straight green cardigan. She also bought me a pair of black casual shoes.

Do you know – Father never even noticed. For my birthday Jane had a special dinner, a squeaking little white rat, and Father gave me a book on butterflies. Actually I wasn't interested in butterflies and had hardly ever seen one as Jane ate them all.

About this time Jeremy began to change.

He found it increasingly difficult to get over the wall to me because his jeans were so tight and he was even more hampered by the pointed toes of his shoes which were amazingly longer than his foot. He said it was fashion. His light brown hair began to grow a different way, very long and curly at the back, very long and curly at the front, and, indeed, very long and curly at the sides. He wore red or black shirts open at the neck, with the collars up, and the sleeves rolled to above his elbows. The type of book he brought me also began to change. And, funnily enough, after all this time, he got back to talking about the facts of life. He said I was pretty. After that every night I would gaze at my face in the mirror. And dream.

I saw less and less of my father, and rather less of Jane, and a lot more of Jeremy, and that was how I wanted it.

And one day Jeremy – Jemmy I always called him – said to be all ready tomorrow for him to take me out.

'Out?'

'Over the garden wall. Your Dad won't know. Tock will pretend not to. I'll take you down the club. I'll teach you to jive.'

'Jive?'

'It's wicked,' Jemmy said, 'the way they keep you bricked up.'

Shyly I did not remind him that, as I knew and accepted the fact, people like me just weren't let out amongst Real people. I felt light-headed and delirious just thinking about tomorrow evening. It would be only the fifth time I had really left my house. Father wouldn't know? I was sure Jane would tell him and he would beat me again.

I sat breathlessly facing Jemmy amongst the nettles.

I thought, I'll wash my hair tomorrow, and brush and brush it. My hair, which was very fair and long, I always left loose since I did not want to remind myself of my mother with her long hair tied back. I looked up into Jeremy's eyes.

He smiled down at me. Then he slipped off the St Christopher that hung round his neck, and put it over my head so it hung at my throat. Immediately my fingers went up to grasp it in delight. Then suddenly I remembered – I could not wear anything round my neck lest it strangle me when I had a fit.

I muttered, 'Oh no,' and tried to take it off, but Jemmy stopped me, and taking my hand in his, kissed it very gently. From a tree Jane watched us without blinking or turning away.

'It's an appointment,' he said, 'tomorrow at this same time.'

The setting sun sent long rays against the convolvulus as he vaulted over the high crumbling wall.

The next day as I went to get the stool to stand on to reach up to the bathroom cupboard for the shampoo, Miss Tock with shining eyes came all beaming with the surprise she was giving me, to tell me the taxi was here to take me away. She led me to the hall where she'd packed my case all waiting ready.

She had nagged and cajoled Father till he agreed to let me go to school. She had meant it for the best. But sudden sobs burned up into my throat as I looked round at the familiar safe things, Jane coiled shining coil on coil in the empty fireplace, the long heavy curtains pulled back and outside a weak sun trying to brighten the bleak picture of West Kensington with all her trees bare and her streets empty. 'But Jeremy,' I cried. 'There'll be *lots* of little friends for you at school, it's just what you've always needed, not just one Jeremy,' bustled Miss Tock and bundled me into the taxi.

The taxi rattled off and I thought desolate thoughts of Jeremy turning up this evening in his new suit over the wall and only Jane hanging shining in the tree in the dying light of the sun.

For two years I was miserable.

I learnt nothing except how to be miserable. The girls would torment
me and sometimes they would steal my letters before I could read them.
From her new job Miss Tock wrote, telling nothing, asking much.
Father never wrote. Jeremy wrote about twice a month usually – though
often less for I believe it took him about a week to write his badly-spelled
notes.

I wrote back every time.

It was a big school: so I did not fit in well. Crowds were so unnatural
to me.

'Fit in' is not a phrase I like to use. My fits were now less violent and
often I remained conscious through them, being just aware of a disarming melancholy when all I could do was to cry. I screamed rarely
and mostly stayed still. Ever since I had worn Jemmy's St Christopher
I had been so afraid of choking myself that by strength of will I kept
my fits in a manageable state. But my father had not liked to think of
me as even remotely normal and the school he'd sent me to was for
unbalanced children.

I was away two years. I wrote to Father when I was coming home
and of course I wrote to Jeremy too.

He had hardly written at all for some months now. But I was so
miserable that nothing could make me more so. Yet as soon as the thrill
of returning to Jemmy – and maybe that date so long postponed – was
on me, the fact of Jeremy's scanty writing began to trouble me.

It was late autumn.

Once again the West Kensington trees were bare.

The sky was pale yellow, mist was at the end of each side street, and
the wind was harsh, noisy and bitter. I travelled home, huddled cold
in the back of a taxi, my small case under my knees. My homecoming
was not at all cosy – I could not recognize even the streets very near my
house as I had so rarely seen them anyway.

The old house was as ugly as ever – it was Jeremy's house I gazed at
hardest. The creepers over our old drum were thicker than I could
have believed. The wind whipped my skirt hard around my legs as I
paid the taxi-driver. Matron had given me the fare before I left – the
last of the £2 pocket money Father had given me those two years before.

I entered the house hesitatingly, my case suddenly heavy in my hand,
my fingers sticking together, and my heart beat so loud in the silent hall.

If I run to Father, I thought, If I run to him, and even perhaps steel
myself to throw my arms around him, will it start our new relationship
off on a new good footing? Has he perhaps been almost lonely here with
just his encyclopaedia and Jane, affectionate though she sometimes is to
him when on a firelit evening she loops around his neck and shoulders?

The flights of creaking stairs were dark. There was no bulb in the light
socket.

Grabbing my case, I slipped quietly into the living room. It was empty. Softly, I called my father, then again – there was no answer. I searched the ground floor – it was empty. The house was cold and unlived-in. Then I noticed Father's pipe in the old bakelite ashtray – it was half-filled, but cold and unlit. I went upstairs. I went into every room – searching carefully. Then I went up to the top floor and searched the bedrooms – there was no one. As I entered my own bedroom a cold draught ruffled my hair. One of the long windows was part-open. Father would never go out and leave the windows open. The long, thick blue curtains swung threateningly in the wind. The bed was unmade – even after all these years. I disliked the room and left quickly.

I could not find Father. I wandered half-frightened along the passage. As I came to the end I noticed the little old staircase up to the attic that had once, in my baby days, been my bedroom. Slowly, creakingly, steadily I went upwards, my suitcase still held fast in one hand. The draught followed me up. Here the pale green wallpaper was damp and discoloured, the wooden steps chipping, cackling.

Up – up to the top – there was the little door before me, very slightly open. I dared move no farther. Now terrified – I could not have opened that door – my hand would not have stretched forward – but the draught, the tiny, sneaking cold little draught gave a sudden shove and the door squeaked open – so slowly.

There, sitting on the floor, was Jane.

Her massive brown coils were glutted, her tiny black eyes red-shot and maddened. Her tongue flicked in-out, in-out like a knife. She was still bloated with the last meal she had digested. A more intoxicating treat than the usual rodent. In the two years that had gone by, it had been Jane's reason, not mine after all, that had foundered. I stood there, hypnotized, there on the landing. Her evil little eyes stared, glazed, at me. I stepped, step by step, forward, into the room. I stood submissively in front of Jane as she rose before me, her nasal little face jutting out at me, and back, out again and back to a horrible rhythm – then her tongue joined in this ghastly game – the peak of her great tail twitched jerkily. Through the sloping window of the little box-room the last light of the sun trembled on our family pet. Unable to move, my eyes held by hers, I saw her slither forward until she was uncoiled – her head up as high as mine. Slowly then she swung her head back and all her horrible body was taut. And then – I broke the spell and as with all her strength Jane struck at me I feebly lifted my case before my face.

It was Jane's strength, not mine, that broke her skull.

As I watched, with a vile fascination, her tiny grey and bloody twisted mass of brain slip cold down my arm and drip on to Father's jacket at my feet – my nerves were jolted awake again. Looking up, I saw jerking unevenly towards me – the little eyes twisted sideways in that dead head

– I saw tense and muscular all the length of her massive body jerk up to come swinging over her head at me. She was thrown violently into the air by her great post-death lunge and as all the strength slithered down upon me I stumbled backwards and fell straight down the stairs.

Injured, in pain, my feet doubled back under me – I lay, my head bleeding, my arm broken I knew – on the landing. Jane, still tortured and not able to die in peace, lashed about until my tiny cot was in splinters, most of which flew wildly down the stairs after me. But in my own mad tumble down all those stairs I'd made even more noise. And so it was, unmercifully not even unconscious, that Jeremy found me.

The Quiet Man

Terry Gisbourne

Gibbet Terrace, Chingford, was never quite the same after that nasty business at No. 37. What veneer of suburban respectability it once had was now pitted and stained by the corrosive events which made the headlines in January 1936.

The *Daily Pictorial*, having voiced the nation's grief at the death of King George V, leapt back with characteristic vigour the next day, proclaiming 'Bloodbath in Gibbet Terrace – Family Victims of "Ritual Slaughter".' Later the case became known generally as 'The Animal Atrocities'. Some residents, anxious to preserve their lily-white reputations, left for cosier, more decent regions of Chingford. House values slumped. For many years those who stayed had to endure the intrusions of bizarre sightseers. But even today, some of the elderly living nearby can't help feeling a vestige of sympathy for their one-time neighbour at No. 35 who was hanged for the killings – quiet and dapper Jack Prince.

'Oh, Jack, I'm glad you're home.'

Violet Prince motioned her husband to come into the kitchen. Her sturdy build and ruddy complexion was proof that much of her life had been spent in the country. That evening, however, her friendly face had a brighter hue than usual.

'It's them next door again, Jack,' she whispered. 'I've been at my wits' end all afternoon. They haven't given me a minute's peace, banging on the walls and shouting. I'm afraid to think what they'll do next.'

Jack paused for an excuse but it found it hard to hide his agitation.

'Perhaps they're moving some furniture about, having a spring clean. You know what some people are like, always shifting things around. Never satisfied with things the way they are.'

Violet gave him a knowing look.

'Let's not kid ourselves, love. We've been here for two months now and they've made trouble right from the start.'

Jack had never been one to make a scene. Like most retiring types he preferred the easy way out. But he had to admit that the Witlows were beginning to get on his nerves.

Jack Prince was a friendly, neat-looking northerner. Tidiness showed in his work and in the way he dressed. A creature of clean living but dominated by habit, some might say. He was tall and fairly well built, with brown eyes and short black hair parted so well you could see the white of his scalp. Jack was thirty-six and in eight years of marriage he and Violet had struggled to save enough to move south. They came from West Tadcaster, near Leeds, where Jack had kept a shop. The chance of buying bigger premises brought them to Chingford where Jack now had his shop in nearby Buchanan Street. Both were determined to get the business on its feet within a year. They planned to build a good customer relationship, to go through the books every night, and for Violet to help Jack out behind the counter four days a week. In the last few weeks their efforts were being rewarded. Trade was becoming more regular and customers quickly got to like their cheerful ways.

But Jack wished he could see some improvement in matters at home. The Witlows, it seemed, were bent on making their life a misery. At first the Princes had simply put the noise down to harmless high spirits. After two weeks, however, they were forced to the conclusion that the problem was more than just rowdy neighbours. Every evening when the Princes settled down in the lounge to some paperwork, the interruptions would start. A chorus of bangings and scrapings invariably gave way to what at first seemed like a row between the Witlows, only the astonished Princes learned later that the muffled verbal abuse was being directed at them. Then the bangings, like a poker being thrown against a grate, would resume with a new intensity.

A month later the trouble increased. The Princes moved to other rooms to escape the noise, but this did not stop the Witlows. Somehow they would find out where the Princes were and proceed to create noise in whichever room was nearest. Faced with this impossible situation, Jack was now being forced to stay late at the shop some nights and finish his balancing there.

'What on earth can we do to reason with the bloody family?' Jack had once shouted in a rare moment of exasperation. Twice he had called next door to protest. On the first occasion he had simply got a blank 'don't know what you're talking about' response from Mrs Witlow, a squat, big-breasted woman with wide, staring eyes like a cow. She claimed her husband was out and wouldn't hear of such wild accusations, anyway. The second visit was even more negative – no one bothered to answer the door.

Despite Violet's requests, Jack flatly refused to call the police.

'Look at it this way, love,' he stressed. 'We've just got to consider the

business. It won't be worth a ha'p'orth to us if we get tangled up in a
court case. It'd be just like hanging dirty washing out in public. No, Vi,
we've got to make the best of it for the time being, until the business is
more on its feet, like. Then, who knows, we might be able to buy another
house, a better place.'

'But for heaven's sake, Jack, aren't we going to do anything? We can't
go on being treated like this. It'll get worse, I know it will.'

He tried reassuring her.

'There's no point getting worked up, Vi. We've got to stay calm no
matter what. If it'll make you feel any better, I've decided to go round
again tonight and thrash this thing out once and for all. I'll make them
see sense even if I have to ... Well, they're going to get a piece of my
mind, anyway.'

But Jack didn't dare tell her what he really thought. That talk and
reason wouldn't stand a chance in hell. That the Witlows were a bunch
of nutters who had it in for them. But why? Jack had thought long and
hard about this and couldn't come up with any sane explanation. Mrs
Witlow was the only member of the family he had seen, and that made
it even more incredible. From talking to customers, he learned there
were three in the family altogether – Mr and Mrs Witlow and a grown-
up daughter named Audrey. Old man Witlow was a storeman at a local
factory, while the daughter stayed at home all day with her mother. Jack
had only seen Mrs Witlow to talk to just that once, but two or three times
he had spotted her passing by his shop on the other side of the street.
Perhaps he had seen the others before without realizing it. Perhaps they
had even been to the shop. No, they wouldn't do that, he assured himself.
In any case, he'd have noticed any strange-looking person like that,
for they must look a bit insane to do what they've done, mustn't they?

What Violet couldn't appreciate was that they would have a very
difficult job proving anything against the Witlows in court. They would
deny everything, that was for sure. And any possibility of getting witnesses looked extremely remote. Jack had checked on the neighbours at
No. 39 and found they were an old couple – as deaf as posts. Everyone
he had spoken to described the Witlows as decent folk – 'good for a
laugh, boisterous but well meaning.' So calling the law was out of the
question, unless Jack was willing to risk the threat of losing the custom
they had built up. And he just wasn't prepared to sacrifice that.

Initially, it was a silent confrontation on the Witlows' doorstep. The
two of them stood there weighing each other up. Jack had this awkward
feeling that he was the pursued finally facing the pursuer. Mr Witlow
simply glared insolently as if to say, 'Right, we'll have a bit of fun with
the bugger.'

He was a burly, balding brick of a man, a little shorter than Jack but
wider. His big belly swelled out over the leather belt which held up his

soiled corduroys. Jack noted the small eyes, the pinky pigmentation of his hairless skin, and half expected Mr Witlow to let out a snort rather than say, 'Clear off'. He had one hand on the half-open door as if he was about to bang it shut in Jack's face. Jack gave a little nervous cough, but his voice was calm and possessed authority.

'Well, Mr Witlow, I don't have to tell you why I have called, do I ... ?'

Before he could finish what he had to say, Mr Witlow bawled for 'Else', his wife, to come to the door. Jack, a bit taken aback by the vehemence of the interruption, began to falter.

'I'm asking you to pack it in, stop this stupid troublemaking. It won't get you anywhere.'

By this time Else and her daughter Audrey, a long-necked girl with a prominent nose, were at the door.

Mr Witlow sucked on his teeth. The glint in his eyes was beginning to irritate Jack. 'Else, is this the bloke who troubled you that time? Came making all kinds of accusations and insinuations? This him?'

She nodded. 'Yes, that's him.'

'Well then, mister, you'd be best off making yourself scarce. If there's one thing I can't stand it's bloody busybodies making a nuisance of themselves.'

Jack butted in. 'Look here, hold on a minute. Let's get this straight. I've a damn good right to be a nuisance as you call it after what we've had to put up with from you lot. What have you got against us, tell me that? Where's the sense? If you can't see reason, at least give me an explanation.'

Too late, Jack realized that he had slipped up. He hadn't meant to get excited, but they had cunningly succeeded in baiting him. His plan had been to play it calm and cool and not get too emotional.

'Do you know what he's talking about Else, because I'm blowed if I do. I'd say he's got a screw loose.'

Else, her arms folded across her wide bosom, looked upwards mournfully and tossed her head in bovine fashion. 'Don't know what the world's coming to when it can't take care of nosey-parkers. Ought to be locked up.'

Jack gave a gasp of disgust. 'Well, that's a laugh and no mistake. Anyway, let's not beat about the bush. You've had your bit of fun. Now try to be rational and see our side of it. How would you like it if we were to play hell every night you came home. You'd want some peace and quiet the same as any other person. It's not much to ask.'

Was it Jack's imagination or did the arrogant gleam in Mr Witlow's eyes suddenly become brighter? He turned and grinned at his wife, then relaxed his hold on the door. 'Seeing how you put it that way ... what's it worth?'

Jack paused. 'I don't understand ... What do you mean by "what's it worth"?'

'What I say.' Mr Witlow proceeded to measure his words carefully. 'You're a man of means ... a man of property ... Got a shop, haven't you? Now we might, and I say might, just show a little consideration to you and your wife ... for a little consideration in return. But if you can't see your way to, how shall we say, obliging us, then we might just let it slip among the folk round here that we have to put up with terrible goings-on next door.' Mr Witlow beamed. 'How's trade, then? Not too slack I hope.'

Jack managed to look calm, but underneath he was boiling with anger. So that was their game. A blatant piece of nasty, sordid, old-fashioned blackmail. Oh yes, he got the picture all right. A bit of free stuff from the shop in return for a little peace and quiet. Not complete peace and quiet, you understand, but just a little. Jack struggled to control his wild, pent-up emotions. For two pins he would belt Witlow and tell him what to do with his foul suggestions. But no, that wouldn't be playing their game, would it? Cunning needed to be matched with cunning. He also needed time to think. So for now he would play along with the Witlows. Make them think they had him licked. A little humility was called for.

'Well yes, Mr Witlow ... I take your point. I've no doubts that I can arrange something. Say tomorrow night? I could drop something by on the way home.'

A smug smile of satisfaction settled on Mr Witlow's face. 'Now he's talking, eh, Else? I knew he'd come round to our way of thinking.'

Jack returned home nursing alien feelings of extreme unpleasantness. His right hand was shaking as he turned the key in the lock. If they thought they could do this to Jack Prince and get away with it ... Who did they take him for? A country yokel who didn't know better? A half-baked northerner out of his depth? He was sure of one thing – that Violet would never be told of the 'arrangement' with the Witlows. She at least would be spared the pain of being forced to bargain with them. Less than an hour ago he would have laughed at any mention of 'peace at a price'.

His thoughts were interrupted by Violet's voice coming from the front room 'Quick, Jack, is that you?'

He turned round and she ran into the hall.

'They're at it again, Jack, making horrible noises.'

Jack strode past her into the room and was greeted by a cacophonous assault on the eardrums. The wall by the fireplace sounded as if it was being rubbed and scored with rough sandpaper. In the corner near the writing bureau came the tap, tap of something striking cold metal. But, despite this confusion of sound, Jack's hearing was also aware of a new and even more ghastly din. The rhythm and pitch came unmistakably from human voices chanting.

'Oink, oink, oink . . . moo, moo, moo . . . quack, quack, quack . . . oink, oink, oink . . .' And so it went on. Jack turned to Violet in exasperation.

'I don't believe it . . . I just don't believe it.'

Two weeks passed and the Witlows' troublemaking continued, but to a lesser degree. Jack, true to his word, had twice called on the family with 'peace offerings' and they, surprisingly, had responded by cutting down on the noise.

They seemed content at present just to hammer away on the wall for about twenty minutes every evening. But that was followed by the new, bizarre display of animal noises. The grunts and snorts and similar farmyard impressions always lasted for exactly ten minutes, and then sweet silence would reign again.

Violet, however, lived in dread of the ritual. Whenever the Witlows started, she would retreat to the kitchen to be out of earshot. It wasn't just the noise, she told Jack, but a feeling at the back of her mind that it meant something evil.

The whole business was also having a big effect on Jack, but he would never admit to it. That was his trouble. He would simply say they were a damned nuisance, and that they'd soon get tired of it. He didn't mention the sleepless nights he was having, the 'arrangement' he'd struck with the Witlows, the dark thoughts he was entertaining. Violet had noticed that Jack wasn't his even-tempered self. He was nervy, irritable, inclined to argue on small matters which normally would have been dismissed lightly. She wasn't to know that Jack had entered the critical stage of a nervous condition. His resistance to stress had sunk to a low ebb. Bottled-up feelings were fighting for possession of his mind.

Even Jack wasn't aware of the dangerous undercurrents. The only warning appeared to be occasional bouts of headache, but these he put down to overwork. It was true he had put in more time at the shop, mainly to take his mind off the business at home. But he found it exceedingly hard to concentrate, and invariably his thoughts lingered on the knotty problem of the Witlows.

Paradoxically, Jack's nervous state was brought about by himself. He was completely unable to feel anything but absolute loathing for the family. Had he joked or even remarked about the idiot antics to one of his regular customers, the intensity of bad feeling may have subsided. But to Jack this wasn't a matter to be talked about. His mind had now told him that it was a very personal insult, something so offensive he wouldn't even discuss it properly with Violet. And so the rot within was nibbling slowly but inexorably away at brittle, taut nerves. It needed just a little more aggravation to accelerate the process.

He was walking down a narrow, winding country lane. The stillness of that hot summer's day was broken only by the sounds of bees searching for pollen in the hedgerows. There wasn't even a wisp of breeze to temper the golden warmth that bathed meadow and valley. And this is how Jack liked it. He was completely at peace with the world. Everyone, it seemed, had been lulled to sleep by the sheer tranquillity of warm, unspoilt, undisturbed open space. No one to bother you. Just left to dream of rural havens like this, far away from the confined, noisy hustle and bustle of town.

Then a noise intruded in his thoughts and he looked up. There was nothing in sight, but the sound was unmistakably that of a pig. The grunts and snorts continued at such a rate that it seemed as if the poor animal was in distress. It must be round the next corner in the lane. And the farther Jack walked, the louder the noise became. Thinking it may have injured itself, he increased his step and rounded the bend. The sight which greeted his eyes froze him to the spot. For there, standing in the middle of the lane was not only a pig but also a cow and a duck. His appearance prompted a burst of noise from all of them. To Jack it appeared that they were chanting at him, but what he couldn't believe as he stared at them was that each one looked like one of the Witlows. Elsie Witlow's face could be seen in the cow as it tossed its head in apparent contempt. There was Audrey Witlow, wings flapping wildly and feathers bristling. And who could mistake old man Witlow as he snorted and screamed on all fours? They advanced towards him and their chant became louder. Jack stumbled backwards, still not able to believe it. No amount of blinking and rubbing of eyes could remove the frightening sight.

He turned and retreated, but as he did so they came after him. He broke into a run with them in hot pursuit. The snorts, mooings and quacks were barely a yard behind. But the horror of it all was that he couldn't shake them off. No matter how fast he ran, the noises were always a few feet away and getting louder all the time. Sweat was pouring down Jack's terrified face as he gasped and panted. They were getting closer and he couldn't do a thing about it. His lungs felt as though they were about to burst. Mist was forming over his eyes. He had to give up. 'Can't go on ... can't go on ... can't go ...'

Jack lay in darkness, trying to get his breath back. Blurred shapes seemed vaguely familiar to him. He struggled to raise himself and his eyes caught sight of the dressing-table next to him. Giving a low groan he lay back on the bed. It had all been a horrible nightmare ... But had it?

Jack listened. He could still hear the noises. The chant seemed more distant yet strangely near to hand. He stared upwards. But no, it couldn't be ... the sounds were definitely coming from above ... from the loft. He heard something shuffling and then a noise like plaster being kicked on to the loft floor. That confirmed Jack's suspicions.

'The bastards ... the bloody ...'

The door of the bedroom opened and Violet switched on the light. She was holding a bottle of tablets and a glass of water. Her voice trembled.

'Are you all right, Jack? This'll make you feel better. For heaven's sake, what are we going to do?'

A little over a day later, there was a knock at the Witlows' front door. It was just after ten o'clock.

Every Monday morning, Florrie Hebditch called on Elsie Witlow for a cup of tea and a natter. It was a little custom of theirs. Mrs Witlow would pop round to Mrs Hebditch one Monday and vice versa the next Monday and so on. If one of them had to go shopping, the other would have a key to let themselves in and wait.

Mrs Hebditch pulled a face. There was no reply. This was the second time running Elsie had gone out and, besides, Florrie was dying to tell her a bit of gossip she couldn't have heard. Mr Brown, from Summerland Terrace, had gone and left his wife for a gypsy woman that very morning.

'Came right out of the blue, Elsie. Talking to Mrs Travers, I was. Then who should come storming out of No. 23 but Mr Brown with a suitcase. "I'm going," he says, "and I'm not coming back." Yelling at her from the gate. She just shouts something I wouldn't repeat and throws a couple of cups and saucers after him. Then she spots me across the street. Honestly, Elsie, if looks could have killed ...' Mrs Hebditch had the tale off pat. She had never liked Mrs Brown and her stuck-up ways anyway.

Using the key from her handbag, Mrs Hebditch fiddled with the lock and opened the front door.

Drip ...

It opened into a black-and-white tiled hall that swept past the stairs and into the kitchen.

Drip ...

Where could that woman have got to? Mrs Hebditch frowned and shut the door behind her.

Drip ...

Well, a nice cup of tea won't go amiss. Elsie will be ready for one.

Drip ...

What's that dripping noise? Must be one of the taps.

Drip ...

Mrs Hebditch turned round in the hall and her mouth sagged wide open. Red swamped her vision. The passageway was bathed in it, the walls and stairs splashed, streaked, daubed and dotted with it. She stepped forward blindly and felt her feet slipping on the stuff.

'Elsie . . .' She gave an involuntary cry.

Can't be paint . . . didn't tell me they were decorating . . . oh, my God. Mrs Hebditch began to panic and shiver. Then her eyes caught sight of red blobs dripping into the pool by the stairs. Instinctively, she raised her head slowly upwards even though something was telling her not to. She wished she hadn't.

That afternoon there were quite a few comings and goings at Chingford police station. News of the Witlow killings had shaken the local constabulary out of their lethargy and produced a burst of activity, the likes of which had never before been witnessed. A passer-by had raised the alarm after finding Mrs Hebditch in a collapsed state on the Witlows' doorstep. Chingford police, faced with a massacre, decided it was a job for Scotland Yard. And the Yard, after a cursory examination of the gruesome findings, surmised with unusual haste that it could be a ritual slaughter linked with witchcraft.

But while detectives sifted the evidence at No. 37, a major if less colourful event was taking place at the police station. Amid all the excitement, no one noticed the dapper, passive-looking man waiting at the station counter. He kept looking from one officer to another, trying to attract their attention.

'Excuse me,' he called. One of the officers turned round.

'Oh, I'm sorry, sir. Bit of a panic going on. What can I do for you?'

'My name's Jack Prince. I'd like to see someone about the business at 37, Gibbet Terrace.'

Detective-Inspector Robert Sanders sat down at the desk facing Jack Prince. He was absent-mindedly fingering a pencil. 'Now, tell me why you think you killed the Witlow family.'

The undertone of sarcasm in the officer's voice was deliberate. Damn it, he was busy. He had a meeting with the forensic boys in an hour's time, and the Commissioner was breathing down his neck for a progress report on the case that evening.

It was equally irritating to him that he couldn't unload this customer on to one of his men because they were working on more important aspects of the case. Cranks were a thorn in the thumb to Detective-Inspector Sanders, and he feared he was looking at one now.

'I'm waiting, Mr Prince,' he snapped impatiently. Jack looked up in surprise.

'What . . . ? Oh yes, I'm sorry. I have a job to concentrate just lately.' He moved restlessly in the chair. 'Well, I'd just had as much as I could stand from them. They were our neighbours, you see. Noisy lot right from the start. Driving the wife out of her mind they were. So I put paid to their little games for good.'

'And how exactly did you put paid to their little games?' said the detective, still refusing to believe the tale.

'I stayed up Sunday night and waited for them to go to bed. Vi had taken something to make her sleep. I must have waited until about three on the Monday morning, and then I decided the time had come. I'd even sharpened my knife for the job.

'I climbed over the back garden fence and got in through a kitchen window they had left open. The stairs squeaked a bit but it didn't worry me. I could still hear snoring coming from the bedrooms. I made a quick guess that the back bedroom was Audrey Witlow's because it was the smallest. So I settled for her first. I didn't mess about. I crept in and switched on the light just in time to see her turning over. I struck once, severing her jugular.'

Detective-Inspector Sanders stopped playing with the pencil. His pulse was starting to race. He leaned forward gently. 'What happened next?'

'Well, I came back out of the bedroom on to the landing. I went to open the front bedroom door. I had my hand on the handle and felt it turning. The next thing who should I come face to face with but old man Witlow standing there in his pyjamas, staring at me as if he was seeing things. I didn't have much time to play with, so his heart got my knife, all ten inches of it. Don't worry, he didn't suffer. I don't make mistakes like that.

'There was still Mrs Witlow, of course. I switched on the light and she was just getting out of bed. She screamed but it didn't last long. I cut her off in mid-stream, again slashing the jugular.' Jack sighed. 'That was it . . . I'd done it. But I wasn't finished yet.' He gave a chuckle. 'I'd brought some meat hooks and twine with me. I lashed their feet together and hung them side by side from the landing. Then I took my knife and ripped their stomachs open. Oh, it was a mess, all right.

'It's a bit of a laugh now when I think about it, but it was just what they deserved. Kind of fitting, I thought. You see they were pigs . . . animals . . . didn't know any different. They needed to be slaughtered like pigs.

'I almost forgot about the knife. You'll find it on the table in my shop . . . the butcher's in Buchanan Street.'

The Cocoon

John B. L. Goodwin

Whereas downstairs his father had a room the walls of which were studded with the trophies of his aggressive quests – heads of ibex, chamois, eland, keitloa, peccary, and ounce – upstairs Denny had pinned upon his playroom walls the fragile bodies of Swallowtails, Nymphs, Fritillaries, Meadow Browns, and Anglewings.

Although his father had manoeuvred expeditions, experienced privation, waded through jungles, climbed upon crags for his specimens, Denny had blithely gathered within the fields and gardens close to home. It was likely that his father's day as a collector was over; Denny's had just begun.

Denny was eleven and his father forty-six, and the house in which they lived was a hundred or more years old, though no one could be exact about it. Mr Peatybog, the postmaster in the shrivelled village, said as how he could recall when the circular window on the second-storey landing hadn't been there; and Mrs Bliss said she knew that at one time what was now the kitchen had been a taproom, because her father had told her about it. The heart of the house, as Denny's father put it, was very old, but people had altered it and added on and covered up. Denny's father had added the room where his heads were hung; but Denny's playroom must have been the original attic, because where the rafters of its high, abrupt ceiling were visible the nails in them were square-headed, and here and there the timbers were still held together with wooden pegs.

But the playroom, where Denny also slept, appeared to the casual glance anything but old. The floor was carpeted in blue, the curtains were yellow, and the bedspread blue and white. The wallpaper, which his mother had chosen for him before she left, was yellow willow trees on a pale-blue ground, and to an alien eye the butterflies pinned on the walls seemed part of the design. It had been a long time since Denny's father had been up in the room; and although he knew that his son's collection of Lepidoptera, as he called them, was pinned upon the walls, he did not know and therefore could not reprimand his son for the damage they had done the pretty wallpaper. Under each specimen a putty-coloured blot was spreading over the blue paper. It was the oil exuding from the drying bodies of the dead insects.

In one corner of the room was a chintz-covered chest in which lay the remains of Denny's earlier loves: battered trains and sections of track, an old transformer, batteries covered with cavernlike crystals of zinc salts, trucks, and windmills no longer recognizable as much more than haphazard, wooden arrangements of fitted blocks and sticks; books crumpled and torn with Denny's name or current dream scrawled aggressively in crayon across the print and pictures; a gyroscope; a rubber ball, its cracked paint making a mosaic of antique red and gold around its sphere; and somewhere at the bottom, weighed down with tin and lead and wood more than any corpse with earth and grass, lay a bear, a monkey, and a boy doll with a scar across one cheek where Denny had kicked it with a skate. In another corner the symbols of his present were proudly displayed. The butterfly net leaned against the wall, and close to the floor on a wooden box turned upside down stood Denny's cyanide bottle, tweezers, and pins, the last shining as dangerously bright as minute surgical instruments in their packet of black paper.

After almost a year of collecting butterflies, Denny had found that a certain equivocal quality could be added to his pursuit if he were to collect not only the butterflies but also the earlier stages of their mutations. By cramming milk bottles, shoeboxes, and whatever other receptacle the house might offer with caterpillars and pupae, he was, in the cases of those that survived, able to participate in a sort of alchemy. Intently he would squat on his haunches and gaze into the receptacles, studying the laborious transformations, the caterpillar shedding skin, the exudation that it used to hitch its shroudlike chrysalid to twigs or undersides of leaves, and then the final unpredictable attainment of the imago. It was like opening a surprise package, for as yet Denny had not learned to tell what colour, size, or shape worm would turn into a Dog's Head Sulphur, Mourning Cloak, or Tiger Swallowtail.

As late summer approached, Denny insisted that the servant girl refrain from opening the windows wide in order to air out his room. The sudden change in temperature, he said, would disturb the caterpillars and pupae. Even though the girl reported to his father that Denny's room smelled unhealthily from all the bugs and things, the man did no more than mention it to Denny in an off-hand manner, Denny grunted to show that he had heard, and did no more about it; and as his father was writing a book on his jungles and crags and beasts, he had really little concern about what went on upstairs.

So it was that an acrid smell of decaying vegetable matter resolving itself into insect flesh pervaded Denny's bright attic room, and the oily blotches on the walls beneath his specimens spread ever so slightly, discolouring the paper more and more.

In a book, *Butterflies You Ought to Know Better*, which an aunt had sent him for Christmas, Denny read that a suitable 'castle' for a caterpillar could be made by placing a lamp chimney, closed at the top, upon a flowerpot filled with earth. He prepared this enclosure, purchasing the lamp chimney from the village store with his own money. It was such an elegant contrivance and yet so magical that he decided to save it for an especially unusual specimen. It was not until a late afternoon in October that Denny found one worthy of the castle.

He was exploring a copse between two fields. Because of the stoniness of the ground, it had never been cultivated and lay like a sword between the fertility of the fields on either side. Denny had never trespassed on it before, and dared to now only because of his growing self-confidence in his power over nature. A month ago he would have shied away from the area entirely, even taking the precaution to circumvent the two fields enclosing it. But he felt a little now the way he thought God must feel when, abject within its glass and cardboard world, the life he watched took form, changed, and ceased. Protected from unpleasant touch or any unpredictable action, Denny watched the metamorphosis from worm to chrysalid to miraculously vibrant petal. It lay within his power to sever abruptly the magical chain of their evolution at any point he chose. In a little way he *was* a little like God. It was this conceit that now gave him the courage to climb over the stones of the old wall and enter the half acre of dense woodland.

The autumn sun, already low, ogled the brittle landscape like some improbable jack-o'-lantern hanging in the west. What birds were still in that country spoke in the rasping tone of the herd; the more mellifluous and prosperous had already gone south. Although the leaves on the trees displayed the incautious yellows of senility and ochres of decay, the underbrush such as cat briar and wild grapes were mostly green. Armed with his forceps and his omnipotence, Denny explored each living leaf and twig.

Brambles tore his stockings and scratched his knees, but except for vulgar tent caterpillars in the wild cherry trees, Denny's efforts were unrewarded. It was dusk when, searching among the speculatively shaped leaves of a sassafras, Denny found a specimen beyond his most arrogant expectations. At first sight, owing in part to the twilight, it looked more like some shrivelled dragon than a caterpillar. Between it and the twig a filament stretched; and this, added to the fact that when Denny touched it gingerly he could feel its puffy flesh contract the way caterpillars do, convinced them that it was no freak of nature – or if it was, it was a caterpillar freak and therefore nothing to fear. Tearing it cautiously with his tweezers from the twig, he put the monster in the Diamond Match box he always carried with him and, running breathlessly, blind to briar and brambles, Denny headed home.

It was suppertime when he got there, and his father was already at the table, his left hand turning the pages of a book while with his right hand he ladled soup into his mouth. Denny had clattered up the stairs before his father was aware of his presence.

'You're late, son,' he said in the moment between two printed sentences and two spoonfuls of soup.

'I know, Father,' Denny replied without stopping, 'But I got something.'

Another sentence and another spoonful.

'How many times have I told you to be explicit? "Something" can be anything from a captive balloon to a case of mumps.'

From the second landing Denny called down, 'It's just *something*. I don't know what it is.'

His father mumbled, and by the time he had finished a paragraph, and scooped up the last nugget of meat out of his soup, and had addressed his son with the words, 'Whatever it is it will wait until you have your supper,' Denny was peering at it through the glass of the lamp chimney.

Even in the bright electric glare it was reptilian. It was large for a caterpillar – between four and five inches long Denny guessed – and was a muddy purple colour, its underside a yellowish black. At either extremity it bore a series of three horny protuberances of a vermilion shade; they were curved sharply inward, and stiff little hairs grew from them. From its mouth there protruded a set of small grasping claws like those of a crustacean. Its skin was wrinkled like that of a tortoise, and the abdominal segments were sharply defined. The feet lacked the usual suctionlike apparatuses caterpillars have, but were scaly and shaped like tiny claws.

It was indeed worthy of its castle. It was not to be found in any of the illustrated books Denny had. He would guard it and keep it a secret, and finally, when he presented its metamorphosis into a winged thing to the world, his father's renown as the captor of extraordinary beasts would pale beside his own. The only thing he could guess at, and that because of its size, was that it was the larva of a moth rather than that of a butterfly.

He was still peering at it when the servant girl brought up a tray. 'Here,' she said, 'if you're such a busy little gentleman that you can't spare time for supper like an ordinary boy. If I had my way, you'd go hungry.' She set the tray down on the table. 'Pugh!' she added. 'The smell in this room is something awful. What have you got there now?'

And she was about to peer over Denny's shoulder.

'Get out!' he shrieked, turning on her. 'Get out!'

'I'm not so sure I will if you speak like that.'

He arose, and in his fury pushed her hulk out of the door, slamming it and locking it after her.

She started to say something on the other side, but what it was Denny never knew or cared, for his own voice screaming, 'And stay out!' sent the young girl scurrying down the stairs to his father.

It was typical of the man that he merely commiserated with the girl, agreed with her on the urgency of some sort of discipline for his son, and then, settling back to his pipe and his manuscript, dismissed the matter from his mind.

The following day Denny told the girl that henceforth she was not to enter his room, neither to make the bed nor to clean.

'We shall see about that,' she said, 'though it would be a pleasure such as I never hoped for this side of heaven were I never to enter that horrid-smelling room again.'

Again his father was approached, and this time he reluctantly called his son to him.

'Ethel tells me something about you not wanting her to go into your room,' he said, peering over his glasses.

'I'd rather she didn't, Father,' Denny replied, humble as pie. 'You see, she doesn't understand about caterpillars and cocoons and things, and she messes everything up.'

'But who will see to the making of your bed and dusting and such?'

'I will,' asserted Denny. 'There's no reason why, if I don't want anyone to go into my room, I shouldn't have to make up for it somehow, like making my own bed and clearing up.'

'Spoken like a soldier, son,' the father said. 'I know the way you feel, and if you're willing to pay the price in responsibility I see no reason why you shouldn't have your wish. But,' and he pointed a paper knife of walrus tusk at the boy, 'if it isn't kept neat and tidy we'll have to rescind the privilege, remember that.'

His father, grateful that the interview had not been as tedious as he had anticipated, told his son he could go. From then on Denny always kept the key to his room in his pocket.

Because caterpillars cease to eat prior to their chrysalis stage and Denny's caterpillar refused to eat whatever assortment of leaves he tried to tempt it with, Denny knew that it had definitely been preparing its cocoon when he had plucked it from the sassafras branch. It was very restless, almost convulsive now, and within the lamp chimney it humped itself aimlessly from twig to twig, its scaly little claws searching for something to settle upon. After a day of such meanderings the caterpillar

settled upon a particular crotch of the twig and commenced to spin its
cocoon. By the end of twenty-four hours the silken alembic was
complete.

Though there was nothing for Denny to observe, he still squatted for
hours on end staring at the cocoon that hung like some parasitic growth
from the sassafras twig. His concentration upon the shape was so great
as he sat hunched over it that his eyes seemed to tear the silken shroud
apart, and to be intimately exploring the secret that was taking place
within.

Now Denny spent less and less of the days out in the open searching
for the more common types of chrysalid with which he was acquainted.
Such were for him as garnets would be to a connoisseur of emeralds. His
lean, tanned face became puffy, and the palms of his hands were pale
and moist.

The winter months dragged on, and Denny was as listlessly impatient
as what was inside the cocoon. His room was cold and airless, for a
constant low temperature must be kept if the cocoon was to lie dormant
until spring. His bed was seldom made, and the floor was thick with dust
and mud. Once a week the girl left the broom and dustpan along with
the clean sheets outside his door, but Denny took only the sheets into
his room, where they would collect into a stack on the floor for weeks
at a time. His father took no notice of his condition other than to write
in a postscript to what was otherwise a legal and splenetic letter to his
wife that their son looked peaked, and upon receiving an apprehensive
reply he casually asked Denny if he was feeling all right. The boy's
affirmative though noncommittal answer seemed to satisfy him and,
dropping a card to his wife to the effect that their son professed to be
in sound health, he considered himself released from any further
responsibility.

When April was about gone, Denny moved his treasure close to the
window, where the sun would induce the dormant thing within it into
life. In a few days Denny was sure that it was struggling for release, for
the cocoon seemed to dance up and down idiotically upon its thread.
All that night he kept vigil, his red and swollen eyes focused on the
cocoon as upon some hypnotic object. His father ate breakfast alone,
and by nine o'clock showed enough concern to send the servant girl up
to see if everything was all right. She hurried back to report that his son
was at least still alive enough to be rude to her. The father mumbled
something in reply about the boy's mother having shirked her respon-
sibilities. The girl said that if it pleased him, she would like to give notice.
She was very willing to enumerate the reasons why, but the man
dismissed her casually with the request that she stay until she found
someone to take her place.

At ten, Denny was positive that the cocoon was about to break; by ten thirty there was no longer any doubt in his mind. Somewhat before eleven the eclosion took place. There was a convulsive movement inside, and the cocoon opened at the top with the faint rustle of silk. The feathery antennae and the two forelegs issued forth, the legs clutching the cocoon in order to hoist the body through the narrow aperture. The furry and distended abdomen, upon which were hinged the crumpled wings, was drawn out with effort. Immediately the creature commenced awkwardly to climb the twig from which the cocoon was suspended. Denny watched the procedure in a trance. Having gained the tip of the branch and unable to proceed further, the insect rested, its wings hanging moist and heavy from its bloated body. The abdomen, with each pulsation, shrank visibly; and gradually, very gradually, the antennae unfurled and the wings expanded with the juices pumped into them from the body.

Within an hour the metamorphosis of many months was complete. The beast, its wings still slightly damp though fully spread, fluttered gently before the eyes of the boy. Though escaped from its cocoon, it lay imprisoned still behind the glass.

Denny's pallor was suddenly flushed. He grasped the lamp chimney, as if he would hold the insect to him. This was his miracle, his alone. He watched with a possessive awe as the creature flexed its wings, although it was still too weak to attempt flight. Surely this specimen before him was unique. The wings were easily ten inches across, and their colour was so subtly gradated that it was impossible to say where black turned to purple and purple to green and green back into black. The only definite delineations were a crablike simulacrum centred on each hind wing and upon each fore wing, the imitation of an open mouth with teeth bared. Both the crabs and the mouths were chalked in white and vermilion.

By noon Denny was hungry, yet so overcome with nervous exhaustion that he almost decided to forego the midday meal. Aware, however, that an absence from two meals running would surely precipitate an intrusion by his father with the servant girl as proxy, he reluctantly left his room and went downstairs to face his father over luncheon.

Despite his complaisance, the father was immediately aware of the transformation in his son.

'Spring seems to have put a new life into the lad,' he said, turning over the page of a book. 'You're like your mother in that respect – and in that respect only, thank heaven. She never did do well in cold weather.'

It was the first time he had mentioned the mother to the son since he had been forced to explain her departure obliquely some five years before. The boy was shocked. But as the opportunity had arisen, he hastily decided to follow up the mention of his mother. It was unseemly that he should disclose any sentiment, so he hesitated and calculated before putting his question. 'Why doesn't she write or send me presents?' he asked.

His father's pause made him almost unbearably aware of the man's chagrin in having opened the subject. He didn't look up at the boy as he answered, 'Because legally she is not allowed to.'

The remainder of the meal was passed in silent and mutual embarrassment.

Denny returned to his room as soon as he could respectfully quit the table; and while unlocking the door, for an awful moment the possibility that the moth might have escaped, might never really have been there, scorched Denny's mind. But it was there, almost as he had left it – only now it had changed its position, the spread of its wings being nearly horizontal, and in this position Denny realized that the lamp chimney was too narrow to allow it free movement.

There was no receptacle in the room any larger, and in Denny's mind there paraded the various jars, the vases, and other vessels in the house that had from time to time in the past served as enclosures for his specimens. None of them was large enough. Without sufficient room, the moth, as soon as it attempted flight, would in no time at all damage its wings. In a kind of frenzy, Denny racked his brains for the memory of some container that would satisfy his need. Like a ferret his thoughts suddenly pounced on what had eluded them. In his father's room a huge crystal tobacco jar, with a lid of repoussé silver, stood on an ebony taboret beneath the smirking head of a tiger.

There was no time to lose, for within five hours after emerging from the cocoon a moth will try its wings in flight. Breathlessly, Denny bounded down the stairs, and for a moment only hesitated before he knocked upon his father's door.

'Yes?' his father asked querulously, and Denny turned the knob and walked in.

'Father——' he began, but he had not as yet caught his breath.

'Speak up, boy, and stop shaking. Why, even confronted by a rogue elephant I never shook so.'

'I want to b-b-borrow something,' the boy managed to stammer.

'Be more explicit! Be more explicit! What do you want? A ticket to Fall River? A hundred-dollar bill? A dose of ipecac? The last would seem the most logical, to judge from your looks.'

Hating his father as he had never hated him before, the boy spoke up. 'I want to borrow your tobacco jar.'

'Which one?' the father parried. 'The elephant foot the President gave me? The Benares brass? The Dutch pottery one? The music box?'

The boy could bear this bantering no longer. 'I want that one.' And he pointed directly where it stood, half full of tobacco.

'What for?' his father asked.

The boy's bravura was suddenly extinguished.

'Speak up. If you make an extraordinary request, you must be ready to back it up with a motive.'

'I want it for a specimen.'

'What's wrong with all the containers you have already appropriated from the kitchen, pantry and parlour?'

Denny would not say they were not big enough. It might arouse sufficient interest within his father so that he would insist on seeing for himself what this monster was. Denny had a vision of his father grabbing the moth and hastening to impale it upon the study wall, adding it to his other conquests.

'They won't do,' Denny said.

'Why won't they do?'

'They just won't.'

'Be explicit!' his father thundered at him.

'I want to put some stuff in it that won't fit in the others.'

'You will stand where you are without moving until you can tell me what do you mean by "stuff".' His father laid down his glasses and settled back in his chair to underscore the fact that he was prepared to wait all day if need be.

'Chrysalids and dirt and sticks and food for them,' the boy mumbled.

The man stared at Denny as if he were an animal he had at bay.

'You intend to put *that* filth into *that* jar?'

Denny made no answer. His father continued.

'Are you by any chance aware that that jar was a gift from the Maharajah of Udaipur? Have you any faintest conception of its intrinsic value aside from the sentimental one? And can you see from where you stand that, beside any other objections I might have, the jar is being employed for what it was intended for? And if for one moment you think I am going to remove my best tobacco from my best jar so that you can use it for a worm bowl, you are, my lad, very much mistaken.'

The man waited for the effect of his speech and then added, 'Go and ask Ethel for a crock.'

It was useless for Denny to attempt to explain that he wouldn't be able to see through a crock. Without a word he turned and walked out of the room, leaving the door open behind him.

His father called him back, but he paid no mind. As he reached the second landing, Denny heard the door slam downstairs.

A half hour had been wasted and, as he had been sure it would, the moth, having gained control over itself, was in the first struggles of flight.

There was only one thing to do. Denny went to the corner where he kept his equipment. Returning, he lifted the lid from the lamp chimney, and reaching inside with his forceps, he clenched the moth with a certain brutality, though he took pains to avoid injury to its wings. Lifting it out, the beauty of so few hours, Denny once again felt his omnipotence. Without hesitation he plunged the moth into the cyanide jar and screwed down the lid.

The wings beat frantically with the effort that should have carried the moth on its first flight through the spring air. Breathless, Denny watched for fear the wings would be injured. The dusty abdomen throbbed faster and faster, the antennae twitched from side to side; with a spasm the abdomen formed a curve to meet the thorax. The eyes, still bearing the unenlightened glaze of birth, turned suddenly into the unknowing glaze of death. But in the moment that they turned Denny thought he saw his distorted image gleaming on their black, china surfaces, as if in that instant the moth had stored his image in its memory.

Denny unscrewed the cap, plucked out the moth, and piercing its body with a pin from the black paper packet, he pinned the moth to the wall at the foot of his bed. He gave it a place of honour, centring it upon a yellow willow tree. From his bed he would see it first thing in the morning and last thing at night.

A few days and nights passed, and Denny, though still on edge, felt somewhat as a hero must returning from a labour. The untimely death of the moth had perhaps been fortuitous, because now in its death the creature was irrevocably his.

The meadows were already filled with cabbage butterflies, and Denny would go out with his net and catch them, but they were too common to preserve and so, having captured them, he would reach his hand into the net and squash them, wiping the mess in his palm off on the grass.

It was less than a week after the death of the moth that Denny was awakened in the night by a persistent beating on his windowpane. He jumped from bed, switched on the light, and peered outside. With the light on he could see nothing, and whatever it had been was gone. Realizing that though the light made anything outside invisible to him it would also act as a lure to whatever had tried to come in, he went back to bed, leaving the light on and the window open. He tried to stay awake but soon fell back into sleep.

In the morning he looked about the room, but there was no sign of anything having entered. It must have been a June bug or possibly a lunar moth, though it had sounded too heavy for one, thought Denny. He went over to look at the moth on the wall, a morning ritual with him. Although he could not be sure, the dust of one wing seemed to be smudged, and the oily stain from the body had soaked into the wallpaper considerably since the day before. He put his face close to the insect to inspect it more fully. Instinctively he drew back; the odour was unbearable.

The following night Denny left his window wide open, and shortly before midnight he was awakened by a beating of wings upon his face. Terrified and not fully conscious, he hit out with his open hands. He touched something, and it wasn't pleasant. It was yielding and at the same time viscid. And something scratched against the palm of his hand, like a tiny spur or horn.

Leaping from bed, Denny switched on the light. There was nothing in the room. It must have been a bat, and the distasteful thought made him shudder. Whatever it had been, it left a stench behind not unlike the spot on the wall. Denny slammed the window shut and went back to bed and tried to sleep.

In the morning his red-rimmed eyes inspecting the moth plainly saw that not only were the wings smudged, but the simulacra of crabs and mouths upon the wings seemed to have grown more definite. The oily spot had spread still farther and the smell was stronger.

That night Denny slept with his window closed, but in his dreams he was beset by horned and squashy things that pounded his flesh with their fragile wings, and wakening in fright he heard the same sound as he had heard the previous night: something beating against the window-pane. All night it beat against the closed window and Denny lay rigid and sleepless in his bed, and the smell within the room grew into something almost tangible.

At dawn Denny arose and forced himself to look at the moth. He held his nose as he did so, and with horror he saw the stain on the paper and the crabs and the mouths which now not only seemed more definite but also considerably enlarged.

For the first time in months Denny left his room and did not return to it until it was his bedtime. Even that hour he contrived to postpone a little by asking his father to read to him. It was the lesser of two evils.

The stench in the room was such that although Denny dared not leave the window open, he was forced to leave the door from the landing into his room ajar. What was left of the light below, after it had wormed its way up and around the stairs, crawled exhaustedly into the room. For some perverse reason it shone most brightly upon the wall where the moth was transfixed. From his bed Denny could not take his eyes off it. Though they made no progress, the two crabs on the hind wings appeared to be attempting to climb up into the two mouths on the fore wings. The mouths seemed to be very open and ready for them.

That night, no sooner had the beating of wings upon the window awakened Denny, than it abruptly ceased. The light downstairs was out and the room was now in darkness. Curling himself up into a ball and pulling the sheet over his head, Denny at length went off to sleep.

Sometime shortly afterwards something came through the door and half crawled and half fluttered to the bed. Denny awoke with a scream, but it was too muffled for either his father or Ethel to hear, because what caused him to scream had wormed its way beneath the sheet and was resting like a sticky pulp upon Denny's mouth.

Floundering like a drowning person, the boy threw back the covers and managed to dislodge whatever had been upon his mouth. When he dared to, he reached out and turned on the light. There was nothing in the room, but upon his sheets there were smudges of glistening dust, almost black, almost purple, almost green, but not quite any of them.

Denny went down to breakfast without looking at the moth.

'No wonder you look ghastly,' his father said to him, 'if the smell in this house is half of what it must be in your room, it's a wonder you're not suffocated. What are you running up there, a potters' field for Lepidoptera? I'll give you until noon to get them out.'

All day Denny left the window of his room wide open. It was the first of May and the sun was bright. As a sop to his father, he brought down a box of duplicate specimens. He showed them to his father before disposing of them.

'Pugh!' said his father. 'Dump them far away from the house.'

That night Denny went to bed with both the door and the window locked tight, in spite of the smell. The moon was bright and shone all night unimpaired upon the wall. Denny could not keep his eyes off the moth.

By now both crabs and mouths were nearly as large as the wings themselves, and the crabs were moving, Denny could swear. They appeared in relief, perhaps through some trick of chiaroscuro induced by the moonlight upon the dusty white and red markings. The claws seemed upon the verge of attacking the mouths, or were the so terribly white teeth of the mouths waiting to clamp down upon the crabs? Denny shuddered and closed his eyes.

Sleep came eventually, only to be broken in upon by the beating of wings against the window-pane. And no sooner had that ceased and Denny become less rigid than the thing was at the door beating urgently, as though it must be let in. The only relief from the tap-tapping was an occasional, more solid thud against the panel of the door. It was, Denny guessed, caused by the soft and fleshy body of the thing.

If he survived the night, Denny vowed he would destroy the thing upon the wall or, better than losing it entirely, he would give it to his father and he in turn would present it to some museum in Denny's name. Denny for a moment was able to forget the persistent rapping which had now returned to the window, for in his mind he saw a glass case with the moth in it and a little card below upon which was printed UNIQUE SPECIMEN LEPIDOPTERA. GIFT OF MR DENNY LONGWOOD, AGED 12.

All through the night – first at the window, then at the door – the beating of wings continued, relieved only by the occasional plop of the soft, heavy body.

Though having dozed for only an hour or two, with the bright light of day Denny felt his decision of the night before indefensible. The moth smelled; that was undeniable. The matter of the crab and mouthlike markings seeming to expand and become more intense in their colour could probably be explained by somebody who knew about such things. As for the beating against the window and the door, it was probably as he had at first surmised; a bat or, if need be, two bats. The moth on the wall was dead, was his. He had hatched it, and he knew the limitations of a moth dead or alive. He looked at it. The stain had spread so that now its diameter was as great as the spread of the wings. It was no longer exactly a stain, either. It looked as if a spoonful of dirty cereal had adhered to the wall; it was just about the colour of mush. It will stop in time like the others; just as soon as the abdomen dries up, thought Denny.

At breakfast his father remarked that the smell as yet hadn't left the house, that it was in fact stronger if anything. Denny admitted it might take a day or two more before it was completely gone.

Before the meal was over, his father told Denny that he was looking so badly that he had better see Dr Phipps.

'How much do you weigh?' he asked.

Denny didn't know.

'You look,' his father said, 'all dried up, like one of those pupae you had upstairs.'

The moon shone bright again that night. In spite of his logic of the morning, Denny felt sure that the movement of the white and vermilion crabs up to the white teeth and vermilion lips was more than just hallucination. And the beating of wings started at the window again. Then at the door. Then back to the window. And, in a way, worse than that was the plop now and then of the body against the barrier. Though he tried to rise and look out when it was at the window, his limbs would not obey him. Hopelessly, his eyes turned to the wall again. The crablike spots clicked their tiny claws together each time the wings struck against the window-pane. And each time the plump, squashy body went plop, the teeth snapped together between the thin-lipped mouths.

All at once the stench within the room became nauseating. There was nothing for Denny to do but make for the door while whatever it was still pounded at the window. As much as he feared and hated his father, his cynical disbelief was to be preferred to this terror.

Denny refrained from switching on the light for fear that it would reveal his movements to the thing outside. Halfway across the room and shivering, he involuntarily turned his head, and for a moment his feverish eyes saw what was outside before it disappeared.

Denny rushed for the door and unlocked it, but as he twisted the knob something beat against the other side of the door, pushing it open before Denny could shut the door against it.

When luncheon was over, Ethel was sent upstairs to see what had happened. She was so hysterical when she came down that Denny's father went up to see himself.

Denny lay in his pyjamas on the floor just inside the door. The skin of his lonely and somewhat arrogant face was marred by the marks of something pincerlike, and from nose, eyes, ears, and mouth a network of viscid filaments stretched across his face and to the floor as though something had tried to bind his head up in them. His father had some trouble in lifting him up, because the threads adhered so stubbornly to the nap of the blue carpet.

The body was feather-light in the father's arms. The thought that the boy had certainly been under-weight passed inanely through his father's mind.

As he carried his son out, his eyes fell upon a spot on the wall at the foot of the bed. The pattern of a willow tree was completely obliterated by a creeping growth that looked like fungus. Still carrying his son, the man crossed over to it. A pin protruded from its centre, and it was from this spot, Mr Longwood could tell, that the terrible smell came.

The Snail-Watcher

Patricia Highsmith

When Mr Peter Knoppert began to make a hobby of snail watching, he had no idea that his handful of specimens would become hundreds in no time. Only two months after the original snails were carried up to the Knoppert study, some thirty glass tanks and bowls, all teeming with snails, lined the walls, rested on the desk and window-sills, and were beginning even to cover the floor. Mrs Knoppert disapproved strongly, and would no longer enter the room. It smelled, she said, and besides she had once stepped on a snail by accident, a horrible sensation she would never forget. But the more his wife and friends deplored his unusual and vaguely repellent pastime, the more pleasure Mr Knoppert seemed to find in it.

'I never cared for nature before in my life,' Mr Knoppert often remarked – he was a partner in a brokerage firm, a man who had devoted all his life to the science of finance – 'but snails have opened my eyes to the beauty of the animal world.'

If his friends commented that snails were not really animals, and their slimy habitats hardly the best example of the beauty of nature, Mr Knoppert would tell them with a superior smile that they simply didn't know all that he knew about snails.

And it was true. Mr Knoppert had witnessed an exhibition that was not described, certainly not adequately described, in any encyclopaedia or zoology book that he had been able to find. Mr Knoppert had wandered into the kitchen one evening for a bite of something before dinner, and had happened to notice that a couple of snails in the china bowl on the draining board were behaving very oddly. Standing more or less on their tails, they were weaving before each other for all the world like a pair of snakes hypnotized by a flute player. A moment later, their faces came together in a kiss of voluptuous intensity. Mr Knoppert bent closer and studied them from all angles. Something else was happening: a protuberance like an ear was appearing on the right side of the head of both snails. His instinct told him that he was watching a sexual activity of some sort.

The cook came in and said something to him, but Mr Knoppert silenced her with an impatient wave of his hand. He couldn't take his eyes from the enchanted little creatures in the bowl.

When the earlike excrescences were precisely together rim to rim, a whitish rod like another small tentacle shot out from one ear and arched over towards the ear of the other snail. Mr Knoppert's first surmise was dashed when a tentacle sallied from the other snail's, too. Most peculiar, he thought. The two tentacles withdrew, then came forth again, and as if they had found some invisible mark, remained fixed in either snail. Mr Knoppert peered intently closer. So did the cook.

'Did you ever see anything like this?' Mr Knoppert asked.

'No. They must be fighting,' the cook said indifferently and went away.

That was a sample of the ignorance on the subject of snails that he was later to discover everywhere.

Mr Knoppert continued to observe the pair of snails off and on for more than an hour, until first the ears, then the rods withdrew, and the snails themselves relaxed their attitudes and paid no further attention to each other. But by that time, a different pair of snails had begun a flirtation, and were slowly rearing themselves to get into a position for kissing. Mr Knoppert told the cook that the snails were not to be served that evening. He took the bowl of them up to his study. And snails were never again served in the Knoppert household.

That night, he searched his encyclopaedias and a few general science books he happened to possess, but there was absolutely nothing on snails' breeding habits, though the oyster's dull reproductive cycle was described in detail. Perhaps it hadn't been a mating he had seen after all, Mr Knoppert decided after a day or two. His wife Edna told him either to eat the snails or get rid of them – it was at this time that she stepped upon a snail that had crawled out on to the floor – and Mr Knoppert might have, if he hadn't come across a sentence in Darwin's *Origin of Species* on a page given to gastropoda. The sentence was in French, a language Mr Knoppert did not know, but the word *sensualité* made him tense like a bloodhound that has suddenly found the scent. He was in the public library at the time, and laboriously he translated the sentence with the aid of a French–English dictionary. It was a statement of less than a hundred words, saying that snails manifested a sensuality in their mating that was not to be found elsewhere in the animal kingdom. That was all. It was from the notebooks of Henri Fabre. Obviously Darwin had decided not to translate it for the average reader, but to leave it in its original language for the scholarly few who really cared. Mr Knoppert considered himself one of the scholarly few now, and his round, pink face beamed with self-esteem.

He had learned that his snails were the fresh water type that laid their eggs in sand or earth, so he put moist earth and a little saucer of water into a big washpan and transferred his snails into it. Then he waited for something to happen. Not even another mating happened. He picked up the snails one by one and looked at them, without seeing anything suggestive of pregnancy. But one snail he couldn't pick up. The shell might have been glued to the earth. Mr Knoppert suspected the snail had buried its head in the ground to die. Two more days went by, and on the morning of the third, Mr Knoppert found a spot of crumbly earth where the snail had been. Curious, he investigated the crumbles with a match stem, and to his delight discovered a pit full of shiny new eggs. Snail eggs! He hadn't been wrong. Mr Knoppert called his wife and the cook to look at them. The eggs looked very much like big caviar, only they were white instead of black or red.

'Well, naturally they have to breed some way,' was his wife's comment.

Mr Knoppert couldn't understand her lack of interest. He had to go look at the eggs every hour that he was at home. He looked at them every morning to see if any change had taken place, and the eggs were his last thought every night before he went to bed. Moreover, another snail was now digging a pit. And another pair of snails was mating! The first batch of eggs turned a greyish colour, and minuscule spirals of shells became discernible on one side of each egg. Mr Knoppert's anticipation rose to higher pitch. At last a morning arrived – the eighteenth after laying, according to Mr Knoppert's careful count – when he looked down into the egg pit and saw the first tiny moving head, the first stubby little antennae uncertainly exploring its nest. Mr Knoppert was as happy as the father of a new child. Every one of the seventy or more eggs in the pit came miraculously to life. He had seen the entire reproductive cycle evolve to a successful conclusion. And the fact that no one, at least no one that he knew of, was acquainted with a fraction of what he knew, lent his knowledge a thrill of discovery, the piquancy of the esoteric. Mr Knoppert made notes on successive matings and egg hatchings. He narrated snail biology to fascinated, more often shocked friends and guests, until his wife squirmed with embarrassment.

'But where is it going to stop, Peter? If they keep on reproducing at this rate, they'll take over the house!' his wife told him after fifteen or twenty pits had hatched.

'There's no stopping nature,' he replied good-humouredly. 'They've only taken over the study. There's plenty of room there.'

So more and more glass tanks and bowls were moved in. Mr Knoppert went to the market and chose several of the more lively looking snails, and also a pair he found mating, unobserved by the rest of the world. More and more egg pits appeared in the dirt floors of the tanks, and out of each pit crept finally from seventy to ninety baby snails, transparent as dewdrops, gliding up rather than down the strips of fresh lettuce that Mr Knoppert was quick to give all the pits as edible ladders for the climb. Matings went on so often that he no longer bothered to watch them. A mating could last twenty-four hours. But the thrill of seeing the white caviar become shells and start to move – that never diminished however often he witnessed it.

His colleagues in the brokerage office noticed a new zest for life in Peter Knoppert. He became more daring in his moves, more brilliant in his calculations, became in fact a little vicious in his schemes, but he brought money in for his company. By unanimous vote, his basic salary was raised from forty to sixty thousand per year. When anyone congratulated him on his achievements, Mr Knoppert gave all the credit to his snails and the beneficial relaxation he derived from watching them.

He spent all his evenings with his snails in the room that was no longer a study but a kind of aquarium. He loved to strew the tanks with fresh lettuce and pieces of boiled potatoes and beets, then turn on the sprinkler system that he had installed in the tanks to simulate natural rainfall. Then all the snails would liven up and begin eating, mating, or merely gliding through the shallow water with obvious pleasure. Mr Knoppert often let a snail crawl on to his forefinger – he fancied his snails enjoyed this human contact – and he would feed it a piece of lettuce by hand, would observe the snail from all sides, finding as much aesthetic satisfaction as another man might from contemplating a Japanese print.

By now, Mr Knoppert did not allow anyone to set foot in his study. Too many snails had the habit of crawling around on the floor, of going to sleep glued to chair bottoms and to the backs of books on the shelves. Snails spent much of their time sleeping, especially the older snails. But there were enough less indolent snails who preferred love-making. Mr Knoppert estimated that about a dozen pairs of snails must be kissing all the time. And certainly there was a multitude of baby and adolescent snails. They were impossible to count. But Mr Knoppert did count the snails sleeping and creeping on the ceiling alone, and arrived at something between eleven and twelve hundred. The tanks, the bowls, the underside of his desk and the bookshelves must surely have held fifty times that number. Mr Knoppert meant to scrape the snails off the ceiling one day soon. Some of them had been up there for weeks, and he was afraid they were not taking enough nourishment. But of late he had been a little too busy, and too much in need of the tranquillity that he got simply from sitting in the study in his favourite chair.

During the month of June he was so busy, he often worked late into the evening at his office. Reports were piling in at the end of the fiscal year. He made calculations, spotted a half dozen possibilities of gain, and reserved the most daring, the least obvious moves for his private operations. By this time next year, he thought, he should be three or four times as well off as now. He saw his bank account multiplying as easily and rapidly as his snails. He told his wife this, and she was overjoyed. She even forgave him the ruination of the study, and the stale, fishy smell that was spreading throughout the whole upstairs.

'Still, I do wish you'd take a look just to see if anything's happening, Peter,' she said to him rather anxiously one morning. 'A tank might have overturned or something, and I wouldn't want the rug to be spoilt. You haven't been in the study for nearly a week, have you?'

Mr Knoppert hadn't been in for nearly two weeks. He didn't tell his wife that the rug was pretty much gone already. 'I'll go up tonight,' he said.

But it was three more days before he found time. He went in one evening just before bedtime and was surprised to find the floor quite covered with snails, with three or four layers of snails. He had difficulty closing the door without mashing any. The dense clusters of snails in the corners made the room look positively round, as if he stood inside some huge, conglomerate stone. Mr Knoppert cracked his knuckles and gazed around him in astonishment. They had not only covered every surface, but thousands of snails hung down into the room from the chandelier in a grotesque clump.

Mr Knoppert felt for the back of a chair to steady himself. He felt only a lot of shells under his hand. He had to smile a little: there were snails in the chair seat, piled up on one another like a lumpy cushion. He really must do something about the ceiling, and immediately. He took an umbrella from the corner, brushed some of the snails off it, and cleared a place on his desk to stand. The umbrella point tore the wallpaper, and then the weight of the snails pulled down a long strip that hung almost to the floor. Mr Knoppert felt suddenly frustrated and angry. The sprinklers would make them move. He pulled the lever.

The sprinklers came on in all the tanks, and the seething activity of the entire room increased at once. Mr Knoppert slid his feet along the floor, through tumbling snail shells that made a sound like pebbles on a beach, and directed a couple of the sprinklers at the ceiling. This was a mistake, he saw at once. The softened paper began to tear, and he dodged one slowly falling mass only to be hit by a swinging festoon of snails, really hit quite a stunning blow on the side of the head. He went down on one knee, dazed. He should open a window, he thought, the air was stifling. And there were snails crawling over his shoes and up his trouser legs. He shook his feet irritably. He was just going to the door, intending to call for one of the servants to help him, when the chandelier fell on him. Mr Knoppert sat down heavily on the floor. He saw now that he couldn't possibly get a window open, because the snails were fastened thick and deep over the windowsills. For a moment, he felt he couldn't get up, felt as if he were suffocating. It was not only the musty smell of the room, but everywhere he looked long wallpaper strips covered with snails blocked his vision as if he were in a prison.

'Edna!' he called, and was amazed at the muffled, ineffectual sound of his voice. The room might have been soundproof.

He crawled to the door, heedless of the sea of snails he crushed under hands and knees. He could not get the door open. There were so many snails on it, crossing and recrossing the crack of the door on all four sides, they actually resisted his strength.

'Edna!' A snail crawled into his mouth. He spat it out in disgust. Mr Knoppert tried to brush the snails off his arms. But for every hundred he dislodged, four hundred seemed to slide upon him and fasten to him again, as if they deliberately sought him out as the only comparative snail-free surface in the room. There were snails crawling over his eyes. Then just as he staggered to his feet, something else hit him – Mr Knoppert couldn't even see what. He was fainting! At any rate, he was on the floor. His arms felt like leaden weights as he tried to reach his nostrils, his eyes, to free them from the sealing, murderous snail bodies.

'Help!' He swallowed a snail. Choking, he widened his mouth for air and felt a snail crawl over his lips on to his tongue. He was in hell! He could feel them gliding over his legs like a glutenous river, pinning his legs to the floor. 'Ugh!' Mr Knoppert's breath came in feeble gasps. His vision grew black, a horrible, undulating black. He could not breathe at all, because he could not reach his nostrils, could not move his hands. Then through the slit of one eye, he saw directly in front of him, only inches away, what had been, he knew, the rubber plant that stood in its pot near the door. A pair of snails were quietly making love in it. And right beside them, tiny snails as pure as dewdrops were emerging from a pit like an infinite army into their widening world.

Guilty

Fannie Hurst

To the swift hiss of rain down soot-greasy window panes and through a medley of the smells of steam off wet overcoats and a pale stench of fish, a judge turned rather tired Friday-afternoon eyes upon the prisoner at the bar, a smallish man in a decent-enough salt-and-pepper suit and more salt than pepper in his hair and moustache.

'You have heard the charge against you,' intoned the judge in the holy and righteous key of justice about to be administered. 'Do you plead guilty or not guilty?'

'I – I plead guilty of not having told her facts that would have helped her to struggle against the – the thing – her inheritance.'

'You must answer the Court directly. Do you——'

'You see, Your Honour – my little girl – so little – my promise. Yes, yes, I – I plead guilty of keeping her in ignorance of what she should have known, but you see, Your Honour, my little gi——'

'Order! Answer to the point. Do you,' began the judge again, 'plead guilty or not guilty?' his tongue chiming the repetition into the waiting silence like a clapper into a bell.

The prisoner at the bar thumbed his derby hat after the immemorial dry-fingered fashion of the hunted meek, his mouth like an open wound puckering to close.

'Guilty or not guilty, my man? Out with it.'

Actually it was not more than a minute or two before the prisoner found reply, but it was long enough for his tortured eye to flash inwards and backwards with terrible focus ...

On its long cross-town block, Mrs Plush's boarding-house repeated itself no less than thirty-odd times. Every front hall of them smelled like cold boiled potato, and the gilt chair in the parlour like banana. At dinner hour thirty-odd basement dining-rooms reverberated, not uncheerfully, to the ironstone clatter of the canary-bird bathtub of succotash, the three stewed prunes, or the redolent boiled potato, and on Saturday mornings, almost to the thirty-odd of them, wasp-waisted, oiled-haired young Negro girls in white cotton stockings and cut-down high shoes enormously run down of heel, tilted pints of water over steep stone stoops and scratched at the trickle with old broom runts.

If Mrs Plush's house broke rank at all, it did so by praise-worthy omission. In that row of the fly-by-night and the van-by-day, the moving or the express wagon seldom backed up before No 28, except immediately preceding a wedding or following a funeral. And never, in twenty-two years of respectable tenancy, had the furtive lodger oozed, under darkness, through the Plush front door by night, or a huddle of sidewalk trunks and trappings staged the drab domestic tragedy of the dispossessed.

The Kellers (second-story back) had eaten their satisfied way through fourteen years of the breakfasts of applesauce or cereal; choice of ham and eggs, any style or country, sausage and buckwheat cakes.

Jeanette Peopping, born in the back parlour, was married out of the front.

On the night that marked the seventeenth anniversary of the Dangs into the third-floor alcove room, there was frozen pudding with hot fudge sauce for dessert, and a red paper bell ringing silently from the dining-room chandelier.

For the eight years of their placid connubiality Mr and Mrs Henry Jett had occupied the second-story front.

Stability, that was the word. Why, Mrs Plush had dealt with her corner butcher for so long that on crowded Saturday mornings it was her custom to step without challenge into the icy zone of the huge refrigerator, herself pinching and tearing back the cold-storage-bitten wings of fowls, weighing them with a fidelity to the ounce, except for a few extra giblets (Mr Keller loved them), hers, anyhow, most of the time, for the asking.

Even the nearest drugstore, wary of that row of the transient hat-on-the-peg, off-the-peg, would deliver to No. 28 a mustard plaster or a deck of cards and charge without question.

To the Jett Fish Company – *Steamers, Hotels, and Restaurants Supplied – If It Swims We Have it* – Mrs Plush paid her bills quarterly only, Mr Jett then deducting the sum delicately from his board.

So it may be seen that Mrs Plush's boarding-house offered scanty palette to the dauber in local colour.

On each of the three floors was a bathroom, spotlessly clean, with a neat hand-lettered sign over each tin tub:

DO UNTO OTHERS AS YOU WOULD HAVE THEM DO UNTO YOU. PLEASE WASH OUT THE TUB AFTER YOU

Upon the outstanding occasion of the fly in the soup and Mr Keller's
subsequent deathly illness, the regrettable immersion had been directly
traceable, not to the kitchen, but to the dining-room ceiling. It was
November, a season of heavy dipterous mortality. Besides Mrs Peopping
had seen it fall.

Nor entered here the dirge of the soggy towel; Mrs Plush placed fluffy
stacks of them outside each door each morning. Nor groggy coffee; Mrs
Plush was famous for hers. Drip coffee, boiled up to an angry sea, and
half an eggshell dropped in like a fairy barque, to settle it.

The Jetts, with whom we have really to do, drank two cups apiece
at breakfast. Mrs Jett, to the slight aid and abetment of one of her two
rolls, stopped right there; Mr Jett plunging on into choice of——

The second roll Mrs Jett usually carried away with her from the
table. Along about ten o'clock she was apt to feel faint rather than
hungry.

'Gone,' she called it. 'Feeling a little gone.'

Not that there was a suggestion of frailty about Mrs Jett. Anything
but that. On the contrary, in all the eight years in the boarding-house,
she held the clean record of not a day in bed, and although her history
previous to that time showed as many as fifteen hours a day on duty in
the little fancy-goods store of her own proprietorship, those years
showed her guilty of only two incapacitated days, and then because she
ran an embroidery needle under her fingernail and suffered a slight
infection.

Yet there was something about Emma Jett – eight years of married
life had not dissipated it – that was not eupeptic; something of the sear
and yellow leaf of perpetual spinsterhood. She was a wintry little body
whose wide marriage band always hung loosely on her finger with an
air of not belonging; wore an invariable knitted shawl iced with beads
across her rounded shoulders, and frizzed her greying bangs, which,
although fruit of her scalp, had a set-on look. Even the softness to her
kind grey eyes was cosy rather than warm.

She could look out tabbily from above a lap of handiwork, but in her
boudoir wrapper of grey flannelette scalloped in black she was scrawny,
almost rangy, like a horse whose ribs show.

'I can no more imagine those two courting,' Mrs Keller, a proud twin
herself and proud mother of twins, remarked one afternoon to a euchre
group. 'They must have sat company by correspondence. Why, they
won't even kiss when he comes home if there's anybody in the room!'

'They kiss, all right,' volunteered Mrs Dang of the bay-window alcove
room, 'and she waves him good-bye every morning clear down the
block.'

But in the end the consensus of opinion, unanimous to the vote was:
Lovely woman, Mrs Jett. Nice couple; so unassuming. The goodness

looks out of her face; and so reserved!

But it was this aura of reserve that kept Mrs Jett, not without a bit of secret heartache about it, as remote from the little world about her as the yolk of an egg is remote from the white. Surrounded, yet no part of those surroundings. No osmosis took place.

Almost daily, in someone's room, over Honiton lace or the making of steel-bead chatelaine bags, then so much in vogue, those immediate, plushy-voiced gatherings of the members of the plain-gold circle took place. Delicious hours of confidence, confab, and the exchanges of the connubially loquacious.

The supreme *lèse majesté* of the married woman who wears her state of wedlock like the crown of blessed thorns; bleeds ecstatically and swaps afternoon-long intimacies, made nasty by the plush in her voice, with her sisters of the matrimonial dynasty.

Mrs Jett was also bidden, by her divine right, to those conclaves of the wives, and faithfully she attended, but on the rim, as it were. Bitterly silent she sat to the swap of:

'That's nothing. After Jeanette was born my hair began to fall out just as if I had had typhoid', or, 'Both mine, I am proud to say, were bottle babies'; and, once, as she listened, her heart might have been a persimmon, puckering: 'The idea of a woman of forty-five to have her first! It's not fair to the child.'

They could not, of course, articulate it, but the fact of the matter was not alone that Mrs Jett was childless (so was Mrs Dang, who somehow belonged), it was that they sensed, with all the antennae of their busy little intuitions, the ascetic odour of spinsterhood which clung to Mrs Jett. She was a little 'too nice'. Would flush at some of the innuendoes of the *contes intimes*, tales of no lustre and dulled by soot, but in spite of an inner shrinkage would loop up her mouth to smile, because not to do so was to linger even more remotely outside the privileged rim of the wedding band.

Evenings, after these gatherings, Mrs Jett was invariably even a bit gentler than her wont in her greetings to Mr Jett.

Of course, they kissed upon his arrival home, comment to the contrary notwithstanding, in a taken-for-granted fashion, perhaps, but there was something sweet about their utter unexcitement; and had the afternoon session twisted her heart more than usual, Mrs Jett was apt to place a second kiss lightly upon the black and ever so slightly white moustache, or lay her cheek momentarily to his, as if to atone by thus yearning over him for the one aching and silent void between them.

But in the main Henry Jett was a contented and happy man.

His wife, whom he had met at a church social and wooed in the front of the embroidery and fancy-goods store, fitted him like the proverbial glove – a suède one. In the eight years since, his fish business had almost doubled, and his expenses, if anything, decreased, because more and more it became pleasanter to join in the evening game of no-stakes euchre down in the front parlour or to remain quietly upstairs, a gas lamp on the table between them, Mr Jett in a dressing gown of hand-embroidered Persian design and a newspaper which he read from first to last; Mrs Jett at her tranquil process of fine needlework.

Their room abounded in specimens of it, Centrepieces of rose design. Mounds of cushions stamped in bulldog's head and pipe and appropriately etched in coloured floss. A poker hand, upheld by realistic five fingers embroidered to the life, and the cuff button denoted by a blue glass jewel. Across their bed, making it a dais of incongruous splendour, was flung a great counterpane of embroidered linen, in design as narrative as a battle-surging tapestry and every thread in it woven out of these long, quiet evenings by the lampside.

He was exceedingly proud of her cunning with a needle, so fine that its stab through the cloth was too slight to be seen, and would lose no occasion to show off the many evidences of her delicate workmanship that were everywhere about the room.

'It's like being able to create a book or a piece of music, Em, to say all that on a piece of cloth with nothing but a needle.'

'It's a good thing I am able to create something, Henry,' placing her thimbled hand on his shoulder and smiling down. She was slightly the taller.

It was remarkable how quick and how tender his intuitions could be. An innuendo from her, faint as the brush of a wing, and he would immediately cluck with his tongue and throw out quite a bravado of chest.

'You're all right, Em. You suit me.'

'And you suit me, Henry,' stroking his hand.

This he withdrew. It was apt to smell of fish and he thought that once or twice he had noticed her draw back from it, and, anyway, he was exceedingly delicate about the cling of the rottenly pungent fish odour of his workadays.

Not that he minded personally. He had long ago ceased to have any consciousness of the vapours that poured from the bins and the incoming catches into his little partitioned-off office. But occasionally, he noticed that in streetcars noses would begin to crinkle around him, and every once in a while, even in a crowded conveyance he would find himself the centre of a little oasis of vacant seats which he had created around himself.

Immediately upon his arrival home, although his hands seldom touched the fish, he would wash them in a solution of warm water and carbolic acid, and most of the time he changed his suit before dinner, from a salt-and-pepper to a pepper-and-salt, the only sartorial variety in which he ever indulged.

His wife was invariably touched by this little nicety of his, and sometimes bravely forced his hand to her cheek to prove her lack of repugnance.

Boarding-house lore had it correctly. They were an exceedingly nice couple, the Jetts.

One day in autumn, with the sky the colour and heaviness of a Lynnhaven oyster, Mrs Jett sat quite unusually forward on her chair at one of the afternoon congresses of the wives, convened in Mrs Peopping's back parlour, Jeanette Peopping, aged four, sweet and blonde, whom the Jetts loved to borrow Sunday mornings while she was still in her little nightdress, playing paper dolls in the background.

Her embroidery hoop, with a large shaded pink rose in the working, had, contrary to her custom, fallen from idle hands, and instead of following the dart of the infinitesimal needle, Mrs Jett's eyes were burningly upon Mrs Peopping, following, with almost lip-reading intensity, that worthy lady's somewhat voluptuous mouthings.

She was a large, light person with protuberant blue eyes that looked as if at some time they had been two-thirds choked from their sockets and a characteristic of opening every sentence with her mouth shaped to an explosive O, which she filled with as much breath as it would hold.

It had been a long tale of obstetrical fact and fancy, told plushily, of course, against the dangerous little ears of Jeanette, and at its conclusion Mrs Peopping's steel-bead bag, half finished, lay at her feet, her pink and flabby face turned reminiscently towards the fire.

'– and for three days six doctors gave me up. Why, I didn't see Jeanette until the fourteenth day, when most women are up and out. The crisis, you know. My night nurse, an awful sweet girl – I send her a Christmas present to this day – said if I had been six years younger it wouldn't have gone so hard with me. I always say if the men knew what we women go through – Maybe if some of them had to endure real pain themselves they would have something to do besides walk up and down the hall and turn pale at the smell of ether coming through the keyhole. Ah me! I've been a great sufferer in my day.'

It was then that Mrs Jett sat forward on the edge of the straight chair, and put her question.

There was a pause after it, as if an intruder had poked her head in through the door, and it brought only the most negligible answer from Mrs Peopping.

'Forty-three.'

Almost immediately Mrs Dang caught at the pause for a case in point that had been trembling on her lips all during Mrs Peopping's recital.

'A doctor once told a second cousin of my sister-in-law's——' and so on *ad infinitum, ad lib.*, and *ad nauseam.*

That night Mrs Jett did an unprecedented thing. She crept into the crevice of her husband's arm from behind as he stood in his waistcoat, washing his hands in the carbolic solution at the bowl and washstand. He turned, surprised, unconsciously placing himself between her and the reeky water.

'Henry,' she said, rubbing up against the alpaca back to his vest like an ingratiating Maltese tabby, 'Hen-ery.'

'In a minute, Em,' he said, rather puzzled and wishing she would wait.

'Hen-ery, I haven't words sweet enough to tell you.'

'Em, tell what?' And stopped. He could see suddenly that her eyes were full of new pins of light and his lightning intuition performed a miracle of understanding.

'Emmy!' he cried, jerking her so that her breath jumped, and at the sudden drench of tears down her face sat her down, supporting her roundish back with his wet hands, although he himself felt weak.

'I – can't say – what I feel, Henry – only – God is good and – I'm not afraid.'

He held her to his shoulder and let her tears rain down into his watch pocket, so shaken that he found himself mouthing silent words.

'God is good, Henry, isn't He?'

'Yes, Emmy, yes. Oh, my Emmy!'

'It must have been our prayers, Henry.'

'Well,' sheepishly, 'not exactly mine, Emmy; you're the saint of this family. But I – I've wished.'

'Henry. I'm so happy – Mrs Peopping had Jeanette at forty-three. Three years older than me. I'm not afraid.'

It was then he looked down at her greying head there, prone against his chest, and a dart of fear smote him.

'Emmy,' he cried, dragging her tear-happy face up to his, 'if you're afraid – not for anything in the world! Your *first*, Em.'

She looked at him with her eyes two lamps.

'Afraid? That's the beautiful part, Henry. I'm not. Only happy. Why afraid, Henry – if others dare it at – forty-three – You mean because it was her second?'

He faced her with a scorch of embarrassment in his face.

'You – We – Well, we're not spring chickens any more, Em. If you are sure it's not too——'

She hugged him, laughing her tears.

'I'm all right, Henry – we've been too happy not to – to – perpetuate – it.'

This time he did not answer. His cheek was against the crochet of her yoke and she could hear his sobs with her heart.

Miraculously, like an amoeba reaching out to enclose unto itself, the circle opened with a gasp of astonishment that filled Mrs Peopping's O to its final stretch and took unto its innermost Emma Jett.

Nor did she wear her initiation lightly. There was a new tint out in her long cheeks, and now her chair, a rocker, was but one removed from Mrs Peopping's.

Oh, the long, sweet afternoons over garments that made needlework sublime. No longer the padded rose on the centrepiece or the futile doily, but absurd little dresses with sleeves that she measured to the length of her hand, and yokes cut out to the pattern of a playing card, and all fretted over with feather stitching that was frailer than maidenhair fern and must have cost many an eyeache, which, because of its source, was easy to bear.

And there happened to Mrs Jett that queer juvenescence that sometimes comes to men and women in middle life. She who had enjoyed no particular youth (her father had died in a ferryboat crash two weeks before her birth, and her mother three years after) came suddenly to acquire comeliness which her youth had never boasted.

The round-shouldered, long-cheeked girl had matured gingerly to rather sparse womanhood that now at forty relented back to a fulsome thirty.

Perhaps it was the tint of light out in her face, perhaps the splendour of the vision; but at any rate, in those precious months to come, Mrs Jett came to look herself as she should have looked ten years back.

They were timid and really very beautiful together, she and Henry Jett. He came to regard her as a vase of porcelain, and, in his ignorance, regarded the doctor's mandates harsh; would not permit her to walk, but ordered a cab every day from three to four, Mrs Jett alternating punctiliously with each of the boarding-house ladies for driving companion.

Every noon, for her delectation at luncheon, he sent a boy from the store with a carton of her special favourites – Blue Point oysters. She suddenly liked them small because, as she put it, they went down easier, and he thought that charming.

Long evenings they spent at names, exercizing their predetermination as to sex. 'Ann' was her choice, and he was all for cancelling his preference for 'Elizabeth', until one morning she awakened to the white light of inspiration.

'I have it! Why not Ann Elizabeth?'

'Great!' And whistled so through his shaving that his mouth was rayed with a dark sunburst of beard where the razor had not found surface.

They talked of housekeeping, reluctantly, it is true, because Mrs Plush herself was fitting up, of hard-to-spare evenings, a basinette of pink and white. They even talked of schools.

Then came the inevitable time when Mrs Jett lost interest. Quite out of the clear sky even the Blue Points were taboo, and instead of joining this or that card or sewing circle, there were long afternoons of stitching away alone, sometimes the smile out on her face, sometimes not.

'Em, is it all right with you?' Henry asked her once or twice, anxiously.

'Of course it is! If I weren't this way – now – it wouldn't be natural. You don't understand.'

He didn't, so could only be vaguely and futilely sorry.

Then one day something quite horrible, in a small way, happened to Mrs Jett. Sitting, sewing, suddenly it seemed to her that through the very fluid of her eyeballs, as it were, floated a school of fish. Small ones – young smelts, perhaps – with oval lips, fillips to their tails, and sides that glistened.

She laid down her bit of linen lawn, fingers to her lids as if to squeeze out their tiredness. She was trembling from the unpleasantness, and for a frightened moment could not swallow. Then she rose, shook out her skirts, and to be rid of the moment carried her sewing up to Mrs Dang's where a euchre game was in session, and by a few adroit questions in between deals gained the reassurance that a nervous state in her 'condition' was highly normal.

She felt easier, but there was the same horrid recurrence three times that week. Once during an evening of lotto down in the front parlour she pushed back from the table suddenly, hand flashing up to her throat.

'Em!' said Mr Jett, who was calling the numbers.

'It's nothing,' she faltered.

The women exchanged knowing glances.

'She's all right,' said Mrs Peopping, ominisciently. 'Those things pass.'

Going upstairs that evening, alone in the hallway, they flung an arm each across the other's shoulder, crowding playfully up the narrow flight.

'Emmy,' he said, 'poor Em, everything will be all right.'

She restrained an impulse to cry. 'Poor nothing,' she said.

But neither the next evening, which was Friday, nor for Fridays thereafter, would she venture down for fish dinner, dining cosily up in her room off milk toast and a fluffy meringue dessert prepared especially by Mrs Plush. It was floating-island night downstairs.

Henry puzzled a bit over the Fridays. It was his heaviest day at the business, and it was upsetting to come home tired and feel her place beside him at the basement dinner-table vacant.

But the women's nods were more knowing than ever, the reassuring insinuations more and more delicate.

But one night, out of one of those stilly cisterns of darkness that between two and four are deepest with sleep, Henry was awakened on the crest of such a blow and yell that he swam up to consciousness in a ready-made armour of high-napped gooseflesh.

A regrettable thing had happened. Awakened, too, on the high tide of what must have been a disturbing dream, Mrs Jett flung out her arm as if to ward off something. That arm encountered Henry, snoring lightly at her side. But, unfortunately, to that frightened fling of her arm Henry did not translate himself to her as Henry.

That was a fish lying there beside her! A man-sized fish with its mouth jerked open to the shape of a gasp and the fillip still through its enormous body, as if its flanks were uncomfortably dry. A fish!

With a shriek that tore a jagged rent through the darkness, Mrs Jett began pounding at the slippery flanks, her hands sliding off its shininess.

'Out! Out! Henry, where are you? Help me! Oh God, don't let him get me. Take him away, Henry! Where are you? My hands – slippery! Where are you——'

Stunned, feeling for her in the darkness, he wanted to take her shuddering form into his arms and waken her out of this horror, but with each groping move of his her hurtling shrieks came faster, and finally, dragging the bedclothing with her, she was down on the floor at the bedside, blobbering. That is the only word for it – blobbering.

He found a light, and by this time there were already other lights flashing up in the startled household. When he saw her there on the floor beside the bed, a cold sweat broke out over him so that he could almost feel each little explosion from the pores.

'Why, Emmy – Emmy – my Emmy——'

She saw him now and knew him, and tried in her poor and already burningly ashamed way to force her chattering jaws together.

'Hen-ery – dream – bad – fish – Hen-ery——'

He drew her up to the side of the bed, covering her shivering knees as she sat there, and throwing a blanket across her shoulders. Fortunately he was aware that the soothing note in his voice helped, and so he sat down beside her, stroking her hand, stroking, almost as if to hypnotize her into quiet.

'Henry,' she said, closing her fingers into his wrists, 'I must have dreamed – a horrible dream. Get back to bed, dear. I – I don't know what ails me, waking up like that. That – fish! Oh God! Henry, hold me, hold me.'

He did, lulling her with a thousand repetitions of his limited store of endearments, and he could feel the jerk of sobs in her breathing subside and she seemed almost to doze.

Then came knocks at the door, and hurried explanations through the slit that he opened, and Mrs Peopping's eye close to the crack.

'Everything is all right ... Just a little bad dream the missus had ...

All right now ... To be expected, of course ... No, nothing anyone can do ... Good night. Sorry ... No, thank you. Everything is all right.'

The remainder of the night the Jetts kept a small light burning, after a while Henry dropping off into exhausted and heavy sleep. For hours Mrs Jett lay staring at the small bud of light, no larger than a human eye. It seemed to stare back at her, warning, Now don't you go dropping off to sleep and misbehaving again.

And holding herself tense against a growing drowsiness, she didn't – for fear——

The morning broke clear, and for Mrs Jett full of small reassurances. It was good to hear the clatter of milk deliveries, and the first bar of sunshine came in through the hand-embroidered window curtains like a smile, and she could smile back. Later she ventured down shame-facedly for the two cups of coffee, which she drank bravely, facing the inevitable potpourri of comment from this one and that one.

'That was a fine scare you gave us last night, Mrs Jett.'

'I woke up stiff with fright. Didn't I, Will? Gracious! That first yell was a curdler!'

'Just before Jeanette was born I used to have bad dreams, too, but nothing like that. My!'

'My mother had a friend whose sister-in-law walked in her sleep right out of a third-storey window and was dashed to——'

'Shh-h-h!'

'It's natural, Mrs Jett. Don't you worry.'

She really tried not to, and after some subsequent and private reassurance from Mrs Peopping and Mrs Keller, went for her ride in the Park, Mrs Plush, in a brocade cape with ball fringe, sitting erect beside her.

One day, in the presence of Mrs Peopping, Mrs Jett jumped to her feet with a violent shaking of her right hand, as if to dash off something that had crawled across its back.

'Ugh!' she cried. 'It flopped right on my hand. A minnow! Ugh!'

'A what?' cried Mrs Peopping, jumping to her feet and her flesh seeming to crawl up.

'A minnow. I mean a bug – a June bug. It was a bug, Mrs Peopping.'

There ensued a mock search for the thing, the two women, on all fours, peering beneath the chairs. In that position they met levelly, eye to eye. Then without more ado rose, brushing their knees and reseating themselves.

'Maybe if you would read books you would feel better,' said Mrs Peopping, scooping up a needleful of steel beads. 'I know a woman who made it her business to read all the poetry books she could lay hands on, and went to all the bandstand concerts in the Park the whole time, and now her daughter sings in the choir out in Saginaw, Michigan.'

'I know some believe in that,' said Mrs Jett, trying to force a smile through her pallor. 'I must try it.'

But the infinitesimal stitching kept her so busy.

It was inevitable, though, that in time Henry should begin to shoulder more than a normal share of unease.

One evening she leaned across the little lamplit table between them as he sat reading in the Persian-design dressing-gown and said, as rapidly as her lips could form the dreadful repetition, 'The fish, the fish, the fish.' And then, almost impudently for her, disclaimed having said it.

He urged her to visit her doctor and she would not, and so, secretly, he did, and came away better satisfied, and with directions for keeping her diverted, which punctiliously he tried to observe.

He began by committing sly acts of discretion on his own accord. Was careful not to handle the fish. Changed his suit now before coming home, behind a screen in his office, and, feeling foolish, went out and purchased a bottle of violet eau de Cologne, which he rubbed into his palms and for some inexplicable reason on his half-bald spot.

Of course that was futile, because the indescribably and faintly rotten smell of the sea came through, nonetheless.

One Sunday morning, Mr Jett climbed into his dressing-gown and padded downstairs for the loan of little Jeanette Peopping, with whom he returned, the delicious nub of her goldilocks head showing just above the blanket which enveloped her, eyes and all.

He deposited her in bed beside Mrs Jett, the little pink feet peeping out from her nightdress and her baby teeth showing in a smile that Mr Jett loved to pinch together with thumb and forefinger.

'Cover her up quick, Em, it's chilly this morning.'

Quite without precedent, Jeanette puckered up to cry, holding herself rigidly to Mr Jett's dressing-gown.

'Why, Jeanette baby, don't you want to go to Aunty Em?'

'No! No! No!' Trying to ingratiate herself back into Mr Jett's arms.

'Baby, you'll take cold. Come under covers with Aunty Em?'

'No! No! No! Take me back.'

'Oh, Jeanette, that isn't nice! What ails the child? She's always so eager to come to me. Shame on Jeanette! Come, baby, to Aunty Em?'

'No! No! No! My mamma says you're crazy. Take me back – take me.'

For a frozen moment Henry regarded his wife above the glittering fluff of little-girl curls. It seemed to him he could almost see her face become smaller, like a bit of ice under sun.

'Naughty little Jeanette,' he said, shouldering her and carrying her down the stairs: 'naughty little girl.'

When he returned his wife was sitting locked in the attitude in which he had left her.

'Henry!' she whispered, reaching out, and closing her hand over his so that the nails bit in. 'Not that, Henry! Tell me not that!'

'Why, Em,' he said, sitting down and trembling. 'I'm surprised at you, listening to baby talk!'

She leaned over, shaking him by the shoulder.

'I know. They're saying it about me. I'm not that, Henry. I swear I'm not that! Always protect me against their saying that, Henry. Not crazy – not that! It's natural for me to feel queer at times – now. Every woman in this house who says that – about me has had her nervous feelings. It's not quite so easy for me, as if I were a bit younger. That's all. The doctor said that. But nothing to worry about. Mrs Peopping had Jeanette—— Oh, Henry, promise me you'll always protect me against their saying that! I'm not that – I swear to you, Henry – not that!'

'I know you're not, Emmy. It's too ridiculous to talk about. Pshaw!'

'And you'll always protect me against anyone saying it? They'll believe you, Henry, not me. Promise to protect me against our little Ann Elizabeth ever thinking that of – of her mother.'

'Why, Emmy!' he said. 'Why, Emmy! I just promise a thousand times——' and could not go on, working his mouth rather foolishly as if he had no teeth and were rubbing empty gums together.

But through her hot gaze of tears she saw and understood and, satisfied, rubbed her cheek against his arm.

The rest is cataclysmic.

When he returned home one evening in a nice glow from a January out-of-doors, his moustache glistening with little frozen drops and his hands (he never wore gloves) unbending of cold, Mrs Jett rose at her husband's entrance from her low chair beside the lamp.

'Well, well!' he said, exhaling heartily, the scent of violet denying the pungency of fish. 'How's the busy bee this evening?'

For answer Mrs Jett met him with the crescendo yell of a gale sweeping around a chimney.

'Ya-a-ah! Keep out – you! Fish! Fish!' she cried, springing towards him; and in the struggle that ensued the tubing wrenched off the gas lamp and plunged them into darkness. 'Fish! I'll fix you! Ya-a-ah!'

'Emmy! For God's sake, it's Henry! Em!'

'Ya-a-ah! I'll fix you! Fish! Fish!'

Two days later Ann Elizabeth was born, beautiful, but premature by two weeks.

Emma Jett died holding her tight against her newly rich breasts, for a few of the most precious and most fleeting moments of her life.

All her absurd fears washed away, her free hand could lie without spasm in Henry's, and it was as if she found in her last words a secret euphony that delighted her.

'Ann-Elizabeth. Sweet-beautiful. Ann-Elizabeth. Sweet-beautiful.'

Later in his bewildered and almost ludicrous widowerhood, tears would sometimes galumph down on his daughter's face as Henry rocked her of evenings and Sunday mornings.

'Sweet-beautiful,' came so absurdly from under his swiftly greying moustache, but often, when sure he was quite alone, he would say it over and over again.

'Sweet-beautiful. Ann-Elizabeth. Sweet-beautiful. Ann-Elizabeth.'

Of course the years puttied in and healed and softened, until for Henry almost a Turner haze hung between him and some of the stark facts of Emma Jett's death, turping out horror, which is always the first to fade from memory, and leaving a dear sepia outline of the woman who had been his.

At seventeen, Ann Elizabeth was the sun, the sky, the west wind, and the summer of spring – all gone into the making of her a rosebud off the stock of his being.

His way of putting it was, 'You're my all Annie, closer to me than I am to myself.'

She hated the voweling of her name, and because she was so nimble with youth could dance from these moods of his rather than plumb them.

'I won't be "Annie". Please, Daddy, I'm your Ann Elizabeth.'

'Ann Elizabeth, then. My Ann Elizabeth,' an inner rhythm in him echoing: Sweet-Beautiful. Sweet-Beautiful.

There was actually something of the lark about her. She awoke with a song, sometimes kneeling up in bed, with her pretty brown hair tousling down over her shoulders and chirruping softly to herself into the little birdseye-maple dressing-table mirror, before she flung her feet over the side of the bed.

And then, innate little housekeeper that she was, it was to the preparing of breakfast with a song, her early morning full of antics. Tiptoeing in to awaken her father to the tickle of a broom straw. Spreading his breakfast piping hot, and then concealing herself behind a screen, that he might marvel at the magic of it. And once she put salt in his coffee, a fresh cup concealed behind the toast rack, and knee to knee they rocked in merriment at his grimace.

She loved thus to tease him, probably because he was so stolid that each new adventure came to him with something of a shock. He was for ever being taken unawares, as if he could never become entirely accustomed to the wonder of her, and that delighted her. Even the obviousness of his slippers stuffed out with carrots could catch him napping. To her dance of glee behind him he kept poking and poking to get into them, only the peck of her kiss upon his neck finally initiating him into the absurdity.

There was a little apartment of five rooms, twenty minutes removed by subway from the fish store; her bedroom, all pink and yellow maple; his; a kitchen, parlour, and dining-room worked out happily in white muslin curtains, spindle-legged parlour chairs, Henry's newfangled chifferobe and bed with a fine depth of mattress, and a kitchen with eight shining pots above the sink and a border of geese, cut out to the snip of Ann's own scissors, waddling across the wall.

It was two and a half years since Mrs Plush had died, and the boarders, as if spilled from an ark on rough seas, had struck out for diverse shores. The marvel to them now was that they had delayed so long.

'A home of our own, Ann. Pretty sweet, isn't it?'

'Oh, Daddy, it is!'

'You mustn't overdo, though, baby. Sometimes we're not so strong as we think we are. A little hired girl would be best.'

'But I love doing it alone, Dad. It – it's the next best thing to a home of – my own.'

He looked startled into her dreaming eyes.

'Your own? Why, Annie, isn't this – your own?'

She laid fingers against his eyes so that he could not see the pinkiness of her.

'You know what I mean, Daddy – my – very – own.'

At that timid phrasing of hers Henry felt that his heart was actually strangling, as if someone were holding it back on its systolic swing, like a caught pendulum.

'Why, Annie,' he said, 'I never thought——'

But of course it had happened.

The young man's name was Willis – Fred E. Willis – already credit man in a large wholesale grocery firm and two feet well on the road to advancement. A square-faced, clean-faced fellow, with a clean love of life and of Ann Elizabeth in his heart.

Henry liked him.

Ann Elizabeth loved him.

And yet, what must have been a long-smouldering flame of fear shot up through the very core of Henry's being.

'Why, Ann Elizabeth,' he kept repeating, in his slow and always inarticulate manner, 'I – You – Mine – I just never thought.'

She wound the softest of arms about his neck.

'I know, Daddy-darlums, and I'll never leave you. Never. Fred has promised we will always be together. We'll live right here with you, or you with us.'

'Annie,' he cried, 'you mustn't ever – marry. I mean, leave Daddy
– that way – anyway. You hear me? You're Daddy's own. Just his by
himself. Nobody is good enough for my girl.'

'But, Daddy,' clouding up for tears, 'I thought you liked Fred so
much!'

'I do, but it's you I'm talking about. Nobody can have you.'

'But I love him, Daddy!'

'Oh, Ann, Ann! Daddy hasn't done right, perhaps, but he meant well.
There are *reasons* why he wants to keep his little girl with him always
– alone – his.'

'But, Daddy dear, I promise you we'll never let you be lonely. Why,
I couldn't stand leaving you any more than you could——'

'Not those reasons alone, Ann.'

'Then what?'

'You're so young,' he tried to procrastinate.

'I'll be eighteen. A woman.'

All his faculties were cornered.

'You're – so—— Oh, I don't know – I——'

'You haven't any reasons, Dad, except silly ones. You can't keep me
a little girl all the time, dear. I love Fred. It's all planned. Don't ruin
my life, Daddy – don't ruin my life.'

She was lovely in her tears and surprisingly resolute in her mind, and
he was more helpless than ever with her.

'Ann – you're not strong.'

'Strong!' she cried, flinging back her curls and out her chest. 'That's
a fine excuse. I'm stronger than most. All youngsters have measles and
scarlet fever and Fred says his sister Lucile out in Des Moines had St
Vitus' dance when she was eleven, just like I did. I'm stronger than you
are, Dad. I didn't get the flu and you did.'

'You're nervous, Annie. That's why I want always to keep you at
home – quiet – with me.'

She sat back, her pretty eyes troubled-up lakes.

'You mean the dreams and the scared feeling, once in a while, that
I can't swallow. That's nothing. I know now why I was so frightened
in my sleep the other night. I told Fred, and he said it was the peach
sundae on top of the crazy old movie we saw that evening. Why,
Jeanette Peopping had to take a rest cure the year before she was
married. Girls are always more nervous than fellows. Daddy – you – you
frighten me when you look at me like that! I don't know what you mean!
What-do-you-mean?'

He was helpless and at bay and took her in his arms and kissed her
hair.

'I guess your old Daddy is a jealous pig and can't bear to share his girl with anyone. Can't bear to – to give her up.'

'You won't be giving up, Daddums. I couldn't stand that, either. It will be three of us then. You'll see. Look up and smile at your Ann Elizabeth.'

And of course he did.

It was typical of her that she should be the busiest of brides-to-be, her completed little trousseau, every piece down to the dishcloths, mono-grammed by her – A. E. W.

Skilful with her needle and thrifty in her purchases, the outfit when completed might have represented twice the outlay that Henry expended on it. Then there were 'showers' – linen, stocking, and even a tin one; gifts from her girl friends – cup, face, bath, and guest towels; all the tremendous trifles and addenda that go to gladden the chattel-loving heart of a woman. A little secret society of her erstwhile school friends presented her with a luncheon set; the Keller twins with a silver gravy boat; and Jeanette Peopping Gruman, who occupied an apart-ment in the same building, spent as many as three afternoons a week with her, helping to piece out a really lovely tulip-design quilt of pink and white sateen.

'Jeanette,' said Ann Elizabeth one afternoon, 'how did you feel that time when you had the nerv – the breakdown?'

Jeanette, pretty after a high-cheekboned fashion and her still bright hair worn coronet fashion about her head, bit off a thread with sharp white teeth, only too eager to reminisce her ills.

'I was just about gone, that's what I was. Let anybody so much as look at me twice and, pop! I'd want to cry about it.'

'And?'

'For six weeks I didn't even have enough interest to ask after Gruman, who was courting me then. Oh, it was no fun, I can tell you, that nervous breakdown of mine!'

'What – else?'

'Isn't that enough?'

'Did it – was it ever hard to swallow, Jeanette?'

'To swallow?'

'Yes. I mean – did you ever dream or – think – or feel so frightened you couldn't swallow?'

'I felt lots of ways, but that wasn't one of them. Swallow! Who ever heard of not swallowing?'

'But didn't you ever dream, Jeanette – terrible things – such terrible things – and get to thinking and couldn't stop yourself? Silly, ghostly – things.'

Jeanette put down her sewing.

'Ann, are you quizzing me about – your mother?'

'My mother? Why my mother? Jeanette, what do you mean? Why

do you ask me a thing like that? What has my mother got to do with it? Jeanette!'

Conscious that she had erred, Jeanette veered carefully back.

'Why, nothing, only I remember Mamma telling me when I was just a kiddie how your mamma used to – to imagine all sorts of things just to pass the time away while she embroidered the loveliest pieces. You're like her, Mamma used to say – a handy little body. Poor Mamma, to think she had to be taken before Gruman, junior, was born! Ah me!'

That evening, before Fred came for his two hours with her in the little parlour, Ann flew from a ring at the door-bell with a good-sized special-delivery box from a silversmith, untying it with eager, fumbling fingers, her father laying aside his newspaper to venture three guesses as to its contents.

'Another one of those syrup pitchers.'

'Oh dear!' – plucking the twine – 'I hope not!'

'Some more nut picks.'

'Daddy, stop calamity howling. Here's the card. Des Moines, Iowa. *From Lucile Willis, with love to her new sister.* Isn't that the sweetest! It's something with a pearl handle.'

'I know. Another one of those pie-spade things.'

'Wrong! Wrong! It's two pieces. Oh!'

It was a fish set of silver and mother-of-pearl. A large-bowled spoon and a sort of Neptune's fork, set up in a white-sateen bed.

'Say now, that *is* neat,' said Henry, appraising each piece with a show of critical appreciation not really his. All this spread of the gewgaws of approaching nuptials seemed meaningless to him; bored him. Butter knives. Berry spoons. An embarrassment of nut picks and silver pitchers. A sliver of silver paper cutter with a hilt and a dog's-head handle. And now, for Fred's delectation this evening, the newly added fish set, so appropriately inscribed from his sister.

Tilting it against the lamp in the place of honour, Ann Elizabeth turned away suddenly, looking up at her father in a sudden dumb panic of which he knew nothing, her two hands at her fair, bare throat. It was so hard again to swallow. Impossible.

But finally, as was always the case, she did swallow, with a great surge of relief. A little later, seated on her father's knee and plucking at his tie in a futile fashion that he loved, she asked him:

'Daddy – about Mother——'

They seldom talked of her, but always during these rare moments a beautiful mood shaped itself between them. It was as if the mere breath of his daughter's sweetly lipped use of 'Mother' swayed the bittersweet memory of the woman he carried so faithfully in the cradle of his heart.

'Yes, baby – about Mother?'

'Daddy' – still fingering at the tie – 'was Mother – was everything all

right with her up – to the very – end? I mean – no nerv – no pain? Just
all of a sudden the end – quietly. Or have you told me that just to – spare
me?'

She could feel him stiffen, but when his voice came it was even.

'Why, Ann, what a – question! Haven't I told you so often how
Mother just peacefully passed on, holding a little pink you.'

Sweet-Beautiful – his heart was tolling through a sense of panic –
Sweet-Beautiful.

'I know, Daddy, but before – wasn't there any nerv – any sickness?'

'No,' he said, rather harshly for him. 'No. No. What put such ideas
into your head?'

You see, he was shielding Emma way back there, and a typhoon of
her words was raging through his head: *Oh, Henry, protect me against anyone
ever saying – that. Promise me.*

And now, with no sense of his terrible ruthlessness, he was protecting
her with her own daughter.

'Then, Daddy, just one more thing,' and her underlip caught while
she waited for answer. 'There is no other reason except your own dear
silly one of loneliness – why you keep wanting me to put off my
marriage?'

'No, baby,' he said, finally, his words with no more depth than if his
body were a hollow gourd. 'What else could there be?'

Immediately, and with all the resilience of youth, she was her happy
self again, kissing him through his moustache and on his now frankly
bald head, which gave off the incongruous odour of violet eau de
Cologne.

'Old dude Daddy!' she cried, and wanted to kiss his hands, which he
held suddenly very still and far from her reach.

Then the bell rang again and Fred Willis arrived. All the evening,
long after Henry lay on his deep-mattressed bed, staring, the little
apartment trilled to her laughter and the basso of Fred's.

A few weeks later there occurred a strike of the delivery men and truck
drivers of the city, and Henry, especially hard hit because of the perish-
able nature of his product, worked early and late, often-times loading
the wagons himself.

Frequently he was as much as an hour or two late to dinner, and upon
one or two occasions had tiptoed out of the house before the usual hour
when Ann opened her eyes to the consciousness of his breakfast to be
prepared.

They were trying days, the scheme of his universe broken into, and
Henry thrived on routine.

The third week of the strike there were street riots, some of them
directly in front of the fish store, and Henry came home after a day of

the unaccustomed labour of loading and unloading hampers of fish, really quite shaken.

When he arrived Ann Elizabeth was cutting around the scalloped edge of a doily with embroidery scissors, the litter of cut glass and silver things out on the table and throwing up quite a brilliance under the electric lamp, and from the kitchen the slow sizzle of waiting chops.

'Whew!' he said, as he entered, both from the whiff he emanated as he shook out of his overcoat, and from a great sense of his weariness.

Ann Elizabeth started violently, first at the whiff which preceded him and at his approach into the room; then sat forward, her hand closing into the arm of the chair, body thrust forward and her eyes widening like two flowers opening.

Then she rose slowly and slyly, and edged behind the table, her two hands up about her throat.

'Don't you come in here,' she said, lowly and evenly. 'I know you, but I'm not afraid. I'm only afraid of you at night, but not by light. You let me swallow, you hear! Get out! Get out!'

Rooted, Henry stood.

'Why, Annie!' he said in the soothing voice from out of his long ago, 'Annie – it's Daddy!'

'No, you don't,' she cried, springing back as he took the step forward. 'My Daddy'll kill you if he finds you here. He'll slit you up from your tail right up to your gill. He knows how. I'm going to tell him and Fred of you. You won't let me swallow. You're slippery. I can't stand it. Don't you come near me! Don't!'

'Annie!' he cried. 'Good God! Annie, it's Daddy who loves you!' Poor Henry – her voice was still under a whisper and in his agony he committed the error of rushing at her. 'Annie, it's Daddy! See, your own dear Daddy!'

But she was too quick. Her head thrown back so that the neck muscles strained out like an outraged deer's cornered in the hunt and her eyes rolled up, Ann felt for and grasped the paper knife off the trinket-littered table.

'Don't you touch me – slit you up from tail to your gills.'

'Annie, it's Daddy! Papa! For God's sake look at Daddy – Ann! God!' And caught her wrist in the very act of its plumb-line rush for his heart.

He was sweating in his struggle with her, and most of all her strength appalled him – she was so little for her terrible unaccountable power.

'Don't touch me! You can't! You haven't any arms! Horrible gills!'

She was talking as she struggled, still under the hoarse and frantic whisper, but her breath coming in long soughs. 'Slit-you-up-from-tail. Slit – you – up – from – tail – to – gills.'

'Annie! Annie!' still obsessed by his anguished desire to reassure her with the normality of his touch. 'See, Annie, it's Daddy. Ann Elizabeth's

Daddy.' With a flash her arm and the glint of the paper cutter eluded him again and again, but finally he caught her by the waist, struggling, in his dreadful mistake, to calm her down into the chair again.

'Now I've got you, darling. Now – sit – down——'

'No, you haven't,' she said, a sort of wild joy coming out in her whisper, and cunningly twisting the upper half of her body back from his, the hand still held high. 'You'll never get me – you *fish!*'

And plunged with her high hand in a straight line down into her throat.

It was only when the coroner withdrew the sliver of paper knife from its whiteness that, coagulated, the dead and waiting blood began to ooze.

'Do you,' intoned the judge for the third and slightly more impatient time, 'plead guilty or not guilty to the charge of murder against you?'

This time the lips of the prisoner's wound of a mouth moved stiffly together:

'Guilty.'

The Romance of Certain Old Clothes

Henry James

I

Towards the middle of the eighteenth century there lived in the Province of Massachusetts a widowed gentlewoman, the mother of three children, by name Mrs Veronica Wingrave. She had lost her husband early in life, and had devoted herself to the care of her progeny. These young persons grew up in a manner to reward her tenderness and to gratify her highest hopes. The first-born was a son, whom she had called Bernard, after his father. The others were daughters – born at an interval of three years apart. Good looks were traditional in the family, and this youthful trio were not likely to allow the tradition to perish. The boy was of that fair and ruddy complexion and that athletic structure which in those days (as in these) were the sign of good English descent – a frank, affectionate young fellow, a deferential son, a patronizing brother, a steadfast friend. Clever, however, he was not; the wit of the family had been apportioned chiefly to his sisters. The late Mr Wingrave had been a great reader of Shakespeare, at a time when this pursuit implied more freedom of thought than at the present day, and in a community where it required much courage to patronize the drama even in the closet: and he had wished to call attention to his admiration of the great poet by calling his daughters out of his favourite plays. Upon the elder he had bestowed the romantic name of Rosalind, and the younger he had called Perdita, in memory of a little girl born between them, who had lived but a few weeks.

When Bernard Wingrave came to his sixteenth year his mother put a brave face upon it and prepared to execute her husband's last injunction. This had been a formal command that, at the proper age, his son should be sent out to England, to complete his education at the university of Oxford, where he himself had acquired his taste for elegant literature. It was Mrs Wingrave's belief that the lad's equal was not to be found in the two hemispheres, but she had the old traditions of literal obedience. She swallowed her sobs, and made up her boy's trunk and his simple provincial outfit, and sent him on his way across the seas. Bernard presented himself at his father's college, and spent five years in England, without great honour, indeed, but with a vast deal of pleasure and no discredit. On leaving the university he made the journey to France. In his twenty-fourth year he took ship for home, prepared to find poor little New England (New England was very small in those days) a very dull, unfashionable residence. But there had been changes at home, as well as in Mr Bernard's opinions. He found his mother's house quite habitable, and his sisters grown into two very charming young ladies, with all the accomplishments and graces of the young women of Britain, and a certain native-grown originality and wildness, which, if it was not an accomplishment, was certainly a grace the more. Bernard privately assured his mother that his sisters were fully a match for the most genteel young women in the old country; whereupon poor Mrs Wingrave, you may be sure, bade them hold up their heads. Such was Bernard's opinion, and such, in a tenfold higher degree, was the opinion of Mr Arthur Lloyd. This gentleman was a college-mate of Mr Bernard, a young man of reputable family, of a good person and a handsome inheritance; which latter appurtenance he proposed to invest in trade in the flourishing colony. He and Bernard were sworn friends; they had crossed the ocean together, and the young American had lost no time in presenting him at his mother's house, where he had made quite as good an impression as that which he had received and of which I have just given a hint.

The two sisters were at this time in all the freshness of their youthful bloom; each wearing, of course, this natural brilliancy in the manner that became her best. They were equally dissimilar in appearance and character. Rosalind, the elder – now in her twenty-second year – was tall and white, with calm grey eyes and auburn tresses; a very faint likeness to the Rosalind of Shakespeare's comedy, whom I imagine a brunette (if you will), but a slender, airy creature, full of the softest, quickest impulses. Miss Wingrave, with her slightly lymphatic fairness, her fine arms, her majestic height, her slow utterance, was not cut out for adventures. She would never have put on a man's jacket and hose; and, indeed, being a very plump beauty, she may have had reasons apart from her natural dignity. Perdita, too, might very well have exchanged the sweet melancholy of her name against something more in consonance with her aspect and disposition. She had the cheek of a gypsy and the eye of an eager child, as well as the smallest waist and lightest foot in all the country of the Puritans. When you spoke to her she never made you wait, as her handsome sister was wont to do (while she looked at you with a cold fine eye), but gave you your choice of a dozen answers before you had uttered half your thought.

The young girls were very glad to see their brother once more; but they found themselves quite able to spare part of their attention for their brother's friend. Among the young men their friends and neighbours, the *belle jeunesse* of the Colony, there were many excellent fellows, several devoted swains, and some two or three who enjoyed the reputation of universal charmers and conquerors. But the homebred arts and somewhat boisterous gallantry of these honest colonists were completely eclipsed by the good looks, the fine clothes, the punctilious courtesy, the perfect elegance, the immense information, of Mr Arthur Lloyd. He was in reality no paragon; he was a capable, honourable, civil youth, rich in pounds sterling, in his health and complacency and his little capital of uninvested affections. But he was a gentleman; he had a handsome person; he had studied and travelled; he spoke French, he played the flute, and he read verses aloud with very great taste. There were a dozen reasons why Miss Wingrave and her sister should have thought their other male acquaintance made but a poor figure before such a perfect man of the world. Mr Lloyd's anecdotes told our little New England maidens a great deal more of the ways and means of people of fashion in European capitals than he had any idea of doing. It was delightful to sit by and hear him and Bernard talk about the fine people and fine things they had seen. They would all gather round the fire after tea, in the little wainscoted parlour, and the two young men would remind each other, across the rug, of this, that and the other adventure. Rosalind and Perdita would often have given their ears to know exactly what adventure it was, and where it happened, and who was there, and what the ladies had on; but in those days a well-bred young woman was not expected to break into the conversation of her elders, or to ask too many questions; and the poor girls used therefore to sit fluttering behind the more languid – or more discreet – curiosity of their mother.

II

That they were both very fine girls Arthur Lloyd was not slow to discover; but it took him some time to make up his mind whether he liked the big sister or the little sister best. He had a strong presentiment – an emotion of a nature entirely too cheerful to be called a foreboding – that he was destined to stand up before the parson with one of them; yet he was unable to arrive at a preference, and for such a consummation a preference was certainly necessary, for Lloyd had too much young blood in his veins to make a choice by lot and be cheated of the satisfaction of falling in love. He resolved to take things as they came – to let his heart speak. Meanwhile he was on a very pleasant footing. Mrs Wingrave showed a dignified indifference to his 'intentions', equally remote from a carelessness of her daughter's honour and from

that sharp alacrity to make him come to the point, which, in his quality
of young man of property, he had too often encountered in the worldly
matrons of his native islands. As for Bernard, all that he asked was that
his friend should treat his sisters as his own; and as for the poor girls
themselves, however each may have secretly longed that their visitor
should do or say something 'marked', they kept a very modest and
contented demeanour.

   Towards each other, however, they were somewhat more on the
offensive. They were good friends enough, and accommodating bed-
fellows (they shared the same four-poster), betwixt whom it would take
more than a day for the seeds of jealousy to sprout and bear fruit; but
they felt that the seeds had been sown on the day that Mr Lloyd came
into the house. Each made up her mind that, if she should be slighted,
she would bear her grief in silence, and that no one should be any the
wiser; for if they had a great deal of ambition, they had also a large share
of pride. But each prayed in secret, nevertheless, that upon *her* the
selection, the distinction, might fall. They had need of a vast deal of
patience, of self-control, of dissimulation. In those days a young girl of
decent breeding could make no advances whatever, and barely respond,
indeed, to those that were made. She was expected to sit still in her chair,
with her eyes on the carpet, watching the spot where the mystic handkerchief should fall. Poor Arthur Lloyd was obliged to carry on
his wooing in the little wainscoted parlour, before the eyes of Mrs
Wingrave, her son, and his prospective sister-in-law. But youth and love
are so cunning that a hundred signs and tokens might travel to and fro,
and not one of these three pairs of eyes detect them in their passage. The
two maidens were almost always together, and had plenty of chances
to betray themselves. That each knew she was being watched, made not
a grain of difference in the little offices they mutually rendered, or in
the various household tasks they performed in common. Neither
flinched nor fluttered beneath the silent battery of her sister's eyes. The
only apparent change in their habits was that they had less to say to each
other. It was impossible to talk about Mr Lloyd, and it was ridiculous
to talk about anything else. By tacit agreement they began to wear all
their choice finery, and to devise such little implements of conquest, in
the way of ribbons and top-knots and kerchiefs, as were sanctioned by
indubitable modesty. They executed in the same inarticulate fashion a
contract of fair play in this exciting game. 'Is it better so?' Rosalind
would ask, tying a bunch of ribbons on her bosom, and turning about
from her glass to her sister. Perdita would look up gravely from her work
and examine the decoration. 'I think you had better give it another
loop,' she would say, with great solemnity, looking hard at her sister
with eyes that added, 'upon my honour!' So they were for ever stitching
and trimming their petticoats, and pressing out their muslins, and

contriving washes and ointments and cosmetics, like the ladies in the household of the vicar of Wakefield. Some three or four months went by; it grew to be midwinter, and as yet Rosalind knew that if Perdita had nothing more to boast of than she, there was not much to be feared from her rivalry. But Perdita by this time – the charming Perdita – felt that her secret had grown to be tenfold more precious than her sister's.

One afternoon Miss Wingrave sat alone – that was a rare accident – before her toilet-glass, combing out her long hair. It was getting too dark to see; she lit the two candles in their sockets, on the frame of her mirror, and then went to the window to draw her curtains. It was a grey December evening; the landscape was bare and bleak, and the sky heavy with snow-clouds. At the end of the large garden into which her window looked was a wall with a little postern door, opening into a lane. The door stood ajar, as she could vaguely see in the gathering darkness, and moved slowly to and fro, as if someone were swaying it from the lane without. It was doubtless a servant-maid who had been having a tryst with her sweetheart. But as she was about to drop her curtain Rosalind saw her sister step into the garden and hurry along the path which led to the house. She dropped the curtain, all save a little crevice for her eyes. As Perdita came up the path she seemed to be examining something in her hand, holding it close to her eyes. When she reached the house she stopped a moment, looked intently at the object, and pressed it to her lips.

Poor Rosalind slowly came back to her chair and sat down before her glass where, if she had looked at it less abstractedly, she would have seen her handsome features sadly disfigured by jealousy. A moment afterwards the door opened behind her and her sister came into the room, out of breath, her cheeks aglow with the chilly air.

Perdita started. 'Ah,' said she, 'I thought you were with our mother.' The ladies were to go to a tea-party, and on such occasions it was the habit of one of the girls to help their mother to dress. Instead of coming in, Perdita lingered at the door.

'Come in, come in,' said Rosalind. 'We have more than an hour yet. I should like you very much to give a few strokes to my hair.' She knew that her sister wished to retreat, and that she could see in the glass all her movements in the room. 'Nay, just help me with my hair,' she said, 'and I will go to mamma.'

Perdita came reluctantly, and took the brush. She saw her sister's eyes, in the glass, fastened hard upon her hands. She had not made three passes when Rosalind clapped her own right hand upon her sister's left, and started out of her chair. 'Whose ring is that?' she cried, passionately, drawing her towards the light.

On the young girl's third finger glistened a little gold ring, adorned with a very small sapphire. Perdita felt that she need no longer keep her secret, yet that she must put a bold face on her avowal. 'It's mine,' she said proudly.

'Who gave it to you?' cried the other.

Perdita hesitated a moment. 'Mr Lloyd.'

'Mr Lloyd is generous, all of a sudden.'

'Ah no,' cried Perdita, with spirit, 'not all of a sudden! He offered it to me a month ago.'

'And you needed a month's begging to take it?' said Rosalind, looking at the little trinket, which indeed was not especially elegant, although it was the best that the jeweller of the Province could furnish. 'I wouldn't have taken it in less than two.'

'It isn't the ring,' Perdita answered, 'it's what it means!'

'It means that you are not a modest girl!' cried Rosalind. 'Pray, does your mother know of your intrigue? does Bernard?'

'My mother has approved my "intrigue", as you call it. Mr Lloyd has asked for my hand, and mamma has given it. Would you have had him apply to you, dearest sister?'

Rosalind gave her companion a long look, full of passionate envy and sorrow. Then she dropped her lashes on her pale cheeks and turned away. Perdita felt that it had not been a pretty scene; but it was her sister's fault. However, the elder girl rapidly called back her pride, and turned herself about again. 'You have my very best wishes,' she said, with a low curtsey. 'I wish you every happiness, and a very long life.'

Perdita gave a bitter laugh. 'Don't speak in that tone!' she cried. 'I would rather you should curse me outright. Come, Rosy,' she added, 'he couldn't marry both of us.'

'I wish you very great joy,' Rosalind repeated, mechanically, sitting down to her glass again, 'and a very long life, and plenty of children.'

There was something in the sound of these words not at all to Perdita's taste. 'Will you give me a year to live at least?' she said. 'In a year I can have one little boy – or one little girl at least. If you will give me your brush again I will do your hair.'

'Thank you,' said Rosalind. 'You had better go to mamma. It isn't becoming that a young lady with a promised husband should wait on a girl with none.'

'Nay,' said Perdita good-humouredly, 'I have Arthur to wait upon me. You need my service more than I need yours.'

But her sister motioned her away, and she left the room. When she had gone poor Rosalind fell on her knees before her dressing-table, buried her head in her arms, and poured out a flood of tears and sobs. She felt very much the better for this effusion of sorrow. When her sister came back she insisted on helping her to dress – on her wearing her prettiest things. She forced upon her acceptance a bit of lace of her own, and declared that now that she was to be married she should do her best to appear worthy of her lover's choice. She discharged these offices in stern silence; but, such as they were, they had to do duty as an apology and an atonement; she never made any other.

Now that Lloyd was received by the family as an accepted suitor nothing remained but to fix the wedding-day. It was appointed for the following April, and in the interval preparations were diligently made for the marriage. Lloyd, on his side, was busy with his commercial arrangements, and with establishing a correspondence with the great mercantile house to which he had attached himself in England. He was therefore not so frequent a visitor at Mrs Wingrave's as during the months of his diffidence and irresolution, and poor Rosalind had less to suffer than she had feared from the sight of the mutual endearments of the young lovers. Touching his future sister-in-law Lloyd had a perfectly clear conscience. There had not been a particle of love-making between them, and he had not the slightest suspicion that he had dealt her a terrible blow. He was quite at his ease; life promised so well, both domestically and financially. The great revolt of the Colonies was not yet in the air, and that his connubial felicity should take a tragic turn it was absurd, it was blasphemous, to apprehend. Meanwhile, at Mrs Wingrave's, there was a greater rustling of silks, a more rapid clicking of scissors and flying of needles, than ever. The good lady had determined that her daughter should carry from home the genteelest outfit that her money could buy or that the country could furnish. All the sage women in the Province were convened, and their united taste was brought to bear on Perdita's wardrobe. Rosalind's situation, at this moment, was assuredly not to be envied. The poor girl had an inordinate love of dress, and the very best taste in the world, as her sister perfectly well knew. Rosalind was tall, she was stately and sweeping, she was made to carry stiff brocade and masses of heavy lace, such as belong to the toilet of a rich man's wife. But Rosalind sat aloof, with her beautiful arms folded and her head averted, while her mother and sister and the venerable women aforesaid worried and wondered over their materials, oppressed by the multitude of their resources. One day there came in a beautiful piece of white silk, brocaded with heavenly blue and silver sent by the bridegroom himself – it not being thought amiss in those days that the husband-elect should contribute to the bride's trousseau. Perdita could think of no form or fashion which would do sufficient honour to the splendour of the material.

'Blue's your colour, sister, more than mine,' she said, with appealing eyes. 'It's a pity it's not for you. You would know what to do with it.'

Rosalind got up from her place and looked at the great shining fabric, as it lay spread over the back of a chair. Then she took it up in her hands and felt it – lovingly, as Perdita could see – and turned about towards the mirror with it. She let it roll down to her feet, and flung the other

end over her shoulder, gathering it in about her waist with her white
arm, which was bare to the elbow. She threw back her head, and looked
at her image, and a hanging tress of her auburn hair fell upon the
gorgeous surface of the silk. It made a dazzling picture. The women
standing about uttered a little 'Look, look!' of admiration. 'Yes, indeed,'
said Rosalind, quietly, 'blue is my colour.' But Perdita could see that
her fancy had been stirred, and that she would now fall to work and solve
all their silken riddles. And indeed she behaved very well, as Perdita,
knowing her insatiable love of millinery, was quite ready to declare.
Innumerable yards of lustrous silk and satin, of muslin, velvet and lace,
passed through her cunning hands, without a jealous word coming
from her lips. Thanks to her industry, when the wedding-day came
Perdita was prepared to espouse more of the vanities of life than any
fluttering young bride who had yet received the sacramental blessing
of a New England divine.

It had been arranged that the young couple should go out and spend
the first days of their wedded life at the country-house of an English
gentleman – a man of rank and a very kind friend to Arthur Lloyd. He
was a bachelor; he declared he should be delighted to give up the place
to the influence of Hymen. After the ceremony at church – it had been
performed by an English clergyman – young Mrs Lloyd hastened back
to her mother's house to change her nuptial robes for a riding-dress.
Rosalind helped her to effect the change, in the little homely room in
which they had spent their undivided younger years. Perdita then
hurried off to bid farewell to her mother, leaving Rosalind to follow. The
parting was short; the horses were at the door, and Arthur was impatient
to start. But Rosalind had not followed, and Perdita hastened back to
her room, opening the door abruptly. Rosalind, as usual, was before the
glass, but in a position which caused the other to stand still, amazed.
She had dressed herself in Perdita's cast-off wedding veil and wreath,
and on her neck she had hung the full string of pearls which the young
girl had received from her husband as a wedding-gift. These things had
been hastily laid aside, to await their possessor's disposal on her return
from the country. Bedizened by this unnatural garb Rosalind stood
before the mirror, plunging a long look into its depths and reading
heaven knows what audacious visions. Perdita was horrified. It was a
hideous image of their old rivalry come to life again. She made a step
towards her sister, as if to pull off the veil and the flowers. But catching
her eyes in the glass, she stopped.

'Farewell, sweetheart,' she said. 'You might at least have waited till
I had got out of the house!' And she hurried away from the room.

Mr Lloyd had purchased in Boston a house which to the taste of those
days appeared as elegant as it was commodious; and here he very soon
established himself with his young wife. He was thus separated by a

distance of twenty miles from the residence of his mother-in-law. Twenty miles, in that primitive era of roads and conveyances, were as serious a matter as a hundred at the present day, and Mrs Wingrave saw but little of her daughter during the first twelvemonth of her marriage. She suffered in no small degree from Perdita's absence; and her affliction was not diminished by the fact that Rosalind had fallen into terribly low spirits and was not to be roused or cheered but by change of air and company. The real cause of the young lady's dejection the reader will not be slow to suspect. Mrs Wingrave and her gossips, however, deemed her complaint a mere bodily ill, and doubted not that she would obtain relief from the remedy just mentioned. Her mother accordingly proposed, on her behalf, a visit to certain relatives on the paternal side, established in New York, who had long complained that they were able to see so little of their New England cousins. Rosalind was despatched to these good people, under a suitable escort, and remained with them for several months. In the interval her brother Bernard, who had begun the practice of the law, made up his mind to take a wife. Rosalind came home to the wedding, apparently cured of her heartache, with bright roses and lilies in her face and a proud smile on her lips. Arthur Lloyd came over from Boston to see his brother-in-law married, but without his wife, who was expecting very soon to present him with an heir. It was nearly a year since Rosalind had seen him. She was glad – she hardly knew why – that Perdita had stayed at home. Arthur looked happy, but he was more grave and important than before his marriage. She thought he looked 'interesting' – for although the word, in its modern sense, was not then invented, we may be sure that the idea was. The truth is, he was simply anxious about his wife and her coming ordeal. Nevertheless, he by no means failed to observe Rosalind's beauty and splendour, and to note how she effaced the poor little bride. The allowance that Perdita had enjoyed for her dress had now been transferred to her sister, who turned it to wonderful account. On the morning after the wedding he had a lady's saddle put on the horse of the servant who had come with him from town, and went out with the young girl for a ride. It was a keen, clear morning in January; the ground was bare and hard, and the horses in good condition – to say nothing of Rosalind, who was charming in her hat and plume, and her dark blue riding coat, trimmed with fur. They rode all the morning, lost their way and were obliged to stop for dinner at a farm-house. The early winter dusk had fallen when they got home. Mrs Wingrave met them with a long face. A messenger had arrived at noon from Mrs Lloyd; she was beginning to be ill, she desired her husband's immediate return. The young man, at the thought that he had lost several hours, and that by hard riding he might already have been with his wife, uttered a passionate oath. He barely consented to stop for a mouthful of supper, but mounted the messenger's horse and started off at a gallop.

He reached home at midnight. His wife had been delivered of a little girl. 'Ah, why weren't you with me?' she said, as he came to her bedside.

'I was out of the house when the man came. I was with Rosalind,' said Lloyd, innocently.

Mrs Lloyd made a little moan, and turned away. But she continued to do very well, and for a week her improvement was uninterrupted. Finally, however, through some indiscretion in the way of diet or exposure, it was checked, and the poor lady grew rapidly worse. Lloyd was in despair. It very soon became evident that she was breathing her last. Mrs Lloyd came to a sense of her approaching end, and declared that she was reconciled with death. On the third evening after the change took place she told her husband that she felt she should not get through the night. She dismissed her servants, and also requested her mother to withdraw – Mrs Wingrave having arrived on the preceding day. She had had her infant placed on the bed beside her, and she lay on her side, with the child against her breast, holding her husband's hands. The night-lamp was hidden behind the heavy curtains of the bed, but the room was illumined with a red glow from the immense fire of logs on the hearth.

'It seems strange not to be warmed into life by such a fire as that,' the young woman said, feebly trying to smile. 'If I had but a little of it in my veins! But I have given all *my* fire to this little spark of mortality.' And she dropped her eyes on her child. Then raising them she looked at her husband with a long, penetrating gaze. The last feeling which lingered in her heart was one of suspicion. She had not recovered from the shock which Arthur had given her by telling her that in the hour of her agony he had been with Rosalind. She trusted her husband very nearly as well as she loved him; but now that she was called away forever she felt a cold horror of her sister. She felt in her soul that Rosalind had never ceased to be jealous of her good fortune; and a year of happy security had not effaced the young girl's image, dressed in her wedding-garments, and smiling with simulated triumph. Now that Arthur was to be alone, what might not Rosalind attempt? She was beautiful, she was engaging; what arts might she not use, what impression might she not make upon the young man's saddened heart? Mrs Lloyd looked at her husband in silence. It seemed hard, after all, to doubt of his constancy. His fine eyes were filled with tears; his face was convulsed with weeping; the clasp of his hands was warm and passionate. How noble he looked, how tender, how faithful and devoted! 'Nay,' thought Perdita, 'he's not for such a one as Rosalind. He'll never forget me. Nor does Rosalind truly care for him; she cares only for vanities and finery and jewels.' And she lowered her eyes on her white hands, which her husband's liberality had covered with rings, and on the lace ruffles which trimmed the edge of her nightdress. 'She covets my rings and my laces more than she covets my husband.'

At this moment the thought of her sister's rapacity seemed to cast a dark shadow between her and the helpless figure of her little girl. 'Arthur,' she said, 'you must take off my rings. I shall not be buried in them. One of these days my daughter shall wear them – my rings and my laces and silks. I had them all brought out and shown me today. It's a great wardrobe – there's not such another in the Province; I can say it without vanity, now that I have done with it. It will be a great inheritance for my daughter when she grows into a young woman. There are things there that a man never buys twice, and if they are lost you will never again see the like. So you will watch them well. Some dozen things I have left to Rosalind; I have named them to my mother. I have given her that blue and silver; it was meant for her; I wore it only once, I looked ill in it. But the rest are to be sacredly kept for this little innocent. It's such a providence that she should be my colour; she can wear my gowns; she has her mother's eyes. You know the same fashions come back every twenty years. She can wear my gowns as they are. They will lie there quietly waiting till she grows into them – wrapped in camphor and rose-leaves, and keeping their colours in the sweet-scented darkness. She shall have black hair, she shall wear my carnation satin. Do you promise me, Arthur?'

'Promise you what, dearest?'

'Promise me to keep your poor little wife's old gowns.'

'Are you afraid I shall sell them?'

'No, but that they may get scattered. My mother will have them properly wrapped up, and you shall lay them away under a double-lock. Do you know the great chest in the attic, with the iron bands? There is no end to what it will hold. You can put them all there. My mother and the housekeeper will do it, and give you the key. And you will keep the key in your secretary, and never give it to anyone but your child. Do you promise me?'

'Ah, yes, I promise you,' said Lloyd, puzzled at the intensity with which his wife appeared to cling to this idea.

'Will you swear?' repeated Perdita.

'Yes, I swear.'

'Well – I trust you – I trust you,' said the poor lady, looking into his eyes with eyes in which, if he had suspected her vague apprehensions, he might have read an appeal quite as much as an assurance.

Lloyd bore his bereavement rationally and manfully. A month after his wife's death, in the course of business, circumstances arose which offered him an opportunity of going to England. He took advantage of it, to change the current of his thoughts. He was absent nearly a year, during which his little girl was tenderly nursed and guarded by her grandmother. On his return he had his house again thrown open, and announced his intention of keeping the same state as during his wife's lifetime. It very soon came to be predicted that he would marry again, and there were at least a dozen young women of whom one may say that it was by no fault of theirs that, for six months after his return, the prediction did not come true. During this interval he still left his little daughter in Mrs Wingrave's hands, the latter assuring him that a change of residence at so tender an age would be full of danger for her health. Finally, however, he declared that his heart longed for his daughter's presence and that she must be brought up to town. He sent his coach and his housekeeper to fetch her home. Mrs Wingrave was in terror lest something should befall her on the road; and, in accordance with this feeling, Rosalind offered to accompany her. She could return the next day. So she went up to town with her little niece, and Mr Lloyd met her on the threshold of his house, overcome with her kindness and with paternal joy. Instead of returning the next day Rosalind stayed out the week; and when at last she reappeared, she had only come for her clothes. Arthur would not hear of her coming home nor would the baby. That little person cried and choked if Rosalind left her; and at the sight of her grief Arthur lost his wits, and swore that she was going to die. In fine, nothing would suit them but that the aunt should remain until the little niece had grown used to strange faces.

It took two months to bring this consummation about; for it was not until this period had elapsed that Rosalind took leave of her brother-in-law. Mrs Wingrave had shaken her head over her daughter's absence; she had declared that it was not becoming, that it was the talk of the whole country. She had reconciled herself to it only because, during the girl's visit, the household enjoyed an unwonted term of peace. Bernard Wingrave had brought his wife home to live, between whom and her sister-in-law there was as little love as you please. Rosalind was perhaps no angel; but in the daily practice of life she was a sufficiently good-natured girl, and if she quarrelled with Mrs Bernard, it was not without provocation. Quarrel, however, she did, to the great annoyance not only of her antagonist, but of the two spectators of these constant altercations. Her stay in the household of her brother-in-law, therefore, would have been delightful, if only because it removed her from contact with the object of her antipathy at home. It was doubly – it was ten times – delightful, in that it kept her near the object of her early passion. Mrs Lloyd's sharp suspicions had fallen very far short of the truth. Rosalind's sentiment had been a passion at first, and a passion it remained – a passion of whose radiant heat, tempered to the delicate state of his feelings, Mr Lloyd very soon felt the influence. Lloyd, as I have hinted, was not a modern Petrarch; it was not in his nature to practise an ideal constancy. He had not been many days in the house with his sister-in-law before he began to assure himself that she was, in the language of that day, a devilish fine woman. Whether Rosalind really practised those insidious arts that her sister had been tempted to impute to her it is needless to inquire. It is enough to say that she found means to appear to the very best advantage. She used to seat herself every morning before the big fireplace in the dining-room, at work upon a piece of tapestry, with her little niece disporting herself on the carpet at her feet, or on the train of her dress, and playing with her woollen balls. Lloyd would have been a very stupid fellow if he had remained insensible to the rich suggestions of this charming picture. He was exceedingly fond of his little girl, and was never weary of taking her in his arms and tossing her up and down, and making her crow with delight. Very often, however, he would venture upon greater liberties than the young lady was yet prepared to allow, and then she would suddenly vociferate her displeasure. Rosalind, at this, would drop her tapestry, and put out her handsome hands with the serious smile of the young girl whose virgin fancy has revealed to her all a mother's healing arts. Lloyd would give up the child, their eyes would meet, their hands would touch, and Rosalind would extinguish the little girl's sobs upon the snowy folds of the kerchief that crossed her bosom. Her dignity was perfect, and nothing could be more discreet than the manner in which she accepted her brother-in-law's hospitality. It may almost be said, perhaps, that there was something harsh in her reserve. Lloyd had a provoking feeling that she was in the house and yet was unapproachable. Half-an-hour after supper, at the very outset of the long winter evenings, she would light her candle, make the young man a most respectful curtsey, and march off to bed. If these were arts, Rosalind was a great artist. But their effect was so gentle, so gradual, they were calculated to work upon the young widower's fancy with a *crescendo* so finely shaded, that, as the reader has seen, several weeks elapsed before Rosalind began to feel sure that her returns would cover her outlay. When this became morally certain she packed up her trunk and returned to her mother's house. For three days she waited: on the fourth Mr Lloyd made his appearance – a respectful but pressing suitor. Rosalind heard him to the end, with great humility, and accepted him with infinite modesty. It is hard to imagine that Mrs Lloyd would have forgiven her husband; but if anything might have disarmed her resentment it would have been the ceremonious continence of this interview. Rosalind imposed upon her lover but a short probation. They were married, as was becoming, with great privacy – almost with secrecy – in the hope perhaps, as was waggishly remarked at the time, that the late Mrs Lloyd wouldn't hear of it.

The marriage was to all appearance a happy one, and each party obtained what each had desired – Lloyd 'a devilish fine woman', and Rosalind – but Rosalind's desires, as the reader will have observed, had remained a good deal of a mystery. There were, indeed, two blots upon their felicity, but time would perhaps efface them. During the first three years of her marriage Mrs Lloyd failed to become a mother, and her husband on his side suffered heavy losses of money. This latter circumstance compelled a material retrenchment in his expenditure, and Rosalind was perforce less of a fine lady than her sister had been. She contrived, however, to carry it like a woman of considerable fashion. She had long since ascertained that her sister's copious wardrobe had been sequestrated for the benefit of her daughter, and that it lay languishing in thankless gloom in the dusty attic. It was a revolting thought that these exquisite fabrics should await the good pleasure of a little girl who sat in a high chair and ate bread-and-milk with a wooden spoon. Rosalind had the good taste, however, to say nothing about the matter until several months had expired. Then, at last, she timidly broached it to her husband. Was it not a pity that so much finery should be lost? – for lost it would be, what with colours fading, and moths eating it up, and the change of fashions. But Lloyd gave her so abrupt and peremptory a refusal, that she saw, for the present, her attempt was vain. Six months went by, however, and brought with them new needs and new visions. Rosalind's thoughts hovered lovingly about her sister's relics. She went up and looked at the chest in which they lay imprisoned. There was a sullen defiance in its three great padlocks and its iron bands which only quickened her cupidity. There was something exasperating in its incorruptible immobility. It was like a grim and grizzled old household servant, who locks his jaws over a family secret. And then there was a look of capacity in its vast extent, and a sound as of dense fullness, when Rosalind knocked its side with the toe of her little shoe, which caused her to flush with baffled longing. 'It's absurd,' she cried; 'it's improper, it's wicked'; and she forthwith resolved upon another attack upon her husband. On the following day, after dinner, when he had had his wine, she boldly began it. But he cut her short with great sternness.

'Once for all, Rosalind,' said he, 'it's out of the question. I shall be gravely displeased if you return to the matter.'

'Very good,' said Rosalind. 'I am glad to learn the esteem in which I am held. Gracious heaven,' she cried, 'I am a very happy woman! It's an agreeable thing to feel one's self sacrificed to a caprice!' And her eyes filled with tears of anger and disappointment.

Lloyd had a good-natured man's horror of a woman's sobs, and he attempted – I may say he condescended – to explain. 'It's not a caprice, dear, it's a promise,' he said – 'an oath.'

'An oath? It's a pretty matter for oaths! and to whom, pray?'

'To Perdita,' said the young man, raising his eyes for an instant, and immediately dropping them.

'Perdita – ah, Perdita!' and Rosalind's tears broke forth. Her bosom heaved with stormy sobs – sobs which were the long-deferred sequel of the violent fit of weeping in which she had indulged herself on the night when she discovered her sister's betrothal. She had hoped, in her better moments, that she had done with her jealousy; but her temper, on that occasion, had taken an ineffaceable hold. 'And pray, what right had Perdita to dispose of my future?' she cried. 'What right had she to bind you to meanness and cruelty? Ah, I occupy a dignified place, and I make a very fine figure! I am welcome to what Perdita has left! And what has she left? I never knew till now how little! Nothing, nothing, nothing.'

This was very poor logic, but it was very good as a 'scene'. Lloyd put his arm around his wife's waist and tried to kiss her, but she shook him off with magnificent scorn. Poor fellow! he had coveted a 'devilish fine woman', and he had got one. Her scorn was intolerable. He walked away with his ears tingling – irresolute, distracted. Before him was his secretary, and in it the sacred key which with his own hand he had turned in the triple lock. He marched up and opened it, and took the key from a secret drawer, wrapped in a little packet which he had sealed with his own honest bit of glazonry. *Je garde*, said the motto – 'I keep.' But he was ashamed to put it back. He flung it upon the table beside his wife.

'Put it back!' she cried. 'I want it not. I hate it!'

'I wash my hands of it,' cried her husband. 'God forgive me!'

Mrs Lloyd gave an indignant shrug of her shoulders, and swept out of the room, while the young man retreated by another door. Ten minutes later Mrs Lloyd returned, and found the room occupied by her little step-daughter and the nursery-maid. The key was not on the table. She glanced at the child. Her little niece was perched on a chair, with the packet in her hands. She had broken the seal with her own small fingers. Mrs Lloyd hastily took possession of the key.

At the habitual supper-hour Arthur Lloyd came back from his counting-room. It was the month of June, and supper was served by daylight. The meal was placed on the table, but Mrs Lloyd failed to make her appearance. The servant whom his master sent to call her came back with the assurance that her room was empty, and that the women informed him that she had not been seen since dinner. They had, in truth, observed her to have been in tears, and, supposing her to be shut up in her chamber, had not disturbed her. Her husband called her name in various parts of the house, but without response. At last it occurred to him that he might find her by taking the way to the attic. The thought gave him a strange feeling of discomfort, and he bade his servants remain behind, wishing no witness in his quest. He reached the foot of the staircase leading to the topmost flat, and stood with his hand on the banisters, pronouncing his wife's name. His voice trembled. He called again louder and more firmly. The only sound which disturbed the absolute silence was a faint echo of his own tones, repeating his question under the great eaves. He nevertheless felt irresistibly moved to ascend the staircase. It opened upon a wide hall, lined with wooden closets, and terminating in a window which looked westward, and admitted the last rays of the sun. Before the window stood the great chest. Before the chest, on her knees, the young man saw with amazement and horror the figure of his wife. In an instant he crossed the interval between them, bereft of utterance. The lid of the chest stood open, exposing, amid their perfumed napkins, its treasure of stuffs and jewels. Rosalind had fallen backward from a kneeling posture, with one hand supporting her on the floor and the other pressed to her heart. On her limbs was the stiffness of death, and on her face, in the fading light of the sun, the terror of something more than death. Her lips were parted in entreaty, in dismay, in agony; and on her blanched brow and cheeks there glowed the marks of ten hideous wounds from two vengeful ghostly hands.

Comrade Death

Gerald Kersh

Sarek was a master-eavesdropper, but in order to hear the conversation of the two men at the adjoining table, he had to concentrate. The street was full of noise – clattering hoofs and heels, and the rumbling wheels of innumerable cabs.

Sarek forgot to puff at his cigar; the smoke stung his eyes. He even forgot to blink: his eyes became inflamed; they stared through a blue cloud, preoccupied and expressionless – eyes of blood and iron. He sat still. Only once, when he caught the words: *We can achieve power only through propaganda*, did Sarek show some sign of life – he grinned. And at last, when the conversation ended and one of the men went away, Sarek turned his head and addressed the other:

'Pardon me; but you are Joseph Pashenka, aren't you?'

'Yes.'

'The leader of the Workers' Party?'

'Yes. What can I do for you?'

'My name is Sarek, Hector Sarek, representative of the Skyrocket Ironmongery Company. You will think me very rude, but you spoke so loudly that I couldn't help overhearing what you said just now.'

'Well, all right. What about it?'

'My dear Mr Pashenka,' said Sarek, 'how you jump at a man! ... So you're the workers' leader! The gentleman who wants to start a revolution, just by talking. Achieve power only through propaganda. Well, well. I read some of your pamphlets, once, I think. Very enlightening, very instructive; but when all is said and done, nothing but *words*. Well, words aren't enough. One bullet, my dear sir——' Sarek flicked out his fingers in a gesture which symbolized scattered brains.

'Well what do you want?'

'I just want to put it to you that words aren't enough. Bullets speak louder. What you need is bullets.'

Pashenka laughed. 'If you're an *agent-provocateur*, you're very clumsy at the job!' he said.

'No, no, no! I have no politics. I'm just a plain business man. There's my card: *Sarek, Skyrocket Ironmongery.* No politics; I haven't the talent. But for political purposes, bullets are better. Now, why don't you do something in the Russian style – just one or two little acts of terrorism. You'd be surprised at the money and support it would bring in. Assassinate one or two unpopular Ministers——'

'You're just a common *agent-provocateur!*'

'– bombs are spectacular, but clumsy. A bomb is not infallible; it may kill the wrong person. But a revolver, in the hands of a practical man – now that's what I call a reliable weapon!'

'And what should I want with bombs and revolvers?'

'Not bombs; only revolvers. I merely offered a suggestion. Arm your supporters with good, reliable small-arms. Then you're ready for absolutely any emergency. The political situation is unstable – unlike Krieger revolvers. It is to them that I should like to call your attention. I may mention, in passing, that President Sadko was shot with a Krieger revolver. They're made in three calibres: .32, .38, and .44. There is a small model, firing a .22 bullet; an elegant little weapon, with a mother-o'-pearl handle; suitable for ladies. There are two varieties of bullet – soft lead, or nickel-coated. The nickel-coated bullets have a superior power of penetration, but the soft lead bullets expand, and inflict a wound which makes up for any slight inaccuracy of aim. You may always trust a Krieger bullet to reach a vital part. Poor President Sadko was killed with a Krieger nickel-coated – it passed through his body, and injured a gendarme standing twenty feet behind him. That speaks for itself. There are special rates for large quantities, and a solid cowhide holster is included, free of charge. Just think! With each pistol, a solid cowhide——'

'I don't know whether you're mad, or what!' exclaimed Pashenka.

'Not at all,' said Sarek. 'I'm just a practical man. You can't overthrow your enemies with words alone. You've got to have arms. And the advantage of arming with Krieger——'

'You don't mean to tell me——'

'Let me quote you——'

Pashenka's solemn face suddenly broke into a network of humorous wrinkles. He began to laugh.

'Ha-ha-ha-ha-ha! No! You don't really mean to say that you're a traveller in fire-arms?'

'Why not?' said Sarek. 'They're a commodity, aren't they?'

'A traveller in fire-arms!' cried Pashenka, who seemed to find something humorous in it. 'Oh Lord! Pistols! Bullets! A traveller in pistols! I never heard of anything so ridiculous in all my life! Ha-ha-ha-ha-ha!'

'Not so ridiculous,' said Sarek, without emotion. 'You'd better pick up my card; you may need it yet; you never know.'

'Thanks.' Pashenka rose, buttoning his frock-coat. He looked closely at Sarek, but in the flat and nondescript Slavonic face, the pursed lips, and the lifeless grey eyes, he could read nothing. Pashenka paused; the inclination to laugh gave place to a vague uneasiness.

'If you are an arms salesman,' he said at length, 'I can tell you one thing – you'll end up in the workhouse or the asylum.'

'Perhaps,' said Sarek, calmly.

Just then a girl approached the café, and Sarek, taking off his hat, went to greet her.

They sat down.

'You look tired,' said Sarek; 'have you just come from the workshop?'

'Yes,' said the girl, 'I had a hard day.'

'Well, listen, Cosima; you must have an egg, beaten up in sherry; that takes away the tiredness. Yes? Then you'll come with me to Grigorieff's and have dinner. Yes?' Sarek's voice had become less impersonal; he looked more alive. But Cosima shook her head.

'I'm sorry, but I came here to meet Janos,' she said.

Sarek's scanty eyebrows contracted.

'I shouldn't persist,' he said, 'it's a waste of energy. You told me once you don't love me at all. Is that so?'

Cosima nodded.

'All right. You don't love me. Good. You love Janos?'

Cosima nodded.

'You like herbs?' asked Sarek.

'What d'you mean?'

'Well, you'll have a meal of herbs where love is,' said Sarek, with an undertone of mockery.

'You shouldn't speak like that. One day Janos will be a great artist, Hector.'

'Hm! One day I shall be even greater.' He stared at her through the smoke of his cigar.

Janos appeared, and flung himself into a chair.

'What was that I heard about "greatness"?' he asked.

'Cosima said you were going to be a great artist,' said Sarek, 'and I said that I should be even greater.'

'As an artist?' asked Janos, with a smile.

'No. I haven't the talent.'

'And how goes the ironmongery business?'

'Very well, thank you. Kriegers have bought up Skyrocket Iron-mongery. Now, I travel for Kriegers.'

'Kriegers?' said Janos. 'They make all the guns, don't they?'

'That's right.'

'And you will still be selling ploughs and tools?'

'No. I'm on something much more progressive, now – arms.'

'Progressive!' cried Janos, with some irritation, 'I can't see that. Ploughs and tools give you comfort, and life. Guns give you nothing but pain and death.'

'You're an idealist,' said Sarek, 'and that's all very nice. But there are things you don't realize. The world moves: movement is life. Nations go to war – that's bad for some and good for others, like everything else. Nations have got to arm, so as to keep their power. Guns are power. I like guns. You always talk about the triumph of mind over matter; well, you see that expressed in a gun. You have your finger on the trigger, and an enemy over the sights – that's the triumph of mind over matter. Not long ago they only had the old muzzle-loading guns. Now, they've got Krieger machine-guns——'

'And what's a Krieger machine-gun?'

'Oh, something quite new. It fires bullets at the rate of hundreds a minute, all in a stream – *rat-at-at-at-at-at-at*! – like that. You could mow down men like corn with one.'

'Is that the gun that's going to be demonstrated in the Park on Wednesday?'

'Well, not quite. A French manufacturer got in first; he's demonstrating the Circonflex gun. All the officials of the War Office will be there. He'll make a fortune out of it. What an advertisement! How the newspapers will talk! What——'

'Beastly weapon, I think,' said Janos. 'Who wants to mow down men like corn, anyway?'

'I don't know,' said Sarek, 'but if you want to mow down an army why not do it efficiently, in the modern style?'

'And don't you *care*?' asked Cosima.

'No,' said Sarek; and Janos uttered an exclamation of disgust.

'Say "Ugh!" as much as you like, but it's the coming thing,' said Sarek. 'There's big money in machine-guns. Why not come and see the demonstration? There's to be a big military band——'

'I'm not interested,' said Janos; 'I like creation, not destruction.'

'And you, Cosima?' asked Sarek.

'Me, too.'

Sarek spat venom: 'Ha! A machine-gun hasn't got to be created, I suppose? Good God, Hiram Maxim had more creation in his little finger than you've got in your whole body – you painters! Copying a naked woman in paint on a bit of canvas – that's what you call creation!'

'Come on, Cosima,' said Janos.

They went away. Sarek sat perfectly still; again the smoke of his cigar curled up into his eyes and made them bloodshot.

*

On the following Wednesday, Sarek stood in the Constantine Park and watched the activities of the salesman of the Circonflex gun. An immense white target had been erected. Now they were fitting the barrel to the tripod.

The pressmen and the Government officials were assembling. Sarek stood near Kovas, the War Minister, and listened to his conversations. Kovas, the centre of a ring of generals, protested, with some petulance:

'Seeing is believing. This gun is too good to be true. It will revolutionize war if it works.'

'*If* it works,' said an aged officer, '*if*. Did this man invent the gun?'

'Heaven knows,' said Kovas. 'It's quite impossible to understand him. He gabbles on and on in his infernal French. He goes too fast for me. Whether he invented it, or sells it, or what, the devil only knows. One says, "*Oui monsieur*," out of politeness. If it works, I buy it; if the devil himself invented it that's all I know.'

Sarek glanced about him. The demonstrator's hired brass band was forming a semicircle. One of the players, with a mighty brazen tuba, blew a deep, tentative note, and tinkered with the mouthpiece of his instrument ...

In that moment Sarek was struck by an inspiration. It paralysed him, for a moment, as if he had been struck by lightning. He spat out his cigar, darted through the crowd, and tugged at the arm of the band conductor.

'When are you going to start playing?' he asked.

'The minute the gentleman finishes his speech.'

'And when is the speech?'

'As soon as the demonstration is over.'

'Listen,' whispered Sarek, 'do you want to earn five hundred *kronen*?'

'Well . . . how?'

'You have instructions to start playing just *after* the speech? Well, listen. Start playing *just as the man starts to talk*. A loud military march! Keep it up for five minutes, and I'll give you five hundred *kronen*!'

The conductor hesitated.

'Six hundred,' said Sarek.

'Make it eight.'

'All right.' Sarek took out a banknote. 'Five hundred now; the rest afterwards.'

'Very good, sir.' The conductor furtively pocketed the note.

'You won't fail me? Play the *Skobeleff March* – as loud as the devil! – *crescendo*, all the time! – blow your trombones out straight! blow their hats off! Keep it up for five minutes. Do it well, and I'll make it a thousand *kronen*.'

'You leave it to me.'

'As he utters the first words.'

'Trust me!'

Gerald Kersh

Sarek went back to his place. He wriggled into a strategic position, between the newspaper reporters and the War Minister. His heart was thumping; he felt that his collar was decapitating him.

Suddenly the crowd became silent.

Sweat poured down into Sarek's eyes.

The demonstrator knelt, aimed his gun, and squeezed the trigger.

With shocking abruptness, and a noise reminiscent of an iron bar drawn over corrugated iron, the gun began to fire. The cartridge belt ran through. A cloud of smoke drifted back into the faces of the spectators, and the white target quivered under the impact of the bullets. A line of bullet holes appeared; then another, and a third.

The demonstrator was, in fact, drawing an enormous letter K – the initial letter of the name of Kovas. He gave point to his delicate compliment of bowing in the direction of the War Minister.

'Amazing!' said Kovas, smiling with pleasure.

Sarek caught his breath. The demonstrator shouted:

'Now, my lords, ladies and gentlemen, it is my honour to write – in one thousand bullets – the Sign of the Cross!'

The gun roared again: the barrel crept upwards, paused, descended, and then swept from left to right. A crude, perforated cross became plainly visible on the blank white boards. Men began to take off their hats.

The demonstrator rose, waving his grease-blackened hands. There was a bellow of applause. He cleared his throat.

'My lords, ladies and gentlemen, I have had the honour of demonstrating——'

(Sarek flung an agonized glance towards the band – the conductor was raising his baton——)

'– what I may term, with all the modesty, the greatest military invention since the days of Schwartz——'

(Sarek ground on his teeth – a fat horn-player filled his lungs with air; his chest bulged——)

'A weapon which will revolutionize warfare! The——'

Down came the conductor's baton, and instantly the band began to force out the ear-splitting bars of the *Skobeleff March*:

Mighty, mighty are our mountains,
Mighty is the rushing river –

Sarek stood on tip-toe and shouted, in a tremendous voice:

'The Krieger Machine-gun!' He turned to Kovas: 'Your Highness has seen the letter K written in lead. That stands for Krieger! The Krieger Machine-gun, which gives one man the strength of a company. The Krieger Machine-gun, which fires at the rate of three hundred bullets a minute! Long may it stand between you and your enemies!'

Through packed masses of people the reporters bored their way to the offices of their papers. The band blared. Twenty yards away the demonstrator screamed at the conductor, but his voice was drowned in the uproar.

'Krieger? I thought Circonflex,' said Kovas.

'An error,' said Sarek.

'Krieger or Circonflex – I buy,' said Kovas.

In the career of any successful man the first skilful stroke – always in conjunction with good fortune – is half the battle. Since the day when Kovas had placed the first great order for Krieger machine-guns, Sarek had never looked back. And now, ten years after, walking with the firm and confident step of the conqueror, Sarek came into the presence of Pancho Pablo, President of Gaudeama in South America.

In a little while they came down to business.

'The position is grave,' said Pancho Pablo, 'soon it will be war. *Guerra al cuchillo*! War to the knife – them or us – Gaudeama or Contrabono. The world is too small for both.'

'You are the weaker,' said Sarek.

'That is so – much weaker. We are badly armed. They have good rifles. We have only eight field guns. They have seventeen. They will eat us alive.'

'It is an elementary rule, in strategy, that the weaker should strike first,' said Sarek. 'The longer you wait the weaker you get. In the end, they simply take you, without a battle. Declare war.'

'I daren't. Say I increase my army, mobilize a few thousand peons? Shall I arm them with machetes and reaping-hooks? I have no money to buy arms.'

'And say I arm you with Krieger rifles, Krieger machine-guns, and Krieger cannons? Say I supply unlimited ammunition? Say, in short, that I win you this war?'

'Oh, Señor! if you would!'

'Let us come to a friendly arrangement,' said Sarek, smoothly. 'I need one or two commodities. I need nitrates; give me the Perro Nitrate Beds for ten years. I need rubber; give me the Aguilar Rubber Forest for five years or so, plus a concession on the Contrabono Copper Mines, after you have won the war. Then I'll arm you to the teeth. I'll give you guns and ammunition enough to blow Contrabono off the map. I'll even send you skilled technicians and officers. Yes?'

'You are asking a great deal,' said the President.

'I never haggle,' said Sarek. 'If you accept my offer you will be sure to beat Contrabono within three months; if you refuse, Contrabono will be certain to beat you within three weeks. Take it or leave it; it is merely a friendly offer. Don't let me persuade you one way or the other.'

'Hm ...'

'A hundred thousand rifles; two hundred machine-guns; twenty field-guns of the latest model; ammunition unlimited – enough to kill a continent!'

'You guarantee me the war, in effect?'

'Oh, absolutely,' said Sarek. 'I will definitely guarantee that no war will start until you are fully equipped.'

'And then I will march on Contrabono,' said Pancho Pablo, with relief. 'Ah, Señor Sarek. I was on the verge of despair; but you come to me like an angel from heaven. God bless you! You are an angel of mercy. Now I shall be able to blow Contrabono into the Pacific.'

Three days later, Sarek sat in the office of Juan Amarillo, President of Contrabono.

Sarek said: 'Let me be quite frank with you. I am in South America for my health, but, seeing the state of affairs between Gaudeama and Contrabono, I felt that some business might be done. I intended to call on Pancho Pablo, but I have received information that he is already arming with Circonflex——'

'*What?*'

'Oh yes. He has ordered about 50,000 rifles, a few machine-guns, and some cannons, I think.'

'How do you know?'

'What I tell you is fact. You will need to strengthen yourself.'

'I shall march on him immediately.'

'You should have thought of that six months ago. You are too late now; he is already well enough equipped to stand against you until the remainder of his equipment arrives. He has, in fact, arranged to hand Circonflex concessions on your copper mines.'

'Good God!'

'Yes, it is rather bad. Some firms do business that way – arms in exchange for commodities. Kriegers, however, keep clear of such dirty transactions.'

'But this is outrageous! What do you advise me to do? As the active partner in one of the greatest armaments firms in Europe?'

'Well ... You might import a dozen field-guns or so, and a few thousand rifles. Krieger guns are superior to Circonflex. Try some machine-guns; they are the modern weapons. Wars are won on equipment nowadays. Get good, reliable machine-guns and cannons. I will arrange quick delivery. For a few million dollars you make yourself secure. Arms are a kind of insurance policy against war, or against defeat. Guns are power. Buy Krieger guns.'

'We have very little ready money.'

'That should be a simple matter. Impose an additional tax on the land; a few cents here and there on various necessities. Get about a dollar and a half from every peasant and the trick is done. Then, again, Kuhnberg will pay you half a million for the match monopoly. It is simple.'

'Wait. As a matter of fact I have been considering buying more arms. Say I buy about enough rifles to bring my infantry up to 175,000; a few of these machine-guns ...'

'Then bring a few thousand of your best able-bodied peons off the land, drill them, and arm them with the old rifles——'

'Requisition a few hundred horses for cavalry; call up my *vaqueros*, and put them into uniform ...'

'Then you would be sure of beating Gaudeama, Señor Amarillo.'

Just then there came the sound of angry voices in the square below. A fat little secretary popped his head in at the door, and said:

'Your Excellency, they have caught a spy.'

Amarillo became blue with rage.

'A spy! Again a spy? From Gaudeama? A dirty Gaudeama spy! Where did they catch him?'

'In the Guayacum Pass, Excellency. He was drawing plans.'

'Bring him in here!' shouted Amarillo. 'Bring him before me. Damn him, I'll shoot him like a dog – I'll shoot him down like a mad dog, I say. Bring him in.'

'Yes, Excellency.'

There was a pause. Then footsteps in the passage.

'That will make eight spies in three months,' said Amarillo.

The door opened.

Dirty, dishevelled, bleeding at the nose, his wrists cut by a chain handcuff, Janos the artist was prodded into the room at the point of a bayonet.

'What the devil is all this?' demanded Janos. 'I was sketching peacefully in the Pass over there, when half a dozen of these infernal louts grabbed hold of me and brought me here. I demand an explanation.'

'Oh, you demand an explanation!' screamed Amarillo. 'Oh, you were sketching peacefully! Spying peacefully, you mean, you dirty spy. What were you after?'

'I——'

'Silence, dog! Juan, show me that sketching-block. Aah! Sketching peacefully! Peacefully sketching an important strategic point! Pancho Pablo sent you, did he? I'll show you! I'll have you shot in the back, like a dog.'

'Nobody sent me,' said Janos. 'I'm an artist.'

'What an excuse! Artist! You liar. You don't even look like one. I've

never seen such a clumsy disguise. That coat! That beard! Bah! Do you
want a priest?'

Janos turned pale. He glanced wildly round the room. Then he
caught sight of Sarek, smiled with relief, and uttered a cry of joy:

'Why, Sarek! Sarek, you recognize me? You remember me, Janos?
Hector Sarek! You remember me – me and Cosima? We're married. We
have a boy, nine years old. You wouldn't let them shoot me, would you,
Sarek?'

Everybody looked at Sarek.

'Do you know this man?' asked Amarillo.

'Of course he does,' said Janos.

Sarek puffed out smoke and said with a shrug: 'I pay the penalty of
being fairly well-known. So many people have my name pat. I don't
know him from Adam.'

'Sarek!' shouted Janos. 'You do! You remember Cosima – you used
to be in love with her – we're married – we have a son——'

'Spare me these ravings,' said Sarek.

'Take him away. Send him a priest if he fancies one. Then a firing-
squad,' said Amarillo. And when the echoes of Janos's last cry of despair
had died away in the passage he turned to Sarek, and added: 'Even if
the fellow isn't a spy we daren't take chances in times like these . . . Now,
let us discuss the delivery of these guns . . .'

When he returned to Europe Sarek called on Cosima.

When he saw her something inside his heart seemed to swell. In
maturing her the years had made her more beautiful. The black dress
of widowhood accentuated the slimness of her waist. Above the high
black collar, like some exotic firework, burst the superb golden cascade
of her hair, fastened in a large loose knot.

'I have never been able to forget you,' said Sarek, in his dry, toneless
voice.

'You've heard about poor Janos?'

'I was in Contrabono when they shot him. I did my best to save him.
I spent ten thousand dollars in bribes, but I didn't begrudge anything,
I was thinking of you.'

'It was awfully kind of you, Hector. It was like you. You always did
have a good heart.'

Sarek stuck to his point: 'I thought of you. I've been thinking of you
for years.' The vague swelling in his heart became oppressive: it was the
repressed passion of a lifetime, struggling to find expression.

'Tell me, how do you live now?'

'I've gone back to the millinery business. It's quite nice.'

'Hard.'

'I don't mind it. I earn enough for little Otto and myself.'

'Listen to me, Cosima. I've got a lot of money, now – hundreds of thousands. But I don't care. Two meals a day, a bed, and a handful of "Virginia" cigars, and I'm satisfied. I've got power; influence. I only use it to make more money. And I don't care about money, actually. I'm alone. I'm a lonely man. Listen; why not marry me?'

'Marry ... But you're joking!'

'No, I never joke – I haven't the talent.'

'But, Hector – surely there are plenty of other nice girls——'

'I want to make you understand, Cosima, that I love you very much. I don't know how to put these things nicely; I haven't the knack. You say "plenty of other nice girls". Listen. I'm a narrow-minded man. I have only single purposes. I want a thing: I try to get it. I have wanted you for over ten years. I haven't been able to get you out of my mind. When I wanted to sell guns, then ploughs didn't exist any more for me; when I fell in love with you, other women didn't exist any more. I want you to marry me.'

'Hector, I can't take you seriously.'

'Cosima!' cried Sarek, with a desperate gesture. 'I'm not joking. I want you to marry me.'

'But I can't. I don't love you.'

'Why not?'

'I love Janos.'

'But he's dead. He doesn't exist any more. You can't love somebody that doesn't exist.'

'You don't understand. I still love him, even though ... I shan't see him any more ...'

Sarek felt a murderous rage surge up inside him. He controlled himself, however, and said:

'Don't cry. No use crying. Listen, Cosima. You've got a son. Think of all the things I could do for him. Even if you don't love me much, you can still marry me. People marry like that every day. You want to be faithful to Janos's memory? All right. Don't love me. But why not marry me, just the same?'

'No.'

Sarek paused. He stared at the floor, and when he looked up again there was something in his eyes that made Cosima shudder.

'Very well,' he said, 'now listen. With me, it's one thing, or the other. You don't love me. Very well. Then you'll hate me. I'll tell you something. I told you that I tried to save Janos? Well, it was a lie. I didn't – I sent him to his death. He was arrested while I was with the President; a word from me might have saved him. But no. I knew that my time was coming. He insulted me once ... besides, he had you, and I was determined to get you. Are you listening? Well, they said: "Do you know him?" and I said "No". Do you hear? Janos went on his bended knees

and begged for mercy. I just went on smoking my cigar. And I'm glad
I did it! ... Well? Well? What are you shaking your head like that for?
Now do you hate me?'

'No,' said Cosima. 'Because I don't believe you.'

'But it's true.'

'No, it isn't, Hector. It can't possibly be. You'd never do a terrible
thing like that. No, no, no! Say what you like, you'd never get me to
believe it. I believe that you tried to save him – yes. But kill him? No.
You always did have a good, kind heart, Hector, so I don't believe you.'

For the first time in his life Sarek tore his hair. Tears of exasperation
appeared in his eyes. He stamped on the floor in a frenzy of impotent
rage. And then Cosima said something which took his breath away like
ice-cold water:

'Poor Hector! Poor man, how you must be suffering, to say such awful
things.'

Sarek was suffering the hellish agonies of the strong man who sees
himself overcome by the weak: the clever man who experiences defeat
at the hands of the stupid: the wicked man vanquished by simplicity –
an exquisite mental torture. A Krieger soft-lead bullet could not have
hurt him more. He felt that he was going mad.

He finally managed to say:

'How ... how *dare* you pity me? How dare *you* pity *me*? How dare you?'

'You see,' said Cosima, sweetly, 'I understand you so well, Hector.
You have a sweet nature and a heart of gold, only you try not to show
it——'

Defeated and utterly humiliated, Sarek pressed his hands over his ears
and rushed out.

He rarely drank alcohol, but now he went to the nearest café and hastily
swallowed a double cognac. Then he lit a cigar and sat thinking, with
the smoke lapping at his face ...

He smiled slightly and blinked his smoke-stung eyes.

'Sarek, representing Comrade Death.'

He ordered another cognac.

Forty red years have passed, with the drone of flying lead. Sarek has
aged, in a horrible kind of way. He seems to have introverted, physically.
His external parts seem to be trying to creep inwards and hide themselves: his stomach yearns towards his spine, and his cheeks endeavour
to meet in his mouth. His head is a death's-head, with prominent ears.
He is covered with honours. European Powers have made a nobleman
of him. On special occasions, when he wears all his orders and medals,
he looks like some little Chinese God of Fear hung with offerings, and
moves with a golden jingling sound. He is unspeakably rich; he has far

more money than he knows what to do with. He has become a universal provider in the realms of the macabre. He endows hospitals and asylums, and fills them up. Not only does he build orphanages: he even provides the orphans. He lives in palaces of incredible splendour; Rolls-Royces are not good enough for him. He owns half of Europe. He is still alone. He goes to his offices at eight every morning; he lives on boiled fish and bismuth, with an occasional purgative; and still smokes twopenny cigars. Sarek sits at the head of a long table, presiding over a meeting of six directors of different nationalities. Half buried in his deep chair, without bothering to take his cigar out of his mouth, he addresses them in a squeaky voice:

'Yes, gentlemen. Half a century has passed since I took the first big order for Krieger machine-guns. Since then how civilization has progressed! Weapons which were highly modern ten years ago are now as obsolete as if they had existed in the Middle Ages. Rifles begin to fall into disuse. Soon the most efficient modern machine-gun will be placed in a glass case and ticketed: "Ancient History". For civilization progresses inexorably. Let us consider: The Franco-Prussian War was considered quite a war in 1870——'

'Ha-ha-ha-ha!'

'But it was mere milk and water. The Boer War was a mere interchange of bullets. Bang! – a man falls over. Skittles – coconut-shies – child's play! The Russo-Japanese affair was better, but not very much; it was relatively unproductive. Those wars were barbaric. Only between 1914 and 1918 did modern civilization begin to justify itself.'

'Hear, hear!'

'Then,' Sarek went on, 'nations fought in quite commendable manner: guns burnt ammunition day and night – thousands of tons an hour – for quite a while.

'But the first real stride towards ideal conditions was – if I may say so – brought about by myself, forty years ago. The Gaudeama-Contrabono affair, in which they reduced each other to pulp in a two-years' war. Krieger guns were used on both sides. It was a vigorous little war; it taught us a lesson.' Sarek cleared his throat, and slipped a bismuth tablet into his mouth. 'It was the first step towards the abolition of the cruel and merciless warfare of the rival armament firms. We came to our senses. We asked ourselves: "Why should we manufacturers cut one another's throats in rivalry? Let us strive towards a world peace between the makers of guns." We became united, controlled, international. By 1914 we were at peace.'

There was a respectful murmur.

'Yes, we were at peace. The air was black with our projectiles. Krieger shells flew both ways. There was nothing one-sided about us; we were free from the follies of morbid nationalism. Krieger cannons fired

Krieger shells into Krieger batteries; Krieger hand-grenades silenced sectors armed with Krieger machine-guns. Krieger tanks squashed Krieger riflemen. Krieger star-shells threw light on Krieger-armed combatants; Krieger bullets mowed them down, the Krieger shrapnel disembowelled them. Krieger torpedoes blew up Krieger battleships. Krieger submarines were blown to atoms by Krieger mines. Krieger searchlights picked out Krieger 'planes: *pom-pom*! went the Krieger anti-aircraft guns; and more orders poured into the factories. Then I breathed a sigh of satisfaction. It was no longer a case of dog eat dog. We were united.'

'Hear, hear!'

'Then, at the end of the War, the late Baron Krieger said to me: "Sarek, this is the end. There will be no more war. The nations have had a frightful lesson. They are tired of slaughter." But I told him: "Wait, my friend. There is still a great deal to hope for. Things are not half as bad as you say." Events are proving me right.'

'So they are.'

'There is one important thing which I have not yet mentioned.'

The Japanese representative raised his head and uttered one sibilant word:

'Gas!'

'Exactly,' said Sarek, 'gas. After the War, people became air-minded. That could have only one outcome, since it is obvious that the primary function of an aeroplane is bombardment. An aeroplane is mainly something to drop things out of. Thus, I concentrated on gas.'

There was a grating of chairs; the directors drew closer.

'From air-mindedness it is only a short step to gas-consciousness,' said Sarek. 'Now the public is gas-conscious. They are terrified of the War in the Air which they know is coming. Hence the colossal sales of our gas mask, the Krieger Impenetrable. Orders are pouring in from all parts of Europe. I leave it to you, gentlemen, to fix retail prices for your respective countries. Soon the Krieger Impenetrable Mask will be on sale in every hardware store. We are introducing three new sizes – the O_2, for babies up to two years old; the O_3, for children up to five; and the X_{13}, outsize, for obese people. Gas-mask clubs are being organized in every town.'

'Have you considered making the Omega gas in the form of pocket-grenades?' asked the Italian representative.

'They will be ready soon,' said Sarek.

'The Omega gas is a good gas,' said the German representative. 'The Krieger Mask is the only mask that can keep it out.'

'Hence the popularity of the Krieger Mask,' said the American representative.

Sarek cut him short:

'Well. You have your instructions. There is no more, for today. Now
you must excuse me ...'

Sarek rested for a while. His personal attendant, a lean Croat, brought
him a glass of milk, which he handed to him without a word.

'Marko,' said Sarek wearily, 'I'm tired out. I'm old. I'm tired. Why
do I go on? What the devil do I do it for? I don't get any pleasure out
of it. Why?'

Marko said nothing.

'I'm big!' shouted Sarek. 'I'm boss of the whole world! I'm guns. Guns
are power. I'm power. Kings and Presidents crawl on their bellies at my
feet. I speak to Governments as I speak to a dog. But what do I want
with it? I don't *feel* big. I feel small. I was beaten by a woman. Marko;
a damned blonde woman. I schemed. I plotted. I swore I'd get her. And
in the end she wouldn't have me – after I'd prostrated myself in front
of her. I was beaten. I was ashamed. I waited. Years after she came to
me. See? She came to me. She said: 'My dear friend Hector, they're
taking my grandson Janos to the front. Stop them. He's all I have in
the world." I said: "No. I'll not lift a finger. Let him die, then you'll
stop pitying me, perhaps, and start to hate me a little." The boy was
killed. She said: "You would have helped me if you could, Hector; you
always did have a kind heart." And she went away still pitying me. And
to this day she pities me. So, you see, I'm not big; I'm small. It eats my
heart up, I feel so small. I'm alone. I'm old. I'm tired. I wish to God
I could die.'

Marko said nothing. He was a deaf-mute. He had never heard nor
spoken. And to his ear alone Sarek confided all the agonies of his soul,
as a child talks to a doll.

Sarek rang a bell, and told his secretary:

'As soon as President Rozma comes, show him in.'

President Rozma turned a haggard gaze to Sarek and complained:

'I tell you, war looms. Incidents are occurring on the frontiers ... there
have been revolver shots ... Our flag was insulted ... We are in danger.'

'You have a belligerent neighbour,' said Sarek.

'Feuerbauch? He is not a man – he is a Mills-bomb with the pin
removed,' said Rozma.

'Feuerbauch is an ambitious man.'

'Not only has he made himself Dictator of his own country, he wants
to be Dictator of the Earth. See the result of making a man of the people
a Dictator! He started with nothing. He does not consider the consequences of what he does. He has nothing to lose——'

'Well?' said Sarek.

'I am concerned mainly with defence,' said Rozma. 'I understand that Feuerbauch has been accumulating enormous supplies of the Omega gas.'

'Yes. You are afraid of a gas attack?'

'I am.' Rozma shuddered. 'Consider. Clouds of the Omega gas in my congested industrial districts! My God!'

'Put your trust in Providence, and keep your gas-masks air-tight. How are you off for masks?'

'We are fully equipped with your Number Three Masks.'

'Against the Omega gas the Number Three Mask is useless. It is obsolete. The only mask worth having, now, is the Krieger Impenetrable, which is proof against every gas known to science.'

'It is rather hard. Two years ago I spent millions on masks. Now I must throw that money into the sea.'

'You needn't, if you don't want to,' said Sarek. 'Just retain your old masks, and when the Omega gas comes over sniff deeply, and all your troubles will be over.'

'That is no argument,' said Rozma. 'I must buy. A million of your Impenetrable Masks. They are proof against the Omega gas?'

'They are.'

'I, also shall buy Omega gas.'

'Why not buy Moribot?'

'What is Moribot?'

'It is a new chemical – a powder. A little on a cornfield, and the crop is destroyed; a little on a meadow, and the cattle die. It is a good thing for paralysing a food supply. It's dear.'

'I'll make a test. If it is good, I will buy that also. I am a man of peace; but this Feuerbauch is a madman, a devil.'

'Well, we will find you some holy water to sprinkle on his tail ...'

After Rozma was gone the secretary informed Sarek:

'Herr Feuerbauch is here.'

A spark of excitement kindled in Sarek's eyes. He sat upright, and lit another cigar.

'Show him in,' he said.

The colossal figure of Feuerbauch, the Dictator, loomed in the doorway.

Helmuth von Feuerbauch was a man of might. He had the physique and the mentality of a rogue elephant. There was ferocity in his little blue eyes, and a tigerish curve to his mouth. Absolute force was expressed in the set of his shoulders. He had a back like a door. His blond head was made more for butting than thinking, like the head of an ox. He extended to Sarek a fist that might have strangled a bullock.'

'Sit down,' said Sarek, 'there are important things I want to tell you.'

'Well, what?' said Feuerbauch. 'If it's about that poor fool of a

Rozma, don't bother. I know already. He's frightened.'

'Oh, Rozma's afraid, all right,' said Sarek. 'He wants gas-masks – Krieger Impenetrables.'

'And you're selling them to him?'

'Yes, why not?'

'But, damn it, what about all my Omega gas? What am I going to do with all my lovely Omega gas? Your masks resist it.'

'That wasn't what I wanted to tell you about,' said Sarek.

'Then what?'

'Listen,' said Sarek. 'I'm a man who has interested himself in chemical warfare. I've got money unlimited. I've bought the finest brains on earth. Do you know what there is in the cellar under this building? A laboratory.'

'A laboratory!'

'Yes. A secret place. Some of the greatest scientists in the world are at work down there at this moment. They work day and night. They've been discovering things – frightful things. You couldn't imagine what things! My finest official products are rubbish compared with two or three that I have up my sleeve——'

'What are they?'

'Wait a minute. What do you think is the deadliest gas known to man?'

'The Omega gas.'

'Wrong. Necrogene. Compared with the gas Necrogene Omega is fresh air. No mask can keep it out. There is no anti-gas.'

'Good Lord!'

The Krieger Impenetrable is useless against it. One sniff and you're dead. Nothing on earth can save you. Nausea, vomiting, coma; and death within five minutes.'

'Great God! With a gas like that I could hold the world in my hand!'

'So you could. It's going to the highest bidder——'

'I'll be the highest bidder. Name the price – anything you like, reasonable or otherwise – but give me that gas.'

'Well, I might. I like your methods, Feuerbauch; there's no sentiment about self-defence about you. Yes, I think I will——'

'Then——'

'One moment, please. If you insist on banging the table with your fist like that I shall ask you to leave. My nerves are not good ... Now tell me, what is the most powerful explosive you know of?'

'There is nothing more violent than Ultimon,' said Feuerbauch.

Sarek laughed. 'Ultimon! *Pfui!* And what if I tell you that I have an explosive beside which Ultimon looks like a penny squib?'

'What? *What?* What is it?'

'Disintegrol.'

'What's that?'

'What the name implies – Oil of Disintegration. It is more than an explosive: it is a kind of explosive principle. The way it works is a mystery. We know how to use it and how to control it; but how it works we don't know.'

'What happens?'

'It combines with most substances to form an extremely unstable high explosive. That's Disintegrol. We've made tests. One milligramme dropped on a common brick turned the brick into something equal to about seven kilos of Ammonal.'

'God!'

'We made some amusing tests. We put a milligramme on a hairbrush, and waited. The hairbrush exploded and blew a hole eight feet deep and twenty feet in diameter. We put half a milligramme on a ballistite cartridge and buried it in a field. There was nearly an earthquake! And as for the field – it no longer exists. There is only a huge pit.'

'What an explosive!'

'You know that little island in Lake Kraken? We sprayed it with Disintegrol, in a fine vapour. Ten minutes later the island ceased to be. Showers of powdered earth fell ten miles away.'

'No!'

'Unhappily, one of our technicians had a pin-prick in his insulated glove. His hand exploded like a bomb and blew him to pieces.'

Feuerbauch actually shuddered.

'If,' said Sarek, 'if you sprayed a city with Disintegrol from an aeroplane you would turn that city into a gigantic bomb. Nothing could be done. Bang! – no more city! Stone and brick are excellent mediums for it. Organic matter also. If you swallowed a capsule of Disintegrol, my friend, I can guarantee that you'd never again be troubled with internal irregularities. What a magnificent bomb you'd make!'

Feuerbauch trembled. His little blue eyes, staring past Sarek, seemed to contemplate some terrible triumphs.

'Disintegrol!' he said. 'Why talk of gases when there is Disintegrol? By God and the devil, I could blow the world out of the solar system.'

'We have special insulating material for aeroplanes and a spraying apparatus by means of which Disintegrol can be sent on the wind in the form of a vapour. That simply means that all of a sudden a city blows up.'

'Give it to me,' said Feuerbauch, with dilated eyes.

'I should be a fool to do that,' said Sarek.

'Then what are you going to do with it?'

'Keep it up my sleeve,' said Sarek. 'In the meantime, I am going to let you have the gas Necrogene. Later on, I may let you blow up the world. You must look after my interests. Meanwhile, I prefer to hold one or two of the trump cards. You understand my attitude?'

'I think I understand. But you will give me Necrogene?'

'I'll sell you Necrogene.' Sarek paused. From a case of gold studded with jewels he took another of his twopenny cigars, and lit it. He went on, in a faint, dreamy voice: 'I'm an old man. I'm very, very old; and very, very tired; and very, very bored. Yes. One day I'll let you have Disintegrol, and then ... then, my friend, there will be such a bang! Yes, one day ...'

'Why not now? demanded Feuerbauch.

'Well ... I don't know,' murmured Sarek. 'Why not? Why not now? ... I have so many things, downstairs. I have brought destruction to a fine art. Why not let you have it now? Why not ...'

'Now!' shouted Feuerbauch.

'Perhaps now,' said Sarek.

'Let me, at least, see it,' said Feuerbauch.

Sarek pressed a button. A minute or two passed. Sarek sat still, limp as a man in a faint. Feuerbauch took out a bent black pipe, filled it, and sucked out big blue clouds. He watched the smoke curling vividly across the sunbeams, and there came into his mind a vision of great open plains ... Men advanced, dressed in gas-proof suits, grotesquely masked in Krieger Impenetrables, which resembled the distorted bones of a face. Suddenly a cloud crept across the plain – a sneaking, curling cloud, which writhed and darted with the wind; and, like toy soldiers stricken by a wind the men fell, in lines, writhing. Then, from the west, behind a blinding barrage of Necrogene, Disintegrol, and liquid fire, a padded army swept forward, dumbly, to a bloody victory ... and, through the shattered streets of blood-besprinkled cities he, Feuerbauch, rode like a god in his huge black armoured limousine, while multitudes under the truncheons of his Guards forced their mournful faces into wry smiles, and uttered feeble cheers ...

'Ah!' said Feuerbauch.

A man in a white coat came in. Sarek said: 'Is all clear?'

'Yes, Excellency.'

'Then conduct us to the laboratory.'

The white-coated man bowed and conducted them out. In another room he helped them to put on great, flapping white suits, triple-sealed at the seams; and curious gas-masks with double respirators and immense, goggling eyes which made them look like unheard-of fishes from some unattainable dark depths of a tropic sea. Feuerbauch was instantly enclosed by a horrible silence. He began to sweat. To him, silence was death. But as he opened his mouth to speak the man in the white coat attached a little black disc to the side of his head, and into the Dictator's ear broke the voice of Sarek, enormously amplified:

'This is necessary. Our laboratories are dangerous, terribly dangerous. Even with all our precautions we lose five men every week. We are playing with the destructive forces of Nature.'

'I fear nothing!' said Feuerbauch, shouting to break down the trembling of his voice.

The doors of a lift clicked behind them. They sank down quickly, down and down: the well of the lift seemed to have no bottom.

'We have tunnelled down right below the city,' said Sarek, 'the whole world knows the city above – that is my city, the Arms City; what the stupid newspapers call Death City. But down here, I have my own secrets. This is the Under World ...'

'Perhaps I had better go back,' said Feuerbauch.

'As you wish,' said Sarek, 'but I hate a coward.'

'I fear nothing,' said Feuerbauch. 'In any case, I have taken the usual precautions. If I do not return within three hours you will be asked why I have not communicated. If, then, I do not communicate, three hundred aeroplanes will ask further questions.'

The lift stopped.

Sarek's Under World was a place of utter silence over which there brooded an atmosphere of horror. 'I don't see why you can't work above ground,' said Feuerbauch. Then he stopped abruptly with a gasp. Staring at him through the lenses of his goggles stood something that resembled a hippopotamus.

Was it a man? His jaws were blackened and swollen beyond the bounds of fantasy. His nose was gone: the horrible enlargement of his face had swallowed it. His eyes bulged, bright red, under hideously distorted brow-ridges. As he opened his mouth to speak, Feuerbauch could see that he had no teeth.

'Our Doctor Krok,' said Sarek. 'Don't be alarmed. He is the result of a slight accident. He can claim the honour of discovering the Krok Poison. But, unhappily, the good doctor was so careless as to permit one imperceptible drop to touch his skin. Observe the result.'

'One imperceptible drop!' said Feuerbauch. 'And what, in God's name, if the drop had been larger?'

'The unfortunate Doctor Krok would have disintegrated, within twenty-four hours, into a sort of liquid,' said Sarek.

Sweat misted the insides of the Dictator's goggles. Sarek added, in a low voice: 'But you ought to see him without any clothes on!'

Feuerbauch followed him, blindly. Soon, Sarek's voice said: 'In this room, you are in the presence of eternal death.'

'Death?'

'Most certain death. Here we store Necrogene.' Sarek pointed. Feuerbauch could see innumerable black containers lying in nests of wood-shavings – smooth, shining, fat, oval, like eggs. 'Necrogene. There lies, on this floor, enough poison to kill the whole of this city within fifteen minutes.'

'God!'

'But wait. All this is nothing.'

'Nothing, you say? Nothing?'

'Well, next to nothing. To look at, those cylinders might be harmless. Would you like to see my museum? I have some curious specimens.'

'Of what?'

'Human remains. They are rather entertaining. There is, for example, all that was left of three men after an accident with the Krok Poison – one coffee-spoonful in a small test tube; a sort of liquid carbon ... And then, again, gas; I can show you some quite amazing things the Necrogene has done to men. They have twisted themselves into positions – well, I tell you, if they had studied acrobatics all their lives they could never have achieved such contortions! Amazing! One poor fellow bit himself in the small of the back. But you'd never believe. Come, let me show you——'

'No. No. I take your word. No. I don't want to see.'

'You may as well see the effects of the gas you are going to employ.'

'My experts will attend to that. I ...'

'You prefer to come in afterwards as the conqueror?' Sarek laughed. 'Good. Now I will show you Disintegrol.'

They passed through a long, white room, padded with felt. Sarek pointed to rows of small brown bottles. 'Disintegrol. We have even invented a special insulating substance, Sekurite. That is the material of which those bottles is made.' He picked one up. The Dictator leapt away. 'Oh, don't be alarmed, Feuerbauch; look——' Sarek dropped a bottle, which bounced a little and then lay still; he kicked it aside. 'As long as it is not exposed to air you can give it to the baby to cut his teeth on ... Come ,,,'

'I want to go,' said Feuerbauch.

'And I say come!' said Sarek.

Feuerbauch looked behind him. The immense sliding doors had automatically closed. He wanted to be sick. Sarek beckoned again; he followed. Another door slid back. 'Gas Department,' said Sarek.

The room was lit by hidden blue lamps. It was high and long, and cut by the gleaming white lengths of glass benches at which masked men, quite still and silent, stood staring into bottles. Above hung glass tubes in terrifying coils. 'You would not think so, but these men have all the technique of hidden death at their fingertips,' said Sarek. 'Look.' He beckoned. A little man came forward under the blue lights – a minutely-proportioned man, with the figure of a schoolboy. Through the clear glass of his goggles gleamed a pair of large, blue, childish eyes. 'Necros,' said Sarek, 'inventor of Necrogene, and my greatest research-worker.'

Necros bowed. 'Thank you, Excellency,' he said in a high, penetrating voice which, in Feuerbauch's microphone sounded like the crowing of a young cock.

'And how goes the new gas, Necros?'

'Very well, Excellency.'

'Near completion?'

'Complete, Excellency. I suggest that we call it Sarek's Last Word.'

'But why haven't you told me before?'

'Excellency, I finished work today. Besides——'

'Is it good?'

'Good? Excellency, it is frightful!'

'Excellent.'

'Compared with this, Excellency, Necrogene is no more poisonous than a night mist.'

'Indeed!' Sarek laughed. 'There is no end. What are its effects?'

'Excellency, I tried it on a mouse, a guinea-pig, a chimpanzee, and – by accident – on a man.'

'What man?'

'Mischa, your Excellency. Poor Mischa.'

'What happened?'

'Excellency, the effects of the gas are like this: it attacks the higher centres. Thus, the mouse, on inhaling it, walked in circles for five minutes, and then began to eat itself.'

'Ah! And the other animals?'

'The guinea-pig also walked in circles, and scratched itself to death. The chimpanzee walked also in circles and then destroyed itself by beating its head against the bars of its cage.'

'And Mischa?'

'He walked in circles for an hour and then began to tear himself to pieces with his hands.'

'Quite spectacular! What did you do?'

'Mischa was my good friend, Excellency, so I put him out of his misery. The reason why I did not tell you before is that I am not quite sure of it.'

'How, not sure?'

'Excellency, I can't hold it.'

'What do you mean?'

'It penetrates everything, even glass.'

'Then how do you keep it?'

'Excellency,' said Necros, bursting into tears, 'that is the trouble – I can't keep it. It is all gone!'

There was silence. Then, suddenly, Feuerbauch – about whose head the laboratory was spinning like a wheel – heard Sarek's voice saying: 'Feuerbauch ... you are walking in circles!'

Feuerbauch blinked. Sarek was before him. Then Sarek was gone; then Sarek was there again. He turned his head. Carefully picking his footsteps, Sarek was walking round and round, followed by Necros and the hideous Doctor Krok. A door opened. Sarek began to laugh uproariously – a piercing, shrieking laugh. Then the others laughed too ... Feuerbauch was becoming giddy, and inside his head there was a sensation of prickling, like soda-water bubbles on a sore tongue ... He began to laugh, too; and when he looked again, Sarek had an armful of brown bottles, Disintegrol bottles, which he was hastening to uncork.

Feuerbauch had a sudden impulse to tear off his clothes and dance. His mask fell away; then his gas-proof suit. He snatched a bottle from Sarek, shouting: 'Give me some, too!'

Disintegrol tasted bitter. He drank a little, and spat it out; then poured it on his hair.

The last thing he ever heard was the voice of Sarek:

'Look! look! look! look! look! look! look! Now they're all walking in circles! Ha-ha-ha-ha-ha-ha-hahahahahahaaah! Oh, what a bang we shall make!'

Then he was seized by an overwhelming desire to pull out his fingers and throw them away ...

At three o'clock that afternoon, Seismographs in distant cities recorded a terrible earthquake. At three-thirty, news came through that, where there had been a city, there was now a pit a mile deep. For three months afterwards, there were beautiful vivid red sunsets, due to the action of the sunlight passing through the high-floating clouds of infinitesimally fine dust.

Among this dust, presumably, there floated all that was left of Sarek.

The Salem Horror

Henry Kuttner

When Carson first noticed the sounds in his cellar, he ascribed them
to the rats. Later he began to hear the tales which were whispered
by the superstitious Polish mill workers in Derby Street regarding the
first occupant of the ancient house, Abigail Prinn. There was none living
today who could remember the diabolical old hag, but the morbid
legends which thrive in the 'witch district' of Salem like rank weeds
on a neglected grave gave disturbing particulars of her activities, and
were unpleasantly explicit regarding the detestable sacrifices she was
known to have made to a worm-eating, crescent-horned image of
dubious origin. The oldsters still muttered of Abbie Prinn and her
monstrous boasts that she was high priestess of a fearfully potent god
which dwelt deep in the hills. Indeed, it was the old witch's reckless
boasting which had led to her abrupt and mysterious death in 1692,
about the time of the famous hangings on Gallows Hill. No one liked
to talk about it, but occasionally a toothless crone would mumble
fearfully that the flames could not burn her, for her whole body had
taken on the peculiar anaesthesia of her witchmark.

Abbie Prinn and her anomalous statue had long since vanished, but
it was still difficult to find tenants for her decrepit, gabled house, with
its overhanging second storey and curious diamond-paned casement
windows. The house's evil notoriety had spread throughout Salem.
Nothing had actually happened there of recent years which might
give rise to the inexplicable tales, but those who rented the house had
a habit of moving out hastily, generally with vague and unsatisfactory
explanations connected with the rats.

And it was a rat which led Carson to the Witch Room. The squealing
and muffled pattering within the rotting walls had disturbed
Carson more than once during the nights of his first week in the house,
which he had rented to obtain the solitude that would enable
him to complete a novel for which his publishers had been asking –
another light romance to add to Carson's long string of popular
successes. But it was not until some time later that he began to entertain

certain wildly fantastic surmises regarding the intelligence of the rat that scurried from under his feet in the dark hallway one evening.

The house had been wired for electricity, but the bulb in the hall was small and gave a dim light. The rat was a misshapen, black shadow as it darted a few feet away and paused, apparently watching him.

At another time Carson might have dismissed the animal with a threatening gesture and returned to his work. But the traffic on Derby Street had been unusually noisy, and he had found it difficult to concentrate upon his novel. His nerves, for no apparent reason, were taut; and somehow it seemed that the rat, watching just beyond his reach, was eyeing him with sardonic amusement.

Smiling at the conceit, he took a few steps towards the rat, and it rushed away to the cellar door, which he saw with surprise was ajar. He must have neglected to close it the last time he had been in the cellar, although he generally took care to keep the doors shut, for the ancient house was draughty. The rat waited in the doorway.

Unreasonably annoyed, Carson hurried forward, sending the rat scurrying down the stairway. He switched on the cellar light and observed the rat in a corner. It watched him keenly out of glittering little eyes.

As he descended the stairs he could not help feeling that he was acting like a fool. But his work had been tiring, and subconsciously he welcomed any interruption. He moved across the cellar to the rat, seeing with astonishment that the creature remained unmoving, staring at him. A strange feeling of uneasiness began to grow within him. The rat was acting abnormally, he felt; and the unwinking gaze of its cold shoe-button eyes was somehow disturbing.

Then he laughed to himself, for the rat had suddenly whisked aside and disappeared into a little hole in the cellar wall. Idly he scratched a cross with his toe in the dirt before the burrow, deciding that he would set a trap there in the morning.

The rat's snout and ragged whiskers protruded cautiously. It moved forward and then hesitated, drew back. Then the animal began to act in a singular and unaccountable manner – almost as though it were dancing, Carson thought. It moved tentatively forward, retreated again. It would give a little dart forward and be brought up short, then leap back hastily, as though – the simile flashed into Carson's mind – a snake were coiled before the burrow, alert to prevent the rat's escape. But there was nothing there save the little cross Carson had scratched in the dust.

No doubt it was Carson himself who blocked the rat's escape, for he was standing within a few feet of the burrow. He moved forward, and the animal hurriedly retreated out of sight.

His interest piqued, Carson found a stick and poked it exploringly into the hole. As he did so his eye, close to the wall, detected something strange about the stone slab just above the rat burrow. A quick glance around its edge confirmed his suspicion. The slab was apparently movable.

Carson examined it closely, noticed a depression on its edge which would afford a handhold. His fingers fitted easily into the groove, and he pulled tentatively. The stone moved a trifle and stopped. He pulled harder, and with a sprinkling of dry earth the slab swung away from the wall as though on hinges.

A black rectangle, shoulder-high, gaped in the wall. From its depths a musty, unpleasant stench of dead air welled out, and involuntarily Carson retreated a step. Suddenly he remembered the monstrous tales of Abbie Prinn and the hideous secrets she was supposed to have kept hidden in her house. Had he stumbled upon some hidden retreat of the long-dead witch?

Before entering the dark gap he took the precaution of obtaining a flashlight from upstairs. Then he cautiously bent his head and stepped into the narrow, evil-smelling passage, sending the flashlight's beam probing out before him.

He was in a narrow tunnel, scarcely higher than his head, and walled and paved with stone slabs. It ran straight ahead for perhaps fifteen feet, and then broadened out into a roomy chamber. As Carson stepped into the underground room – no doubt a hidden retreat of Abbie Prinn's, a hiding-place, he thought, which nevertheless could not save her on the day the fright-crazed mob had come raging along Derby Street – he caught his breath in a gasp of amazement. The room was fantastic, astonishing.

It was the floor which held Carson's gaze. The dull grey of the circular wall gave place here to a mosaic of varicoloured stone, in which blues and greens and purples predominated – indeed, there were none of the warmer colours. There must have been thousands of bits of coloured stone making up that pattern, for none was larger than a walnut. And the mosaic seemed to follow some definite pattern, unfamiliar to Carson; there were curves of purple and violet mingled with angled lines of green and blue, intertwining in fantastic arabesques. There were circles, triangles, a pentagram, and other, less familiar, figures. Most of the lines and figures radiated from a definite point: the centre of the chamber, where there was a circular disc of dead black stone perhaps two feet in diameter.

It was very silent. The sounds of the cars that occasionally went past overhead in Derby Street could not be heard. In a shallow alcove in the wall Carson caught a glimpse of markings on the walls, and he moved slowly in that direction, the beam of his light travelling up and down the walls of the niche.

The marks, whatever they were, had been daubed upon the stone long ago, for what was left of the cryptic symbols was indecipherable. Carson saw several partly-effaced hieroglyphics which reminded him of Arabic, but he could not be sure. On the floor of the alcove was a corroded metal disc about eight feet in diameter, and Carson received the distinct impression that it was movable. But there seemed no way to lift it.

He became conscious that he was standing in the exact centre of the chamber, in the circle of black stone where the odd design centred. Again he noticed the utter silence. On an impulse he clicked off the ray of his flashlight. Instantly he was in dead blackness.

At that moment a curious idea entered his mind. He pictured himself at the bottom of a pit, and from above a flood was descending, pouring down the shaft to engulf him. So strong was this impression that he actually fancied he could hear a muffled thundering, the roar of the cataract. Then, oddly shaken, he clicked on the light, glanced around swiftly. The drumming, of course, was the pounding of his blood, made audible in the complete silence – a familiar phenomenon. But, if the place was so still——

The thought leaped into his mind, as though suddenly thrust into his consciousness. This would be an ideal place to work. He could have the place wired for electricity, have a table and chair brought down, use an electric fan if necessary – although the musty odour he had first noticed seemed to have disappeared completely. He moved to the tunnel mouth, and as he stepped from the room he felt an inexplicable relaxation of his muscles, although he had not realized that they had been contracted. He ascribed it to nervousness, and went upstairs to brew black coffee and write to his landlord in Boston about his discovery.

The visitor stared curiously about the hallway after Carson had opened the door, nodding to himself as though with satisfaction. He was a lean, tall figure of a man, with thick steel-grey eyebrows overhanging keen grey eyes. His face, although strongly marked and gaunt, was unwrinkled.

'About the Witch Room, I suppose?' Carson said ungraciously. His landlord had talked, and for the last week he had been unwillingly entertaining antiquaries and occultists anxious to glimpse the secret chamber in which Abbie Prinn had mumbled her spells. Carson's annoyance had grown, and he had considered moving to a quieter place; but his inherent stubbornness had made him stay on, determined to finish his novel in spite of interruptions. Now, eyeing his guest coldly, he said, 'I'm sorry, but it's not on exhibition any more.'

The other looked startled, but almost immediately a gleam of comprehension came into his eyes. He extracted a card and offered it to Carson.

'Michael Leigh ... occultist, eh?' Carson repeated. He drew a deep breath. The occultists, he had found, were the worst, with their dark hints of nameless things and their profound interest in the mosaic pattern on the floor of the Witch Room. 'I'm sorry, Mr Leigh, but – I'm really quite busy. You'll excuse me.'

Ungraciously he turned back to the door.

'Just a moment,' Leigh said swiftly.

Before Carson could protest he had caught the writer by the shoulders and was peering closely into his eyes. Startled, Carson drew back, but not before he had seen an extraordinary expression of mingled apprehension and satisfaction appear on Leigh's gaunt face. It was as though the occultist had seen something unpleasant – but not unexpected.

'What's the idea?' Carson asked harshly. 'I'm not accustomed——'

'I'm very sorry,' Leigh said. His voice was deep, pleasant. 'I must apologize. I thought – well, again I apologize. I'm rather excited, I'm afraid. You see, I've come from San Francisco to see this Witch Room of yours. Would you really mind letting me see it? I should be glad to pay any sum——'

Carson made a deprecatory gesture.

'No,' he said, feeling a perverse liking for this man growing within him – his well-modulated, pleasant voice, his powerful face, his magnetic personality. 'No, I merely want a little peace – you have no idea how I've been bothered,' he went on, vaguely surprised to find himself speaking apologetically. 'It's a frightful nuisance. I almost wish I'd never found the room.'

Leigh leaned forward anxiously. 'May I see it? It means a great deal to me – I'm vitally interested in these things. I promise not to take up more than ten minutes of your time.'

Carson hesitated, then assented. As he led his guest into the cellar he found himself telling the circumstances of his discovery of the Witch Room. Leigh listened intently, occasionally interrupting with questions.

'The rat – did you see what became of it?' he asked.

Carson looked surprised. 'Why, no. I suppose it hid in its burrow. Why?'

'One never knows,' Leigh said cryptically as they came into the Witch Room.

Carson switched on the light. He had had an electrical extension installed, and there were a few chairs and a table, but otherwise the chamber was unchanged. Carson watched the occultist's face, and with surprise saw it become grim, almost angry.

Leigh strode to the centre of the room, staring at the chair that stood on the black circle of stone.

'You work here?' he asked slowly.

'Yes. It's quiet – I found I couldn't work upstairs. Too noisy. But this is ideal – somehow I find it very easy to write here. My mind feels' –

he hesitated – 'free; that is, disassociated with other things. It's quite an unusual feeling.'

Leigh nodded as though Carson's words had confirmed some idea in his own mind. He turned towards the alcove and the metal disc in the floor. Carson followed him. The occultist moved close to the wall, tracing out the faded symbols with a long forefinger. He muttered something under his breath – words that sounded like gibberish to Carson.

'*Nyogtha . . . k'yarnak . . .*'

He swung about, his face grim and pale. 'I've seen enough,' he said softly. 'Shall we go?'

Surprised, Carson nodded and led the way back into the cellar.

Upstairs Leigh hesitated, as though finding it difficult to broach his subject. At length he asked, 'Mr Carson – would you mind telling me if you have had any peculiar dreams lately.'

Carson stared at him, mirth dancing in his eyes. 'Dreams?' he repeated. 'Oh – I see. Well, Mr Leigh, I may as well tell you that you can't frighten me. Your compatriots – the other occultists I've entertained – have already tried it.'

Leigh raised his thick eyebrows. 'Yes? Did they ask you whether you'd dreamed?'

'Several did – yes.'

'And you told them?'

'No.' Then as Leigh leaned back in his chair, a puzzled expression on his face, Carson went on slowly, 'Although, really, I'm not quite sure.'

'You mean?'

'I *think* – I have a vague impression – that I have dreamed lately. But I can't be sure. I can't remember anything of the dream, you see. And – oh, very probably your brother occultists put the idea into my mind!'

'Perhaps,' Leigh said non-committally, getting up. He hesitated. 'Mr Carson, I'm going to ask you a rather presumptuous question. Is it necessary for you to live in this house?'

Carson sighed resignedly. 'When I was first asked that question I explained that I wanted a quiet place to work on a novel, and that any quiet place would do. But it isn't easy to find 'em. Now that I have this Witch Room, and I'm turning out my work so easily, I see no reason why I should move and perhaps upset my programme. I'll vacate this house when I finish my novel, and then you occultists can come in and turn it into a museum or do whatever you want with it. I don't care. But until the novel is finished I intend to stay here.'

Leigh rubbed his chin. 'Indeed. I can understand your point of view. But – is there no other place in the house where you can work?'

He watched Carson's face for a moment, and then went on swiftly. 'I don't expect you to believe me. You are a materialist. Most people are. But there are a few of us who know that above and beyond what men call science there is a greater science that is built on laws and principles which to the average man would be almost incomprehensible. If you have read Machen you will remember that he speaks of the gulf between the world of consciousness and the world of matter. It is possible to bridge that gulf. The Witch Room is such a bridge! Do you know what a whispering-gallery is?'

'Eh?' Carson said, staring. 'But there's no——'

'An analogy – merely an analogy. A man may whisper a word in a gallery – or a cave – and if you are standing in a certain spot a hundred feet away you will hear that whisper, although someone ten feet away will not. It's a simple trick of acoustics – bringing the sound to a focal point. And this principle can be applied to other things besides sound. To any wave impulse – *even to thought!*'

Carson tried to interrupt, but Leigh kept on.

'That black stone in the centre of your Witch Room is one of those focal points. The design on the floor – when you sit on the black circle there you are abnormally sensitive to certain vibrations – certain thought commands – dangerously sensitive! Why do you suppose your mind is so clear when you are working there? A deception, a false feeling of lucidity – for you are merely an instrument, a microphone, tuned to pick up certain malign vibrations the nature of which you could not comprehend!'

Carson's face was a study in amazement and incredulity. 'But – you don't mean you actually *believe*——'

Leigh drew back, the intensity fading from his eyes, leaving them grim and cold. 'Very well. But I have studied the history of your Abigail Prinn. She too, understood this super-science of which I speak. She used it for evil purposes – the black art, as it is called. I have read that she cursed Salem in the old days – and a witch's curse can be a frightful thing. Will you——' He got up, gnawing at his lip. 'Will you, at least, allow me to call on you tomorrow?'

Almost involuntarily Carson nodded. 'But I'm afraid you'll be wasting your time. I don't believe – I mean, I have no——' He stumbled, at a loss for words.

'I merely wish to assure myself that you – oh, another thing. If you dream tonight, will you try to remember the dream? If you attempt to recapture it immediately after waking, it is often possible to recall it.'

'All right. If I dream——'

That night Carson dreamed. He awoke just before dawn with his heart racing furiously and a curious feeling of uneasiness. Within the walls and from below he could hear the furtive scurrying of the rats. He got out of bed hastily, shivering in the cold greyness of early morning. A wan moon still shone faintly in a paling sky.

Then he remembered Leigh's words. He *had* dreamed – there was no question of that. But the content of his dream – that was another matter. He absolutely could not recall it to his mind, much as he tried, although there was a very vague impression of running frantically in darkness.

He dressed quickly, and because the stillness of early morning in the old house got on his nerves, went out to buy a newspaper. It was too early for shops to be open, however, and in search of a news-boy he set off westward, turning at the first corner. And as he walked a curious and inexplicable feeling began to take possession of him: a feeling of – familiarity! He had walked here before, and there was a dim and disturbing familiarity about the shapes of the houses, the outline of the roofs. But – and this was the fantastic part of it – to his knowledge he had never been on this street before. He had spent little time walking about this region of Salem, for he was indolent by nature; yet there was this extraordinary feeling of remembrance, and it grew more vivid as he went on.

He reached a corner, turned unthinkingly to the left. The odd sensation increased. He walked on slowly, pondering.

No doubt he *had* travelled by this way before – and very probably he had done so in a brown study, so that he had not been conscious of his route. Undoubtedly that was the explanation. Yet as Carson turned into Charter Street he felt a nameless uneasy waking within him. Salem was rousing; with daylight impassive Polish workers began to hurry past him towards the mills. An occasional automobile went by.

Before him a crowd was gathered on the sidewalk. He hastened his steps, conscious of a feeling of impending calamity. With an extraordinary sense of shock he saw that he was passing the Charter Street Burying Ground, the ancient, evilly famous 'Burying Point'. Hastily he pushed his way into the crowd.

Comments in a muffled undertone came to Carson's ears, and a bulky blue-clad back loomed up before him. He peered over the policeman's shoulder and caught his breath in a horrified gasp.

A man leaned against the iron railing that fenced the old graveyard. He wore a cheap, gaudy suit, and he gripped the rusty bars in a clutch that made the muscles stand out in ridges on the hairy back of his hands. He was dead, and on his face, staring up at the sky at a crazy angle, was frozen an expression of abysmal and utterly shocking horror. His eyes, all whites, were bulging hideously; his mouth was a twisted, mirthless grin.

A man at Carson's side turned a white face towards him. 'Looks as if he was scared to death,' he said somewhat hoarsely. 'I'd hate to have seen what he saw. Ugh – look at that face!'

Mechanically Carson backed away, feeling an icy breath of nameless things chill him. He rubbed his hand across his eyes, but still that contorted, dead face swam in his vision. He began to retrace his steps, shaken and trembling a little. Involuntarily his glance moved aside, rested on the tombs and monuments that dotted the old graveyard. No one had been buried there for over a century, and the lichen-stained tombstones, with their winged skulls, fat-cheeked cherubs, and funeral urns, seemed to breathe out an indefinable miasma of antiquity. What had frightened the man to death?

Carson drew a deep breath. True, the corpse had been a frightful spectacle, but he must not allow it to upset his nerves. He could not – his novel would suffer. Besides, he argued grimly to himself, the affair was obvious enough in its explanation. The dead man was apparently a Pole, one of the group of immigrants who dwell about Salem Harbor. Passing by the graveyard at night, a spot about which eldritch legends had clung for nearly three centuries, his drink-befuddled eyes must have given reality to the hazy phantoms of a superstitious mind. These Poles were notoriously unstable emotionally, prone to mob hysteria and wild imaginings. The great Immigrant Panic of 1853, in which three witch-houses had been burned to the ground, had grown from an old woman's confused and hysterical statement that she had seen a mysterious white-clad foreigner 'take off his face'. What else could be expected of such people, Carson thought?

Nevertheless he remained in a nervous state, and did not return home until nearly noon. When on his arrival he found Leigh, the occultist, waiting, he was glad to see the man, and invited him in with cordiality.

Leigh was very serious. 'Did you hear about your friend Abigail Prinn?' he asked without preamble, and Carson stared, pausing in the act of siphoning charged water into a glass. After a long moment he pressed the lever, sent the liquid sizzling and foaming into the whisky. He handed Leigh the drink and took one himself – neat – before answering the question.

'I don't know what you're talking about. Has – what's she been up to?' he asked, with an air of forced levity.

'I've been checking up the records,' Leigh said, 'and I find Abigail Prinn was buried on December 14th 1690, in the Charter Street Burying Ground – with a stake through her heart. What's the matter?'

'Nothing,' Carson said tonelessly. 'Well?'

'Well – her grave's been opened and robbed, that's all. The stake was found uprooted near by, and there were footprints all around the grave. Shoe-prints. Did you dream last night, Carson?' Leigh snapped out the question, his grey eyes hard.

'I don't know,' Carson said confusedly, rubbing his forehead. 'I can't remember. I was at the Charter Street graveyard this morning.'

'Oh. Then you must have heard something about the man who——'

'I saw him,' Carson interrupted, shuddering. 'It upset me.'

He downed the whisky at a gulp.

Leigh watched him. 'Well,' he said presently, 'are you still determined to stay in this house?'

Carson put down the glass and stood up.

'Why not?' he snapped. 'Is there any reason why I shouldn't? Eh?'

'After what happened last night——'

'After *what* happened? A grave was robbed. A superstitious Pole saw the robbers and died of fright. Well?'

'You're trying to convince yourself,' Leigh said calmly. 'In your heart you know – you must know – the truth. You've become a tool in the hands of tremendous and terrible forces, Carson. For three centuries Abbie Prinn has lain in her grave – *undead* – waiting for someone to fall into her trap – the Witch Room. Perhaps she foresaw the future when she built it, foresaw that some day someone would blunder into that hellish chamber and be caught by the trap of the mosaic pattern. It caught you, Carson – and enabled that undead horror to bridge the gulf between consciousness and matter, to get *en rapport* with you. Hypnotism is child's play to a being with Abigail Prinn's frightful powers. She could very easily force you to go to her grave and uproot the stake that held her captive, and then erase the memory of that act from your mind so that you could not remember it even as a dream!'

Carson was on his feet, his eyes burning with a strange light. 'In God's name, man, do you know what you're saying?'

Leigh laughed harshly. 'God's name! The devil's name rather – the devil that menaces Salem at this moment; for Salem is in danger, terrible danger. The men and women and children of the town Abbie Prinn cursed when they bound her to the stake – and found they couldn't burn her! I've been going through certain secret archives this morning, and I've come to ask you, for the last time, to leave this house.'

'Are you through?' Carson asked coldly. 'Very well. I shall stay here. You're either insane or drunk, but you can't impress me with your poppycock.'

'Would you leave if I offered you a thousand dollars?' Leigh asked. 'Or more, then – ten thousand? I have a considerable sum at my command.'

'No, damn it!' Carson snapped in a sudden blaze of anger. 'All I want is to be left alone to finish my novel. I can't work anywhere else – I don't want to, I won't——'

'I expected this,' Leigh said, his voice suddenly quiet, and with a strange note of sympathy. 'Man, you can't get away! You're caught in the trap, and it's too late for you to extricate yourself so long as Abbie Prinn's brain controls you through the Witch Room. And the worst part of it is that she can only manifest herself with your aid – she drains your life forces, Carson, feeds on you like a vampire.'

'You're mad,' Carson said dully.

'I'm afraid. That iron disc in the Witch Room – I'm afraid of that, and what's under it. Abbie Prinn served strange gods, Carson – and I read something on the wall of that alcove that gave me a hint. Have you ever heard of Nyogtha?'

Carson shook his head impatiently. Leigh fumbled in a pocket, drew out a scrap of paper. 'I copied this from a book in the Kester Library,' he said, 'a book called the *Necronomicon*, written by a man who delved so deeply into forbidden secrets that men called him mad. Read this.'

Carson's brows drew together as he read the excerpt:

Men know him as the Dweller in Darkness, that brother of the Old Ones called Nyogtha, the Thing that should not be. He can be summoned to Earth's surface through certain secret caverns and fissures, and sorcerers have seen him in Syria and below the black tower of Leng; from the Thang Grotto of Tartary he has come ravening to bring terror and destruction among the pavilions of the great Khan. Only by the looped cross, by the Vach-Viraj incantation and by the Tikkoun elixir may he be driven back to the nighted caverns of hidden foulness where he dwelleth.

Leigh met Carson's puzzled gaze calmly. 'Do you understand now?'

'Incantations and elixirs!' Carson said, handing back the paper. 'Fiddle-sticks!'

'Far from it. That incantation and that elixir have been known to occultists and adepts for thousands of years. I've had occasion to use them myself in the past on certain – occasions. And if I'm right about this thing——' He turned to the door, his lips compressed in a bloodless line. 'Such manifestations have been defeated before, but the difficulty lies in obtaining the elixir – it's very hard to get. But I hope ... I'll be back. Can you stay out of the Witch Room until then?'

'I'll promise nothing,' Carson said. He had a dull headache, which had been steadily growing until it obtruded upon his consciousness, and he felt vaguely nauseated. 'Goodbye.'

He saw Leigh to the door and waited on the steps, with an odd reluctance to return to the house. As he watched the tall occultist hurry down the street, a woman came out of the adjoining house. She caught sight of him, and her huge breasts heaved. She burst into a shrill, angry tirade.

Carson turned, staring at her with astonished eyes. His head throbbed painfully. The woman was approaching, shaking a fat fist threateningly.

'Why you scare my Sarah?' she cried, her swarthy face flushed. 'Why you scare her wit' your fool tricks, eh?'

Carson moistened his lips.

'I'm sorry,' he said slowly. 'Very sorry. I didn't frighten your Sarah. I haven't been home all day. What frightened her?'

'T'e brown t'ing – it ran in your house, Sarah say——'

The woman paused, and her jaw dropped. Her eyes widened. She made a peculiar sign with her right hand – pointing her index and little fingers at Carson, while her thumb was crossed over the other fingers. 'T'e old witch!'

She retreated hastily, muttering in Polish in a frightened voice.

Carson turned, went back into the house. He poured some whisky into a tumbler, considered, and then set it aside untasted. He began to pace the floor, occasionally rubbing his forehead with fingers that felt dry and hot. Vague, confused thoughts raced through his mind. His head was throbbing and feverish.

At length he went down to the Witch Room. He remained there, although he did not work; for his headache was not so oppressive in the dead quiet of the underground chamber. After a time he slept.

How long he slumbered he did not know. He dreamed of Salem, and of a dimly-glimpsed, gelatinous black thing that hurtled with frightful speed through the streets, a thing like an incredibly huge, jet-black amoeba that pursued and engulfed men and women who shrieked and fled vainly. He dreamed of a skull-face peering into his own, a withered and shrunken countenance in which only the eyes seemed alive, and they shone with a hellish evil light.

He awoke at last, sat up with a start. He was very cold.

It was utterly silent. In the light of the electric bulb the green and purple mosaic seemed to writhe and contract towards him, an illusion which disappeared as his sleep-fogged vision cleared. He glanced at his wrist-watch. It was two o'clock. He had slept through the afternoon and the better part of the night.

He felt oddly weak, and a lassitude held him motionless in his chair. The strength seemed to have been drained from him. The piercing cold seemed to strike through to his brain, but his headache was gone. His mind was very clear – expectant, as though waiting for something to happen. A movement near by caught his eye.

A slab of stone in the wall was moving. He heard a gentle grating sound, and slowly a black cavity widened from a narrow rectangle to a square. There was something crouching there in the shadow. Stark, blind horror struck through Carson as the thing moved and crept forward into the light.

It looked like a mummy. For an intolerable, age-long second the thought pounded frightfully at Carson's brain: *It looked like a mummy!* It was a skeleton-thin, parchment-brown corpse, and it looked like a skeleton with the hide of some great lizard stretched over its bones. It stirred, it crept forward, and its long nails scratched audibly against the stone. It crawled out into the Witch Room, its passionless face pitilessly revealed in the white light, and its eyes were gleaming with charnel life. He could see the serrated ridge of its brown, shrunken back ...

Carson sat motionless. Abysmal horror had robbed him of the power to move. He seemed to be caught in the fetters of dream-paralysis, in which the brain, an aloof spectator, is unable or unwilling to transmit the nerve-impulses to the muscles. He told himself frantically that he was dreaming, that he would presently awaken.

The withered horror arose. It stood upright, skeleton-thin, and moved to the alcove where the iron disc lay embedded in the floor. Standing with its back to Carson it paused, and a dry and sere whisper rustled out in the dead stillness. At the sound Carson would have screamed, but he could not. Still the dreadful whisper went on, in a language Carson knew was not of Earth, and as though in response an almost imperceptible quiver shook the iron disc.

It quivered and began to rise, very slowly, and as if in triumph the shrivelled horror lifted its pipestem arms. The disc was nearly a foot thick, but presently as it continued to rise above the level of the floor an insidious odour began to penetrate the room. It was vaguely reptilian, musky and nauseating. The disc lifted inexorably, and a little finger of blackness crept out from beneath its edge. Abruptly Carson remembered his dream of a gelatinous black creature that hurtled through the Salem streets. He tried vainly to break the fetters of paralysis that held him motionless. The chamber was darkening, and a black vertigo was creeping up to engulf him. The room seemed to rock.

Still the iron disc lifted; still the withered horror stood with its skeleton arms raised in blasphemous benediction; still the blackness oozed out in slow amoeboid movement.

There came a sound breaking through the sere whisper of the mummy, the quick patter of racing footsteps. Out of the corner of his eye Carson saw a man come racing into the Witch Room. It was the occultist, Leigh, and his eyes were blazing in a face of deathly pallor. He flung himself past Carson to the alcove where the black horror was surging into view.

The withered thing turned with dreadful slowness. Leigh carried some implement in his left hand, Carson saw, a *crux ansata* of gold and ivory. His right hand was clenched at his side. His voice rolled out, sonorous and commanding. There were little beads of perspiration on his white face.

'*Ya na kadishtu nilgh'ri ... stell'bsna kn'aa Nyogtha ... k'yarnak phlegethor ...*'

The fantastic, unearthly syllables thundered out, echoing from the walls of the vault. Leigh advanced slowly, the *crux ansata* held high. And from beneath the iron disc black horror came surging!

The disc was lifted, flung aside, and a great wave of irridescent blackness, neither liquid nor solid, a frightful gelatinous mass, came pouring straight for Leigh. Without pausing in his advance he made a quick gesture with his right hand, and a little glass tube hurtled at the black thing was engulfed.

The formless horror paused. It hesitated, with a dreadful air of indecision, and then swiftly drew back. A choking stench of burning corruption began to pervade the air, and Carson saw great pieces of the black thing flake off, shrivelling as though destroyed with corroding acid. It fled back in a liquescent rush, hideous black flesh dropping as it retreated.

A pseudopod of blackness elongated itself from the central mass and like a great tentacle clutched the corpse-like being, dragged it back to the pit and over the brink. Another tentacle seized the iron disc, pulled it effortlessly across the floor, and as the horror sank from sight, the disc fell into place with a thunderous crash.

The room swung in wide circles about Carson, and a frightful nausea clutched him. He made a tremendous effort to get to his feet, and then the light faded swiftly and was gone. Darkness took him.

Carson's novel was never finished. He burned it, but continued to write, although none of his later work was ever published. His publishers shook their heads and wondered why such a brilliant writer of popular fiction had suddenly become infatuated with the weird and ghastly.

'It's powerful stuff,' one man told Carson, as he handed back his novel, *Black God of Madness*. 'It's remarkable in its way, but it's morbid and horrible. Nobody would read it. Carson, why don't you write the type of novel you used to do, the kind that made you famous?'

It was then that Carson broke his vow never to speak of the Witch Room, and he poured out the entire story, hoping for understanding and belief. But as he finished, his heart sank as he saw the other's face, sympathetic but sceptical.

'You dreamed it, didn't you?' the man asked, and Carson laughed bitterly.

'Yes – I dreamed it.'

'It must have made a terribly vivid impression on your mind. Some dreams do. But you'll forget about it in time,' he predicted, and Carson nodded.

And because he knew that he would only be arousing doubts of his sanity, he did not mention the thing that was burned indelibly on his brain, the horror he had seen in the Witch Room after wakening from his faint. Before he and Leigh had hurried, white-faced and trembling, from the chamber, Carson had cast a quick glance behind him. The shrivelled and corroded patches that he had seen slough off from that being of insane blasphemy had unaccountably disappeared, although they had left black stains upon the stones. Abbie Prinn, perhaps, had returned to the hell she had served, and her inhuman god had withdrawn to hidden abysses beyond man's comprehension, routed by powerful forces of elder magic which the occultist had commanded. But the witch had left a memento behind her, a hideous thing which Carson, in that last backward glance, had seen protruding from the edge of the iron disc, as though raised in ironic salute – *a withered, claw-like hand!*

Cold Spell

David Langford

The handkerchiefs whirled and wove their lacy patterns in the sky; there was a tinkle of bells and a muffled sound of feet on stone as the men swung easily through their last dance. Stephen Carling tried to hide his impatience; for the last quarter-hour he had been eyeing the red-lit windows of the 'Olde Coach-House', wishing he were on the inside instead of making an olde-world fool of himself in its freezing olde-world courtyard. But Hubbard, prancing about in the role of Fool, tapped him with the bladder. He fought down his shivers and concentrated on the swirling handkerchief, so graceful to watch and so bloody difficult to control.

The landlord had done his best by the dancers, training improvised spotlights from his upper windows and drumming up a respectable crowd for the solstice performance. On this freezing night, by some occult tradition, Hubbard's team were not simply dancing but enacting 'The Lambertstow Morris'. It made no difference that Carling could see, but the rest of the team had an intense look, almost a religious look, somewhere in the eyes. Back and forth, back and forth, in and out. Why didn't the others turn blue with cold? The watchers were well muffled up (which was an injustice) and supplied with drinks (which was intolerable).

And now Hubbard was muttering dirge-like fragments which Carling had never heard in the Morris before. *This ae night, this ae night, everie night and alle* ... It was not the full lyke-wake song, the corpse-chant, but scrappy extracts now heard and now inaudible. *If ever thou gavest roof and flame, Everie night and alle, Pass thee by the standing stane* ...

And then, in a blossoming flourish of white linen, the pattern was complete. An informal nod to their audience, and the Morris-dancers marched smartly into the pub's rosy warmth. On one side old Bell was struggling out of his costume as 'Twig' — an all-enclosing leafy cone in which he frisked about to symbolize boundless fertility or something of the sort. Carling chafed his fingers and recalled that Bell was well over sixty ...

The 'Olde Coach-House' provided drinks on the house for the Morris team. Carling was well into his second pint by the time Hubbard ran a hand through his thick white hair and said, as he always did, 'Not a bad performance, that.' He looked around the other seven with a sort of weary patience. 'But there were one or two little things. It's the twenty-first, remember, the twenty-first! John, you must swing gentler in the sword piece. You're trying to tap Dick's sword neatly, not disarm him like ruddy d'Artagnan. And you, Bell, you stay further from the poor sodding audience – they don't want Twig knocking drinks out of their hands and irrigating their trousers ... And *you*, Stephen, what were you at? Consumed by fires of apathy, I'd say, and an attack of shivers with it. I've said it before, if you get cold it means you're holding back. Do it properly and you'll be warm enough.'

These indictments caused Dr Sims to practise swordsweeps of ex- aggerated daintiness, and Bell to grin over his tankard, and Carling to stalk mutinously off for another drink. He was doing them a favour, wasn't he, standing in when his father went sick? He coughed in the thick and smoky air of the bar. Hubbard picked on him as the only one who wasn't past it. Even Forester, the other 'kid', must be way past thirty.

Sure enough, when he came back, Hubbard was at it again. 'Hey, Stephen! Watch your step with the ale! Shivering's better than stagger- ing, y'know.'

Carling swigged a third of his pint in a pointed way before forcing a return smile. 'Be staggering home pretty soon, won't we?'

They all looked at him. He'd said the wrong thing again. Cautiously he said, 'Look, I haven't got any of the bloody tradition wrong, have I? We go and prance about at Coldrock for a few minutes and then we go home ... surely?'

It was odd to see some of the expressions. Old Bell, in particular, was looking as if someone had been swearing in church.

'It's an *important* tradition, you know,' said Hubbard. 'And of course we'll be doing the whole Morris again, right the way through, starting at midnight. Didn't your father tell you? Or weren't you listening, as usual?'

Carling didn't know. He'd just assumed that no one would be so cretinous as to dance on the open moor at Coldrock for longer than five minutes – especially on a night when the whole countryside was cracking and squeaking with ice. He shrugged in beery acquiescence and drank again.

Dr Sims passed a few bland comments about how alcohol cooled you down, really, and only made you *feel* warm. Carling was happy to settle for the feeling.

Coldrock was a mere ten minutes out of Lambertstow village. But the

cold was bitter, the clear sky frozen into a single huge crystal in which
the trapped stars could scarcely twinkle; it seemed that the icy night
must crack open and scatter them as frosty points of fire. Carling's coat
did not help. By the time they neared the rock itself the whole sky seemed
a lens which concentrated upon him all the chill of space.

Coldrock was a great nub of granite, man-high, of rough and undistinguished shape. Some said it had once been carved, though nobody
knew into what form. Shallow pools lay around, now sealed with ice.
The tradition was that the Lambertstow Morris-dancers performed by
the rock on the night of the winter solstice. By this, no doubt, the old
gods of winter cold were appeased and Bell was free to fertilize birds and
bees for spring ... But the icy pain in Carling's feet was inimical to such
thoughts. He stumbled, not for the first time. *Pass thee by the standing
stane* ...

Miller, landlord of the 'Olde Coach-House', was already present. He
had sensibly travelled by car (no doubt tradition decreed that the stupid
dancers had to walk) and was unloading the properties: wooden swords,
a battered cardboard box overflowing with giant handkerchiefs, the
Fool's worn bladder and 'Twig'. The 'Twig' costume was something like
a vast crinoline to which innumerable sprays of foliage had been wired;
it concealed the wearer in a cone of prickly green.

The dancers removed their coats to reveal again the thin white shirts,
embroidered waistcoats and black breeches.

'Fine,' said Hubbard, his head cocked on one side. 'Now there's just
one thing. This is an old dance, and maybe it'd be better to have the
most experienced men for the dancing, if you see what I mean. Besides,
Stephen is a bit the worse for wear. So if he and Bell change places we'll
do just fine. All right?'

Carling thought of the scratchy interior of 'Twig' and grimaced. The
absurd fertility symbol might be the most interesting part of the
Lambertstow Morris to students of folkways, but it was the most uncomfortable role for the dancers And the leafy symbol spent most of its
time lurking on the sidelines. There would only be the occasional
improvised frisk-about to keep him warm.

'No,' he said. 'It's OK, I'm fine. I just tripped because my feet are
cold.' But his lips seemed frozen, too, and the words came out stiff and
slurred.

'Don't you worry,' said Hubbard with infuriating tact. 'We do understand. Mind you, you should have been more careful – *tried* to
tell you. You'll be fine in Twig.'

'No,' said Carling again. 'I ... I'm going home.'

All the others looked shocked again. The shock of the unthinkable.
'Doesn't tradition mean anything to you at all?' said Hubbard.

'Bloody tradition ... Look, you call yourself a Christian – it's a *Pagan*

tradition. You'll be at Christmas service in a few days. Isn't that
hypocrisy or something?'

Hubbard said: 'Christmas was a pagan tradition as well.' Which was
no answer.

'I'm a science student,' Carling pointed out. 'I don't believe in any
of it. And *I* won't be at the Christmas service.'

'You stay,' said Bell with a sort of desperate insistence.

'I'm going,' said Carling. And went.

He walked for a while and looked back. They were limbering up for
the dance ... but Hubbard kept staring after him.

A breeze sprang up and whispered in the frozen grass; the night grew
colder and colder still, until Carling almost ran along the frosted lane.
The stale beer swilled in his stomach, weighing him down like a chill,
flopping bag of mercury. His feet were unfeeling lumps when he reached
his father's house; and then followed the slow, burning pain of warming
them up again before the electric fire.

All this could have been avoided if only his father hadn't been ill.
Must visit the hospital some time, Carling thought as he drank hot
coffee. He wondered about the dancers out by the stone. Perhaps by now
they were frozen into grotesque positions, a sacrifice to the strange gods
that Hubbard half-believed in. He chuckled, but the chill was leaking
into the room. It was a good time to go to bed, snug beneath the electric
blanket. It was better still to lie in warm darkness, with the fatigue of
dancing transmuted to pleasant heaviness. It was better to forget the
odd moments of the night: a muttered verse, a ring of shocked faces, a
feeling of dreadful intensity ... Some thoughts of future recriminations
from his father for 'letting the side down' (Carling knew it would be
phrased thus) chased themselves about his head, but not for long.

Through his dreams stalked fantastically garbed dancers, weighted
with frightful significance. Even in dream he stubbornly did not join the
midnight dance, though tenuous threads of ice held him close and
tugged him slowly towards the ugly bulk of Coldrock. But the sluggish-
ness of the beer was with him still, and he stood as if rooted while the
wild dancers whirled and spangles of ice flew from beneath their feet,
on and on and on ...

He awoke with a hangover. He swore at himself for not having
remembered to drink pints of water and take an aspirin before going to
bed. Chill mists hung over the village. Disinclined to venture outside,
Carling dosed himself with coffee and pills, and began a studied attempt
to read Zemansky's *Heat and Thermodynamics* through the blurring,
throbbing pain which would not leave his head.

The doorbell rang. He was glad to set aside the book; less glad when the visitor proved to be Hubbard.

'Look here,' said Hubbard, almost pushing him over as he stormed in. 'I want a word with you about last night.'

'Bloody hell, it's all over now,' Carling protested.

'It is not.' Hubbard dropped uninvited into an armchair. Carling, still labouring under the vast, formless guilt which accompanies many a hangover, did likewise, and Hubbard began to speak.

'Never you mind your ruddy atheism and humanism and I don't know what. This is important. And hard to explain. Look, did you ever hear that Eastern story about the loony who was doing something really mad, and they asked him why, and he said, "To scare off the tigers"? And of course they said, "There aren't any tigers", and he came right back with "See! It works!" '

Carling blinked. 'So what?'

'I'm asking you to get out there to Coldrock tonight and fill in the missing part of the Morris. You can skip the costume, I reckon: just do a Twig sort of improvisation and that'll be fine. Because of the tigers, that's why. Because ... well, I *don't* ask you to believe a word of it, but there's one or two of us who think our Morris and a very few old things like it are important. Some say they dance the dance as a festival at the turn of winter; some think maybe the winter only turns because of the dance, but you bet they keep ruddy quiet about it. Until now. We've done our loony dance all these years and, maybe, kept away the tigers. Now will you humour us – c'mon, be as condescending as you like – and dance on your own tonight?'

'Good grief,' said Carling, amazed and contemptuous. 'You think I'm an easy mark, don't you? Screw up your precious dance one night and you come here with this load of rubbish ... Laugh yourselves sick, won't you, if I fall for it and go prancing in the cold on my own! No thanks. The winter's always come to an end before and it can manage it this year without my help.'

'We've never missed a dance before,' said Hubbard seriously, and repeated: ' "See! It works!" '

'Oh, go *away*,' returned Carling, whose head was beginning to feel worse.

Hubbard went. Carling picked up Zemansky again and stared dully at the exposition of the Maxwell equations; after a little time, the doorbell rang again.

'Good morning to you,' said Dr Sims. He brushed ice-crystals from his lapels and shot a keen glance at Carling's bleary face. 'We don't normally make house calls for a head like yours, but I just happened to be passing.'

'Thanks, I've taken a pill,' said Carling warily.

'Good, good. Oh, just one thing ... I hear Hubbard's been round telling you off. These local boys are really sincere about the dancing, you know. Absolute dens of superstition, villages like this. Don't you think, just as a favour to me, you could see your way to humouring Hubbard and the rest? Lot of ill-feeling if you don't ... and though I say it as shouldn't, I'll slip you ten quid for a warming bottle of scotch if you do. How about it?'

Carling still felt ill and obstinate. 'No,' he said. 'They'll have to lump it.'

The doctor put his hands on Carling's shoulders with sudden, terrible sincerity. *'Please,'* he whispered. 'Please do it.'

'You believe it all, too,' said Carling in disgust. 'You're scared of ghosts, like the others. I'm staying by the fire, thanks very much.'

The doctor left, slamming the door without another word. Carling was left to consider how, each time he said 'No', it became more final. His own pride in rationality now held him to his word, so that nothing would make him back down by dancing the dance ... which was surely irrational?

He had no time to pick up Zemansky before, for the third time, the doorbell rang.

'Thankee, I won't come in,' said Bell before being either invited in or told to go away. 'It is a warning I've come to give you. Don't think old Coldrock'll muck up the springcoming just for one young fool. If you are not thinking to dance this night, *this ae night*, then you'll think again. Little birds as can't sing and won't sing will be made to sing, they say – remember that, my lad. The rock's a trickster and it'll have its way.'

Carling was so dumbfounded by the words from doddery old Bell that he found himself literally unable to reply before the old man (with a brusque nod) had left him standing there. Bell's breath was a plume of white in the freezing air; he did not look back.

Made to dance, eh? The notion roused Carling's obstinacy to something close to fury. Though he stared at Zemansky all the afternoon, his mind was on nothing but the determination not to give in – not to pander to Hubbard's idiotic superstition, nor fall for the doctor's fake reasonableness, and most specially to spit in the eye of anyone who dared tell Carling what to do.

Tigers! Humour them for ten pounds! *Made* to dance!

When he had made and eaten his dinner that evening, and drunk most of a bottle of wine, he took special pains to ensure that every window was fastened and every door firmly bolted. It was difficult to imagine a mob of irate villagers storming the house and carrying him forth to dance the wretched dance ... but when he finally went to bed, he was careful to load up his father's old .22 rifle and leave it beside the bed. Just in case, he told himself. In case of ... tigers. The weapon's presence was a comfort as he relaxed and sank gradually into sleep.

... So there he was at Coldrock once more, walking away, but now through sparkling countryside, where all the lanes ran together in a maze of ice. At every turning and blind alley the road gave a wriggle in 'Looking-Glass' fashion and became an inviting path which led to that shapeless grey rock. Voices shouted distant warnings or exhortations; Hubbard and Dr Sims and old Bell were all trying to tell him something which they could not quite express nor Carling quite comprehend, as Coldrock loomed obscenely at the end of every path, until at last there were no more paths and he stood upon a featureless plain with only the granite thing for company. Its shape was charged with a terrible significance. Although indubitably the same old rock, it now stood on every side of him, with all space twisted to exclude everything which was not Carling or the cold, cold rock ...

It pressed in, encircling, unspeakable——

And if thou holdest to any thinge, Everie night and alle, The Ende thou canst not enter in, And

– and he touched it.

There was a soundless flash. Cold fire dripped over the universe, and icicle-fangs gnawed at Carling's flesh, everywhere, agonizing.

He woke then, and found it *was* cold. The wine had left a lingering acridity in his mouth. He swore at himself for succumbing to silly dreams, but the bed was absurdly chilly, his teeth were chattering beyond control. The luminous clockface at the bedside told him it was some while before midnight.

'Oh hell,' he said aloud.

He slid from the bed, to find the unheated room mysteriously warmer than the bed. Oddly enough, the electric blanket's control light still burnt: the thing must be faulty. Carling decided on more coffee, and slipped downstairs in dressing-gown and slippers. It was warmer below, in a silence disturbed only by the wind which leant from time to time against the house, and by the tiny gobbling of the refrigerator. He sloshed water into the kettle and clicked it on; then retreated to turn on the living-room fire. It was then that he realized something was most definitely wrong. As the heater's spiral elements began to glow, Carling began to shiver. It seemed that waves of cold were rolling towards him.

He blinked – for some reason he didn't seem to be thinking too clearly – and switched off the fire. The chill receded until he was merely cold, not frozen. 'Bloody hell,' he said with renewed shivers, and walked out to the kitchen. There he found the kettle bubbling furiously ... and icy cold.

'Fight fire with fire,' he said aloud (this seemed very funny) and opened the refrigerator door. Waves of warmth lapped out across his legs. He hesitated for a while before unlocking the door between him and the night outside – but there, too, all was warm and pleasant. For a moment he frowned at a dim memory of someone who was a trickster: no, it was gone.

As he walked about the garden in a breeze as cosy as central heating, he knew this must be another dream. He deserved a pleasant dream to offset the one he'd just had, where Coldrock caught him ... The sparkling lanes around Lambertstow were warm beneath his slippered feet. He walked at random, enjoying the clear beauty of the night (not a cloud in the sky!), and was somehow not surprised to find himself on the path to Coldrock. He was stumbling again; he was almost prepared to admit he'd had a few too many in the 'Olde Coach-House' ... but no, that was last night. Though the stars shone hard and clear, a mist of unreality drifted behind his eyes. Nothing was quite as it should be; nothing was quite important ...

His feet were numb with fatigue, but the strangely pleasing shape of Coldrock reminded him why he was here. (How strange to have forgotten!) Clumsily, his slippers flapping until he kicked them off, his dressing-gown flying wildly in the wind, he began to dance ...

Dimly he realized that Coldrock and its power had tricked him indeed, in spite of all his scepticism and folly, into doing the right thing at last and fulfilling the ancient requirements of the dance. He found his lips moving in the lyke-wake song which mourned the passing year ...

From empty airt when thou'rt past, Everie night and alle, To Alleman's Ende thou comest at last ...

He danced there in the delicious drowsy warmth before Coldrock, as the brittle grass snapped underfoot, and the ice burst crackling from the pools, and slowly his toes and stiffened fingers turned black.

The Meerschaum Pipe

L. A. Lewis

November 17th.

Never having tried keeping a diary before, it will be amusing to see whether I have enough mental energy to go on with it. At all events my new-found leisure will not give me the excuse of being too busy. The only question about it is – shall I find anything worth recording in this quiet, country existence? Well, it pleases me to begin with such a trifle as my own enjoyment in this property I have bought, and, after all, I am writing for myself and not for others.

My ability to retire and settle down at the early age of forty is a cause of gratitude to the Gods of Chance, who gave me such rapid commercial success in the 'slump' years when so many others were feeling the pinch. I just happened to strike the right propositions all the time, and now I can play the Squire in my new 'domain' and look forward to the idyllic life which next summer will bring, fishing and pottering about these beautiful, unspoilt backwaters. Not that I despise the country and its pursuits in winter – being country-bred – particularly in this fine old house. I shall find all the entertainment I need for the long evenings sorting through the books and all the lumber with which it is stocked, and by next winter I hope to have made friends who will come round for billiards or cards.

Perhaps I may marry again, for 'Heronay' should possess a hostess, but I fear I could never bring to another union the zeal of my first romantic attachment so quickly ended in one of the London air raids.

I feel myself lucky to have got 'Heronay' at such a bargain price, and suppose it would have cost me a good few thousands more, but for the bad name it derives from its former occupant. After standing empty, however, for so many years, the dilapidation was great, and I could see how the agents jumped at my offer.

It is rather strange how a house can continue to bear an ill repute from the misdemeanours of a tenant, even years after his or her death, though no doubt this place holds very gruesome associations for many of the local residents. One can excuse Harper his crimes on the ground of his undeniable lunacy, but his 'reign of terror', conducted from here, must have been a ghastly period for the neighbourhood, especially in view of the shocking mutilations he always practised. Still, he died long ago in Broadmoor, and it is thought that the ground was cleared of all his victims. I have had the exterior entirely re-faced, and I think 'Heronay' may now claim to be purged of his influence.

Well, I seem to be rambling on – a good start for the diary, anyway, if I can keep it up! Now I will close for today, and spend the rest of the evening looking over my new possessions.

November 18th.

A bright day for the time of year, crisp and frosty. Had a call from the Vicar, who asked, among other things, if I proposed to join the local Hunt. Told him that I was no horseman, but hoped to do a bit of shooting when more completely settled. He then touched on the poor maniac, my predecessor, and I asked him if he thought the dreadful record of the place would affect my welcome in the village. He replied that he was sure the people in the other big houses would soon forget Harper when they realized the hospitality of the new owner and saw how the whole estate had been cleansed of its former unkempt appearance. The villagers, though, would take longer to accept me to their confidence, and I must not be surprised if tradesmen refused to deliver goods after dark, as the grounds of 'Heronay' were popularly supposed to be haunted. He made his exit, after inviting me to dinner next week, when he promised I should meet some of my new neighbours at the Vicarage. I shall welcome the change from solitude, although my evenings here will not be dull while I have so many of Harper's belongings to look through. He appears to have had no next-of-kin, which accounts for all the furniture being sold with the house. Before his dementia overtook him he must have been a man of refinement. His library is a book-lover's paradise, and his personal knick-knacks and ornaments mostly of quite intrinsic value. While rummaging in the drawers of the study desk last night I found a remarkably fine meerschaum pipe, which he must have smoked for many years, to judge by the degree of coloration of the bowl. It has an amber mouthpiece set in gold, and is, in fact, quite an ornament. I intend to clean it up and give it a place of honour on the mantel-shelf. My man can polish it when he starts on the china. As an ex-army batsman, polishing is a hobby with him.

Incidentally, I must consider engaging a staff of servants now that I am about to meet new people. Jobson can manage quite well in a flat, as he has done for so long during my City career, but we shall need more than occasional daily help if we are to entertain as I hope to be entertained. That's all for today. I shall consult the local registry – if any – in the morning.

November 19th.
An irritating set-back today. Called on Miss Simms the post-mistress, who acts as domestic registrar, and she promised to send round some applicants for my household jobs. Left her, thinking the matter as good as settled, and stayed at home till lunch-time, but nobody called. Now she has rung up to say that she 'can find no one suitable at the moment'. On reflection, I thought her a bit evasive during the interview, and am inclined to suspect the cause is all this superstitious rubbish the Vicar mentioned. Suppose I shall have to get servants from elsewhere, but it is very ridiculous. My alterations have given the place quite a modern appearance, and there is nothing sinister about the grounds at night. Evidently the local proletariat keep dwelling on the secret burials that used to take place, and imagination has done the rest.

Spent the earlier part of the evening thinking things over, and planning for the future. I must seriously consider taking another wife. She might solve the servant problem more readily, and a hostess is really essential for entertaining married guests; but I don't fancy the notion a bit. Mary's memory is still too fresh even after all these years ... Perhaps a lady housekeeper?

Jobson has made a splendid job of the meerschaum, which looks, as I said before, definitely ornamental. I have a great fancy for this class of pipe myself, though I have never achieved such superb 'colour' in any of my own. I am, in fact, tempted to sterilize the stem of this one and see how it tastes. It should prove a ripe smoke. It has never occurred to me before to smoke another man's pipe – much less that of a homicidal maniac – but I think washing the mouthpiece with lysol and scouring the bowl-stem with a hot wire should destroy any possible germs ...

November 20th.
I carried out my intention before retiring last night, and so enjoyed my smoke that I felt disinclined for writing up any more of this diary. With a load of my favourite tobacco, and a good fire in the study, the time passed like lightning. Really speaking, I think I must have dozed, though the meerschaum was still burning well when I saw by the clock that it was well past my usual bedtime. Today I feel rather unrested, though I was sleeping soundly when Jobson called me. Most likely I have spent too much time indoors lately browsing among the relics of Harper's tenancy. When I am getting daily fresh air and exercise I never dream – but I am under the impression that my sleep was disturbed last night, though I cannot recall any details. I shall take a walk round the grounds now and blow the cobwebs away before lunch.

Later.

My morning walk very beneficial and brightened by parading my new acquisition. Saw the Vicar and Dr Corbett, the local GP, passing my drive gates, and they complimented me on the 'colour' of it. As they made no reference to Harper I took it they did not recognize it as his, and I did not choose to enlighten them. My ramble took me to a strip of waste ground enclosed by a shrubbery and a walk where, I am told, two of Harper's victims were buried – their trunks at least. It seemed an ideal spot for a murder, and I could almost enter into his distorted point of view – at least as far as the spice of secrecy was concerned.

There must be a grim fascination in committing a crime that rouses the countryside and then watching the police go off on false scents. Harper went about his butchery for months without attracting the least suspicion. Evidently he can have shown no outward symptom of insanity between the attacks, and must have exercised amazing caution in executing his horrible tasks; yet his dementia was of an extreme kind, as was shown by the distorted artistry of his mutilations.

Employed the afternoon and evening in a fruitless journey to the County town – twenty miles away – in search of domestics. Interviewed several candidates who happened to be at the Registry Office, but as soon as I mentioned my address they made various excuses not to accept service with me. The popular aversion to 'Heronay' is very widespread, it seems, and it looks as if I shall have to engage my staff in London. Most annoying.

Found some newspaper cuttings in the course of my evening's exploring among Harper's belongings. They all related to his criminal career, and I could picture him gloating over the horror which his monstrous 'recreation' was instilling in the public mind. Having been abroad at the time I was not 'well up' in the history of this butcher, and so took the trouble to read the cuttings through. Apparently he was actuated by no personal motives but from a general lust to kill, and his victims were invariably women. The most revolting feature of the murders was his habit of severing the head and limbs with a sharp hatchet and leaving them on the scene for identification, while carrying away the trunk for addition to a sort of 'musaeam' which is supposed to have been kept in some room of the house.

The subsequent interring seems only to have been affected when decomposition rendered it necessary, as the police deduced from the remains.

November 21st.

Another disturbed night, judging by this morning's lassitude – though again I have no clear recollection of my dreams beyond the feeling that they were of a distressing and even frightening nature. Also I am convinced that I did – for me – quite an unprecedented thing. I noticed earth stains on my feet when getting into my bath, and Jobson found more of them on the bed-linen, from which it is clear that I must have walked in my sleep. I have always regarded this as a sign of mental unbalance, so told Jobson I had gone down to the garden, fancying I heard an intruder. He must have wondered why I did not wear my slippers, but is too well trained to offer such criticism. I have never had a day's illness in my life, and I do not like this symptom of nerve trouble – especially as I spent most of yesterday out-of-doors. I shall spend today on the links and get my lunch at the Club House.

Later.

A splendid game of golf with a member to whom the Secretary introduced me, and another round, by myself, in the afternoon. I should sleep well tonight. Meanwhile a sensation has arisen in the village by the discovery of a dead body in Arningham Woods. It appears to be a case of murder, the victim being a young girl from a gypsy encampment nearby. The postman told me that her throat had been cut and that one of the hands, severed at the wrist, was missing.

The last I take to be a piece of village gossip originating in Harper's dismembering proclivities. I understand the affair is regarded as probably a crime of jealousy and that the police are looking for a young basket-maker who left the camp this morning.

Enough diary for today. Just half an hour's smoke, and I shall not want any rocking.

November 22nd.

Once more a shockingly restless night – this time caused by definite nightmares. Though I fell asleep at once and do not remember awakening until Jobson brought my tea, I feel as if I had been 'on the tiles'. Most of the time I seemed to be pacing endless corridors and clambering up and down stairs burdened by some weighty object which I was trying to conceal. What it was I cannot remember, except that it seemed both precious and repulsive simultaneously, and that I was in a panic in case anyone find me with it. I examined my feet on rising for any traces of sleep-walking, but could find no such evidence. One thing, however, puzzled me – namely, that I appeared to be wearing different pyjamas from those in which I went to bed. Still, most of my sleeping-suits resemble each other, being all black silk and varying only in the braiding, so I may have been mistaken. Somnambulism apart, though, if these exhausting dreams continue I must ask Corbett for a tonic. It will be a good opportunity to mention the matter if I can persuade him to a round of golf this afternoon.

Later.

I was wrong, it would seem, to start this diary wondering if I should find enough to write about in so rural a spot. The murder of the gypsy girl has now been followed by the mysterious disappearance of a cottager's daughter. By a coincidence she is one of the prospective maids I interviewed two days ago, and, although in service in the County Town, was spending the weekend here with her family.

Apparently she went out for a solitary walk late last evening and she has not been seen since, nor has she returned to her employer's residence. The discovery of blood-stains in a little-used lane near the village has, of course, given rise to a crop of ugly rumours, but as none of the girl's clothing or belongings has come to light I see no reason to connect the two facts. Quite probably a case of elopement ...

I was about to close my diary for the day when Jobson entered my study in a great state of agitation. He had been taking a moonlight walk in the grounds near one of the boundary walls when he noticed some unusual object in a tussock of grass. Stooping to examine it, he saw, to his horror, that it was a human hand! As he finished describing the finding of it he produced the horrible thing from a roll of newspaper and laid it on my desk, when, overcoming my natural revulsion, I inspected it under a powerful reading-lamp. Though no student of anatomy, I judged it to be the hand of a woman, I dare say, on account of the cheap and gaudy rings which adorned two of the fingers. These baubles seemed, in a vague way, familiar, and I supposed that I had seen their wearer at some time in the village. Naturally, I rang up the Police without loss of time, and have spent the last hour talking with the Inspector – a very capable man who, as a young member of the Force, was instrumental in Harper's arrest. He not only confirmed the rumour of the gypsy's hand having been cut off, but positively identified it with Jobson's grim 'find'. He thinks that the basket-maker, an unsuccessful suitor, must have taken the hand as a keepsake and then, fearing to keep so terrible a reminder, have thrown it over my wall in his flight. This theory gives them a clue to the direction in which he was travelling, and the Inspector spoke hopefully of an early arrest.

November 26th.

The events of the past few days have occupied my mind to the exclusion of all other matters. My diary has been neglected, and I must re-capitulate. So far from rustic uneventfulness, I seem to have landed myself in the middle of a Grand Guignol play.

A fresh series of crimes identical with those of my perverted pre-decessor has broken out in the neighbourhood, and the surrounding country is teeming with police, press men, and morbid sightseers. By having the gates locked I have been able to keep most of them off this property, but I caught two reporters astride the wall near Harper's 'cemetery' yesterday, and had Jobson turn them away. The village is in a state of siege, as no woman will venture out after dark, and even by daylight they go in twos and threes. A rumour that Harper had not died at Broadmoor, but had escaped, rapidly gained ground, and I found myself wondering if this were the case. The police, however, assure me that he died years ago and that so far from any such escape being 'hushed up' a warning would be broadcast to all districts. Hard upon the heels of Jobson's discovery of the hand came news of a second mutilation during the ensuing night. The head, arms, and legs of Dr Corbett's cook were found lying on a tombstone in the churchyard. The torso was missing. The night after, another woman's head and limbs were left neatly piled by the roadside not far from the Assembly Rooms. They must have been placed there in the early morning hours, as a local dance held there was not over till well after midnight. It is very disturbing to have this dangerous lunatic on one's doorstep, apart from the noisy crowd of sightseers who came to pry around – and even picnic on! – the sites of his crimes. To add to all this discord (and perhaps resulting from it) my own health is causing me serious anxiety. It seems impossible for me to get a decent night's rest even with the sedative that Corbett prescribed. My sleep is constantly broken by the most hideous nightmares, in one of which, last night, I even dreamt that I was accompanying Harper on one of his nocturnal escapades. The beginning of the dream remains utterly chaotic, but I distinctly remember standing in a field over the corpse of a woman whom he had dismembered.

Though I could not see the man distinctly he seemed to be constantly at my side compelling me to busy myself hiding the traces of his handiwork. As often, I believe, happens in dreams when we do things as a matter of course that are completely foreign to our natures, I felt myself lacking all volition to resist Harper's influence and, in fact, quite entering into the spirit of his requirements. I buried the woman's clothes in a ditch, covering them carefully with earth and dead bracken, and arranged parts of the body on a gate, balancing the head on one post and hanging the limbs in a row on the bars. The rest of the nightmare is like a fogged photographic plate, save that I repeated my former impression of tramping great distances with a heavy burden – in this instance a nude female torso.

Such ghastly dreams must indicate some kind of ill-health, and if Corbett cannot stop them I shall consult a specialist.

Later.

Jobson has just come back from the village with fresh news which, to me at any rate, appears horribly significant. Another woman's head and limbs have been found, balanced on a gate dividing two nearby pastures. Jobson's description corresponds unpleasantly with my dream. Is it possible that I am somehow spiritually *en rapport* with Harper's ghost through the medium of a common dwelling-place? I have never imagined myself in the least 'psychic'. And then, how explain the finding of an actual corpse (or, at any rate, parts of one) in view of Harper's decease? No: obviously a different maniac, but with similar tendencies, must be at large, and I do not see why the 'aura' of Harper's possessions should bring me in touch with *him* – unless, perhaps, there is some malignant 'elemental' native to these parts which prompts the killings and which may, to some extent, influence anybody living locally. But this is too wild a speculation. I have never believed in such things. Jobson, by the way, found a telegram for him at the Post-Office telling him of a sister's illness. He is a sterling friend and servant, so I told him that he must, of course, take a few days off to see her. He demurred at first on the ground that I should be unable to get local help, but I could see he really wanted to go. He has accordingly left to catch a late train, and I have the house to myself.

November 27th.
Another outrage last night, and another nightmare for me! This time it is Miss Simms, the post-mistress, whose remains were found on her own counter by her daily help, who arrives to make early tea at seven o'clock. The unfortunate woman can have had no chance to resist her attacker as, though she had neighbours on both sides, no outcry was heard. The trunk, as usual, had been carried off. Whether my nightmare had, again, any connection with this crime I cannot recall. I am only aware of the sensation, to which I have now grown accustomed, of carrying things about and of being a fugitive. Towards morning however, I had an amazingly vivid dream to the effect that I came down the stairs from an upper floor at present disused, entered the bathroom and carefully washed my hands and feet, without, for some reason, turning on the light. This recollection came back as soon as I opened my eyes, and, being convinced that I had been guilty of actual sleep-walking on at least one previous occasion, I went at once to the bathroom to look for traces of my suspected earlier visit. But nothing turned out to be disarranged, and I was left in doubt until, after preparing and eating a light breakfast, I decided to explore the upstairs rooms.

One of the first things to catch my eye was a black tassel, similar to those of my pyjama girdles, projecting from under a locked door. I remembered having seen the key to this door hanging in a cupboard under the main staircase, but on going to get it found it had disappeared, and I am now forced to a conclusion that I hate to face. Apart from the evidence of somnambulism, which, in itself, I resent as a weakness, I cannot overlook the connection between my dreams and the nightly butchery that is being enacted.

Is it conceivable that, in my sleeping state, I have been actually present at one or more of these murders, and even – dreadful thought! – handled the dismembered cadavers? My whole mind shrinks from this theory; but it is otherwise hard to explain the subconscious urge to wash, the locking up of a (possibly *stained*) pyjama suit, and the hiding of the keys. Good God! I must be under hypnotic suggestion, and if I am seen and recognized in this state I shall be thought guilty of the actual crimes themselves!

It has occurred to me that my bad nights may be due to excessive smoking – for I have lately been inseparable from my – or rather Harper's – meerschaum. To test this I shall abstain from it tonight and make do with a couple of cigarettes.

November 28th.
It is finished. And the meerschaum pipe is burnt in the largest fire I could build into my grate! I only write this last page of my diary for the sake of my next-of-kin – to assure them that, whatever my own condition, there is no *hereditary* taint. The pipe alone was to blame. When my writing is done I shall go out into the grounds and shoot myself under God's clean daylit sky!

I stuck to my intention of smoking nothing stronger than cigarettes, and for the first time in a week passed the early hours of the night in untroubled repose. Later, however, the restlessness must have returned, for a falling log awoke me to find myself sitting by the study fire – smoking the meerschaum. As I came to full consciousness I experienced the sudden waning of an abstract horror – indefinable but intense. It passed so quickly, though, that within a few seconds I doubted its very existence. Everything seemed normal, the room was still comfortably warm, and I felt too wide awake to seek my bed at once. Instead I said aloud and quite cheerfully, 'Well, if my sleep-walking only brings me down here for a smoke, there's no great harm done', and as the meerschaum was drawing satisfactorily I decided to sit up and finish it. If only I had suspected and burned the damnable thing then! An habitual smoker always derives a soothing effect from puffing at a pipe, and it was the marked superiority of the meerschaum in this respect that had attached me to it so strongly. Now, within a few moments, so pleasant a drowsiness crept over me that I heaped more logs on the fire, determined to finish the night where I sat rather than risk finally arousing myself by a journey back to bed. But if sleep came back – and it did, heavily – it was not the revitalizing, dreamless slumber that I wanted, but a fantastic string of the disjointed nightmare scenes in which I was constantly hunted from place to place by unseen pursuers and carrying in my arms a naked torso. At length these visions gave way to a sort of silent, oppressive darkness, and that, in turn, to pictures of my own earlier life, so that I shook off the menace of the former and looked happily at sane and wholesome things.

I forgot that Mary had long been dead, and thought that she lay beside me in our old room at Hampstead. She was asleep, to judge by her quietness, and I had just awakened; but she lay very still in my arms. I bent my head forward and tried to touch her face with my lips – but it eluded me – and, with an effort, I opened my eyes. I was back in my own bed at 'Heronay', and, of course, there was no face on the pillow beside me.

Yet I did indeed hold something in my arms down under the bedclothes – something that felt like the body of a woman, *but it was very cold and still*. I slid my feet out to the floor *sideways without turning back the sheet*.

The missing bunch of keys lay on my pedestal cupboard, but I shall not belatedly explore that upper room. I know too well what it contains.

The Hound

H. P. Lovecraft

In my tortured ears there sounds unceasingly a nightmare whirring and flapping, and a faint distant baying as of some gigantic hound. It is not dream – it is not, I fear, even madness – for too much has already happened to give me these merciful doubts.

St John is a mangled corpse; I alone know why, and such is my knowledge that I am about to blow out my brains for fear I shall be mangled in the same way. Down unlit and illimitable corridors of eldritch phantasy sweeps the black, shapeless Nemesis that drives me to self-annihilation.

May heaven forgive the folly and morbidity which led us both to so monstrous a fate! Wearied with the commonplaces of a prosaic world; where even the joys of romance and adventure soon grow stale, St John and I had followed enthusiastically every aesthetic and intellectual movement which promised respite from our devastating ennui. The enigmas of the symbolists and the ecstasies of the pre-Raphaelites all were ours in their time, but each new mood was drained too soon, of its diverting novelty and appeal.

Only the sombre philosophy of the decadents could help us, and this we found potent only by increasing gradually the depth and diabolism of our penetrations. Baudelaire and Huysmans were soon exhausted of thrills, till finally there remained for us only the more direct stimuli of unnatural personal experiences and adventures. It was this frightful emotional need which led us eventually to that detestable course which even in my present fear I mention with shame and timidity – that hideous extremity of human outrage, the abhorred practice of grave-robbing.

I cannot reveal the details of our shocking expeditions, or catalogue even partly the worst of the trophies adorning the nameless museum we prepared in the great stone house where we jointly dwelt, alone and servantless. Our museum was a blasphemous, unthinkable place, where with the satanic taste of neurotic virtuosi we had assembled an universe of terror and decay to excite our jaded sensibilities. It was a secret room, far, far, underground; where huge winged daemons carven of basalt and onyx vomited from wide grinning mouths weird green and orange light, and hidden pneumatic pipes ruffled into kaleidoscopic dances of death the lines of red charnel things hand in hand woven in voluminous black hangings. Through these pipes came at will the odours our moods most craved; sometimes the scent of pale funeral lilies; sometimes the narcotic incense of imagined Eastern shrines of the kingly dead, and sometimes – how I shudder to recall it! – the frightful, soul-upheaving stenches of the uncovered grave.

Around the walls of this repellent chamber were cases of antique mummies alternating with comely, lifelike bodies perfectly stuffed and cured by the taxidermist's art, and with headstones snatched from the oldest churchyards of the world. Niches here and there contained skulls of all shapes, and heads preserved in various stages of dissolution. There one might find the rotting, bald pates of famous noblemen, and the fresh and radiantly golden heads of new-buried children.

Statues and paintings there were, all of fiendish subjects and some executed by St John and myself. A locked portfolio, bound in tanned human skin, held certain unknown and unnameable drawings which it was rumoured Goya had perpetrated but dared not acknowledge. There were nauseous musical instruments, stringed, brass, and wood-wind, on which St John and I sometimes produced dissonances of exquisite morbidity and cacodaemoniacal ghastliness; whilst in a multitude of inlaid ebony cabinets reposed the most incredible and unimaginable variety of tomb-loot ever assembled by human madness and perversity. It is of this loot in particular that I must not speak – thank God I had the courage to destroy it long before I thought of destroying myself!

The predatory excursions on which we collected our unmentionable treasures were always artistically memorable events. We were no vulgar ghouls, but worked only under certain conditions of mood, landscape, environment, weather, season, and moonlight. These pastimes were to us the most exquisite form of aesthetic expression, and we gave their details a fastidious technical care. An inappropriate hour, a jarring lighting effect, or a clumsy manipulation of the damp sod, would almost totally destroy for us that ecstatic titillation which followed the exhumation of some ominous, grinning secret of the earth. Our quest for novel scenes and piquant conditions was feverish and insatiate – St John was always the leader, and he it was who led the way at last to that mocking, accursed spot which brought us our hideous and inevitable doom.

By what malign fatality were we lured to that terrible Holland churchyard? I think it was the dark rumour and legendry, the tales of one buried for five centuries, who had himself been a ghoul in his time and had stolen a potent thing from a mighty sepulchre. I can recall the scene in these final moments – the pale autumnal moon over the graves, casting long horrible shadows; the grotesque trees, drooping sullenly to meet the neglected grass and the crumbling slabs; the vast legions of strangely colossal bats that flew against the moon; the antique ivied church pointing a huge spectral finger at the livid sky; the phosphorescent insects that danced like death-fires under the yews in a distant corner; the odours of mould, vegetation, and less explicable things that mingled feebly with the night-wind from over far swamps and seas; and, worst of all, the faint deep-toned baying of some gigantic hound which we could neither see nor definitely place. As we heard this suggestion of baying we shuddered, remembering the tales of the peasantry; for he whom we sought had centuries before been found in this selfsame spot, torn and mangled by the claws and teeth of some unspeakable beast.

I remember how we delved in the ghoul's grave with our spades, and how we thrilled at the picture of ourselves, the grave, the pale watching moon, the horrible shadows, the grotesque trees, the titanic bats, the antique church, the dancing death-fires, the sickening odours, the gently moaning night-wind, and the strange, half-heard directionless baying of whose objective existence we could scarcely be sure.

Then we struck a substance harder than the damp mould, and beheld a rotting oblong box crusted with mineral deposits from the long undisturbed ground. It was incredibly tough and thick, but so old that we finally pried it open and feasted our eyes on what it held.

Much – amazingly much – was left of the object despite the lapse of five hundred years. The skeleton, though crushed in places by the jaws of the thing that had killed it, held together with surprising firmness, and we gloated over the clean white skull and its long, firm teeth and its eyeless sockets that once had glowed with a charnel fever like our own. In the coffin lay an amulet of curious and exotic design, which had apparently been worn around the sleeper's neck. It was the oddly conventionalized figure of a crouching winged hound, or sphinx with a semi-canine face, and was exquisitely carved in antique Oriental fashion from a small piece of green jade. The expression of its features was repellent in the extreme, savouring at once of death, bestiality, and malevolence. Around the base was an inscription in characters which neither St John nor I could identify; and on the bottom, like a maker's seal, was graven a grotesque and formidable skull.

Immediately upon beholding this amulet we knew that we must possess it; that this treasure alone was our logical pelf from the centuried grave. Even had its outlines been unfamiliar we would have desired it, but as we looked more closely we saw that it was not wholly unfamiliar. Alien it indeed was to all art and literature which sane and balanced readers know, but we recognized it as the thing hinted of in the forbidden *Necronomicon* of the mad Arab Abdul Alhazred; the ghastly soul-symbol of the corpse-eating cult of inaccessible Leng, in Central Asia. All too well did we trace the sinister lineaments described by the old Arab daemonologist; lineaments, he wrote, drawn from some obscure supernatural manifestation of the souls of those who vexed and gnawed at the dead.

Seizing the green jade object, we gave a last glance at the bleached and cavern-eyed face of its owner and closed up the grave as we found it. As we hastened from the abhorrent spot, the stolen amulet in St John's pocket, we thought we saw the bats descend in a body to the earth we had so lately rifled, as if seeking for some cursed and unholy nourishment. But the autumn moon shone weak and pale, and we could not be sure.

So, too, as we sailed the next day from Holland to our home, we thought we heard the faint distant baying of some gigantic hound in the background. But the autumn wind moaned sad and wan, and we could not be sure.

Less than a week after our return to England, strange things began to happen. We lived as recluses; devoid of friends, alone, and without servants in a few rooms of an ancient manor-house on a bleak and unfrequented moor; so that our doors were seldom disturbed by the knock of the visitor.

Now, however, we were troubled by what seemed to be a frequent fumbling in the night, not only around the doors but around the windows also, upper as well as lower. Once we fancied that a large, opaque body darkened the library window when the moon was shining against it, and another time we thought we heard a whirring or flapping sound not far off. On each occasion investigation revealed nothing, and we began to ascribe the occurrences to imagination which still prolonged in our ears the faint far baying we thought we had heard in the Holland churchyard. The jade amulet now reposed in a niche in our museum, and sometimes we burned a strangely scented candle before it. We read much in Alhazred's *Necronomicon* about its properties, and about the relation of ghosts' souls to the objects it symbolized; and were disturbed by what we read.

Then terror came.

On the night of September 24th, 19—, I heard a knock at my chamber door. Fancying it St John's, I bade the knocker enter, but was answered only by a shrill laugn. There was no one in the corridor. When I aroused St John from his sleep, he professed entire ignorance of the event, and became as worried as I. It was the night that the faint, distant baying over the moor became to us a certain and dreaded reality.

Four days later, whilst we were both in the hidden museum, there came a low, cautious scratching at the single door which led to the secret library staircase. Our alarm was now divided, for, besides our fear of the unknown, we had always entertained a dread that our grisly collection might be discovered. Extinguishing all lights, we proceeded to the door and threw it suddenly open; whereupon we felt an unaccountable rush of air, and heard, as if receding far away, a queer combination of rustling, tittering, and articulate chatter. Whether we were mad, dreaming, or in our senses, we did not try to determine. We only realized, with the blackest of apprehensions, that the apparently disembodied chatter was beyond a doubt *in the Dutch language.*

After that we lived in growing horror and fascination. Mostly we held to the theory that we were jointly going mad from our life of unnatural excitements, but sometimes it pleased us more to dramatize ourselves as the victims of some creeping and appalling doom. Bizarre manifestations were now too frequent to count. Our lonely house was seemingly alive with the presence of some malign being whose nature we could not guess, and every night that daemoniac baying rolled over the wind-swept moor, always louder and louder. On October 29th we found in the soft earth underneath the library window a series of footprints utterly impossible to describe. They were as baffling as the hordes of great bats which haunted the old manor-house in unprecedented and increasing numbers.

The horror reached a culmination on November 18th, when St John, walking home after dark from the dismal railway station, was seized by some frightful carnivorous thing and torn to ribbons. His screams had reached the house, and I had hastened to the terrible scene in time to hear a whir of wings and see a vague black cloudy thing silhouetted against the rising moon.

My friend was dying when I spoke to him, and he could not answer coherently. All he could do was to whisper, 'The amulet — that damned thing——.'

Then he collapsed, an inert mass of mangled flesh.

I buried him the next midnight in one of our neglected gardens, and mumbled over his body one of the devilish rituals he had loved in life. And as I pronounced the last daemoniac sentence I heard afar on the moor the faint baying of some gigantic hound. The moon was up, but I dared not look at it. And when I saw on the dim-lighted moor a wide nebulous shadow sweeping from mound to mound, I shut my eyes and threw myself face down upon the ground. When I arose, trembling, I know not how much later, I staggered into the house and made shocking obeisance before the enshrined amulet of green jade.

Being now afraid to live alone in the ancient house on the moor, I departed on the following day for London, taking with me the amulet after destroying by fire and burial the rest of the impious collection in the museum. But after three nights I heard the baying again, and before a week was over felt strange eyes upon me whenever it was dark. One evening as I strolled on Victoria Embankment for some needed air, I saw a black shape obscure one of the reflections of the lamps in the water. A wind, stronger than the night-wind, rushed by, and I knew that what had befallen St John must soon befall me.

The next day I carefully wrapped the green jade amulet and sailed for Holland. What mercy I might gain by returning the thing to its silent, sleeping owner I knew not; but I felt that I must try any step conceivably logical. What the hound was, and why it had pursued me, were questions still vague; but I had first heard the baying in that ancient churchyard, and every subsequent event including St John's dying whisper had served to connect the curse with the stealing of the amulet. Accordingly I sank into the nethermost abysses of despair when, at an inn in Rotterdam, I discovered that thieves had despoiled me of this sole means of salvation.

The baying was loud that evening, and in the morning I read of a nameless deed in the vilest quarter of the city. The rabble were in terror, for upon an evil tenement had fallen a red death beyond the foulest previous crime of the neighbourhood. In a squalid thieves' den an entire family had been torn to shreds by an unknown thing which left no trace, and those around had heard all night a faint, deep, insistent note as of a gigantic hound.

So at last I stood again in the unwholesome churchyard where a pale winter moon cast hideous shadows, and leafless trees drooped sullenly to meet the withered, frosty grass and cracking slabs, and the ivied church pointed a jeering finger at the unfriendly sky, and the night-wind howled maniacally from over frozen swamps and frigid seas. The baying was very faint now, and it ceased altogether as I approached the ancient grave I had once violated, and frightened away an abnormally large horde of bats which had been hovering curiously around it.

I know not why I went thither unless to pray, or gibber out insane pleas and apologies to the calm white thing that lay within; but, whatever my reason, I attacked the half-frozen sod with a desperation partly mine and partly that of a dominating will outside myself. Excavation was much easier than I expected, though at one point I encountered a queer interruption; when a lean vulture darted down out of the cold sky and pecked frantically at the grave-earth until I killed him with a blow of my spade. Finally I reached the rotting oblong box and removed the damp nitrous cover. This is the last rational act I ever performed.

For crouched within that centuried coffin, embraced by a closepacked nightmare retinue of huge, sinewy, sleeping bats, was the bony thing my friend and I had robbed; not clean and placid as we had seen it then, but covered with caked blood and shreds of alien flesh and hair, and leering sentiently at me with phosphorescent sockets and sharp ensanguined fangs yawning twistedly in mockery of my inevitable doom. And when it gave from those grinning jaws a deep, sardonic bay as of some gigantic hound, and I saw that it held in its gory filthy claw the lost and fateful amulet of green jade, I merely screamed and ran away idiotically, my screams soon dissolving into peals of hysterical laughter.

Madness rides the star-wind ... claws and teeth sharpened on centuries of corpses ... dripping death astride a bacchanale of bats from night-black ruins of buried temples of Belial ... Now, as the baying of that dead fleshless monstrosity grows louder and louder, and the stealthy whirring and flapping of those accursed web-wings circles closer and closer, I shall seek with my revolver the oblivion which is my only refuge from the unnamed and unnameable.

Our Feathered Friends

Philip MacDonald

The hot, hard August sunshine poured its pale and glazing gold over the countryside. At the crest of the hill, which overlooked a county and a half, the tiny motor car drawn up to the side of the dusty road which wound up the hill like a white riband looked not so much mechanical as insectile. It looked like a Brobdingnagian bee which, wings folded, has settled for a moment's sleepy basking in the fierce sunshine.

Beside the car, seeming almost ludicrously out of proportion with it, stood a man and a woman. The sum of their ages could not have exceeded forty-five. The dress of the girl, which was silken and slight, would not, at all events upon her charming body, have done aught save grace a car as large and costly as this one was minute and cheap. But the clothes of the boy, despite his youth and erect comeliness, were somehow eloquent of Norwood, a careful and not unintelligent clerkliness pursued in the City of London, and a pseudo-charitable arrangement whereby the bee-like motor car should be purchased, for many pounds more than its actual worth, in small but almost eternal slices.

The girl was hatless, and her clipped, golden poll glittered in the sun-rays. She looked, and was, cool, despite the great heat of the afternoon. The boy, in his tweed jacket, thick flannel trousers, and over-tight collar, at whose front blazed a tie which hoped to look like that of some famous school or college, was hot, and very hot. He pulled his hat from his dark head, and mopped at his brow with a vivid handkerchief.

'Coo!' he said. 'Hot enough for you, Vi?'

She wriggled slim, half-covered shoulders. 'It's a treat!' she said. She gazed about her with wide, blue eyes; she looked down and round at the county-and-a-half. 'Where's this, Jack?'

The boy continued to puff and mop. He said:

'Blessed if *I* know ... I lost me bearings after that big village place – what was it? ...'

'Greyne, or some such,' said the girl absently. Her gaze was now directed down the hillside to her right, where the emerald roof of a dense wood shone through the sun's gold. There was no breath of wind, even right up upon this hill, and the green of the leaves showed smooth and unbroken.

The boy put on his hat again. 'Better be getting on, I s'pose. You've had that leg-stretch you were wanting.'

'Ooh! Not *yet*, Jack. Don't let's yet.' She put the fingers of her left hand upon his sleeve. On the third of these fingers there sparkled a ring of doubtful brilliance. 'Don't let's go on yet, Jack!' she said. She looked up into his face, her lips pouted in a way which was not the least of reasons for the flashing ring.

He slid an arm about the slim shoulders; he bent his head and kissed thoroughly the red mouth. 'Just's *you* like, Vi ... But what you want to do?' He looked about him with curling lip. 'Sit around up here on this dusty grass and frizzle?'

'Silly!' she said, pulling herself away from him. She pointed down to the green roof. 'I want to go down there ... Into that wood. Jest to see what it's like. Haven't been in a reel wood since the summer holidays before last, when Effie an' me went to Hastings ... Cummon! Bet it's lovely and cool down there ...'

This last sentence floated up to him, for already she was off the narrow road and beginning a slipping descent of the short rough grass of the hillside's first twenty feet.

He went sliding and stumbling after her. But he could not catch up with the light, fragile little figure in its absurdly enchanting wisp of blue silk. The soles of his thick shoes were of leather, and, growing polished by the brushing of the close, arid grass, were treacherous. Forty feet down, on the suddenly jutting and only gently sloping plateau where the wood began, he did come up with her: he ended a stumbling, sliding rush with an imperfect and involuntary somersault which landed him asprawl at her feet.

He sat up, shouting with laughter. With a shock of surprise greater than any of his short life, he felt a little foot kick sharply – nearly savagely – at his arm, and heard a tensely whispered 'ssh!'

He scrambled to his feet, to see that she was standing facing the trees, her shining golden head thrust forward, her whole body tense as that of a sprinter waiting for the pistol's crack. As, wonderingly, he shuffled to take his stand at her shoulder, she said:

'*Listen* ... Birds! ... Jever hear the like? ...' Her tone was a hushed yet clear whisper – like none he had ever heard her use before.

He said nothing. He stood scowling sulkily down at the grass beneath his feet and rubbing the spot where her shoe had met his arm.

It seemed to him an hour before she turned. But turn at last she did. He still had his hand at the kicked arm, for all the world as if it really were causing him pain. From beneath his brows he watched her, covertly. He saw the odd rapt look leave the small face once more its

pertly pretty self; saw the blue eyes suddenly widen with memory of
what she had done ...

And then soft warm arms came about his neck and by their pressure
pulled down his head so that, close pressed against him and standing
upon tiptoe, she might smother his face with the kisses of contrition.

He said, in answer to the pleas for forgiveness with which the caresses
were interspersed:

'Never known you do a thing like that before, Vi!'

'No,' she said. 'And you never won't again! Reely, Jack darling! ...
It ... it ...' – a cloud came over her blue eyes – 'it ... I don't rightly
know what came over me ... I was listening to the birds ... I never heard
the like ... and ... and I never heard you till you laughed ... and I
dunno *what* it was, but it seemed 's if I jest *had* to go on hearing what
the birds were ... 's if it was ... was *wrong* to listen to anything else ...
Oh, *I* dunno!'

The small face was troubled and the eyes desperate with the realization of explanation's impossibility. But the mouth pouted. The boy
kissed it. He laughed and said:

'Funny kid, you!' He drew her arm through the crook of his and began
to walk towards the first ranks of the trees. He put up his free hand and
felt tenderly at the back of his neck. He said:

'Shan't be sorry for some shade. Neck's gettin' all sore.'

They walked on, finding that the trees were strangely farther away
than they had seemed. They did not speak, but every now and then the
slim naked arm would squeeze the thick, clothed arm and have its
pressure returned.

They had only some ten paces to go to reach the fringe of the wood
when the girl halted. He turned his head to look down at her and found
that once more she was tense in every muscle, and thrusting the golden
head forward as if the better to hear. He frowned; then smiled; then
again bent his brows. He sensed that there was somewhere an oddness
which he knew he would never understand – a feeling abhorrent to him,
as, indeed, to most men. He found that he, too, was straining to listen.

He supposed it must be birds that he was listening for. And quite
suddenly he laughed. For he had realized that he was listening for
something which had been for the last few moments so incessantly in his
ears that he had forgotten he was hearing it. He explained this to the
girl. She seemed to listen to him with only half an ear, and for a moment
he came near to losing his temper. But only for a moment. He was a
good-natured boy, with sensitive instincts serving him well in place of
realized tact.

He felt a little tugging at his arm and fell into step with her as she
began to go forward again. He went on with his theme, ignoring her
patently half-hearted attention.

'Like at a dance,' he said. 'You know, Vi – you never hear the noise of the people's feet on the floor unless you happen to listen for it, an' when you do listen for it an' hear that sort of *shishing* – then you know you've been hearing it all the time, see? That's what we were doing about the birds ...' He became suddenly conscious that, in order to make himself clearly heard above the chattering, twittering flood of bird-song, he was speaking in a tone at least twice as loud as the normal. He said:

'Coo! ... You're right, Vi. *I* never heard anything like it!'

They were passing now through the ranks of the outer line of trees. To the boy, a little worried by the strangeness of his adored, and more than a little discomfited by the truly abnormal heat of the sun, it seemed that he passed from an inferno to a paradise at one step. No more did the sun beat implacably down upon the world. In here, under the roof of green which no ray pierced but only a gentle, pervading, filtered softness of light, there was a cool peacefulness which seemed to bathe him, instantly, in a placid bath of contentment.

But the girl shivered a little. She said:

'Oh! It's almost cold in here!'

He did not catch the words. The chirping and carolling which was going on all about and above them seemed to catch up and absorb the sound of her voice.

'Drat the birds!' he said. 'What you say?'

He saw her lips move, but though he bent his head, did not catch a sound. There had come, from immediately above their heads, the furious squeaks and flutterings of a bird-quarrel.

'Drat the birds!' he said again.

They were quite deep in the wood now. Looking round, he could not see at all the sun-drenched grass plateau from which they had come. He felt a tugging at his arm. The girl was pointing to a gently sloping bed of thick moss which was like a carpet spread at the foot of an old and twisted tree.

They sauntered to this carpet and sat down upon it, the boy sprawling at his ease, the girl very straight of back, with her hands clasped tightly about her raised knees. Had he been looking at her, rather than at the pipe he was filling, he would have seen again that craning forward of her head.

He did not finish the filling of his pipe. The singing of the birds went on. It seemed to gather volume until the whole world was filled with its chaotic whistling. The boy found, now that he had once consciously listened for and to it, that he could not again make his ears unconscious of the sound; the sound which, with its seemingly momentarily increased volume, was now so plucking at the nerves within his head – indeed over his whole body – that he felt he could not much longer endure it. He thrust pipe and pouch savagely back into his pocket and turned to say to the girl that the quicker they got away from this blinking twittering the better he'd be pleased.

But the words died upon his lips. For even as he turned he became aware of a diminution of the reedy babel. He saw, too, calmer now with the decrease of irritation, that the girl was still in rapt attention.

So he held his tongue. The singing of the birds grew less and less with each moment. He began to feel drowsy, and once caught himself with a startled jerk from the edge of actual slumber. He peered sideways at his companion, and saw that still she sat rigid; not by the breadth of a hair had she altered her first attentive pose. He felt again for pipe and pouch.

His fingers idle in the jacket pocket, he found himself listening again. Only this time he listened because he wanted to listen. There was now but one bird who sang. And the boy was curiously conscious, hearing these liquid notes alone and in the fullness of their uninterrupted and almost unbearable beauty, that the reason for his hatred of that full and somehow discordant chorus which a few moments ago had nearly driven him from the trees and their lovely shelter, had been his inability to hear more than an isolated note or two of this song whose existence then he had realized only subconsciously.

The full, deep notes ceased their rapid and incredible trilling, cutting their sound off sharply, almost in the manner of an operatic singer. There was, then, only silence in the wood. It lasted, for the town-bred boy and girl caught suddenly in this placid whirlpool of natural beauty, for moments which seemed strained and incalculable ages. And then into this pool of pregnant no-sound were dropped, one by one, six exquisite jewels of sound, each pause between these isolated lovelinesses being of twice the duration of its predecessor.

After the last of these notes – deep and varying and crystal-pure, yet misty with unimaginable beauties – the silence fell again; a silence not pregnant, as the last, with the vibrant foreshadowings of the magic to come, but a silence which had in it the utter and miserable quietness of endings and nothingness.

The boy's arm went up and wrapped itself gently about slim, barely-covered shoulders. Two heads turned, and dark eyes looked into blue. The blue were abrim with unshed tears. She whispered:

'It was *him* I was listening to all the while. I could hear *that* all . . . all through the others . . .'

A tear brimmed over and rolled down the pale cheek. The arm about her shoulders tightened, and at last she relaxed. The little body grew limp and lay against his strength.

'You lay quiet, darling,' he said. His voice trembled a little. And he spoke in the hushed voice of a man who knows himself in a holy or enchanted place.

Then silence. Silence which weighed and pressed upon a man's soul. Silence which seemed a living deadness about them. From the boy's shoulder came a hushed, small voice which endeavoured to conceal its shaking. It said:

'I ... I ... felt all along ... we shouldn't ... shouldn't be here ... We didn't ought to 've come ...'

Despite its quietness there was something like panic in the voice.

He spoke reassuring words. To shake her from this queer, repressed hysteria, he said these words in a loud and virile tone. But this had only the effect of conveying to himself something of the odd disquiet which had possessed the girl.

'It's cold in here,' she whispered suddenly. Her body pressed itself against him.

He laughed; an odd sound. He said hastily:

'Cold! You're talking out of the back of your neck, Vi.'

'It is,' she said. But her voice was more natural now. 'We better be getting along, hadn't we?'

He nodded. 'Think we had,' he said. He stirred as if to get to his feet. But a small hand suddenly gripped his arm, and her voice whispered:

'Look! *Look!*' It was her own voice again, so that even while he started a little at her sudden clutch and the urgency of her tone, he felt a wave of relief and a sudden quietening of his own vague but discomfortable uneasiness.

His gaze followed the line of her pointing finger. He saw, upon the carpeting of rotten twigs and brown mouldering leaves, just at the point where this brown and the dark cool green of their moss-bank met, a small bird. It stood upon its slender sticks of legs and gazed up at them, over the plump bright-hued breast, with shining little eyes. Its head was cocked to one side.

'D'you know,' said the girl's whisper, 'that's the first one we've *seen*?'

The boy pondered for a moment. 'Gosh!' he said at last. 'So it is and all!'

They watched in silence. The bird hopped nearer.

'Isn't he *sweet*, Jack?' Her whisper was a delighted chuckle.

'Talk about tame!' said the boy softly. 'Cunning little beggar!'

Her elbow nudged his ribs. She said, her lips barely moving:

'Keep still. If we don't move, I believe he'll come right up to us.'

Almost on her words, the bird hopped nearer. Now he was actually upon the moss, and thus less than an inch from the toe of the girl's left shoe. His little pert head, which was of a shining green with a rather comically long beak of yellow, was still cocked to one side. His bright, small eyes still surveyed them with the unwinking stare of his kind.

The girl's fascinated eyes were upon the small creature. She saw nothing else. Not so the boy. There was a nudge, this time from his elbow.

'Look there!' he whispered, pointing. 'And there!'

She took, reluctantly enough, her eyes from the small intruder by her foot. She gazed in the directions he had indicated. She gasped in wonder. She whispered:

'Why, they're *all* coming to see us!'

Everywhere between the boles of the close-growing trees were birds. Some stood singly, some in pairs, some in little clumps of four and more. Some seemed, even to urban eyes, patently of the same family as their first visitor, who still stood by the white shoe, staring up at the face of its owner. But there were many more families. There were very small birds, and birds of sparrow size but unsparrowlike plumage, and birds which were a little bigger than this, and birds which were twice and three times the size. But one and all faced the carpet of moss and stared with their shining eyes at the two humans who lay upon it.

'This,' said the boy, 'is the rummest start *I* ever . . .'

The girl's elbow nudged him to silence. He followed the nod of her head and, looking down, saw that the first visitor was now perched actually upon her instep. He seemed very much at his ease there. But he was no longer looking up at them with those bright little eyes. And his head was no longer cocked to one side: it was level, so that he appeared to be in contemplation of a silk-clad shin.

Something – perhaps it was a little whispering, pattering rustle among the rotting leaves of the wood's carpet – took the boy's fascinated eyes from this strange sight. He lifted them to see a stranger; a sight perhaps more fascinating, but with by no means the same fascination.

The birds were nearer. Much, much nearer. And their line was solid now; an unbroken semi-circle with bounding-line so wide-flung that he felt rather than saw its extent. One little corner of his brain for an instant busied itself with wild essays at numerical computation, but reeled back defeated by the impossibility of the task. Even as he stared, his face pale now, and his eyes wide with something like terror, that semi-circle drew yet nearer, each unit of it taking four hops and four hops only. Now, its line unmarred, it was close upon the edge of the moss.

But was it only a semi-circle? A dread doubt of this flashed into his mind.

One horrified glance across his shoulder told him that semi-circle it was not. Full circle it was.

Birds, birds, birds! Was it possible that the world itself should hold such numbers of birds?

Eyes! Small, shining, myriad button-points of glittering eyes. All fixed upon him . . . and – God! upon *her* . . .

In one wild glance he saw that as yet she had not seen. Still she was rapt in silent ecstasy over her one bird. And this now sat upon the outspread palm of her hand. Close to her face she was holding this hand . . .

Through the pall of silence he could feel those countless eyes upon him. Little eyes; bright, glittering eyes ...

His breath came in shuddering gasps. He tried to get himself in hand; tried, until the sweat ran off him with the intensity of his effort, to master his fear. To some extent he succeeded. He would no longer sit idle while the circle ... while the circle ...

The silence was again ruffled upon its surface by a rustling patter ... It was one hop this time. It brought the semi-circle fronting him so near that there were birds within an inch of his feet.

He leapt up. He waved his arms and kicked out and uttered one shout which somehow cracked and was half-strangled in his throat.

Nothing happened. At the edge of the moss a small bird, crushed by his kick, lay in a soft, small heap.

Not one of the birds moved. Still their eyes were upon him.

The girl sat like a statue in living stone. She had seen, and terror held her. Her palm, the one bird still motionless upon it, still was outspread near her face.

From high above them there dropped slowly into the black depths of the silence one note of a sweetness ineffable. It lingered upon the breathless air, dying slowly until it fused with the silence.

And then the girl screamed. Suddenly and dreadfully. The small green poll had darted forward. The yellow beak had struck and sunk. A scarlet runnel coursed down the tender cheek.

Above the lingering echo of that scream there came another of those single notes from on high.

The silence died then. There was a whirring which filled the air. That circle was no more.

There were two feathered mounds which screamed and ran and leapt, and at last lay and were silent.

The Thirteenth Kestrel

Roger Malisson

Stanley Davis eased back the joystick and went into a steep climb, watching the toy-and-patchwork countryside falling away beneath him. He made for the coast and flew above the sea, where the waves looked like wrinkled metal. A couple of yachtsmen waved at him but he only smiled back, too happy and too numb to lift his hand from the Kestrel's controls.

Lulled by the engine's steady roar, a half-forgotten Zen story drifted into his mind about a man clinging to a cliff, knowing that he would plunge to his death in a few seconds, and plucking a wild strawberry with his free hand: 'How sweet it tasted!' He felt he understood that now. Climbing into sunlit cumulus, his throat contracted at the beauty of the pearly, snowy cloud.

One by one his friends came to say goodbye. He dismissed them kindly, with affection and humour. Even Lucy, the one woman who could have helped him out of his emotional mess and hadn't; and his Managing Director, who would discover the missing thousands on Monday. In his euphoric detachment, he wished them all well.

His two-seater Kestrel monoplane was his best friend, though. It was a pity he was going to destroy it. He knew its every quirk, he thought with a maudlin smile, and it wouldn't fly straight, sometimes wouldn't even start, for anyone else. To it he owed the happiest hours of his life.

Well, it would all be over soon. Idly he remembered the hundred or so aspirins he had washed down with sips of Guinness. The black beer and the white pills . . .

Stanley Davis was nearly ready to enter his final sleep. There was one more decision to be made. The Kestrel seemed to be heading out to sea of its own volition; but no, he would not destroy it. Gently he banked left, towards the land. On a deserted stretch of countryside in Northumberland – or was it Scotland by this time? – he made his last and most perfect landing, which was odd because he knew his reactions were becoming erratic.

The Kestrel seemed to be cradling him to sleep, and he smiled faintly as he drifted into the coma from which he never awoke.

'Have you heard about Stan Davis's Kestrel?' Mike Bennett asked as he walked into the club. 'Bill Rogerson's bought it.'

'Bill has?' His friend Geoff Matlock looked surprised, then chuckled. 'I wonder what Lucy thinks about that. How much?'

'Two thousand. A gift, might I remind you.'

Mike went to order coffee, and Geoff felt slightly guilty. Mike had wanted them to buy half-shares in the Kestrel when it came on the market after Davis's suicide, but Geoff already had his eye on a Piper, a type he preferred to Kestrels.

Ironic that Bill should buy it, though. It was common knowledge that his wife Lucy had been a great friend of Davis. Whether they'd had an affair or not Geoff didn't know, and didn't want to know. He liked Lucy, but nervy, china-doll blondes weren't really his type. She had stayed with Bill throughout, which was just as well considering the unstable sort Davis had been.

'I thought Bill didn't get on too well when he flew that Kestrel a few months back?' he asked when Mike returned with the coffee.

'He didn't. The engine stalled and he reckoned it needed a complete overhaul. Says it's A1 now, though. He's arranged for hangarage here at Southland.'

The Kestrel had a reputation for awkwardness at the flying club where Davis had kept it. Rumours grew from trivia, and some swore it was unlucky.

'Isn't there someting quaint about its registration?' asked Geoff.

Mike laughed. 'Yes X-ray India India India. XIII. Thirteen in Roman numerals, see? Helps the legend no end, as you can imagine.'

It was not until the following Saturday that Geoff and Mike had their first look at the thirteenth Kestrel. They clustered round it with James Sharples, the chief flying instructor. Bill was full of his new acquisition, but Lucy stood back a little, frowning.

'Not the most beautiful design I've ever seen, but it's in great shape,' Geoff said to her conversationally.

'I suppose so. I really know very little about them.'

The Kestrels were large, inelegant-looking aircraft, with horizontally opposed engines in the blunt noses, and sharply angled wings. This one was painted a dull blue and white and, though by no means the biggest plane in the hangar, it seemed strangely dominant. An illusion because it was a newcomer, thought Geoff.

'She's a beauty.' Bill climbed into the plane and sat in the pilot's seat with all the legitimate pride of his ownership. 'Come on, Lucy, see what you think.'

Lucy complied, obviously unwillingly. Geoff wondered whether Bill hadn't been trying to prove some point to her by buying the Kestrel.

'Got your Certificate of Airworthiness renewed yet, Bill?' James was asking.

'Yes, it came this morning. I'm planning a flight for tomorrow if the rain stops.'

Geoff watched Lucy. She looked drawn and strained, and she seemed to be trembling. Abruptly she stood up and began to climb uncertainly out of the plane. Stepping on to the wing she nearly stumbled, and Geoff ran forward to help her.

'Steady on, that's a great way to sprain your ankle. Hold my hand.'

'Oh, thank you, Geoff.' Her hands were icy. He was about to join in the others' discussion of the Kestrel's engine but, still talking nervously to him, Lucy began walking away to the back of the hangar. Reluctantly, he followed her.

'I really don't like that plane. It gives me such an odd feeling every time I see it, and sitting in it just now was really sort of frightening. Do you know what I mean?' she continued rapidly. 'As if it had some kind of life of its own. No, that's not right, I mean ... some sort of will.'

'Really?' said Geoff politely.

She must, of course, be associating the Kestrel with Davis's death.

'Yes. Can't you feel it?' she asked anxiously. 'Sort of – emanations, unfriendly vibrations?'

Geoff laughed. She really should stop these fancies before they started. 'No, Lucy, I'm afraid I can't.'

A sharp cry of pain distracted them. James Sharples was shaking his hand and trying not to swear.

'Blasted bit of metal sticking up there,' he said, pointing at the fuselage.

'Here, James, wrap this around it.' Mike produced a clean hanky. The cut was small but deep and bled profusely.

'Thanks,' said James. 'I'll get some Dettol on it back at the club.'

'Here it is,' said Bill, running his hands carefully along the body of the plane. 'It's jagged, just along here. Funny I didn't notice it when I got in.'

Geoff glanced round at Lucy. She was staring white-faced at the Kestrel, hands clenched. No doubt, he thought wryly, she was reading some sinister significance into this little accident.

Dr Harry Levers breezed into the flying club the following day.

'Lovely morning,' he remarked to everybody. 'Ready for the Midlands flight, James?'

' 'Fraid not, Harry.' James displayed his swollen hand.

'Oh, hell,' Harry groaned. 'Let's have a look at it.' He unwound the bandage and grimaced. 'What did you do with this, wrap it in an oily rag?'

Bill Rogerson strolled over to Geoff.

'Coming to see me off?' he asked. 'It's my first flight in the Kestrel today.'

'Sure. I'm going up myself later in Joe's Cessna. Where's Lucy?'

Bill stopped smiling. 'She wouldn't come. She's got some weird idea that the plane's not safe. Said it was jinxed, or some damn thing!' He gave a short, mirthless laugh. 'You know what women are, once they've got an idea in their heads.'

Geoff helped him wheel the Kestrel out of the hangar and on to the concrete path outside.

'Thanks, Geoff. See you later.'

'Good luck.' said Geoff involuntarily.

Bill laughed and closed the Kestrel's perspex top. For an ugly second the action reminded Geoff of a man unwittingly sealing himself into his own tomb. He shrugged off the morbid thought impatiently. Lucy's nerves were infectious.

From the club windows he watched the Kestrel taxi down the runway, stop for its final checks, and take off without hazard.

Airborne, the Kestrel flew straight and steady. Bill grinned to himself. Jinx plane indeed. He'd show Lucy. Probably it did need skilled handling, but once one was used to it there were no problems. It's a perfect day for flying, he thought complacently, drifting through the warm azure haze. Strange how, at height, one had the illusion of scarcely moving ... At height? The altimeter showed 5,500 feet – how had he managed that? Startled and shaken, he went into a moderate dive, reducing the throttle as the Kestrel picked up speed.

Something fell against the side of the plane and he glanced down. Christ, his safety harness was unfastened! How in hell had that happened? He struggled one-handed to refasten it as the plane levelled out. Then suddenly, smoothly, the stick pressed back against his hand and the throttle opened as the plane began to climb. Bill fought against panic as the horizon disappeared below the nose. The thing was out of control, flying itself! He tried desperately to force the stick forward but it wouldn't move. Clinging helplessly to his harness, Bill crouched low in his seat, but he blacked out as the Kestrel executed a neat loop and began another.

At the top of the second loop the inverted aeroplane flicked out and went into a horizontal spin, then accelerated into a barrel roll.

'What the bloody hell does he think he's doing?' shouted James Sharples, running out of the club house with a forgotten sandwich in his good hand.

'Looks like a stall turn,' suggested a parachutist who had gathered with others to watch what appeared to be a brilliant display of acrobatics. James elbowed him aside and pushed his way over to Geoff, who had never seen the instructor so furious.

'Wait till he gets back,' James muttered, '——*if* he gets back. Two thousand feet above the blasted club – he's lost his reason!'

'Look out – he's going to crash!'

It might have been during a simple slow roll that Bill died, or during the heart-stopping tail slide. The Kestrel came in to land almost lazily on the grass, ploughing its nose in the soft, deep mud. One wing was warped, a propeller blade snapped and there was minor structural and engine damage, but all things considered it had a miraculous escape from the scrap-heap.

The autopsy showed that Bill had died from a broken neck and skull fracture. Because of the unfastened safety harness, the inquest returned an open verdict. Lucy was brave and said little, beyond denying that her husband had been suicidal. But then, Geoff knew, she had half-expected him to have an accident in the Kestrel. Not like this, though, he thought with revulsion, not to be rattled and battered to death like a fly in a matchbox.

To cheers, boos and catcalls, Joe Nolan climbed on to a table, swaying precariously but holding his pint straight, and began to bawl:

'If I were the marrying kind,

Which thank the Lord I'm not, sir——'

'That'll do, Joe. Lady present, you know,' called Mike, who was acting as barman that evening.

'They never complain at the rugger club,' grumbled Joe, climbing down again. 'Sorry, Mrs Rogerson,' he said, and Lucy nodded acknowledgement.

When Geoff arrived he was quite happy that the Saturday night drink at the flying club had developed into a binge, because he was quietly celebrating the acquisition of a brown belt in Judo, his main interest after flying. Joe was apparently drowning his sorrows over a crash he'd had that afternoon, the first at the club since poor Bill Rogerson had died nearly a month ago. It was a surprise to see Lucy there with a couple of old friends of Bill's; probably the first time she'd had an evening out since the accident, Geoff surmised.

'Where's James tonight?' he asked Harry Levers.

'At the hospital having his dressing changed,' said Harry. 'He'll be here later. Worst case of sepsis I've seen for a long time, that hand. He's damn lucky he didn't lose it.'

'You're joking,' protested Geoff. 'A tiny cut like that?'

'I'm telling you,' the doctor began impressively, then changed his mind. 'Oh, well, we're not here to talk shop, are we? Come and have a drink.'

'Congratulations,' said Mike as they pushed their way up to the bar. 'Black belt in Origami, wasn't it?'

'Something like that,' Geoff grinned.

'Listen, Geoff, what about the Kestrel?' Mike asked, pushing a pint towards him.

'What about it?'

'Well, Lucy's bound to be selling it now that Bill's gone. We'd probably get it for eighteen hundred. What do you say we make her an offer?'

Geoff considered. It was a tempting idea, as he only had a third share in a Turbulent at the moment, and he preferred two-seaters. In fact, it was probably an ideal opportunity.

'So we ignore the curse, or jinx, or whatever?' he said, half-jokingly. 'The Thirteenth Kestrel, you know, Mike ...'

'Oh, come on, Geoff, you can't believe all that rubbish. It's a snip!'

'Is it that Kestrel of Stan Davis's you're talking about?' Joe laid a heavy hand of Geoff's shoulder.

'You weren't thinking about buying it yourself, surely, Joe?' Mike asked anxiously.

'Wouldn't have it as a gift. Wouldn't fly it for a kingdom,' said Joe emphatically, swaying against the bar. 'Something all wrong about that kite. Pardon,' he hiccupped.

'Oh, now look here, Joe – coming!' called Mike to someone farther down the bar. 'It's all superstitious rot about the Kestrel. It's as sound as any in this club, and – oh, all right,' he shouted to the impatient customer. 'I'll be back in a second. Don't let him put you off, Geoff.'

'Is there anything wrong with it mechanically, Joe?' Geoff asked when Joe emerged from his drink. He respected the older man's opinion; Joe had been flying before he was out of nappies.

'It's just a feeling. Nothing rational, I'm afraid.' Joe was suddenly serious. 'It was said to be the thirteenth of that particular series, and an engineer was supposed to have been killed when it was being made. Unpleasant things seem to happen around it ... There's something wrong about it.' He shook his head helplessly. 'There was only Stan Davis could ever handle it. Yes, I know I sound as if I'm rambling, but all I can say to you, son, is – is....' He swayed close to Geoff, staring intently into his eyes. '... Don't touch it. Don't have anything to do with it. D'you understand? Because it's ev——' He broke off as if embarrassed, and turned back to his drink, muttering to himself.

Despite the fact that Joe was tight, Geoff was impressed. A scientist by profession, Geoff couldn't bring himself to believe in anything metaphysical. Still, if people believed in something firmly enough, it might be possible to bring disaster upon themselves through that outside agency. Voodoo cults worked on that sort of principle. Privately he had rationalized Bill's death as some compulsive, buried fear which had made him loose his seatbelt at some traumatic moment during his aerobatics. Like people with vertigo who were tempted to jump from heights to realize their fear. Perhaps a full-scale psychoanalysis would one day be a condition of obtaining one's Private Pilot's Licence.

Half-smiling at the thought, he went to join Lucy's group. She must be bored with all the endless talk of aeroplanes about her; a penalty, at the flying club, for non-enthusiasts.

'Hello, Lucy, Tony.' He nodded to the other man whose name he did not know.

'Hi, Geoff. Come and join us,' said Tony, who was ex-RAF. 'So anyway, he panicked and pressed the OCB.'

'What's an OCB?' asked Lucy.

'The ejector seat control. We used to call it the Oh Christ Button.'

'I see,' said Lucy primly.

'So this chap, now, he wasn't much of a parachutist, and he ...'

'Are you fed up with all this, Lucy?' Geoff led her aside from the group.

'Yes, Geoff, but I must stay, to see about the – the Kestrel.' She shuddered as she mentioned the plane.

'Leave it,' Geoff advised. 'Get someone else to sell it. You'll only get upset with all the associations around here. I should go away for a holiday if I were you.'

'I can't.' She looked almost angry. 'How can I go away without – without ...'

For a moment Geoff thought she was going to faint, and caught her arm.

'Lucy, you look ill. You'd better come outside for some fresh air. Or would you like me to get Dr Levers?'

'No, I'll be all right.'

Once outside in the cool, brilliant evening, Lucy began to walk automatically towards the hangar where the Kestrel was housed.

'I can't believe it was an accident,' she said, half to herself. 'Bill was too careful ... Stanley loved that plane. He used to talk about it like a ... lover, almost. Nobody else could do much with it ...'

At the hangar, Geoff opened the doors and she stepped inside the cavernous building towards the Kestrel. The effect on her was devastating.

'There it is,' she whispered, clutching his arm, and her eyes grew huge with fascinated hate as she stared at the dark, hulking shape.

'It's malignant. Can't you feel it? It would kill us all if it could. I'd like to smash it ...'

'Lucy, stop it.' He grasped her shoulders, turning her round to face him. 'It's only an aeroplane. I can understand you loathing it, but you must keep a sense of proportion. It's just a piece of machinery, and it functions as efficiently or otherwise as the person who handles it.'

He was wasting his breath.

'Geoff,' she said urgently. 'Promise me you'll never fly it. It carries death! It will kill you, too.'

'For crying out loud, Lucy, you sound like something out of a melodrama.' He hadn't meant to speak so sharply, but her breathless, terrified tension scraped at his nerves.

She looked at him with wild eyes for a moment, then broke away and ran outside to her car.

He closed the hangar doors and walked slowly back to the club.

It was an hour later that James Sharples arrived. Sounds of merriment echoed from the club as he parked his car, and he paused to take a breath of air before joining the fray.

He glanced around the lonely, windswept airfield and a dark moving shape over by the hangar caught his eye. He knew instinctively that something was wrong. Was someone trying to steal a plane? He strained his eyes through the dusk, and what he saw made him start at a run towards the hangar.

Lucy knew what she had to do. She had driven home for an axe, as fast as she dared, and back again to the airfield. With the axe in her hand she entered the hangar and walked steadily towards the thirteenth Kestrel. I'm not afraid, she told herself, her heart thumping loudly in the darkness. I can feel it's evil but I will not be afraid.

The hangar was full; she did not dare risk wrecking the aircraft there, for fear of damaging the other planes. Approaching the Kestrel's sinister, looming bulk she quailed for an instant, and then she threw the axe into the pilot's seat and kicked the chocks from under the wheels.

The Kestrel was almost too heavy for one girl to move, but she managed it, pushing and pulling on alternate wings until she had it in the fresh air. There was a slight downward gradient on the concrete outside which made moving it easier.

Lucy did not see James running towards her along the path, and she cursed under her breath as the plane stopped dead. She gave a strong heave at the offside wing and suddenly the great machine rolled into motion. Before she could step aside it swung sideways, and she felt a stunning crack across her temple as the front fuselage knocked her down.

James couldn't believe what happened next. Continuing its sideways swing, the Kestrel, wheels twisted almost to right angles, ran smoothly over Lucy's body, and its half-ton weight crushed the life out of her as easily as a man might step on a beetle.

The Kestrel rolled gently to a halt against the grass verge. Fifty yards away, James dropped to his knees and vomited, with Lucy's last choked screams ringing in his ears.

'Well, somebody's got to break the jinx.' It was the day after Lucy's death, and Mike spoke with assumed cheerfulness.

'Look here, Mike, you are not going to fly the Kestrel today,' said Geoff hotly. 'It's bloody dangerous. Three people have died in that plane very recently.'

'Yes – one suicide, one lunatic, and one downright incompetent,' snapped Mike, who had a temper to match his red hair. 'Look, Geoff,' he continued in a quieter tone, 'all these deaths are pure coincidence. You only have to look at statistics to see that. Give a dog a bad name ... ! Davis had women and money worries, or maybe he was trying out some stupid trick that didn't work, and Lucy – well, poor girl, she was asking for trouble, messing about like that.'

'And more than trouble she got,' Geoff reminded him. 'You know damn well the odds must be millions to one against a plane rolling up and over a body, several inches high, on as slight a gradient as that. And what about James's hand?'

'Geoff, you're supposed to be a scientist, a rational being. Infection can happen in any open wound, Levers said that. As to Lucy – maybe the angles and impetus and all that were such that the unlikely had to happen. Now all I'm going to do is prove to you and everybody else around here that there's no jinx or any of that nonsense on a perfectly good aeroplane. Or would you rather get it exorcized? Come on, man, see sense.'

'Well, I can't stop you, I suppose,' said Geoff, only half convinced. 'But I wish you'd forget the damned thing. There's an Emeraud for sale over at Newcastle——'

'Great.' Mike grinned and clapped him on the shoulder. 'We'll talk about your Emeraud after I land the Kestrel, OK?'

Geoff felt absurdly anxious as he watched Mike taxiing down the runway for take-off. When they were airborne he went back inside the clubhouse for a drink, knowing full well that he wouldn't be able to relax until Mike was back safe.

It was with relief and excitement that, an hour and a half later, he spotted the Kestrel circling overhead and heard Mike's voice crackling to the control tower over his portable radio.

'Southland Tower, this is Golf X-ray India double India. Request landing instructions ...'

More crackle.

'Golf double India you are cleared to runway 25 ... Wind velocity 260 degrees, 13 knots ... QFE 1019 ...'

He confirmed, and was given further instructions. Geoff listened avidly for Mike's last clear broadcast:

'Southland Tower. Golf double India finals.'

Thank God for that. Now for the landing. Geoff realized that his fingers were crossed in his pocket and his heart was racing. The approach was good – perhaps a little high – God, he was going to overshoot! No – the Kestrel's wheels skimmed over the runway, bounced a little, made contact, and the plane ran out of sight.

He's made it! Nearly jumping with excitement, Geoff caught himself almost laughing aloud and calmed down. He's made it, indeed, he thought ironically. Biggles rides again.

He walked out of the clubhouse and towards the hangar, where the Kestrel taxied slowly up to meet him. The aeroplane stopped and Geoff helped to push back the perspex top.

'Southland Tower. Golf double India finals.' Mike said.

'That was damn good, Mike,' Geoff said warmly. 'Come on, stop fooling. You realize you've broken the jinx?'

Mike pushed back his goggles and it was only when his blue eyes roved vacantly over him that Geoff realized with a chill that there was something badly wrong.

'Southland Tower. Golf double India finals.' He gave a hideous, babbling laugh and pushed his gloved hands before his face as if to ward something off.

Mike never recovered his reason.

Geoff grasped the wing and pushed and dragged the Kestrel out of the hangar. He wheeled it carefully away from the airfield, across the road and a mile or so over the meadows. It was a long, exhausting job and he was sweating profusely by the time he had positioned it in the middle of a deserted field. He stood back and lit a cigarette.

The Kestrel stood back and menacing against the evening sky. The disappearing sun left streaks of blood and gold in the massing rain clouds.

Geoff threw his cigarette away.

He climbed into the plane and unscrewed the top of the petrol can. He threw the reeking liquid all over the controls and back down the fuselage. Unwrapping a twenty-yard length of oil-soaked rope from a polythene cover, he tied one end to the joystick for a fuse. That done, he smiled grimly.

'Your turn now. Three you've destroyed so far, isn't it? Well, that's your lot. It's your turn now.'

Just for a second he felt the absurdity of what he was doing. Alone in a field, about to destroy two thousand pounds' worth of excellent modern aircraft, and talking to himself into the bargain. Then he remembered what had happened to Lucy and Bill and Mike, and his actions didn't seem so foolish.

He stepped out onto the wing and jumped to the ground from the leading edge, turning back to play out the oily rope.

Without warning, the inconceivable happened. Of its own accord, the Kestrel's engine began to purr into life. Geoff's head jerked upwards at the familiar, impossible noise, and he stepped back automatically.

'What the hell . . . ?'

Suddenly, in one blinding split-second, he knew the inevitable. Even before he could fling his arms to his head in a useless protective reflex, the first incisive blow of the Kestrel's rotating propeller cut him down.

The great blades continued to whirr viciously for perhaps twenty seconds, then spun slowly to a halt.

The engine shut off with a quiet click, and the aeroplane stood passive in the middle of the darkening field, with the body prone before it like a sacrifice.

The Werewolf

Frederick Marryat

Before noon Philip and Krantz had embarked, and made sail in the peroqua.

They had no difficulty in steering their course; the islands by day, and the clear stars by night, were their compass. It is true that they did not follow the more direct track, but they followed the more secure, working up the smooth waters, and gaining to the northward more than to the west. Many times they were chased by the Malay proas which infested the islands, but the swiftness of their little peroqua was their security; indeed, the chase was, generally speaking, abandoned as soon as the smallness of the vessel was made out by the pirates, who expected that little or no booty was to be gained.

One morning, as they were sailing between the isles, with less wind than usual, Philip observed:

'Krantz, you said that there were events in your own life, or connected with it, which would corroborate the mysterious tale I confided to you. Will you now tell me to what you referred?'

'Certainly,' replied Krantz; 'I have often thought of doing so, but one circumstance or another has hitherto prevented me; this is, however, a fitting opportunity. Prepare therefore to listen to a strange story, quite as strange, perhaps, as your own.

'I take it for granted that you have heard people speak of the Hartz Mountains,' observed Krantz.

'I have never heard people speak of them that I can recollect,' replied Philip; 'but I have read of them in some book, and of the strange things which have occurred there.'

'It is indeed a wild region,' rejoined Krantz, 'and many strange tales are told of it; but strange as they are, I have good reason for believing them to be true.

'My father was not born, or originally a resident in the Hartz Mountains; he was a serf of a Hungarian nobleman, of great possessions, in Transylvania; but although a serf, he was not by any means a poor or illiterate man. In fact, he was rich, and his intelligence and respectability were such, that he had been raised by his lord to the stewardship; but whoever may happen to be a born serf, a serf must he remain, even though he become a wealthy man: such was the condition of my father. My father had been married for about five years; and by his marriage had three children – my eldest brother Caesar, myself (Hermann), and a sister named Marcella. You know, Philip, that Latin is still the language spoken in that country; and that will account for our high-sounding names. My mother was a very beautiful woman, unfortunately more beautiful than virtuous: she was seen and admired by the lord of the soil; my father was sent away upon some mission; and during his absence, my mother, flattered by the attentions and won by the assiduities of this nobleman, yielded to his wishes. It so happened that my father returned very unexpectedly, and discovered the intrigue. The evidence of my mother's shame was positive; he surprised her in the company of her seducer! Carried away by the impetuosity of his feelings, he watched the opportunity of a meeting taking place between them, and murdered both his wife and her seducer. Conscious that, as a serf, not even the provocation which he had received would be allowed as a justification of his conduct, he hastily collected together what money he could lay his hands upon, and, as we were then in the depths of winter, he put his horses to the sleigh, and taking his children with him, he set off in the middle of the night, and was far away before the tragical circumstance had transpired. Aware that he would be pursued, and that he had no chance of escape if he remained in any portion of his native country (in which the authorities could lay hold of him), he continued his flight without intermission until he had buried himself in the intricacies and seclusion of the Hartz Mountains. Of course, all that I have told you I learned afterwards. My oldest recollections are knit to a rude, comfortable cottage, in which I lived with my father, brother, and sister. It was on the confines of one of those vast forests which cover the northern part of Germany; around it were a few acres of ground, which, during the summer months, my father cultivated, and which, though they yielded a doubtful harvest, were sufficient for our support. In the winter we remained much indoors, for, as my father followed the chase, we were left alone, and the wolves during that season incessantly prowled about. My father had purchased the cottage, and land about it, of one of the rude foresters, who gain their livelihood partly by hunting, and partly by burning charcoal, for the purpose of smelting the ore from the neighbouring mines; it was distant about two miles from any other habitation. I can call to mind the whole landscape now; the tall pines which rose up on the mountain above us, and the wide expanse of the forest beneath, on the topmost boughs and heads of whose trees we looked down from our cottage as the mountain below us rapidly descended into the distant valley. In summer time the prospect was beautiful: but during the severe winter a more desolate scene could not well be imagined.

'I said that, in the winter, my father occupied himself with the chase; every day he left us, and often would he lock the door, that we might not leave the cottage. He had no one to assist him or to take care of us – indeed, it was not easy to find a female servant who would live in such a solitude; but, could he have found one, my father would not have received her, for he had imbibed a horror of the sex, as the difference of his conduct towards us, his two boys, and my poor little sister Marcella evidently proved. You may suppose we were sadly neglected; indeed, we suffered much, for my father, fearful that we might come to some harm, would not allow us fuel when he left the cottage; and we were obliged, therefore, to creep under the heaps of bears' skins, and there to keep ourselves as warm as we could until he returned in the evening, when a blazing fire was our delight. That my father chose this restless sort of life may appear strange, but the fact was, that he could not remain quiet; whether from the remorse for having committed murder or from the misery consequent on his change of situation, or from both combined, he was never happy unless he was in a state of activity. Children, however, when left so much to themselves, acquire a thoughtfulness not common to their age. So it was with us; and during the short cold days of winter, we would sit silent, longing for the happy hours when the snow would melt and the leaves burst out, and the birds begin their songs, and when we should again be set at liberty.

'Such was our peculiar and savage sort of life until my brother Caesar was nine, myself seven, and my sister five years old, when the circumstances occurred on which is based the extraordinary narrative which I am about to relate.

'One evening my father returned home rather later than usual; he had been unsuccessful, and as the weather was very severe, and many feet of snow were upon the ground, he was not only very cold, but in a very bad humour. He had brought in wood, and we were all three gladly assisting each other in blowing on the embers to create a blaze, when he caught poor little Marcella by the arm and threw her aside; the child fell, struck her mouth, and bled very much. My brother ran to raise her up. Accustomed to ill-usage, and afraid of my father, she did not dare to cry, but looked up in his face very piteously. My father drew his stool nearer to the hearth, muttered something in abuse of women, and busied himself with the fire, which both my brother and I had deserted when our sister was so unkindly treated. A cheerful blaze was soon the result of his exertions; but we did not, as usual, crowd round it. Marcella, still bleeding, retired to a corner, and my brother and I took our seats beside her, while my father hung over the fire gloomily and alone. Such had been our position for about half an hour, when the howl of a wolf, close under the window of the cottage, fell on our ears. My father started up, and seized his gun; the howl was repeated; he examined the priming, and then hastily left the cottage, shutting the door after him. We all waited (anxiously listening), for we thought that if he succeeded in shooting the wolf, he would return in a better humour; and, although he was harsh to all of us, and particularly so to our little sister, still we loved our father, and loved to see him cheerful and happy, for what else had we to look up to? And I may here observe that perhaps there never were three children who were fonder of each other; we did not, like other children, fight and dispute together; and if, by chance, any disagreement did arise, between my elder brother and me, little Marcella would run to us, and kissing us both, seal, through her entreaties, the peace between us. Marcella was a lovely, amiable child; I can recall her beautiful features even now. Alas! poor little Marcella.'

'She is dead, then?' observed Philip.

'Dead! yes, dead! but how did she die? – But I must not anticipate, Philip; let me tell my story.

'We waited for some time, but the report of the gun did not reach us, and my elder brother then said, "Our father has followed the wolf, and will not be back for some time. Marcella, let us wash the blood from your mouth, and then we will leave this corner and go to the fire to warm ourselves."

'We did so, and remained there until near midnight, every minute wondering, as it grew later, why our father did not return. We had no idea that he was in any danger, but we thought that he must have chased the wolf for a very long time. "I will look out and see if father is coming," said my brother Caesar, going to the door. "Take care," said Marcella, "the wolves must be about now, and we cannot kill them, brother." My brother opened the door very cautiously, and but a few inches; he peeped out. "I see nothing," said he, after a time, and once more he joined us at the fire. "We have had no supper," said I, for my father usually cooked the meat as soon as he came home; and during his absence we had nothing but the fragments of the preceding day.

'"And if our father comes home after his hunt, Caesar," said Marcella, "he will be pleased to have some supper; let us cook it for him and for ourselves." Caesar climbed upon the stool, and reached down some meat – I forget now whether it was venison or bear's meat, but we cut off the usual quantity and proceeded to dress it, as we used to do under our father's superintendence. We were all busy putting it into platters before the fire, to await his coming, when we heard the sound of a horn. We listened – there was a noise outside, and a minute afterwards my father entered, ushered in a young female and a large dark man in a hunter's dress.

'Perhaps I had better now relate what was only known to me many years afterwards. When my father had left the cottage, he perceived a large white wolf about thirty yards from him; as soon as the animal saw my father, it retreated slowly growling and snarling. My father followed; the animal did not run, but always kept at some distance; and my father did not like to fire until he was pretty certain that his ball would take effect; thus they went on for some time, the wolf now leaving my father far behind, and then stopping and snarling defiance at him, and then, again, on his approach, setting off at speed.

'Anxious to shoot the animal (for the white wolf is very rare), my father continued the pursuit for several hours, during which he continually ascended the mountain.

'You must know, Philip, that there are peculiar spots on those mountains which are supposed, and, as my story will prove, truly supposed, to be inhabited by the evil influences: they are well known to the huntsmen, who invariably avoid them. Now, one of these spots, an open space in the pine forest above us, had been pointed out to my father as dangerous on that account. But whether he disbelieved these wild stories, or whether, in his eager pursuit of the chase, he disregarded them, I know not; certain, however, it is, that he was decoyed by the white wolf to this open space, when the animal appeared to slacken her speed. My father approached, came closer up to her, raised his gun to his shoulder, and was about to fire, when the wolf suddenly disappeared. He thought that the snow on the ground must have dazzled his sight, and he let down his gun to look for the beast – but she was gone; how she could have escaped over the clearance, without his seeing her, was beyond his comprehension. Mortified at the ill-success of his chase, he was about to retrace his steps, when he heard the distant sound of a horn. Astonishment at such a sound – at such an hour – in such a wilderness, made him forget for the moment his disappointment, and he remained riveted to the spot. In a minute the horn was blown a second time, and at no great distance; my father stood still, and listened; a third time it was blown. I forget the term used to express it, but it was the signal which, my father well knew, implied that the party was lost in the woods. In a few minutes more my father beheld a man on horseback, with a female seated on the crupper, enter the cleared space, and ride up to him. At first, my father called to mind the strange stories which he had heard of the supernatural beings who were said to frequent these mountains; but the nearer approach of the parties satisfied him that they were mortals like himself. As soon as they came up to him, the man who guided the horse accosted him. "Friend hunter, you are out late, the better fortune for us; we have ridden far, and are in fear of our lives, which are eagerly sought after. These mountains have enabled us to elude our pursuers; but if we find not shelter and refreshment, that will avail us little, as we must perish from hunger and the inclemency of the night. My daughter, who rides behind me, is more dead than alive – say, can you assist us in our difficulty?"

' "My cottage is some few miles distant," replied my father, "but I have little to offer you besides a shelter from the weather; to the little I have you are welcome. May I ask whence you come?"

' "Yes, friend, it is no secret now; we have escaped from Transylvania, where my daughter's honour and my life were equally in jeopardy!"

'This information was quite enough to raise an interest in my father's heart. He remembered his own escape: he remembered the loss of his wife's honour, and the tragedy by which it was wound up. He immediately, and warmly, offered all the assistance which he could afford them.

' "There is no time to be lost then, good sir," observed the horseman; "my daughter is chilled with the frost, and cannot hold out much longer against the severity of the weather."

' "Follow me," replied my father, leading the way towards his home.

' "I was lured away in pursuit of a large white wolf," observed my father; "it came to the very window of my hut, or I should not have been out at this time of night."

' "The creature passed by us just as we came out of the wood," said the female, in a silvery tone.

' "I was nearly discharging my piece at it," observed the hunter; "but since it did us such good service, I'm glad that I allowed it to escape."

'In about an hour and a half, during which my father walked at a rapid pace, the party arrived at the cottage, and, as I said before, came in.

' "We are in good time, apparently," observed the dark hunter, catching the smell of the roasted meat, as he walked to the fire and surveyed my brother and sister and myself. "You have young cooks here, Meinheer." "I am glad that we shall not have to wait," replied my father. "Come, mistress, seat yourself by the fire; you require warmth after your cold ride." "And where can I put up my horse, Meinheer?" observed the huntsman. "I will take care of him," replied my father, going out of the cottage door.

'The female, must, however, be particularly described. She was young, and apparently twenty years of age. She was dressed in a travelling dress, deeply bordered with white fur, and wore a cap of white ermine on her head. Her features were very beautiful, at least I thought so, and so my father has since declared. Her hair was flaxen, glossy, and shining, and bright as a mirror; and her mouth, although somewhat large when it was open, showed the most brilliant teeth I have ever beheld. But there was something about her eyes, bright as they were, which made us children afraid; they were so restless, so furtive; I could not at that time tell why, but I felt as if there was cruelty in her eye;

and when she beckoned us to come to her, we approached her with fear and trembling. Still she was beautiful, very beautiful. She spoke kindly to my brother and myself, patted our heads and caressed us; but Marcella would not come near her; on the contrary, she slunk away, and hid herself in the bed, and would not wait for the supper, which half an hour before she had been so anxious for.

'My father, having put the horse into a close shed, soon returned, and supper was placed on the table. When it was over, my father requested the young lady would take possession of the bed, and he would remain at the fire, and sit up with her father. After some hesitation on her part, this arrangement was agreed to, and I and my brother crept into the other bed with Marcella, for we had as yet always slept together.

'But we could not sleep; there was something so unusual, not only in seeing strange people, but in having those people sleep at the cottage, that we were bewildered. As for poor little Marcella, she was quiet, but I perceived that she trembled during the whole night, and sometimes I thought that she was checking a sob. My father had brought out some spirits, which he rarely used, and he and the strange hunter remained drinking and talking before the fire. Our ears were ready to catch the slightest whisper – so much was our curiosity excited.

' "You said you came from Transylvania?" observed my father.

' "Even so, Meinheer," replied the hunter. "I was a serf to the noble house of——; my master would insist upon my surrendering up my fair girl to his wishes; it ended in my giving him a few inches of my hunting-knife."

' "We are countrymen and brothers in misfortune," replied my father, taking the huntsman's hand and pressing it warmly.

' "Indeed! Are you then from that country?"

' "Yes; and I too fled for my life. But mine is a melancholy tale."

' "Your name?" inquired the hunter.

' "Krantz."

' "What! Krantz of——? I have heard your tale; you need not renew your grief by repeating it now. Welcome, most welcome, Meinheer, and, I may say, my worthy kinsman. I am your second cousin, Wilfred of Barnsdorf," cried the hunter, rising up and embracing my father.

'They filled their horn-mugs to the brim, and drank to one another after the German fashion. The conversation was then carried on in a low tone; all that we could collect from it was that our new relative and his daughter were to take up their abode in our cottage, at least for the present. In about an hour they both fell back in their chairs and appeared to sleep.

' "Marcella, dear, did you hear?" said my brother, in a low tone.

' "Yes," replied Marcella, in a whisper, "I heard all. Oh! brother, I cannot bear to look upon that woman – I feel so frightened."

'My brother made no reply, and shortly afterwards we were all three fast asleep.

'When we awoke the next morning, we found that the hunter's daughter had risen before us. I thought she looked more beautiful than ever. She came up to little Marcella and caressed her: the child burst into tears, and sobbed as if her heart would break.

'But not to detain you with too long a story, the huntsman and his daughter were accommodated in the cottage. My father and he went out hunting daily, leaving Christina with us children; and gradually the dislike even of little Marcella wore away. But a great change took place in my father; he appeared to have conquered his aversion to the sex, and was most attentive to Christina. Often, after her father and we were in bed, he would sit up with her, conversing in a low tone by the fire. I ought to have mentioned that my father and the huntsman Wilfred slept in another portion of the cottage, and that the bed which he formerly occupied, and which was in the same room as ours, had been given up to the use of Christina. These visitors had been about three weeks at the cottage, when, one night, after we children had been sent to bed, a consultation was held. My father had asked Christina in marriage, and had obtained both her consent and that of Wilfred; after this, a conversation took place, which was, as near as I can recollect, as follows:

'"You may take my child, Meinheer Krantz, and my blessing with her, and I shall then leave you and seek some other habitation – it matters little where."

'"Why not remain here, Wilfred?"

'"No, no, I am called elsewhere; let that suffice, and ask no more questions. You have my child."

'"I thank you for her, and will duly value her; but there is one difficulty."

'"I know what you would say; there is no priest here in this wild country; true; neither is there any law to bind. Still must some ceremony pass between you to satisfy a father. Will you consent to marry her after my fashion? If so I will marry you directly."

'"I will," replied my father.

'"Then take her by the hand. Now, Meinheer, swear."

'"I swear," repeated my father.

'"By all the spirits of the Hartz Mountains——"

'"Nay, why not by Heaven?" interrupted my father.

'"Because it is not my humour," rejoined Wilfred. "If I prefer that oath, less binding, perhaps, than another, surely you will not thwart me."

'"Well, be it so, then; have your humour. Will you make me swear by that in which I do not believe?"

'"Yet many do so, who in outward appearance are Christians," rejoined Wilfred; "say, will you be married, or shall I take my daughter away with me?"

' "Proceed," replied my father impatiently.

' "I swear by all the spirits of the Hartz Mountains, by all the power for good or for evil, that I take Christina for my wedded wife; that I will ever protect her, cherish her, and love her; that my hand shall never be raised against her to harm her."

'My father repeated the words after Wilfred.

' "And if I fail in this my vow, may all the vengeance of the spirits fall upon me and upon my children; may they perish by the vulture, by the wolf, or other beasts of the forest; may their flesh be torn from their limbs, and their bones blanch in the wilderness: all this I swear."

' "My father hesitated, as he repeated the last words; little Marcella could not restrain herself, and as my father repeated the last sentence, she burst into tears. This sudden interruption appeared to discompose the party, particularly my father; he spoke harshly to the child, who controlled her sobs, burying her face under the bedclothes.

'Such was the second marriage of my father. The next morning, the hunter Wilfred mounted his horse and rode away.

'My father resumed his bed, which was in the same room as ours; and things went on much as before the marriage, except that our new mother-in-law did not show any kindness towards us; indeed, during my father's absence, she would often beat us, particularly little Marcella, and her eyes would flash fire, as she looked eagerly upon the fair and lovely child.

'One night my sister awoke me and my brother.

' "What is the matter?" said Caesar.

' "She has gone out," whispered Marcella.

' "Gone out!"

' "Yes, gone out at the door, in her nightclothes," replied the child; "I saw her get out of bed, look at my father to see if he slept, and then she went out at the door."

'What could induce her to leave her bed, and all undressed, to go out, in such bitter wintry weather, with the snow deep on the ground, was to us incomprehensible; we lay awake, and in about an hour we heard the growl of a wolf close under the window.

' "There is a wolf," said Caesar. "She will be torn to pieces."

' "Oh no!" cried Marcella.

'In a few minutes afterwards our mother-in-law appeared; she was in her night-dress, as Marcella had stated. She let down the latch of the door, so as to make no noise, went to a pail of water, and washed her face and hands, and then slipped into bed where my father lay.

' "We all three trembled – we hardly knew why; but we resolved to watch the next night. We did so; and not only on the ensuing night, but on many others, and always at about the same hour, would our mother-in-law rise from her bed and leave the cottage; and after she was gone we invariably heard the growl of a wolf under our window, and always saw her on her return wash herself before she retired to bed. We observed also that she seldom sat down to meals, and that when she did she appeared to eat with dislike; but when the meat was taken down to be prepared for dinner, she would often furtively put a raw piece into her mouth.

'My brother Caesar was a courageous boy; he did not like to speak to my father until he knew more. He resolved that he would follow her out, and ascertain what she did. Marcella and I endeavoured to dissuade him from the project; but he would not be controlled; and the very next night he lay down in his clothes, and as soon as our mother-in-law had left the cottage he jumped up, took down my father's gun, and followed her.

'You may imagine in what a state of suspense Marcella and I remained during his absence. After a few minutes we heard the report of a gun. It did not awaken my father; and we lay trembling with anxiety. In a minute afterwards we saw our mother-in-law enter the cottage – her dress was bloody. I put my hand to Marcella's mouth to prevent her crying out, although I was myself in great alarm. Our mother-in-law approached my father's bed, looked to see if he was asleep, and then went to the chimney and blew up the embers into a blaze.

' "Who is there?" said my father, waking up.

' "Lie still, dearest," replied my mother-in-law; "it is only me; I have lighted the fire to warm some water; I am not quite well."

'My father turned round, and was soon asleep; but we watched our mother-in-law. She changed her linen, and threw the garments she had worn into the fire; and we then perceived that her right leg was bleeding profusely, as if from a gun-shot wound. She bandaged it up, and then dressing herself, remained before the fire until the break of day.

'Poor little Marcella, her heart beat quick as she pressed me to her side – so indeed did mine. Where was our brother Caesar? How did my mother-in-law receive the wound unless from his gun? At last my father rose, and then for the first time I spoke, saying, "Father, where is my brother Caesar?"

' "Your brother?" exclaimed he; "why, where can he be?"

' "Merciful Heaven! I thought as I lay very restless last night," observed our mother-in-law, "that I heard somebody open the latch of the door; and, dear me, husband, what has become of your gun?"

'My father cast his eyes up above the chimney, and perceived that his gun was missing. For a moment he looked perplexed; then, seizing a broad axe, he went out of the cottage without saying another word.

'He did not remain away from us long; in a few minutes he returned, bearing in his arms the mangled body of my poor brother; he laid it down, and covered up his face.

'My mother-in-law rose up, and looked at the body, while Marcella and I threw ourselves by its side, wailing and sobbing bitterly.

'"Go to bed again, children," said she sharply. "Husband," continued she, "your boy must have taken the gun down to shoot a wolf, and the animal has been too powerful for him. Poor boy! he has paid dearly for his rashness."

'My father made no reply. I wished to speak – to tell all – but Marcella, who perceived my intention, held me by the arm, and looked at me so imploringly, that I desisted.

'My father, therefore, was left in his error; but Marcella and I, although we could not comprehend it, were conscious that our mother-in-law was in some way connected with my brother's death.

'That day my father went out and dug a grave; and when he laid the body in the earth, he piled stones over it, so that the wolves should not be able to dig it up. The shock of this catastrophe was to my poor father very severe; for several days he never went to the chase, although at times he would utter bitter anathemas and vengeance against the wolves.

'But during this time of mourning on his part, my mother-in-law's nocturnal wanderings continued with the same regularity as before.

'At last my father took down his gun to repair to the forest; but he soon returned, and appeared much annoyed.

'Would you believe it, Christina, that the wolves – perdition to the whole race! – have actually contrived to dig up the body of my poor boy, and now there is nothing left of him but his bones."

'"Indeed!" replied my mother-in-law. Marcella looked at me, and I saw in her intelligent eye all she would have uttered.

'"A wolf growls under our window every night, father," said I.

'"Ay, indeed! Why did you not tell me, boy? Wake me the next time you hear it."

'I saw my mother-in-law turn away; her eyes flashed fire, and she gnashed her teeth.

'My father went out again, and covered up with a larger pile of stones the little remains of my poor brother which the wolves had spared. Such was the first act of the tragedy.

'The spring now came on; the snow disappeared, and we were permitted to leave the cottage; but never would I quit for one moment my dear little sister, to whom, since the death of my brother, I was more ardently attached than ever; indeed, I was afraid to leave her alone with my mother-in-law, who appeared to have a particular pleasure in ill-treating the child. My father was now employed upon his little farm, and I was able to render him some assistance.

'Marcella used to sit by us while we were at work, leaving my mother-in-law alone in the cottage. I ought to observe that, as the spring advanced, so did my mother-in-law decrease her nocturnal rambles, and that we never heard the growl of the wolf under the window after I had spoken of it to my father.

'One day, when my father and I were in the field, Marcella being with us, my mother-in-law came out, saying that she was going into the forest to collect some herbs my father wanted, and that Marcella must go to the cottage and watch the dinner. Marcella went; and my mother-in-law soon disappeared in the forest, taking a direction quite contrary to that in which the cottage stood, and leaving my father and me, as it were, between her and Marcella.

'About an hour afterwards we were startled by shrieks from the cottage – evidently the shrieks of little Marcella. "Marcella has burnt herself, father," said I, throwing down my spade. My father threw down his, and we both hastened to the cottage. Before we could gain the door, out darted a large white wolf, which fled with the utmost celerity. My father had no weapon; he rushed into the cottage, and there saw poor little Marcella expiring. Her body was dreadfully mangled and the blood pouring from it had formed a large pool on the cottage floor. My father's first intention had been to seize his gun and pursue; but he was checked by this horrid spectacle; he knelt down by his dying child, and burst into tears. Marcella could just look kindly on us for a few seconds, and then her eyes were closed in death.

'My father and I were still hanging over my poor sister's body, when my mother-in-law came in. At the dreadful sight she expressed much concern; but she did not appear to recoil from the sight of blood, as most women do.

'"Poor child!" said she, "it must have been that great white wolf which passed me just now, and frightened me so. She's quite dead, Krantz."

'"I know it! – I know it!" cried my father, in agony.

'I thought my father would never recover from the effects of this second tragedy; he mourned bitterly over the body of his sweet child, and for several days would not consign it to its grave, although frequently requested by my mother-in-law to do so. At last he yielded, and dug a grave for her close by that of my poor brother, and took every precaution that the wolves should not violate her remains.

'I was now really miserable as I lay alone in the bed which I had formerly shared with my brother and sister. I could not help thinking that my mother-in-law was implicated in both their deaths, although I could not account for the manner; but I no longer felt afraid of her; my little heart was full of hatred and revenge.

'The night after my sister had been buried, as I lay awake, I perceived my mother-in-law get up and go out of the cottage. I waited some time, then dressed myself, and looked out through the door, which I half opened. The moon shone bright, and I could see the spot where my brother and sister had been buried; and what was my horror when I perceived my mother-in-law busily removing the stones from Marcella's grave!

'She was in her white night-dress, and the moon shone full upon her. She was digging with her hands, and throwing away the stones behind her with all the ferocity of a wild beast. It was some time before I could collect my senses and decide what I should do. At last I perceived that she had arrived at the body, and raised it up to the side of the grave. I could bear it no longer: I ran to my father and awoke him.

'"Father, father!" cried I, "dress yourself, and get your gun."

'"What!" cried my father, "the wolves are there, are they?"

'He jumped out of bed, threw on his clothes, and in his anxiety did not appear to perceive the absence of his wife. As soon as he was ready I opened the door, he went out, and I followed him.

'Imagine his horror, when (unprepared as he was for such a sight) he beheld, as he advanced towards the grave, not a wolf, but his wife, in her night-dress, on her hands and knees, crouching by the body of my sister, and tearing off large pieces of the flesh, and devouring them with all the avidity of a wolf. She was too busy to be aware of our approach. My father dropped his gun; his hair stood on end, so did mine; he breathed heavily, and then his breath for a time stopped. I picked up the gun and put it into his hand. Suddenly he appeared as if concentrated rage had restored him to double vigour; he levelled his piece, fired, and with a loud shriek down fell the wretch whom he had fostered in his bosom.

'"God of heaven!" cried my father, sinking down upon the earth in a swoon, as soon as he had discharged his gun.

'I remained some time by his side before he recovered. "Where am I?" said he, "what has happened? Oh! – yes, yes! I recollect now. Heaven forgive me!"

'He rose and we walked up to the grave; what again was our astonishment and horror to find that, instead of the dead body of my mother-in-law, as we expected, there was lying over the remains of my poor sister a large white she-wolf.

'"The white wolf," exclaimed my father, "the white wolf which decoyed me into the forest – I see it all now – I have dealt with the spirits of the Hartz Mountains."

'For some time my father remained in silence and deep thought. He then carefully lifted up the body of my sister, replaced it in the grave, and covered it over as before, having struck the head of the dead animal with the heel of his boot, and raving like a madman. He walked back to the cottage, shut the door, and threw himself on the bed; I did the same, for I was in a stupor of amazement.

'Early in the morning we were both roused by a loud knocking at the door, and in rushed the hunter Wilfred.

' "My daughter – man – my daughter! – where is my daughter?" cried he in a rage.

' "Where the wretch, the fiend should be, I trust," replied my father, starting up, and displaying equal choler: "where she should be – in hell! Leave this cottage, or you may fare worse."

' "Ha – ha!" replied the hunter, "would you harm a potent spirit of the Hartz Mountains? Poor mortal, who must needs wed a werewolf."

' "Out, demon! I defy thee and thy power."

' "Yet shall you feel it; remember your oath – your solemn oath – never to raise your hand against her to harm her."

' "I made no compact with evil spirits."

' "You did, and if you failed in your vow, you were to meet the vengeance of the spirits. Your children were to perish by the vulture, the wolf——"

' "Out, out, demon!"

' "And their bones blanch in the wilderness. Ha! – ha!"

'My father, frantic with rage, seized his axe and raised it over Wilfred's head to strike.

' "All this I swear," continued the huntsman mockingly.

'The axe descended; but it passed through the form of the hunter, and my father lost his balance, and fell heavily on the floor.

' "Mortal!" said the hunter, striding over my father's body, "we have power over those only who have committed murder. You have been guilty of a double murder: you shall pay the penalty attached to your marriage vow. Two of your children are gone, the third is yet to follow – and follow them he will, for your oath is registered. Go – it were kindness to kill thee – your punishment is, that you live!"

'With these words the spirit disappeared. My father rose from the floor, embraced me tenderly, and knelt down in prayer.

'The next morning he quitted the cottage for ever. He took me with him, and bent his steps to Holland, where we safely arrived. He had some little money with him; but he had not been many days in Amsterdam before he was seized with a brain fever, and died raving mad. I was put into the asylum, and afterwards was sent to sea before the mast. You now know all my history. The question is, whether I am to pay the penalty of my father's oath? I am myself perfectly convinced that, in some way or another, I shall.'

II

On the twenty-second day the high land of the south of Sumatra was in view: as there were no vessels in sight, they resolved to keep their course through the Straits, and run for Pulo Penang, which they expected, as their vessel lay so close to the wind, to reach in seven or eight days. By constant exposure Philip and Krantz were now so bronzed, that with their long beards and Mussulman dresses, they might easily have passed off for natives. They had steered during the whole of the days exposed to a burning sun; they had lain down and slept in the dew of the night; but their health had not suffered. But for several days, since he had confided the history of his family to Philip, Krantz had become silent and melancholy; his usual flow of spirits had vanished, and Philip had often questioned him as to the cause. As they entered the Straits, Philip talked of what they should do upon their arrival at Goa; when Krantz gravely replied, 'For some days, Philip, I have had a presentiment that I shall never see that city.'

'You are out of health, Krantz,' replied Philip.

'No, I am in sound health, body and mind. I have endeavoured to shake off the presentiment, but in vain; there is a warning voice that continually tells me that I shall not be long with you. Philip, will you oblige me by making me content on one point? I have gold about my person which may be useful to you; oblige me by taking it, and securing it on your own.'

'What nonsense, Krantz.'

'It is no nonsense, Philip. Have you not had your warnings? Why should I not have mine? You know that I have little fear in my composition, and that I care not about death; but I feel the presentiment which I speak of more strongly every hour ...'

'These are the imaginings of a disturbed brain, Krantz; why you, young, in full health and vigour, should not pass your days in peace, and live to a good old age, there is no cause for believing. You will be better tomorrow.'

'Perhaps so,' replied Krantz; 'but still you must yield to my whim, and take the gold. If I am wrong, and we do arrive safe, you know, Philip, you can let me have it back,' observed Krantz, with a faint smile – 'but you forget, out water is nearly out, and we must look out for a rill on the coast to obtain a fresh supply.'

'I was thinking of that when you commenced this unwelcome topic. We had better look out for the water before dark, and as soon as we have replenished our jars, we will make sail again.'

At the time that this conversation took place, they were on the eastern side of the Strait, about forty miles to the northward. The interior of the coast was rocky and mountainous, but it slowly descended to low land of alternate forest and jungles, which continued to the beach; the country appeared to be uninhabited. Keeping close in to the shore, they discovered, after two hours' run, a fresh stream which burst in a cascade from the mountains, and swept its devious course through the jungle, until it poured its tribute into the waters of the Strait.

They ran close into the mouth of the stream, lowered the sails, and pulled the peroqua against the current, until they had advanced far enough to assure them that the water was quite fresh. The jars were soon filled, and they were again thinking of pushing off, when, enticed by the beauty of the spot, the coolness of the fresh water, and wearied with their long confinement on board of the peroqua, they proposed to bathe – a luxury hardly to be appreciated by those who have not been in a similar situation. They threw off their Mussulman dresses, and plunged into the stream, where they remained for some time. Krantz was the first to get out; he complained of feeling chilled, and he walked on to the banks where their clothes had been laid. Philip also approached nearer to the beach, intending to follow him.

'And now, Philip,' said Krantz, 'this will be a good opportunity for me to give you the money. I will open my sash and pour it out and you can put it into your own before you put it on.'

Philip was standing in the water, which was about level with his waist.

'Well, Krantz,' said he, 'I suppose if it must be so, it must; but it appears to me an idea so ridiculous – however, you shall have your own way.'

Philip quitted the run, and sat down by Krantz, who was already busy in shaking the doubloons out of the folds of his sash; at last he said——

'I believe, Philip, you have got them all, now! – I feel satisfied.'

'What danger there can be to you, which I am not equally exposed to, I cannot conceive,' replied Philip; 'however——'

Hardly had he said these words, when there was a tremendous roar – a rush like a mighty wind through the air – a blow which threw him on his back – a loud cry – and a contention. Philip recovered himself, and perceived the naked form of Krantz carried off with the speed of an arrow by an enormous tiger through the jungle. He watched with distended eyeballs; in a few seconds the animal and Krantz had disappeared.

'God of heaven! would that thou hadst spared me this,' cried Philip, throwing himself down in agony on his face. 'O Krantz! my friend – my brother – too sure was your presentiment. Merciful God! have pity – but Thy will be done;' and Philip burst into a flood of tears.

For more than an hour did he remain fixed upon the spot, careless and indifferent to the danger by which he was surrounded. At last, somewhat recovered, he rose, dressed himself, and then again sat down – his eyes fixed upon the clothes of Krantz, and the gold which still lay on the sand.

'He would give me that gold. He foretold his doom. Yes! yes! it was his destiny, and it has been fulfilled. *His bones will bleach in the wilderness*, and the spirit-hunter and his wolfish daughter are avenged.'

No Such Thing as a Vampire

Richard Matheson

In the early autumn, Madame Alexis Gheria awoke one morning to a sense of utmost torpor. For more than a minute, she lay inertly on her back, her dark eyes staring upward. How wasted she felt. It seemed as if her limbs were sheathed in lead. Perhaps she was ill. Petre must examine her and see.

Drawing in a faint breath, she pressed up slowly on an elbow. As she did, her nightdress slid, rustling to her waist. How had it come unfastened? she wondered, looking down at herself.

Quite suddenly, Madame Gheria began to scream.

In the breakfast-room, Dr Petre Gheria looked up, startled, from his morning paper. In an instant, he had pushed his chair back, slung his napkin on the table and was rushing for the hallway. He dashed across its carpeted breadth and mounted the staircase two steps at a time.

It was a near hysterical Madame Gheria he found sitting on the edge of her bed looking down in horror at her breasts. Across the dilated whiteness of them, a smear of blood lay drying.

Dr Gheria dismissed the upstairs maid who stood frozen in the open doorway, gaping at her mistress. He locked the door and hurried to his wife.

'Petre!' she gasped.

'Gently.' He helped her lie back across the bloodstained pillow.

'Petre, what *is* it?' she begged.

'Lie still, my dear.' His practised hands moved in swift search over her breasts. Suddenly, his breath choked off. Pressing aside her head, he stared down dumbly at the pinprick lancinations on her neck, the ribbon of tacky blood that twisted downward from them.

'My *throat*,' Alexis said.

'No, it's just a——' Dr Gheria did not complete the sentence. He knew exactly what it was.

Madame Gheria began to tremble. 'Oh, my God, my *God*,' she said.

Dr Gheria rose and foundered to the wash basin. Pouring in water, he returned to his wife and washed away the blood. The wound was clearly visible now – two tiny punctures close to the jugular. A grimacing Dr Gheria touched the mounds of inflamed tissue in which they lay. As he did, his wife groaned terribly and turned her face away.

'Now listen to me,' he said, his voice apparently calm. 'We will not succumb, immediately, to superstition, do you hear? There are any number of——'

'I'm going to die,' she said.

'Alexis, do you hear me?' He caught her harshly by the shoulders.

She turned her head and stared at him with vacant eyes. 'You know what it is,' she said.

Dr Gheria swallowed. He could still taste coffee in his mouth.

'I know what it appears to be,' he said, 'and we shall – not ignore the possibility. However——'

'I'm going to die,' she said.

'Alexis!' Dr Gheria took her hand and gripped it fiercely. '*You shall not be taken from me,*' he said.

Solta was a village of some thousand inhabitants situated in the foothills of Romania's Bihor Mountains. It was a place of dark traditions. People, hearing the bay of distant wolves, would cross themselves without a thought. Children would gather garlic buds as other children gather flowers, bringing them home for the windows. On every door there was a painted cross, at every throat a metal one. Dread of the vampire's blighting was as normal as the dread of fatal sickness. It was always in the air.

Dr Gheria thought about that as he bolted shut the windows of Alexis' room. Far off, molten twilight hung above the mountains. Soon it would be dark again. Soon the citizens of Solta would be barricaded in their garlic-reeking houses. He had no doubt that every soul of them knew exactly what had happened to his wife. Already the cook and upstairs maid were pleading for discharge. Only the inflexible discipline of the butler, Karel, kept them at their jobs. Soon, even that would not suffice. Before the horror of the vampire, reason fled.

He'd seen the evidence of it that very morning when he'd ordered Madame's room stripped to the walls and searched for rodents or venomous insects. The servants had moved about the room as if on a floor of eggs, their eyes more white than pupil, their fingers twitching constantly to their crosses. They had known full well no rodents or insects would be found. And Gheria had known it. Still, he'd raged at them for their timidity, succeeding only in frightening them further.

He turned from the window with a smile.

'There now,' he said, 'nothing alive will enter this room tonight.'

He caught himself immediately, seeing the flare of terror in her eyes.

'Nothing at *all* will enter,' he amended.

Alexis lay motionless on her bed, one pale hand at her breast, clutching at the worn silver cross she'd taken from her jewel box. She hadn't worn it since he'd given her the diamond studded one when they were married. How typical of her village background that, in this moment of dread, she should seek protection from the unadorned cross of her church. She was such a child. Gheria smiled down gently at her.

'You won't be needing that, my dear,' he said, 'you'll be safe tonight.'

Her fingers tightened on the crucifix.

'No, no, wear it if you will,' he said. 'I only meant that I'll be at your side all night.'

'You'll stay with me?'

He sat on the bed and held her hand.

'Do you think I'd leave you for a moment?' he said.

Thirty minutes later, she was sleeping. Dr Gheria drew a chair beside the bed and seated himself. Removing his glasses, he massaged the bridge of his nose with the thumb and forefinger of his left hand. Then, sighing, he began to watch his wife. How incredibly beautiful she was. Dr Gheria's breath grew strained.

'There is no such thing as a vampire,' he whispered to himself.

There was a distant pounding. Dr Gheria muttered in his sleep, his fingers twitching. The pounding increased; an agitated voice came swirling from the darkness. 'Doctor!' it called.

Gheria snapped awake. For a moment, he looked confusedly towards the locked door.

'Dr Gheria?' demanded Karel.

'What?'

'Is everything all right?'

'Yes, everything is——'

Dr Gheria cried out hoarsely, springing for the bed. Alexis' nightdress had been torn away again. A hideous dew of blood covered her chest and neck.

Karel shook his head.

'Bolted windows cannot hold away the creature, sir,' he said.

He stood, tall and lean, beside the kitchen table on which lay the cluster of silver he'd been polishing when Gheria had entered.

'The creature has the power to make itself a vapour which can pass through any opening however small,' he said.

'But the cross!' cried Gheria. 'It was still at her throat – untouched! Except by – blood,' he added in a sickened voice.

'This I cannot understand,' said Karel, grimly. 'The cross should have protected her.'

'But why did I see nothing?'

'You were drugged by its mephitic presence,' Karel said. 'Count yourself fortunate that you were not, also, attacked.'

'I do not count myself fortunate!' Dr Gheria struck his palm, a look of anguish on his face. 'What am I to do, Karel?' he asked.

'Hang garlic,' said the old man. 'Hang it at the windows, at the doors. Let there be no opening unblocked by garlic.'

Gheria nodded distractedly. 'Never in my life have I seen this thing,' he said, brokenly. 'Now, my own wife...'

'I have seen it,' said Karel. 'I have, myself, put to its rest one of these monsters from the grave.'

'The stake——?' Gheria looked revolted.

The old man nodded slowly.

Gheria swallowed. 'Pray God you may put this one to rest as well,' he said.

'Petre?'

She was weaker now, her voice a toneless murmur. Gheria bent over her. 'Yes, my dear,' he said.

'It will come again tonight,' she said.

'No.' He shook his head determinedly. 'It cannot come. The garlic will repel it.'

'My cross didn't,' she said. 'You didn't.'

'The garlic will,' he said. 'And see?' He pointed at the bedside table. 'I've had black coffee brought for me. I won't sleep tonight.'

She closed her eyes, a look of pain across her sallow features.

'I don't want to die,' she said. 'Please don't let me die, Petre.'

'You won't,' he said. 'I promise you; the monster shall be destroyed.'

Alexis shuddered feebly. 'But if there is no way, Petre,' she murmured.

'There is always a way,' he answered.

Outside, the darkness, cold and heavy, pressed around the house. Dr Gheria took his place beside the bed and began to wait. Within the hour, Alexis slipped into a heavy slumber. Gently, Dr Gheria released her hand and poured himself a cup of steaming coffee. As he sipped it, hotly bitter, he looked around the room. Door locked, windows bolted, every opening sealed with garlic, the cross at Alexis' throat. He nodded slowly to himself. It will work, he thought. The monster would be thwarted.

He sat there, waiting, listening to his breath.

Dr Gheria was at the door before the second knock.

'Michael!' He embraced the younger man. 'Dear Michael, I was sure you'd come!'

Anxiously, he ushered Dr Vares towards his study. Outside, darkness was just falling.

'Where on earth are all the people of the village?' asked Vares. 'I swear I didn't see a soul as I rode in.'

'Huddling, terror-stricken, in their houses,' Gheria said, 'and all my servants with them save for one.'

'Who is that?'

'My butler, Karel,' Gheria answered. 'He didn't answer the door because he's sleeping. Poor fellow, he is very old and has been doing the work of five.' He gripped Vares' arm. 'Dear Michael,' he said, 'you have no idea how glad I am to see you.'

Vares looked at him worriedly. 'I came as soon as I received your message,' he said.

'And I appreciate it,' Gheria said. 'I know how long and hard a ride it is from Cluj.'

'What's wrong?' asked Vares. 'Your letter only said——'

Quickly, Gheria told him what had happened in the past week.

'I tell you, Michael, I stumble at the brink of madness,' he said. 'Nothing works! Garlic, wolfsbane, crosses, mirrors, running water – useless! No, don't say it! This isn't superstition nor imagination! This is *happening*! A vampire is destroying her! Each day she sinks yet deeper into that – deadly torpor from which——'

Gheria clenched his hands. 'And yet I cannot understand it,' he muttered, brokenly, 'I simply cannot understand it.'

'Come sit, sit.' Doctor Vares pressed the older man into a chair, grimacing at the pallor of him. Nervously, his fingers sought for Gheria's pulse beat.

'Never mind me,' protested Gheria. 'It's Alexis we must help.' He pressed a sudden, trembling hand across his eyes. 'Yet how?' he said.

He made no resistance as the younger man undid his collar and examined his neck.

'You, too,' said Vares, sickened.

'What does that matter?' Gheria clutched at the younger man's hand. 'My friend, my dearest friend,' he said, 'tell me that it is not I! Do *I* do this hideous thing to her?'

Vares looked confounded. '*You?*' he said. 'But——'

'I know, I know,' said Gheria, 'I, myself, have been attacked. Yet nothing follows, Michael! What breed of horror is this which cannot be impeded? From what unholy place does it emerge? I've had the countryside examined foot by foot, every graveyard ransacked, every crypt inspected! There is no house within the village that has not been subjected to my search. I tell you, Michael, there is nothing! Yet, there *is* something – something which assaults us nightly, draining us of life. The village is engulfed by terror – and I as well! I never see this creature, never hear it! Yet, every morning, I find my beloved wife——'

Vares' face was drawn and pallid now. He stared intently at the older man.

'What am I to do, my friend?' pleaded Gheria. 'How am I to save her?'

Vares had no answer.

'How long has she – been like this?' asked Vares. He could not remove his stricken gaze from the whiteness of Alexis' face.

'For days,' said Gheria. 'The retrogression has been constant.'

Dr Vares put down Alexis' flaccid hand. 'Why did you not tell me sooner?' he asked.

'I thought the matter could be handled,' Gheria answered, faintly. 'I know now that it – cannot.'

Vares shuddered. 'But, surely——' he began.

'There is nothing left to be done,' said Gheria. 'Everything has been tried, *everything*!' He stumbled to the window and stared out bleakly into the deepening night. 'And now it comes again,' he murmured, 'and we are helpless before it.'

'Not helpless, Petre.' Vares forced a cheering smile to his lips and laid his hand upon the older man's shoulder. 'I will watch her tonight.'

'It's useless.'

'Not at all, my friend,' said Vares, nervously. 'And now you must sleep.'

'I will not leave her,' said Gheria.

'But you need rest.'

'I cannot leave,' said Gheria. 'I will not be separated from her.'

Vares nodded. 'Of course,' he said. 'We will share the hours of watching then.'

Gheria sighed. 'We can try,' he said, but there was no sound of hope in his voice.

Some twenty minutes later, he returned with an urn of steaming coffee which it was barely possible to smell through the heavy mist of garlic fumes which hung in the air. Trudging to the bed, Gheria set down the tray. Dr Vares had drawn a chair up beside the bed.

'I'll watch first,' he said. 'You sleep, Petre.'

'It would do no good to try,' said Gheria. He held a cup beneath the spigot and the coffee gurgled out like smoking ebony.

'Thank you,' murmured Vares as the cup was handed to him. Gheria nodded once and drew himself a cupful before he sat.

'I do not know what will happen to Solta if this creature is not destroyed,' he said. 'The people are paralysed by terror.'

'Has it – been elsewhere in the village?' Vares asked him.

Gheria sighed exhaustedly. 'Why need it go elsewhere?' he said. 'It is finding all it – craves within these walls.' He stared despondently at Alexis. 'When we are gone,' he said, 'it will go elsewhere. The people know that and are waiting for it.'

Vares set down his cup and rubbed his eyes.

'It seems impossible,' he said, 'that we, practitioners of a science, should be unable to——'

'What can science effect against it?' said Gheria. 'Science which will not even admit its existence? We could bring, into this very room, the foremost scientists of the world and they would say – my friends, you have been deluded. There is no vampire. All is mere trickery.'

Gheria stopped and looked intently at the younger man. He said, 'Michael?'

Vares' breath was slow and heavy. Putting down his cup of untouched coffee, Gheria stood and moved to where Vares sat slumped in his chair. He pressed back an eyelid, looked down briefly at the sightless pupil, then withdrew his hand. The drug was quick, he thought. And most effective. Vares would be insensible for more than time enough.

Moving to the closet, Gheria drew down his bag and carried it to the bed. He tore Alexis' nightdress from her upper body and, within seconds, had drawn another syringe full of her blood; this would be the last withdrawal, fortunately. Stanching the wound, he took the syringe to Vares and emptied it into the young man's mouth, smearing it across his lips and teeth.

That done, he strode to the door and unlocked it. Returning to Vares, he raised and carried him into the hall. Karel would not awaken; a small amount of opiate in his food had seen to that. Gheria laboured down the steps beneath the weight of Vares' body. In the darkest corner of the cellar, a wooden casket waited for the younger man. There he would lie until the following morning when the distraught Dr Petre Gheria would, with sudden inspiration, order Karel to search the attic and cellar on the remote, nay fantastic possibility that ——

Ten minutes later, Gheria was back in the bedroom checking Alexis' pulse beat. It was active enough; she would survive. The pain and torturing horror she had undergone would be punishment enough for her. As for Vares...

Dr Gheria smiled in pleasure for the first time since Alexis and he had returned from Cluj at the end of the summer. Dear spirits in heaven, would it not be sheer enchantment to watch old Karel drive a stake through Michael Vares' damned cuckolding heart!

The Hand

Guy de Maupassant

A circle had formed round Monsieur Bermutier, the Examining Magistrate, who was giving his opinion about the mysterious Saint-Cloud affair. For the past month this unsolved crime had been the talk of Paris. No one could explain it.

Monsieur Bermutier was standing with his back to the fireplace, talking. He marshalled the evidence, discussed a variety of theories, but could reach no conclusion.

Several ladies had left their chairs to get closer to him, and they remained standing, with their eyes on the magistrate's clean-shaven lips, from which fell words of the utmost gravity. They shuddered and were thrilled. That strange fear had hold of them, that avid and insatiable love of being frightened which haunts all women and torments them like a physical hunger.

A brief silence had fallen, and one of these ladies, who looked paler than the others, broke it.

'It is positively horrifying,' she said. 'There is something almost supernatural about it. I don't suppose we shall ever know what really happened.'

The magistrate turned to her:

'That is extremely probable, Madame. But this I can tell you, that the word *supernatural*, which you have just used, is entirely out of place in this connection. We are dealing with a crime which was skilfully planned, most adroitly carried out, and so wrapped in mystery that we have completely failed to free it from the impenetrable circumstances which surround it. But I once had to inquire into an affair about which there really was an element of the fantastic. There, too, the investigation had to be abandoned, for lack of evidence.'

Several of the ladies exclaimed, with such unanimity that their voices sounded as one:

'Oh, do tell us about it!'

Monsieur Bermutier's smile was sober and serious, as the smile of an Examining Magistrate should be. He continued:

'Please do not think for a single moment that I suppose there to have been anything supernatural about the case in question. I believe only in natural causes. It would be a great deal better if we used the word "inexplicable" rather than "supernatural" to describe matters we know nothing of. Be that as it may, what really interested me in the occurrence I am about to describe, were the attendant, the preparatory circumstances. Here are the facts.

'At the time of which I am speaking I was Examining Magistrate at Ajaccio, a small white town standing on the shore of a lovely bay surrounded on all sides by high mountains.

'I was chiefly concerned with matters having to do with *vendetta*. This tradition of private warfare is rich in superb, infinitely dramatic, fierce and heroic incidents. It provides us with the most wonderful stories of vengeance imaginable – hatred kept alive from generation to genera-tion, momentarily appeased but never allowed to die, stratagems of the most horrible description, murders on such a scale as to deserve the name of massacres, and almost epic deeds. For two years I heard of nothing but blood-feuds, of that terrible Corsican obsession which insists that a man must take vengeance not only on an enemy, but on his descendants and his relatives. I have known of old men, children, cousins having their throats cut in the name of that bloodstained doctrine. I have heard more stories of *vendetta* than I care to remember.

'I learned one day that an Englishman had taken the lease of a house, at the far end of the bay, for several years. He had brought with him a French servant whom he had engaged when passing through Marseilles.

'It was not long before the whole neighbourhood was buzzing with gossip about this strange character, who lived all alone in his house and never left it except to shoot and fish. He talked to nobody, never went into the town, and spent an hour or two every morning practising with a revolver and a carbine.

'He became the subject of many legends. Some said that he was a man of high rank who had fled from his country for political reasons; others, that he was hiding in order to escape the consequences of a detestable crime. People went so far as to give details of a more than usually blood-curdling nature.

'It was natural that, as an Examining Magistrate, I should wish to find out all I could about the fellow. But to learn much turned out to be impossible. He went by the name of Sir John Rowell.

'I had to be content with keeping such watch as I could upon him, but, even so, I could discover nothing in any way suspicious in his activities.

'Since, however, rumours continued to circulate, to grow and to become widespread, I thought it my duty to make personal contact with this foreigner, and, with this end in view, I took to shooting regularly near his property. I had to wait some time for the chance I needed. But it came at last, in the form of a partridge at which I took a pot shot and happened to bring down under the very nose of the Englishman. My dog recovered it, and I went at once, with the bird in my hand, to apologize for my bad manners and to ask Sir John to accept the victim of my gun.

'He was a big man, with red hair and beard, very tall, very broad, in fact, a sort of urbane and quiet-mannered Hercules. There was nothing of the traditional British stiffness about him, and he thanked me warmly for my civility. He spoke French with an accent which undoubtedly hailed from across the Channel. By the end of a month, we had chattered together on five or six occasions.

'Then one evening, when I happened to be passing his door, I saw him sitting astride a chair in his garden, smoking his pipe. I raised my hat, and he asked me in for a glass of beer. Needless to say, I did not wait to be asked twice. He received me with scrupulous English courtesy, was loud in his praise of France and of Corsica, and declared that he had developed a great fondness for "this country" and "this stretch of coast".

'With the utmost care, and pretending a lively interest, I questioned him about his life and his plans. He showed no embarrassment, and told me that he had travelled a great deal in Africa, India, and America, adding with a laugh:

' "I have had my full share of adventures."

'Then I started to talk shooting with him, and he told me many curious details about his experiences when hunting hippopotamuses, tigers, elephants, and even gorillas.

' "Those are all very dangerous animals," I said.

'He smiled: "But there is none more dangerous than man."

'All of a sudden, he laughed outright, and his laugh was that of a solid, satisfied Englishman.

' "I have hunted a good many men, too, in my time."

'Then he switched the talk to firearms, and asked me into the house to look at his collection of guns and rifles.

'The hangings in his drawing-room were black – black silk embroidered in gold. Great yellow flowers sprawled all over the dark material, glittering like flame.

' "It is a Japanese fabric," he said.

'But, in the middle of the largest panel, a strange object caught my eye. On a square of red velvet something black stood out in strong relief. I went closer. It was a hand, a human hand, not the hand of a skeleton, white and clean, but a shrivelled black hand with yellow nails. The sinews had been laid bare, and there were traces of dried blood, like a scab, on the bones, which had been cleanly severed about half way up the forearm.

'Round the wrist was an enormous iron chain, riveted and soldered to the unsavoury limb, and attached to the wall. It looked strong enough to tether an elephant.

' "What is that?" I asked.

'With complete composure the Englishman replied: "That belonged to my best enemy. Comes from America – cut off with a sabre, and the skin scraped away with a sharp stone. Left to dry in the sun for eight days. It was a bit of luck for me, I can tell you."

'I touched the grisly relic, which must have belonged to a man of tremendous size. The abnormally long fingers were attached to enormous sinews to which, in places, strips of skin were still adhering. Flayed like that, the hand was a disgusting sight, and seemingly bore witness to some act of savage vengeance.

'I said: "He must have been very strong."

Very quietly, my host replied: "He was: but I was stronger. I put that chain on to hold him down."

'I thought he was joking, and said: "But there is no reason for the chain now. That hand isn't going to run away!"

'In a perfectly serious voice, Sir John Rowell said: "It was always trying to get free: I had to chain it."

'I shot a quick inquiring look at him. Was he, I wondered, a madman or just a practical joker?

'But his face remained inscrutable, calm, and benignant. I changed the subject, and much admired his collection of guns.

'I noticed however, that there were three loaded revolvers lying about on various pieces of furniture, as though the man were living in constant fear of attack.

'I revisited him on several occasions. Then I stopped going. The locals had grown used to him, and nobody now gave him a thought.'

'A year went by, and then, one morning towards the end of November, my servant woke me with the news that Sir John Rowell had been murdered during the night.

'I went to the Englishman's house with the Chief Constable and the Captain of Gendarmes. The dazed and distracted valet was blubbering in front of the door. I immediately suspected him, but he was, as it turned out, innocent.

'The identity of the murderer was never established.

'On going into the drawing-room, the first thing I saw was the body of Sir John lying in the middle of the floor.

'His waistcoat was torn open, and one sleeve of the coat was hanging by a thread. There had obviously been a fierce struggle.

'The Englishman had been strangled. His black and swollen face was horrible to see and, in his eyes, there was a look of the most appalling terror. There was something between his clenched teeth, and his neck, pierced in five places by some sharp instrument, was covered in blood.

'A doctor joined us. He made a prolonged examination of the finger-marks on the dead man's neck, and then uttered these strange words:

' "Looks to me as though he'd been strangled by a skeleton!"

'A shiver went down my back, and I looked at the wall where I had once seen that dreadful flayed hand. It was no longer there. The chain had been broken and was hanging loose.

'Then I bent over the corpse. The object between its teeth was one of the fingers of the vanished hand, but cut, or rather bitten through at the second joint.

'A search was made but without producing any new evidence. Not a door, nor a window, had been forced. None of the furniture showed signs of violence. The two watch-dogs seemed to have slept through whatever had happened.

'Here in brief, is the gist of the servant's deposition.

'For the last month, he said, his master had seemed to be uneasy and on edge. He had received a number of letters which he had thrown on the fire as soon as they arrived.

'He frequently took a hunting-crop, and, in a fit more of madness than of rage, had lashed blindly at the withered hand, which, at the moment of the crime, had been spirited away from its place on the wall, no one could say how.

'He went to bed very late, and was careful to lock all the doors and windows. He always had some weapon within easy reach. He would frequently speak in a loud voice during the night. He seemed to be quarrelling with somebody.

'On the night in question, however, he made no noise, and it was only when his servant went into his room to open the shutters, that he found Sir John murdered. He could think of no possible suspect.

'I communicated all I knew about the dead man to the civil authorities and the police. The whole island was combed, but without result.

'About three months after the crime, I had a most terrifying nightmare. I dreamed that I saw that horrible hand scuttling like a scorpion or a spider along my walls and curtains. Three times I woke up: three times I fell asleep again, and three times I saw that hideous relic galloping round the room, moving its fingers like legs.

'Next morning it was brought to me. It had been found in the churchyard on Sir John Rowell's grave – for in the absence of any discoverable relative, he had been buried on the spot. The index finger was missing.

'And that, ladies, is my story. I know nothing more.'

The ladies were horror-stricken, pale, and trembling. One of them exclaimed:

'But you have suggested no solution, no explanation of the mystery! I am sure none of us will sleep unless you tell us at least what you *think* happened!'

The Magistrate smiled, but his eyes remained severe.

'I fear that, so far as dreams are concerned, I shall be a wet blanket. My theory, such as it is, is very simple, namely that the owner of the hand was not dead at all, but came to look for it. What he did, I have no idea, but I am inclined to think that the whole affair had something to do with a *vendetta*.'

'No,' murmured one of the ladies: 'that *can't* be the explanation!'

The Magistrate, still smiling, concluded:

'I told you that you would not like my theory.'

The Will of Luke Carlowe

Clive Pemberton

Mr Jonas Fenwick, the lawyer, unclasped his bony, wrinkled hands as he came to the end of the short document he had perused for the third time, and carefully placing it in a convenient pigeon-hole in his bureau, peered sharply over his gold-rimmed *pince-nez* at Mr Reuben Tunny, his confidential clerk.

'It is quite the most extraordinary document that has ever come under my notice,' he said, slowly. 'A little more than eccentric, eh, Reuben, eh?' and the lawyer chuckled – a dry, eminently legal chuckle in which mirth found no place. Mr Reuben Tunny – an angular, sallow-faced man of middle age who had grown up in Mr Fenwick's service – slowly and gravely shook his head.

'I don't understand it, sir,' he said, solemnly. 'I don't understand it at all.'

'What don't you understand, Reuben?' returned the lawyer quizzically. 'This' – laying his hand on the document under discussion – 'is plain enough for a child to comprehend.'

'I did not mean that I could not understand the meaning of Professor Luke Carlowe's last written words, sir,' said Mr Tunny slowly. 'As you rightly say, a child could comprehend the meaning of that document, for it is a perfectly plain statement. No, what I *cannot understand* is a sane man doing such an extraordinary thing. It – it is almost uncanny!'

'*Almost* uncanny!' echoed the lawyer, laying a strong emphasis on the first word. 'I call it *very* uncanny, and with a hint of the devilish in it, too, Reuben! Of course, I – in common with everybody acquainted with Luke Carlowe – knew that he was very eccentric, and expected him to do something extraordinary before he died; but this matter relating to his will—. Well, well! we will hear presently what the young man has to say about it.'

'You appointed twelve o'clock in your letter, and I do not doubt that he will be punctual,' and with a dry smile at his employer, the sedate old clerk withdrew to the outer office with a sheaf of parchments. Precisely at twelve o'clock the outer door of Mr Fenwick's office opened, and a tall, good-looking young man of about twenty-five years of age entered quickly.

'I have an appointment with Mr Fenwick,' he said, handing Mr Tunny a card on which was neatly engraved the name 'Cyril Carlowe.' 'I suppose – I presume he is in?'

'If you will be so good as to wait one moment, I will inform Mr Fenwick that you are here,' returned Mr Tunny, and a moment later he ushered Mr Cyril Carlowe into the lawyer's presence.

'Good morning, Mr Carlowe,' said Mr Fenwick briskly, bowing his visitor to a chair. 'I daresay – I expect you are wondering why I have asked you to see me this morning?'

The other shifted in his chair a little; then he gave the lawyer a frank, clear look.

'I will confess that I am most curious to learn the reason, Mr Fenwick,' he replied quickly, 'for I can think of nothing to – to——'

'Well, well, Mr Carlowe, I will set the matter before you at once. I have sent for you with regard to your uncle's will. You are aware, of course,' he went on, slightly hesitating as he looked at the other, 'that your uncle Professor Carlowe, died just a month ago?'

Cyril Carlowe nodded disinterestedly, and the lawyer proceeded:

'I think I may say that I enjoyed the fullest confidence of my late client, and I never knew him take any step or do anything important without first consulting me. Of course, I need not say that I am cognizant of the strange and, now that I have seen you' – with a courtly little bow – 'inexplicable dislike he bore towards his brother – your father – and you.'

Cyril Carlowe nodded gloomily.

'I always told the guv'nor he was mad,' he rejoined slowly. 'Before he refused to see either of us again, he used to talk the wildest rot you ever heard by the hour. All about the spirits of the dead returning from the grave – supernatural agencies and intermediate states – that kind of mad foolery! I verily believe it was our scepticism and – and ridicule that turned him so violently against us, Mr Fenwick.'

The lawyer nodded quietly.

'He was eccentric – most eccentric, I agree with you; but to return to what I was saying. With regard to his will, I drew it up, but he kept it, and——'

'And, of course, left all his money – a good bit it must be too – to some society for the furthering of his mad theories, eh?'

'Yes – and no,' answered the lawyer, paradoxically. He took a paper from the pigeon-hole and turned it about thoughtfully in his hand. 'That will he left in my care, and in it he bequeathed his fortune to a – a society. This paper,' – holding it up – 'contains his last written instructions, and leads me to believe that he made a later will, leaving everything instead to – to you.'

'To me?' If a thunderbolt had fallen at his feet, Cyril Carlowe could not have looked more astounded. 'Good heavens Mr Fenwick, what do you mean? What – what is that paper? Where is the last will?'

'Ah! where, indeed?' rejoined the lawyer, handing him the paper. 'Just read that, Mr Carlowe, and you will know as much as I know.'

There was a space of silence, while Cyril Carlowe, with amazed eyes, read the following few lines – the last words of the late Professor Luke Carlowe, written but a few hours before his death.

'This message, which I leave in the care of my trusted friend and lawyer, Jonas Fenwick, is to be read by him one month after my decease, and then handed to my nephew, Cyril Carlowe. I now state that I have made a later will, in which I leave everything I possess to my nephew, Cyril Carlowe, on certain conditions. The whereabouts of this will I alone know, and it is to prove my life theory – that is, that there is a means of communication between the dead and the living – that I have planned this proof. On a certain night – to be arranged by the members of the "Occult Association" – my nephew, Cyril Carlowe, is to descend into the vault where I am buried, and I – from the spirit world – will return and reveal where the will is. A committee of ten of my colleagues will wait outside, and a lasting proof will be given to the world of that which is now treated with ignorant scepticism. If the said Cyril Carlowe will not undertake the test, the will now existent, which Jonas Fenwick holds, will be proved.'

'He must have been mad when he wrote this, Mr Fenwick,' said Cyril Carlowe, looking up from the amazing document. 'I can't quite grasp it. He says here that in his last will he has left me everything. That will, nobody, save himself, knows the whereabouts of, and unless I – I – Good heavens! Am I awake or dreaming?'

'What it means is this, Mr Carlowe,' replied the lawyer, looking keenly at him. 'The will which I hold, and which I thought was the only one and the last, is evidently not so. That document distinctly states that he drew up a fresh will, leaving you his sole heir. To find that will and establish your right, he states what I candidly confess is beyond my powers of credulity – that is, that he himself will reveal to you – alone – where it is.'

'But – but it is too – too monstrously fantastic!' cried the other excitedly. 'A dead man reveal where his will is hidden?'

'It was his pet theory, remember,' put in the lawyer, 'the theory that there is a means of communicating between the dead and the living – a bridge of communication I think they call it.'

There was another long silence. Professor Carlowe had ended an eccentric life by an eccentricity which almost passed belief.

Cyril Carlowe spoke at last, slowly and thoughtfully.

'What is your opinion about it, Mr Fenwick?' he said. The lawyer coughed and deliberated carefully before replying.

'If you were rich, I would say, "don't do it," ' he replied slowly; 'but as things are – you are young; you don't seem nervous——'

'What is the law on the point?'

The lawyer chuckled.

'There is no point of law in it,' he said drily. 'It is purely an optional matter as far as you are concerned. You can carry out the – er – instructions, or – you need not.'

'And if I don't?'

'Then the will I hold – in which everything is left to the "Occult Association" – will be proved, and the money will go to further more – ahem! – extraordinary theories.'

'I see!'

There was another long silence – a thoughtful one on Mr Cyril Carlowe's part, judging from his facial expression.

He looked up suddenly, and his firm chin set in a determined manner. 'I shall do it, Mr Fenwick,' he said in a decisive tone.

The lawyer looked sharply at him.

'You will——?' he began, then stopped abruptly.

'I shall carry out the instructions left in that document,' said Cyril Carlowe firmly. 'I am not afraid, and to show I am not afraid I will do it. You will make all the formal arrangements?'

'I will,' replied the lawyer, and a strange light – a light of admiration – flickered in his dull eyes for one moment.

In the large, comfortably-appointed room where the 'Occult Association' held its spiritualistic and psychological séances, a group of men were gathered round the solid mahogany table. At one end sat the chairman – Professor Michael Andover – and ranged along either side were six of the association's foremost members. At the other end, facing the chairman, sat Mr Fenwick, the lawyer, and Cyril Carlowe. The former's face was expressive of dry cynicism; the latter looked slightly pale, but perfectly calm and self-possessed. The room was very still, for the hour was late – ten o'clock – and the quiet street was empty and deserted. Amid perfect silence, the chairman rose to speak.

'Gentlemen,' he began, 'the purpose for which we are gathered together here tonight is known to you all. Our valued and deeply lamented colleague, Professor Luke Carlowe, has left in our hands the proving of a much discussed and – and scepticized theory. Everything is arranged, and I have only to ask Mr Cyril Carlowe if he wishes to – to say anything before a start is made.'

'I have nothing to say – no comment to make,' replied Cyril Carlowe, 'save to have done with this matter as speedily as possible.'

'Very good! Then a start had better be made, for the drive to the cemetery will occupy a full hour.'

Four carriages were waiting without, and in a few minutes they were progressing at a fair speed towards the distant cemetery. The night was heavy and overcast – a sullen sky and a peculiar oppressiveness in the air suggesting that thunder was not far distant. Indeed, before the cemetery was reached, a few large drops of rain fell, and a distant muttering of thunder joined the rumbling of the carriage wheels.

'This is a strange project, Mr Fenwick,' said Cyril Carlowe, breaking the silence for the first time. He and the lawyer had the last carriage to themselves. 'Even now, I half wish——'

The lawyer looked sharply at him.

'It is not too late to draw back if you wish,' he said, quietly. 'As you say, the whole thing is – er – very strange!'

'I cannot understand how they have arranged it,' went on the other, thoughtfully. 'The access to the vault at this time of night, I mean.'

The lawyer shrugged his shoulders.

'Enthusiasts can do anything with money to help them,' he said, drily. 'I don't know how they have worked it – it is no concern of yours and mine. Suffice to say they have, by bribing the keeper, I suppose.'

At that moment the carriages came to a stop, and the party alighted. The cemetery, dark and gloomy, was barred by heavy gates; but, as the carriages withdrew, a man came quickly out of the lodge and unlocked the side gate. The party quickly filed through, and the gate clanged behind them. Led by Professor Andover, they proceeded down a side path which led to the vault. The silence of death was over everything, and only the pattering of the hurrying rain and the crunching of their footsteps broke the intense hush. Now and again, arrows of lightning darted from the black sky, lighting up the white stones and lending an added weirdness to the scene. In a few minutes they were standing opposite the vault wherein the body of Professor Luke Carlowe was interred. It was a huge stone mausoleum, square in shape, and guarded by a massive black iron-studded door. Lighting a lamp, the leader of the party unlocked the door, and all descended the short flight of stone steps. In a niche on a level with their heads was the massive coffin with its velvet pall. Flowers still withered on the ledge of the stained-glass window, and a dank atmosphere pervaded the echoing interior.

'We shall now leave you, Mr Carlowe,' said Professor Andover, in a hushed voice. 'The conditions you know – that you wait here until the last stroke of twelve has sounded. It is now a quarter to twelve.'

The young man inclined his head, but said nothing, and one by one they filed up the steps. Mr Fenwick, with the lantern, was the last to go, and he hung back to say a last word.

'I feel that I advised you wrong,' he said in a hurried whisper. 'Have done with this mad business – no good can come of it!'

But Cyril Carlowe shook his head.

'I shall go through with it now, Mr Fenwick,' he said, firmly. 'I am not afraid. I have my revolver, and I will see it through.'

The lawyer said nothing further, but holding his hand for a moment, hurried up the steps. The gate shut with a dull clang, and Cyril Carlowe found himself in the dank darkness – alone!

The moments passed slowly – very slowly. Without, the storm was coming up fast. The rain rattled dully on the roof of the vault; a bright flash of lightning darted through the stained-glass window and revealed the coffin for a fleeting second. High up in the domed space of the roof, a harsh screech sounded, followed by the whirr of beating wings as a bat flew round and round, and then clung panting to the groin. Strange, wild fancies crowded on his brain. With the revolver gripped in his hand, he turned slowly round, and once he was certain something touched him. Yet he was alone, save for the dead in the massive casket. Alone! was he alone? A strange shrinking sensation suddenly crept over him; a deadly nausea shook him, and he slowly sank on the stone floor. A crash of thunder split the air – a blinding flash of lightning suddenly illumined the whole vault as with the light of day, and in that moment he saw——

Above the war of thunder, the waiting group heard it – a cry that none had ever heard the like of before, and that would ring in their ears for ever.

'Great heaven!' cried the lawyer, looking into the others' white faces; 'That was – that was Cyril Carlowe's voice!'

He waited for no reply, but dashed headlong into the open, and made for the vault at frantic speed. In less than ten seconds he was at the gate and tugging at the iron handle. Holding the lamp high above his head, he paused and peered into the darkness below with a horrible presage of evil.

'Carlowe!' he cried, 'are you all right?'

No answer – only the dull, reverberating echo of his own voice. With the others pressing behind him, he cleared the steps in two bounds, then fell back, half fainting with a horrible dread, for this is what he saw.

A huddled body on the stone floor – the body of Cyril Carlowe – dead! He knelt down beside him and looked into a face so distorted as to be hardly recognizable. But it was not that which sent the creeping chill of fear – the one frantic desire to be clear of the place – pressing on him. In the clenched hand of the dead man was a roll of paper – the missing will of Professor Luke Carlowe!

The Screaming Plant

Hal Pink

'Look!'

Barker held out a tiny cardboard box for my inspection. Inside, on a nest of cotton-wool, was a large, shrivelled seed, similar in appearance to a dead and curled-up maggot.

'What is it?' I asked.

'That's what I am wondering,' smiled Barker, 'but the man from whom I got it said that it was a genuine mandrake seed!'

He made this pronouncement with such marked emphasis and enthusiasm that my interest was quickened, though I was still no wiser. Barker, my lifelong friend, is a botanist of repute, the discoverer of several new varieties of orchid, and his researches have led him through many lands, to the fringes of civilization and beyond. He had recently returned from an expedition to the Matto Grosso forests of Brazil, and after a re-union dinner and two seats at a cinema to celebrate the occasion, we were smoking a final pipe of tobacco in his cosy study.

'And what on earth is a mandrake?' I handed back the box.

For answer, Barker leaned over the arm of his chair, jerked open the glass door of a bookcase, and selected a battered volume from the jumble of books on the shelves. Opening it, he read aloud the words '*Nomen Herbae Mandragora ...*'

'This,' said Barker, tapping the book with his pipe-stem, 'is a herbal book much prized 500 years ago when housewives brewed the families' medicines from plants and flowers gathered in the fields. It contains the legend of the mandrake. I will not weary you with the tedious and badly-phrased Latin version given here, but the illustration will give you the idea at once.'

He handed the book to me. It was dated 1433, and looked its age. The calfskin binding was worn into holes; the leaves were yellowed with the light of five centuries; and the crude type, irregular composition and faded brown ink combined to render the pages more picturesque than readable.

The illustration of the mandrake was a rough drawing showing a

figure with the body, arms, and legs of a man, but with roots instead
of hands and feet and a cluster of leaves where the head should have
been. A small dog was depicted, attached by a cord to the mandrake's
right leg.

'There you have it,' said Barker. 'An early artist's idea of the human
plant of the legend. The mandrake was supposed to be a plant with
human form and the voracity of a carnivorous animal, which reached
out with its root-tentacles to seize unsuspecting herb-gatherers and
crush them to death, gaining strength from their blood. As uprooting
a mandrake was believed to be tantamount to committing suicide, dogs
were employed for this purpose, as the drawing shows.'

'What nonsense!' I laughed. 'Do you actually believe that such a
monstrosity existed?'

'Why not?' replied Barker. 'Why shouldn't the missing link between
man and the sub-world be a plant? Plants have always stood upright
and never moved on their bellies like animals. And there do exist in the
tropics today jungle plants with tentacles and suckers which catch small
flies.'

'Well, why not try to germinate your so-called mandrake seed?' I
suggested, laughingly. 'And see what happens.'

To my surprise, he took me seriously. 'It would need colossal heat,'
he mused, 'moist heat ... swamp heat ...'

A sudden scratching noise at the door interrupted him.

Barker's face lit up.

'That's Tom.'

Tom was his greatest pet, a magnificent Persian cat, which stayed
under my charge many times when its master was off on a journey to
the wilds. As Barker opened the door it stalked in, purring with delight.

'He's been hunting rats in the cellar, as usual,' said Barker, stooping
to make a fuss of his pet, 'and now he wants his milk.'

A month passed. I had been very busy, and had seen little of Barker
since our night of celebration. Then he telephoned to me.

'Can you come round here?' His usually calm voice was quivering
with excitement. 'Something incredible to show you! That mandrake
seed——'

'What? It has germinated?' I gasped.

'Yes – the application of terrific heat – it is sprouting in my cellar –
come and see——'

I slammed the telephone receiver on its hook and ran for my hat.

Barker greeted me at the door with shining eyes. He was elated as a
schoolboy.

'Man, you ought to see it! As big as my arm, with shoots, tentacles,
suckers and everything! Do you realize what this means? It is the
greatest botanical discovery of all time! At one stroke thousands of years

have been wiped off the calendar! Here is a plant which in history has only existed in legend, which vanished from this earth before primitive men became articulate – alive – growing – in my cellar——'

I caught his infection. As eager to see the phenomenon as he was to display it, I hurried after him to the cellar. It was the bottom cellar of three, far underground, and as we descended the stairs a cloud of hot steam swirled to meet us.

'Moist heat,' explained Barker. 'Hot steam and electric arc-lights. I had a copper boiler from the wash-house installed down here, and it has been boiling away for three weeks now. Water is fed into the boiler through a hose-pipe, and I build up the fire every four hours. The steam gives the temperature and humidity of the swamps in which these plants lived. The electric arcs provide light and additional warmth.'

We reached the bottom cellar. It was difficult to breathe in the super-heated atmosphere, but I peered through the mist of steam and there, swaying in a bed of soft, oozy mud, was the strangest plant I had ever set eyes on.

I said *swaying*. I mean it. Although no wind blew in the cellar, to cause motion, the plant writhed slowly from side to side! It was, as Barker had said, about the length of his arm in height. The stem was thick and two thick branches with a mass of thin roots at their ends, stuck out near the leaf cluster at the top. It was white in colour, but the stem of the plant was blotched with patches of light-grey fungus.

'You see?' said Barker. 'True, there are no legs such as were shown in the illustration, but there are arms, and tentacles. Look closer. You will see the suckers at the end of each tentacle.'

I looked. Flower-shaped suckers there were indeed, opening and shutting like so many gasping mouths waiting for food. I shuddered. There was something indescribably evil, loathsome, about the creature.

'See! It seems to be growing every minute!' cried Barker, clutching me by the arm. The plant was swelling and then subsiding, swelling again, and each time it seemed to increase its stature.

I could stand it no longer. 'Come on, let us get out of this!' I said thickly; 'this heat is overpowering.'

He was loath to leave, and at last I had to take him by the arm and literally drag him out of that cellar. The sweet air up above was good after that sweltering oven below.

'Isn't it a beauty?' said Barker, enthusiastically. 'Why, it is the greatest——'

'Yes, yes, I know – I agree,' was my hasty rejoinder, but though I tried to change the subject he kept me talking about that foul thing down in the cellar for nearly an hour before I left.

For two days after that I tried to forget about Barker's cellar and the plant that was sprouting there, but always the Thing came uppermost

in my thoughts. It was on the morning of the third day that it began
to worry me. I could not concentrate on my work, for mentally I was
visualizing that writhing creature in its artificially-created tropical
swamp, and Barker peering lovingly at it through the miasma ... Barker
building up the boiler fires ... Barker tending the arc-lights like an
acolyte at the altar of an evil god ... Barker reaching out to touch the
tentacles ...

I went to his house. I had to go. Something stronger than reason,
something bigger than myself forced me to go.

There was no reply to my knock. Was he out? I thundered at the
door. I went through the garden and round to the back of the house,
shouting his name.

At last I broke in a window. Never in a sane moment would I have
done such a thing, but the strange absence of my friend had crystallized
my vague misgivings into one overwhelming fear for his safety.

I entered by the window, calling his name.

'Where are you?' I shouted. But the words came echoing back to me,
mockingly.

The door leading to the cellar was open. I dashed down the steps.
Then——

'Help!'

Barker's voice. My heart was pounding like a trip-hammer as I
thundered down the last flight of steps and into the hot mist.

There was Barker, in the farthest corner of the cellar, crouching
against the wall, and looming over him was that dreadful Thing, now
grown to the size of a man.

A low humming noise filled the air. The plant was waving from side
to side, its tentacle arms outstretched towards the cowering man. On
the bed of mud was a mangled heap of fur – Tom, the Persian cat,
crushed to death.

'For God's sake, get an axe!' cried Barker, as he saw me. 'Quickly!'

I turned and ran. In one of the upper cellars I found a short-handled
chopper and a garden spade. Armed with these, I dashed below again.
Only just in time. The roots of the arms were reaching out towards my
friend, nearer and nearer, the suckers dripping with a wet, sticky mass.
Barker gave a despairing shout, and——

Whack! I brought down the blade of the spade with all my force on
the monster's trunk.

It screamed.

Shrill as the shriek of a siren was that cry of agony.

One set of suckers had already fastened on Barker's shoulder,
but now they fell away as the plant writhed backwards towards
me.

I struck again and again, and still the shrill screams of the Thing rent the air. I tossed the short chopper to Barker, and reaching out he slashed at the tentacles.

It took us five minutes to cut it to pieces. When it was safe for him to move, Barker came round the bed of mud and joined me, wiping the sweat from his face. He was trembling.

'By Heaven, you only just got here in time!' he gasped. 'I've been down here four hours. Came down early this morning to see to the fires, and was amazed to see how the plant had grown overnight. I was round in that corner, examining one of the arc-lights, when poor Tom came down. I had shut him out of the cellars while this – this Thing was growing. He stood over there – the nearest point to it – and it seemed to me that the cat was hypnotized by the plant, for he made no move as the tentacles came slowly down towards him. Then – it got him.'

He shuddered at the memory.

'Before I could snatch him clear, it had crushed him with its root-fingers, and the suckers were drinking the blood. That was what it wanted – blood. Blood gave it power. Even as I stood there, astounded, it grew and grew, and the humming noise developed. I realized then that I was trapped. I could not get past. The blood of the cat had given just the impetus it needed to become dangerous. I was cut off. And I remained cut off until your arrival. You saved my life——'

'Don't let's talk about it,' I muttered, and hurried him upstairs for a stiff glass of whisky.

We sprayed the battered stump and the hacked pieces of the mandrake, if such it was, with acid, and burnt the foul thing into oblivion. Barker locked up that bottom cellar after the mud and the apparatus had been removed. The terrible death of his pet cat hurt him deeply, and when last I went to see him I noticed that the faded old volume containing the legend of the mandrake had disappeared from the shelves of his bookcase.

The Black Cat

Edgar Allan Poe

For the most wild yet most homely narrative which I am about to pen, I neither expect nor solicit belief. Mad indeed would I be to expect it, in a case where my very senses reject their own evidence. Yet, mad am I not – and very surely do I not dream. But tomorrow I die, and today I would unburden my soul. My immediate purpose is to place before the world, plainly, succinctly, and without comment, a series of mere household events. In their consequences, these events have terrified – have tortured – have destroyed me. Yet I will not attempt to expound them. To me, they have presented little but horror – to many they will seem less terrible than *baroques*. Hereafter, perhaps, some intellect may be found which will reduce my phantasm to the commonplace – some intellect more calm, more logical, and far less excitable than my own, which will perceive, in the circumstances I detail with awe, nothing more than an ordinary succession of very natural causes and effects.

From my infancy I was noted for the docility and humanity of my disposition. My tenderness of heart was even so conspicuous as to make me the jest of my companions. I was especially fond of animals, and was indulged by my parents with a great variety of pets. With these I spent most of my time, and never was so happy as when feeding and caressing them. This peculiarity of character grew with my growth, and, in my manhood, I derived from it one of my principal sources of pleasure. To those who have cherished an affection for a faithful and sagacious dog, I need hardly be at the trouble of explaining the nature or the intensity of the gratification thus derivable. There is something in the unselfish and self-sacrificing love of a brute, which goes directly to the heart of him who has had frequent occasion to test the paltry friendship and gossamer fidelity of mere *Man*.

I married early, and was happy to find in my wife a disposition not uncongenial with my own. Observing my partiality for domestic pets, she lost no opportunity of procuring those of the most agreeable kind.

We had birds, gold-fish, a fine dog, rabbits, a small monkey, and a *cat*.

This latter was a remarkably large and beautiful animal, entirely black, and sagacious to an astonishing degree. In speaking of his intelligence, my wife, who at heart was not a little tinctured with superstition, made frequent allusion to the ancient popular notion, which regarded all black cats as witches in disguise. Not that she was ever *serious* upon this point – and I mention the matter at all for no better reason than that it happens, just now, to be remembered.

Pluto – this was the cat's name – was my favourite pet and playmate. I alone fed him, and he attended me wherever I went about the house. It was even with difficulty that I could prevent him from following me through the streets.

Our friendship lasted, in this manner, for several years, during which my general temperament and character – through the instrumentality of the Fiend Intemperance – had (I blush to confess it) experienced a radical alteration for the worse. I grew, day by day, more moody, more irritable, more regardless of the feelings of others. I suffered myself to use intemperate language to my wife. At length, I even offered her personal violence. My pets, of course, were made to feel the change in my disposition. I not only neglected, but ill-used them. For Pluto, however, I still retained sufficient regard to restrain me from maltreating him, as I made no scruple of maltreating the rabbits, the monkey, or even the dog, when, by accident, or through affection, they came in my way. But my disease grew upon me – for what disease is like Alcohol! – and at length even Pluto, who was now becoming old, and consequently somewhat peevish – even Pluto began to experience the effects of my ill temper.

One night, returning home, much intoxicated, from one of my haunts about town, I fancied that the cat avoided my presence. I seized him; when, in his fright at my violence, he inflicted a slight wound upon my hand with his teeth. The fury of a demon instantly possessed me. I knew myself no longer. My original soul seemed, at once, to take its flight from my body; and a more than fiendish malevolence, gin-nurtured, thrilled every fibre of my frame. I took from my waistcoat-pocket a penknife, opened it, grasped the poor beast by the throat, and deliberately cut one of its eyes from the socket! I blush, I burn, I shudder, while I pen the damnable atrocity.

When reason returned with the morning – when I had slept off the fumes of the night's debauch – I experienced a sentiment half of horror, half of remorse, for the crime of which I had been guilty; but it was, at best, a feeble and equivocal feeling, and the soul remained untouched. I again plunged into excess, and soon drowned in wine all memory of the deed.

In the meantime the cat slowly recovered. The socket of the lost eye presented, it is true, a frightful appearance, but he no longer appeared to suffer any pain. He went about the house as usual, but, as might be expected, fled in extreme terror at my approach. I had so much of my old heart left, as to be first grieved by this evident dislike on the part of a creature which had once so loved me. But this feeling soon gave place to irritation. And then came, as if to my final and irrevocable overthrow, the spirit of PERVERSENESS. Of this spirit philosophy takes no account. Yet I am not more sure that my soul lives, than I am that perverseness is one of the primitive impulses of the human heart – one of the indivisible primary faculties, or sentiments, which give direction to the character of Man. Who has not, a hundred times, found himself committing a vile or a stupid action, for no other reason than because he knows he should *not?* Have we not a perpetual inclination, in the teeth of our best judgement, to violate that which is *Law*, merely because we understand it to be such? This spirit of perverseness, I say, came to my final overthrow. It was this unfathomable longing of the soul to *vex itself* – to offer violence to its own nature – to do wrong for the wrong's sake only – that urged me to continue and finally to consummate the injury I had inflicted upon the unoffending brute. One morning, in cold blood, I slipped a noose about its neck and hung it to the limb of a tree; – hung it with the tears streaming from my eyes, and with the bitterest remorse at my heart; – hung it *because* I knew that it had loved me, and *because* I felt it had given me no reason of offence; – hung it *because* I knew that in so doing I was committing a sin – a deadly sin that would so jeopardize my immortal soul as to place it – if such a thing were possible – even beyond the reach of the infinite mercy of the Most Merciful and Most Terrible God.

On the night of the day on which this most cruel deed was done, I was aroused from sleep by the cry of fire. The curtains of my bed were in flames. The whole house was blazing. It was with great difficulty that my wife, a servant, and myself, made our escape from the conflagration. The destruction was complete. My entire wordly wealth was swallowed up, and I resigned myself thenceforward to despair.

I am above the weakness of seeking to establish a sequence of cause and effect, between the disaster and the atrocity. But I am detailing a chain of facts – and wish not to leave even a possible link imperfect. On the day succeeding the fire, I visited the ruins. The walls, with one exception, had fallen in. This exception was found in a compartment wall, not very thick, which stood about the middle of the house, and against which had rested the head of my bed. The plastering had here, in great measure, resisted the action of the fire – a fact which I attributed to its having been recently spread. About this wall a dense crowd were collected, and many persons seemed to be examining a particular portion of it with very minute and eager attention. The words 'strange!'

'singular!' and other similar expressions, excited my curiosity. I approached and saw, as if graven in *bas-relief* upon the white surface, the figure of a gigantic *cat*. The impression was given with an accuracy truly marvellous. There was a rope about the animal's neck.

When I first beheld this apparition – for I could scarcely regard it as less – my wonder and my terror were extreme. But at length reflection came to my aid. The cat, I remembered, had been hung in a garden adjacent to the house. Upon the alarm of fire, this garden had been immediately filled by the crowd – by someone of whom the animal must have been cut from the tree and thrown, through an open window, into my chamber. This had probably been done with the view of arousing me from sleep. The falling of other walls had compressed the victim of my cruelty into the substance of the freshly-spread plaster; the lime of which, with the flames, and the *ammonia* from the carcass, had then accomplished the portraiture as I saw it.

Although I thus readily accounted to my reason, if not altogether to my conscience, for the startling fact just detailed, it did not the less fail to make a deep impression upon my fancy. For months I could not rid myself of the phantasm of the cat; and, during this period, there came back into my spirit a half-sentiment that seemed, but was not, remorse. I went so far as to regret the loss of the animal, and to look about me, among the vile haunts which I now habitually frequented, for another pet of the same species, and of somewhat similar appearance, with which to supply its place.

One night as I sat, half stupefied, in a den of more than infamy, my attention was suddenly drawn to some black object, reposing upon the head of one of the immense hogsheads of gin, or of rum, which con-stituted the chief furniture of the apartment. I had been looking steadily at the top of this hogshead for some minutes, and what now caused me surprise was the fact that I had not sooner perceived the object there-upon. I approached it, and touched it with my hand. It was a black cat – a very large one – fully as large as Pluto, and closely resembling him in every respect but one. Pluto had not a white hair upon any portion of his body; but this cat had a large, although indefinite splotch of white, covering nearly the whole region of the breast.

Upon my touching him, he immediately arose, purred loudly, rubbed against my hand, and appeared delighted with my notice. This, then, was the very creature of which I was in search. I at once offered to purchase it of the landlord; but this person made no claim to it – knew nothing of it – had never seen it before.

I continued my caresses, and when I prepared to go home, the animal evinced a disposition to accompany me. I permitted it to do so; occasion-ally stooping and patting it as I proceeded. When it reached the house it domesticated itself at once, and became immediately a great favourite with my wife.

For my own part, I soon found a dislike to it arising within me. This was just the reverse of what I had anticipated; but – I know not how or why it was – its evident fondness for myself rather disgusted and annoyed me. By slow degrees these feelings of disgust and annoyance rose into the bitterness of hatred. I avoided the creature; a certain sense of shame, and the remembrance of my former deed of cruelty, preventing me from physically abusing it. I did not, for some weeks, strike, or otherwise violently ill use it; but gradually – very gradually – I came to look upon it with unutterable loathing, and to flee silently from its odious presence, as from the breath of a pestilence.

What added, no doubt, to my hatred of the beast, was the discovery, on the morning after I brought it home, that, like Pluto, it also had been deprived of one of its eyes. This circumstance, however, only endeared it to my wife, who, as I have already said, possessed, in a high degree, that humanity of feeling which had once been my distinguishing trait, and the source of many of my simplest and purest pleasures.

With my aversion to this cat, however, its partiality for myself seemed to increase. It followed my footsteps with a pertinacity which it would be difficult to make the reader comprehend. Whenever I sat, it would crouch beneath my chair, or spring upon my knees, covering me with its loathsome caresses. If I arose to walk it would get between my feet and thus nearly throw me down, or, fastening its long and sharp claws in my dress, clamber, in this manner, to my breast. At such times, although I longed to destroy it with a blow, I was yet withheld from so doing, partly by a memory of my former crime, but chiefly – let me confess it at once – by absolute *dread* of the beast.

This dread was not exactly a dread of physical evil – and yet I should be at a loss how otherwise to define it. I am almost ashamed to own – yes, even in this felon's cell, I am almost ashamed to own – that the terror and horror with which the animal inspired me, had been heightened by one of the merest chimeras it would be possible to conceive. My wife had called my attention, more than once, to the character of the mark of white hair, of which I have spoken, and which constituted the sole visible difference between the strange beast and the one I had destroyed. The reader will remember that this mark, although large, had been originally very indefinite; but, by slow degrees – degrees nearly imperceptible, and which for a long time my reason struggled to reject as fanciful – it had, at length, assumed a rigorous distinctness of outline. It was now the representation of an object that I shudder to name – and for this, above all, I loathed, and dreaded, and would have rid myself of the monster *had I dared* – it was now, I say, the image of a hideous – of a ghastly thing – of the GALLOWS! – oh, mournful and terrible engine of Horror and of Crime – of Agony and of Death!

And now was I indeed wretched beyond the wretchedness of mere Humanity. And *a brute beast* – whose fellow I had contemptuously destroyed – *a brute beast* to work out for *me* – for me, a man fashioned in the image of the High God – so much of insufferable woe! Alas! neither by day nor by night knew I the blessing of rest any more! During the former the creature left me no moment alone, and in the latter I started hourly from dreams of unutterable fear to find the hot breath of *the thing* upon my face, and its vast weight – an incarnate nightmare that I had no power to shake off – incumbent eternally upon my *heart!*

Beneath the pressure of torments such as these the feeble remnant of the good within me succumbed. Evil thoughts became my sole intimates – the darkest and most evil of thoughts. The moodiness of my usual temper increased to hatred of all things and of all mankind; while from the sudden, frequent, and ungovernable outbursts of a fury to which I now blindly abandoned myself, my uncomplaining wife, alas, was the most usual and the most patient of sufferers.

One day she accompanied me, upon some household errand, into the cellar of the old building which our poverty compelled us to inhabit. The cat followed me down the steep stairs, and, nearly throwing me headlong, exasperated me to madness. Uplifting an axe, and forgetting in my wrath the childish dread which had hitherto stayed my hand, I aimed a blow at the animal, which, of course, would have proved instantly fatal had it descended as I wished. But this blow was arrested by the hand of my wife. Goaded by the interference into a rage more than demoniacal, I withdrew my arm from her grasp and buried the axe in her brain. She fell dead upon the spot without a groan.

This hideous murder accomplished, I set myself forthwith, and with entire deliberation, to the task of concealing the body. I knew that I could not remove it from the house, either by day or by night, without the risk of being observed by the neighbours. Many projects entered my mind. At one period I thought of cutting the corpse into minute fragments, and destroying them by fire. At another, I resolved to dig a grave for it in the floor of the cellar. Again, I deliberated about casting it in the well in the yard – about packing it in a box, as if merchandise, with the usual arrangements, and so getting a porter to take it from the house. Finally I hit upon what I considered a far better expedient than either of these. I determined to wall it up in the cellar, as the monks of the Middle Ages are recorded to have walled up their victims.

For a purpose such as this the cellar was well adapted. Its walls were loosely constructed, and had lately been plastered throughout with a rough plaster, which the dampness of the atmosphere had prevented from hardening. Moreover, in one of the walls was a projection, caused by a false chimney, or fireplace, that had been filled up and made to resemble the rest of the cellar. I made no doubt that I could readily displace the bricks at this point, insert the corpse, and wall the whole up as before, so that no eye could detect any thing suspicious.

And in this calculation I was not deceived. By means of a crowbar I easily dislodged the bricks, and, having carefully deposited the body against the inner wall, I propped it in that position, while with little trouble I relaid the whole structure as it originally stood. Having procured mortar, sand, and hair, with every possible precaution, I prepared a plaster which could not be distinguished from the old, and with this I very carefully went over the new brick-work. When I had finished, I felt satisfied that all was right. The wall did not present the slightest appearance of having been disturbed. The rubbish on the floor was picked up with the minutest care. I looked around triumphantly, and said to myself: 'Here at least, then, my labour has not been in vain.'

My next step was to look for the beast which had been the cause of so much wretchedness; for I had, at length, firmly resolved to put it to death. Had I been able to meet with it at the moment, there could have been no doubt of its fate; but it appeared that the crafty animal had been alarmed at the violence of my previous anger, and forbore to present itself in my present mood. It is impossible to describe or to imagine the deep, the blissful sense of relief which the absence of the detested creature occasioned in my bosom. It did not make its appearance during the night; and thus for one night, at least, since its introduction into the house, I soundly and tranquilly slept; aye, *slept* even with the burden of murder upon my soul.

The second and the third day passed, and still my tormentor came not. Once again I breathed as a freeman. The monster, in terror, had fled the premises for ever! I should behold it no more! My happiness was supreme! The guilt of my dark deed disturbed me but little. Some few inquiries had been made, but these had been readily answered. Even a search had been instituted – but of course nothing was to be discovered. I looked upon my future felicity as secured.

Upon the fourth day of the assassination, a party of the police came, very unexpectedly, into the house, and proceeded again to make rigorous investigation of the premises. Secure, however, in the inscrutability of my place of concealment, I felt no embarrassment whatever. The officers bade me accompany them in their search. They left no nook or corner unexplored. At length, for the third or fourth time, they descended into the cellar. I quivered not in a muscle. My heart beat calmly as that of one who slumbers in innocence. I walked the cellar from end to end. I folded my arms upon my bosom, and roamed easily to and fro. The police were thoroughly satisfied and prepared to depart. The glee at my heart was too strong to be restrained. I burned to say if but one word, by way of triumph, and to render doubly sure their assurance of my guiltlessness.

'Gentlemen,' I said at last, as the party ascended the steps, 'I delight to have allayed your suspicions. I wish you all health and a little more courtesy. By the bye, gentlemen, this – this is a very well-constructed house,' (in the rabid desire to say something easily, I scarcely knew what I uttered at all) – 'I may say an *excellently* well-constructed house. These walls – are you going, gentlemen? – these walls are solidly put together'; and here, through the mere frenzy of bravado, I rapped heavily with a cane which I held in my hand, upon that very portion of the brickwork behind which stood the corpse of the wife of my bosom.

But may God shield and deliver me from the fangs of the Arch-Fiend! No sooner had the reverberation of my blows sunk into silence, than I was answered by a voice from within the tomb! – by a cry, at first muffled and broken, like the sobbing of a child, and then quickly swelling into one long, loud, and continuous scream, utterly anomalous and inhuman – a howl – a wailing shriek, half of horror and half of triumph, such as might have arisen only out of hell, conjointly from the throats of the damned in their agony and of the demons that exult in the damnation.

Of my own thoughts it is folly to speak. Swooning, I staggered to the opposite wall. For one instant the party on the stairs remained motionless, through extremity of terror and awe. In the next a dozen stout arms were toiling at the wall. It fell bodily. The corpse, already greatly decayed and clotted with gore, stood erect before the eyes of the spectators. Upon its head, with red extended mouth and solitary eye of fire, sat the hideous beast whose craft had seduced me into murder, and whose informing voice had consigned me to the hangman. I had walled the monster up within the tomb.

The House of Horror

Seabury Quinn

'Morbleu, Friend Trowbridge, have a care,' Jules de Grandin warned as my lurching motor car almost ran into the brimming ditch beside the rain-soaked road.

I wrenched the steering wheel viciously and swore softly under my breath as I leaned forward, striving vainly to pierce the curtains of rain which shut us in.

'No use, old fellow,' I confessed, turning to my companion, 'we're lost; that's all there is to it.'

'Ha,' he laughed shortly, 'do you just begin to discover that fact, my friend? *Parbleu*, I have known it this last half hour.'

Throttling my engine down, I crept along the concrete roadway, peering through my streaming windscreen and storm curtains for some familiar landmark, but nothing but blackness, wet and impenetrable, met my eyes.

Two hours before, answering an insistent phone call, de Grandin and I had left the security of my warm office to administer a dose of toxin antitoxin to an Italian labourer's child who lay choking with diphtheria in a hut at the workmen's settlement where the new branch of the railway was being put through. The cold, driving rain and the Stygian darkness of the night had misled me when I made the detour round the railway cut, and for the past hour and a half I had been feeling my way over unfamiliar roads as futilely as a lost child wandering in the woods.

'*Grâce à Dieu*,' de Grandin exclaimed, seizing my arm with both his small, strong hands, 'a light! See, there it shines in the night. Come, let us go to it. Even the meanest hovel is preferable to this so villainous rain.'

I peeped through a joint in the curtains and saw a faint, intermittent light flickering through the driving rain some two hundred yards away.

'All right,' I acquiesced, climbing from the car; 'we've lost so much time already we probably couldn't do anything for the Vivianti child, and maybe these people can put us on the right road, anyway.'

Plunging through puddles like miniature lakes, soaked by the wind-driven rain, barking our shins again and again on invisible obstacles, we made for the light, finally drawing up to a large square house of red brick fronted by an imposing white-pillared porch. Light streamed out through the fan-light over the white door and from the two tall windows flanking the portal.

'*Parbleu*, a house of circumstance, this,' de Grandin commented, mounting the porch and banging lustily at the polished brass knocker.

I wrinkled my forehead in thought while he rattled the knocker a second time. 'Strange, I can't remember this place,' I muttered. 'I thought I knew every building within thirty miles, but this is a new one——'

'Ah, bah!' de Grandin interrupted. 'Always you must be casting a wet blanket on the parade, Friend Trowbridge. First you insist on losing us in the midst of a *sacré* rainstorm, then when I, Jules de Grandin, find us a shelter from the weather, you must needs waste time in wondering why it is you know not the place. *Morbleu,* you will refuse shelter because you have never been presented to the master of the house, if I do not watch you, I fear.'

'But I ought to know the place, de Grandin,' I protested. 'It's certainly imposing enough to——'

My defence was cut short by the sharp click of a lock, and the wide, white door swung inwards before us.

We strode over the threshold, removing our dripping hats as we did so, and turned to address the person who had opened the door.

'Why——' I began, and stared about me in open-mouthed surprise.

'Name of a little blue man!' said Jules de Grandin, and added his incredulous stare to mine.

As far as we could see, we were alone in the mansion's imposing hall. Straight before us, perhaps for forty feet, ran a corridor of parquetry flooring, covered here and there by rich-hued Oriental rugs. White-panelled walls, adorned with oil paintings of imposing-looking individuals, rose for eighteen feet or so to a beautifully frescoed ceiling, and a graceful, curving staircase swept upwards from the farther end of the room. Candles in cut-glass sconces lighted the high-ceilinged apartment, the hospitable glow from a log fire burning under the high white marble mantel lent an air of homely cosiness to the place, but of anything living, human or animal, there was no faintest trace or sign.

Click! Behind us the heavy outer door swung to silently on well-oiled hinges and the automatic lock latched firmly.

'Death of my life!' de Grandin murmured, reaching for the door's silver-plated knob and giving it a vigorous twist. '*Par la moustache du diable*, Friend Trowbridge, it is locked! Truly, perhaps it had been better if we had remained outside in the rain!'

'Not at all, I assure you, my dear sir,' a rich, mellow voice answered him from the curve of the stairs. 'Your arrival was nothing less than providential, gentlemen.'

Coming towards us, walking heavily with the aid of a stout cane, was an unusually handsome man attired in pyjamas and dressing gown, a sort of nightcap of flowered silk on his white head, slippers of softest Morocco on his feet.

'You are a physician, sir?' he asked, glancing inquiringly at the medicine case in my hand.

'Yes,' I answered. 'I am Dr Samuel Trowbridge, from Harrisonville, and this is Dr Jules de Grandin, of Paris, who is my guest.'

'Ah,' replied our host, 'I am very, very glad to welcome you to Marston Hall, gentlemen. It so happens that one – er – my daughter, is quite ill, and I have been unable to obtain medical aid for her on account of my infirmities and the lack of a telephone. If I may trespass on your charity to attend my poor child, I shall be delighted to have you as my guests for the night. If you will lay aside your coats ...' He paused expectantly. 'Ah, thank you' – as we hung our dripping garments over a chair. 'You will come this way, please?'

We followed him up the broad stairs and down an upper corridor to a tastefully furnished chamber, where a young girl – fifteen years of age, perhaps – lay propped up with a pile of diminutive pillows.

'Anabel, Anabel, my love, here are two doctors to see you,' the old gentleman called softly.

The girl moved her fair head with a weary, peevish motion and whimpered softly in her sleep, but gave no further recognition of our presence.

'And what have been her symptoms, if you please, monsieur?' de Grandin asked, as he rolled back the cuffs of his jacket and prepared to make an examination.

'Sleep,' replied our host; 'just sleep. Some time ago she suffered from influenza; lately she has been given to fits of protracted slumber from which I cannot waken her. I fear she may have contracted sleeping sickness, sir. I am told it sometimes follows influenza.'

'H'm.' De Grandin passed his small, pliable hands rapidly over the girl's cheeks in the region of the ears, felt rapidly along her neck over the jugular vein, then raised a puzzled glance to me. 'Have you some laudanum and aconite in your bag, Friend Trowbridge?' he asked.

'There's some morphine,' I answered, 'and aconite; but no laudanum.'

'No matter.' He waved his hand impatiently, bustling over to the medicine case and extracting two small phials from it. 'No matter – this will do as well. Some water, if you please, monsieur' – he turned to the father, a medicine bottle in each hand.

'But, de Grandin——' I began, when a sudden kick from one of his slender, heavily shod feet nearly broke my shin. 'De Grandin, do you think that's the proper medication?' I finished lamely.

'Oh, *mais oui*, undoubtedly,' he replied. 'Nothing else would do in this case. Water, if you please, monsieur,' he repeated, again addressing the father.

I stared at him in ill-disguised amazement as he extracted a pellet from each of the bottles and quickly ground them to powder while the old gentleman filled a tumbler with water from the porcelain pitcher which stood on the chintz-draped washstand in the corner of the chamber. He was as familiar with the arrangement of my medicine case as I was, I knew, and knew that my phials were arranged by numbers instead of being labelled. Deliberately, I saw, he had passed over the morphine and aconite, and had chosen two bottles of plain, un-medicated sugar-of-milk pills. What his object was I had no idea, but I watched him measure out four teaspoonful of water, dissolve the powder in it, and pour the sham medication down the unconscious girl's throat.

'Good,' he proclaimed as he washed the glass with meticulous care. 'She will rest easily until the morning, monsieur. When daylight comes we shall decide on further treatment. Will you now permit that we retire?' He bowed politely to the master of the house, who returned his courtesy and led us to a comfortably furnished room farther down the corridor.

'See here, de Grandin,' I demanded, when our host had wished us a pleasant good night and closed the door upon us, 'what was your idea in giving that child an impotent dose like that——?'

'S-s-sh!' he cut me short with a fierce whisper. 'That young girl, *mon ami*, is no more suffering from encephalitis than you and I. There is no characteristic swelling of the face or neck, no diagnostic hardening of the jugular vein. Her temperature was a bit subnormal, it is true – but upon her breath I detected the odour of chloral hydrate. For some reason – good, I hope, but bad I fear – she is drugged, and I thought it best to play the fool and pretend I believed the man's statements. *Pardieu*, the fool who knows himself no fool has an immense advantage over the fool who believes him one, my friend.'

'But——'

'But me no buts, Friend Trowbridge; remember how the door of this house opened with none to touch it; recall how it closed behind us in the same way, and observe this, if you will.' Stepping softly, he crossed the room, pulled aside the chintz curtains at the window, and tapped lightly on the frame which held the thick plate-glass panes. '*Regardez vous*,' he ordered, tapping the frame a second time.

Like every other window I had seen in the house, this one was of the casement type, small panes of heavy glass being sunk into lattice-like frames. Under de Grandin's directions I tapped the latter, and found them not painted wood, as I had supposed, but stoutly welded and bolted metal. Also to my surprise, I found the turn buckles for opening

the casement were only dummies, the metal frames being actually
securely bolted to the stone sills. To all intents, we were as firmly
incarcerated as though serving a sentence in the state penitentiary.

'The door——' I began, but he shook his head.

Obeying his gesture, I crossed the room and turned the handle lightly.
It twisted under the pressure of my fingers, but, though we had heard
no warning click of lock or bolt, the door itself was as firmly fastened
as though nailed shut.

'Wh – why,' I asked stupidly, 'what's it all mean, de Grandin?'

'*Je ne sais quoi,*' he answered with a shrug; 'but one thing I know: I
like not this house, Friend Trowbridge. I——'

Above the hissing of the rain against the windows and the howl of the
sea-wind about the gables there suddenly rose a scream, wire-edged
with inarticulate terror, freighted with utter, transcendental anguish of
body and soul.

'*Cordieu!*' He threw up his head like a hound hearing the call of the
pack from far away. 'Did you hear it, too, Friend Trowbridge?'

'Of course,' I answered, every nerve in my body trembling in
horripilation with the echo of the hopeless wail.

'*Pardieu,*' he repeated, 'I like this house less than ever now. Come, let
us move this dresser before our door. It is safer that we sleep behind
barricades this night, I think.'

We blocked the door, and I was soon sound asleep.

'Trowbridge, Trowbridge, my friend' – de Grandin drove a sharp
elbow into my ribs – 'wake up, I beseech you, Name of a green goat,
you lie like one dead, save for your so abominable snoring!'

'Eh?' I answered sleepily, thrusting myself deeper beneath the
voluminous bedclothes. Despite the unusual occurrences of the night, I
was tired to the point of exhaustion, and fairly drunk with sleep.

'Up; arise, my friend,' he ordered, shaking me excitedly. 'The coast
is clear, I think, and it is high time we did some exploring.'

'Rats!' I scoffed, disinclined to leave my comfortable couch. 'What's
the use of wandering about a strange house to gratify a few unfounded
suspicions? The girl might have been given a dose of chloral hydrate,
but the chances are her father thought he was helping her when he gave
it. As for these trick devices for opening and locking doors, the old man
apparently lives here alone and has installed these mechanical aids to
lessen his work. He has to hobble around with a cane, you know.'

'Ah!' my companion assented sarcastically. 'And that scream we
heard, did he install that as an aid to his infirmities, also?'

'Perhaps the girl woke up with a nightmare,' I hazarded, but he made
an impatient gesture.

'Perhaps the moon is composed of green cheese also,' he replied. 'Up,
up and dress, my friend. This house should be investigated while yet

there is time. Attend me: But five minutes ago, through this very window, I did observe monsieur our host, attired in a raincoat, depart from his own front door, and without his cane. *Parbleu*, he did skip as agilely as any boy, I assure you. Even now he is almost at the spot where we abandoned your automobile. What he intends doing there, I know not. What I intend doing I know full well. Do you accompany me or not?'

'Oh, I suppose so,' I agreed, crawling from the bed and slipping into my clothes. 'How are you going to get past that locked door?'

He flashed me one of his sudden smiles, shooting the points of his little blond moustache upwards like the horns of an inverted crescent. 'Observe,' he ordered, displaying a short length of thin wire. 'In the days when woman's hair was still her crowning glory, what mighty deeds a lady could encompass with a hairpin! *Pardieu*, there was one little *grisette* in Paris who showed me some tricks in the days before the war! *Regard* me, if you please.'

Deftly he thrust the pliable loop of wire into the keyhole, twisting it tentatively back and forth, at length pulling it out and regarding it carefully. '*Très bien*,' he muttered, as he reached into an inside pocket, bringing out a heavier bit of wire.

'See' – he displayed the finer wire – 'with this I take an impression of that lock's tumblers, now' – quickly he bent the heavier wire to conform to the waved outline of the lighter loop – '*voilà*, I have a key!'

And he had. The lock gave readily to the pressure of his improvised key, and we stood in the long, dark hall, staring about us half curiously, half fearfully.

'This way, if you please,' de Grandin ordered; 'first we will look in upon *la jeunesse*, to see how it goes with her.'

We walked on tiptoe down the corridor, entered the chamber where the girl lay, and approached the bed.

She was lying with her hands folded upon her breast in the manner of those composed for their final rest, her wide, periwinkle-blue eyes staring sightlessly before her, the short, tightly curled ringlets of her blonde, bobbed hair surrounding her drawn, pallid face like a golden nimbus encircling the ivory features of a saint in some carved icon.

My companion approached the bed softly, placing one hand on the girl's wrist with professional precision. 'Temperature low, pulse weak,' he murmured, checking off her symptoms. 'Complexion pale to the point of lividity – ha, now for the eyes; sleeping, her pupils should have been contracted, while they should now be dilate – *Dieu de Dieu!* Trowbridge, my friend, come here.'

'Look!' he commanded, pointing to the apathetic girl's face. 'Those eyes – *grand Dieu*, those eyes! It is sacrilege, nothing less.'

I looked into the girl's face, then started back with a half suppressed cry of horror. Asleep, as she had been when we first saw her, the child had been pretty to the point of loveliness. Her features were small and regular, clean-cut as those of a face in a cameo, the tendrils of her light-yellow hair had lent her a dainty, ethereal charm comparable to that of a Dresden-china shepherdess. It had needed but the raising of her delicate, long-lashed eyelids to give her face the animation of some laughing sprite playing truant from fairyland.

Her lids were raised now, but the eyes they unveiled were no clear, joyous windows of a tranquil soul. Rather they were the peepholes of a spirit in torment. The irises were a lovely shade of blue, it is true, but the optics themselves were things of horror. Rolling grotesquely to right and left, they peered futilely in opposite directions, lending to her sweet, pale face the half ludicrous, wholly hideous expression of a bloating frog.

'Good heavens!' I exclaimed, turning from the deformed girl with a feeling of disgust akin to nausea. 'What a terrible affliction!'

De Grandin made no reply, but bent over the girl's still form, gazing intently at her malformed eyes. 'It is not natural,' he announced. 'The muscles have been tampered with, and tampered with by someone who is a master hand at surgery. Will you get me your syringe and some strychnine, Friend Trowbridge? This poor one is still unconscious.'

I hastened to our bedroom and returned with the hypodermic and stimulant, then stood beside him, watching eagerly, as he administered a strong injection.

The girl's narrow chest fluttered as the powerful drug took effect, and the pale lids dropped for a second over her repulsive eyes. Then, with a sob which was half moan, she attempted to raise herself on her elbow, fell back again, and, with apparent effort, gasped. 'The mirror, let me have the mirror! Oh, tell me it isn't true; tell me it was a trick of some sort. Oh, the horrible thing I saw in the glass couldn't have been I. Was it?'

'*Tiens, ma petite,*' de Grandin replied; 'but you speak in riddles. What is it you would know?'

'He – he,' the girl faltered weakly, forcing her trembling lips to frame the words – 'that horrible old man showed me a mirror a little while ago and said the face in it was mine. Oh, it was horrible, horrible!'

'Eh? What is this?' de Grandin demanded on a rising note. '"He"? "Horrible old man"? Are you not his daughter? Is he not your father?'

'No,' the girl gasped, so low her denial was scarcely audible. 'I was driving home from Mackettsdale last – oh, I forget when it was, but it was at night – and my tyres punctured. I – I think there must have been glass on the road, for the shoes were cut to ribbons. I saw the light in this house and came to ask for help. An old man – oh, I thought he was so nice and kind! – let me in and said he was all alone here and about to eat dinner, and asked me to join him. I ate some – some – oh, I don't

remember what it was – and the next thing I knew he was standing by
my bed, holding a mirror up to me and telling me it was my face I saw
in the glass. Oh, please, *please* tell me it was some terrible trick he played
on me. I'm not truly hideous, am I?'

'*Morbleu!*' de Grandin muttered softly, tugging at the ends of his
moustache. 'What is all this?'

To the girl he said: 'But of course not. You are like a flower,
mademoiselle. A little flower that dances in the wind. You——'

'And my eyes, they aren't – they aren't' – she interrupted with piteous
eagerness – 'please tell me they aren't——'

'*Mais non, ma chère,*' he assured her. 'Your eyes are like the *pervenche*
that mirrors the sky in springtime. They are——'

'Let – let me see the mirror, please,' she interrupted in an anxious
whisper. 'I'd like to see for myself, if you – oh, I feel all weak
inside——' She lapsed back against the pillow, her lids mercifully veiling
the hideously distorted eyes and restoring her face to tranquil
beauty.

'*Cordieu!*' de Grandin breathed. 'The chloral reasserted itself none too
soon for Jules de Grandin's comfort, Friend Trowbridge. Sooner would
I have gone to the rack than have shown that pitiful child her face in
a mirror.'

'But what's it all mean?' I asked. 'She says she came here, and——'

'And the rest remains for us to find out, I think,' he replied evenly.
'Come, we lose time, and to lose time is to be caught, my friend.'

De Grandin led the way down the hall, peering eagerly into each door
we passed in search of the owner's chamber, but before his quest was
satisfied he stopped abruptly at the head of the stairs. 'Observe, Friend
Trowbridge,' he ordered, pointing a carefully manicured forefinger to
a pair of buttons, one white, one black, set in the wall. 'Unless I am more
mistaken than I think I am, we have here the key to the situation – or
at least to the front door.'

He pushed vigorously at the white button, then ran to the curve of
the stairs to note the result.

Sure enough, the heavy door swung open on its hinges of cast bronze,
letting gusts of rain drive into the lower hall.

'*Pardieu,*' he ejaculated, 'we have here the open sesame; let us see if
we possess the closing secret as well! Press the black button, Trowbridge,
my friend, while I watch.'

I did his bidding, and a delighted exclamation told me the door had
closed.

'Now what?' I asked, joining him on the staircase.

'U'm' – he pulled first one end, then the other, of his diminutive
moustache meditatively – 'the house possesses its attractions, Friend
Trowbridge, but I believe it would be well if we went out to observe

what our friend, *le vieillard horrible*, does. I like not to have one who shows young girls their disfigured faces in mirrors near our conveyance.'

Slipping into our raincoats, we opened the door, taking care to place a wad of paper on the sill to prevent its closing tightly enough to latch, and scurried out into the storm.

As we left the shelter of the porch a shaft of indistinct light shone through the rain, as my car was swung from the highway and headed towards a depression to the left of the house.

'*Parbleu*, he is a thief, this one!' de Grandin exclaimed excitedly. '*Hola, monsieur!*' He ran forward swinging his arms like a pair of semaphores. 'What sort of business is it you make with our auto?'

The wailing of the storm tore the words from his lips and hurled them away, but the little Frenchman was not to be thwarted. '*Pardieu,*' he gasped, bending his head against the wind-driven rain, 'I will stop the scoundrel if – *nom d'un coq*, he has done it!'

Even as he spoke the old man flung open the car's forward door and leaped, allowing the machine to go crashing down a steep embankment into a lake of slimy swamp-mud.

For a moment the vandal stood contemplating his work, then burst into a peal of wild laughter more malignant than any profanity.

'*Parbleu*, robber! *Apache!* You shall laugh from the other side of your mouth!' de Grandin promised, as he made for the old man.

But the other seemed oblivious of our presence. Still chuckling at his work, he turned towards the house, stopped short as a sudden heavy gust of wind shook the trees along the roadway, then started forward with a yell of terror as a great branch, torn bodily from a towering oaktree, came crashing towards the earth.

He might as well have attempted to dodge a meteorite. Like an arrow from the bow of divine justice the great timber hurtled down, pinning his frail body to the ground like a worm beneath a labourer's brogan.

'Trowbridge, my friend,' de Grandin announced matter-of-factly, 'observe the evil effects of stealing motor cars.'

We lifted the heavy bough from the prostrate man and turned him over on his back. De Grandin on one side, I on the other, we made a hasty examination, arriving at the same finding simultaneously. His spinal column was snapped like a pipe stem.

'You have some last statement to make, monsieur?' de Grandin asked curtly. 'If so, you had best be about it, your time is short.'

'Y – yes,' the stricken man replied weakly. 'I – I meant to kill you, for you might have hit upon my secret. As it is, you may publish it to the world, that all may know what it meant to offend a Marston. In my room you will find the documents. My – my pets – are – in – the – cellar. She – was – to – have – been – one – of – them.' The pauses between his words became longer and longer, his voice grew weaker with each laboured syllable. As he whispered the last sentence painfully there was a gurgling sound, and a tiny stream of blood welled up at the corner of his mouth. His narrow chest rose and fell once with a convulsive movement, then his jaw dropped limply. He was dead.

'Oh-ho,' de Grandin remarked, 'it is a haemorrhage which finished him. A broken rib piercing his lung. U'm? I should have guessed it. Come, my friend, let us carry him to the house, then see what it was he meant by that talk of documents and pets. A pest upon the fellow for dying with his riddle half explained! Did he not know that Jules de Grandin cannot resist the challenge of a riddle? *Parbleu*, we will solve this mystery, *Monsieur le Mort*, if we have to hold an autopsy to do so!'

'Oh, for heaven's sake, hush, de Grandin!' I besought, shocked at his heartlessness. 'The man is dead.'

'Ah, bah!' he returned scornfully. 'Dead or not, did he not steal your motor car?'

We laid our gruesome burden on the hall couch and mounted the stairs to the second floor. With de Grandin in the lead we found the dead man's room and began a systematic search for the papers he had mentioned, almost with his last breath. After some time my companion unearthed a thick, leather-bound portfolio from the lower drawer of a beautiful old mahogany highboy, and spread its wide leaves open on the white-counterpaned bed.

'Ah' – he drew forth several papers and held them to the light – 'we begin to make the progress, Friend Trowbridge. What is this?'

He held out a newspaper-clipping cracked from long folding and yellowed with age. It read:

ACTRESS JILTS SURGEON'S CRIPPLED SON ON EVE OF WEDDING

Declaring she could not stand the sight of his deformity, and that she had engaged herself to him only in a moment of thoughtless pity, Dora Lee, well-known variety actress, last night repudiated her promise to marry John Biersfield Marston, Jr, hopelessly crippled son of Dr John Biersfield Marston, the well-known surgeon and expert osteologist. Neither the abandoned bridegroom nor his father could be seen by reporters from the *Planet* last night.

'Very good,' de Grandin nodded, 'we need go no farther with that account. A young woman, it would seem, once broke her promise to marry a cripple, and, judging from this paper's date, that was in 1896. Here is another; what do you make of it?'

The clipping he handed me read as follows:

SURGEON'S SON A SUICIDE

Still sitting in the wheel chair, from which he has not moved during his waking hours since he was hopelessly crippled while playing polo in England ten years ago, John Biersfield Marston, son of the famous surgeon of the same name, was found in his bedroom this morning by his valet. A rubber hose was connected with a gas jet, the other end being held in the young man's mouth.

Young Marston was jilted by Dora Lee, well-known vaudeville actress, on the day before the date set for their wedding, one month ago. He is reported to have been extremely low-spirited since his desertion by his fiancée.

Dr Marston, the bereaved father, when seen by reporters from the *Planet* this morning, declared the actress was responsible for his son's death, and announced his intention of holding her accountable. When asked if legal proceedings were contemplated, he declined further information.

'So?' de Grandin nodded shortly. 'Now this one, if you please.'

The third clipping was brief to the point of curtness:

WELL-KNOWN SURGEON RETIRES

Dr John Biersfield Marston, widely known throughout this section of the country as an expert in operations concerning the bones, has announced his intention of retiring from practice. His house has been sold, and he will move from the city.

'The record is clear so far,' de Grandin asserted, studying the first clipping with raised eyebrows, 'but – *morbleu*, my friend, look – look at this picture. This Dora Lee, of whom does she remind you? Eh?'

I took the clipping again and looked intently at the illustration of the article announcing young Marston's broken engagement. The woman in the picture was young and inclined to be overdressed in the voluminous, fluffy mode of the days before the Spanish–American War.

'U'm, no one whom I know——' I began, but halted abruptly as a sudden likeness struck me. Despite the towering pompadour arrangement of her blonde hair, and the unbecoming straw sailor hat above the coiffure, the woman in the picture bore a certain resemblance to the disfigured girl we had seen a half hour before.

The Frenchman saw recognition dawn in my face, and nodded agreement. 'But of course,' he said. 'Now, the question is, is this young girl whose eyes are so out of alignment a relative of this Dora Lee, or is the resemblance a coincidence, and, if so, what lies behind it? *Hein?*'

'I don't know,' I admitted, 'but there must be some connection——'

'Connection? Of course there is a connection,' de Grandin affirmed, rummaging deeper in the portfolio. 'A-a-ah! What is this *Nom d'un nom*, Friend Trowbridge, I think I smell the daylight! Look!'

He held a full-page story from one of the sensational New York dailies before him, his eyes glued to the flowing type and crude, coarse-screen half-tones of half a dozen young women which composed the article.

'WHAT HAS BECOME OF THE MISSING GIRLS?'

I read in bold-faced type across the top of the page.

'Are sinister, unseen hands reaching out from the darkness to seize our girls from palace and hovel, shop, stage, and office?' the article asked rhetorically. 'Where are Ellen Munro and Dorothy Sawyer and Phyllis Bouchet and three other lovely light-haired girls who have walked into oblivion during the past year?'

I read to the end the sensational account of the girls' disappearances. The cases seemed fairly similar; each of the vanished young women had failed to return to her home and had never been accounted for in any manner, and in no instance, according to the newspaper, had there been any assignable reason for voluntary departure.

'*Parbleu*, but he was stupid, even for a journalist!' de Grandin asserted as I completed my inspection of the story. 'Why, I wager even my good Friend Trowbridge has already noticed one important fact which this writer has treated as though it were as commonplace as the nose on his face.'

'Sorry to disappoint you, old chap,' I answered, 'but it looks to me as though the reporter had covered the case from every possible angle.'

'Ah? So?' he replied sarcastically. '*Morbleu*, we shall have to consult the oculist in your behalf when we return home, my friend. Look, look, I beseech you, upon the pictures of these so totally absent and un-accounted-for young women, *cher ami*, and tell me if you do not observe a certain likeness among them; not only a resemblance to each other, but to that Mademoiselle Lee who jilted the son of Dr Marston? Can you see it, now I have pointed it out?'

'No – wh – why, yes – yes of course!' I responded, running my eye over the pictures accompanying the story. 'By the Lord Harry, de Grandin, you're right; you might almost say there is a family resemblance between these girls! You've put your finger on it, I do believe.'

'*Hélas*, no!' he answered with a shrug. 'I have put my finger on nothing as yet, my friend. I reach, I grope, I feel about me like a blind man tormented by a crowd of naughty little boys, but nothing do the poor fingers of my mind encounter. Pah! Jules de Grandin, you are one great fool! Think, think, stupid one!'

He sat on the edge of the bed, cupping his face in his hands and leaning forward till his elbows rested on his knees.

Suddenly he sprang erect, one of his elfish smiles passing across his small, regular features. '*Nom d'un chat rouge*, my friend, I have it – I have it!' he announced. 'The pets – the pets that old stealer of motor cars spoke of! They are in the basement! *Pardieu*, we will see those pets, *cher* Trowbridge; with our four collective eyes we will see them. Did not that so execrable stealer declare she was to have been one of them? Now, in the name of Satan and brimstone, whom could he have meant by "she" if not that unfortunate child with eyes like *la grenouille*? Eh?'

'Why——' I began, but he waved me forward.

'Come, come; let us go,' he urged. 'I am impatient, I am restless, I am not to be restrained. We shall investigate and see for ourselves what sort of pets are kept by one who shows young girls their deformed faces in mirrors and – *parbleu!* – steals motor cars from my friends.'

Hurrying down the main staircase, we hunted about for the cellar entrance, finally located the door, and, holding above our heads a pair of candles from the hall, began descending a flight of rickety steps into a pitch-black basement, rock walled and, judging by its damp, mouldy odour, unfloored save by the bare, moist earth beneath the house.

'*Parbleu*, the dungeons of the château at Carcassonne are more cheerful than this,' de Grandin commented as he paused at the stairs' foot, holding his candle aloft to make a better inspection of the dismal place.

I suppressed a shudder of mingled chill and apprehension as I stared at the blank stone walls, unpierced by windows or other openings of any sort, and made ready to retrace my steps. 'Nothing here,' I announced. 'You can see that with half an eye. The place is as empty as——'

'Perhaps, Friend Trowbridge,' he agreed, 'but Jules de Grandin does not look with half an eye. He uses both eyes, and uses them more than once if his first glance does not prove sufficient. Behold that bit of wood on the earth yonder. What do you make of it?'

'U'm – a piece of flooring, maybe,' I hazarded.

'Maybe yes, maybe no,' he answered. 'Let us see.'

Crossing the cellar, he bent above the planks, then turned to me with a satisfied smile. 'Flooring does not ordinarily have ring bolts in it, my friend,' he remarked, bending to seize the iron ring which was made fast to the boards by a stout staple.

'Ha!' As he heaved upwards the planks came away from the black earth, disclosing a board-lined well about three feet square and of uncertain depth. An almost vertical ladder of two-by-four timbers led downward from the trapdoor to the well's impenetrable blackness.

'*Allons*, we descend,' he commented, turning about and setting his foot on the topmost rung of the ladder.

'Don't be a fool,' I advised. 'You don't know what's down there.'

'True' – his head was level with the floor as he answered – 'but I shall know, with luck, in a few moments. Do you come?'

I sighed with vexation as I prepared to follow him.

At the ladder's foot he paused, raising his candle and looking about inquiringly. Directly before us was a passageway through the earth, ceiled with heavy planks and shored up with timbers like the lateral workings of a primitive mine.

'Ah, the plot shows complications,' he murmured, stepping briskly into the dark tunnel. 'Do you come, Friend Trowbridge?'

I followed, wondering what manner of thing might be at the end of the black, musty passage, but nothing but fungus-grown timbers and walls of moist, black earth met my questing gaze.

De Grandin preceded me by some paces, and I suppose we had gone fifteen feet through the passage when a gasp of mingled surprise and horror from my companion brought me beside him in two long strides. Fastened with nails to the timbers at each side of the tunnel were a number of white, glistening objects – objects which, because of their very familiarity, denied their identity to my wondering eyes. There was no mistaking the things; even a layman could not have failed to recognize them for what they were. I, as a physician, knew them even better. To the right of the passage hung fourteen perfectly articulated skeletons of human legs, complete from foot to ilium, gleaming white and ghostly in the flickering light of the candles.

'Good heavens!' I exclaimed.

'*Sang du diable!*' Jules de Grandin commented. 'Behold what is there, my friend.' He pointed to the opposite wall. Fourteen bony arms, complete from hand to shoulder joint, hung pendulously from the tunnel's upright timbers.

'*Pardieu,*' de Grandin muttered, 'I have known men who collected stuffed birds and dried insects; I have known those who stored away Egyptian mummies – even the skulls of men long dead – but never before have I seen a collection of arms and legs! *Parbleu,* he was *caduo* – mad as a hatter, this one, or I am much mistaken!'

'So these were his pets,' I answered. 'Yes, the man was undoubtedly mad to keep such a collection, and in a place like this. Poor fellow——'

'*Nom d'un canon!*' de Grandin broke in; 'what was that?'

From the darkness before us there came a queer, inarticulate sound such as a man might make attempting to speak with a mouth half filled with food, and, as though the noise had wakened an echo slumbering in the cavern, the sound was repeated, multiplied again and again till it resembled the babbling of half a dozen overgrown infants – or an equal number of full-grown imbeciles.

'Onward!' Responding to the challenge of the unknown like a warrior obeying the trumpet's call to charge, de Grandin dashed towards the strange noise, swung about, flashing his candle this side and that, then:

'*Nom de Dieu de nom de Dieu!*' he almost shrieked. 'Look, Friend Trowbridge – look and say that you see what I see, or have I, too, gone mad?'

Lined up against the wall was a series of seven small wooden boxes, each with a door composed of upright slats before it, similar in construction to the coops in which country-folk pen brooding hens – and no larger. In each of the hutches huddled an object the like of which I had never before seen, even in the terrors of nightmare.

The things had the torsos of human beings, though hideously shrunken from starvation and incrusted with scales of filth, but there all resemblance to mankind ceased. From shoulders and waist there twisted flaccid tentacles of unsupported flesh, the upper ones terminating in flat, paddle-like flippers which had some remote resemblance to hands, the lower ones ending in almost shapeless stubs which resembled feet only in that each had a fringe of five shrivelled, unsupported protuberances of withered flesh.

On scrawny necks were balanced caricatures of faces, flat, noseless, chinless countenances with horrible crossed or divergent eyes, mouths widened almost beyond resemblance to buccal orifices, and – horror of horrors! – elongated, *split* tongues protruding several inches from the lips and wagging impotently in vain efforts to form words.

'Satan, thou art outdone!' de Grandin cried, as he held his candle before a scrap of paper decorating one of the cages after the manner of a sign before an animal's den at the Zoo. 'Observe!' he ordered, pointing a shaking finger at the notice.

I looked, then recoiled, sick with horror. The paper bore the picture and name of Ellen Munro, one of the girls mentioned as missing in the newspaper article we had found in the dead man's bedroom.

Beneath the photograph was scribbled in an irregular hand: 'Paid 12–5–97'.

Sick at heart, we walked down the line of pens. Each was labelled with the picture of a young and pretty girl with the notation, 'Paid', followed by a date. Every girl named as missing in the newspaper was represented in the cages.

Last of all, in a coop somewhat smaller than the rest, we found a body more terribly mutilated than any. This was marked with the photograph and name of Dora Lee. Beneath her name was the date of her 'payment', written in bold red figures.

'*Parbleu*, what are we to do, my friend?' de Grandin asked in an hysterical whisper. 'We cannot return these poor ones to the world; that would be the worst form of cruelty; yet – yet I shrink from the act of mercy I know they would ask me to perform if they could speak.'

'Let's go up,' I begged. 'We must think this thing over, de Grandin, and if I stay here any longer I shall faint.'

'*Bien*,' he agreed, and turned to follow me from the cavern of horrors.

'It is to consider,' he began as we reached the upper hall once more. 'If we give those so pitiful ones the stroke of mercy we are murderers before the law, yet what service could we render them by bringing them once more into the world? Our choice is a hard one, my friend.'

I nodded.

'*Morbleu*, but he was clever, that one,' the Frenchman continued, half to me, half to himself. 'What a surgeon! Fourteen instances of Wyeth's amputation of the hip and as many more of the shoulder – and every patient lived, lived to suffer the tortures of that hell-hole down there! But it is marvellous! None but a madman could have done it.

'Bethink you, Friend Trowbridge. Think how the mighty man of medicine brooded over the suicide of his crippled son, meditating hatred and vengeance for the heartless woman who had jilted him. Then – snap, went his great mentality, and from hating one woman he fell to hating all, to plotting vengeance against the many for the sin of the one. And, *cordieu*, what a vengeance! How he must have laid his plans to secure his victims; how he must have worked to prepare that hell-under-the-earth to house those poor, broken bodies which were his handiwork, and how he must have drawn upon the great surgical skill which was his, even in his madness, to transform those once lovely ones into the visions of horror we have just beheld! Horror of horrors! To remove the bones and let the girls still live!'

He rose, pacing impatiently across the hall. 'What to do? What to do?' he demanded, striking his open hands against his forehead.

I followed his nervous steps with my eyes, but my brain was too numbed by the hideous things I had just seen to be able to respond to his question.

I looked hopelessly past him at the angle of the wall by the great fireplace, rubbed my eyes, and looked again. Slowly, but surely, the wall was declining from the perpendicular.

'De Grandin,' I shouted, glad of some new phenomenon to command my thoughts, 'the wall – the wall's leaning!'

'Eh, the wall?' he queried. '*Pardieu*, yes! It is the rain; the foundations are undermined. Quick, quick, my friend! To the cellars, or those unfortunate ones are undone!'

We scrambled down the stairs leading to the basement, but already the earth floor was sopping with water. The well leading to the madman's sub-cellar was more than half full of bubbling, earthy ooze.

'Mary, have pity!' de Grandin exclaimed. 'Like rats in a trap, they did die. God rest their tired souls' – he shrugged his shoulders as he turned to retrace his steps – 'it is better so. Now, Friend Trowbridge, do you hasten aloft and bring down that young girl from the room above. We must run for it if we do not wish to be crushed under the falling timbers of this house of abominations!'

The storm had spent itself, and a red, springtime sun was peeping over the horizon as de Grandin and I trudged up my front steps with the mutilated girl stumbling wearily between us.

'Put her to bed, my excellent one,' de Grandin ordered Nora, my housekeeper, who came to meet us enveloped in righteous indignation and an outsize flannel nightgown. '*Parbleu*, she has had many troubles!'

In the study, a glass of steaming whisky and hot water in one hand, a vile-smelling French cigarette in the other, he faced me across the desk. 'How was it you knew not that house, my friend?' he demanded.

I grinned sheepishly. 'I took the wrong turning at the detour,' I explained, 'and got on the Yerbyshire Road. It's just recently been hard-surfaced, and I haven't used it for years because it was always impassable. Thinking we were on the Andover Pike all the while, I never connected the place with the old Olmsted Mansion I'd seen hundreds of times from the road.'

'Ah yes,' he agreed, nodding thoughtfully, 'a little turn from the right way, and – pouf – what a distance we have to retrace!'

'Now, about the girl upstairs . . .' I began; but he waved the question aside.

'The mad one had but begun his devil's work on her,' he replied. 'I, Jules de Grandin, will operate on her eyes and make them as straight as before, nor will I accept one penny for my work. Meantime, we must find her kindred and notify them she is safe and in good hands.

'And now' – he handed me his empty tumbler – 'a little more whisky, if you please, Friend Trowbridge.'

The Refugee

Jane Rice

The trouble with the war, Milli Cushman thought as she stared sulkily through streaming french windows into her rain-drenched garden, was that it was so frightfully boring. There weren't any men, any more. Interesting ones, that is. Or parties. Or little pink cocktails. Or café royale. Or long-stemmed roses wrapped in crackly green wax paper. There wasn't even a decent hairdresser left.

She had been a fool to stay on. But it had seemed so exciting. Everyone was listening to the radio broadcasts; the streets blossoming with uniforms; an air of feverish gaiety, heady as Moselle wine, over all the city; the conversations that made one feel so important – so in the thick of things. Would the Maginot Line hold? Would the British come? Would the Low Countries be invaded? Was it true that America had issued an ultimatum? Subjects that, now, were outdated as Gatling guns.

It had been terrifically stimulating being asked for her opinion, as an American. Of course, she hadn't been home for a number of years and considered herself a true cosmopolite freed from the provincialities of her own country – but, still, it had been nice, in those first flurried jack-in-the-box days of the war to be able to discourse so intelligently on Americana. It had been such *fun*.

Momentarily, Milli's eyes sparkled – remembering. The sparkle faded and died.

Then, unexpectedly, the city had become a gaunt, grey ghost. No, not a ghost, a cat. A gaunt grey cat with its bones showing through, as it crouched on silent haunches and stared unwinkingly before it. Like one of those cats that hung around the alley barrels of the better hotels. Or used to hang. Cooked, a cat bore a striking resemblance to a rabbit.

Overnight, a hush had fallen on everything. It was as though the city had gasped in one long, last, laboured, dying breath. And had held it. One could feel it in the atmosphere. Almost like a desperate pounding.

For some inexplicable reason, it reminded her of her childhood when she had played a game as the street lights began to bloom in the gathering dusk. 'If I can hold my eyes opening without blinking,' she would tell herself, 'until the last one is lighted, I'll get a new doll' – or a new muff – or a new hair ribbon – or whatever it might be she wanted. She could still recall that exhausted sense of time running out as the final lights went on. Most always she had won. Sometimes she hadn't, but most always she had. By the skin of her teeth.

It would be perfectly horrid, if this was one of the times when she *didn't* win. If she had to stay on and on, trotting back and forth seeing about that idiotic visa, and saving her hairpins and soap ends and things, it was going to be too utterly stultifying. It was fortunate she had had the perception to realize, before it was too late, who were the 'right people' to know. It helped. Although, in these days, the right people didn't fare much better than the 'wrong' ones.

Milli used 'fare' in its strictest interpretation. Often, of late, she found herself dwelling, with an aching nostalgia, on her father's butcher shop in Pittsburgh. That had been before he'd invented a new de-boner, or meat cleaver, or something, and had amassed an unbelievable amount of money and before he strangled to death on a loose gold filling at Tim O'Toole's clambake.

Milli's recollection of her father was but a dim blur of red face and handle-bar moustaches and a deep booming voice that Milli had associated with the line 'the curfew tolls the knell of parting day', which she had been forced to learn and recite at P.S. 46. Her mother she didn't remember at all, as she had been called to pastures greener than anything Pittsburgh had to offer while Milli was yet wearing swaddling clothes in a perpetual state of dampness.

However, sharpened by adversity, Milli's recollections of the butcher shop were crystal clear. The refrigerator with whole sides of beef hanging from hooks, legs of lamb like fat tallow candles, plump chickens with thick drumsticks and their heads wrapped in brown paper, slabs of pork and veal, and, at Thanksgiving and Christmas, short-legged ducks, and high-breasted turkeys, and big, yellow geese. In the showcase had been chops, and steaks, and huge roasts, and all sorts of sausages and spiced meats laid out in white enamelled trays with carrot tops in between for 'dressing'.

It was hopeless to dream of these things, but practically impossible to stop. The main topics of conversation no longer were of 'major developments' but of where one could buy an extra ration of tea of questionable ingredients, or a gristly chop of dubious origin, or a few eggs of doubtful age – if one could pay the whopping price.

Well, as long as she had liqueur-filled chocolates, and she had had enough foresight to lay in quite a supply, she could be assured of her 'share'. They were better than money, at the present exchange.

The clock on the mantelpiece tinkled out the hours and Milli sighed. She should bathe and dress for dinner. But what was the use of keeping up appearances when there wasn't anyone to see. And it was dreadful curling the ends of one's hair on an iron. It was tedious and it didn't really *do* a great deal for one. And it had an unmistakable scent of burning shoe leather about it. The water would be tepid, if not actually cold. The soap wouldn't lather. The bathroom would be clammy, and the dinner, when it was forthcoming, would be a ragoût of God knew what, a potato that had gouged-out areas in it, a limp salad, and a compote of dried fruit. And Maria grumbled so about serving it in courses. It was positively useless to diagram for her the jumbled-up indecencies of a table d'hôte. Maria was almost worse than no help at all. Definitely a bourgeois.

Milli yawned and stretched her arms above her head. She arose and, going over to the windows, stood looking out. A shaft of sunlight broke through the clouds and angered the tiny charms that dangled from her 'war bracelet'. An aeroplane studded with rhinestones, a miniature cannon with gold-leaf wheels, a toy soldier whose diamond chip eyes winked red and blue and green in the sun as he twirled helplessly on his silver chain. Ten or twelve of these baubles hung from the bracelet and it is indicative of Milli's character that she had bought them as a gift to herself to 'celebrate' the last Bastille Day.

The sun's watery radiance turned the slackening rain into shining strings of quicksilver and made a drowned seascape of the garden. The faun that once had been a fountain, gleamed wetly in the pale, unearthly light and about its feet, in the cracked basin, the pelting raindrops danced and bubbled like antiphonic memories of long-gone grace notes. The flower heads were heavy with sodden, brown-edged petals and their stalks bent wearily as if cognizant of the fact that their lives were held by a tenuous thread that was about to be snapped between the chill, biting teeth of an early frost.

Milli looked at the rain intermingled with sun and thought, The devil is beating his wife. That was what Savannah used to say, back in Pittsburgh. 'The devil's beatin' his wife, sho nuff.' Savannah, who made such luscious mince pies and cherry tarts, and whose baked hams were always brown and crunchy on top and stuck with cloves and criss-crossed with a knife so that the juice ran down in between the cracks and – Milli's culinary recollections suffered a complete collapse and her eyes opened very wide as they alighted on a head poking out inquisitively from the leafy seclusion of the tall hedge that bounded the garden.

Two brown hands pushed aside the foliage to allow a pair of broad, brown shoulders to come through.

Milli gave an infinitesimal gasp. A man was in her garden! A man

who, judging from the visible portion of his excellent anatomy, had –
literally – lost his shirt.

Instinctively, she opened her mouth to make some sort of an outcry.
Whether she meant to call for aid, or to scare the interloper away, or
merely to give vent to a belated exclamation of surprise, will forever be
debatable, for the object of her scrutiny chose that moment to turn his
extraordinarily well-shaped head and his glance fixed itself on Milli.
Milli's outcry died a-borning.

To begin with, it wasn't a man. It was a youth. And to end with, there
was something about him, some queer, indefinable quality, that was
absolutely fascinating.

He was, Milli thought, rather like a young panther, or a half-
awakened leopard. He was, Milli admitted, entranced, beautiful.
Perfectly *beautiful*, as an animal is beautiful, and, automatically, she
raised her chin so that the almost unnoticeable pouch under it became
one with the line of her throat.

The youth was unabashed. If the discovery of his presence in a private
garden left him in a difficult position, he effectively concealed his
embarrassment. He regarded Milli steadfastly, and unwaveringly, and
admiringly, and Milli, like a mesmerised bird, watched the rippling play
of his muscles beneath his skin as he shoved the hedge apart still farther
to obtain a better view of his erstwhile hostess.

Confusedly, Milli thought that it was lucky that the windows were
locked and, in the same mental breath, what a pity that they were.

The two peered at one another. Milli knew only that his hair was
pasted flat to his head with the rain, and that his arms shone like sepia
satin, and his eyes were tawny and filled with a flickering inward fire
that made suet pudding of her knees.

For a long moment they remained so – their eyes locked. Milli's like
those of an amazed china doll's; his like those of an untamed animal that
was slightly underfed and resented the resulting gastric disturbances. The
kitchen door banged and Milli could hear Maria calling a neighbourly
greeting to someone, as she emptied a bucket of water in the yard. At that
instant the last vestiges of sun began to sink behind the horizon, and the
youth was gone. There was just the garden, and the rain, and the hedge.

Dimly, as through a fog, Milli heard Maria come in, heard the latch
shoot home, the metallic clatter of the bucket as she set it down under
the sink and, from somewhere outside, the long, diminishing, mournful
howl of a dog.

Milli shook herself out of her trance. She brushed a hand across her
eyelids as if to clear them of cobwebs and, unbolting one of the windows,
went out into the garden. There was no one. Only a footprint by the
hedge, a bare footprint filling in with water.

She went back into the house. Maria was there, turning on the lamps. She looked at Milli curiously and Milli realized that she must be an odd sight, indeed, her hair liberally besprinkled with raindrops, her shoes muddy, her dress streaked with moisture.

'I thought I saw someone out there, just now,' she explained. 'Someone looking in.'

'The police, probably,' Maria said dourly. 'The police have no notion of privacy.'

'No,' Milli said. 'No, it wasn't the police. Didn't I hear you go out a few moments ago?'

'I wasn't looking in,' Maria said in a peevish voice. 'For why should I look in? I have other things to do besides looking in the windows.' She drew herself up to list vocally and with accompanying gestures the numberless things she had to do.

'Did you see anyone?' Milli asked quickly.

'Old Phillipe,' Maria answered. 'I saw old Phillipe. On his way to the inn in the pouring rain and he with a cough since last April. When one has a cough and it is raining, one does not look in windows. Anyway, Phillipe is too old. When one is as old as Phillipe one is no longer interested. Anyhow, his son was killed at Avignon. Phillipe would not look in the windows.'

'You saw no one else?'

Maria's eyes narrowed. 'Madame was expecting someone, no?'

'No,' Milli said. 'No, I just thought ... it was nothing.'

'If madame is expecting someone, perhaps it would be well to save the beverage for later in the evening?'

'I am expecting no one.'

It was, Milli thought as she let the curling iron rest in the gaseous flame, next to impossible to tell which side of the fence Maria was on. She could easily be reporting things to *both* sides. One had to be careful. So very careful.

This chap in the garden, for example. He must have escaped from somewhere. That would account for the absence of clothes. He was a refugee of some sort. And refugees of any sort were dangerous. It was best to stick to the beaten path and those who trod thereon. But he was so beautiful. Like a stripling god. No more than twenty, surely. It was delightful to see again someone as young as twenty. It was – Milli swore fluently as the iron began to smoke; she waved it in the air to cool it and, testing it gingerly with a moistened forefinger, applied it to her coiffure – it was not only delightful, it was heavenly. It was, really, rather like one of those little, long ago, pink cocktails. It *did* something for one.

A faint aroma of singeing hair made itself manifest in the damp, wall-papery-smelling room.

Milli considered the refugee from every angle as she ate her solitary dinner and, afterward, as she reclined on her chaise-longue idly turning the pages of a book selected at random, and while she was disrobing for bed, and even when she was giving the underpart of her chin the regulation number of backhanded slaps, a ritual that as a rule occupied her entire attention.

Slipping into her dressing-gown, she opened her window and leaned out, chin in hands, elbows on the sill. The moon rode in the sky – a hunted thing dodging behind wisps of tattered cloud, and the air was heavy and wet and redolent of dying leaves.

'The moon was a ghostly galleon,' Milli quoted, feeling somehow frail and immensely poetic. She smiled a sad, fragile smile in keeping with her mood and wondered if the refugee also was having a lonely rendez-vous with the moon. Lying on his back in some hidden spot thinking, possibly, of—— Her reverie was broken sharply by Maria's voice, shattering the stillness of the night. It was followed by a cascade of water.

'What on earth are you *doing*!' Milli called down exasperatedly.

'There was an animal out here,' Maria yelled back, equally as exasperated. 'Trampling in my mulch pile.'

Milli started to say, 'Don't be ridiculous, go to bed,' but the sentence froze on her lips as she remembered the refugee. He had come back! Maria had thrown water on him! He had returned full of . . . of – well, hope for refuge, maybe, and Maria, the dolt, had chased him away!

'Wait,' she called frenziedly into the darkness. 'Wait! Oh, please, wait!'

Maria, thinking the command was for her, had waited, although the 'please' had astonished her somewhat. Muttering under her breath, she had led her strangely overwrought mistress into the kitchen garden and had pointed out with pardonable pride the footprints in her mulch pile. Padded footprints. With claws.

'I saw the eyes,' she said, 'great, gleaming, yellow ones shining in the light when I started to pull the scullery blinds. Luckily I had a pot of water handy and I jerked open the door and——'

But her mistress wasn't listening. In truth, for one originally so upset, she had regained her composure with remarkable rapidity.

'Undoubtedly, the Trudeaus' dog,' she said with a total lack of interest.

'The Trudeaus' dog is a Pomeranian,' Maria said determinedly.

'No matter,' Milli said. 'Go to bed, Maria.'

Maria went, mumbling to herself a querulous litany in which the word Pomeranian was, ever and anon, distinguishable – and pro-nounced with expletive force.

Milli awakened to find her room bright with sun, which was regrett-able as it drew attention to the pattern of the rug and the well-worn condition of the curtains. It, likewise, did various things to Milli

Cushman's face, which were little short of libellous. Libellous, that is, after Milli had painted herself a new one with painstaking care and the touch of an inspired, if jaded, master.

Downstairs, she found her breakfast ready and, because of its readiness, a trifle cold. She also found Maria, while not openly weeping, puffy as to eyes, and pink as to nose, and quite snuffly – a state that Milli found deplorable in servants.

A series of sharp questions brought to light the fact that old Phillipe was dead. Old Phillipe, it seemed, was not only dead but a bit mangled. To make a long story short, old Phillipe had been discovered in a condition that bordered on the skeletal. Identification had been made through particles of clothing and a pair of broken spectacles.

'You mean to say he was *eaten*!' Milli cried, which caused Maria to go off into a paroxysm of near hysterics from which Milli gathered, obscurely, that Maria blamed herself for old Phillipe's untimely demise.

By degrees, Milli drew it out of her. The footprints in the mulch pile. The kettle of water. The withdrawal of the animal to more congenial surroundings. Surroundings, doubtless, that were adjacent to the inn from whence old Phillipe, subsequently, plodded homeward. The stealthy pad of marauding feet. The encounter. The shriek. The awful ensuing silence.

Maria's detail was so graphic that it made Milli slightly ill, although it didn't prevent her from being firm about the matter of the wolf.

'Nonsense,' Milli said. 'Ridiculous. A *wolf*. Preposterous.'

Maria explained about the bloody footprints leading away from the scene of slaughter. Footprints much too large for a dog. *Enormous* footprints.

'No doubt it was an enormous dog,' Milli said coldly. 'The natural habitat of a wolf is a forest, not a paved street.'

Maria opened her mouth to go even further into detail, but Milli effectively shut it for her by a reprimand that, like the porridge of the smallest of the three bears, was neither too hot nor too cold, but just right.

After all, Milli thought, old Phillipe was better off. In all probability, he hadn't suffered a great deal. Most likely he had died of shock first. One more, one less, what difference did it make. Especially when one was as old as Phillipe. At least he had lived his life while *she*, with so much life yet to be lived, was embalmed in a wretched sort of flypaper existence that adhered to every inch of her no matter how hard she pulled. That visa. She would have to see about it again tomorrow. And the tea supply was disastrously low. And this horrible toast made of horrible bread that was crumbly and dry and tasted of sawdust. And her last bottle of eau de cologne practically *gone*, and she *couldn't* eat this mess in front of her.

Milli got up and went into the parlour. She flung wide the french windows and petulantly surveyed the garden. She had rented the place *because* of the garden – such a lovely setting for informal teas, she had thought, and impromptu chafing-dish suppers on the flagstones with candlelight and thin, graceful-stemmed glasses. She had pictured herself in appropriate attire, cutting flowers and doing whatever it was one did with peat moss and now look at the thing. Just *look* at it!

Milli looked at it. Her breath went out of her. She drew it in again with an unbecoming wheeze. One hand flew to her throat.

In the garden, fast asleep, curled up in a ball under the hedge, was the refugee, all dappled with shadows and naked as the day he was born.

This time, it must be noted in all fairness, Milli didn't open her chops. If an outcry was in her, it wasn't strong enough to register on her reflexes. Her eyes blinked rapidly, as they always did when Milli was thinking fast and, when she recrossed the parlour and walked down the hallway into the kitchen her heels made hard staccato sounds on the flooring, as they always did when Milli had reached a decision.

Milli's decision made Maria as happy as could be, under the circumstances, and ten minutes later, reticule in hand, Maria departed for the domicile of her married niece's husband's aunt who was a friend of old Phillipe's widow and, consequently, would be in possession of all the particulars and would more than appreciate a helping hand and an attentive ear over the weekend.

Milli turned the key behind her. Lightly, she ran to the scullery closet and took down from a nail a pair of grass-stained pants that had belonged to a gardener who had been liquidated before he had had a chance to return for his garment. Carrying the trousers over her arm, she retraced her steps to the parlour and through the double french windows.

Quiet as she was, her unbidden guest was awake as soon as her foot touched the first flagstone. He didn't move a muscle. He just opened his eyes and watched her with the easy assurance of one who knows he can leave whenever he wants to and several jumps ahead of the nearest competitor.

Milli stopped. She held out the pants.

'For you,' she said. She gave them a toss. The boy, his queer, light eyes watching her every movement, made no attempt to catch them.

'Put them on,' Milli said. She hesitated. 'Please,' she said, adding, 'I am your friend.'

The boy sat up. Milli hastily turned her back.

'Tell me when you get them on,' she ordered.

She waited, and waited, and waited, and, hearing not the faintest rustle, cautiously swivelled her head around. Once again she drew in her breath and the wheeze was very nearly an eek for, not six inches away, was her visitor – his lips pulled over his teeth in a rather disconcerting smile, his eyes like glittering nuggets of amber.

The thought raced through Milli's head that he was going to 'spring' at her, as the boy's eyes enumerated her charms one by one. She promptly elevated her chin and tried to keep her consternation from becoming obvious.

The boy laughed softly. A laugh that, somehow, was like a musical sort of a snarl. He stepped back. He bowed. Mockingly.

'What are you doing in my garden?' Milli asked, thinking it best to put him in his place, first and foremost. It wouldn't do to let him get out of hand. So soon, anyway.

'Sleeping,' the boy said.

'Don't you have any place to sleep?'

'Yes. Many places. But I like this place.'

'What happened to your clothes?'

The boy shrugged. He didn't answer.

'Are you a refugee?'

'In a way, I suppose, yes.'

'You're hiding, aren't you?'

'Until you came out, I was simply sleeping. After I have eaten I sleep until a short while before sundown.'

'You're not hungry?' Milli elevated her eyebrows in surprise.

'Not now.' The boy let his glance rove fleetingly over his hostess's neck. 'I will be later.'

'What do you mean "until a short while before sundown"? Have you been travelling by night?'

'Yes.'

Milli made an ineffectual motion towards the trousers. 'Wasn't it ... I mean, going around without any ... that is, I should think—— Weren't you cold?'

'No.'

'It's a wonder you didn't catch pneumonia.'

The boy grinned. He patted his flat stomach. 'Not pneumonia,' he said. 'But it wasn't much better. Old and stringy and without flavour.'

Milli regarded him with a puzzled frown. She didn't like being 'taken in'. She decided to let it go.

'My name is Milli Cushman,' she said. 'You are more than welcome to stay here until you are rested. You won't be bothered. I have sent my maid away.'

'You're most kind,' the boy said with exaggerated politeness. 'Until tonight will be sufficient.' If he realized that Milli was expecting him to introduce himself, he gave no sign.

After a pause, she spoke, a shade irritably. 'No doubt, you *do* have a name?'

'I have lots of names. Even Latin ones.'

'Well, what is one? I can't just go about calling you "you", you know.'

'You might call me Lupus,' the boy said. 'It's one of the Latin ones. It means wolf.'

'Do they call you The Wolf?'

'Yes.'

'How intriguing. But why?'

The boy smiled at her. 'I daresay you'll find out,' he said.

'You mean you're one of the ones who ... well, like the affair of that German officer last week ... that is to say, in a manner of speaking, you're one of those who're *still* going at it hammer and tongs?'

'Tooth and nail,' the boy said.

'It seems so *silly*,' Milli said. 'What *good* does it do? It doesn't scare them. It just makes them angrier. And that makes it harder on *us*.'

'Oh, but it *does* scare them,' the boy said with an ironic lilt to his voice. 'It scares them to death. Or at any rate it helps.' He yawned, his tongue curling out like a cat's. And suddenly, he was sullen. He glared at Milli with remote hostility.

'I'm sleepy,' he growled. 'I'm tired of talking. I want to go to sleep. Go away.'

'Come inside,' Milli said. 'You can have Maria's bed.' She gave him her most delectable glance. The one that involved the upsweeping and downsweeping of her eyelashes with the slimmest trace of a roguish quirk about the lips.

'I won't disturb you,' she said. 'And, besides, you might be caught if you stay in the garden. There was a man killed last night by some kind of creature, or so they say, and Maria is sure to spread the news abroad that she threw water at something, and police just *might* investigate, and it *could* be very awkward for us both. Won't you come in, please?'

The boy looked at her in surly silence.

'Please, Lupus. For me?'

Once more he laughed softly. And this time the laugh was definitely a snarl. He reached out and pinched her. 'For you, I will.'

It was, Milli thought, not at all a flirtatious pinch. It was the kind of pinch her father used to give chickens to see if they were filled out in the proper places.

But Lupus wouldn't sleep in Maria's bed. He curled up on the floor of the parlour. Which, Milli thought, was just as well. It would save remaking Maria's bed so Maria wouldn't notice anything.

While her caller slept, Milli busied herself with pots and pans in the kitchen. It was tedious, but worth it. Tonight, there would be supper on the flagstones, with candles, and starlight, and all the accessories. A chance like this might not come her way for many another moon. She was resolved to make the most of it. As Savannah would have said, she was going to 'do herself proud'. For Lupus, the best was none too good. She nibbled a sandwich for luncheon, not wanting to spoil her appetite – not waking Lupus, for fear of spoiling his.

She got out her precious hoard of condiments. She scanned the fine printed directions on boxes. Meticulously she read the instructive leaflet enclosed in her paper bag of tanbarky-appearing flour. She took off her bracelet, rolled up her sleeves, and went to work – humming happily to herself, a thing which she hadn't done for months.

She scraped, peeled, measured, sifted, chopped, stirred, beat and folded. Some fairly creditable muffins emerged from under her unaccustomed and amateurish fingers, a dessert that wasn't bad at all, and a salad that managed to give the impression of actually *being* a salad, which bordered on the miraculous.

The day slowly drew to a close and Milli was quite startled to find the hours had passed with such swiftness. So swiftly, that her initial awareness of their passing was caused by the advent of a patently ill-humoured Lupus.

'Oh, dear,' Milli said, 'I didn't realize ... is it late?'

'No,' Lupus said. 'It's growing early. The sun is going down.'

'Are you hungry? I'm fixing some things I think will be rather good.'

'I'm ravenous,' Lupus said. 'Let's go watch the sunset.'

Milli put her hands up to her coiffure, coquettishly, allowing her sleeves to fall away from her round, white arms.

'Wait till I fix my hair. I must be a sight.'

'You are,' Lupus agreed, his eyes glistening. 'And I won't have to wait much longer.' Effortlessly he moved across and stood over Milli, devouring her with an all-encompassing gaze.

'Won't you have one of these?' Milli asked hurriedly, hoping his impetuosity wouldn't brim over *too* abruptly. She shoved a box of liqueur-filled chocolates at him. 'There's no such thing as a cocktail any more. Come along, we'll eat them on the sofa. It's ... it's cosier.'

But Lupus wasn't interested in the chocolates. In the parlour he stretched his long, supple length on the floor and contemplated the garden, ablaze in the last rays of a dying sun.

Milli plopped down beside him and began to rub his back, gently with long, smooth, even strokes. Lupus rolled his head over in a lazy, indifferent pleasure, and looked up at her with a hunger that would have been voluptuous, if it hadn't been so stark.

'Do you like that?' Milli whispered.

For a reply, Lupus opened his mouth and yawned. And into it Milli dropped a chocolate, while at the same instant she jabbed him savagely with a hairpin.

The boy sucked in his breath with a pained howl, and a full eight minutes before the sun went down, Lupus had neatly choked to death on a chocolate whose liqueur-filled insides contained a silver bullet from Milli Cushman's 'war bracelet'.

It had been, Milli told herself later, a near thing. And it would have been *ghastly* if it hadn't worked. But it *had* worked, tra la. Of course, it stood to reason that it *would*. After all, if, at death, a werewolf changed back into human form, why, logically, the human form would – if in close personal contact with a silver bullet *before* sundown – metamorphose into a wolf.

It was marvellous that she'd happened to pick up *The Werewolf of Paris* yesterday – had given her an insight, so to speak, and it was *extremely* handy that she'd had all that butcher shop background.

Milli wiped her mouth daintily with a napkin. How divinely *full* she was. And with Maria gone she could have Lupus all to herself.

Down to the last, delicious morsel.

Back from the Grave

Robert Silverberg

Massey woke slowly, as if the return to awareness were almost painful to him. He had the ghastly sensation of being closed in. The air around him was warm and moist and faintly foul-tasting as it passed into his lungs, and everything was dark.

He yawned, tried to stretch. Probably the windows were closed in the bedroom, that was all. That was why everything seemed so muggy in here. All he had to do was to call his wife, have her get the maid or someone else to draw back the curtains and let some fresh air into the room ...

'Louise! Louise!'

His voice sounded oddly muffled, flat and indistinct in his own ears. It seemed to bounce back at him from the walls and ceiling of his bedroom.

'Louise? I'm calling you!'

Massey suddenly became conscious of the noxious humidity all about him. *Very well*, he thought, *if there's no one else here I'll have to open the windows myself!* He levered himself up on his elbows, tried to swing himself out of bed.

He realized that he was not in bed at all.

A pallid quiver of fear lanced through him as he discovered he did not have room to rise to a sitting position. Above him, only inches above his head, he felt the smooth sheen of satin. There was satin all about. He reached to his left in the darkness and felt satin again, barely an inch from his shoulder. It was the same to his right.

Moment after moment, the air was growing murkier and harder to breathe. And he did not have room to move. He seemed to be in a container just about the length and width of his own body.

There is only one purpose for a container of such dimensions.

Massey felt the clammy hand of panic brush his cheeks. *My God*, he thought. *They've made a mistake! They thought I was dead and they buried me!*

I'm not dead! I'm – I'm – buried alive!

Massey lay quite still for several moments after the terrible truth had become apparent. He did not want to panic. He was a reasonable man; he knew that to panic now would mean certain death. He had to be calm. Think this thing out. Don't panic.

The first fact to consider was that he was in a coffin. Coffins are not built with much air-space. Massey was a heavy-set man, and that meant not only that he needed a lot of air but that there could be little air in the coffin to begin with. And that air was rapidly being exhausted. He began taking shallower and less frequent breaths.

Perhaps they had not buried him yet. Maybe he was still lying in state in a funeral parlour somewhere. They had lowered the coffin lid already, but there was still the chance they had not yet placed him in the grave. In that case——

He summoned up his energy and released it in one mighty cry for help. He waited.

Nothing happened.

Massey realized that such shouting was wasteful of oxygen. Probably they could not hear him through the heavy lid of the coffin. Or – he quivered at the possibility – perhaps they had lowered him into the ground already, said the proper words over him, shovelled the soil back into the cavity.

That would mean that five feet of packed-down earth lay above his head. Not even a superman could raise a coffin lid with that kind of weight pressing down. Lying there in the darkness, Massey tried to force himself not to think of that possibility. Despite himself, the vision came – of himself, two yards beneath the ground, wasting his last strength in a desperate and ultimately futile attempt to raise a coffin lid held down by hundreds of pounds of soil. Pushing and pushing, while the moist air around him gradually gave up its life-saving oxygen and became unfit to breathe, until finally he clutched at his purpling throat in agony, unable even to double up because of the dimensions of the coffin.

No, he thought. *I won't think of it!*

The only situation he would allow his numbed mind to consider was a more hopeful one, that he was still above the surface of the ground. Otherwise there would be no hope, and he might as well lie back and die.

But . . .

How could such a thing happen to me?

He had heard cases of premature burial before. Most of them were apocryphal, of course – tales out of Poe, placed in real life by glib-tongued liars. But this was no lie, nor was it a story by Poe. Here he was: James Ronald Massey, forty-four years old, assets better than five

hundred thousand dollars, holding responsible positions in no less than
seven important corporations – here he was, lying in a coffin hardly
bigger than his own body, while his life flickered like a dying candle.

It was like a dream – a nightmare. But it was real.

Massey allowed himself the luxury of a deep breath and raised his
arms until his hands pressed against the satin-lined lid of the coffin.
Tensing his body, he pushed upwards until his wrists ached. Nothing
happened; not even the smallest upwards motion of the coffin lid was
apparent.

He let his hands drop.

Droplets of sweat broke out all over his body. His clothes itched; he
was wearing, not one of his own costly suits, but some cheap outfit
supplied by the undertaker, and the coarse fabric felt rough and unfamiliar against his skin.

He wondered how much more time he had, before the air would be
totally vitiated. Ten minutes? An hour? A day, perhaps?

He wondered how he could possibly have been buried alive at all.

As he lay there, gathering his strength for another attempt to raise the
lid, his thoughts drifted back – back over an entire lifetime, really, but
centering on only the last three years, the years of his marriage to
Louise. Massey had been past forty when he married her; she had been
only twenty-three.

He had never had time to marry when he was young. He was always
too busy, involved in complex corporate schemes, pyramiding his
investments, building up his money to provide himself with a luxurious
middle age. Despite himself he smiled ironically, lying in the coffin, as
he recalled his frantic planning, the long hours of pacing the floor at
night to devise yet another investment plan.

For what? Here at the age of forty-four he lay trapped alive in his
coffin – with his life ticking away with every beat of his heart. Unless
he freed himself through a miracle, there would be no old age for him.

And he would not have Louise any more.

The thoughts of Louise made the fear return. He had met her at a
summer resort, one of his rare vacations; she was with her parents, and
they had danced a few times, and before the two weeks were over Massey
had astonished himself by proposing marriage to her. She had astonished him even more by accepting.

They had been married a month later. It was a small ceremony
though he did send announcements to all of his business associates, and
they honeymooned for a month in South America. Massey could not
spare more than a month away from his desk. Louise didn't seem to
object to his devotion to his work, especially when he explained his
financial status to her and their children after he was gone.

Those early married months had been the happiest of his life, Massey thought. To watch Louise moving around the big mansion was a delight; she seemed to bring a glowing radiance wherever she went.

I have to get out of here! The thought took on new urgency as he pictured Louise in his mind, tall, slim, so graceful she seemed to float instead of to walk, with her hair a golden halo round her head. So lovely, so warm, so loving.

Massey's breath came in panicky harsh gasps now, even though he fought for control over his rebellious lungs. There still was plenty of time, he told himself. Just get in the right position and lift. How much can a coffin-lid weigh, anyway?

Plenty, came the answer, *if there's a ton of dirt holding it down.*

'No! It isn't so!' Massey shouted, and the booming sound ricocheted mockingly from the walls of his coffin. 'I'm not underground yet! I can still get out!'

He squirmed around on one hip after a good deal of wriggling, and put his shoulder to the coffin lid. He took a deep breath.

Now – lift!

He pushed upward, anchoring himself with his left hand and pressing up with his right shoulder, until it seemed that his left arm would buckle under the strain. Bands of pain coursed through his body, across his chest, down his back.

The lid would not budge.

Massey's calmness began to desert him. The air was so close it stank now, stank with musty graveyard odours and with his own perspiration and with the killing dankness of the carbon dioxide that was rapidly replacing its oxygen. He began to laugh hysterically, suddenly, without warning. He threw his head back and laughed, not seeming to care that by so laughing he was consuming more of his precious remnant of breathable air.

It was all so funny! He remembered his last day of consciousness. Remembered Louise – in Henry Marshall's arms!

Henry Marshall had arrived on the scene in the first year of Massey's marriage to Louise. She had told Massey, one night, in that casual way of hers, 'I'm having a guest for dinner.'

'Oh? Anyone I know?'

'A boy named Henry Marshall. An old playmate of mine; I haven't seen him for years.'

Massey had smiled indulgently. Above all else, he wanted Louise to be happy, and never to fear that because she had married a husband nearly twice her age she was condemned to a life of solemn loneliness.

Henry Marshall arrived at the dot of six that night. He was a boy of about twenty-five, tall and handsome, with wavy blond hair and an easy, likeable manner about him. Something in his very charm made

Massey dislike him almost on sight, He was too casual, took things too much for granted. Massey noticed that Henry Marshall was dressed rather shabbily, too.

It was not a pleasant evening. Louise and Henry Marshall reminisced together, chuckled over old times that meant nothing to Massey, told stories of friends long since unseen. Henry Marshall stayed late, past eleven, and when he finally left and Massey held Louise tightly in the quiet of her bedroom he sensed a certain remoteness about her that he had never felt before. It was as if she were making love mechanically, not really caring.

Massey brooded about that in the days that followed, though he never spoke a word to Louise. And Henry Marshall became a frequent visitor at the Massey's, coming sometimes for dinner, occasionally remaining as a house guest for two or three days. Massey resented the younger man's presence, but, as always, he remained silent out of deference to his wife's happiness.

He had almost come to accept Marshall's regular visits, even though they were occurring more frequently now, twice a month where they had been only once a month. But, thought Massey as he lay in the clammy darkness of the coffin where he had been interred alive, this final visit – only a few days ago, was it, or had years gone by? – this final visit had been too much.

Young Marshall had arrived on Friday night in time for dinner, as usual. By now he was well known among the servants, and they gave him his usual room in the north wing of the building. He was gay and amusing at dinner and afterwards.

Massey retired early that night, pleading a headache. But he lay awake, tossing restlessly in his bed, perturbed half by the problems involved in a large steel manoeuvre coming up on Monday, half by the presence of this flippant youngster under his own roof.

Half the sleepless night went by, and visions danced before him: Louise, lovely, tempting, belonging to him. A current of excitement rose in Massey. He left his bed, donned a housecoat, and made his way down the hallway to his wife's bedroom. The great clock in the corridor told him that the time was past three in the morning, and the big house was quiet.

Louise had left the 'do not disturb' sign on her bedroom door. Massey opened the door gently, silently, thinking that if she were asleep he would not awaken her, but hoping that perhaps she, too, had tossed and turned this evening, and would welcome him into her bed, into her arms.

He tiptoed towards the canopied bed.

Louise was not asleep. She was looking up at him, eyes bright with fear (or was it defiance?).

Louise was not alone.

Henry Marshall lay beside her, an arm thrown negligently over her bare shoulders.

In one stunned instant of understanding, Massey saw confirmed what he had barely dared to suspect, these past years when Henry Marshall had visited them so many times. Louise was deceiving him!

A hot ribbon of pain coursed across the front of his body, centering like a cauterizing knife just behind his ribs. He gasped in agony and confusion.

'Louise – I didn't know——'

They were sitting up in bed, both of them, smiling at him. They were unafraid.

'Well, now you *do* know,' Henry Marshall said. 'And it's been going on for years. What are you going to do about it old boy?'

Massey's heart thundered agonizingly. He staggered, nearly fell, grabbed a bedpost to support himself. His arms and legs felt cold with a deadly chill.

Louise said quietly, 'You were bound to find out about us sooner or later. Henry and I have been in love for years ever since we were nineteen. But we couldn't afford to marry – and he agreed to wait a few years, when I met you. Only a few years; that's what your doctor told me, privately. He didn't want you to know.'

Massey put his hands to the fiery ball of palpitating hell that his heart had abruptly become. He could almost feel the blood circulating through his body, pounding at his brain.

Louise said, 'Dr Robinson said you had a serious heart defect – any shock was likely to carry you off. But he didn't want you to know about it; he said your days were numbered anyway, so you might as well live them out in peace. But *I* knew – and Henry knew! And now we'll inherit your money, James. We're both still young, and we'll have each other for years to come!'

Massey took two uncertain steps towards the couple in the bed. Red flashes of light were interfering with his vision, and his legs were numb.

'Louise – it isn't so, Louise – this is all a dream, isn't it?'

'You're wide awake! It's actually happening! Why don't you die, you old fool? Die! Die!'

And then he had started to fall, toppling into the thick wine-red carpet of Louise's bedroom, lying there with his hands dug deep into the high pile rug, while eddies of pain ripped through him, and above him sounded their mocking laughter and Louise's repeated cry of 'Die, you old fool! Die! Die.'

So that was the way it had been. Massey recalled everything, now, and he understood. The shock of finding Louise and Henry Marshall that way had touched off the heart attack that had been inevitable for so long. He had lain on the floor in Louise's bedroom, unconscious, in a coma, perhaps, and somehow – somehow – the doctors had decided he was dead.

It was incredible. Had life indeed been flickering so feebly in him that the high-priced medicos had failed to realize he still lived? Or – the thought chilled Massey there in the darkness – had Louise and her lover found some complacent doctor who, for a fee, would certify death when death had not really come? What if Louise had known he was still alive, though unconscious, and had knowingly placed him in this coffin and sent him to the darkness of the grave?

A terrible passion came to life in Massey. He *would* get out! He had won before, in corporation matters, in proxy fights, in struggles of every kind. He was a mild-mannered man on the surface, but his will was all-consuming once it was aroused.

He would free himself.

Somehow.

Massey vowed to escape from his grave, whether he lay under a ton of soil or not. He would return to life, come back from the grave. Punish Louise for her crime, make her atone for her mocking infidelity.

I'll get out, he swore to himself. *I won't die here like a trapped rat.*

The word 'rat' brought a new and even more ghastly thought to mind. He had heard legends of the graveyard rats, great slug-shaped creatures with blazing red eyes and tails like scaled serpents, who tunnelled under the graveyards and gnawed their way into the new graves to devour the flesh of recent corpses.

Suppose they came for him? Suppose, even now as he lay here, the graveyard beasts squatted in their unmentionable tunnels below his coffin, nibbling at the wood with yellowed teeth, gnawing, biting, scratching, boring ominously inward.

How the rats would rejoice when they found a living man within the coffin!

Massey had always had a vivid imagination. Now, with darkness settled like a cloak about him, he found himself unable to make that imagination cease functioning. Sharply in the eye of his mind he saw the gleeful cascade of rats pouring through the breach in the coffin wall, saw dozens of the foul beasts launching themselves on him with more burrowing greedily in from all sides. He pictured the rats madly joyous at the discovery of a live being, of fresh meat.

He saw their bristly snouts nuzzling at the soft pink flesh of his throat. He could picture their razor-keen teeth meeting beneath his chin, while his outraged blood spurted out over them. He could feel the animals quarrelling with each other for the right to devour the tender morsels that were his eyes.

'What was that? That sound?

A fitful champing and chewing sound, was it? As of hundreds of rats patiently gnawing at the sleek fresh wood of his coffin?

No, he thought. More imagination. There was no sound. Everything was utterly silent. It was, he thought, the silence of – the grave.

Then he wondered how he could still retain a sense of humour. How, for that matter, he could still retain any shred of his sanity, trapped like this.

He could no longer preserve the fiction that he was still lying in state in some undertaker's parlour. Coffins do not normally have locks; the only reason why he had been unable to lift the lid was that he was already in the ground. No doubt Louise and her lover had rushed him into the ground as fast as they could.

They would be in for a surprise, Massey thought with calmness that surprised himself. Calmness was what he needed now. In the same way as he had piloted so many complicated financial manoeuvres, James Ronald Massey now set to work to think of a way to escape from the living grave to which he had been condemned.

Pushing at the lid was futile. He had already tried that a dozen unsuccessful times. But perhaps he could break the lid, claw his way upward through the dirt till he reached the surface.

He felt in the darkness for the satin lining of the coffin. The air hung like a moist cloth around him now. He realized he had no more than a few minutes' air left, and then the hideous slow death of strangulation would start.

Better that than the rats, he told himself. I don't want to be alive if the rats break into the coffin. I'd rather choke to death than be eaten alive. Yes. Much better to choke.

His hands clawed at the satin and ripped it away, shredding the expensive cloth. Now he could feel the smooth, cool pine boards from which his coffin had been made. The wood had been planed and sanded to a perfect finish. He laughed, a little wildly. Probably Louise had bought him the most expensive coffin that could be found. 'Nothing but the best for my poor dead darling husband,' she must have told the undertaker.

He began to pound at the wood, hoping he would hear it splinter. But the wood held. He gasped for breath, knowing just a bit of fresh air remained, that now the torture would begin. He could barely fill his lungs. He drew in a deep breath and nearly retched at the nauseous taste of the stale air.

Weirdly he wondered if perhaps they had laid him in his grave upside-down. Perhaps he did not face the sky, and perhaps he was really digging at the bottom of his coffin instead of the top. In that case, even if he did succeed in breaking through the solid wood he would be far from free.

Impossible, he thought. *A joke of my tired mind.* He had to keep trying. Couldn't give up now. Not now, when the air would be gone in minutes, and the rats lay waiting for him.

His hands, which had never done any kind of manual labour, now clawed and scraped desperately at the unyielding wood of the coffin lid. His nails raked the mocking pine boards again and again, as if he thought to dig his way through the wood splinter by splinter. His nails ripped away one by one and blood streamed down his fingers, and he felt the bright hotness of the terrible pain, but still he clawed.

And screamed.

'Help me! Can't you hear me? I'm buried alive in here! Alive! I'll give ten thousand dollars to any man who gets me out! Twenty thousand! Fifty thousand! Do you hear me, fifty thousand dollars!'

He might just as well have offered the moon and the stars. No one heard his call; no one answered him. The funeral was probably long since over, the mourners dispersed. At this moment perhaps Louise and Henry Marshall were making love and laughing to each other about the fortune that was now theirs.

'Help me! Help me!'

His broken fingers clawed futilely at the wooden barrier above him, clawed until his nerves were numbed by constant agony and he could feel no more pain. The air was all but gone, now.

Part of his mind was still clear. Part was still engaged in formulating plans. Break a hole in the coffin lid, he thought. Widen it. Claw through the dirt to the surface. The soil will still be loose and soft. You can push it to one side if you can only get out of this coffin. Get your head above air, breath the fresh air again, call for help.

Then settle with Louise and Henry.

It was all so simple – all but the first step. He could not get a purchase on the wood. The air was a vile moist thing now, and he could feel the cold hand of asphyxiation tightening steadily round his throat. The staleness of the air was making thought more difficult; he could barely think clearly any more. And he seemed to hear the rats again, chewing tirelessly at the wood, as if they knew that a living being lay in the wooden box, as if they yearned to get to Massey while the warm blood still pulsed in his veins.

And his heart, the heart whose sudden failure had been mistaken for death – his heart now pounded wildly from his exertions, and the pain that shot through him was ten times the torment he had experienced that night in Louise's bedroom. He wondered how long he could stand the combined assault.

The rats . . . the rats coming to get me . . . and the air almost gone . . . the darkness

... my heart, my heart! ... I'll need a miracle to get out of here now ... my heart! The pain!

The pain!

Suddenly tranquillity stole over Massey. He smiled, and realized that the pain had diminished. He felt calm and assured now.

How foolish he had been to work so hard to get out of his coffin! There was such an easier way to do it!

All he had to do was drift. He drifted upwards, passed lightly through the sturdy wood he had failed to break, drifted up through five feet of dark earth, and stood once more on the surface of the green land.

Free!

It was mid-afternoon. The sun glinted brightly, the sun Massey had thought never to see again. Fifty feet away, a group of people were gathered round a marble headstone, placing a wreath. Massey shouted to them.

'I'm free! They buried me, but I escaped from the grave! Get the sexton! Tell him there's been a mistake, please!'

Curiously, they ignored him. They did not even turn around to see who called. Massey repeated the words, to no avail.

He took a deep breath – and discovered for the first time that he could not taste the spring-like freshness of the air. He felt no cool fragrance in his nostrils.

Massey looked down. Then, suddenly, it was as if the ground parted beneath him, and he could see clearly the coffin lying deep in the earth, and he could see into the coffin, where the dead body of a middle-aged man lay – his fingers torn and bloodied, his face mottled with the discolouration of asphyxiation and the redness of a sudden and fatal heart attack.

Claws

Frances Stephens

Terry Price never meant to stay long on a remote Hebridean island. At thirty, he didn't have much time for mist and mountains. He only went there on impulse anyway.

The fact was, things had got too sticky in the Welsh seaside town where he ran a one-man souvenir shop, latest in a long line of bids for easy money. Some of the people to whom he was in debt had turned awkward, and the gullible tourists with open wallets hadn't flocked around in the numbers he had anticipated.

So one night he locked the shop door, having first removed anything of value, which wasn't much. Then, carrying a useful bunch of keys, he went round to the ill-lit car park behind a large hotel. Extravaganza Night at the Metropole.

He stole a plushy number – after all, why stint when someone else was footing the bill? A previous arrangement with a crony, plus an exchange of cash, secured him different number-plates.

Price was over the border into Scotland by the time the car owner sauntered out after his breakfast coffee.

He kept moving. It seemed sense to get as far away as possible. Soon he crossed on a ferry to the islands, with the idea of putting a stretch of water between himself and the mainland. Some nights he slept in the car, others he booked a bed at a wayside farm.

One morning he was lounging against the car in the sunshine, staring moodily over an unbelievable vista of rocks and islands. The loneliness of the place made him uneasy, yet there was a pull he could not ignore, for Price's father had been a sailor, and the sea ran strong in his blood.

A small boat was working its way towards a rough jetty. Soon two brawny fishermen thumped boxes of live lobsters on to the concrete, alongside a waiting van, where a man in dungarees stood counting. Cash changed hands.

Price moved forward. In a box on the ground, snapping, stalk-eyed shellfish blundered and bumped against each other. Blue-black bodies arched as tentacles waved. The claws were fastened with rubber bands, closing them tightly, and rendering them impotent.

The man in dungarees, completing the job, brought out a padlock for the back of the van. Price stared.

'Business good, then?'

'You could say that.'

'What's it worth, this little lot?'

The man's eyes flicked over Price's car, parked further along.

'I've got more inside here than you've got over there.'

The car would have cost a cool two thousand plus.

Dungarees was ready to leave. He stared calmly at Price.

'My name's Frazer. Come and see us if you're round our way.'

On the side of the van were painted the words Island Shellfish, with the name of a place twenty miles farther north.

The next day it rained, cold cruel steel rods of water that penetrated layers of clothing and lambasted the skin from your face. Terry Price squelched across vile-smelling mud to where raw-faced men in streaming oilskins stood inside a fair-sized shed waiting to collect what they had earned for their catch.

Crude fish odours slapped against his nostrils, stinging his eyes. The stench made him gasp. A couple of youths were busy with weighing scales. Negligently they discarded certain specimens, tossing them on to the wet concrete floor with a sickening crack. Segments of lobsters mutilated in transit littered the ground.

A girl in a rubber apron shovelled living creatures into a boiling cauldron. A hiss of steam arose. Another girl, big and blonde, idled in the doorway of a workroom off the main shed, unashamedly staring.

Frazer detached himself. 'Just look around. I'll be with you later.'

Price climbed three steps, then walked along the wet slimy boards that ran between the running salt-water tanks, where he could gaze down on hundreds of sea creatures, groping around like something left over from a primeval nightmare.

One tank contained specimens that had lost a limb or claw. Others were graded in size. The largest were gross and monstrous.

'Want a job?'

Price turned to see Frazer beside him.

'We're short of a man. McInnes got drunk and fell off the quay. Fractured hip.'

It was as easy as that. A room in a local cottage, hand-me-down oilskins, dungarees and rubber boots. Price, for all his streak of scrounging, had physical strength and fanatical zest when the mood took him.

He stood in wind and driving rain until his hands were numb and his eyes were swollen. He drove in the van out to piers and landing points bleak beyond his worst imagining. He fell into bed each night, half dead from sheer exhaustion. But the money. Ye gods, the money. Pleasure throbbed and bubbled inside him. He had never known anything like it.

Logan was the fly in the ointment. The other men, a group of half a dozen, some truculent, some foul-mouthed, observed that Price did his fair whack, and let him be. Not Logan. It needled him that a rank outsider should walk in here and be accepted.

Logan was island born and bred, and he didn't make much of dirty upstarts from the south, particularly when they moved in and took a share of the profits. He was lean but he was wiry, living hard, drinking hard. Price would turn round and find a pair of hostile eyes burning into him, a silence that said more than a spate of words.

Frazer was the go-between. Handling the office work, as well as a hundred other things, he had an easy friendliness that prevented trouble flaring.

One cold afternoon, Price was in the shed grading lobsters, eyeing them for size, then tossing them into the appropriate tanks where they were kept until they could be moved out. His hands were stiff, for care in getting a correct grip on the creatures was essential. Given a chance, the shellfish could arch their tails and bodies, twisting to give a vicious nip. Drastic enough to sever a man's finger.

Price had developed a healthy respect for the lobsters he handled. Their habits were scarcely dainty. Sometimes a blind impulse would unite them so that they turned sadistically on a small, weaker brother, tearing and trampling to death. After the massacre, the bottom of the pool would be speckled with frayed and mangled pieces.

They were cannibals, eating each other, sometimes even their own limbs, detached as a result of frequent fights.

Logan stood glowering.

'You should keep your mind on your work and not expect us to pay for your mistakes.'

Price frowned.

'What the hell——?'

Logan gestured with a stringy thumb at the lobsters.

'Look at those three. They're too big for the medium-sized tank. We could sell them for more money.'

Price breathed hard. He was still a newcomer, and Logan knew what he was talking about, but it left a sour taste, particularly as a couple of other men were listening. And the girl Sheena. Big-boned and indolent, with twine-coloured hair and breasts of no particular interest, her pale, crafty eyes were on Price now. Talk had it she was Logan's girl-friend. They deserved each other.

Irritated, Price turned away. He knew that Sheena and the other girl who packed the cooked meat often had slack periods. Now they would nudge each other, gossiping and giggling about the clash between the two men. Stupid bitches!

Logan stumped off along the slimy boards, and Price started whistling, glad now that he had bitten his tongue. Let the surly devil say what he liked. Price's palm itched with the feel of money.

Later that week he had a small accident with the company van. Nothing serious, but as yet he was not familiar with every bend and twist on the long stretches of one-track road, and he grazed a wall, denting one panel.

The van still functioned, so there need be no hold-up, and Price was prepared if necessary to make good the damage, although the islanders were notoriously careless with their cars, flogging the last spark of life out of their rusty frames.

Predictably, Logan was antagonistic and bitter. Gritty fragments of his conversation floated across the shed to Price: '. . . our property he's damaging. Upstart southerner. And that car he's supposed to own. Fit for some prancing nancy-boy.'

That car he's supposed to own. Supposed to own. What did Logan mean? What was going on in the dark and twisted passages of his mind?

For the first time since he came to the island, Price felt a stab of doubt. Could Logan suspect? *How* could Logan suspect?

Frazer was busy packing stores into the deep-freeze room with its massive door. Deliberately he maintained neutrality. Price worked late. He was a loner, never wanted to be anything else, but it seemed to him now that he was in a highly vulnerable position. An outsider. Damn them. He did his whack, didn't he?

It was dark when he left, and he noticed with surprise that Sheena was waiting. Everyone else had gone.

She walked beside him across the yard and got into his car. Price was beginning to tumble, although he could scarcely believe it.

Inside, she settled herself, smoothing the skirt back from her knees with deliberate gestures. She had strong, stocky legs, as attractive as a kitchen table.

'You don't want to worry about Andy. It's just his way.'

Andy? It must be Logan she was talking about.

'Everybody else likes you.'

There was a meaning note in her voice, and Price felt his palms beginning to sweat at the look on her bold, brazen face. She moved inches nearer, and in her eyes was the reflection of his own animal strength.

He kissed her, because only a blind imbecile would have refused, but it wasn't good enough, and she knew. Sensed that she roused his instincts as little as a worm crawling about on the ground. She pulled away, and flung out of the car, slamming the door.

Price smoked cigarette after cigarette. He had blundered badly. Surprise had slowed his reactions to an electric situation. But the fact was, he had no time for women. Money was a more exciting mistress.

He did not know what tale she spun to Logan, obviously not the truth, but the island man's activities now became deliberate persecution. Price found the upholstery of his car slashed and tattered. A can of engine oil was poured, accidentally of course, over his oikskins. The meanest, filthiest jobs came his way.

The situation was bothering him now, rubbing away at a patch of his mind like sandpaper on sore flesh. Logan had friends, there was no doubt of that, and if it came to a showdown, the locals, bound by centuries of tradition, would stick together. Damn them. Price ground his teeth. The irony of it. All he wanted was to earn his fair whack.

He worked doggedly, avoiding the others when possible. He was conscious of Sheena, her cold, fish-like eyes watching him, always watching. He had lost out there, half-baked moron that he was. What harm would it have done to drive her off along one of those deserted roads and lay her in the back of the car? He would have gained an ally then. Instead of which, Sheena and Logan made a vindictive pair of enemies.

Frazer had dropped into the habit of leaving Terry Price on the premises in the evening when everyone else had gone. Price preferred it that way. There was a certain fascination in wandering around the dimness of the shed, the whole place empty except for hundreds and hundreds of creeping, crawling shellfish groping their way along the floors of the tanks. The bubble and swish of the ever-flowing water was a ghostly symphony. Small waves lapped on the sodden floor boards of the wooden platforms.

Price avoided the refrigerated store-room. Once Frazer had invited him to look inside, explaining the system of storage. A chill like death had immediately clamped down. The door had been standing open, and a foggy, vaporous cloud had engulfed them. Rock-hard supplies of shellfish stood row on row, a hoary film on the clear polythene bags. Frazer kept talking, but Price's teeth were chattering as he plunged out into the normal atmosphere.

Tonight the rest had gone. Logan loomed up out of the shadows.

Sensing trouble, Price turned on his heel and strode along the wooden planks between the lobster tanks. Logan followed.

It was a stupid move on Price's part, because there was no other way back. Logan leaned forward and insolently prodded his arm.

'We've taken enough from you. It's time you got into your fancy car and drove away.'

A slow and terrible anger was building in Price, so that he could scarcely contain his revulsion for the narrow, twisted face thrust near his own. There was a physical ache in controlling his fists as they itched to flash out, but the memory of a hundred backstreet brawls told him Logan would be a mean and vicious fighter. And a crack on the jaw was too good for this loathsome enemy.

Logan's face was seamed with hatred. The silence of the other man goaded him.

'Did ye hear what I said?'

Price's quick eyes flicked over the boards on which they were standing. A mere six inches or so separated Logan from the heaving tanks.

'Ask me that tomorrow,' he said smoothly.

It worked. Logan flung away, his mind seeking out ways of inflicting pain and shame on his adversary. He would be back. Late, the next day, when the rest had gone.

Price lay awake, making his plans, checking and counter-checking each detail. Fate had played into his hands. The tanks would be teeming. One would contain gigantic specimens, menacing and obscene.

The day dragged through, but eventually the last man went home. Price sprang to work. He had little time, and an exacting job to do. Swiftly he donned a pair of tough industrial gloves. Clippers he had already selected. The gloves made his fingers clumsy, but cold clear hatred sang in his blood, making him oblivious of the fifteen inches of water that lapped his long rubber boots.

Already an aggressive leader was tearing into a less belligerent neighbour. Water in the tank swirled and heaved with the mass movement of the lobsters. Eyes waving on stalks, intoxicated with the new-found freedom, they turned on each other, snapping, crushing, fighting. Price stood back. He hurried outside, where he dumped the gloves in an overflowing bin and piled other rubbish on top.

He was standing on the wooden platform when Logan appeared. The Scotsman wore a jacket over a frayed shirt open at the neck. Price held his ground. Now he could smell the whisky on Logan's breath.

'So it's a fight you want, is it?' Price's voice was mocking.

'Why, you bloody upstart, you——'

'Take your jacket off, then.'

With deliberate insolence, Price leaned forward and tore at the unstylish lapel. Material ripped.

Logan's eyes had suddenly spotted something very wrong in the lobster tank.

'What in hell's name——'

His eyes were still on the tank as he pulled his jacket half off, and Price didn't intend to let him get any further than that. There was a sickening sound as fist crunched on jaw-bone at the crucial point. Stunned, Logan collapsed on to the wet platform. It took but a moment for Price to rip off the jacket. With a shove, he heaved Logan into the tank. Face upward, water closed over.

A froth of bubbles rose, but already blue-black shapes were converging, fighting, clawing forward, groping, feelers conveying hot messages of excitement. Blood from a gash on Logan's face already stained the water. It spread, palely pink, like a rosy cloud.

Claws snapped at the pulpy flesh, nibbling, tasting, as shellfish blundered and climbed all over the motionless form. Two lobsters had pulled off a finger and were fighting for possession. A claw ripped an eyeball from its socket, leaving fronds of jelly wafting in the water like a rare and exotic plant.

Price stood for an hour, listening to the bubbling and churning of the water. He tossed the jacket into the tank. Making sure he was unobserved, he went home.

It took a lot of nerve to turn up as usual next morning, but ignorance seemed the best defence. A group of men stood talking in subdued voices, looking down into the tank containing lobsters of top-grade size. Frazer hurried forward.

'Here you are Price. Come and look at this.'

He had to look, but there wasn't enough left of Logan's face to reveal any evidence of a fight. His stomach was ripped open. Grey-green intestines bobbed in the lapping water, vaguely putrescent, with a weird and repellent shine.

Only the jacket was a real clue to identity. Price assumed a horrified tone.

'He must have come back looking for me when I'd gone. Missed his footing maybe, if he'd had a drop too much.'

Several people had access to the building, and no one could prove Price was a liar. He stuck to his tale, crafty enough not to embroider it with extra detail.

A mate of Logan's stooped down and picked up a slashed rubber band. He glanced meaningly around. Nobody spoke.

'Drunk,' said Price clearly. 'He must have been very drunk.'

The remains were hauled out of the water and covered with a tarpaulin. To contact the mainland police would take both time and effort. Too much time and effort for a severely local matter. The men went into a conclave.

A throbbing disquiet pervaded the shed. Deliberately Price set about his work, for he was to take the van out today.

Later, when he returned, the remains had been removed. A weight dropped from him. Watch his step now, and he had won.

He stayed on that evening, for he needed to be on his own. The whole thing had knocked the stuffing out of him. Ye gods, he could sleep for a month.

He was ready to leave when Sheena appeared.

'Frazer wants a word with ye.'

Price was under the impression that everyone else had gone, but perhaps his nerves were playing him tricks. He stared, perplexed, into the bland eyes of the whey-faced girl. She smiled.

'It'll no take a minute.'

Appeasement was his policy until he was entirely sure of his ground. He followed her across the yard, in the direction of the refrigerated storeroom. The door stood open. Row upon row of stiff-scarlet rock-hard lobsters leered at him from the shelves. Boiling in the cauldron had reduced them to harmless titbits.

Price peered inside.

'Frazer?'

A hefty shove jerked him forward, stars swum before his eyes, glittering in the pitch-black darkness as he crashed on to the floor. The door slammed behind him. A whimper rose to his lips as his hands groped out, feeling nothing around but that icy chill that would grow and grow until it froze the very blood in his veins, until his eyeballs glazed.

Gibbering with helpless fury, he flung himself here and there, bruising his body on the hard wooden shelves. Now they would be snapping the latch on the padlock, for the stores in the refrigerated room were valuable, and only the most trusted had access to the key.

Frazer pulled up the collar of his mackintosh, preparing to leave. He glanced at Sheena.

'Going to be a cold night.'

'A long, cold night,' she said.

Dracula

An extract

Bram Stoker

(Continuing Jonathan Harker's journal ...)

I only slept a few hours when I went to bed, and feeling that I could not sleep any more, got up. I had hung my shaving-glass by the window, and was just beginning to shave. Suddenly I felt a hand on my shoulder, and heard the Count's voice saying to me, 'Good morning.' I started, for it amazed me that I had not seen him, since the reflection of the glass covered the whole room behind me. In starting I had cut myself slightly, but did not notice it at the moment. Having answered the Count's salutation, I turned to the glass again to see how I had been mistaken. This time there could be no error, for the man was close to me, and I could see him over my shoulder. But there was no reflection of him in the mirror! The whole room behind me was displayed; but there was no sign of a man in it, except myself. This was startling, and, coming on the top of so many strange things, was beginning to increase that vague feeling of uneasiness which I always have when the Count is near; but at that instant I saw that the cut had bled a little, and the blood was trickling over my chin. I laid down the razor, turning as I did so half-round to look for some sticking-plaster. When the Count saw my face, his eyes blazed with a sort of demoniac fury, and he suddenly made a grab at my throat. I drew away, and his hand touched the string of beads which held the crucifix. It made an instant change in him, for the fury passed so quickly that I could hardly believe that it was ever there.

'Take care,' he said, 'take care how you cut yourself. It is more dangerous than you think in this country.' Then seizing the shaving-glass, he went on: 'And this is the wretched thing that has done the mischief. It is a foul bauble of man's vanity. Away with it!' and opening the heavy window with one wrench of his terrible hand, he flung out the glass, which was shattered into a thousand pieces on the stones of the courtyard far below. Then he withdrew without a word. It is very annoying, for I do not see how I am to shave, unless in my watch-case or the bottom of the shaving-pot, which is, fortunately, of metal.

When I went into the dining-room, breakfast was prepared; but I could not find the Count anywhere. So I breakfasted alone. It is strange that as yet I have not seen the Count eat or drink. He must be a very peculiar man! After breakfast I did a little exploring in the castle. I went out on the stairs and found a room looking towards the south. The view was magnificent, and from where I stood there was every opportunity of seeing it. The castle is on the very edge of a terrible precipice. A stone falling from the window would fall a thousand feet without touching anything! As far as the eye can reach is a sea of green tree-tops, with occasionally a deep rift where there is a chasm. Here and there are silver threads where the rivers wind in deep gorges through the forests.

But I am not in heart to describe beauty, for when I had seen the view I explored further; doors, doors, doors everywhere, and all locked and bolted. In no place save from the windows in the castle walls is there an available exit.

The castle is a veritable prison, and I am a prisoner!

When I found that I was a prisoner a sort of wild feeling came over me. I rushed up and down the stairs, trying every door and peering out of every window I could find; but after a little the conviction of my helplessness overpowered all other things. When I look back after a few hours I think I must have been mad for the time, for I behaved much as a rat does in a trap. When, however, the conviction had come to me that I was helpless I sat down quietly – as quietly as I have ever done anything in my life – and began to think over what was best to be done. I am thinking still, and as yet have come to no definite conclusion. Of one thing only am I certain: that it is no use making my ideas known to the Count. He knows well that I am imprisoned; and as he has done it himself, and has doubtless his own motives for it, he would only deceive me if I trusted him fully with the facts. So far as I can see, my only plan will be to keep my knowledge and my fears to myself, and my eyes open. I am, I know, either being deceived, like a baby, by my own fears, or else I am in desperate straits; and if the latter be so, I need, and shall need, all my brains to get through. I had hardly come to this conclusion when I heard the great door below shut, and knew that the Count had returned. He did not come at once into the library, so I went cautiously to my own room and found him making the bed. This was odd, but only confirmed what I had all along thought – that there were no servants in the house. When later I saw him through the chink of the hinges of the door laying the table in the dining-room, I was assured of it; for if he does himself all these menial offices, surely it is proof that there is no one else to do them. This gave me a fright, for if there is no one else in the castle, it must have been the Count himself who was the driver of the coach that brought me here. This is a terrible thought; for if so, what does it mean that he could control the wolves, as he did, by only holding up his hand in silence? How was it that all the people at Bistritz and on the coach had some terrible fear for me? What meant the giving of the crucifix, of the garlic, of the wild rose, of the mountain ash? Bless that good, good woman who hung the crucifix round my neck! for it is a comfort and a strength to me whenever I touch it. It is odd that a thing which I have been taught to regard with disfavour and as idolatrous should in a time of loneliness and trouble be of help. Is it that there is something in the essence of the thing itself, or that it is a medium, a tangible help, in conveying memories of sympathy and comfort? Some time, if it may be, I must examine this matter and try to make up my mind about it. In the meantime I must find out all I can about Count Dracula, as it may help me to understand. Tonight he may talk to himself, if I turn the conversation that way. I must be very careful, however, not to awake his suspicion.

Midnight – I have had a long talk with the Count. I asked him a few questions on Transylvanian history, and he warmed up to the subject wonderfully. In his speaking of things and people, and especially of battles, he spoke as if he had been present at them all. This he afterwards explained by saying that to a *boyar* the pride of his house and name is his own pride, that their glory is his glory, that their fate is his fate. Whenever he spoke of his house he always said 'we', and spoke almost in the plural, like a king speaking. I wish I could put down all he said exactly as he said it, for to me it was most fascinating. It seemed to have in it a whole history of the country. He grew excited as he spoke, and walked about the room pulling his great white moustache and grasping anything on which he laid his hands as though he would crush it by main strength. One thing he said which I shall put down as nearly as I can; for it tells in its way the story of his race:

'We Szekelys have a right to be proud, for in our veins flows the blood of many brave faces who fought as the lion fights, for lordship. Here, in the whirlpool of European races, the Ugric tribe bore down from Iceland the fighting spirit which Thor and Wodin gave them, which their Berserkers displayed to such fell intent on the seaboards of Europe, aye, and of Asia and Africa, too, till the peoples thought that the were-wolves themselves had come. Here, too, when they came, they found the Huns, whose warlike fury had swept the earth like a living flame, till the dying peoples held that in their veins ran the blood of those old witches, who, expelled from Scythia, had mated with the devils in the desert. Fools, fools! What devil or what witch was ever so great as Attila, whose blood is in these veins?' He held up his arms. 'Is it a wonder that we were a conquering race; that we were proud; that when the Magyar, the Lombard, the Avar, the Bulgar, or the Turk poured his thousands on our frontiers, we drove them back? Is it strange that when Arpad and his legions swept through the Hungarian fatherland he found us here when he reached the frontier; that the Honfoglalas was completed there? And when the Hungarian flood swept eastward, the Szekelys were claimed as kindred by the victorious Magyars, and to us for centuries was trusted the guarding of the frontier of Turkey-land; aye, and more than that, endless duty of the frontier guard, for, as the Turks say, "water sleeps, and enemy is sleepless." Who more gladly than we throughout the Four Nations received the "bloody sword", or at its warlike call flocked quicker to the standard of the King? When was redeemed that great shame of my nation, the shame of Cassova, when the flags of the Wallach and the Magyar went down beneath the Crescent; who was it but one of my own race who as Voivode crossed the Danube and beat the Turk on his own ground! This was a Dracula indeed. Who was it that his own unworthy brother, when he had fallen, sold his people to the Turk and brought the shame of slavery on them! Was it not this Dracula, indeed, who inspired that other of his race who in a later age again and again brought his forces over the great river into Turkey-land; who, when he was beaten back, came again, and again, and again, though he had to come alone from the bloody-field where his troops were being slaughtered, since he knew that he alone could ultimately triumph? They said that he thought only of himself. Bah! what good are peasants without a leader? Where ends the war without a brain and heart to conduct it? Again, when, after the battle of Mohacs, we threw off the Hungarian yoke, we of the Dracula blood were amongst their leaders, for our spirit would not brook that we were not free. Ah, young sir, the Szekelys – and the Dracula as their heart's blood, their brains, and their swords – can boast a record that mushroom growths like the Hapsburgs and the Romanoffs can never reach. The warlike days are over. Blood is too precious a thing in these days of dishonourable peace; and the glories of the great races are as a tale that is told.'

It was by this time close on morning, and we went to bed. (*Mem.*, this diary seems horribly like the beginning of the 'Arabian Nights', for everything has to break off at cockcrow – or like the ghost of Hamlet's father.)

12 *May* – Let me begin with facts – bare, meagre facts, verified by books and figures, and of which there can be no doubt. I must not confuse them with experiences which will have to rest on my own observation or my memory of them. Last evening when the Count came from his room he began by asking me questions on legal matters and on the doing of certain kinds of business. I had spent the day wearily over books, and, simply to keep my mind occupied, went over some of the matters I had been examined in at Lincoln's Inn. There was a certain method in the Count's inquiries, so I shall try to put them down in sequence; the knowledge may somehow or some time be useful to me.

First, he asked if a man in England might have two solicitors, or more.
I told him he might have a dozen if he wished, but that it would not
be wise to have more than one solicitor engaged in one transaction, as
only one could act at a time, and that to change would be certain to
militate against his interest. He seemed thoroughly to understand, and
went on to ask if there would be any practical difficulty in having one
man to attend, say, to banking, and another to look after shipping, in
case local help were needed in a place far from the home of the banking
solicitor. I asked him to explain more fully, so that I might not by any
chance mislead him, so he said:

'I shall illustrate. Your friend and mine, Mr Peter Hawkins, from
under the shadow of your beautiful cathedral at Exeter, which is far
from London, buys for me through your good self my place at London.
Good! Now here let me say frankly, lest you should think it strange that
I have sought the services of one so far off from London instead of
someone resident there, that my motive was that no local interest might
be served save my wish only; and as one of London resident might,
perhaps, have some purpose of himself or friend to serve I went thus
afield to seek my agent, whose labours should be only to my interest.
Now, suppose I, who have much of affairs, wish to ship goods, say, to
Newcastle, or Durham, or Harwich, or Dover, might it not be that it
could with more ease be done by consigning to one in these ports?' I
answered that certainly it would be most easy, but that we solicitors had
a system of agency one for the other, so that local work could be done
locally on instruction from any solicitor, so that the client, simply
placing himself in the hands of one man, could have his wishes carried
out by him without further trouble.

'But,' said he, 'I could be at liberty to direct myself. Is it not so?'

'Of course,' I replied; 'and such is often done by men of business, who
do not like the whole of their affairs to be known by any one person.'

'Good!' he said, and then went on to ask about the means of making
consignments and the forms to be gone through, and of all sorts of
difficulties which might arise, but by forethought could be guarded
against. I explained all these things to him to the best of my ability, and
he certainly left me under the impression that he would have made a
wonderful solicitor, for there was nothing that he did not think of or
foresee. For a man who was never in the country, and who did not
evidently do much in the way of business, his knowledge and acumen
were wonderful. When he had satisfied himself on these points of which
he had spoken, and I had verified all as well as I could by the books
available, he suddenly stood up and said:

'Have you written since your first letter to our friend Mr Peter
Hawkins, or to any other?' It was with some bitterness in my heart that
I answered that I had not, that as yet I had not seen any opportunity

of sending letters to anybody.

'Then write now, my young friend,' he said, laying a heavy hand on my shoulder; 'write to our friend and to any other; and say, if it will please you, that you shall stay with me until a month from now.'

'Do you wish me to stay so long?' I asked, for my heart grew cold at the thought.

'I desire it much; nay, I will take no refusal. When your master, employer, what you will, engaged that someone should come on his behalf, it was understood that my needs only were to be consulted. I have not stinted. Is it not so?'

What could I do but bow acceptance? It was Mr Hawkins's interest, not mine, and I had to think of him, not myself; and besides, while Count Dracula was speaking, there was that in his eyes and in his bearing which made me remember that I was a prisoner, and that if I wished it I could have no choice. The Count saw his victory in my bow, and his mastery in the trouble of my face, for he began at once to use them, but in his own smooth, resistless way:

'I pray you, my good young friend, that you will not discourse of things other than business in your letters. It will doubtless please your friends to know that you are well, and that you look forward to getting home to them. Is it not so?' As he spoke he handed me three sheets of notepaper and three envelopes. They were all of the thinnest foreign post, and looking at them, then at him, and noticing his quiet smile, with the sharp, canine teeth lying over the red under-lip, I understood as well as if he had spoken that I should be careful what I wrote, for he would be able to read it. So I determined to write only formal notes now, but to write fully to Mr Hawkins in secret, and also to Mina, for to her I could write in shorthand, which would puzzle the Count, if he did see it. When I had written my two letters I sat quiet, reading a book whilst the Count wrote several notes, referring as he wrote them to some books on his table. Then he took up my two and placed them with his own, and put by his writing materials, after which, the instant the door had closed behind him, I leaned over and looked at the letters, which were face down on the table. I felt no compunction in doing so, for under the circumstances I felt that I should protect myself in every way I could.

One of the letters was directed to Samuel F. Billington, No. 7, The Crescent, Whitby; another to Herr Leutner, Varna; the third was to Coutts & Co., London, and the fourth to Herren Klopstock & Billreuth, bankers, Buda-Pesth. The second and fourth were unsealed. I was just about to look at them when I saw the door-handle move. I sank back in my seat, having just had time to replace the letters as they had been and to resume my book before the Count, holding still another letter in his hand, entered the room. He took up the letters on the table and stamped them carefully, and then, turning to me, said:

'I trust you will forgive me, but I have much work to do in private this evening. You will, I hope, find all things as you wish.' At the door he turned, and after a moment's pause said:

'Let me advise you, my dear young friend – nay, let me warn you with all seriousness, that should you leave these rooms you will not by any chance go to sleep in any other part of the castle. It is old, and has many memories, and there are bad dreams for those who sleep unwisely. Be warned! Should sleep now or ever overcome you, or be like to do, then haste to your own chamber or to these rooms, for your rest will then be safe. But if you be not careful in this respect, then——' He finished his speech in a gruesome way, for he motioned with his hands as if he were washing them. I quite understood; my only doubt was as to whether any dream could be more terrible than the unnatural, horrible net of gloom and mystery which seemed closing round me.

Later – I endorse the last words written, but this time there is no doubt in question. I shall not fear to sleep in any place where he is not. I have placed the crucifix over the head of my bed – I imagine that my rest is thus freer from dreams; and there it shall remain.

When he left me I went to my room. After a little while, not hearing any sound, I came out and went up the stone stair to where I could look out towards the south. There was some sense of freedom in the vast expanse, inaccessible though it was to me, as compared with the narrow darkness of the courtyard. Looking out on this, I felt that I was indeed in prison, and I seemed to want a breath of fresh air, though it were of the night. I am beginning to feel this nocturnal existence tell on me. It is destroying my nerve. I start at my own shadow, and am full of all sorts of horrible imaginings. God knows that there is ground for any terrible fear in this accursed place! I looked out over the beautiful expanse, bathed in soft yellow moonlight till it was almost as light as day. In the soft light the distant hills became melted, and the shadows in the valleys and gorges of velvety blackness. The mere beauty seemed to cheer me; there was peace and comfort in every breath I drew. As I leaned from the window my eye was caught by something moving a storey below me, and somewhat to my left, where I imagined, from the lie of the rooms, that the windows of the Count's own room would look out. The window at which I stood was tall and deep, stone-mullioned, and though weather-worn, was still complete; but it was evidently many a day since the case had been there. I drew back behind the stonework, and looked carefully out.

What I saw was the Count's head coming out from the window. I did not see the face, but I knew the man by the neck and the movement of his back and arms. In any case, I could not mistake the hands which I had had so many opportunities of studying. I was at first interested and somewhat amused, for it is wonderful how small a matter will interest

and amuse a man when he is a prisoner. But my very feelings changed
to repulsion and terror when I saw the whole man slowly emerge from
the window and begin to crawl down the castle wall over that dreadful
abyss, *face down*, with his cloak spreading out around him like great
wings. At first I could not believe my eyes. I thought it was some trick
of the moonlight, some weird effect of shadow; but I kept looking, and
it could be no delusion. I saw the fingers and toes grasp the corners of
the stones, worn clear of the mortar by the stress of years, and by thus
using every projection and inequality move downwards with considerable speed, just as a lizard moves along a wall.

What manner of man is this, or what manner of creature is it in the
semblance of man? I feel the dread of this horrible place overpowering
me; I am in fear – in awful fear – and there is no escape for me; I am
encompassed about with terrors that I dare not think of . . .

15 *May* – Once more have I seen the Count go out in his lizard fashion.
He moved downwards in a sidelong way, some hundred feet down, and
a good deal to the left. He vanished into some hole or window. When
his head had disappeared I leaned out to try and see more, but without
avail – the distance was too great to allow a proper angle of sight. I knew
he had left the castle now, and thought to use the opportunity to explore
more than I had dared to do as yet. I went back to the room, and taking
a lamp, tried all the doors. They were all locked as I had expected, and
the locks were comparatively new; but I went down the stone stairs to
the hall where I had entered originally. I found I could pull back the
bolts easily enough and unhook the great chains; but the door was
locked, and the key was gone! That key must be in the Count's room;
I must watch should his door be unlocked, so that I may get it and
escape. I went on to make a thorough examination of the various stairs
and passages, and to try the doors that opened from them. One or two
small rooms near the hall were open, but there was nothing to see in
them except old furniture, dusty with age and moth-eaten. At last,
however, I found one door at the top of a stairway which, though it
seemed to be locked, gave a little under pressure. I tried it harder, and
found that it was not really locked, but that the resistance came from
the fact that the hinges had fallen somewhat, and the heavy door rested
on the floor. Here was an opportunity which I might not have again,
so I exerted myself, and with many efforts forced it back so that I could
enter. I was now in a wing of the castle further to the right than the
rooms I knew and a storey lower down. From the windows I could see
that the suite of rooms lay along to the south of the castle, the windows
of the end room looking out both west and south. On the latter side, as
well as to the former, there was a great precipice. The castle was built
on the corner of a great rock, so that on three sides it was quite
impregnable, and great windows were placed here where sling, or bow,

or culverin could not reach, and consequently light and comfort, impossible to a position which had to be guarded, were secured. To the
west was a great valley, and then, rising far away, great jagged
mountain fastnesses, rising peak on peak, the sheer rock studded with
mountain ash and thorn, whose roots clung in cracks and crevices and
crannies of the stone. This was evidently the portion of the castle
occupied in bygone days, for the furniture had more air of comfort than
any I had seen. The windows were curtainless, and the yellow moonlight, flooding in through the diamond panes, enabled one to see even
colours, whilst it softened the wealth of dust which lay over all and
disguised in some measure the ravages of time and the moth. My lamp
seemed to be of little effect in the brilliant moonlight, but I was glad to
have it with me, for there was a dread loneliness in the place which
chilled my heart and made my nerves tremble. Still, it was better than
living alone in the rooms which I had come to hate from the presence
of the Count, and after trying a little to school my nerves, I found a soft
quietude come over me. Here I am, sitting at a little oak table where
in old times possibly some fair lady sat to pen, with much thought and
many blushes, her ill-spelt love-letter, and writing in my diary in shorthand all that has happened since I closed it last. It is nineteenth century
up-to-date with a vengeance. And yet, unless my senses deceive me, the
old centuries had, and have, powers of their own which mere 'modernity'
cannot kill.

  Later: the Morning of 16 *May* – God preserve my sanity, for to this I
am reduced. Safety and the assurance of safety are things of the past.
Whilst I live on here there is but one thing to hope for: that I may not
go mad, if, indeed, I be not mad already. If I be sane, then surely it is
maddening to think that of all the foul things that lurk in this hateful
place the Count is the least dreadful to me; that to him alone I can look
for safety, even though this be only whilst I can serve his purpose. Great
God! merciful God! Let me be calm, for out of that way lies madness
indeed. I begin to get new lights on certain things which have puzzled
me. Up to now I never quite knew what Shakespeare meant when he
made Hamlet say:

> 'My tablets! quick, my tablets!
> 'Tis meet that I put it down,' etc.,

for now, feeling as though my own brain were unhinged or as if the shock
had come which must end in its undoing, I turn to my diary for repose.
The habit of entering accurately must help to soothe me.

  The Count's mysterious warning frightened me at the time; it
frightens me more now when I think of it, for in future he has a fearful
hold upon me. I shall fear to doubt what he may say!

When I had written in my diary and had fortunately replaced the book and pen in my pocket, I felt sleepy. The Count's warning came into my mind, but I took a pleasure in disobeying it. The sense of sleep was upon me, and with it the obstinacy which sleep brings as outrider. The soft moonlight soothed, and the wide expanse without gave a sense of freedom which refreshed me. I determined not to return tonight to the gloom-haunted rooms, but to sleep here, where of old ladies had sat and sung and lived sweet lives whilst their gentle breasts were sad for their menfolk away in the midst of remorseless wars. I drew a great couch out of its place near the corner, so that, as I lay, I could look at the lovely view to east and south, and unthinking of and uncaring for the dust, composed myself for sleep.

I suppose I must have fallen asleep; I hope so, but I fear, for all that followed was startlingly real – so real that now, sitting here in the broad, full sunlight of the morning, I cannot in the least believe that it was all sleep.

I was not alone. The room was the same, unchanged in any way since I came into it; I could see along the floor, in the brilliant moonlight, my own footsteps marked where I had disturbed the long accumulation of dust. In the moonlight opposite me were three young women, ladies by their dress and manner. I thought at the time that I must be dreaming when I saw them, for, though the moonlight was behind them, they threw no shadow on the floor. They came close to me and looked at me for some time and then whispered together. Two were dark, and had high aquiline noses, like the Count's, and great dark, piercing eyes, that seemed to be almost red when contrasted with the pale yellow moon. The other was fair, as fair as can be, with great, wavy masses of golden hair and eyes like pale sapphires. I seemed somehow to know her face, and to know it in connection with some dreamy fear, but I could not recollect at the moment how or where. All three had brilliant white teeth, that shone like pearls against the ruby of their voluptuous lips. There was something about them that made me uneasy, some longing and at the same time some deadly fear. I felt in my heart a wicked, burning desire that they would kiss me with those red lips. It is not good to note this down, lest some day it should meet Mina's eyes and cause her pain; but it is the truth. They whispered together, and then they all three laughed – such a silvery, musical laugh, but as hard as though the sound never could have come through the softness of human lips. It was like the intolerable, tingling sweetness of water-glasses when played on by a cunning hand. The fair girl shook her head coquettishly, and the other two urged her on. One said:

'Go on! You are first, and we shall follow; yours is the right to begin.' The other added:

'He is young and strong; there are kisses for us all.' I lay quiet, looking out under my eyelashes in an agony of delightful anticipation. The fair girl advanced and bent over me till I could feel the movement of her breath upon me. Sweet it was in one sense, honey-sweet, and sent the same tingling through the nerves as her voice, but with a bitter underlying the sweet, a bitter offensiveness, as one smells in blood.

I was afraid to raise my eyelids, but looked out and saw perfectly under the lashes. The fair girl went on her knees and bent over me, fairly gloating. There was a deliberate voluptuousness which was both thrilling and repulsive, and as she arched her neck she actually licked her lips like an animal, till I could see in the moonlight the moisture shining on the scarlet lips and on the red tongue as it lapped the white sharp teeth. Lower and lower went her head as the lips went below the range of my mouth and chin and seemed about to fasten on my throat. Then she paused, and I could hear the churning sound of her tongue as it licked her teeth and lips, and could feel the hot breath on my neck. Then the skin of my throat began to tingle as one's flesh does when the hand that is to tickle it approaches nearer – nearer. I could feel the soft, shivering touch of the lips on the supersensitive skin of my throat, and the hard dents of two sharp teeth, just touching and pausing there. I closed my eyes in a languorous ecstasy and waited – waited with beating heart.

But at that instant another sensation swept through me as quick as lightning. I was conscious of the presence of the Count, and of his being as if lapped in a storm of fury. As my eyes opened involuntarily I saw his strong hand grasp the slender neck of the fair woman and with giant's power draw it back, the blue eyes transformed with fury, the white teeth champing with rage, and the fair cheeks blazing red with passion. But the Count! Never did I imagine such wrath and fury, even in the demons of the pit. His eyes were positively blazing. The red light in them was lurid, as if the flames of hell-fire blazed behind them. His face was deathly pale, and the lines of it were hard like drawn wires; the thick eyebrows that met over the nose now seemed like a heaving bar of white-hot metal. With a fierce sweep of his arm, he hurled the woman from him, and then motioned to the others, as though he were beating them back; it was the same imperious gesture that I had seen used to the wolves. In a voice which, though low and almost a whisper, seemed to cut through the air and then ring round the room, he exclaimed:

'How dare you touch him, any of you? How dare you cast eyes on him when I had forbidden it? Back, I tell you all! This man belongs to me! Beware how you meddle with him, or you'll have to deal with me.' The fair girl, with a laugh of ribald coquetry, turned to answer him:

'You yourself never loved; you never love!' On this the other women joined, and such a mirthless, hard, soulless laughter rang through the room that it almost made me faint to hear; it seemed like the pleasure of fiends. Then the Count turned, after looking at my face attentively, and said in a soft whisper:

'Yes, I too can love; you yourselves can tell it from the past. Is it not so? Well, now I promise you that when I am done with him, you shall kiss him at your will. Now go! go! I must awaken him, for there is work to be done.'

'Are we to have nothing tonight?' said one of them, with a low laugh, as she pointed to the bag which he had thrown upon the floor, and which moved as though there were some living thing within it. For answer he nodded his head. One of the women jumped forward and opened it. If my ears did not deceive me there was a gasp and a low wail, as of a half-smothered child. The women closed round, whilst I was aghast with horror; but as I looked they disappeared, and with them the dreadful bag. There was no door near them, and they could not have passed me without my noticing. They simply seemed to fade into the rays of the moonlight and pass out through the window, for I could see outside the dim, shadowy forms for a moment before they entirely faded away.

Then the horror overcame me, and I sank down unconscious.

I awoke in my own bed. If it be that I had not dreamt, the Count must have carried me here. I tried to satisfy myself on the subject, but could not arrive at any unquestionable result. To be sure, there were certain small evidences, such as that my clothes were folded and laid by in a manner which was not my habit. My watch was still unwound, and I am rigorously accustomed to wind it the last thing going to bed, and many such details. But these things are no proof, for they may have been evidences that my mind was not as usual, and, from some cause or another, I had certainly been much upset. I must watch for proof. Of one thing I am glad: if it was the Count that carried me here and undressed me, he must have been hurried in his task, for my pockets are intact. I am sure this diary would have been a mystery to him which he would not have brooked. He would have taken or destroyed it. As I look round this room, although it has been to me so full of fear, it is now a sort of sanctuary, for nothing can be more dreadful than those awful women, who were – who *are* – waiting to suck my blood.

18 *May* – I have been down to look at that room again in daylight, for I *must* know the truth. When I got to the doorway at the top of the stairs, I found it closed. It had been so forcibly driven against the jamb that part of the woodwork was splintered. I could see that the bolt of the lock had not been shot, but the door is fastened from the inside. I fear it was no dream, and must act on this surmise.

19 *May* – I am surely in the toils. Last night the Count asked me in the suavest tones to write three letters, one saying that my work there was nearly done and that I should start for home within a few days, another that I was starting on the next morning from the time of the

letter, and the third that I had left the castle and arrived at Bistritz. I would fain have rebelled, but felt that in the present state of things it would be madness to quarrel openly with the Count whilst I am so absolutely in his power; and to refuse would be to excite his suspicion and to arouse his anger. He knows that I know too much, and that I must not live, lest I be dangerous to him; my only chance is to prolong my opportunities. Something may occur which will give me a chance to escape. I saw in his eyes something of that gathering wrath which was manifest when he hurled that fair woman from him. He explained to me that posts were few and uncertain, and that my writing now would ensure ease of mind to my friends; and he assured me with so much impressiveness that he could countermand the later letters, which would be held over at Bistritz until due time in case chance would admit of my prolonging my stay, that to oppose him would have been to create new suspicion. I therefore pretended to fall in with his views, and asked him what dates I should put on the letters. He calculated a minute, and then said:

'The first should be June 12, the second June 19, and the third June 29.'

I know now the span of my life. God help me!

28 *May* – There is a chance of escape, or at any rate of being able to send word home. A band of Szgany have come to the castle, and are encamped in the courtyard. These Szgany are gipsies; I have notes of them in my book. They are peculiar to this part of the world, though allied to the ordinary gipsies all the world over. There are thousands of them in Hungary and Transylvania who are almost outside all law. They attach themselves as a rule to some great noble or *boyar*, and call themselves by his name. They are fearless and without religion, save superstition, and they talk only their own varieties of the Romany tongue.

I shall write some letters home, and shall try to get them to have them posted. I have already spoken to them through my window to begin an acquaintanceship. They took their hats off and made obeisance and many signs, which, however, I could not understand any more than I could their spoken language ...

I have written the letters. Mina's is in shorthand, and I simply ask Mr Hawkins to communicate with her. To her I have explained my situation, but without the horrors which I may only surmise. It would shock and frighten her to death were I to expose my heart to her. Should the letters not carry, then the Count shall not yet know my secret or the extent of my knowledge ...

I have given the letters; I threw them through the bars of my window with a gold piece, and made what signs I could to have them posted. The man who took them pressed them to his heart and bowed, and then put them in his cap. I could do no more. I stole back to the study and began to read. As the Count did not come in, I have written here ...

The Count has come. He sat down beside me, and said in his smoothest voice as he opened two letters:

'The Szgany has given me these, of which, though I know not whence they come, I shall, of course, take care. See!' – he must have looked at it – 'one is from you, and to my friend Peter Hawkins; the other' – here he caught sight of the strange symbols as he opened the envelope, and the dark look came into his face, and his eyes blazed wickedly – 'the other is a vile thing, an outrage upon friendship and hospitality! It is not signed. Well! so it cannot matter to us.' And he calmly held letter and envelope in the flame of the lamp till they were consumed. Then he went on:

'The letter to Hawkins – that I shall, of course, send on, since it is yours. Your letters are sacred to me. Your pardon, my friend, that unknowingly I did break the seal. Will you not cover it again?' He held out the letter to me, and with a courteous bow handed me a clean envelope. I could only redirect it and hand it to him in silence. When he went out of the room I could hear the key turn softly. A minute later I went over and tried it, and the door was locked.

When, an hour or two after, the Count came quietly into the room, his coming wakened me, for I had gone to sleep on the sofa. He was very courteous and very cheery in his manner, and seeing that I had been sleeping, he said:

'So, my friend, you are tired? Get to bed. There is the surest rest. I may not have the pleasure to talk tonight, since there are many labours to me; but you will sleep, I pray.' I passed to my room and went to bed, and, strange to say, slept without dreaming. Despair has its own calms.

31 *May* – This morning when I woke I thought I would provide myself with some paper and envelopes from my bag and keep them in my pocket, so that I might write in case I should get an opportunity; but again a surprise, again a shock!

Every scrap of paper was gone, and with it all my notes, my memoranda relating to railways and travel, my letter of credit, in fact, all that might be useful to me were I once outside the castle. I sat and pondered a while, and then some thought occurred to me, and I made search of my portmanteau and in the wardrobe where I had placed my clothes.

The suit in which I had travelled was gone, and also my overcoat and rug; I could find no trace of them anywhere. This looked like some new scheme of villainy ...

17 *June* – This morning, as I was sitting on the edge of my bed cudgelling my brains, I heard without a cracking of whips and pounding and scraping of horses' feet up the rocky path beyond the courtyard.

With joy I hurried to the window, and saw drive into the yard two great leiter-wagons, each drawn by eight sturdy horses, and at the head of each pair a Slovak, with his wide hat, great, nail-studded belt, dirty sheepskin, and high boots. They had also their long staves in hand. I ran to the door, intending to descend and try and join them through the main hall, as I thought that way might be opened for them. Again a shock: my door was fastened on the outside.

Then I ran to the window and cried to them. They looked up at me stupidly and pointed, but just then the 'hetman' of the Szgany came out, and seeing them pointing to my window, said something, at which they laughed. Henceforth, no effort of mine, no piteous cry or agonized entreaty, would make them even look at me. They resolutely turned away. The leiter-wagons contained great, square boxes, with handles of thick rope; these were evidently empty by the ease with which the Slovaks handled them, and by their resonance as they were roughly moved. When they were all unloaded and packed in a great heap in one corner of the yard, the Slovaks were given some money by the Szgany, and spitting on it for luck, lazily went each to his horse's head. Shortly afterwards I heard the cracking of their whips die away in the distance.

24 *June, before morning* – Last night the Count left me early, and locked himself into his own room. As soon as I dared, I ran up the winding stair, and looked out of the window which opened south. I thought I would watch for the Count, for there is something going on. The Szgany are quartered somewhere in the castle, and are doing work of some kind. I know it, for now and then I hear a far-away, muffled sound as of mattock and spade, and, whatever it is, it must be to the end of some ruthless villainy.

I had been at the window somewhat less than half an hour, when I saw something coming out of the Count's window. I drew back and watched carefully, and saw the whole man emerge. It was a new shock to me to find that he had on the suit of clothes which I had worn whilst travelling here, and slung over his shoulder the terrible bag which I had seen the women take away. There could be no doubt as to his quest, and in my garb, too! This, then, is his new scheme of evil: that he will allow others to see me, as they think, so that he may both leave evidence that I have been seen in the towns or villages posting my own letters, and that any wickedness which he may do shall by the local people be attributed to me.

It makes me rage to think that this can go on, and whilst I am shut up here, a veritable prisoner, but without that protection of the law which is even a criminal's right and consolation.

I thought I would watch for the Count's return, and for a long time sat doggedly at the window. Then I began to notice that there were some quaint little specks floating in the rays of the moonlight. They were like the tiniest grains of dust, and they whirled round and gathered in clusters in a nebulous sort of way. I watched them with a sense of soothing, and a sort of calm stole over me. I leaned back in the embrasure in a more comfortable position, so that I could enjoy more fully the aerial gambolling.

Something made me start up, a low, piteous howling of dogs somewhere far below in the valley, which was hidden from my sight. Louder it seemed to ring in my ears, and the floating motes of dust to take new shapes to the sound as they danced in the moonlight. I felt myself struggling to awake to some call of my instincts; nay, my very soul was struggling, and my half-remembered sensibilities were striving to answer the call. I was becoming hypnotized! Quicker and quicker danced the dust, and the moonbeams seemed to quiver as they went by me into the mass of gloom beyond. More and more they gathered till they seemed to take dim phantom shapes. And then I started, broad awake and in full possession of my senses, and ran screaming from the place. The phantom shapes, which were becoming gradually materialized from the moonbeams, were those of the three ghostly women to whom I was doomed. I fled, and felt somewhat safer in my own room, where there was no moonlight and where the lamp was burning brightly.

When a couple of hours had passed I heard something stirring in the Count's room, something like a sharp wail quickly suppressed; and then there was silence, deep, awful silence, which chilled me. With a beating heart, I tried the door; but I was locked in my prison, and could do nothing. I sat down and simply cried.

As I sat I heard a sound in the courtyard without – the agonized cry of a woman. I rushed to the window, and throwing it up, peered out between the bars. There, indeed, was a woman with dishevelled hair, holding her hands over her heart as one distressed with running. She was leaning against a corner of the gateway. When she saw my face at the window she threw herself forward, and shouted in a voice laden with menace:

'Monster, give me my child!'

She threw herself on her knees, and raising up her hands, cried the same words in tones which wrung my heart. Then she tore her hair and beat her breast, and abandoned herself to all the violences of extravagant emotion. Finally, she threw herself forward, and, though I could not see her, I could hear the beating of her naked hands against the door.

Somewhere high overhead, probably on the tower, I heard the voice of the Count calling in his harsh, metallic whisper. His call seemed to be answered from far and wide by the howling of wolves. Before many minutes had passed a pack of them poured, like a pent-up dam when liberated, through the wide entrance into the courtyard.

There was no cry from the woman, and the howling of the wolves was but short. Before long they streamed away singly, licking their lips.

I could not pity her, for I knew now what had become of her child, and she was better dead.

What shall I do? what can I do? How can I escape from this dreadful thrall of night and gloom and fear?

25 *June, morning* – No man knows till he has suffered from the night how sweet and how dear to his heart and eye the morning can be. When the sun grew so high this morning that it struck the top of the great gateway opposite my window, the high spot which it touched seemed to me as if the dove from the ark had lighted there. My fear fell from me as if it had been a vaporous garment which dissolved in the warmth. I must take action of some sort while the courage of the day is upon me. Last night one of my post-dated letters went to post, the first of that fatal series which is to blot out the very traces of my existence from the earth.

Let me not think of it. Action!

It has always been at night-time that I have been molested or threatened, or in some way in danger or in fear. I have not yet seen the Count in the daylight. Can it be that he sleeps when others wake, that he may be awake whilst they sleep! If I could only get into his room! But there is no possible way. The door is always locked, no way for me.

Yes, there is a way, if one dares to take it. Where his body has gone why not may another body go? I have seen him myself crawl from his window; why should not I imitate him, and go in by his window? The chances are desperate, but my need is more desperate still. I shall risk it. At the worst it can only be death. And a man's death is not a calf's, and the dread Hereafter may still be open to me. God help me in my task! Goodbye, Mina, if I fail; goodbye, my faithful friend and second father; goodbye, all, and last of all Mina!

Same day, later – I have made the effort, and, God helping me, have come safely back to this room. I must put down every detail in order. I went whilst my courage was fresh straight to the window on the south side, and at once got outside on the narrow ledge of stone which runs round the building on this side. The stones were big and roughly cut, and the mortar had by process of time been washed away between them. I took off my boots, and ventured out on the desperate way. I looked down once, so as to make sure that sudden glimpse of the awful depth would not overcome me, but after that kept my eyes away from it. I knew pretty well the direction and distance of the Count's window, and made for it as well as I could, having regard to the opportunities available. I did not feel dizzy – I suppose I was too excited – and the time seemed ridiculously short till I found myself standing on the window-sill and trying to raise up the sash. I was filled with agitation, however, when I bent down and slid feet foremost in through the window. Then

I looked around for the Count, but, with surprise and gladness, made a discovery. The room was empty! It was barely furnished with odd things, which seemed to have never been used; the furniture was something the same style as that in the south rooms, and was covered with dust. I looked for the key, but it was not in the lock, and I could not find it anywhere. The only thing I found was a great heap of gold in one corner – gold of all kinds, Roman, and British, and Austrian and Hungarian, and Greek and Turkish money, covered with a film of dust, as though it had lain long in the ground. None of it that I noticed was less than three hundred years old. There were also chains and ornaments, some jewelled, but all of them old and stained.

At one corner of the room was a heavy door. I tried it, for, since I could not find the key of the room or the key of the outer door, which was the main object of my search, I must make further examination, or all my efforts would be in vain. It was open, and led through a stone passage to a circular stairway, which went steeply down. I descended, minding carefully where I went, for the stairs were dark, being only lit by loopholes in the heavy masonry. At the bottom there was a dark, tunnel-like passage, through which came a deathly, sickly odour, the odour of old earth newly turned. As I went through the passage the smell grew closer and heavier. At last I pulled open a heavy door which stood ajar, and found myself in an old, ruined chapel, which had evidently been used as a graveyard. The roof was broken, and in two places were steps leading to vaults, but the ground had recently been dug over, and the earth placed in great wooden boxes, manifestly those which had been brought by the Slovaks. There was nobody about, and I made search for any further outlet, but there was none. Then I went over every inch of the ground, so as not to lose a chance. I went down even into the vaults, where the dim light struggled, although to do so was a dread to my very soul. Into two of these I went, but saw nothing except fragments of old coffins and piles of dust; in the third however, I made a discovery.

There, in one of the great boxes, of which there were fifty in all, on a pile of newly dug earth, lay the Count! He was either dead or asleep, I could not say which – for the eyes were open and stony, but without the glassiness of death – and the cheeks had the warmth of life through all their pallor, and the lips were as red as ever. But there was no sign of movement, no pulse, no breath, no beating of the heart. I bent over him, and tried to find any sign of life, but in vain. He could not have lain there long, for the earthy smell would have passed away in a few hours. By the side of the box was its cover, pierced with holes here and there. I thought he might have the keys on him, but when I went to search I saw the dead eyes, and in them, dead though they were, such a look of hate, though unconscious of me or my presence, that I fled from the place, and leaving the Count's room by the window, crawled again up the castle wall. Regaining my own chamber, I threw myself panting upon the bed and tried to think ...

29 *June* – Today is the date of my last letter, and the Count has taken steps to prove that it was genuine, for again I saw him leave the castle by the same window, and in my clothes. As he went down the wall, lizard fashion, I wished I had a gun or some lethal weapon, that I might destroy him; but I fear that no weapon wrought alone by man's hand would have any effect on him. I dared not wait to see him return, for I feared to see those weird sisters. I came back to the library, and read there till I fell asleep.

I was awakened by the Count, who looked at me as grimly as a man can look as he said:

'Tomorrow, my friend, we must part. You return to your beautiful England, I to some work which may have such an end that we may never meet. Your letter home has been despatched; tomorrow I shall not be here, but all shall be ready for your journey. In the morning come the Szgany, who have some labours of their own here, and also come some Slovaks. When they have gone, my carriage shall come for you, and shall bear you to the Borgo Pass to meet the diligence from Bukovina to Bistritz. But I am in hopes that I shall see more of you at Castle Dracula.' I suspected him, and determined to test his sincerity. Sincerity! It seems like a profanation of the word to write it in connection with such a monster, so I asked him point-blank:

'Why may I not go tonight?'

'Because, dear sir, my coachman and horses are away on a mission.'

'But I would walk with pleasure. I want to get away at once.' He smiled, such a soft, smooth, diabolical smile that I knew there was some trick behind his smoothness. He said:

'And your baggage?'

'I do not care about it. I can send for it some other time.'

The Count stood up, and said, with a sweet courtesy which made me rub my eyes, it seemed so real:

'You English have a saying which is close to my heart, for its spirit is that which rules our *boyars*: "Welcome the coming, speed the parting guest." Come with me, my dear young friend. Not an hour shall you wait in my house against your will, though sad am I at your going, and that you so suddenly desire it. Come!' With a stately gravity, he, with the lamp, preceded me down the stairs and along the hall. Suddenly he stopped.

'Hark!'

Close at hand came the howling of many wolves. It was almost as if the sound sprang up at the raising of his hand, just as the music of a great orchestra seems to leap under the baton of the conductor. After a pause

of a moment, he proceeded, in his stately way, to the door, drew back
the ponderous bolts, unhooked the heavy chains, and began to draw it
open.

To my intense astonishment I saw that it was unlocked. Suspiciously
I looked all round, but could see no key of any kind.

As the door began to open, the howling of the wolves without grew
louder and angrier; their red jaws, with champing teeth, and their
blunt-clawed feet as they leaped, came in through the opening door. I
knew that to struggle at the moment against the Count was useless. With
such allies as these at his command, I could do nothing. But still the door
continued slowly to open, and only the Count's body stood in the gap.
Suddenly it struck me that this might be the moment and the means of
my doom; I was to be given to the wolves, and at my own instigation.
There was a diabolical wickedness in the idea great enough for the
Count, and as a last chance I cried out:

'Shut the door; I shall wait till morning!' and covered my face with
my hands to hide my tears of bitter disappointment. With one sweep
of his powerful arm, the Count threw the door shut, and the great bolts
clanged and echoed through the hall as they shot back into their places.

In silence we returned to the library, and after a minute or two I went
to my own room. The last I saw of Count Dracula was his kissing his
hand to me, with a red light of triumph in his eyes, and with a smile
that Judas in hell might be proud of.

When I was in my room and about to lie down, I thought I heard
a whispering at my door. I went to it softly and listened. Unless my ears
deceived me, I heard the voice of the Count:

'Back, back, to your own place! Your time is not yet come. Wait. Have
patience. Tomorrow night, tomorrow night, is yours!' There was a low,
sweet ripple of laughter, and in a rage I threw open the door, and saw
without the three terrible women licking their lips. As I appeared they
all joined in a horrible laugh, and ran away.

I came back to my room and threw myself on my knees. Is it then
so near the end? Tomorrow! tomorrow! Lord, help me, and those to
whom I am dear!

30 *June, morning* – These may be the last words I ever write in this
diary. I slept till just before the dawn, and when I woke threw myself
on my knees, for I determined that if Death came he should find me
ready.

At last I felt that subtle change in the air and knew that the morning
had come. Then came the welcome cock-crow, and I felt that I was safe.
With a glad heart, I opened my door and ran down to the hall. I had
seen that the door was unlocked and now escape was before me. With
hands that trembled with eagerness, I unhooked the chains and drew
back the massive bolts.

But the door would not move. Despair seized me. I pulled and pulled at the door, and shook it till, massive as it was, it rattled in its casement. I could see the bolt-shot. It had been locked after I left the Count.

Then a wild desire took me to obtain that key at any risk, and I determined then and there to scale the wall again and gain the Count's room. He might kill me, but death now seemed the happier choice of evils. Without a pause I rushed up to the east window and scrambled down the wall, as before, into the Count's room. It was empty, but that was as I expected. I could not see a key anywhere, but the heap of gold remained. I went through the door in the corner and down the winding stair and along the dark passage to the old chapel. I knew now well enough where to find the monster I sought.

The great box was in the same place, close against the wall, but the lid was laid on it, not fastened down, but with the nails ready in their places to be hammered home. I knew I must search the body for the key, so I raised the lid and laid it back against the wall; and then I saw something which filled my very soul with horror. There lay the Count, but looking as if his youth had been half-renewed, for the white hair and moustache were changed to dark iron-grey; the cheeks were fuller, and the white skin seemed ruby-red underneath; the mouth was redder than ever, for on the lips were gouts of fresh blood, which trickled from the corners of the mouth and ran over the chin and neck. Even the deep, burning eyes seemed set amongst swollen flesh, for the lids and pouches underneath were bloated. It seemed as if the whole awful creature were simply gorged with blood; he lay like a filthy leech, exhausted with his repletion. I shuddered as I bent over to touch him, and every sense in me revolted at the contact; but I had to search, or I was lost. The coming night might see my own body a banquet in a similar way to those horrid three. I felt all over the body, but no sign could I find of the key. Then I stopped and looked at the Count. There was a mocking smile on the bloated face which seemed to drive me mad. This was the being I was helping to transfer to London, where, perhaps for centuries to come, he might, amongst its teeming millions, satiate his lust for blood, and create a new and ever widening circle of semi-demons to batten on the helpless. The very thought drove me mad. A terrible desire came upon me to rid the world of such a monster. There was no lethal weapon at hand, but I seized a shovel which the workmen had been using to fill the cases, and lifting it high, struck with the edge downward, at the hateful face. But as I did so the head turned, and the eyes fell full upon me, with all their blaze of basilisk horror. The sight seemed to paralyse me, and the shovel turned in my hand and glanced from the face, merely making a deep gash above the forehead. The shovel fell from my hand across the box, and as I pulled it away the flange of the blade caught the edge of the lid, which fell over again, and hid the horrid thing from my sight. The last glimpse I had was of the bloated face, bloodstained and fixed with a grin of malice which would have held its own in the nethermost hell.

I thought and thought what should be my next move, but my brain seemed on fire, and I waited with a despairing feeling growing over me. As I waited I heard in the distance a gipsy song sung by merry voices coming closer, and through their song the rolling of heavy wheels and the cracking of whips; the Szgany and the Slovaks of whom the Count had spoken were coming. With a last look around and at the box which contained the vile body, I ran from the place and gained the Count's room, determined to rush out at the moment the door should be opened. With strained ears I listened, and heard downstairs the grinding of the key in the great lock and the falling back of the heavy door. There must have been some other means of entry, or someone had a key for one of the locked doors. Then there came the sound of many feet tramping and dying away in some passage which sent up a clanging echo. I turned to run down again towards the vault, where I might find the new entrance; but at that moment there seemed to come a violent puff of wind, and the door to the winding stair blew to with a shock that set the dust from the lintels flying. When I ran to push it open, I found that it was hopelessly fast. I was again a prisoner, and the net of doom was closing round me more closely.

As I write there is in the passage below a sound of many tramping feet and the crash of weights being set down heavily, doubtless the boxes, with their freight of earth. There is a sound of hammering; it is the box being nailed down. Now I can hear the heavy feet tramping again along the hall, with many other idle feet coming behind them.

The door is shut, and the chains rattle; there is a grinding of the key in the lock; I can hear the key withdrawn; then another door opens and shuts; I hear the creaking of lock and bolt.

Hark! in the courtyard and down the rocky way the roll of heavy wheels, the crack of whips, and the chorus of the Szgany as they pass into the distance.

I am alone in the castle with those awful women. Faugh! Mina is a woman, and there is naught in common. They are devils of the Pit!

I shall not remain alone with them; I shall try to scale the castle wall farther than I have yet attempted. I shall take some of the gold with me, lest I want it later. I may find a way from this dreadful place.

And then away for home! away to the quickest and nearest train! away from this cursed spot, from this cursed land, where the devil and his children still walk with earthly feet!

At least God's mercy is better than that of these monsters, and the precipice is steep and high. At its foot a man may sleep – as a man. Goodbye, all! Mina!

It

Theodore Sturgeon

It walked in the woods.

It was never born. It existed. Under the pine needles the fires burn, deep and smokeless in the mould. In heat and in darkness and decay there is growth. There is life and there is growth. It grew, but it was not alive. It walked unbreathing through the woods, and thought and saw and was hideous and strong, and it was not born and it did not live. It grew and moved about without living.

It crawled out of the darkness and hot damp mould into the cool of a morning. It was huge. It was lumped and crusted with its own hateful substances, and pieces of it dropped off as it went its way, dropped off and lay writhing, and stilled, and sank putrescent into the forest loam.

It had no mercy, no laughter, no beauty. It had strength and great intelligence. And – perhaps it could not be destroyed. It crawled out of its mound in the wood and lay pulsing in the sunlight for a long moment. Patches of it shone wetly in the golden glow, parts of it were nubbled and flaked. And whose dead bones had given it the form of a man?

It scrabbled painfully with its half-formed hands, beating the ground and the bole of a tree. It rolled and lifted itself up on its crumbling elbows, and it tore up a great handful of herbs and shredded them against its chest, and it paused and gazed at the grey-green juices with intelligent calm. It wavered to its feet, and seized a young sapling and destroyed it, folding the slender trunk back on itself again and again, watching attentively the useless, fibred splinters. And it snatched up a fear-frozen field-creature, crushing it slowly, letting blood and pulpy flesh and fur ooze from between its fingers, run down and rot on the forearms.

It began searching.

Kimbo drifted through the tall grasses like a puff of dust, his busy tail curled tightly over his back and his long jaws agape. He ran with an easy lope, loving his freedom and the power of his flanks and furry shoulders. His tongue lolled listlessly over his lips. His lips were black and serrated, and each tiny pointed liplet swayed with his doggy gallop. Kimbo was all dog, all healthy animal.

He leaped high over a boulder and landed with a startled yelp as a long-eared cony shot from its hiding place under the rock. Kimbo hurtled after it, grunting with each great thrust of his legs. The rabbit bounced just ahead of him, keeping its distance, its ears flattened on its curving back and its little legs nibbling away at distance hungrily. It stopped, and Kimbo pounced, and the rabbit shot away at a tangent and popped into a hollow log. Kimbo yelped again and rushed snuffling at the log, and knowing his failure, curveted but once around the stump and ran on into the forest. The thing that watched from the wood raised its crusted arms and waited for Kimbo.

Kimbo sensed it there, standing dead-still by the path. To him it was a bulk which smelled of carrion not fit to roll in, and he snuffled distastefully and ran to pass it.

The thing let him come abreast and dropped a heavy twisted fist on him. Kimbo saw it coming and curled up tight as he ran, and the hand clipped stunningly on his rump, sending him rolling and yipping down the slope. Kimbo straddled to his feet, shook his head, shook his body with a deep growl, came back to the silent thing with green murder in his eyes. He walked stiffly, straight-legged, his tail as low as his lowered head and a ruff of fury round his neck. The thing raised its arm again, waited.

Kimbo slowed, then flipped himself through the air at the monster's throat. His jaws closed on it, his teeth clicked together through a mass of filth, and he fell choking and snarling at its feet. The thing leaned down and struck twice, and after the dog's back was broken, it sat beside him and began to tear him apart.

'Be back in an hour or so,' said Alton Drew, picking up his rifle from behind the wood box. His brother laughed.

'Old Kimbo 'bout runs your life, Alton,' he said.

'Ah, I know the ol' devil,' said Alton. 'When I whistle for him for half an hour and he don't show up, he's in a jam or he's treed something wuth shootin' at. The ol' son of a gun calls me by not answerin'.'

Cory Drew shoved a full glass of milk over to his nine-year-old daughter and smiled. 'You think as much o' that houn' dog o' yours as I do of Babe here.'

Babe slid off her chair and ran to her uncle. 'Gonna catch me the bad fella, Uncle Alton?' she shrilled. The 'bad fella' was Cory's invention – the one who lurked in corners ready to pounce on little girls who chased the chickens and played around mowing machines and hurled green apples with powerful young arms at the sides of the hogs, to hear the synchronized thud and grunt; little girls who swore with an Austrian accent like an ex-hired man they had had; who dug caves in haystacks till they tipped over, and kept pet crawfish in tomorrow's milk cans, and rode work horses to a lather in the night pasture.

'Get back here and keep away from Uncle Alton's gun!' said Cory. 'If you see the bad fella, Alton, chase him back here. He has a date with Babe here for that stunt of hers last night.' The preceding evening, Babe had kindheartedly poured pepper on the cows' salt block.

'Don't worry, kiddo,' grinned her uncle, 'I'll bring you the bad fella's hide if he don't get me first.'

Alton Drew walked up the path towards the wood, thinking about Babe. She was a phenomenon – a pampered farm child. Ah well – she had to be. They'd both loved Clissa Drew, and she'd married Cory, and they had to love Clissa's child. Funny thing, love. Alton was a man's man, and thought things out that way; and his reaction to love was a strong and frightened one. He knew what love was because he felt it still for his brother's wife and would feel it as long as he lived for Babe. It led him through his life, and yet he embarrassed himself by thinking of it. Loving a dog was an easy thing, because you and the old devil could love one another completely without talking about it. The smell of gun smoke and wet fur in the rain were perfume enough for Alton Drew, a grunt of satisfaction and the scream of something hunted and hit were poetry enough. They weren't like love for a human, that choked his throat so he could not say words he could not have thought of anyway. So Alton loved his dog Kimbo and his Winchester for all to see, and let his love for his brother's women, Clissa and Babe, eat at him quietly and unmentioned.

His quick eyes saw the fresh indentations in the soft earth behind the boulder, which showed where Kimbo had turned and leaped with a single surge, chasing the rabbit. Ignoring the tracks, he looked for the nearest place where a rabbit might hide, and strolled over to the stump. Kimbo had been there, he saw, and had been there too late. 'You're an ol' fool,' muttered Alton. 'Y' can't catch a cony by chasin' it. You want to cross him up some way.' He gave a peculiar trilling whistle, sure that Kimbo was digging frantically under some nearby stump for a rabbit that was three counties away by now. No answer. A little puzzled, Alton went back to the path. 'He never done this before,' he said softly.

He cocked his .32-40 and cradled it. At the county fair someone had once said of Alton Drew that he could shoot at a handful of corn and peas thrown in the air and hit only the corn. Once he split a bullet on the blade of a knife and put two candles out. He had no need to fear anything that could be shot at. That's what he believed.

The thing in the woods looked curiously down at what it had done to

Kimbo, and tried to moan the way Kimbo had before he died. It stood a minute storing away facts in its foul, unemotional mind. Blood was warm. The sunlight was warm. Things that moved and bore fur had a muscle to force the thick liquid through tiny tubes in their bodies. The liquid coagulated after a time. The liquid on rooted green things was thinner and the loss of a limb did not mean loss of life. It was very interesting, but the thing, the mould with a mind, was not pleased. Neither was it displeased. Its accidental urge was a thirst for knowledge, and it was only – interested.

It was growing late, and the sun reddened and rested awhile on the hilly horizon, teaching the clouds to be inverted flames. The thing threw up its head suddenly, noticing the dusk. Night was ever a strange thing, even for those of us who have known it in life. It would have been frightening for the monster had it been capable of fright, but it would only be curious; it could only reason from what it had observed.

What was happening? It was getting harder to see. Why? It threw its shapeless head from side to side. It was true – things were dim, and growing dimmer. Things were changing shape, taking on a new and darker colour. What did the creatures it had crushed and torn apart see? How did they see? The larger one, the one that had attacked, had used two organs in its head. That must have been it, because after the thing had torn off two of the dog's legs it had struck at the hairy muzzle; and the dog, seeing the blow coming, had dropped folds of skin over the organs – closed its eyes. Ergo, the dog saw with its eyes. But then after the dog was dead, and its body still, repeated blows had had no effect on the eyes. They remained open and staring. The logical conclusion was, then, that a being that had ceased to live and breathe and move about lost the use of its eyes. It must be that to lose sight was, conversely, to die. Dead things did not walk about. They lay down and did not move. Therefore the thing in the wood concluded it must be dead, and so it lay down by the path, not far away from Kimbo's scattered body, lay down and believed itself dead.

Alton Drew came up through the dusk to the wood. He was frankly worried. He whistled again, and then called, and there was still no response, and he said again, 'The ol' flea-bus never done this before,' and shook his heavy head. It was past milking time, and Cory would need him. 'Kimbo!' he roared. The cry echoed through the shadows, and Alton flipped on the safety catch of his rifle and put the butt on the ground beside the path. Leaning on it, he took off his cap and scratched the back of his head, wondering. The rifle butt sank into what he thought was soft earth; he staggered and stepped into the chest of the thing that lay beside the path. His foot went up to the ankle in its yielding rottenness, and he swore and jumped back.

'*Whew!* Somp'n sure dead as hell there! Ugh!' He swabbed at his boot with a handful of leaves while the monster lay in the growing blackness with the edges of the deep footprint in its chest sliding into it, filling it up. It lay there regarding him dimly out of its muddy eyes, thinking it was dead because of the darkness, watching the articulation of Alton Drew's joints, wondering at this new uncautious creature.

Alton cleaned the butt of his gun with more leaves and went on up the path, whistling anxiously for Kimbo.

Clissa Drew stood in the door of the milk shed, very lovely in red-checked gingham and a blue apron. Her hair was clean yellow, parted in the middle and stretched tautly back to a heavy braided knot. 'Cory! Alton!' she called a little sharply.

'Well?' Cory responded gruffly from the barn, where he was stripping off the Ayrshire. The dwindling streams of milk plopped pleasantly into the froth of a full pail.

'I've called and called,' said Clissa. 'Supper's cold, and Babe won't eat until you come. Why – where's Alton?'

Cory grunted, heaved the stool out of the way, threw over the stanchion lock and slapped the Ayrshire on the rump. The cow backed and filled like a towboat, clattered down the line and out into the barnyard. 'Ain't back yet.'

'Not back?' Clissa came in and stood beside him as he sat by the next cow, put his forehead against the warm flank. 'But, Cory, he said he'd——'

'Yeh, yeh, I know. He said he'd be back fer the milkin'. I heard him. Well, he ain't.'

'And you have to – oh, Cory, I'll help you finish up. Alton would be back if he could. Maybe he's——'

'Maybe he's treed a bluejay,' snapped her husband. 'Him an' that damn dog.' He gestured hugely with one hand while the other went on milking. 'I got twenty-six head o' cows to milk. I got pigs to feed an' chickens to put to bed. I got to toss hay for the mare and turn the team out. I got harness to mend and a wire down in the night pasture. I got wood to split an' carry.' He milked for a moment in silence, chewing on his lip. Clissa stood twisting her hands together, trying to think of something to stem the tide. It wasn't the first time Alton's hunting had interfered with the chores. 'So I got to go ahead with it. I can't interfere with Alton's spoorin'. Every damn time that hound o' his smells out a squirrel I go without my supper. I'm gettin' sick and——'

'Oh, I'll help you!' said Clissa. She was thinking of the spring, when Kimbo had held four hundred pounds of raging black bear at bay until Alton could put a bullet in its brain, the time Babe had found a bear cub and started to carry it home, and had fallen into a freshet, cutting her head. You can't hate a dog that has saved your child for you, she thought.

'You'll do nothin' of the kind!' Cory growled. 'Get back to the house. You'll find work enough there. I'll be along when I can. Dammitt, Clissa, don't cry! I didn't mean to – oh, shucks!' He got up and put his arms around her. 'I'm wrought up,' he said. 'Go on now. I'd no call to speak that way to you. I'm sorry. Go back to Babe. I'll put a stop to this for good tonight. I've had enough. There's work here for four farmers an' all we've got is me an' that ... that huntsman.'

'Go on now, Clissa.'

'All right,' she said into his shoulder. 'But, Cory, hear him out first when he comes back. He might be unable to come back. He might be unable to come back this time. Maybe he ... he——'

'Ain't nothin' kin hurt my brother that a bullet will hit. He can take care of himself. He's got no excuse good enough this time. Go on, now. Make the kid eat.'

Clissa went back to the house, her young face furrowed. If Cory quarrelled with Alton now and drove him away, what with the drought and the creamery about to close and all, they just couldn't manage. Hiring a man was out of the question. Cory'd have to work himself to death, and he just wouldn't be able to make it. No one man could. She sighed and went into the house. 'It was seven o'clock, and the milking not done yet. Oh, why did Alton have to——'

Babe was in bed at nine when Clissa heard Cory in the shed, slinging the wire cutters into a corner. 'Alton back yet?' they both said at once as Cory stepped into the kitchen; and as she shook her head he clumped over to the stove, and lifting a lid, spat into the coals. 'Come to bed,' he said.

She laid down her stitching and looked at his broad back. He was twenty-eight, and he walked and acted like a man ten years older, and looked like a man five years younger. 'I'll be up in a while,' Clissa said.

Cory glanced at the corner behind the wood box where Alton's rifle usually stood, then made an unspellable, disgusted sound and sat down to take off his heavy muddy shoes.

'It's after nine,' Clissa volunteered timidly. Cory said nothing, reaching for house slippers.

'Cory, you're not going to——'

'Not going to what?'

'Oh, nothing. I just thought that maybe Alton——'

'Alton,' Cory flared. 'The dog goes hunting field mice. Alton goes hunting the dog. Now you want me to go hunting Alton. That's what you want?'

'I just – he was never this late before.'

'I won't do it! Go out lookin' for him at nine o'clock in the night? I'll be damned! He has no call to use us so, Clissa.'

Clissa said nothing. She went to the stove, peered into the wash boiler set aside at the back of the range. When she turned around, Cory had his shoes and coat on again.

'I knew you'd go,' she said. Her voice smiled though she did not.

'I'll be back durned soon,' said Cory. 'I don't reckon he's strayed far. It is late. I ain't feared for him, but——' He broke his 12-gauge shotgun, looked through the barrels, slipped two shells in the breech and a box of them into his pocket. 'Don't wait up,' he said over his shoulder as he went out.

'I won't,' Clissa replied to the closed door, and went back to her stitching by the lamp.

The path up the slope to the wood was very dark when Cory went up to it, peering and calling. The air was chill and quiet, and a fetid odour of mould hung in it. Cory blew the taste of it out through impatient nostrils, drew it in again with the next breath, and swore. 'Nonsense,' he muttered. 'Houn' dawg huntin', at ten in th' night, too. Alton!' he bellowed. 'Alton Drew!' Echoes answered him, and he entered the wood. The huddled thing he passed in the dark heard him and felt the vibrations of his footsteps and did not move because it thought it was dead.

Cory strode on, looking around and ahead and not down since his feet knew the path.

'Alton!'

'That you, Cory?'

Cory Drew froze. That corner of the wood was thickly set and as dark as a burial vault. The voice he heard was choked, quiet, penetrating.

'Alton?'

'I found Kimbo, Cory.'

'Where the hell have you been?' shouted Cory furiously. He disliked this pitch-darkness; he was afraid at the tense hopelessness of Alton's voice, and he mistrusted his ability to stay angry at his brother.

'I called him, Cory. I whistled at him, an' the ol' devil didn't answer.'

'I can say the same for you, you ... you louse. Why weren't you to milkin'? Where are you? You caught in a trap?'

'The houn' never missed answerin' me before, you know,' said the tight, monotonous voice from the darkness.

'Alton! What the devil's the matter with you! What do I care if your mutt didn't answer? Where——'

'I guess because he ain't never died before,' said Alton, refusing to be interrupted.

'You *what?*' Cory clicked his lips together twice and then said, 'Alton, you turned crazy? What's that you say?'

'Kimbo's dead,'

'Kim ... oh! Oh!' Cory was seeing that picture again in his mind –

Babe sprawled unconscious in the freshet, and Kimbo raging and
snapping against a monster bear, holding her back until Alton could get
there. 'What happened, Alton?' he asked more quietly.

'I aim to find out. Someone tore him up.'

'*Tore him up?*'

'There ain't a bit of him left tacked together, Cory. Every damn joint
in his body tore apart. Guts out of him.'

'Good God! Bear, you reckon?'

'No bear, nor nothin' on four legs. He's all here. None of him's been
et. Whoever done it just killed him an' – tore him up.'

'Good God!' Cory said again. 'Who could've——' There was a long
silence, then, 'Come 'long home,' he said almost gently. 'There's no call
for you to set up by him all night.'

'I'll set. I aim to be here at sunup, an' I'm going to start trackin', an'
I'm goin' to keep trackin' till I find the one done this job on Kimbo.'

'You're drunk or crazy, Alton.'

'I ain't drunk. You can think what you like about the rest of it. I'm
stickin' here.'

'We got a farm back yonder. Remember? I ain't going to milk twenty-
six head o' cows again in the mornin' like I did jest now, Alton.'

'Somebody's got to. I can't be there. I guess you'll just have to, Cory.'

'You dirty scum!' Cory screamed. 'You'll come back with me now or
I'll know why!'

Alton's voice was still tight, half-sleepy. 'Don't you come no nearer,
bud.'

Cory kept moving towards Alton's voice.

'I said' – the voice was very quiet now – '*stop where you are.*' Cory kept
coming. A sharp click told of the release of the .32-40's safety. Cory
stopped.

'You got your gun on me, Alton?' Cory whispered.

'Thass right, bud. You ain't a-trompin' up these tracks for me. I need
'em at sunup.'

A full minute passed, and the only sound in the blackness was that
of Cory's pained breathing. Finally:

'I got my gun too, Alton. Come home.'

'You can't see to shoot me.'

'We're even on that.'

'We ain't. I know just where you stand, Cory. I been here four hours.'

'My gun scatters.'

'My gun kills.'

Without another word Cory Drew turned on his heel and stamped
back to the farm.

Black and liquidescent it lay in the blackness, not alive, not understanding death, believing itself dead. Things that were alive saw and moved about. Things that were not alive could do neither. It rested its muddy gaze on the line of trees at the crest of the rise, and deep within it thoughts trickled wetly. It lay huddled, dividing its new-found facts, dissecting them as it had dissected live things when there was light; comparing, concluding, pigeon-holing.

The trees at the top of the slope could just be seen, as their trunks were a fraction of a shade lighter than the dark sky behind them. At length, they, too, disappeared, and for a moment sky and trees were a monotone. The thing knew it was dead now, and like many a being before it, it wondered how long it must stay like this. And then the sky beyond the trees grew a little lighter. That was a manifestly impossible occurrence, thought the thing, but it could see it and it must be so. Did dead things live again? That was curious. What about dismembered dead things? It would wait and see.

The sun came hand over hand up a beam of light. A bird somewhere made a high yawning peep, and as an owl killed a shrew, a skunk pounced on another, so that the night-shift deaths and those of the day could go on without cessation. Two flowers nodded archly to each other, comparing their pretty clothes. A dragonfly nymph decided it was tired of looking serious and cracked its back open, to crawl out and dry gauzily. The first golden ray sheared down between the trees, through the grasses, passed over the mass in the shadowed bushes. 'I am alive again,' thought the thing that could not possibly live. 'I am alive, for I see clearly.' It stood up on its thick legs, up into the golden glow. In a little while the wet flakes that had grown during the night dried in the sun, and when it took its first steps, they cracked off and a small shower of them fell away. It walked up the slope to find Kimbo, to see if he, too, were alive again.

Babe let the sun come into her room by opening her eyes. Uncle Alton was gone – that was the first thing that ran through her head. Dad had come home last night and had shouted at mother for an hour. Alton was plumb crazy. He'd turned a gun on his own brother. If Alton ever came ten feet into Cory's land, Cory would fill him so full of holes, he'd look like a tumbleweed. Alton was lazy, shiftless, selfish and one or two other things of questionable taste but undoubted vividness. Babe knew her father. Uncle Alton would never be safe in this county.

She bounced out of bed in the enviable way of the very young, and ran to the window. Cory was trudging down to the night pasture with two bridles over his arm, to get the team. There were kitchen noises from downstairs.

Babe ducked her head in the washbowl and shook off the water like a terrier before she towelled. Trailing clean shirt and dungarees, she

went to the head of the stairs, slid into the shirt, and began her morning
ritual with the trousers. One step down was a step through the right leg.
One more, and she was into the left. Then, bouncing step by step on
both feet, buttoning one button per step, she reached the bottom fully
dressed and ran into the kitchen.

'Didn't Uncle Alton come back a-tall, Mum?'

'Morning, Babe. No, dear.' Clissa was too quiet, smiling too much,
Babe thought shrewdly. Wasn't happy.

'Where'd he go, Mum?'

'We don't know, Babe. Sit down and eat your breakfast.'

'What's a misbegotten, Mum?' the Babe asked suddenly. Her mother
nearly dropped the dish she was drying. 'Babe! You must never say that
again!'

'Oh. Well, why is Uncle Alton, then?'

'Why is he what?'

Babe's mouth muscled around an outsize spoonful of oatmeal. 'A
misbe——'

'Babe!'

'All right, Mum,' said Babe with her mouth full. 'Well, why?'

'I told Cory not to shout last night,' Clissa said half to herself.

'Well, whatever it means, he isn't,' said Babe with finality. 'Did he
go hunting again?'

'He went to look for Kimbo, darling.'

'Kimbo? Oh Mummy, is Kimbo gone, too? Didn't he come back
either?'

'No, dear. Oh, please, Babe, stop asking questions!'

'All right. Where do you think they went?'

'Into the north woods. Be quiet.'

Babe gulped away at her breakfast. An idea struck her; and as she
thought of it she ate slower and slower, and cast more and more glances
at her mother from under the lashes of her tilted eyes. It would be awful
if daddy did anything to Uncle Alton. Someone ought to warn him.

Babe was halfway to the woods when Alton's .32-40 sent echoes
giggling up and down the valley.

Cory was in the south thirty, riding a cultivator and cussing at the team
of greys when he heard the gun. 'Hoa,' he called to the horses, and sat
a moment to listen to the sound. 'One-two-three. Four,' he counted.
'Saw someone, blasted away at him. Had a chance to take aim and give
him another, careful. My God!' He threw up the cultivator points and
steered the team into the shade of three oaks. He hobbled the gelding
with swift tosses of a spare strap, and headed for the woods. 'Alton a
killer,' he murmured, and doubled back to the house for his gun. Clissa
was standing just outside the door.

'Get shells!' he snapped and flung into the house. Clissa followed him. He was strapping his hunting knife on before she could get a box off the shelf. 'Cory——'

'Hear that gun, did you? Alton's off his nut. He don't waste lead. He shot at someone just then, and he wasn't fixin' to shoot pa'tridges when I saw him last. He was out to get a man. Gimme my gun.'

'Cory, Babe——'

'You keep her here. Oh, God, this is a helluva mess. I can't stand much more.' Cory ran out the door.

Clissa caught his arm: 'Cory I'm trying to tell you. Babe isn't here. I've called, and she isn't here.'

Cory's heavy, young-old face tautened. 'Babe – where did you last see her?'

'Breakfast.' Clissa was crying now.

'She say where she was going.'

'No. She asked a lot of questions about Alton and where he'd gone.'

'Did you say?'

Clissa's eyes widened and she nodded, biting the back of her hand.

'You shouldn't ha' done that, Clissa,' he gritted and ran towards the woods, Clissa looking after him, and in that moment she could have killed herself.

Cory ran with his head up, straining with his legs and lungs and eyes at the long path. He puffed up the slope to the woods, agonized for breath after the forty-five minutes' heavy going. He couldn't even notice the damp smell of mould in the air.

He caught a movement in a thicket to his right, and dropped. Struggling to keep his breath, he crept forward until he could see clearly. There was something in there, all right. Something black, keeping still. Cory relaxed his legs and torso completely to make it easier for his heart to pump some strength back into them, and slowly raised the 12-gauge until it bore on the thing hidden in the thicket.

'Come out!' Cory said when he could speak.

Nothing happened.

'Come out or by God I'll shoot!' rasped Cory.

There was a long moment of silence, and his finger tightened on the trigger.

'You asked for it,' he said, and as he fired, the thing leaped sideways into the open, screaming.

It was a thin little man dressed in sepulchral black, and bearing the rosiest baby-face Cory had ever seen. The face was twisted with fright and pain. The man scrambled to his feet and hopped up and down saying over and over, 'Oh, my hand. Don't shoot again! Oh, my hand. Don't shoot again!' He stopped after a bit, when Cory had climbed to his feet, and he regarded the farmer out of sad china-blue eyes. 'You shot me,' he said reproachfully, holding up a little bloody hand. 'Oh, my goodness.'

Cory said, 'Now, who the hell are you?'

The man immediately became hysterical, mouthing such a flood of broken sentences that Cory stepped back a pace and half-raised his gun in self-defence. It seemed to consist mostly of 'I lost my papers,' and 'I didn't do it,' and 'It was horrible. Horrible. Horrible,' and 'The dead man,' and 'Oh, don't shoot again.'

Cory tried twice to ask him a question, and then he stepped over and knocked the man down. He lay on the ground writhing and moaning and blubbering and putting his bloody hand to his mouth where Cory had hit him.

'Now what's going on around here?'

The man rolled over and sat up. 'I didn't do it!' he sobbed. 'I didn't. I was walking along and I heard the gun and I heard some swearing and an awful scream and I went over there and peeped and I saw the dead man and I ran away and you came and I hid and you shot me and——'

'*Shut up!*' The man did, as if a switch had been thrown. 'Now,' said Cory, pointing along the path, 'you say there's a dead man up there?'

The man nodded and began crying in earnest. Cory helped him up. 'Follow this path back to my farmhouse,' he said. 'Tell my wife to fix up your hand. *Don't* tell her anything else. And wait there until I come. Hear?'

'Yes. Thank you. Oh, thank you. *Sniff.*'

'Go on now.' Cory gave him a gentle shove in the right direction and went alone, in cold fear, up the path to the spot where he had found Alton the night before.

He found him here now, too, and Kimbo. Kimbo and Alton had spent several years together in the deepest friendship; they had hunted and fought and slept together, and the lives they owed each other were finished now. They were dead together.

It was terrible that they died the same way. Cory Drew was a strong man, but he gasped and fainted dead away when he saw what the thing of the mould had done to his brother and his brother's dog.

The little man in black hurried down the path, whimpering and holding his injured hand as if he rather wished he could limp with it. After a while the whimper faded away, and the hurried stride changed to a walk as the gibbering terror of the last hour receded. He drew two deep breaths, said: 'My goodness!' and felt almost normal. He bound a linen handkerchief around his wrist, but the hand kept bleeding. He tried the elbow, and that made it hurt. So he stuffed the handkerchief back in his pocket and simply waved the hand stupidly in the air until the blood clotted. He did not see the great moist horror that clumped along behind him, although his nostrils crinkled with its foulness.

The monster had three holes close together on its chest, and one hole in the middle of its slimy forehead. It had three close-set pits in its back and one on the back of its head. These marks were where Alton Drew's bullets had struck and passed through. Half of the monster's shapeless face was sloughed away, and there was a deep indentation on its shoulder. This was what Alton Drew's gun butt had done after he clubbed it and struck at the thing that would not lie down after he put his four bullets through it. When these things happened the monster was not hurt or angry. It only wondered why Alton Drew acted that way. Now it followed the little man without hurrying at all, matching his stride step by step and dropping little particles of muck behind it.

The little man went on out of the wood and stood with his back against a big tree at the forest's edge, and he thought. Enough had happened to him here. What good would it do to stay and face a horrible murder inquest, just to continue this silly, vague search? There was supposed to be the ruin of an old, old hunting lodge deep in this wood somewhere, and perhaps it would hold the evidence he wanted. But it was a vague report – vague enough to be forgotten without regret. It would be the height of foolishness to stay for all the hick-town red tape that would follow that ghastly affair back in the wood. Ergo, it would be ridiculous to follow that farmer's advice, to go to his house and wait for him. He would go back to town.

The monster was leaning against the other side of the big tree.

The little man snuffled disgustedly at a sudden overpowering odour of rot. He reached for his handkerchief, fumbled and dropped it. As he bent to pick it up, the monster's arm *whuffed* heavily in the air where his head had been – a blow that would certainly have removed that baby-face protuberance. The man stood up and would have put the handkerchief to his nose had it not been so bloody. The creature behind the tree lifted its arm again just as the little man tossed the handkerchief away and stepped out into the field, heading across country to the distant highway that would take him back to town. The monster pounced on the handkerchief, picked it up, studied it, tore it across several times and inspected the tattered edges. Then it gazed vacantly at the disappearing figure of the little man, and finding him no longer interesting, turned back into the woods.

Babe broke into a trot at the sound of the shots. It was important to warn Uncle Alton about what her father had said, but it was more interesting to find out what he had bagged. Oh, he'd bagged it, all right. Uncle Alton never fired without killing. This was about the first time she had ever heard him blast away like that. Must be a bear, she thought excitedly, tripping over a root, sprawling, rolling to her feet again, without noticing the tumble. She'd love to have another bearskin in her room. Where would she put it? Maybe they could line it and she could have it for a blanket. Uncle Alton could sit on it and read to her in the evening – oh, no. No. Not with this trouble between him and dad. Oh, if she could only do something! She tried to run faster, worried and anticipating, but she was out of breath and went more slowly instead.

At the top of the rise by the edge of the woods she stopped and looked back. Far down in the valley lay the south thirty. She scanned it carefully, looking for her father. The new furrows and the old were sharply defined, and her keen eyes saw immediately that Cory had left the line with the cultivator and had angled the team over to the shade trees without finishing his row. That wasn't like him. She could see the team now, and Cory's pale-blue denim was nowhere in sight. She giggled lightly to herself as she thought of the way she would fool her father. And the little sound of laughter drowned out, for her, the sound of Alton's hoarse dying scream.

She reached and crossed the path and slid through the brush beside it. The shots came from up around here somewhere. She stopped and listened several times, and then suddenly heard something coming towards her, fast. She ducked under cover, terrified, and a little baby-faced man in black, his blue eyes wide with horror, crashed blindly past her, the leather case he carried catching on the branches. It spun a moment and then fell right in front of her. The man never missed it.

Babe lay there for a long moment and then picked up the case and faded into the woods. Things were happening too fast for her. She wanted Uncle Alton, but she dared not call. She stopped again and strained her ears. Back towards the edge of the wood she heard her father's voice, and another's – probably the man who had dropped the briefcase. She dared not go over there. Filled with enjoyable terror, she thought hard, then snapped her fingers in triumph. She and Alton had played Injun many times up here; they had a whole repertoire of secret signals. She had practised birdcalls until she knew them better than the birds themselves. What would it be? Ah – bluejay. She threw back her head and by some youthful alchemy produced a nerve-shattering screech that would have done justice to any jay that ever flew. She repeated it, and then twice more.

The response was immediate – the call of a bluejay, four times, spaced two and two. Babe nodded to herself happily. That was the signal that they were to meet immediately at The Place. The Place was a hide-out that he had discovered and shared with her, and not another soul knew of it; an angle of rock beside a stream not far away. It wasn't exactly a cave, but almost. Enough so to be entrancing. Babe trotted happily away towards the brook. She had just known that Uncle Alton would remember the call of the bluejay, and what it meant.

In the tree that arched over Alton's scattered body perched a large jay bird, preening itself and shining in the sun. Quite unconscious of the presence of death, hardly noticing the Babe's realistic cry, it screamed again four times, two and two.

It took Cory more than a moment to recover himself from what he had seen. He turned away from it and leaned weakly against a pine. Alton. That was Alton lying there, in – parts.

'God! God, God, God——'

Gradually his strength returned, and he forced himself to turn again. Stepping carefully, he bent and picked up the .32-40. Its barrel was bright and clean, but the butt and stock were smeared with some kind of stinking rottenness. Where had he seen the stuff before? Somewhere – no matter. He cleaned it off absently, throwing the befouled bandanna away afterwards. Through his mind ran Alton's words – was that only last night? – '*I'm goin' to start trackin'. An' I'm goin' to keep trackin' till I find the one done this job on Kimbo.*'

Cory searched shrinkingly until he found Alton's box of shells. The box was wet and sticky. That made it – better, somehow. A bullet wet with Alton's blood was the right thing to use. He went away a short distance, circled around till he found heavy footprints, then came back.

'I'm a-trackin' for you, bud,' he whispered thickly, and began. Through the brush he followed its wavering spoor, amazed at the amount of filthy mould about, gradually associating it with the thing that had killed his brother. There was nothing in the world for him any more but hate and doggedness. Cursing himself for not getting Alton home last night, he followed the tracks to the edge of the woods. They led him to a big tree, and there he saw something else – the footprints of the little city man. Nearby lay some tattered scraps of linen, and – what was that?

Another set of prints – small ones. Small, stub-toed ones.

'Babe!'

No answer. The wind sighed. Somewhere a bluejay called.

Babe stopped and turned when she heard her father's voice, faint with distance, piercing.

'Listen at him holler,' she crooned delightedly. 'Gee, he sounds mad.' She sent a jay bird's call disrespectfully back to him and hurried to The Place.

It consisted of a mammoth boulder beside the brook. Some upheaval in the glacial age had cleft it, cutting out a huge V-shaped chunk. The widest part of the cleft was at the water's edge, and the narrowest was hidden by bushes. It made a little ceilingless room, rough and uneven and full of pot-holes and cavelets inside, and yet with quite a level floor. The open end was the water's edge.

Babe parted the bushes and peered down the cleft.

'Uncle Alton!' she called softly. There was no answer. Oh, well, he'd be along. She scrambled in and slid down to the floor.

She loved it here. It was shaded and cool, and the chattering stream filled it with shifting golden lights and laughing gurgles. She called again, on principle, and then perched on an outcropping to wait. It was only then she realized that she still carried the little man's briefcase.

She turned it over a couple of times and then opened it. It was divided in the middle by a leather wall. On one side were a few papers in a large yellow envelope, and on the other some sandwiches, a candy bar and an apple. With a youngster's complacent acceptance of manna from heaven, Babe fell to. She saved one sandwich for Alton, mainly because she didn't like its highly spiced bologna. The rest made quite a feast.

She was a little worried when Alton hadn't arrived, even after she had consumed the apple core. She got up and tried to skim some flat pebbles across the roiling brook, and she stood on her hands, and she tried to think of a story to tell herself, and she tried just waiting. Finally, in desperation, she turned again to the briefcase, took out the papers, curled up by the rocky wall and began to read them. It was something to do, anyway.

There was an old newspaper clipping that told about strange wills that people had left. An old lady had once left a lot of money to whoever would make the trip from the Earth to the Moon and back. Another had financed a home for cats whose masters and mistresses had died. A man left thousands of dollars to the first person who could solve a certain mathematical problem and prove his solution. But one item was blue-pencilled. It was:

'One of the strangest of wills still in force is that of Thaddeus M. Kirk, who died in 1920. It appears that he built an elaborate mausoleum with burial vaults for all the remains of his family. He collected and removed caskets from all over the country to fill the designated niches. Kirk was the last of his line; there were no relatives when he died. His will stated that the mausoleum was to be kept in repair permanently, and that a certain sum was to be set aside as a reward for whoever could produce the body of his grandfather, Roger Kirk, whose niche is still empty. Anyone finding this body is eligible to receive a substantial fortune.'

Babe yawned vaguely over this, but kept on reading because there was nothing else to do. Next was a thick sheet of business correspondence, bearing the letterhead of a firm of lawyers. The body of it ran:

'In regard to your query regarding the will of Thaddeus Kirk, we are authorized to state that his grandfather was a man about five feet, five inches, whose left arm had been broken and who had a triangular silver plate set into his skull. There is no information as to the whereabouts of his death. He disappeared and was declared legally dead after the lapse of fourteen years.

The amount of the reward as stated in the will, plus accrued interest, now amounts to a fraction over sixty-two thousand dollars. This will be paid to anyone who produces the remains, providing that said remains answer descriptions kept in our private files.

There was more, but Babe was bored. She went on to the little black notebook. There was nothing in it but pencilled and highly abbreviated records of visits to libraries; quotations from books with titles like 'History of Angelina and Tyler Counties' and 'Kirk Family History'. Babe threw that aside, too. Where could Uncle Alton be?

She began to sing tunelessly, 'Tumalumalum tum, ta ta ta,' pretending to dance a minuet with flowing skirts like a girl she had seen in the movies. A rustle of the bushes at the entrance to The Place stopped her. She peeped upwards, saw them being thrust aside. Quickly she ran to a tiny cul-de-sac in the rock wall, just big enough for her to hide in. She giggled at the thought of how surprised Uncle Alton would be when she jumped out at him.

She heard the newcomer come shuffling down the steep slope of the crevice and land heavily on the floor. There was something about the sound – what was it? It occurred to her that though it was a hard job for a big man like Uncle Alton to get through the little opening in the bushes, she could hear no heavy breathing. She heard no breathing at all!

Babe peered out into the main cave and squealed in utmost horror. Standing there was, not Uncle Alton, but a massive caricature of a man: a huge thing like an irregular mud doll, clumsily made. It quivered and parts of it glistened and parts of it were dried and crumbly. Half of the lower left part of its face was gone, giving it a lop-sided look. It had no perceptible mouth or nose, and its eyes were crooked, one higher than the other, both a dingy brown with no whites at all. It stood quite still looking at her, its only movement a steady unalive quivering.

It wondered about the queer little noise Babe had made.

Babe crept far back against a little pocket of stone, her brain running round and round in tiny circles of agony. She opened her mouth to cry out, and could not. Her eyes bulged and her face flamed with the strangling effort, and the two golden ropes of her braided hair twitched and twitched as she hunted hopelessly for a way out. If only she were out in the open – or in the wedge-shaped half-cave where the thing was – or home in bed!

The thing clumped towards her, expressionless, moving with a slow inevitability that was the sheer crux of horror. Babe lay wide-eyed and frozen, mounting pressure of terror stilling her lungs, making her heart shake the whole world. The monster came to the mouth of the little pocket, tried to walk to her and was stopped by the sides. It was such a narrow little fissure, and it was all Babe could do to get in. The thing from the wood stood straining against the rock at its shoulders, pressing harder and harder to get to Babe. She sat up slowly, so near to the thing that its odour was almost thick enough to see, and a wild hope burst through her voiceless fear. It couldn't get in! It couldn't get in because it was too big!

The substance of its feet spread slowly under the tremendous strain and at its shoulder appeared a slight crack. It widened as the monster unfeelingly crushed itself against the rock, and suddenly a large piece of the shoulder came away and the being twisted slushily three feet farther in. It lay quietly with its muddy eyes fixed on her, and then brought one thick arm up over its head and reached.

Babe scrambled in the inch farther she had believed impossible, and the filthy clubbed hand stroked down her back, leaving a trail of muck on the blue denim of the shirt she wore. The monster surged suddenly and, lying full length now, gained that last precious inch. A black hand seized one of her braids, and for Babe the lights went out.

When she came to, she was dangling by her hair from that same crusted paw. The thing held her high, so that her face and its featureless head were not more than a foot apart. It gazed at her with a mild curiosity in its eyes, and it swung her slowly back and forth. The agony of her pulled hair did what fear could not do – gave her a voice. She screamed. She opened her mouth and puffed up her powerful young lungs, and she sounded off. She held her throat in the position of the first scream, and her chest laboured and pumped more air through the frozen throat. Shrill and monotonous and infinitely piercing, her screams.

The thing did not mind. It held her as she was, and watched. When it had learned all it could from this phenomenon, it dropped her jarringly, and looked around the half-cave, ignoring the stunned and huddled Babe. It reached over and picked up the leather brief case and tore it twice across as if it were tissue. It saw the sandwich Babe had left, picked it up, crushed it, dropped it.

Babe opened her eyes, saw she was free, and just as the thing turned back to her she dived between its legs and out into the shallow pool in front of the rock, paddled across and hit the other bank screaming. A vicious little light of fury burned in her; she picked up a grapefruit-sized stone and hurled it with all her frenzied might. It flew low and fast, and struck squashily on the monster's ankle. The thing was just taking a step towards the water; the stone caught it off balance, and its unpractised equilibrium could not save it. It tottered for a long, silent moment at the edge and then splashed into the stream. Without a second look Babe ran shrieking away.

Cory Drew was following the little gobs of mould that somehow indicated the path of the murderer, and he was nearby when he first heard her scream. He broke into a run, dropping his shotgun and holding the .32-40 ready to fire. He ran with such deadly panic in his heart that he ran right past the huge cleft rock and was a hundred yards past it before she burst out through the pool and ran up the bank. He had to run hard and fast to catch her, because anything behind her was that faceless horror in the cave, and she was living for the one idea of getting away from there. He caught her in his arms and swung her to him, and she screamed on and on and on.

Babe didn't see Cory at all, even when he held her and quieted her.

The monster lay in the water. It neither liked nor disliked this new element. It rested on the bottom, its massive head a foot beneath the surface, and it curiously considered the facts that it had garnered. There was the little humming noise of Babe's voice that sent the monster questing into the cave. There was the black material of the briefcase that resisted so much more than green things when he tore it. There was the little two-legged one who sang and brought him near, and who screamed when he came. There was this new cold moving thing he had fallen into. It was washing his body away. That had never happened before. That was interesting. The monster decided to stay and observe this new thing. It felt no urge to save itself; it could only be curious.

The brook came laughing down out of its spring, ran down from its source beckoning to the sunbeams and embracing freshets and helpful brooklets. It shouted and played with streaming little roots, and nudged the minnows and pollywogs about in its tiny backwaters. It was a happy brook. When it came to the pool by the cloven rock it found the monster there, and plucked at it. It soaked the foul substances and smoothed and melted the moulds, and the waters below the thing eddied darkly with its diluted matter. It was a thorough brook. It washed all it touched, persistently. Where it found filth, it removed filth; and if there were layer on layer of foulness, then layer by foul layer it was removed. It was a good brook. It did not mind the poison of the monster, but took it up and thinned it and spread it in little rings round rocks downstream, and let it drift to the rootlets of water plants, that they might grow greener and lovelier. And the monster melted.

'I am smaller,' the thing thought. 'That is interesting. I could not move now. And now this part of me which thinks is going, too. It will stop in just a moment, and drift away with the rest of the body. It will stop thinking and I will stop being, and that, too, is a very interesting thing.'

So the monster melted and dirtied the water, and the water was clean again, washing and washing the skeleton that the monster had left. It was not very big, and there was a badly-healed knot on the left arm. The sunlight flickered on the triangular silver plate set into the pale skull, and the skeleton was very clean now. The brook laughed about it for an age.

They found the skeleton, six grim-lipped men who came to find a killer. No one had believed Babe, when she told her story days later. It had to be days later because Babe had screamed for seven hours without stopping, and had lain like a dead child for a day. No one believed her at all, because her story was all about the bad fella, and they knew that the bad fella was simply a thing that her father had made up to frighten her with. But it was through her that the skeleton was found, and so the men at the bank sent a cheque to the Drews for more money than they had ever dreamed about. It was old Roger Kirk, sure enough, that skeleton, though it was found five miles from where he had died and sank into the forest floor where the hot moulds built around his skeleton and emerged – a monster.

So the Drews had a new barn and fine new livestock and they hired four men. But they didn't have Alton. And they didn't have Kimbo. And Babe screams at night and has grown very thin.

See How They Run

Terry Tapp

Cassie leaned against the porch rail, staring up at the charred night sky, her eyes sweeping down to the distant hills. It was hot. The air was still, taut-strung and wound tight like a spring. She looked across the rock-baked mud of the yard to the open gate, from which the thin thread road snaked away through the cornfield and squirmed between the rocks to join the main highway, where traffic bitched and snarled through the night with flaming headlight eyes.

It was unnaturally silent. The heat closed in around the clapboard house, soaking into the timbers, warping them. Cassie wiped the back of her hand across her forehead and eased her thin cotton dress away from her skin. There would be a storm tonight, she guessed. That would clear the air.

Soon David would be home.

She sighed, clasping her hands over her stomach so that she could feel the kicking and the moving and growing of the child. This time it would be a girl, and she would be tall and slender with yellow hair and she would have David's blue eyes.

The telephone bell rang in the kitchen, and Cassie pulled back the screen door and went through quickly to answer it before the noise could wake up Simon.

'Hello?'

'Cassie?'

She laughed, glad to hear his voice. 'Who else could it be?'

'Cassie – I haven't time to joke about.'

'You're going to be late.' Now her voice was dull and flat.

'Can't help it,' said David. 'The stock-count didn't work out too good and I have to recheck all the main items again. The figures have to be finalized by morning.'

'Come home, David.' She had not meant to say that, but the words were out now. Cassie bit her lip.

'What's wrong?'

'Nothing. Nothing's wrong.'

'I have to see this work through, Cassie. You know how important it is for me to do well just now. It could mean promotion.'

'Yes, I see,' she said.

'We have to get some money from somewhere. Dammit, we can't go on living like we do.'

'There's nothing wrong with the way we live.'

'Maybe you don't notice it,' David said. 'But I do. We have to do more than just pay for the farm, Cassie. The farm needs money spending on it. Fences, stock, some corn, maybe.'

'How long will you be?' Cassie asked.

'An hour or two. No longer.'

'Your dinner's almost cooked.'

'It will keep, Cassie.' There was a long pause, then he spoke in a cheerful voice, and the cheerfulness of it annoyed Cassie. 'How's Simon? Been a rascal today, has he?'

'Did you call in to see Mr Moyce?' Cassie asked. 'I reminded you before you left this morning.'

'Hell – I forgot.'

'I knew you would,' said Cassie. 'Forgetting is what you're best at.'

'Listen, honey, I've got a load of work to get through. The sooner it's finished, the sooner I'll be home.'

'Can you take a few minutes and see Mr Moyce this evening?' Cassie asked. 'We need those traps, David. I found one in Simon's crib this morning.'

'I can't leave the store now,' said David. 'I'll pick the traps up tomorrow.' He let out a sigh. 'Christ, it's hot. I've never known it so hot.'

'It was lying on the coverlet in Simon's crib,' Cassie said. 'Must have been collecting wool to make a nest. Anyway, it had swallowed the wool and choked on it. The wool was spilling out of its mouth.'

'I'll get the traps, Cassie. You have to expect a few mice and rats when you live in the country, especially now we've got the east field sown with corn. It'll soon be harvest.'

'Then you can sell the corn and get the money to pay the interest on the loan.' Her voice was loaded with sarcasm.

'The field is ploughed and fenced, Cassie. Next year we should be able to afford to buy our own seed and— —'

'I won't keep you from your work,' she cut in.

'Cassie?'

'Yes?'

'I love you, Cassie.'

'Yes, I know,' she said. 'Don't pay any attention to me. I'm just tensed up, and hot.'

'See you soon.'

The telephone went dead and she stood there, holding on to it, reluctant to let go of the broken link between them. She glanced up into the mottled mirror, noting that her face was paler than usual, highlighting the intensity of her brown, liquid eyes. Replacing the receiver she combed her fingers through her hair, pulling it this way and that, then piled it high on her head and held it there with one hand, examining the effect critically.

She walked over to the sink and cooled her hands and wrists under the tap, then she bathed her face, allowing the tepid water to trickle down her neck. She went out on to the porch and stood there, her face glistening. The corn was swaying, as if stirred by a breeze, and Cassie longed for the wind and rains of winter. Standing there, she remembered how excited they had been when they first saw the farmhouse. The plans they had made; the promises and the hopes.

Now there was corn, trespassing in the field, growing fat each day, but not so fat as the slick, oil-skinned manager of the bank. He would ride by each week and raise his hat and nod to the corn like he had grown it himself. 'Fine lookin' corn you got there, Cassie,' he would call. Then he would grin, splitting his face open to show his rotting teeth and the two gold fillings he was so proud of.

Last week he had come by and pulled his glittering car in close to the house and he had stepped from the car and mopped his sweaty neck with a red handkerchief. 'Fine crop,' he told her.

'You'll soon have your money,' Cassie had replied.

'Fine, upstanding crop,' he said. He had been looking at Cassie with a new directness in his eyes, rubbing the palms of his hands slowly, slowly on the red handkerchief. 'A beautiful sight,' he continued, staring and staring at her, his eyes travelling over her, exploring.

She shivered.

Suddenly she felt vulnerable out there in the dark with the kitchen light playing on her. Anyone could be watching. Cassie went into the kitchen, pulling the screen door tightly shut, leaving the inner door wide open so that the air could circulate.

Then she saw it.

The tiny creature was sitting on the wooden draining board, resting back on its hind feet, its smaller fore feet held out, like human hands. It was about eight inches from tail to nose, larger than the normal mouse, and covered in coarse grey fur, except for its exposed underside, which was white. Thin, trembling whiskers tasted the air nervously.

Cassie picked up a towel and threw it, but the mouse dodged easily and skittered along the draining board so fast that it fell into the enamel sink and continued to run around the bowl, trying to climb out, its feet slipping and slithering down the glossy sides.

She went over to the sink, turned on the hot water tap and waited for the water to come through. The mouse paused, reared up, then watched the water fizz and hiss from the spluttering tap, swirling around the base of the bowl. Again the mouse ran, but this time straight into the scalding jetstream of water, which fell forcefully on to its grey back, burning through, stunning it, paralysing it with shock. The creature tried to run, then gave up, falling over on its side. The water flooded around it, dragging it towards the waste pipe, then the body blocked the hole and the basin began to fill.

Cassie watched, her face impassive.

It was dead.

Poking the body with the handle of the dishmop, she levered it aside to allow the water to escape, then picked up the mouse by the tail and threw it from the porch into the blackness of the night.

The corn waved, yet was not moved by the breeze, for there was no breeze that night.

Cassie went indoors and sat in the armchair by the fireplace so that she could look out through the screen and watch the road for the first sign of David's car coming.

They moved slowly through the cornfield. Hundreds of them. Slowly, noiselessly they came, from the barns and the houses nearby, from the river bank and from the twisted roots of the trees, from caves and crevices, hundreds joining hundreds, slowly, without hurry.

It was time.

They poured out of the fat belly of the hill, gushed up from the earth like oil, disgorged themselves from the warehouses and the railway yard sheds. They flowed down from the main highway, despite the massive slaughter by the wheels of the traffic, and moved purposefully through the night.

Cassie turned on the radio and listened to some music awhile, then switched stations and tuned to a quiz game.

'Right,' the quizmaster was saying. 'Now for your final question. How many passengers were carried by United States domestic and international airlines last year? Two million? Twenty million? Two hundred million?'

Cassie guessed at two million.

'Twenty,' said the contestant.

'Wrong.' The quizmaster sounded triumphant. 'Two hundred million passengers were estimated to have been carried.'

Two hundred million. Cassie closed her eyes and tried to imagine such a number. A hundred was a whole chapel full of people on Easter day. Two chapels would hold two hundred. But a million! How to think of a million? Why, just about everyone in the world must have used the airlines.

She filled the kettle and placed it on the stove, her mind still wrestling with those figures.

Something rustled by the porch and she went over to look for David's car. The clock chimed seven and she knew it was too early to be watching out for him yet. Then Simon cried out suddenly and Cassie turned to make her way up the stairs.

'I'm coming,' she called.

The hallway was cooler than the kitchen. Cassie stood there, at the foot of the stairs, listening. Simon may have called out in his sleep.

Again she heard that strange, secretive rustling sound and decided that she might as well go up and make sure the child was comfortable for the night.

'Two hundred million,' she said. 'That's how many times I've climbed these stairs, I guess.' Then she saw two mice dart across the landing into the boy's room.

He cried out again, louder this time – more of a scream – and Cassie raced up the last few steps to the bedroom. The door was open, and she could hear rustling and scratching, coming from Simon's bed. The child was now making a high, hysterical, whining noise. She switched on the light, flooding the room.

There were scores of the tiny creatures in the room, swarming over the bedclothes, only temporarily disturbed by the light. They were biting, then retreating, crawling over Simon's flailing body, darting at his face, his eyes, snapping, biting, then retreating, feeding off him, too crazed with hunger to be aware of Cassie.

She ran forward, grasped the bedclothes and tore them from the struggling child, throwing off a shower of frail-boned mice. But they came back, determined now. More were under the bedclothes, secret and warm, teeth bared as the child's legs came near. Cassie dragged the clothes away, then, sick with anger and fear, thrust her hands into the seething mass of frenzied creatures, feeling for Simon's body. She pulled hard, dragging him from the bed by an arm, while the creatures clung to him with teeth and claws, squealing with rage.

Shaking him like a rag doll, she managed to dislocate some of the creatures from him. They were over her feet now, ravenous, scaling her legs, biting deep and savagely. She ran, crushing them underfoot, screaming. Holding Simon close to her she could feel them moving within his clothing. The boy was delirious with pain and fear.

Down the stairs, two and three at a time, into the kitchen. She ripped the telephone off its rest and jabbed her finger in the dial, twisting viciously. The earpiece hummed in her ear. 'Please – please,' she sobbed.

'Emergency. Which service do you require?'

'Help me——' Cassie moaned. 'For God's sake——'

'Which service do you require?' The voice was impatient.

'Please – please,' Cassie moaned. 'Help.'

'I have to know the service you require,' insisted the operator.

Cassie glanced up as she saw a sudden movement at the foot of the stairs. She dropped the telephone and took a backward pace.

A tidal wave of mice tumbled from the stairs and spread out like a stain on the floor in the hall. Squealing with rage and hunger they flowed, like water, everywhere, then seemed to sense the right direction. 'Dear God!' Cassie screamed. 'No!'

Still holding Simon she kicked the door with her foot, just in time to stop the main body of them surging through into the kitchen. She screamed, and Simon sobbed wildly, his head lolling and pitching as Cassie moved.

The kitchen floor was alive with them, scuttling and climbing the thin curtains, dispersing over the floor, slithering on the tiles.

Cassie edged across to the screen door, hooked it back and pressed herself to the wall as several mice ran past her out into the black night. Thrusting Simon into his high chair, she opened the pantry door and reached for the broom. Some of the mice smelled the food and darted into the pantry before she had closed the door.

'Get out of here!' she screamed, sweeping the brush head wildly across the floor. 'Out! Out!'

She tried to sweep them towards the back door, but when she glanced across the floor she noticed that several mice were now coming in from the back yard. Screaming, Cassie dropped the broom and rushed over to pull the screen door shut.

The kitchen light shone out through the screen, pale yellow, making a wedge shape in the yard. And, as she watched, the ground appeared to heave as if broken by the blade of a massive plough.

Cassie gasped as a whole sea of them rose up in the yard, flooding in towards the light, tumbling over each other, squealing and filling the darkness with their awful cries. She felt giddy, nauseated by the sight of them, powerless to resist the onrush.

Somehow she managed to slam the screen door, and she stood there, hypnotized, watching wave after wave of them crashing into the metal like drumrolls. Some were squeezing under the screen, bending the thin wood by the sheer weight of numbers. Cassie closed the inner door, then slid the long metal bolt across. She noticed the telephone dangling crazily by its cord and was about to go over to it when she saw a group of mice gnawing at the feedwire which ran along the skirting. Within seconds they had severed it.

Three creatures had fallen into the shiny bowl of the sink and Cassie knew how to deal with them. She turned the hot water tap fully on.

The water sputtered, then ceased to flow.

She stared at it stupidly, hitting the tap with the heel of her hand. Now she could hear them overhead, between the ceiling plaster and the floorboards, drumming, gnawing. They were in the roof, crawling into the water tank; they were at the window, running across the hardwood frame, gnawing, splintering off chunks of wood with their sharp teeth. Everywhere. They were everywhere.

Simon moaned softly and Cassie wheeled around to see two mice attacking his bare legs. One sat just above his knee, its face fat with feeding, dipping its muzzle into the open wound, gouging, piercing. With a cry Cassie swept them to the floor and stamped down hard, once, twice, again, again, again!

And still they came.

The air was filled with the sound of them, squealing, drumming, scratching, ripping wood to get into the house. They poured over the roof, scaled the walls, squeezed through cracks and ran through the roof space. Below the floor, in the low cellar and in the store room they ran, falling on the few boxes of apples, eating cardboard and fruit alike.

Insanely they hurled their frail bodies at the windows, and Cassie went across to draw the curtains and shut out the light.

Above her head she could hear the thrumming of feet on the plaster; she could hear the sharp teeth tearing at the wood, gnawing everything.

The lights arced.

Then the house was plunged into darkness.

Cassie knew that it was just a matter of time. There were too many of them out there. Too many.

Above the sound of the radio she could hear them, wild, desperately intent on breaking in. She turned up the volume, praying that the battery would last until – until——

Feeling her way through the darkness, she took Simon into her arms and stood by the window. Through the curtains she caught sight of two pinpoints of light.

'David!' She screamed his name over and over. 'David! David!'

Pulling back the curtains she saw the car sweep around the yard, spotlighting the deep waves of scurrying creatures. The wheels threw out showers of tiny bodies, drove down on them, crushing and mangling. 'Cassie!' He shouted above the roar of the engine. 'You'll have to come out! I daren't stop or they'll be all over the car!'

She watched him circle the yard once more.

'I'll slow down as I pass the kitchen door!' David cried. 'Be ready, Cassie. If the car stops I'll never get it going again!'

'I'll try!' she called back.

'You *must* do it!' David yelled.

She could see his stark white face filled with fear. Their eyes met and held for a brief instant, then the car coughed. The engine choked twice, then died. For a few yards the car rolled on, then stopped. David turned the key. 'Come on! Come on!' He cursed the engine.

'David! Your window!'

Cassie saw the look of horror on his face as he saw that they were swarming in through the car window, leaping right on to him, instantly starting to bite and claw.

'No!' Cassie screamed. 'No!'

His arms flailed wildly, brushing them away, struggling to wind up the window. He cried out: 'God, Cassie! I can't see!' His hands went up to his face. More streamed into the car, jumping on to his shoulders, diving down at his legs.

There was nothing Cassie could do. It was hopeless now. Too many of them.

She watched the lights of the car dim, then die, and she sank to the floor, holding her quietly moaning child close to her, waiting and listening.

The radio could not now drown out the clamour outside. They were in the hallway, above her and below her, crowding to the window, scratching and gnawing.

Sounds of laughter came from the radio. A man's voice rumbled some words, but Cassie could not make sense of them. What did it matter, anyway?

'Three or four reported incidents do not make a plague.' The voice was clearer now.

'But is it not true that a pair of mice, or rats, left unmolested for a year could, with all the offspring, produce a population of almost a million?'

'Yes,' replied the rumbling voice. 'In theory this is true, but in practice it could never happen. The same theory applies to houseflies. If left unmolested for a year, without being eaten by birds and insects, or sprayed by chemicals, the common housefly could cover the entire surface of the earth to a depth of forty-seven feet.' The man laughed comfortably 'This, as you know, has not happened yet. Neither will it.'

'We have just had another report come in——' said the announcer.

'Coincidence,' interrupted the first voice. 'Coincidence, that's all.'

'Well, time is running out,' the announcer said ruefully. 'Have you a last word of comfort for the people who have been calling this programme?'

'Yes, I have. If this was a widespread thing – if rats and mice were everywhere, people would have flooded your studio with telephone calls. There is absolutely no need to be alarmed.'

The voice droned on as Cassie watched the dark shadows move across the window.

She tried to visualize a chapel full of mice at Easter-time. Then two hundred such chapels. Then a million – or more.

Too scared to cry, she listened, waiting in the darkness for the dreadful moment she knew would come.

Outside, they moved over the flattened corn and still came down from the highway in floods, tumbling and squeaking. Closing in.

Pat-a-Cake, Pat-a-Cake

Bernard Taylor

I like it here in this place. It's warm and cosy. And the people around me are nice. The face on the dark-haired lady who leans over my cot is especially nice. She has the softest brown eyes. I kept stealing little glances at her as she tucked me in with this beautiful new Rupert Bear eiderdown. I never had anything like this before. It's really nice. Not that I could *tell* them, of course – the man *or* the woman. Well, I *could* tell them, but they just wouldn't understand, and I've learned now that it's quite useless to try, no matter how clear I make myself. I think it must be something they learn – an ability they develop as we grow older and bigger. I hope so. I hope they will learn. There's so much I want to tell them.

I think this place is going to be my new home. Just now the woman leaned over me and said: 'You're going to stay here with your Daddy and me for ever and ever.' Oh, I felt so glad. It's exactly what I wanted. I would have hugged her except that my arms aren't long enough. So I sort of clapped my hands instead. Just think, these two people are going to be my New Mummy and Daddy. They must be.

I had a Mummy before. But the new one is much nicer. I never had a Daddy before, though. I must say I like it. This one's got a faint tobacco-y smell about him. I can recognize it. But it's not unpleasant, and his voice is very kind and gentle. I wonder if all Daddies are like him . . .

I'm going to stay here. I shall. I don't think I'll ever move on again. It's so nice.

I just clapped my hands together again, and the lady – I must always try to think of her as *Mummy* – went all smiley and happy. She said to me: 'That's it! Clever boy! That's it – *Pat-a-cake, pat-a-cake, baker's man* . . . *Go on* . . . *Pat-a-cake, pat-a-cake, baker's man* . . .' So I clapped my hands together even harder – as well as I could – and gave her a big grin. She laughed then, and said again:

Pat-a-cake, pat-a-cake, baker's man,
Bake me a cake as fast as you can.

Pat it and prick it and mark it with B,
And put it in the oven for baby and me!

I think that's how it went. Mind you, I'm not absolutely sure what this pat-a-cake thing is. I think it must be this clapping thing I do – waving my arms around – things like that. Though I'm not all that good at it yet – the clapping, pat-a-cake thing, I mean. It's not always easy to make your hands actually *meet* – hit together, you understand. The New Mummy seems to know this, and she took my hands and held them and gently clapped them together. And all the time she sang about pat-a-cake. I suppose I shall get the hang of it all sooner or later. I hope so. Some people do seem to set such store by these funny things, and I would so like to please her. And Daddy. I wonder what a *baker's man* is ... I expect I'll find that out some time as well. That must have been what I did with my First Mummy – the pat-a-cake, I mean. Well, something like it.

My First Mummy. She was my *real* Mummy.

I didn't like her.

I'm not proud of it. Because she *was* my real Mummy, after all. But she was quite horrid. I've no idea where a Daddy was – if there was one. There was just her. And me. Well, sometimes there were other men around – strangers who'd stay for an odd night or so in her bed – but no one I ever got to like. Oh, I'm so glad I'm not with her any more.

This lady now, this New Mummy, calls me nice names like – like Baby, and – Sweetheart, and Darling, and other things, and the way she says them they sound *nice*. I can tell she's smiling even when I can't see her face. You see, her smile is in her voice. But the other Mummy – the real one – *she* didn't call me nice things. She used to call me things like Bloody Kid, and Bastard, and Snivelling Little Sod. And they didn't sound nice. Not at all. Not the way she said them.

My nose is always clean now. It wasn't before. Before I often had a runny nose. That Mother never bothered at all. Once I got up all my courage and said to her: 'How would you like it if *your* nose was never wiped ... ?' But she just said: 'I'll bloody well goo-goo-goo-goo *you* in a minute!' Oh, it's best to forget her. I must try.

My New Mummy and Daddy are both near me now. *He* just looked down at me. His smile is so wide. He put a hand to my face. And I flinched. I didn't mean to. But his hand turned out to be the softest, gentlest touch you ever felt. So I put my hand up and held on to his thumb. He looked so pleased that I held on even harder. He likes that a lot. It's funny: it's very easy to make some people happy. The New Mummy said:

'Look, Dave. Look at the little love ...'

She never talked like that – the First one.

But I won't think about her. I said I wouldn't. I shall just think about these two. They love me. You can tell; it's easy. They're nice. I think these are the two I would have chosen if I'd had any choice, any say in the matter. I think it's a great pity that babies have to put up with what they get in the way of parents. I mean, without any thought or consideration at all I just got dumped with that awful woman who swore all the time, who had nicotine-stained fingers and bad teeth. And her breath was really terrible. Not that she ever kissed me or anything, I'm glad to say. Most of the time she just left me sitting there in this terrible battered old pram she got from somewhere. And I could be really *filthy*, honestly, and she wouldn't bother in the least. She used to go out to the pub and play darts most evenings, sometimes with one or other of the men who came to the door. Or else she'd go to Bingo. It didn't make much difference to me. Wherever she went, I'd be left. For ages and ages and ages. Sometimes with a woman who lived next door and sometimes – mostly – on my own. Yes, I think it's really unfair that we can't choose our own Mummy and Daddy.

I remember thinking that first of all when I was sitting outside the supermarket one day – in my pram. And I was looking at some of the other babies around me. They were so clean and smelt so lovely. And you should have seen some of the Mummies and Daddies – *beautiful*. Absolutely. And I thought then – how unfair it all was. I felt really ashamed. There I was, covered with this disgusting old blanket (not like my Rupert Bear eiderdown!), and feeling very uncomfortable because I hadn't been changed for ages and I decided, then and there, that I had to do something about it. It couldn't go on. I mean, it just couldn't, could it?

My New Daddy just said to my New Mummy:

'That scar on his arm. Poor little chap. Really must have hurt him. Fancy burning a kid like that – accident or no accident. Still, the doctor says it'll fade in time ...'

They mean that mark where she spilt boiling milk over me from the saucepan. Honest, I just wasn't safe. I *had* to get out.

Anyway, as I said, I'd made up my mind. Now I just had to wait for the right chance. And the right time. And I had to think of a good way. And there weren't that many ways open to me, still being on the little side as people go. But I was sure there'd be something.

All this, of course, was still outside the supermarket. I didn't have much chance to think on the problem then, as she came out loaded down with groceries. The next second I was almost smothered under a whole heap of instant mashed potatoes, tinned beans and tinned spaghetti and sliced bread. I said, before I could stop myself:

'For goodness' sake have a bit of consideration, will you? I mean, I'm not made of *rubber!*'

And she said, crossly:

'Don't you start bleedin' cryin'. If you've got the wind it's your own bloody fault. I wish to Christ I'd never 'ad you.'

You can see what I was up against. One felt totally impotent. It was just so hard to get anything across to anyone. I remember once when I was in my pram outside an off-licence one lunch-time. A policeman came by and stopped and crouched down by me. He said: 'Hello, young fellow. Waiting for your mother, are you? She won't be long.'

I thought, now's my chance. I said to him:

'Look at the state I'm in. You wouldn't believe it. I've had this nappy on since last night. Last night! And she doesn't care. Not a bit. Do you suppose you could report the matter to the proper authorities when you get an opportunity ... ? Do you think you could help to get me moved to someone else ... ? Another Mummy? As you can see, things are just not working out as they are ... *Please* ... ?'

I didn't have a chance to say any more as *she* came out of the shop carrying the bottles. The policeman stood up as she approached and smiled at her.

'I think he's getting impatient for you,' he said. He turned back to me and put his face close up to mine. 'Go on,' he said, 'say it. Mum-mum-mum-mum-mum-mum-mum-mum. You'll be talking next, won't you. Mum-mum-mum-mum ...'

I dribbled and made a rude noise.

That night we went to the pub. It was her darts night. She wheeled me into the shadow of the wall that I knew so well, grabbed her darts and her handbag and went off inside. I was left alone. Just like that.

It's a good job it was summer. Honestly, I could have frozen to death, otherwise, for all the notice she took of me. I was there for ages, and she never once even looked out to see that I was all right. One time some strange woman with breath that smelt of beer and onions came out and stuck her face close to mine. She turned and yelled back through the open pub door:

'Yeh, 'e's all right, love ...'

All right ... ? I tell you. There I was, hungry, thirsty, miserable and dirty. I hadn't been changed *still*. The least she could have done was given me a clean nappy. I mean, supposing I'd got knocked down ...

God, it was boring out there. I had a bit of a chat with a dog for a few minutes, a collie crossed with a spaniel; not the most communicative breed at the best of times, but at least it broke the monotony for a while. Later on, the beery-oniony woman came out again and looked at me. I said to her, as plainly as I could:

'Would you ask her if we can go home, please? Tell her I'm tired and bored, will you? And I'm so *wet*. I want to be *changed*. Please ...'

A look of real concern flashed across the woman's face for a second, and I thought: at last I've got through to somebody. Then she said:

'That's right, darlin'. You cough it up.' And then patted me on the back. What can you do . . . ?

Anyway, at least *she* came out. She flung her stuff on the pram by me and started to wheel me up the street. Looking out I saw this man there. Not nice though. Not like *this Daddy*. And they were talking and talking. We stopped outside the fish and chip shop where the light was very bright and got in my eyes. She braked the pram and joined the end of the queue leading to the counter; the man was with her. They didn't take any notice of me at all, and didn't even look to see what I was up to. Of course, by this time I was really awake. What with all that noise in my ears and that light in my eyes I couldn't very well be *expected* to sleep, could I? Actually it's a good job I didn't. Otherwise I might still be with her today.

I thought she'd never come back to the pram. It seemed ages before I felt her shadow over me and smelt the smell of her – chips, fish and vinegar all mixed up with the beer. I had my eyes closed now and I heard her say:

'Oh, bloody 'ell. Look what the little bastard's gone and done.' Her voice got nearer and louder, and angrier, and all the time I kept my face turned away. 'He's emptied every bleedin' thing out of my 'andbag,' she said. 'Look at that bleedin' mess.'

And then she leaned down, right low, over the pram. And that's when I did the pat-a-cake. But I did it against her neck and as hard as I could. It wasn't easy to aim properly – I'm not that good, as you probably know – but this time I got it *just right*. And the next thing she was straightening up, and clasping her hands to her throat, and I got a sudden glimpse of the red coming out between her fingers. She half shouted, half spoke:

'Oh, my God, what's that little sod done to me? Jesus Christ, I'm *bleedin'*, for God's sake!'

The man went up next to her then and I could see him putting up his hands, trying to stop the blood coming out of her neck. But he couldn't. Of course he couldn't. No one could. And all the time her cries were getting louder and more frightened. Lots of people were gathering around us – I think it must be the blood that does it – and you should have seen and heard the panic going on.

'Quick!' somebody was shouting, '——it's the jugular vein. She's bleeding to death!'

And then more voices:

'Get a tourniquet! That's what she needs.'

'What for?'

'To stop the bleeding——!'

'——A tourniquet? Round her *neck*?'

'Yes! It'll stop the bleeding.'

'Yeh! – stop her breathin' as well ...'

You should have been there, seen them all running around. I was the only calm one there and for a good few minutes nobody took any notice of me ... and all the time I still had the darts in my hand. Then this strange woman came over and took them away from me; she did it anxiously but quite gently.

'Let's have these before you do any *more* damage,' she said. 'We don't want *you* hurt as well.' Her face was close as she bent down to me. She looked very sad. She murmured softly: 'Poor little devil ...'

'Listen,' I said, looking up into her eyes, 'I had to do it. I *had* to. I mean, what kind of a future did I have with her ... ?'

The woman shook her head. 'Listen to him chortling away. Poor little bugger. He thinks it's all a huge joke. Thank God he's too young to understand what he's done ...'

And that's when I *really* started to laugh. I mean, you've *got* to.

The Whispering Gallery

William F. Temple

'Now, if you will just come this way ...'

The voice was sibilant and insinuating. It hinted at wonders which would make all you had seen so far become thin and flat and forgotten. Marvels unmatched lay just around the corner and the voice knew the way.

But Frederic was five years old and therefore he knew what voices really said and it wasn't always what the words would have you believe. This voice said, really, 'I hate you all, especially the boy, and this is the way out and I shall be glad to see the last of you.'

The voice had no intention after all of leading the way up the secret staircase to the golden ball.

This guide was a tall lean fellow, with yellow sunken cheeks and eye-sockets so deep and shadowed you could not be sure whether there were eyes in their recesses or not. Not unless you looked hard into them, that was, and so far Frederic had not found the courage to do so and make sure.

He peeped up at the guide's face only now and again from the corners of his own eyes and the sight of the strangely small nose (as if the original had been paired down to the bone) and the almost lipless mouth, with the big white teeth that seemed set in a sort of sardonic grin that would always be there whatever the outward facial mask expressed, had frightened his timid glance away every time.

If only this man had been like the jolly Beefeater in the fancy dress who had shown him the room in the Tower of London where the little Princes had been murdered. The Beefeater would have taken him up to the golden ball and perhaps given it to him. Especially if he had known that Frederic had wanted if for years. Since yesterday morning.

Yesterday was the magic morning when Jim was driving him around London in the open tourer. Just him and Jim. They were caught for a few minutes in a traffic jam in Fleet Street and their car was facing east.

'Gosh,' said Frederic, pointing over the bonnet, 'that must be the biggest building in the world!'

The chauffeur looked tolerantly up at the Cathedral.

He said, 'It looks big from here because it's standing on top of a hill – Ludgate Hill. But it's not so big really. It's hardly knee-high to the Empire State and you've been up that.'

Frederic craned his neck. The great grey dome swelled up like an enormous bubble above the twin flanking towers and on top of the dome stood another high tower with a golden gallery around its base. And right at the top of this tower was a golden ball with a golden cross planted on it like a tree. All the golden things glittered in the sunlight but the ball gleamed brightest of all. It seemed to give a light of its own rather than reflect.

'Don't be stupid, Jim,' said Frederic, scornfully. 'Anybody can see it's higher than the Empire State. It's the biggest thing I've ever seen. What a lovely golden ball that is! I wish I had it to play with. I wonder if it – comes off?'

'Would you like me to climb up there and unscrew it for you?' Jim asked quizzically.

'Would you?' said Frederic eagerly. '*Would* you?'

Jim laughed. There was a time when he would have sighed and muttered under his breath, 'These rich folk are all alike – big kids and little kids. But all kids. Get me this, get me that – look, the moon shines pretty – get me that.'

But he had served them for a long time now and had grown philosophical. They weren't happy, these people – they were poor. They were always wanting something – not only to have something but to go somewhere, see something new, have someone praise them, reassure them, do things for them. When they were little kids the world was too big for them and they tore around it in deadly fear of missing any of it before they died.

And when they were big kids, with dulled eyes and desensitized palates, the world was too small. It was a pile of cinders which they prodded wearily, hoping against hope that one day they might uncover something that gleamed bright and new and fascinated the attention. Like the dimly-remembered silver ring hanging from the hood of the baby carriage. Like the golden ball atop St Paul's Cathedral on a sunny day in your fifth year.

'*Jim!* You're not listening.'

'Yes I am, Freddy. See here, son, when you're small you get all balled up over sizes and heights and distances. I remember when I was a kid telling my Ma that telegraph posts were just the tallest things in the world, higher than any old church steeple. But when I grew up I saw I hadn't been talking sense.'

'Get me the ball, Jim,' said Frederic gravely.

'I'm trying to tell you, son – it's too big. Why, half a dozen grown-up men could get inside it.'

'Why, it's no bigger than an apple! Perhaps it *is* an apple – a golden apple. The golden apple in the story.'

'What story?'

'Oh,' – impatiently – 'the one Mr George told me about Paris giving Aphro – Aphrodotty' – he hadn't got the name right but it didn't matter – Jim wouldn't know – 'a golden apple for a prize. I've always wanted a golden apple. I wonder if it *is*, Jim? Do you think it is?'

Jim Bates opened his mouth, then closed it again. He had often done that in the service of the Staggs. Mrs Stagg frequently found the truth unpleasant. Her son also obstinately believed what he wanted to believe. There wasn't much use fighting against it. The rich were always right – if you wanted to keep your job.

'I don't know, Freddy. I don't suppose I shall ever know.'

'Why not climb . . . ?'

'Chauffeurs aren't allowed in churches,' said Jim hastily but firmly, as though it were a thing everybody knew. And Frederic, who knew that there were many holy sanctums in his native Boston where chauffeurs weren't allowed entry, said 'Oh,' disappointedly as the jam broke and the car rolled forward.

'Jim, perhaps *I* –'

More haste and firmness. 'We must go back to the hotel now. Your mother said you're to be back at one for lunch.'

And the tourer swung sharply left at Ludgate Circus and angled back through side-streets to Holborn and the straight run to the hotel at Marble Arch, and though he kept looking back, Frederic could not see St Paul's again for the shops and office buildings. He couldn't understand how such little buildings could block out such a towering magnificence as St Paul's.

Perhaps they're jealous, he thought. *They're getting together and trying to stop anyone from seeing St Paul's because it makes them look so unimportant beside it.*

'But I *can't*, Frederic – not this afternoon. We're having tea with Lady Cornford.'

'Can we go tomorrow then, Mom?'

'No. We're going home tomorrow.'

The corners of Frederic's mouth turned down. His eyes began to water.

'Oh, my!' said Mrs Stagg and her self-harassed mind darted about seeking to forestall the shrieks which would have drowned the orchestra in the hotel restaurant.

She consulted the clock-face which was always in that mind's eye by which she lived, by which she moved, always aiming to fit the social events and the sightseeing in so that there would be no awful gaps in which she might be left to reflect upon herself.

'Well, look, I could just spare half an hour – no more. We should have to come away right after that.'

Frederic smiled. 'Thanks, Mom.' Half an hour was an enormously long time – easily long enough to reach the golden apple. For by now he was almost sure that it was an apple.

It was a long time but Skeleton-face, as Frederic silently named the lanky guide, wasted it. When he had taken the little party around the various chapels and the choir and shown them the Grinling Gibbons carvings and the altar, Frederic hoped that now they would go up to the golden ball.

But the quiet cold sibilant voice said, 'Now, if you will just come this way ...'

And it lured them downstairs among the vast piers of the crypt and it seemed reluctant to leave this place. It kept them staring at the huge and horrible iron funeral carriage that had brought Wellington's body here, while it gave them endless precise details about the manufacture of this ugly thing. It hissed over the tomb of Nelson, and of Wren himself, and over the resting places of the silent multitude of bishops, artists, military and naval men.

This cold gloom was the natural habitat of the voice and Frederic felt that it wanted none of them to leave, it wanted them all to stay here. It would talk smoothly and quietly until they were lulled to sleep and then, somehow, it would get them lying stiff and dead with the others under the hard heavy stone floor.

So just as the voice was saying, 'This is the sepulchre of Arch-deacon——' Frederick cut in with a wail.

'I wanna go upstairs!'

That was where the voice began to hate him.

'Now if you will just come this way ...'

They went upstairs, past a notice saying *To the Golden Gallery and Ball* and up some more stairs, up and up and up.

As they mounted behind the steady-paced guide all the party began to lose their breath and make little sighs and smiling grimaces at each other. Except Frederic, who was tense with excitement and antici-pation.

Maybe this guide wouldn't *give* him the ball (which, of course, was really an apple) but if Mom saw how much he wanted it she would buy it for him. It didn't matter how much it cost – Mom was the richest lady in the world. She could buy him the whole Cathedral if she wanted to. But he only wanted the apple.

The richest lady in the world gasped, 'Oh dear! I didn't know it was going to take as long as this.'

They got to the top of the winding staircase and with his heart throbbing in his breast, Frederic followed the guide through the only doorway there.

'*Ooh!*' they all said as they found they were all insects perched precariously on a narrow rim immediately beneath the arching interior of the great dome, that only an iron railing stood between them and the spreading gulf beneath. Far, far below other insects crawled over the black-and-white checkerboard of the floor. They were all in a vast but bounded universe.

Frederic peered up to where the browning murals curved together and met around a spider's gallery and realized that although he was very high up the golden apple was at least as high again above him still. There must be another staircase somewhere that led up through the dome. Perhaps a hidden secret staircase.

He hesitated and tried to go back but the heavy grown-ups pressed all about him and carried him forward. And then they stopped, because the guide had stopped.

Skeleton-face said, 'This is the famous Whispering Gallery. It has peculiar acoustic properties which I shall now demonstrate to you. If you would kindly move around to the opposite side of the Gallery and stand listening against the wall . . .'

'I don't want –' began Frederic. But Mrs Stagg grabbed his hand and said in a low irritated whisper, 'Oh come *on!*'

The group moved slowly along the curving ledge with the fearful drop on its right-hand side, at which some of them dared not look and others only vouchsafed fleeting sidelong glances. There was a hush over everything.

Frederic was impatient and wanted to run. But this was a place where you neither ran nor shouted. The great Cathedral stood impassive and suffered these insects to crawl over it so long as they moved slowly and reverentially Frederic felt that if he shouted the Cathedral would start angrily and shake all these invading creatures out of its crevices.

At last they reached the side of the Gallery opposite the doorway, beside which the guide had remained standing, dwarfed by distance. They arranged themselves in a line, kneeling with one knee on the seat, putting one ear close to the wall.

Frederic did not put his ear very close. He had no wish to hear that voice again. Nevertheless he heard it, distinct and loud, as if the guide were standing beside him – yet he could see him, a thin little shape a long way off, with all the width of the dome between them.

'I am speaking only in a whisper, yet you hear me clearly. The inward diameter of this dome is one hundred and eight feet and the outer diameter one hundred and forty-five feet. The eight murals which you see on the inner surface of the dome were painted by Sir James Thornhill and represented episodes in the life of St Paul ...'

The voice went on about St Paul and Frederic sensed that its owner had no great liking for the saint – there was a new sneering undertone. The voice wanted to have done. So did Frederic. On an impulse, Frederic put his mouth close to the wall and said shrilly, 'We don't want to stay here. We want to go up to the golden apple.'

'Frederic!' exclaimed his mother, shocked and alarmed. Her voice became amplified to that of an angry giantess and boomed hollowly all about them.

The guide's voice had stopped. There was a moment's awful silence, which Mrs Stagg spent with a guilty flush spreading over her cheeks.

Then – 'Now, if you will just come this way ...'

The voice was sibilant and insinuating. It hinted at wonders which could make all you had seen so far become thin and flat.

But Frederic was five years old and therefore he knew that the voice really said, 'I hate you all, especially the boy, and this is the way out and I shall be glad to see the last of you.'

The voice had no intention after all of leading the way up the secret staircase to the golden ball.

The party shuffled round the great semi-circle back to the door – and Skeleton-face, who stood awaiting him like Charon. Frederic kept his eyes on his own feet and would not look up. For he knew that deep in those dark eye-sockets somewhere above his head, animosity burned like a flame and if the other people hadn't been there ... He was glad now that he was in the middle of a bunch of grown-ups. They were his unconscious protectors.

Huddling close he watched his feet and his mother's feet descending the stairs. And presently they were crossing the black-and-white floor, then the dirty black steps outside the Cathedral, and then – hurriedly – the sidewalk.

Then he saw the running-board of the car and looked up and there was Jim grinning at him and the fear in him unfroze.

'Get in, Frederic, don't just stand there,' said his mother, pushing him. 'Go as fast as you dare, Bates – we're ten minutes late now. What *will* Lady Cornford think?'

Frederic had not shone before the Lady. He had been silent and, when pressed, sulky. And, when pressed again, rude – very rude.

When they got back to the hotel Mrs Stagg decided on disciplinary measures. 'You will go straight to bed now, Frederic. And you are *not* to look at your picture books in bed. I've had more than enough of you today.'

The boy who had caused his mother to shout in a cathedral and look small, who had been rude to an English Lady and again made his mother look small, was left alone in the bedroom with his guilt.

He felt no remorse, only an intense aching regret that tomorrow they would be leaving London and the golden apple behind. Forever, probably. Someone else would come along and take the golden apple away while he was on the silly ship or back at silly school in Boston.

He got out of bed and went to the window. The buses swung dizzily in and out of Park Lane and for a while he watched them and the little people down there who dodged them and took sanctuary in green Hyde Park. It was summer and there was still an hour or two of daylight left.

He decided nothing. It was as if someone else had taken over his body suddenly and made it act with purpose. He found himself putting on his street clothes, buttoning them up.

Then he was opening the door quietly, surveying the passage, and then he was at the open window at the rear of the building, scrambling through it, and then he was watching his feet descending the webby iron steps of the fire-escape just as they had descended the staircase in St Paul's.

The feet seemed to know the way though it was easy enough. It was almost a straight road back to St Paul's. But it was a very long road and the feet were very tired when they got there and climbed the dirty steps in the pale rose light coming up the hill from the sinking sun.

He entered to the sound of far-off singing. There, down at the end of the great nave, candles burned on the altar and before them two lines of people in white surplices sang sweetly together and the organ made quiet thunder over their heads. There were other people too, watching them, in the dim pink light reflected from the windows below the dome.

In fact they were so intent on their watching and the choir was so intent on its song that no one noticed him stealing down a side aisle, between the chairs and up the stairs which led to the Whispering Gallery.

The old verger who took the entrance money was no longer there and this gave Frederic heart. All the guides would have gone home by now, Skeleton-face among them. Now all he had to do was to find a place to hide for just a little while until the choir and the congregation had gone home too, leaving St Paul's – and the golden apple – to him alone.

Up the stairs there was a corridor leading to the library and in that corridor he had noticed a certain secluded alcove. He hoped he could reach it soon for his legs were aching and very tired ...

When he awakened, his shoulders and legs were painful with cramp for the alcove was small even for him. Rubbing them he went exploring in the dark. Soon he had other places to rub, for there seemed to be a lot of things to bump into and they were all hard. What chance had he of finding the secret staircase to the apple? It must be well hidden and hard to detect even in the daytime. He wished he had thought to bring his torch. But then he hadn't intended to fall asleep and stay here until after dark.

He was not afraid for the ball shining in the sunlight shone still in his memory and he felt that it was even now shining there in actuality somewhere above him. When he reached it and unscrewed it (but it was an apple, really, and he would just pick it) it would continue to glow and light his way back down the stairs and along the streets to the hotel. He bumped and blundered along the wall like a blow-fly on a window-pane and all at once fell through a doorway. As he lay there, his foot, extended behind him, discovered the top of a stairway.

And then, quite distinctly, he heard slow steady footsteps coming up that dark stairway.

He caught his breath and picked himself up. He must not be dis-covered now. He went on through the doorway and so emerged into a very dim yellow light. He was in the Whispering Gallery, uncertainly lit by a moon striving first to pierce a veil of nimbus cloud and then the dusty windowpanes of the Cathedral.

He hesitated. There was only this one door, which was the sole entrance and exit to the Gallery. The footsteps were louder now and began to echo. He fled from them, keeping close to the seat along the curving wall in a stumbling yet stealthy sort of run, trying to make no noise in a place which he knew magnified sound in a terrifying way.

Yet he was still not really frightened – only excited.

It was a long way around to the place diametrically opposite the door, the place where they had all stood listening in the afternoon, but it did not seem quite so far this time because he could run. There he sat on the seat, hunched up against the wall, trying to make himself so small as to be invisible and holding his breath lest the same treacherous wall caught the small sound of his presence and flung it around in reveal-ment.

A threadbare patch in the flat cloud passed under the moon and the spacious murals on the dome overhead suddenly stood out distinctly with an odd stereoscopic effect. And the dark little oblong of the door-way on the far side of the Gallery became visible.

Below, in the immense well of the Cathedral, he saw now that here and there an electric candelabra glowed, each casting its little circle of light, frayed and thin at the edges – a few tiny wide-scattered oases in a black desert.

But now he watched the distant doorway opposite – and waited.

His vision became a little blurred with the intensity of his gaze. Presently it seemed that a small vertical strip of the dark rectangle had detached itself and floated away from the main body. And then this little black stroke became still. He rubbed his watering eyes and looked again. There was no doubt about it. The thin black shadow was quite separate from the frame of the doorway.

Then the cloud thickened under the moon again, the murals became blurs, the doorway and the shadow merged into common blackness and only the small glints of electric light far below retained their clarity and shape.

He hoped the shadow would go back through the doorway. He sat, still hunched, gripping the edge of the seat. He was trembling a little but was not really afraid.

Then his heart leapt into his throat as the voice spoke right beside him. A sibilant chill voice, cloaking malice with a surface politeness – *'Now, if you will just come this way ...'*

He shrank and cowered. His trembling became a violent shaking as fear passed through him like a series of electric shocks. A pain gripped his stomach and he pressed both hands against the place, doubled up. He could not control his breathing now – it came in loud rapid gasps, as if he had just been plunged into cold water.

For ages, it seemed, he sat tied in a knot of pain, gazing terror-struck through the railing at the points of light below – remote as stars – dreading to look up at Skeleton-face standing over him, unable to face the cavernous eye-sockets and the white fixed grin, shrinking from the imagined touch of a thin hand.

But no hand touched him.

Then the smothered moon broke free to throw a wealth of silvery light about him and it was apparent that there was no one standing over him. He peeped under his eyelids – over there. The shadow remained small and distant by the door. It was so perfectly still that a hope suddenly struck him it was not a man at all but just the shadow of some ordinary thing he had not noticed before. Yet it had seemed to move ...

He watched it, relaxing gradually as the thin shadow remained stiff and stationary as a gatepost.

He told himself, not in so many words but with the rough apprehension of the imperfectly articulate, that he had been frightening himself with an imagined bogey-man.

But he had not imagined that voice. That had been real enough. Still, there was probably an explanation any grown-up could make clear to him. He supposed that everything you said in Whispering Gallery went echoing around the Gallery for ever and ever because there was no way for the sound to get out – it was like a fly caught under an upturned bowl. He expected that the echoes became rarer and rarer as time went on until you hardly heard them at all.

All he had heard was a belated echo of the words Skeleton-face had kept using in the afternoon.

Then he jumped again, as the same freezing voice said right alongside him, *'If you will just come this way . . .'*

The palms of his hands became sticky with sweat, and his scalp prickled. But he told himself that it was all right. The shadow hadn't moved. It was only that old echo again.

He noticed it had dropped a word this time. How could the sound of that word, *'Now,'* have escaped? Why, of course, it would have slipped out through the doorway as the echo went past on its travels. That was how echoes died, losing a piece every time they went slowly round. It would have to be something like that, otherwise everything everybody ever said would have gone on sounding for ever and it would be like a great crowd shouting all the time.

Well, it wasn't any good just sitting there. He'd have to start looking for the staircase to the golden apple. His mother might already have discovered he had left the hotel and she would guess where he had gone and come after him.

He stood up slowly, not taking his eyes off the shadow by the door. It remained still. If he went to the left he would approach the doorway from the side away from the shadow and wouldn't have to go past it at all. *Well,* he thought, *I must go now.* He took a deep breath.

And then the clouds made a sudden rush at the moon and all but extinguished it. The silvery light ceased abruptly as if it had been switched off. It was darker than ever.

He paused, irresolute, his courage evaporating. He could not go around the Gallery in this darkness. He might not be able to distinguish the doorway when he came to it and he might go past it to where the shadow was. But that was silly – if there was no light there could be no shadow.

Nevertheless fear was stronger than reason. He stood there, clutching the iron railing and looking down at the little lights below. Suddenly he wished he were down there in the safe steady light that did not go out and leave you trapped on a high shelf and at the mercy of unseen shadows.

But if he were down there, he would be further away from the shining golden apple. If he were to attain that prize he must be courageous and bear the nervous ordeals that lay on the path to it. To deserve the apple you must be brave.

His fingers tightened on the railing as the mouthless voice said near at hand in the dark, *'You will just come this way . . .'*

This time it sounded less like a request than a command. *'You* will *come this way . . .'* It was as if the voice knew that it was losing some of the words it could use and was trying to counterbalance the loss with greater persuasion.

Frederic thought, *It's quite all right, really. If I stay here long enough the echo will have no more words left, it will die out altogether. Perhaps the shadow will go with it. Perhaps the shadow has nothing to do with it.*

However he was glad when the bright moonlight suddenly flooded the dome again. At least he was glad until——

He screamed as he saw that the shadow had moved in the darkness, had advanced nearly halfway towards him around the Gallery and was still coming on steadily.

He turned and fled in the opposite direction. As he blundered along the curving path, sometimes banging a knee against the endless seat, sometimes slipping and grabbing the railing for support, he cast a terrified glance across the moonlit spaces to see where the shadow had got to.

It had ceased to pursue its original course around the Gallery. It had turned back, was moving swiftly the other way to head him off before he could reach the door. And it was moving faster than he could.

He spun around, choking with terror, little thin screams coming from him as he ran. This time he did not blunder or slip. Self-preservation told him that he could afford no mistakes and the sheer desperate will to live made his feet fly with speed and precision.

For now he knew he did not know how he knew but he knew – that the shadow was the shadow of Death. And Death wanted to take him and put him with the other dead people under the cold floor of the crypt.

He was back to where he had been, diametrically opposite to the doorway. And the shadow too was back to where it had been, by that doorway. He collapsed on the seat, whooping for breath but keeping his staring eyes on the shadow. It seemed to have returned to complete immobility.

Then the voice came again, quietly this time, almost coaxingly, '*Just come this way* . . .'

It seemed to imply that if he were just to go along to it everything would be all right and there would be nothing to worry about.

But he knew it was a trap. He would not go. He would hang on to life as long as he could because there was still hope. The voice had lost two of its words this time. Perhaps it had called after him as he ran from it and haste and terror had deafened him to it.

The great dome overhead was almost radiant now with light from the unshielded moon and the human figures crowded in the arches of the murals were a tense silent audience looking down on the narrow circular track where Frederic had to run for his life.

He believed they were watching him and he wondered whether they were on his side. St Paul seemed to be. He stood up there, one hand pointing upwards towards the spider's gallery at the apex of the dome, towards the golden apple. 'That's the way you want to go, Frederic,' said his expression.

'I know, I know,' whispered the boy. 'But how do I get up there?'

And the voice of Death spoke again, calling, '*Come this way* ...'

'*No!*' cried Frederic, starting to his feet and going a few paces. The shadow glided in the same direction too, coming around to meet him. He ran back and the shadow stopped as if it were watching him, weighing his intention, then moved back to cover the doorway.

And so Frederic stopped again. It was plain that he could never reach the doorway safely whichever way he went, for the shadow had the advantages of position and speed of movement and could always get there first. Was there to be no end to this horrible game?

Yes, he thought desperately, *there must be an end when the echo dies. And that must be soon now.*

He pressed his hot brow against the cool iron railing. There were, he noticed now, mosaics just under the Gallery itself, between the arches which fell away from beneath them into bottomless gloom, and they all pictured angels flying confidently. What mattered it to them that they were at a frightful height. They were borne by their trusted wings.

He thought, *If only I had wings! I could escape Death. More than that — I could fly up there and pick the golden apple.*

His forehead burned and droplets of sweat trickled slowly down the iron bars. His head ached as though a fever had come upon him and the angels seemed to advance and recede before his blurring gaze as if they had come quite away from the wall and were indeed flying over the back wall.

He watched them for some time, feeling dull and heavy-headed, and they seemed to be aware of him and smile at him and indicate by their slow weaving motions that it was quite easy to fly. Anyone could do it. *He* could do it if he only tried.

Then suddenly he remembered the shadow and looked up at the opposite side of the Gallery. And it was gone!

Then he caught a movement away to the right and there was a shadow, much taller, well past the crucial halfway mark on its way to him. It had taken advantage of his preoccupation with the angels to chance leaving the doorway to come around after him.

It had won the awful game. Even if Frederic ran his hardest for the door, the shadow had gained enough ground to overtake him easily before he reached it.

It was too near. It was Skeleton-face, all right. He could see the dark eye-cavities turned steadfastly upon him, the gleam of teeth, as the tall thin figure approached.

He scrambled up on to the rim of the railing before him, which was not easy for the rim was turned back inwards. But he mounted to the top of it and balanced there like a wire-walker. He looked up. Somewhere up there, beyond the dome, was the glittering prize he would never now reach.

But St Paul still pointed upwards like an inspiration. 'Have faith!' he seemed to say. 'Have faith!'

And the angels seemed to be calling in chorus, 'Have faith, Frederic, and you can fly like us. Have faith and you can fly up to the apple.'

Frederic teetered, arms outstretched, on the edge of cavernous space below and above. He took a quick peep sideways. Skeleton-face was almost upon him, lipless mouth open to speak.

'This way ...'

'You can fly. You can fly. Have faith,' called the angels together.

'I have faith. I'm coming,' said Frederic with a new strength and began to extend a foot quite steadily and calmly.

'Frederic!' It was his mother's voice, loud with alarm.

A warm relief flooded right over him. Mom had found him, had got here just in time. She would save him from Skeleton-face – she would pay him to go away. She could pay anything, she was so rich.

He looked eagerly around but he couldn't see her. There was only Skeleton-face reaching for him.

And then he realized with a sudden horrible sinking of all his energies that the cry was only the echo of his mother's exclamation of the afternoon. It must have been slowly circling the Gallery ever since. He was sick with disappointment.

And then bony hands reached for his ankles and he leapt outwards into space.

It wasn't a leap of faith. It was merely a leap to avoid death.

In confusion and wretchedness he fell past the angels, fell into darkness. The lights of the candelabras grew bigger as he fell and they illuminated something that lay below them.

A golden disc.

He was turning as he fell and couldn't obtain more than fleeting glimpses of it but he could see that he was heading straight for it.

Could it be that somehow, in a way he couldn't understand, he was succeeding after all? That he was to reach——

The golden disc flashed up hugely now and dazzled his eyes.

The verger on the night watch had happened just by chance to glance up and catch what looked like a tiny figure balanced on the rail of the Whispering Gallery. He tried to shield his eyes from the immediate light of the candelabra over his head and see past it more clearly up into the moonlit dome.

It *was* a figure and even as he watched it jumped out into space.

'My God!' he said, and rushed forward.

A thin shout came from above – *'Way ...!'*

He stopped, uncertain.

The figure fell down past the mosaics, past the golden organ pipes, past the red canopy over the high pulpit, arching ever outwards to the centre of the floor as it came.

He saw it hit the large circular brass plate set into the floor, immediately over Nelson's tomb, immediately under the ball and cross 365 feet above. And he hid his eyes.

When he looked again a delta of red rivulets was spreading from the crumpled little shape that lay on the brass plate in the centre of the star with the long black and faded pink points – bright red trickles which matched the scarlet of the altar screen.

It was a small child, a boy. Dead – naturally.

He sought his fellow verger on the watch and brought him to the scene. Only it wasn't quite the same. The brass ring shone clean and bright – and clear. There was no body. There was no blood.

The second verger put his arm about the other, who had suddenly begun to shake, and led him to the chairs by the lectern.

'Sit down and rest, Alex,' he said. 'Don't worry. It's all right. It once happened to me.'

Alex looked at him in slow surprise, his lower lip quivering, his hands shaking like those of a very old man.

'Nor are we the only ones,' said the second verger. 'It happens – every so often.'

'When did it first – *really* – happen? Don't tell me it didn't.'

'Over twenty years ago. It was a boy named Stagg – an American boy. He had strayed from his hotel, somehow found his way here and got up – there. His mother was distracted when she found him gone. But he had been here in the afternoon and for some reason wanted very much to return. And he was due to go home the next day. So she guessed he might have come here. But she got here just too late – he was already on the rail, just as you and I saw him. She shouted his name. But he fell.'

'Do you think she startled him? He was performing some idiotic balancing trick and——'

'Did it look like that to you?'

Alex looked unseeingly at the golden lectern with the big golden eagle bearing the Bible on its back and wings outstretched and eyes staring keenly up at the dome.

'He jumped,' he said in a low voice.

'Nobody knows why.'

'But he saw me,' Alex said. 'He must have seen me and thought he was going to hit me. He shouted *"Way!"*'

'*Someone* shouted "Way!" I heard it too when the thing happened to me. But it didn't sound like a boy's voice. He was only five, you know.'

'If it wasn't he, who was it?'

The second verger shrugged his shoulders and became absorbed in removing a few hairs that clung to his black cassock.

Without looking up he said, 'There have been many temples on this site. Before this was Old St Paul's and before that a Saxon church stood on this spot for nearly five hundred years, and long before that the Romans had a temple here – a Roman altar of stone was uncovered here in 1830.'

'I remember reading about that in the chronicles. There was a carved representation of Diana on it, was there not?'

'Yes. Diana, Goddess of the Hunt.'

Alex looked at the other sharply. 'Was it a – sacrificial temple?'

The second verger pursed his lips, picked up a long brown hair carefully by the ends, held it up to the light of the candelabra and regarded it without answering.

'What did you say the name of the boy was?' pursued Alex.

'Stagg,' said the other, letting the hair drift gently down – it floated away under a chair. Then he looked straight at Alex and said firmly, 'Which may be a coincidence or it may not. We shall never know. The one thought that really terrifies me about this affair, the thought I don't want to face, is this – does that poor child have to suffer his frightful experience over and over again, every time it happens? Is he caught in some vicious circle of time and unable to escape?'

'I don't think so,' said Alex. 'What's past is past. We have merely, by some trick of time, been given a glimpse of that past. Like looking at an old film in which the characters go through the motions but are only unfeeling shadows.'

'For our souls' ease,' said the other, soberly, 'we must believe that.'

They sat brooding, two tiny figures side by side under the great dome in the little pool of light from the candelabra. Each was grateful for the other's company. For all around them black shadows filled the enormous arches and the silent chapels and the long, empty passages. Under their feet, spreading beneath the thick walls into the ancient churchyard besieging them in the night and into the burial grounds below that, were the bones of the innumerable dead. The great and the small. The famous and the forgotten. The human and the – possibly non-human.

Before them the golden eagle of the lectern, rising on its claws with excitement, gazed eagerly and unwaveringly up at the Whispering Gallery as if it were absorbed in watching a tense and perpetual drama ...

*

'Now, if you will just come this way ...'

The voice was sibilant and insinuating. It hinted at wonders which would make all you had seen so far become thin and flat and forgotten. Marvels unmatched lay just around the corner and the voice knew the way ...

Now Showing at the Roxy

Harry E. Turner

Stan Rabble was manager and sole proprietor of the Roxy Cinema. It was a crumbling, red-brick building with a domed, quasi-ecclesiastical façade that gave it the appearance of a 1920 synagogue – with Walt Disney additions. It stood, or rather leant, on the rubble-strewn corner of Canal Street on the outskirts of the city.

From his tiny flat above the Dress Circle, Stan had a clear view across the disused motorway to Paradise Street. All the buildings in Paradise Street had long since been condemned, and now provided refuge only for rats and the occasional drunken tramp. But at the top of the street, on an island of concrete, stood the Luxor Palace picture house, owned by Stan's hated rival, Lou Rouser.

The Luxor was, if anything, even more architecturally forlorn than the Roxy – a snubby oblong of concrete with chipped doric columns, and headless stone cherubs prancing along its roofline – but it was about the same size.

Stan pulled his wicker chair up to the window and raised a pair of binoculars to his eyes. He could see Lou Rouser quite clearly now, cigar clenched in his mouth, dinner jacket flapping. He was struggling with a huge cardboard sign. Stan strained his eyes to read the lettering, but it was facing the wrong way.

Eventually, Lou gave up the struggle and left the sign face down on the pavement. He turned and pulled a handkerchief from his pocket. Stan could see his fat, piggy face and glistening head, pink mouth chewing furiously on the cigar. Then, suddenly, Lou extended his right arm and made a 'V' sign in the direction of the Roxy.

Stan pulled back from the window with a volley of curses. How could little Lou see him from there?

He threw down his binoculars and loosened his black bow tie. Well, Lou could make all the rude signs he liked, that wouldn't worry Stan. His next double-feature would really pull 'em in, and no mistake. Lou would laugh on the other side of his face then.

Stan picked up the typewritten sheet of coming attractions and scanned it greedily.

Starting Monday:
THE SON OF THE THING FROM THE SLIME
Treble 'X' certificate   Not for the squeamish

Stan gave a sigh of satisfaction. It was one of the best he'd had for a long time, and by God he needed it. Three hundred seats to fill, rates to pay, debts piling up. It wasn't easy, being a cinema owner in the year 2028. Two-thirds of the population were geriatrics kept alive by drugs in state institutions, and the remaining third were glued to the telly or watching teenage riots in the streets.

Stan rinsed his hands in the plastic bowl beside the gas cooker and selected his lunch from an impressive range of individual fruit pies. As he bit into the soggy crust of a blueberry 'n' apple he heard shouts coming from the open window. Curious, he hurried across the room and peered out. Lou had recruited a couple of tramps, and all three of them were manhandling the huge sign. As it was hoisted upright, revealing its message, Stan's lower jaw fell open, disgorging a hunk of pie.

The letters on the giant sign were six feet high in cyclamen pink. They proclaimed:

Starting Monday:
THE RETURN OF THE CURSE
OF THE HUNCHBACK WEREWOLF
Nauseating! Suitable only for patrons with nerves of steel
Prop.: L. Rouser

'Typical,' said Stan through gritted teeth. 'Right down to the cult of personality – always putting his damn name on the hoardings.'

He snatched up his sheet of coming attractions, and a slow grin spread over his face. Maybe Lou did have a crowd-puller next week – but the week *after* ... oh boy! Did *he* have a shock coming.

Whistling cheerfully, Stan straightened his bow tie and hurried from the room.

Over in the Luxor Palace, Lou Rouser was taking a breather after his exertions with the sign. He was a tubby little man with a round, gleaming face and eyes like hard-boiled eggs. He jammed another cigar into his mouth and set light to it with a Queen Anne table-lighter. What he would have given just to see Stan Rabble's face. There was no doubt about it – poor old Stan was no match for an operator like Lou. Strategy – that was the key – strategy and timing. He sucked at the frayed end of his cigar and laughed aloud.

Things generally, he concluded, were looking up. He had a very good
batch of films booked for the Luxor, *and* a new commissionaire. Found
him cheap, too, swigging paraffin in one of the Paradise Street ruins, and
signed him up on the spot. All that was needed now was to get him
scrubbed and shaved and fitted with the uniform. Lovely uniform it was
– plum-coloured with gold tassels, very musical comedy. Just the right
touch. Some of the yobbos would laugh – and throw stones – but the
regulars, they'd appreciate it. Even today, people liked a bit of respect,
a modicum of dignity.

He heaved himself to his feet and brushed the ash from his jacket.
Time for a spot of lunch. A cold frankfurter perhaps, washed down with
lemon squash.

He shuffled out of his tiny sitting-room with its faded linoleum walls
and on to the Grand Staircase that led to the foyer. Its grandeur had
long since vanished, and the cupola that had once supported a hanging
chandelier of quite brilliant extravagance was now a pock-marked basin
encrusted with filth and cobwebs.

As he descended the stairs painfully, one by one, his right hand
clutching the rickety banister, he saw below in the foyer a scraggy
woman sloshing water from a bucket across the marble floor.

She looked up and grinned when she saw Lou approaching.

'Now then, Mrs Prendergast, no skimping. We want the old Luxor
to be spick and span, don't we?'

The hag nodded vacantly, her tongue flickering over toothless gums.

'Thpick and thpan,' she repeated. 'Thure enough, Mr Routher.'

Lou swept past, Caesar inspecting the legions, and went to the refreshment counter. Behind it stood a huge open freezer stacked with iced
lollies and bottles of cordial. Next to it was a frankfurter dispenser,
scabby with dried mustard.

'I'm at lunch, Mrs Prendergast,' said Lou sternly. 'I don't wish to be
disturbed.'

But the old woman wasn't listening. She was gazing stupidly out
through the open swing doors at something across the street.

'What *is* it, Mrs Prendergast?' said Lou, biting into a large, curved
frankfurter.

The old woman made a croaking noise and pointed. 'Look 'ere, Mr
Routher, look 'ere.'

Lou placed his lunch carefully on the counter and walked across to
her. She seemed transfixed by what she saw. He followed her gaze,
shielding his eyes like Rommel at Tobruk.

What he saw made him stop chewing – a sure sign that he had been
deeply shocked.

'So *that's* his rotten game, is it?' he cried. 'O.K., then. *Two* can play
at this!'

He turned and hurried back up the staircase, the half-consumed frankfurter now a forgotten relic on the refreshment counter.

The old woman was still rooted to the spot, her jaw working slowly to form the words on the gigantic sign across the road.

Outside the Roxy, still glistening with wet paint, was a crudely painted message. It read:

> *The Week After Next. The Ultimate in Entertainment.*
> THE NYMPHOMANIAC MUMMY
> FROM TWENTY THOUSAND FATHOMS
> BENEATH THE EARTH'S CRUST MEETS
> THE BONELESS SNAKE MAN
> Sex, Violence, Blood, Filth, Horror.
> *Old Age Pensioners Half Price*

Lou paused on the staircase and waved a clenched fist. 'This is total war, Mrs Prendergast. No quarter will be asked or given!'

Early the next day, Lou Rouser launched his counter-attack. His platoon of freelance sign-writers, recruited from the vagabond denizens of Paradise Street, had toiled all night in return for soup and cigarettes, and completed a monster hoarding, thirty feet square.

It was cut into sections and manhandled up the staircase to the roof, and, as they reassembled it to Lou's hoarsely shouted instructions, its riveting legend became clear:

> *Coming Next Month at the Luxor Palace –*
> *Lou Rouser is Proud to Present*
> I WAS A SEX MAD TEENAGE VAMPIRE
> DOLLY BIRD FROM OUTER SPACE

Minutes later, Stan Rabble retaliated with a flourish. A flag was hoisted, daubed with 'day-glo' letters. It proclaimed:

> *Special Late Night Movie at the Roxy*
> THE HEART TRANSPLANT, VOODOO DRUG-
> ADDICT, THIGH-BOOTED NUN MEETS
> ABBOTT AND COSTELLO ON ICE
> *Air Conditioning*

The bit about the air conditioning was a lie, but Stan intended to leave a few doors open.

In the days that followed, the battle raged with devastating ferocity.

Lou had by now plastered every available space with posters, advertising all the films on his schedule for the next six months. Stan had followed suit. It was a kind of stalemate.

Audiences ebbed and flowed, were drawn hither and thither like corks in a storm as they switched their allegiance from the Roxy to the Luxor and then back again.

In mid-June it rained heavily, creating havoc with the cardboard signs. In spite of running repairs and a sharp increase in tramp labour, both Lou and Stan had to pull down the hoardings and plan their campaigns anew.

During this lull in the fighting, audiences dwindled to a dangerous, all-time low. No film, it seemed, however sensational, could tickle their jaded palates.

Stan had tried a number of daring combinations – Japanese liver-transplant documentaries coupled with nude Swedish musicals, under-water wrestling sagas featuring homosexual dwarfs, cannibalism and belly-dancing – all to no avail. And Lou's efforts had been no less impressive. He had imported horror movies of mind-boggling variety – also to no avail. The vanishing public remained unmoved.

The summer months dragged on, and by mid-August the city was in the grip of an intense heat wave. So hot did it become that the municipal refuse collectors went on strike, claiming that working in such heat was not conducive to the dignity of labour.

As garbage began to accumulate in the streets, and the already seedy areas, like Paradise Street, took on a nightmarish aspect, the colonies of rats grew bolder, venturing into the city by daylight and scavenging among the refuse.

Street riots were an everyday occurrence, inevitably reported by the television networks, who now provided an hourly digest of violence and bloodshed throughout the metropolis.

With so much in life to disgust and excite the population, Stan's and Lou's cinemas seemed tame by comparison. Like beleaguered generals they withdrew behind the barricades and prayed for a miracle.

Stan's rations were dangerously low. He had broken open the last case of individual rhubarb pie and shared it among his staff: Nora, the cashier, and Culp, the blind Negro commissionaire.

Culp wasn't much use as a commissionaire because, in addition to his blindness, he was eighty-four and lame. Nevertheless, draped in faded velvet, he did add a touch of dignity to the foyer of the Roxy. (Stan was determined not to concede an inch to Lou Rouser, whose own vagabond commissionaire was now in the last, palsied throes of alcoholism.)

Lou, for his own part, was in equally straitened circumstances. Mrs Prendergast had recently expired over her bucket, and, fearful of admitting such a depletion in the ranks, Lou had buried her in the car park.

High up in his room in the Luxor, Lou washed down the fragments of a rancid frankfurter with a cup of Pepsi. Spread out before him on the green baize card-table was a map of the city. If the public refused to come to him, then perhaps he should go to them with – with, yes, a decorated float, extolling the joys of the cinema. He could tour the city and bellow slogans through a loud-hailer ...

Even as he savoured the thought, it curdled in his mind. Was he *mad*? If he as much as set foot outside the Luxor with such an expedition he would be pounced upon by hooligans and beaten to a pulp. Killing for kicks, the TV people called it.

He pushed aside the map with a despairing sigh. He felt limp, exhausted, defeated. Then from the street below he heard a shout, followed by pounding footsteps and then more shouts. He glanced out of the window. A group of youths was kicking another boy, who was shielding his head with his arms. After a few moments they dragged him to his feet and took turns head-butting him in the face.

Lou watched the spectacle without emotion. They were probably all friends, enjoying a bit of horseplay over the affections of a girl. According to the telly, people were so bored with their lives that they had taken to savaging their friends – just to inject drama into what was becoming an increasingly pointless existence.

It was at this precise moment that the idea came to him. Participation – that's what people craved – participation, risk and involvement.

Shaking with excitement, he leapt to his feet and began calling loudly for the commissionaire.

When, the following morning, Stan Rabble raised his binoculars for a routine squint at the Luxor, his heart missed a beat.

The truce, such as it had been, was clearly at an end. Lou's giant poster glistened with fresh paintwork and invited patrons to –

Come to the Luxor – and Live Dangerously!
One in Every Hundred Vanilla Ice-Creams Served in
the Interval has been Injected with Bubonic Plague.
Who Will Be the Unlucky Victim?
Bring All the Family. Have a Sporting Wager
that it Won't Be Your Mother-In-Law.
Also Showing:
I WAS DRACULA'S TRANSVESTITE MASSEUR

The effect of Lou's poster was positively electric. Word spread throughout the city of his latest gimmick, and that evening, for the seven o'clock performance, there was a queue outside the Luxor for the first time in three months.

Providing the necessary germ-infested vanilla was even simpler than Lou had imagined. A retired chemist who occasionally helped Lou out as a free-lance usher produced the ingredients from dead rats and rotting garbage heaps.

It was a crude virus, but it did the trick. Three patrons became violently ill, and one died within a week in excruciating pain.

Even though the other two recovered, the verdict was clear. Lou Rouser and the Luxor had done it again!

Stan was livid. He watched with mounting fury as the queues grew longer outside Lou's crumbling palace.

Within a month, Lou had employed the elderly chemist on a full-time basis and made him an associate director.

But Stan was not the sort of man to concede victory without a bitter struggle. Like the true fighter he was, he counter-attacked with devastating skill.

Only at the Roxy, his advertising blurb read, *Will a*
Genuine Rapist Mingle with the Audience and
Savagely Assault Defenceless Women while they
Innocently Enjoy
BLUEBEARD'S JOURNEY INTO
THE INTESTINES OF A WHALE
Cinemascope

It was with a sense of great pride that Stan saw his plan unfold. The Roxy was besieged by cinema-goers – mostly middle-aged women and the occasional male hairdresser – to savour the thrills of his unique package-deal.

The supply of genuine rapists, however, began to dwindle after six weeks, two of them confessing to be wholly cured and another to be engaged to a nice woman who shared his interest in stamp-collecting.

Lou Rouser, meanwhile, retired to his room above the Luxor, brooding and resentful.

The alcoholic commissionaire made a painful ascent each evening at seven to appraise his employer of the state of play, and with each report Lou grew more outraged, and his screams were awful to hear. He pilloried the wretched commissionaire and bellowed abuse at the retired chemist – accusing him of sloth, treachery, lack of imagination. Desperately, the man tried to introduce additional viruses into the ice-cream – a touch of diphtheria in the chocolate sundae, a soupçon of malaria in the raspberry ripple. But the novelty wore off.

The cinema-going public were on a different kick, and it was Stan Rabble who was providing it.

Encouraged by his success, Stan began embellishing it. Coffin-shaped choc ices in the interval, calves' blood tipped on to the audience from the Dress Circle. The Roxy, he now claimed, was the only cinema in the country that gave its audiences a *real* experience. The queues grew longer, and he was obliged to bring extra rapists in from the suburbs by charabanc in order to keep the audiences in a perpetual state of terror and disgust. But they *loved* it. This was *real*. This was *involvement*.

He doubled his prices, and still they came. By September, he had accumulated enough funds to purchase a new batch of movies for the winter season.

Lou Rouser, it seemed, had thrown in the sponge. There was a brief revival of interest when he set a live tarantula loose among his pitifully small Saturday-night audience, but the creature was a disappointment and failed to generate the naked panic that Lou had hoped for. Instead, it had crawled into the projection room, where the drunken commission-aire had retreated to finish off a flagon of meths, and bitten him in the throat. The sozzled wretch had merely crushed it with a single blow from his bottle and continued drinking, apparently unaffected by its deadly venom.

Over at the Roxy, Stan Rabble was celebrating his success with a bottle of chilled Tizer and an exceptionally large apple-and-black-currant pie. It was just a matter of time now, he reasoned, before the Luxor Palace closed down for ever.

But his euphoria was misplaced. Fortune is a fickle and capricious lady – as any student of history will confirm.

The heat of summer had passed and the cool promise of winter had begun. Street riots were less frequent, and a general apathy had settled over the city. The Roxy was still doing excellent business, but what Stan had failed to notice was the subtle, almost imperceptible change in the mood of his patrons. They filed into his crumbling emporium like bloodless zombies, and even the shrieks of the free-lance rapists failed to stir them. They were, to put it succinctly, ripe for poaching.

The Luxor, meanwhile, had boarded up its windows and displayed a sign announcing

Extensive Renovations

but Stan assumed it was simply a euphemism for bankruptcy and final surrender.

His surprise was considerable, therefore, when on December 13th the Luxor put up another sign, proclaiming:

Grand Re-Opening Saturday.
The Ultimate Experience is at the Luxor.
You Can Trust Lou Rouser. Spectacular Double Feature:

THE SOUND OF MUSIC
&
MARY POPPINS
(*Bring Your Granny*)

Stan could scarcely believe his eyes. Lou must surely be in the last throes of raving lunacy. *The Sound of Music! Mary Poppins!* Nobody, but nobody, would pay good money to see that sort of shmaltz!

In spite of his incredulity, however, a worm of doubt started in his mind, and he determined to keep a close eye upon events.

Saturday came, and against Lou's pallid double feature, Stan was re-running a Cinemascope epic about heroin-crazed necrophiliac giraffe-women.

But, to his utter dismay, people began assembling outside the Luxor Palace, wearing expressions of listless curiosity. At seven there was a healthy queue and the doors were opened by the purple-faced commissionaire who, on encountering the blast of cool street air, promptly collapsed in a drunken heap. He was gently trampled by the first wave of patrons.

By eight o'clock, business was booming. Stan's own audience had dwindled to a handful of elderly priests who were on a package tour of the city from South-East Asia.

Stan threw discretion to the winds, straightened his greasy bow tie and ran as fast as his legs could carry him across the motorway to the Luxor Palace.

People were still filing in, strangely silent and orderly, and he had no trouble in forcing his way into the foyer. No evidence of renovation could be seen – it was still the same old scabby decor and dismal grandeur, so, burning with curiosity, he approached the swing doors that led to the auditorium. From within he could hear a curious mechanical whirring and what appeared to be a series of plopping sounds.

As his hands fell on the ornate handle, an arm was thrust in front of his chest, barring his progress. He turned to meet the sardonic gaze of Lou Rouser, resplendent in a burgundy dinner-jacket and frilled dress shirt.

'Well, well, well,' said Lou, with glacial charm, 'and to what do we owe the honour of this unexpected visit?'

Stan stifled the impulse to kick his rival in the groin. 'All right, Lou,' he said, 'let's talk.'

Lou Rouser adjusted his velvet bow tie and shrugged.

'Talk, Stanley? What do you and I have to talk about?'

Stan gritted his teeth. This was not going to be easy.

'I'm serious, Lou. I want to talk.'

Lou withdrew a long, slim cigar from his breast pocket and chewed off the end. 'In that case, my dear Stanley,' he said smoothly, 'perhaps we should adjourn to my office.'

Stan followed him up the wide staircase and along a narrow corridor until they reached a door marked 'Private'. Lou opened it and waved him inside. He was at once assailed by the reek of stale frankfurters.

Lou closed the door behind them and indicated for Stan to sit down.

'Now then, Stanley,' he said, lighting his cigar, 'what is it I can do for you? A small loan, perhaps? A cup of sugar——'

Stanley was on his feet, fists clenched. 'For pity's sake, Lou!' he cried. 'Stop torturing me – just tell me how the hell you've managed to pack them in like that.'

Lou sucked thoughtfully on the end of his cigar.

'You admit I've beat you, then?'

Stan nodded, already a broken man.

'Yes, yes. You've beat me. Fair and square. But with *Mary Poppins*! I just don't understand it.'

Lou patted his rival's shoulder. 'Because I *like* you, Stan, because you're a *sport*, I'll tell you. Would you like a drink first? Pepsi? Fizzy orange? Bitter lemon? Tizer? I got 'em all, Stan.'

'Just tell me,' said Stan, sinking down into his chair.

'O.K. It's quite simple. People are bored, right? There's nothing in life to look forward to, right? They live in a stinking city with no hope, right? They'll try *anything* for kicks, right?'

'I know all that,' protested Stan weakly. 'Tell me something I don't know.'

Lou went over to the door and opened it. 'Down there, Stanley,' he said dramatically, 'are people queueing up to savour the *ultimate* experience – and I mean the *ultimate*.'

'The ultimate?' repeated Stan. 'What are you talking about?'

Lou was growing excited and his face had started to sweat. 'What is the one experience none of those people has ever savoured? The only one common to all of them. Oh, come on, Stan, *think*! They've been mugged, shocked, abused, outraged, bored, drunk, tired, frightened, conned, robbed, swindled, amused, excited. There's only one thing left, Stan, and *I'm* giving it to them!'

He was already outside the door, beckoning for Stan to follow. 'I'm giving it to them,' he cried again, 'at the Luxor!'

Stan followed him down the stairs to the foyer. It was jammed with people now, many of them singing. The queues outside stretched half across the motorway.

Lou forced his way through the crowd until he reached the entrance to the stalls. Stan was hard on his heels as he prised open one of the swing doors and pointed inside.

'Look, Stan!' he cried triumphantly. 'Look for yourself!'

Stan poked his head round the door and stared hard into the darkness. The whirring and the plopping were quite loud, now. As his eyes adjusted to the gloom, he saw that the floor of the cinema had been excavated and was now a vast crater. At various points around the perimeter, steel escalators were uncoiling downwards into the pit. They were solidly packed with people. From deep down in the darkness came a continuous plop, plop, plop – the sound of bodies falling into liquid.

Lou Rouser was at his side, now, cigar clenched in his teeth.

'Surprisingly enough,' he said in a chatty, conversational tone, 'the escalators weren't so expensive to install. But, Stan old pal, two hundred thousand gallons of sulphuric acid was a real hefty investment – even at wholesale prices.'

The Finless Death

R. E. Vernede

Don Miguel, proprietor of the inn grown about with orange-trees, yellow and green, that grew juicily in the warm airs of the gulf, was flustered.

It could not be the heat that flustered him, for it was still before dawn; and, though at any moment the sun might come blazing out, he was not thinking of it.

'Señores!' he said, appealingly.

The two Englishmen stopped.

'What does the fat fool want?' asked Flackman, impatiently.

'Don't know,' said Kender. 'I'll ask him' – and he put the question fluently in Spanish.

'If I might be permitted,' said the innkeeper, extending the palms of his hands in emphasis, 'I would advise the Señores.'

'The advice of Don Miguel is more precious than pearls,' said Kender, courteously, resting the butt-end of his heavy rod on the ground, 'and, without doubt, the oyster does not contain more. But in what does the advice consist?'

Don Miguel bowed to the compliment, and made answer:

'It is that the Señores should not go fishing today.'

'For what reason?'

Don Miguel had many reasons, apparently.

'The day is warm, yet on land, in the 'arbour, very cool. How pleasant to sit there and sip aguardiente. Also, Rietta will sing to the Señores. She had this morning the voice of a nightingale.'

'She has the voice of six nightingales invariably,' said Kender. 'Also, aguardiente is good. But we came to fish.'

'Consider, Señor, how easily the sun goes to the head of the unaccustomed.'

'True,' said Kender. 'But the heads of both of us are thick as the rinds of pumpkins, and are protected by sombreros.'

'The heads of the Señores are of an excellent proportion' said Don Miguel, hastily. 'And yet – there might be a hurricane.'

'I see no sign of it,' Kender maintained.

The innkeeper became yet more earnest.

'Señor,' he said, 'you will laugh, I know it, or maybe frown, for it is Don Flackman that laughs always, thinking these things but superstitions, and of no account.'

'But what things?'

Don Miguel looked about him anxiously as if he feared the presence of some supernatural agency, and crossed himself, before he answered in a low voice.

'Things that are said – in fear – the Mexicans say them. Without doubt these half-breeds are mad compared to your excellencies, and yet I, who live here and know, who am of the blood of Castile, I also am afraid. Señor, I ask you, where are the German Señores that went fishing yesterday? Them also I warned and' – again he crossed – 'they have not returned.'

'Warned them of what?' said Kender, eager to get to the point.

The innkeeper dropped his voice still lower.

'Of the Finless Death,' he said.

Kender looked at him curiously. The man was evidently earnest in his warnings, for the sweat stood out in his face, and he wrung his fat hands as if in dread of some impending evil. Kender himself, a scientist, a little man, but firm-lipped, unemotional, and with a chin that betokened incredulity, was the last person to take a superstition literally, or to be moved by it. Nevertheless, he hesitated a moment. It seemed to him as if something – some danger perhaps – might underlie this manifest fear.

'Aren't you coming?' said Flackman, impatiently.

He had not understood the conversation, and was longing to reach the fishing-grounds.

'In a minute,' said Kender, and he turned to the innkeeper. 'What is the Finless Death?' he said, tapping him on the arm.

Don Miguel turned up the whites of his eyes.

'Señor, how should I know? Only this I have heard – that at the full moon the Finless Death moves on the lagoons, and makes men stark with fear. Last night it was almost full.'

'True,' said Kender, 'it was undeniably almost full.'

'And twice Pedro, that, as the Señor knows, is an unerring watchdog, bayed violently.'

'At what?'

'At nothing.'

'And therefore at this devil?' said Kender, smiling.

The innkeeper evaded insisting on this sequence.

'The German Señores have not returned,' he repeated significantly.

'Nor paid their bill?' asked Kender.

'That is nothing,' said Don Miguel, with dignity. 'I have warned the Señores.' He turned away hurt.

'And truly I am most grateful,' said Kender; 'but my friend, as you perceive, is not to be persuaded and therefore we go to fish. Maybe we shall catch the finless thing itself.'

The innkeeper threw up his hands in an ecstasy of horror as Kender followed Flackman through the orange-groves that led down to the creek where José, the half-breed, was getting ready the boat. Flackman was highly amused to hear of the innkeeper's alarm.

'You refuse to be warned?'

'Don't you?'

'My dear man,' said Kender, 'I never take warnings – at least in so far as they frighten a man away from what he does know by what he does not know. It's my business to learn, just as it's my business to jest. I only told you because – well – you know you've got an imagination – it might get on your nerves.'

'Nonsense!' said Flackman, and added inconsequently: 'Miguel is a fat man, and all fat men are fools.'

'I incline to think there's something in it.'

'Some Mexican, full of aguardiente, saw a cuttle-fish at the full moon once.'

'Perhaps – but it's descriptive – their name for the terror?'

'Oh, that I grant you,' said Flackman, laughing. 'They make a good case for their demons by giving them a sounding title, but they've got too many of 'em – only they seem to have impressed you, Kender?'

'Not much,' said Kender, 'I'm interested, I admit; I take it to be some water-devil – something connected with fish.'

'But finless.'

'An eel, perhaps – it's quite easy to imagine an eel without fins – or some sort of water-snake.'

'Sea-serpent,' Flackman suggested. He was much amused to see Kender – usually so sceptical – interesting himself in Don Miguel's supernatural absurdity. For his own part, he could think of nothing but the desire to hear his reel run again, and to hold up a fighting fish by his own skilful handling till it should be drawn to the boat-side and the gaff, splashing faintly a hundredweight of tired silver. And it was a day of days for fishing – the sky already full of suppressed brightness, as if the sun were just behind it, and the morning unwontedly fresh. Ahead of them, Flackman could see the creek (solitary, since it was before the time when tarpon-fishing had become a fashionable amusement), and the boat and the Mexican boatman lolling beside it. He was almost annoyed with Kender that with such a view before him he would go on discussing his ridiculous subject, quite gravely too.

'But it might be some kind of sea-serpent,' he was saying, 'or merely a delusion, as you seem to think; for it doesn't take anything tangible to give these fellows a belief in some new devil. But I should like to know. After all, it is strange that the civilized people should be so incurious about fish, which are the ugliest things in earth or sea. Think how they were detested in bygone times! The ancients considered them not only uneatable, but unclean abominations – a part of the devilish things that lived in the sea, that was always the devil!'

'Poor old bats!' said Flackman. 'They never knew what it was to fly fish. And here's José, alive and as energetic as usual. I almost expected to find he'd been swallowed by a whale!'

José's energy was not conspicuous. He began by suggesting that it was not a good day for bites. Asked why, he said because the night before the moon was full. Flackman began to lose his temper.

'It's some trick,' he said, 'that the scamp has got up with Miguel. He wants to slack.'

'It is a possibility,' Kender admitted, thoughtfully, 'but, at the same time ...'

'I don't believe you want to go either.'

'Never wanted to fish more,' Kender said.

'It doesn't look like it.'

'And if we could catch this finless beast, I should be happy for days.'

'Oh! confound it!' said Flackman.

His spirits were mercurial, and this reiteration of an unpleasant topic was getting on his nerves. Doubtless, the whole thing was absurd; but it was unpleasant. Flackman himself thought nothing of it. He kept on assuring himself of that; but, at the same time, he was one of those who, not altogether self-reliant, liked to have their opinion corroborated by their company. And here was Kender frowning over this suggestion of peril as if he were assured there were some bottom in it, if one only knew. He wanted to fish, not to face a mystery. If he had known what they were going to encounter, he might have hung back. But he did not know, and Kender was remorseless in the pursuit of science.

'Hurry up, José,' said Flackman, pettishly.

It was very sullenly that the Mexican pulled seaward, and Flackman was reduced to whistling to keep his own spirits up. The sea ran from creek to creek, lagoon-like reaches, and spaces of the bluest calm, locked in from the gulf by reefs only to be passed at certain tides and points where the rollers had forced an inlet, as sheep force their way through a hedge, by incessant pressing. They had made a good many futile casts in the open, and Flackman's spirits were at zero, before, at Kender's suggestion, they made for one of these lagoons for a last throw. Kender had relieved the Mexican at the oars, and had his back turned to the bows, so that as they shot into that reach of still water, slack and shining, except where it was criss-crossed by dull patches that looked like stains on polished walnut, it was the younger man who saw and sprang to his feet pointing to something ahead: 'What's that?' he cried.

Out in the middle water, immobile, a boat floated, as though anchored in a pond. A single oar, broken at the blade, was caught in the left rollock and suspended.

As Kender stood up, he observed that there were two men in the stern, who seemed to be standing in stiff attitudes.

'H'm,' he said, and he sat himself down again to row for the boat, unconcernedly enough, but with a little extra speed. Flackman remained standing: his eyes moved uneasily.

'Ship your oars,' he said excitedly, as they came bow to bow with the other boat.

Kender shipped his oars, and sat steadying the boat in the expectation that Flackman would step across it, if it were only for curiosity. But Flackman had no curiosity and he had gone very pale.

'Hadn't you better – hadn't we better be getting back?' he said.

Kender carefully refrained from expressing anything, but he picked up his rod which lay in the way, and stepped across past the shrinking Mexican into the other boat. Flackman was flushing now with shame at his own poltroonery.

'What's the matter with them?' he sang out, for the swing of Kender stepping across had sent the two boats apart.

The little man had rammed his rod methodically under the bowseat, the line overboard to prevent a tangle, and was contemplating the two figures. He saw at once they were the Germans of whom Don Miguel had spoken.

'What's the matter?' cried Flackman again.

He was in an agony of uneasiness, and in the merest pretence began making casts. Again he appealed to Kender:

'You might say what's the matter with them.'

'Death!' said Kender, curtly.

'Why do they look like that?'

'I don't know.'

Kender sat on the thwarts and considered them. Never had he seen such dead men – in attitude exaggeratedly alive, rigid as waxworks, and hideous in their mimic intensity! One, a great bearded man, with spectacles, had his hand on the dragging oar and half knelt to it, as if he had been caught by a blinding cramp in the act of pulling; the other, of a slighter build, was bent forward standing, a gaff in his hand, menacing, as it seemed, the empty space in the middle of the boat – at least it should have been empty, but there was a slime over it, as if a great snail had crawled there. The faces of the two were indescribably afraid.

'Now, how did that slime get there?' said Kender to himself.

Almost as if in answer, Flackman gave a shout.

'I've hooked something!' he said. 'By gad! and a heavy one!' he went on, as the thick rod bent nearly double under the weight.

'You'd better cut your line,' said Kender, gruffly. 'It's hardly time to fish.'

'Right,' said Flackman. But he didn't.

Mechanically he had struck, and equally mechanically he began to reel up. He had a semi-conscious idea of saving as much of his line as possible before he cut loose, and as he saw far down the loom of a great white fish, the zeal of sport carried him away. He reeled steadily, the rod seemed strained with a dead weight, but there was no rush or plunging. Quite suddenly, the white mass was on the surface, and as Flackman tightened his hold and yelled for the gaff, it seemed to fly up into the boat. It fell, facing the bows, where the Mexican was sitting, the hook in its mouth, the line broken.

Flackman stared. From its size the fish could not have weighed less than a hundred pounds, yet it had come up without a struggle, and had been landed ungaffed. Now it lay there heaving equably – a white-bellied, shapeless thing, rotund and flabby, with the detestable lidless fish eyes.

'It's a remarkable fish,' said Flackman, curiously.

'Very,' said Kender.

'Did you see how it came up?'

'Yes. What are you going to do with it?'

'Chuck it over, if possible.'

'I should.'

They seemed unanimous in thinking it would be a good riddance.

'Hi, José! give me a hand. Hullo! what's wrong?' Flackman saw that some strange malady had seized the Mexican. He seemed to be stiffening as he crouched in the bows; his arms were stretched out fixedly, like the arms of a sign-post. Kender started.

'What's he pointing at?' he shouted.

'The fish. Ugh! it's oozing slime!'

'Slime!'

'A sort of snail slime.'

Flackman drew back from the fish, disgusted. 'It's too filthy to touch,' he went on. 'It's – by gad – Kender – it's got no fins!' His voice rose nervously. 'What is it? What's it doing, and to José?'

He began to stammer, frightened at he knew not what. The Mexican was growing most rigid.

'José!' shouted Kender, imperiously.

There was no answer but Flackman's.

'He's – he's being poisoned, I think.'

'Go and shake him!'

'I daren't.'

The two Englishmen eyed each other from the boats. Then Flackman, seized with a spasm of shame or horror, snatched up the gaff and stabbed the fish through the grey-skinned back. A white ichor spurted up and took him on the arm. Kender saw him drop the gaff, clutch at his elbow, and begin to mumble wildly. It was then that a fear began to take hold of him also; he could do nothing where he sat, for there were no oars to the boat.

'Flackman!' he said, sharply.

'No fins, no fins!' muttered the other.

'Come here!' commanded Kender.

Flackman looked up in a dazed manner, and took a step towards the oars. Then, as his eye caught the white-bellied fish lying there, he shrank back, crying out:

'No fins, no fins!'

Even while he cried another spurt of the fluid came from the cut in the creature's back, and dribbled over his arm. He cried out, and unsheathed his knife. Before Kender could say anything, he had stuck it into his arm and stabbed again and again. Kender watched the blood stream helplessly, for he could do nothing unless Flackman would bring the boats together. He longed for an oar, longed to be able to swim. Again he shouted sharply:

'Bring her up!'

'No, no, Kender,' the young man spoke in a strange voice. 'I mustn't do that – I mustn't do that.'

'Why not?'

'Because ...' Flackman paused, and looked out of the corner of his eyes slyly. 'You understand, Kender, don't you?'

'I tell you to come here,' said Kender, firmly.

'It's – no – it's impossible.'

It seemed to be, for Flackman was like a child in his obstinacy. Kender changed his tactics accordingly.

'The fish will have you then,' he called.

The effect was magical. Flackman sprang up, looked at the fish, shuddered, and, diving into the sea began to swim to the other boat. Kender watched. Surely it was the most peaceful scene in the world, a man swimming silently in a sea still to the horizon, scattering bubbles like diamonds before him, and leaving behind him the clear curve of his wake – a blue sky, unbeaten by any storm, a swimmer, and two pleasure-boats. And yet Kender was beginning to feel afraid. He tried to argue the fear away, but it would not go. It crept over him jointless, inexplicable, binding as a nightmare. He laughed at himself in sheer bravado, and the laugh stuck in his throat and became a shrill giggling that seemed to carry his reason with it high up above his reach. He clutched after it, to recall it and could not. For he knew that the man that was swimming towards him had a face distorted with terror; that the boat in which he sat and giggled held two men grotesquely dead: that the blue, calm sea was vacant of human help. And in the other boat lay that monstrous fish without fins, staring the life out of the Mexican. It was with a struggle that he drew himself together, shivering, and pulled his friend on board.

Flackman fell in the bottom of the boat exhausted. He muttered continually, and was plainly delirious, for through his multifarious imaginings there ran always the vague thread of terror that haunts delirious men.

'No fins, no fins,' he would moan, and clutch at the arm Kender had bound up.

It was impossible to relieve him. Kender wished for his own sake that anything could be done, for in this feeling of impotence was evil, and he was aware that his own hysteria was growing. Must they wait, then, for ever on that hateful sea? He tried the broken oar, but it would not move the heavy boat an inch. They must lie there, it seemed, and grow to knowledge of what fear could be. He sat and stared before him, and then, without warning, the last horror came. The bows of the other boat lifted suddenly, so that the Mexican rolled over and was seen to sink, while almost imperceptibly the boat itself began to glide towards them, the fish on board. As it came near, throwing no ripples before it, Kender bit his lips in agony.

There was no help – none! The boat was gliding with so swift a motion that it seemed upon them, and yet he could see still far down in the water the corpse of the Mexican, all huddled up and stiff – still twirling head over heels, round and round, deeper and deeper, to the bottom ooze. Not ten yards separated them now from the horror that blinked there in the other boat and heaved its hideous whiteness – not eight – and it was death – the death without fins – not five!

Kender shrieked aloud and ran about the boat, so that it rocked violently. For a moment it seemed an added terror, and then he saw the reason. The rod – his rod – clinched in the bows as he stepped on board, had hooked something with its dangling bait – something that went with jerks and rushes, darting ahead, towing the boat after it – some huge tarpon. It made for the opening by which they had passed into the lagoon and for the open sea. Behind, always quickening, the other boat came, drawn on by its own mysterious power. With tense eyes, Kender watched this strange race, in which he and his friend stood for both prize and spoil. Without reasoning the matter, he somehow knew (so he said afterwards) that that which reached the open sea would win away. The line taken zigzagged for the outlet. Kender dared not stir, but he prayed to reach it, and the boat seemed to go quick with his longing.

The water flew under them – surely the outlet could not be far off – the other boat was gaining – no – yes – ah, but the outlet was before them. Their boat was through it. With a rasping noise, the ghastly boat behind drove on a sunk reef to the left. Kender, as his senses went from him in a swoon, fancied that he saw leap from it, like a great curl of smoke, the great white fish that turned in mid-air and plunged noise-lessly into the sea ...

It was towards dusk, and some seven miles off shore, that the yacht *Swallow* came on a drifting boat, noticeable for a rod bent in its bows like a bowsprit and snapped off as if by a jerk of some fish that had been hooked and had escaped. Besides this, there were on board two dead men, half standing in constrained positions, and two alive, a young man obviously raving, and another man – older – who might have been sane, except that his lips twitched continuously, and he told this story.

The Man Who Liked Dickens

Evelyn Waugh

Although Mr McMaster had lived in Amazonas for nearly sixty years, no one except a few families of Shiriana Indians was aware of his existence. His house stood in a small savannah, one of those little patches of sand and grass that crop up occasionally in that neighbourhood, three miles or so across, bounded on all sides by forest.

The stream which watered it was not marked on any map; it ran through rapids, always dangerous and at most seasons of the year impassable, to join the upper waters of the River Uraricuera, whose course, though boldly delineated in every school atlas, is still largely conjectural. None of the inhabitants of the district, except Mr McMaster, had ever heard of the republic of Colombia, Venezuela, Brazil or Bolivia, each of whom had at one time or another claimed its possession.

Mr McMaster's house was larger than those of his neighbours, but similar in character – a palm-thatch roof, breast-high walls of mud and wattle, and a mud floor. He owned a dozen or so head of puny cattle which grazed in the savannah, a plantation of cassava, some banana and mango trees, a dog, and, unique in the neighbourhood, a single-barrelled, breech-loading shotgun. The few commodities which he employed from the outside world came to him through a long succession of traders, passed from hand to hand, bartered for in a dozen languages at the extreme end of one of the longest threads in the web of commerce that spreads from Manáos into the remote fastness of the forest.

One day, while Mr McMaster was engaged in filling some cartridges, a Shiriana came to him with the news that a white man was approaching through the forest, alone and very sick. He closed the cartridge and loaded his gun with it, put those that were finished into his pocket and set out in the direction indicated.

The man was already clear of the bush when Mr McMaster reached him, sitting on the ground, clearly in a bad way. He was without hat or boots, and his clothes were so torn that it was only by the dampness of his body that they adhered to it; his feet were cut and grossly swollen, every exposed surface of skin was scarred by insect and bat bites;

his eyes were wild with fever. He was talking to himself in delirium, but stopped when Mr McMaster approached and addressed him in English.

'I'm tired,' the man said; then: 'Can't go on any farther. My name is Henty and I'm tired. Anderson died. That was a long time ago. I expect you think I'm very odd.'

'I think you are ill, my friend.'

'Just tired. It must be several months since I had anything to eat.'

Mr McMaster hoisted him to his feet and, supporting him by the arm, led him across the hummocks of grass towards the farm.

'It is a very short way. When we get there I will give you something to make you better.'

'Jolly kind of you.' Presently he said: 'I say, you speak English. I'm English, too. My name is Henty.'

'Well, Mr Henty, you aren't to bother about anything more. You're ill and you've had a rough journey. I'll take care of you.'

They went very slowly, but at length reached the house.

'Lie there in the hammock. I will fetch something for you.'

Mr McMaster went into the back room of the house and dragged a tin canister from under a heap of skins. It was full of a mixture of dried leaf and bark. He took a handful and went outside to the fire. When he returned he put one hand behind Henty's head and held up the concoction of herbs in a calabash for him to drink. He sipped, shuddering slightly at the bitterness. At last he finished it. Mr McMaster threw out the dregs on the floor. Henty lay back in the hammock sobbing quietly. Soon he fell into a deep sleep.

'Ill-fated' was the epithet applied by the Press to the Anderson expedition to the Parima and upper Uraricuera region of Brazil. Every stage of the enterprise from the preliminary arrangements in London to its tragic dissolution in Amazonas was attacked by misfortune. It was due to one of the early setbacks that Paul Henty became connected with it.

He was not by nature an explorer; an even-tempered, good-looking young man of fastidious tastes and enviable possessions, unintellectual, but appreciative of fine architecture and the ballet, well travelled in the more accessible parts of the world, a collector though not a connoisseur, popular among hostesses, revered by his aunts. He was married to a lady of exceptional charm and beauty, and it was she who upset the good order of his life by confessing her affection for another man for the second time in the eight years of their marriage. The first occasion had been a short-lived infatuation with a tennis professional, the second was a captain in the Coldstream Guards, and more serious.

Henty's first thought under the shock of this revelation was to go out and dine alone. He was a member of four clubs, but at three of them he was liable to meet his wife's lover. Accordingly he chose one which he rarely frequented, a semi-intellectual company composed of publishers, barristers, and men of scholarship awaiting election to the Athenaeum.

Here, after dinner, he fell into conversation with Professor Anderson and first heard of the proposed expedition to Brazil. The particular misfortune that was retarding arrangements at the moment was defalcation of the secretary with two-thirds of the expedition's capital. The principals were ready – Professor Anderson, Dr Simmons the anthropologist, Mr Necher the biologist, Mr Brough the surveyor, wireless operator and mechanic – the scientific and sporting apparatus was packed up in crates ready to be embarked, the necessary facilities had been stamped and signed by the proper authorities, but unless twelve hundred pounds was forthcoming the whole thing would have to be abandoned.

Henty, as has been suggested, was a man of comfortable means; the expedition would last from nine months to a year; he could shut his country house – his wife, he reflected, would want to remain in London near her young man – and cover more than the sum required. There was a glamour about the whole journey which might, he felt, move even his wife's sympathies. There and then, over the club fire he decided to accompany Professor Anderson.

When he went home that evening he announced to his wife: 'I have decided what I shall do.'

'Yes, darling?'

'You are certain that you no longer love me?'

'Darling, you *know*, I *adore* you.'

'But you are certain you love this guardsman, Tony whatever-his-name-is, more?'

'Oh, yes, *ever* so much more. Quite a different thing altogether.'

'Very well, then. I do not propose to do anything about a divorce for a year. You shall have time to think it over. I am leaving next week for the Uraricuera.'

'Golly, where's that?'

'I am not perfectly sure. Somewhere in Brazil, I think. It is unexplored. I shall be away a year.'

'But darling, how ordinary! Like people in books – big game, I mean, and all that.'

'You have obviously already discovered that I am a very ordinary person.'

'Now, Paul, don't be disagreeable – oh, there's the telephone. It's probably Tony. If it is, d'you mind terribly if I talk to him alone for a bit?'

But in the ten days of preparation that followed she showed greater

tenderness, putting off her soldier twice in order to accompany Henty
to the shops where he was choosing his equipment and insisting on his
purchasing a worsted cummerbund. On his last evening she gave
a supper-party for him at the Embassy to which she allowed him
to ask any of his friends he liked; he could think of no one except
Professor Anderson, who looked oddly dressed, danced tirelessly and
was something of a failure with everyone. Next day Mrs Henty came
with her husband to the boat train and presented him with a pale blue,
extravagantly soft blanket, in a suède case of the same colour furnished
with a zip fastener and monogram. She kissed him goodbye and said,
'Take care of yourself in wherever it is.'

Had she gone as far as Southampton she might have witnessed
two dramatic passages. Mr Brough got no farther than the gangway
before he was arrested for debt – a matter of £32; the publicity given
to the dangers of the expedition was responsible for the action. Henty
settled the account.

The second difficulty was not to be overcome so easily. Mr Necher's
mother was on the ship before them; she carried a missionary
journal in which she had just read an account of the Brazilian
forests. Nothing would induce her to permit her son's departure; she
would remain on board until he came ashore with her. If necessary, she
would sail with him, but go into those forests alone he should not. All
argument was unavailing with the resolute old lady who eventually, five
minutes before the time of embarkation, bore her son off in
triumph, leaving the company without a biologist.

Nor was Mr Brough's adherence long maintained. The ship in which
they were travelling was a cruising liner taking passengers on a round
voyage. Mr Brough had not been on board a week and had scarcely
accustomed himself to the motion of the ship before he was engaged to
be married; he was still engaged, although to a different lady, when they
reached Manáos and refused all inducements to proceed farther,
borrowing his return fare from Henty and arriving back in Southampton engaged to the lady of his first choice, whom he immediately
married.

In Brazil the officials to whom their credentials were addressed were
all out of power. While Henty and Professor Anderson negotiated with
the new administrators, Dr Simmons proceeded up river to Boa Vista
where he established a base camp with the greater part of the stores.
These were instantly commandeered by the revolutionary garrison, and
he himself imprisoned for some days and subjected to various humilia-
tions which so enraged him that, when released, he made promptly for
the coast, stopping at Manáos only long enough to inform his colleagues
that he insisted on laying his case personally before the central authorities at Rio.

Thus, while they were still a month's journey from the start of their labours, Henty and Professor Anderson found themselves alone and deprived of the greater part of their supplies. The ignominy of immediate return was not to be borne. For a short time they considered the advisability of going into hiding for six months in Madeira or Teneriffe, but even there detection seemed probable, there had been too many photographs in the illustrated papers before they left London. Accordingly, in low spirits, the two explorers at last set out alone for the Uraricuera with little hope of accomplishing anything of any value to anyone.

For seven weeks they paddled through green, humid tunnels of forest. They took a few snapshots of naked, misanthropic Indians, bottled some snakes and later lost them when their canoe capsized in the rapids; they overtaxed their digestions, imbibing nauseous intoxicants at native galas, they were robbed of the last of their sugar by a Guianese prospector. Finally, Professor Anderson fell ill with malignant malaria, chattered feebly for some days in his hammock, lapsed into a coma and died, leaving Henty alone with a dozen Maku oarsmen, none of whom spoke a word of any language known to him. They reversed their course and drifted down stream with a minimum of provisions and no mutual confidence.

One day, a week or so after Professor Anderson's death, Henty awoke to find that his boys and his canoe had disappeared during the night, leaving him with only his hammock and pyjamas some two or three hundred miles from the nearest Brazilian habitation. Nature forbade him to remain where he was although there seemed little purpose in moving. He set himself to follow the course of the stream, at first in the hope of meeting a canoe. But presently the whole forest became peopled for him with frantic apparitions, for no conscious reason at all. He plodded on, now wading in the water, now scrambling through the bush.

Vaguely at the back of his mind he had always believed that the jungle was a place full of food, that there was danger of snakes and savages and wild beasts, but not of starvation. But now he observed that this was far from being the case. The jungle consisted solely of immense tree trunks, embedded in a tangle of thorn and vine rope, all far from nutritious. On the first day he suffered hideously. Later he seemed anaesthetized and was chiefly embarrassed by the behaviour of the inhabitants who came out to meet him in footmen's livery, carrying his dinner, and then irresponsibly disappeared or raised the covers of their dishes and revealed live tortoises. Many people who knew him in London appeared and ran round him with derisive cries, asking him questions to which he could not possibly know the answer. His wife came, too, and he was pleased to see her, assuming that she had got tired of her guardsman and was there to fetch him back, but she soon disappeared, like all the others.

It was then that he remembered that it was imperative for him to reach Manáos; he redoubled his energy, stumbling against boulders in the stream and getting caught up among the vines. 'But I mustn't waste my breath,' he reflected. Then he forgot that, too, and was conscious of nothing more until he found himself lying in a hammock in Mr McMaster's house.

His recovery was slow. At first, days of lucidity alternated with delirium, then his temperature dropped and he was conscious even when most ill. The days of fever grew less frequent, finally occurring in the normal system of the tropics between long periods of comparative health. Mr McMaster dosed him regularly with herbal remedies.

'It's very nasty,' said Henty, 'but it does do good.'

'There is medicine for everything in the forest,' said Mr McMaster, 'to make you well and to make you ill. My mother was an Indian and she taught me many of them. I have learned others from time to time from my wives. There are plants to cure you and give you fever, to kill you and send you mad, to keep away snakes, to intoxicate fish so that you can pick them out of the water with your hands like fruit from a tree. There are medicines even I do not know. They say that it is possible to bring dead people to life after they have begun to stink, but I have not seen it done.'

'But surely you are English?'

'My father was – at least a Barbadian. He came to British Guiana as a missionary. He was married to a white woman but he left her in Guiana to look for gold. Then he took my mother. The Shiriana women are ugly but very devoted. I have had many. Most of the men and women living in this savannah are my children. That is why they obey – for that reason and because I have the gun. My father lived to a great age. It is not twenty years since he died. He was a man of education. Can you read?'

'Yes, of course.'

'It is not everyone who is so fortunate. I cannot.'

Henty laughed apologetically. 'But I suppose you haven't much opportunity here.'

'Oh, yes, that is just it. I have a great many books. I will show you when you are better. Until five years ago there was an Englishman – at least a black man, but he was well educated in Georgetown. He died. He used to read to me every day until he died. You shall read to me when you are better.'

'I shall be delighted to.'

'Yes, you shall read to me,' Mr McMaster repeated, nodding over the calabash.

During the early days of his convalescence Henty had little conversation with his host; he lay in the hammock staring up at the thatched roof and thinking about his wife, rehearsing over and over again different incidents in their life together, including her affairs with the tennis professional and the soldier. The days, exactly twelve hours each, passed without distinction. Mr McMaster retired to sleep at sundown, leaving a little lamp burning – a hand-wove wick drooping from a pot of beef fat – to keep away vampire bats.

The first time that Henty left the house Mr McMaster took him for a little stroll around the farm.

'I will show you the black man's grave,' he said, leading him to a mound between the mango trees. 'He was very kind to me. Every afternoon until he died, for two hours, he used to read to me. I think I will put up a cross – to commemorate his death and your arrival – a pretty idea. Do you believe in God?'

'I've never really thought about it much.'

'You are perfectly right. I have thought about it a *great* deal and I still do not know ... Dickens did.'

'I suppose so.'

'Oh yes, it is apparent in all his books. You will see.'

That afternoon Mr McMaster began the construction of a headpiece for the Negro's grave. He worked with a large spokeshave in a wood so hard that it grated and rang like metal.

At last when Henty had passed six or seven consecutive days without fever, Mr McMaster said, 'Now I think you are well enough to see the books.'

At one end of the hut there was a kind of loft formed by a rough platform erected up in the eaves of the roof. Mr McMaster propped a ladder against it and mounted. Henty followed, still unsteady after his illness. Mr McMaster sat on the platform and Henty stood at the top of the ladder looking over. There was a heap of small bundles there, tied up with rag, palm leaf and raw hide.

'It has been hard to keep out the worms and ants. Two are practically destroyed. But there is an oil the Indians know how to make that is useful.'

He unwrapped the nearest parcel and handed down a calf-bound book. It was an early American edition of *Bleak House*.

'It does not matter which we take first.'

'You are fond of Dickens?'

'Why, yes, of course. More than fond, far more. You see, they are the only books I have ever heard. My father used to read them and then later the black man ... and now you. I have heard them all several times by now but I never get tired; there is always more to be learned and noticed, so many characters, so many changes of scene, so many words

... I have all Dickens's books except those that the ants devoured. It takes a long time to read them all – more than two years.'

'Well,' said Henty lightly, 'they will well last out my visit.'

'Oh, I hope not. It is delightful to start again. Each time I think I find more to enjoy and admire.'

They took down the first volume of *Bleak House* and that afternoon Henty had his first reading.

He had always rather enjoyed reading aloud and in the first year of marriage had shared several books in this way with his wife, until one day, in one of her rare moments of confidence, she remarked that it was torture to her. Sometimes after that he had thought it might be agreeable to have children to read to. But Mr McMaster was a unique audience.

The old man sat astride his hammock opposite Henty, fixing him throughout with his eyes, and following the words, soundlessly, with his lips. Often when a new character was introduced he would say, 'Repeat the name, I have forgotten him,' or, 'Yes, yes, I remember her well. She dies, poor woman.' He would frequently interrupt with questions: not as Henty would have imagined about the circumstances of the story – such things as the procedure of the Lord Chancellor's Court or the social conventions of the time, though they must have been unintelligible, did not concern him – but always about the characters. 'Now, why does she say that? Does she really mean it? Did she feel faint because of the heat of the fire or of something in that paper?' He laughed loudly at all the jokes and at some passages which did not seem humorous to Henty, asking him to repeat them two or three times; and later at the description of the sufferings of the outcasts in 'Tom-all-alone' tears ran down his cheeks into his beard. His comments on the story were usually simple. 'I think that Dedlock is a very proud man,' or 'Mrs Jellyby does not take enough care of her children.' Henty enjoyed the readings almost as much as he did.

At the end of the first day the old man said, 'You read beautifully, with a far better accent than the black man. And you explain better. It is almost as though my father were here again.' And always at the end of a session he thanked his guest courteously. 'I enjoyed that very much. It was an extremely distressing chapter. But, if I remember rightly, it will all turn out well.'

By the time that they were well into the second volume, however, the novelty of the old man's delight had begun to wane, and Henty was feeling strong enough to be restless. He touched more than once on the subject of his departure, asking about canoes and rains and the possibility of finding guides. But Mr McMaster seemed obtuse and paid no attention to these hints.

One day, running his thumb through the pages of *Bleak House* that remained to be read, Henty said, 'We still have a lot to get through. I hope I shall be able to finish it before I go.'

'Oh, yes,' said Mr McMaster. 'Do not disturb yourself about that. You will have time to finish it, my friend.'

For the first time Henty noticed something slightly menacing in his host's manner. That evening at supper, a brief meal of farine and dried beef eaten just before sundown, Henty renewed the subject.

'You know, Mr McMaster, the time has come when I must be thinking about getting back to civilization. I have already imposed myself on your hospitality for too long.'

Mr McMaster bent over his plate, crunching mouthfuls of farine, but made no reply.

'How soon do you think I shall be able to get a boat? ... I said how soon do you think I shall be able to get a boat? I appreciate all your kindness to me more than I can say, but...'

'My friend, any kindness I may have shown is amply repaid by your reading of Dickens. Do not let us mention the subject again.'

'Well, I'm very glad you have enjoyed it. I have, too. But I really must be thinking of getting back...'

'Yes,' said Mr McMaster. 'The black man was like that. He thought of it all the time. But he died here...'

Twice during the next day Henty opened the subject but his host was evasive. Finally he said, 'Forgive me, Mr McMaster, but I really must press the point. When can I get a boat?'

'There is no boat.'

'Well, the Indians can build one.'

'You must wait for the rains. There is not enough water in the river now.'

'How long will that be?'

'A month ... two months...'

They had finished *Bleak House* and were nearing the end of *Dombey and Son* when the rain came.

'Now it is time to make preparations to go.'

'Oh, that is impossible. The Indians will not make a boat during the rainy season – it is one of their superstitions.'

'You might have told me.'

'Did I not mention it? I forgot.'

Next morning Henty went out alone while his host was busy, and, looking as aimless as he could, strolled across the savannah to the group of Indian houses. There were four or five Shirianas sitting in one of the doorways. They did not look up as he approached them. He addressed them in the few words of Maku he had acquired during the journey but they made no sign whether they understood him or not. Then he drew a sketch of a canoe in the sand, he went through some vague motions

of carpentry, pointed from them to him, then made motions of giving
something to them and scratched out the outlines of a gun and a hat
and a few other recognizable articles of trade. One of the women
giggled, but no one gave any sign of comprehension, and he went away
unsatisfied.

At their midday meal Mr McMaster said: 'Mr Henty, the Indians tell
me that you have been trying to speak with them. It is easier that you
say anything you wish through me. You realize, do you not, that they
would do nothing without my authority. They regard themselves, quite
rightly in most cases, as my children.'

'Well, as a matter of fact, I was asking them about a canoe.'

'So they gave me to understand . . . and now if you have finished your
meal perhaps we might have another chapter. I am quite absorbed in
the book.'

They finished *Dombey and Son*; nearly a year had passed since Henty
had left England, and his gloomy foreboding of permanent exile became
suddenly acute when, between the pages of *Martin Chuzzlewit*, he found
a document written in pencil in irregular characters.

Year 1919.

*I James McMaster of Brazil do swear to Barnabas Washington of Georgetown
that if he finish this book in fact Martin Chuzzlewit I will let him go away back
as soon as finished.*

There followed a heavy pencil *X*, and after it: *Mr McMaster made this
mark signed Barnabas Washington.*

'Mr McMaster,' said Henty, 'I must speak frankly. You saved my life,
and when I get back to civilization I will reward you to the best of my
ability. I will give you anything within reason. But at present you are
keeping me here against my will. I demand to be released.'

'But, my friend, what is keeping you? You are under no restraint. Go
when you like.'

'You know very well that I can't get away without your help.'

'In that case you must humour an old man. Read me another chapter.'

'Mr McMaster, I swear by anything you like that when I get to
Manáos I will find someone to take my place. I will pay a man to read
to you all day.'

'But I have no need of another man. You read so well.'

'I have read for the last time.'

'I hope not,' said Mr McMaster politely.

That evening at supper only one plate of dried meat and farine was
brought in and Mr McMaster ate alone. Henty lay without speaking,
staring at the thatch.

Next day at noon a single plate was put before Mr McMaster, but with it lay his gun, cocked, on his knee, as he ate. Henty resumed the reading of *Martin Chuzzlewit* where it had been interrupted.

Weeks passed hopelessly. They read *Nicholas Nickleby* and *Little Dorrit* and *Oliver Twist*. Then a stranger arrived in the savannah, a half-caste prospector, one of that lonely order of men who wander for a lifetime through the forests, tracing the little streams, sifting the gravel and, ounce by ounce, filling the little leather sack of gold dust, more often than not dying of exposure and starvation with five hundred dollars' worth of gold hung round their necks. Mr McMaster was vexed at his arrival, gave him farine and *passo* and sent him on his journey within an hour of his arrival, but in that hour Henty had time to scribble his name on a slip of paper and put it into the man's hand.

From now on there was hope. The days followed their unvarying routine: coffee at sunrise, a morning of inaction while Mr McMaster pottered about on the business of the farm, farine and *passo* at noon, Dickens in the afternoon, farine and *passo* and sometimes some fruit for supper, silence from sunset to dawn with the small wick glowing in the beef fat and the palm thatch overhead dimly discernible; but Henty lived in quiet confidence and expectation.

Some time, this year or the next, the prospector would arrive at a Brazilian village with news of his discovery. The disasters to the Anderson expedition would not have passed unnoticed. Henty could imagine the headlines that must have appeared in the popular Press; even now probably there were search parties working over the country he had crossed; any day English voices might sound over the savannah and a dozen friendly adventurers come crashing through the bush. Even as he was reading, while his lips mechanically followed the printed pages, his mind wandered away from his eager, crazy host opposite, and he began to narrate to himself incidents of his home-coming – the gradual re-encounters with civilization; he shaved and bought new clothes at Manáos, telegraphed for money, received wires of congratulation; he enjoyed the leisurely river journey to Belem, the big liner to Europe; savoured good claret and fresh meat and spring vegetables; he was shy at meeting his wife and uncertain how to address ... '*Darling*, you've been much longer than you said. I quite thought you were lost ...'

And then Mr McMaster interrupted. 'May I trouble you to read that passage again? It is one I particularly enjoy.'

The weeks passed; there was no sign of rescue, but Henty endured the day for hope of what might happen on the morrow; he even felt a slight stirring of cordiality towards his gaoler and was therefore quite willing to join him when, one evening after a long conference with an Indian neighbour, he proposed a celebration.

'It is one of the local feast days,' he explained, 'and they have been making *piwari*. You may not like it, but you should try some. We will go across to this man's home tonight.'

Accordingly after supper they joined a party of Indians that were assembled round the fire in one of the huts at the other side of the savannah. They were singing in an apathetic, monotonous manner and passing a large calabash of liquid from mouth to mouth. Separate bowls were brought for Henty and Mr McMaster, and they were given hammocks to sit in.

'You must drink it all without lowering the cup. That is the etiquette.'

Henty gulped the dark liquid, trying not to taste it. But it was not unpleasant, hard and muddy on the palate like most of the beverages he had been offered in Brazil, but with a flavour of honey and brown bread. He leant back in the hammock feeling unusually contented. Perhaps at that very moment the search party was in camp a few hours' journey from them. Meanwhile he was warm and drowsy. The cadence of song rose and fell interminably, liturgically. Another calabash of *piwari* was offered him and he handed it back empty. He lay full length watching the play of shadows on the thatch as the Shirianas began to dance. Then he shut his eyes and thought of England and his wife and fell asleep.

He awoke, still in the Indian hut, with the impression that he had outslept his usual hour. By the position of the sun he knew it was late afternoon. No one else was about. He looked for his watch and found to his surprise that it was not on his wrist. He had left it in the house, he supposed, before coming to the party.

'I must have been tight last night,' he reflected. 'Treacherous drink, that.' He had a headache and feared a recurrence of fever. He found when he set his feet to the ground that he stood with difficulty; his walk was unsteady and his mind confused as it had been during the first weeks of his convalescence. On the way across the savannah he was obliged to stop more than once, shutting his eyes and breathing deeply. When he reached the house he found Mr McMaster sitting there.

'Ah, my friend, you are late for the reading this afternoon. There is scarcely another half-hour of light. How do you feel?'

'Rotten. That drink doesn't seem to agree with me.'

'I will give you something to make you better. The forest has remedies for everything; to make you awake and to make you sleep.'

'You haven't seen my watch anywhere?'

'You have missed it?'

'Yes. I thought I was wearing it. I say, I've never slept so long.'

'Not since you were a baby. Do you know how long? Two days.'

'Nonsense. I can't have.'

'Yes, indeed. It is a long time. It is a pity because you missed our guests.'

'Guests?'

'Why, yes. I have been quite gay while you were asleep. Three men from outside. Englishmen. It is a pity you missed them. A pity for them, too, as they particularly wished to see you. But what could I do? You were so sound asleep. They had come all the way to find you so – I thought you would not mind – as you could not greet them yourself I gave them a little souvenir, your watch. They wanted something to take home to your wife who is offering a great reward for news of you. They were very pleased with it. And they took some photographs of the little cross I put up to commemorate your coming. They were pleased with that, too. They were very easily pleased. But I do not suppose they will visit us again, our life here is so retired ... no pleasures except reading ... I do not suppose we shall ever have visitors again ... Well, well, I will get you some medicine to make you feel better. Your head aches; does it not...? We will not have any Dickens today ... but tomorrow, and the day after that, and the day after that. Let us read *Little Dorrit* again. There are passages in that book I can never hear without the temptation to weep.'

Buffy

Philip Welby

Number Nine, Acacia Street, is an unlikely address for an alchemist. At the very least, one feels, his dwelling ought to be graced with the magic number seven. However, Nine was the number, Acacia the faded suburban street, where Halliwell the alchemist tended his alembics.

To the youth of the district, even those who knew the word, he was not an alchemist particularly, he was simply Halliwell. Most towns, most neighbourhoods, harbour some such character, an object of amused contempt, of scandal to the civic-minded, a butt for the young. We used to call at him from across the street as he shambled, unwashed, overcoated even in summer, on his rare forays for provisions. Mostly he bought cheap food, but sometimes he would invade the chemist with lists of chemicals.

By the time I was fifteen, I had outgrown these baitings, or at least become sensitive enough to be embarrassed by them, but other boys did not change thus. Particularly Buffy Albright. His real name was Burford, he was a few months younger than me but a good deal bigger, and, it must be said, he was a lout. Not an underprivileged, ill-educated lout, but a well-spoken grammar-school lout, which is even less endearing. He dearly loved Halliwell-harrying, as he called it, but one day he went too far.

We were cycling home from school, Buffy and I and a couple of others, hated caps in our pockets, eyes open for girls to whistle at, or other diversions. Like Halliwell . . .

'Hey, there's the mad alchemist!' shouted Buffy, leading the charge. He was one who did know about alchemy, or at least what it meant. I hung back for a moment, but then shamefacedly joined in.

'How are the gold reserves?' yelled Buffy, swooping past, pretending to grab at the parcels with which the old man was laden.

'Go to hell!' snarled Halliwell shrilly, hopping clumsily out of the way and dropping a package. 'Go to hell, you bloody urchins!'

This was the sort of response Buffy savoured, and he pedalled furiously back, feinting at his quarry.

'I'll have you!' screamed Halliwell.

'Catch me!' cried Buffy, and this time he mounted the pavement. Bell ringing, he bore down on Halliwell, swerving aside at the last instant. But it went wrong ...

Halliwell, confused, caught between dodging and making a half-hearted swipe at his tormentor, slipped and fell heavily. Packages flew, and there was the crunch of breaking glass. Buffy, glancing back, realized this was enough, regained the road and fled.

'Buffy!' I shouted, suddenly scared, concerned for the struggling gnome on the pavement. But Buffy and the others sped away. For a long moment I vacillated, then parked my bike on the kerb and nervously approached Halliwell.

His fall had shaken him out of his fury, and his first venomous glance faded as I helped him up. Mumbling apologies, I gathered his parcels, some clearly spoiled. He stared at me silently, then gave a wintry smile.

'If you've any sense, you'll find better friends. Doesn't that school teach ...' He stopped, and an odd expression crossed his face, to be followed by another smile, and not a pleasant one.

'You called him Buffy, eh? So that's his name ...'

I said nothing, feeling like a betrayer. At least he didn't know the surname.

'Hmm. For him, I think, the black tincture, among other things. I know more than alchemy, my young Buffy!'

And, after a grunt of farewell from him and an awkward response from me, he shuffled away. I cycled home alone and subdued.

Next day Buffy scoffed at my soft-heartedness, though I knew he was relieved to know Halliwell wasn't injured. Not that he'd have been sympathetic, but Major Albright (retd) would have been furious at any scandal. Buffy's mother was dead, and his father was what they call old-fashioned. Whatever the motivation, henceforth he would leave Halliwell alone.

The same day I sought out Meade, a boy not of my immediate circle, whose hobby was chemistry. He used to buy chemicals from the same place as Halliwell, and was friendly with the chemist. (I now wonder how friendly. I was very innocent at fifteen.)

'Does Mr Hallam tell you anything about Halliwell and this alchemy business?'

'A bit,' said Meade. '*He* doesn't know much about Halliwell either – who does? As far as the alchemy goes, Halliwell's dead serious. He really thinks he'll find how to make gold. Mr Hallam says he used to be quite respectable years ago – used to write books about alchemy and magic, stuff like that.'

My curiosity went no deeper then, and it was only years later that I bothered to look for Halliwell in library catalogues. He had indeed written books, limited editions for obscure publishers, books regarded as eccentric.

I was stimulated to find this out by a report of his death, a few lines in an evening paper, three years ago, by which date I'd left the district. Apparently he'd had an accident with his experiments – about which the reporter evidently knew little – and died in a fire that totally destroyed his house. Up to then, if I ever thought about the seedy suburb that had formed me, it was with something of the same tolerant contempt its inhabitants had shown for Halliwell.

But looking at that newspaper, 'That's not far from where I live,' remarked a certain young lady on whom I had designs. Though we were not close, I fancied there was closeness to be achieved, and late one Friday evening I decided, impulsively, to go up and see her. I rang, but there was no reply. I'd go anyway. So, early Saturday morning, I sat in a bus watching the streets of my childhood go past, some familiar, some half-recognized, some in the throes of redevelopment. Then I entered another district, and alighted in a strange street, checking the jotted address.

Of course she wasn't in, had gone away for the weekend, and when I learned with whom, I was effectively discouraged from further pursuit. *That* idiot! Disgruntled, I caught a bus back and got off at my old haunts. While I was up this way, I might as well look round, maybe meet someone I knew.

Even in those three years, the place had changed a lot, edging towards the familiar Anonymous Rebuilt. I was rather saddened, and was glad to take refuge in my old local when it opened. Really, I mean the pub near my former home; I'd left before I was old enough to drink there.

I sat down in a corner and was just reflecting that this at least was one place they hadn't changed, when a young man strolled in, stared at me in surprise, then strode over, grinning.

'Bob Cronin – it is, isn't it? Whatever are *you* doing here?'

'Good God, Del, I didn't recognize you!' I jumped up, welcoming diversion, and we pumped each other's hands. Derek Benson hadn't been a close friend, but we'd known each other fairly well, had even been fellow Halliwell-harriers. We plunged into nostalgic gossip. Derek was a social worker, returned to his home borough. His parents still lived there; mine had moved out of London.

'Do you see any of the old crowd?' I asked over the second pint.

'Well, not many – most of them seem to have moved away. Jack Cartwright's in India, did you know? Oh, I tell you who comes in here sometimes – Buffy. Maybe he'll be in today.'

'How's he getting on?'

'You may well ask. He's gone a bit weird, I think. Wears *gloves* all the time, Lord knows why. His father died, left him enough to live on, so he doesn't work.'

'Lucky!' I said.

'Maybe.' Derek shrugged. 'He didn't seem happy the last time I saw him.'

We talked of other things, and the time and the pints proceeded. Then, half an hour before closing time, Buffy walked in. He looked startled to see both of us and not, I thought, pleased. But he sat down with his drink and we talked of this and that, Derek carefully ignoring Buffy's hands, which were indeed gloved. But when Derek was in the Gents', I took a deep breath and asked:

'Trouble with your hands, Buffy?'

He glared, then took his own deep breath and answered tightly.

'Look, Bob, I don't know what Derek's been saying – I suppose you noticed anyway – but I'd appreciate it if you changed the subject. I don't want to discuss it, and that's that.'

I didn't pursue the matter, and when the pub closed he made off with a perfunctory excuse. I went round to Derek's place for a meal, and when I caught the bus that evening, we arranged to meet again in a few weeks.

It was nice to have bumped into Derek again, but I wondered about Buffy. Obviously something was wrong with his hands, but he must have changed a lot to behave like this. Perhaps his father's death ... After that, to be honest, I forgot about him again.

Time passed, my studies came to an end, and I arrived at the next phase of my life: I took a job. Here again, events conspired to bring me back to my native soil, or rather my native pavements. I looked around, I studied the newspapers, and I was pleased when a vacancy cropped up in that same North London borough. Since my chance visit, I'd been back a few times to see Derek, and I felt better disposed towards the place.

So, one Saturday in May, I sat again in the Blacksmith's Arms with Derek, celebrating my return. I was to lodge with his parents (he was married, with his own house), his father had joined us in the pub, and all was pleasantness. I managed to shadow the conviviality by asking if Buffy still wore gloves. Derek became serious.

'I'm afraid poor old Buffy's got beyond a joke. To tell the truth, he's a real thorn in my professional conscience.'

'They'll have to take him in, one of these days,' said his father.

I felt a chill – I might have been listening to a ten-year-old discussion of Halliwell the alchemist.

'What's happened to him?' I asked.

'Nobody knows, and that's the trouble. He's gone to earth, become a complete recluse. After you saw him in here, he went about still wearing his gloves, getting less and less approachable. Then, about last Christmas, he began muffling his face up, and stopped speaking to anybody except shopkeepers and suchlike. And, as far as I know, the last time anybody saw him was on February the sixth, when he went to the shops. He was wearing dark glasses – in February!'

'Some sort of disfigurement?' I said. 'Starting on his hands, and spreading. He was a good-looking lad, wasn't he, and rather vain.'

Derek nodded.

'That's the general opinion – some skin illness. But nobody *knows*. He hasn't seen his GP in years.'

'I remember,' said his father musingly, 'seeing a book, years ago, about prosthetics for the disfigured. It was mostly masks, of celluloid and stuff – it was before plastics. There were before-and-after pictures. A good lot of them were neglected cases of syphilis, and they were unbelievable – they'd put you off your dinner. But it shows the lengths people will go to, to hide something they're ashamed of. To stay untreated, until your face is eaten right away, until you haven't *got* a face ...'

'Dad's right,' said Derek. 'Though I wouldn't think this case was syphilis. But you never know.'

'How does he live?'

'You remember, I told you his father left him enough to live on. Well, he conducts all his business by phone, has his food delivered. When the gas man calls to empty the meter, he finds the door unlocked, and a note telling him to get finished and get out, but no sign of Buffy. Oh, I've investigated all I can, but if he doesn't request help, we've no legal right to intrude.'

'No *legal* right,' emphasized his father.

'It may come to that,' said Derek grimly. 'After all, he was a friend. Let's talk about something cheerful, Bob. I think it's your round!'

Soon enough I slipped into the routine of my new job, and life went on pleasantly. I made new friends and rediscovered old ones, and only occasionally did the pathetic recluse Buffy creep into conversations. His case continued to bother Derek, both as a kind man and through his professional pride. One day I took a walk with him and looked at Buffy's house. It was a good quality detached house on an avenue, hidden behind its hedges and, surprisingly, both house and garden were reasonably well kept.

'Buffy's not stupid,' said Derek. 'He may be mad but he's not stupid. He's not going to give anyone, council or neighbours, cause to interfere with him. I know the man who does the garden – he's paid by cheque and he never sees Buffy. Mind you, I don't know what it's like inside.'

'And nobody's seen him since February?'

'Not a soul. There haven't even been any of those sinister glimpses of a horrid shape behind the net curtains. But I shouldn't joke. Poor Buffy.'

Poor Buffy.

Summer progressed and became autumn, and the only change in the hermit's life-style was his abandoning the phone for letters, if the term could be applied to those shopping lists or peremptory requests. Derek remained alert for an excuse to invade, but none came. Particularly worrying was the remark by the grocer, that in the last few phone calls, Buffy's voice had grown very hoarse and he obviously found it hard to speak.

I think we all felt it wouldn't be long before we found out what was wrong with Buffy. In that, we were wrong, strictly speaking. Or perhaps *I* was not.

About the end of September Buffy purchased a new electric fire. There was, I should explain, no central heating, because his father had considered it character-sapping. Anyway, it was some reassurance to know he was looking after himself to that extent, and the food he bought indicated that his diet, though simple, was better than that of many old age pensioners.

Winter came . . .

That winter was particularly severe, and from November the handy-man had frequently to clear the snow from the hermitage's front path, though only the delivery boy and, very seldom, the postman, went to the blank, bolted door.

At eight o'clock on the evening of February the third, a Tuesday, there was a power failure. A big electricity plant broke down, and, across a large slice of North London, TV screens faded, fires dulled, cookers cooled. Everywhere was a hunt for candles, and little dim lights flickered in a thousand windows. I was in the lounge chatting to Derek and his wife and parents, and as the house was heated by gas fires we treated the blackout as a joke.

Derek, though, began worrying when, after three hours, the current was still off. What was happening to the old folk who relied on electricity for heating? The borough, like any other, had its grim statistics, every cold spell, of deaths from hypothermia.

In the event, the power was to come back at midnight, but at ten Derek organized a sort of posse to go round checking on his flock. Of course, I had to volunteer, though I found it embarrassing; still, I'm sure it was good for my soul.

Many doors were knocked on, and most of the old people received with good grace the queries about their survival, though a few made salty remarks about youngsters not knowing what cold weather was.

'I'm warm enough in my bed, until you come and drag me out of it, young man!'

The old lady shut the door firmly, and I grinned with relief. That was the last of my calls. Soon after, the electricity back, we were saying tired good nights.

'Christ, we forgot Buffy!' exclaimed Derek, just as he was going.

'Oh, come on, Del,' sighed his wife. 'You're not traipsing out there at this time of night. If all those old folk survived, he should have.'

'But he's a sick man.'

'You don't *know* that. He's probably had twice as much to eat as those old people, so don't invent worries!'

'He'll be all right, Derek,' said his mother. 'His house is warmer, and more weatherproof, too.'

Derek allowed himself to be persuaded, though I suspect he sensed, as I did, a trace of the old intolerance that had once been directed at Halliwell. He went home, and I went to bed.

On Friday evening I went to a party, arrived home in the early hours of Saturday, and naturally had a lie-in. So it was with considerable head-splitting indignation that I clawed my way out of bed when Derek invaded my room at the unearthly hour of ten a.m.

'Come on, Bob, this is urgent. I know you feel rough – so do I – but something's happened to Buffy. I knew I should have checked.'

'What's up?' I demanded, struggling into my trousers.

'The grocer rang me a few minutes ago. The delivery boy couldn't get any answer – remember, the door's always been unlocked for him. And he said there's a parish magazine stuck in the letterbox. They were distributed on Wednesday, and Buffy never leaves anything in the letterbox.'

I didn't argue.

'Are you going to call the police?' I asked as Derek drove through crowded Saturday streets.

'Not if I can avoid it. We owe it to Buffy to keep his secret, whatever it is, if we possibly can. If he's ill, well, that's another matter.'

The avenue was on a hill, and though no snow had fallen for a week, patches lingered in gardens. Buffy's was unbroken white but for the path, up which we hurried, not speaking now. The magazine was still there.

Derek strode resolutely up the steps, wrapped in the mantle of his profession. I hung back. He hammered resoundingly – predictably, there was no response. After more knocking, he knelt and shouted through the letterbox.

'Buffy! Are you there? This is Derek Benson. If you don't answer, I'm going to break in.'

Nothing stirred.

'Right, come on, Bob!' He tried the door briefly. 'Bolted. I'm going to break a window.'

Within a minute, we stood in a puddle of broken glass in the front room. Inside, the distant traffic muted, the house seemed even more oppressively lifeless. This was the lounge, but it couldn't have been used for months. It was bitterly cold, and everything was coated in dust. In a flower bowl, the blooms long withered, a remnant of dirty water was frozen solid.

Derek led the way into the hall. A couple of circulars lay on the mat. Everywhere was that film of dust, and all the downstairs rooms were freezing and deserted.

'I don't believe he's here,' I whispered – somehow the place made you whisper.

'Upstairs,' said Derek briefly.

The stair carpet, like that of the hall, was a trifle less dusty, as if walked on regularly.

'Jesus!'

Derek stopped abruptly at the first-floor landing, and I collided with him. Clinging to the banister rail, I peered round him and saw, partially wrapped in a ragged quilt, a figure sprawled at the foot of the next flight of stairs.

Derek started forward, but halted again, with an odd gasp, then half turned and leaned against the wall as if he were ill. I put a hand on his shoulder and gazed at the prone form. In the pale winter light, filtered through the dusty window, it was not immediately obvious what was wrong.

For something was hideously wrong.

I suppose I'd expected to see Buffy lying there, but this . . . We edged closer and stared at the half-concealed body, then with abrupt decision, Derek flung back the quilt, revealing the monstrosity beneath.

It was a man, but only just a man, naked under the quilt, because normal clothes could not accommodate the swollen body. The skin showed greenish-brown in the dim light – but what skin! From head to foot he – it – was covered with huge warts, excrescences that, on the torso, reached grotesque size, each topped with a small tubercle. There were great swellings behind each ear, or rather where the ears would be, for they were lost in the rough surface. The body was face down. The blunt head, sunk neckless in the shoulders, bore a few scraps of hair.

Mastering our horror somehow, we half turned the body over, handling it through the quilt, unwilling to touch the warty hide.

'Good God almighty – it's Buffy!'

It was. Unbelievably, appallingly changed and distorted, it was yet the face of the man we had known. Small wonder he had hidden from the world.

His head, as I say, seemed sunk into his shoulders, the neck hidden under folds of bossed skin. The skull was flattened, the forehead

receding, the hairless brows projecting. The bulging, unseeing eyes were
open, the irises an inhuman, iridescent gold. No whites showed. The
nose was so flattened it had almost vanished. And the mouth ... Lipless,
chinless, that incredible gash stretched literally from ear to ear, bisecting
the ghastly face.

And yet, in all its shocking metamorphosis, somehow that face was
Buffy's.

I don't know how long Derek and I stood on that landing, staring at
that repulsive carcass, but at length we took our eyes from it and looked
at each other. I suppose I was as pale as he was.

'Are we sure he's dead?' I mumbled, more to break the silence than
from any doubt. Derek produced a small mirror, perhaps brought for
that very purpose, and held it to the frog-like mouth. That was it! A frog!
God, even the hands and the enlarged feet, now I looked at them, were
partially webbed.

'Bob, look!'

Derek showed me the mirror and, stooping close, I just caught the
vanishing trace of a blur on the glass. A second try produced the same
result. He was alive.

Suddenly there was something to do, to break the nightmare. We ran
down to the hall and Derek grabbed the phone. By unspoken agreement, we waited on the doorstep for the ambulance. Neither of us
wanted to see that parody of Buffy again just yet.

When we warned them to be ready for a shock, the ambulance men
smiled politely. They'd seem some unpleasant things in their time, those
smiles said. But they were not smiling when they came down, and they
were careful to cover the Buffy-thing when they bore the stretcher down
the path, so nothing was seen by the neighbours brought out by the noise
of the ambulance.

Derek and I sat inside, watching the unconscious gargoyle. The
ambulance man with us swallowed several times before he could speak.

'I've travelled a bit, I've seen leprosy and things as bad, but nothing
like this. The whole shape is changed, even the bones. How long has –
he, been that way?'

'He was out and about until about thirteen months ago,' said Derek.

'Thirteen months ... my God!'

'Derek!' I interjected. 'Look at his eyes!'

The pupils had contracted to vertical slits.

'It must be the light,' said the ambulance man. 'He must be regaining
consciousness.'

And sure enough, by the time we reached the hospital, the swollen
chest was moving under the blankets, and once or twice I thought a limb
twitched, or was it only the jolting of the ambulance?

We covered Buffy's face again when he was taken into the hospital, and it was not uncovered until we were well out of the public gaze. In the casualty department, the doctor on duty was rendered speechless when he saw what was, officially, a case of exposure. When he recovered he hastily summoned every available colleague to view this phenomenon, and for a couple of minutes we, and the ambulance man who'd accompanied us, were the only people in the room with Buffy.

That was when it happened.

Perhaps he had been shamming for a while, I don't know, but suddenly Buffy sat up, flinging back the blankets, trying shakily to stand. The ambulance man, heroically, stepped forward to restrain him.

'Lie down, old son, everything will be——'

But Buffy was not listening. The huge golden eyes stared at his two friends. Abruptly he thrust out a gnarled arm, flinging aside the ambulance man with surprising strength, and for a moment he stood swaying on his huge feet.

'No, no, NO!'

A harsh, awful bellow, the reiterated word boomed out, then Buffy literally bounded towards the door, and was through it with a blundering leap.

We all three sprang after him, but as we burst through the door, he was at the head of the stairs to the lower ground floor, and with shocking suddenness he flung himself down. He landed with a dreadful thud, striking his head on the wall. Moaning once, he drew in his arms and thrust out his legs behind him. Frozen in this weird posture he lay still.

When he was laid on the stretcher trolley again, there was thin blood coming from his nostrils.

In terms of life, or the pathetic thing his life had become, that day saw Buffy's end. As nearly as a diagnosis could be made on this bizarre creature, he seemed to be suffering from some compression of the brain, consequent on his fall. He was operated on the same afternoon, and died under the anaesthetic.

The postscript is necessarily compounded of speculation and second-hand information. I was not, of course, present at the operation, but I have learned things beyond what the surgeon told, and there is one tiny personal memory that may be the keystone of the whole monstrous edifice.

'I have some little experience of *outré* diseases and disorders,' said the surgeon, as Derek and I sat sombrely with him a week after Buffy's death, 'but I can safely say that I have never even *read* of a case like that of your unfortunate friend.'

'It developed so quickly . . .' said Derek.

'Just so – that is one of a hundred anomalies. In some respects – the papillomatous growths, the changes in the bone itself – one is reminded of neurofibromatosis. You may remember Treves's "Elephant Man".

But the changes were so *symmetrical*, and as for the eyes, and some of the internal ... no, I am bereft of ideas.'

'Quite honestly,' I said, 'it was as though he were changing into a frog.'

The surgeon nodded and drew on his cigar.

'Quite ... or a toad. Did you know, I wonder, that *bufo* is the Latin for toad? A hideous irony, isn't it?'

When I got home that day, I looked up *bufo* in the dictionary. I wasn't too hopeful, since it is a Latin word, but in fact it was there. It seems Ben Jonson used *bufo* for a black tincture in alchemy.

Alchemy!

Clearly as though I had only just heard it, there came back to me, across the intervening years, the remark of old Halliwell as I helped him pick up his scattered parcels:

'You called him Buffy, eh? For him, I think, the black tincture, among other things.'

Great God, was it even faintly *possible*? How could he have done it? Did he contrive to give Buffy something, some substance? Why did it take so long to begin? Both of them are dead, and we can never know. But ... a toad it was, that Buffy was turning into. First his hands ...

A toad, deprived of heat in winter, would sink into hibernal coma. Did I mention, the electric fire in Buffy's room was still on after we found him? He must, I think, have supposed a fuse had blown, gone down to see, succumbed to the cold before he could climb the stairs back. Probably, pathetically, he lived upstairs because from there he could see more of the world he hid from.

At first, I could not help wondering about Buffy's state of mind, his thoughts and feelings, as the grisly metamorphosis progressed, but now I prefer not to dwell on these things. I still remember, though, the closing words of the surgeon, that pompous, pedantic, but kindly man, as he studied the glowing tip of his cigar ...

'I suppose the worst thing of all was the brain.'

'Why,' I asked, 'was it greatly changed?'

He shook his head, grimacing as though the cigar had turned sour.

'No, poor fellow. The brain was still completely human.'

Pollock and the Porroh Man

H. G. Wells

It was in a swampy village on the lagoon river behind the Turner Peninsula that Pollock's first encounter with the Porroh man occurred. The women of that country are famous for their good looks – they are Gallinas with a dash of European blood that dates from the days of Vasco da Gama and the English slave traders, and the Porroh man, too, was possibly inspired by a faint Caucasian taint in his composition. (It's a curious thing to think that some of us may have distant cousins eating men on Sherboro Island or raiding with the Sofas.) At any rate, the Porroh man stabbed the woman to the heart as though he had been a mere low-class Italian, and very narrowly missed Pollock. But Pollock, using his revolver to parry the lightning stab which was aimed at his deltoid muscle, sent the iron dagger flying, and, firing, hit the man in the hand.

He fired again and missed, knocking a sudden window out of the wall of the hut. The Porroh man stooped in the doorway, glancing under his arm at Pollock. Pollock caught a glimpse of his inverted face in the sunlight, and then the Englishman was alone, sick and trembling with the excitement of the affair, in the twilight of the place. It had all happened in less time than it takes to read about it.

The woman was quite dead, and having ascertained this, Pollock went to the entrance of the hut and looked out. Things outside were dazzling bright. Half a dozen of the porters of the expedition were standing up in a group near the green huts they occupied, and staring towards him, wondering what the shots might signify. Behind the little group of men was the broad stretch of black fetid mud by the river, a green carpet of rafts of papyrus and water-grass, and then the leaden water. The mangroves beyond the stream loomed indistinctly through the blue haze. There were no signs of excitement in the squat village, whose fence was just visible above the cane-grass.

Pollock came out of the hut cautiously and walked towards the river, looking over his shoulder at intervals. But the Porroh man had vanished. Pollock clutched his revolver nervously in his hand.

One of his men came to meet him, and as he came, pointed to the bushes behind the hut in which the Porroh man had disappeared. Pollock had an irritating persuasion of having made an absolute fool of himself; he felt bitter, savage, at the turn things had taken. At the same time, he would have to tell Waterhouse – the moral, exemplary, cautious Waterhouse – who would inevitably take the matter seriously. Pollock cursed bitterly at his luck, at Waterhouse, and especially at the West Coast of Africa. He felt consummately sick of the expedition. And in the back of his mind all the time was a speculative doubt where precisely within the visible horizon the Porroh man might be.

It is perhaps rather shocking, but he was not at all upset by the murder that had just happened. He had seen so much brutality during the last three months, so many dead women, burnt huts, drying skeletons, up the Kittam River in the wake of the Sofa cavalry, that his senses were blunted. What disturbed him was the persuasion that this business was only beginning.

He swore savagely at the black, who ventured to ask a question, and went on into the tent under the orange-trees where Waterhouse was lying, feeling exasperatingly like a boy going into the headmaster's study.

Waterhouse was still sleeping off the effects of his last dose of chlorodyne, and Pollock sat down on a packing-case beside him, and, lighting his pipe, waited for him to awake. About him were scattered the pots and weapons Waterhouse had collected from the Mendi people, and which he had been repacking for the canoe voyage to Sulyma.

Presently Waterhouse woke up, and after judicial stretching, decided he was all right again. Pollock got him some tea. Over the tea the incidents of the afternoon were described by Pollock, after some preliminary beating about the bush. Waterhouse took the matter even more seriously than Pollock had anticipated. He did not simply disapprove, he scolded, he insulted.

'You're one of those infernal fools who think a black man isn't a human being,' he said. 'I can't be ill a day without you must get into some dirty scrape or other. This is the third time in a month that you have come crossways-on with a native, and this time you're in for it with a vengeance. Porroh, too! They're down upon you enough as it is, about that idol you wrote your silly name on. And they're the most vindictive devils on earth! You make a man ashamed of civilization. To think you come of a decent family! If ever I cumber myself up with a vicious, stupid young lout like you again——'

'Steady on, now,' snarled Pollock, in the tone that always exasperated Waterhouse; 'steady on.'

At that Waterhouse became speechless. He jumped to his feet.

'Look here, Pollock,' he said, after a struggle to control his breath.

'You must go home. I won't have you any longer. I'm ill enough as it is through——you.'

'Keep your hair on,' said Pollock, staring in front of him. 'I'm ready enough to go.'

Waterhouse became calmer again. He sat down on the camp-stool. 'Very well,' he said. 'I don't want a row, Pollock, you know, but it's confoundedly annoying to have one's plans put out by this kind of thing. I'll come to Sulyma with you, and see you safe aboard——'

'You needn't,' said Pollock. 'I can go alone. From here.'

'Not far,' said Waterhouse. 'You don't understand this Porroh business.'

'How should *I* know she belonged to a Porroh man?' said Pollock bitterly.

'Well, she did,' said Waterhouse; 'and you can't undo the thing. Go alone, indeed! I wonder what they'd do to you? You don't seem to understand that this Porroh hokey-pokey rules this country, is its law, religion, constitution, medicine, magic . . . They appoint the chiefs. The Inquisition, at its best, couldn't hold a candle to these chaps. He will probably set Awajale, the chief here, on to us. It's lucky our porters are Mendis. We shall have to shift this little settlement of ours . . . Confound you, Pollock! And, of course, you must go and miss him.'

He thought, and his thoughts seemed disagreeable. Presently he stood up and took his rifle. 'I'd keep close for a bit, if I were you,' he said, over his shoulder, as he went out. 'I'm going out to see what I can find out about it.'

Pollock remained sitting in the tent, meditating. 'I was meant for a civilized life,' he said to himself regretfully, as he filled his pipe. 'The sooner I get back to London or Paris the better for me.'

His eye fell on the scaled case in which Waterhouse had put the featherless poisoned arrows they had bought in the Mendi country. 'I wish I had hit the beggar somewhere vital,' said Pollock viciously.

Waterhouse came back after a long interval. He was not communicative, though Pollock asked him questions enough. The Porroh man, it seems, was a prominent member of that mystical society. The village was interested, but not threatening. No doubt the witchdoctor had gone into the bush. He was a great witchdoctor. 'Of course, he's up to something,' said Waterhouse, and became silent.

'But what can he do?' asked Pollock, unheeded.

'I must get you out of this. There's something brewing, or things would not be so quiet,' said Waterhouse, after a gap of silence. Pollock wanted to know what the brew might be. 'Dancing in a circle of skulls,' said Waterhouse; 'brewing a stink in a copper pot.' Pollock wanted particulars. Waterhouse was vague. Pollock pressing. At last Waterhouse lost his temper. 'How the devil should *I* know?' he said to Pollock's twentieth inquiry what the Porroh man would do. 'He tried to kill you off-hand in the hut. *Now*, I fancy he will try something more elaborate. But you'll see fast enough. I don't want to help unnerve you. It's probably all nonsense.'

That night, as they were sitting at their fire, Pollock again tried to draw Waterhouse out on the subject of Porroh methods. 'Better get to sleep,' said Waterhouse, when Pollock's bent became apparent: 'we start early tomorrow. You may want all your nerve about you.'

'But what line will he take?'

'Can't say. They're versatile people. They know a lot of rum dodges. You'd better get that copper-devil, Shakespeare, to talk.'

There was a flash and a heavy bang out of the darkness behind the huts, and a clay bullet came whistling close to Pollock's head. This, at least, was crude enough. The blacks and half-breeds sitting and yarning round their own fire jumped up, and someone fired into the dark.

'Better go into one of the huts,' said Waterhouse quietly, still sitting unmoved.

Pollock stood up by the fire, and drew his revolver. Fighting, at least, he was not afraid of. But a man in the dark is in the best of armour. Realizing the wisdom of Waterhouse's advice, Pollock went into the tent and lay down there.

What little sleep he had was disturbed by dreams, variegated dreams, but chiefly of the Porroh man's face, upside down, as he went out of the hut, and looked up under his arm. It was odd that this transitory impression should have stuck so firmly in Pollock's memory. Moreover, he was troubled by queer pains in his limbs.

In the white haze of the early morning, as they were loading the canoes, a barbed arrow suddenly appeared quivering in the ground close to Pollock's foot. The boys made a perfunctory effort to clear out the thicket, but it led to no capture.

After these two occurrences, there was a disposition on the part of the expedition to leave Pollock to himself, and Pollock became, for the first time in his life, anxious to mingle with blacks. Waterhouse took one canoe, and Pollock, in spite of a friendly desire to chat with Waterhouse, had to take the other. He was left all alone in the front part of the canoe, and he had the greatest trouble to make the men – who did not love him – keep to the middle of the river, a clear hundred yards or more from either shore. However, he made Shakespeare, the Freetown half-breed, come up to his own end of the canoe and tell him about Porroh, which Shakespeare, failing in his attempts to leave Pollock alone, presently did with considerable freedom and gusto.

The day passed. The canoe glided swiftly along the ribbon of lagoon water, between the drift of water-figs, fallen trees, papyrus, and palm-wine palms, and with the dark mangrove swamp to the left, through

which one could hear now and then the roar of the Atlantic surf.
Shakespeare told in his soft, blurred English of how the Porroh could
cast spells; how men withered up under their malice; how they could
send dreams and devils; how they tormented and killed the sons of Ijibu;
how they kidnapped a white trader from Sulyma who had maltreated
one of the sect, and how his body looked when it was found. And Pollock
after each narrative cursed under his breath at the want of missionary
enterprise that allowed such things to be, and at the inert British
Government that ruled over this dark heathendom of Sierra Leone. In
the evening they came to the Kasi Lake, and sent a score of crocodiles
lumbering off the island on which the expedition camped for the night.

The next day they reached Sulyma, and smelt the sea breeze, but
Pollock had to put up there for five days before he could get on to
Freetown. Waterhouse, considering him to be comparatively safe here,
and within the pale of Freetown influence, left him and went back with
the expedition to Gbemma, and Pollock became very friendly with
Perea, the only resident white trader at Sulyma – so friendly, indeed,
that he went about with him everywhere. Perea was a little Portuguese
Jew, who had lived in England, and he appreciated the Englishman's
friendliness as a great compliment.

For two days nothing happened out of the ordinary; for the most part
Pollock and Perea played Nap – the only game they had in common
– and Pollock got into debt. Then, on the second evening, Pollock had
a disagreeable intimation of the arrival of the Porroh man in Sulyma
by getting a flesh wound in the shoulder from a lump of filed iron. It
was a long shot, and the missile had nearly spent its force when it hit
him. Still it conveyed its message plainly enough. Pollock sat up in his
hammock, revolver in hand, all that night, and next morning confided,
to some extent, in the Anglo-Portuguese.

Perea took the matter seriously. He knew the local customs pretty
thoroughly. 'It is a personal question, you must know. It is revenge. And
of course he is hurried by your leaving de country. None of de natives
or half-breeds will interfere wid him very much – unless you make it wort
deir while. If you come upon him suddenly you might shoot him. But
den he might shoot you.

'Den dere's dis – infernal magic,' said Perea. 'Of course, I don't
believe in it – superstition – but still it's not nice to tink dat wherever
you are, dere is a black man, who spends a moonlight night now and
den a-dancing about a fire to send you bad dreams ... Had any bad
dreams?'

'Rather,' said Pollock. 'I keep on seeing the beggar's head upside
down grinning at me and showing all his teeth as he did in the hut, and
coming close up to me, and then going ever so far off, and coming back.
It's nothing to be afraid of, but somehow it simply paralyses me with

terror in my sleep. Queer things – dreams. I know it's a dream all the time, and I can't wake up from it.'

'It's probably only fancy,' said Perea. 'Den my niggers say Porroh men can send snakes. Seen any snakes lately?'

'Only one. I killed him this morning, on the floor near my hammock. Almost trod on him as I got up.'

'*Ah!*' said Perea, and then, reassuringly. 'Of course it is a – coincidence. Still I would keep my eyes open. Den dere's pains in de bones.'

'I thought they were due to miasma,' said Pollock.

'Probably dey are. When did dey begin?'

Then Pollock remembered that he first noticed them the night after the fight in the hut. 'It's my opinion he don't want to kill you,' said Perea – 'at least not yet. I've heard deir idea is to scare and worry a man wid deir spells, and narrow misses, and rheumatic pains, and bad dreams, and all dat, until he's sick of life. Of course, it's all talk, you know. You mustn't worry about it ... But I wonder what he'll be up to next.'

'*I* shall have to be up to something first,' said Pollock, staring gloomily at the greasy cards that Perea was putting on the table. 'It don't suit my dignity to be followed about, and shot at, and blighted in this way. I wonder if Porroh hokey-pokey upsets your luck at cards.'

He looked at Perea suspiciously.

'Very likely it does,' said Perea warmly, shuffling. 'Dey are wonderful people.'

That afternoon Pollock killed two snakes in his hammock, and there was also an extraordinary increase in the number of red ants that swarmed over the place; and these annoyances put him in a fit temper to talk over business with a certain Mendi rough he had interviewed before. The Mendi rough showed Pollock a little iron dagger, and demonstrated where one struck in the neck, in a way that made Pollock shiver, and in return for certain considerations Pollock promised him a double-barrelled gun with an ornamental lock.

In the evening, as Pollock and Perea were playing cards, the Mendi rough came in through the doorway, carrying something in a blood-soaked piece of native cloth.

'Not here!' said Pollock very hurriedly. 'Not here!'

But he was not quick enough to prevent the man, who was anxious to get to Pollock's side of the bargain, from opening the cloth and throwing the head of the Porroh man upon the table. It bounded from there on to the floor, leaving a red trail on the cards, and rolled into a corner, where it came to rest upside down, but glaring hard at Pollock.

Perea jumped up as the thing fell among the cards, and began in his excitement to gabble in Portuguese. The Mendi was bowing, with the red cloth in his hand. 'De gun!' he cried. Pollock stared back at the head in the corner. It bore exactly the expression it had in his dreams.

Something seemed to snap in his own brain as he looked at it.

Then Perea found his English again.

'You got him killed?' he said. 'You did not kill him yourself?'

'Why should I?' said Pollock.

'But he will not be able to take it off now!'

'Take *what* off?' said Pollock.

'And all dese cards are spoiled!'

'*What* do you mean by taking off?' said Pollock.

'You must send me a new pack from Freetown. You can buy dem dere.'

'But – "take it off"?'

'It is only superstition. I forgot. De niggers say dat if de witches – he was a witch—— But it is rubbish ... You must make de Porroh man take it off, or kill him yourself ... It is very silly.'

Pollock swore under his breath, still staring hard at the head in the corner.

'I can't stand that glare,' he said. Then suddenly he rushed at the thing and kicked it. It rolled some yards or so, and came to rest in the same position as before, upside down, and looking at him.

'He is ugly,' said the Anglo-Portuguese. 'Very ugly. Dey do it on deir faces with little knives.'

Pollock would have kicked the head again, but the Mendi man touched him on the arm. 'De gun?' he said, looking nervously at the head.

'Two – if you will take that beastly thing away,' said Pollock. The Mendi shook his head, and intimated that he only wanted one gun now due to him, and for which he would be obliged. Pollock found neither cajolery nor bullying any good with him. Perea had a gun to sell (at a profit of three hundred per cent), and with that the man presently departed. Then Pollock's eyes, against his will, were recalled to the thing on the floor.

'It is funny dat his head keeps upside down,' said Perea, with an uneasy laugh. 'His brains must be heavy, like de weight in de little images one sees dat keep always upright wid lead in dem. You will take him wiv you when you go presently. You might take him now. De cards are all spoilt. Dere is a man sell dem in Freetown. De room is in a filthy mess as it is. You should have killed him yourself.'

Pollock pulled himself together, and went and picked up the head. He would hang it up by the lamp hook in the middle of the ceiling in his room, and dig a grave for it at once. He was under the impression that he hung it up by the hair, but that must have been wrong, for when he returned for it, it was hanging by the neck upside down.

He buried it before sunset on the north side of the shed he occupied, so that he should not have to pass the grave after dark when he was returning from Perea's. He killed two snakes before he went to sleep. In the darkest part of the night he awoke with a start, and heard a pattering sound and something scraping on the floor. He sat up noiselessly and felt under his pillow for his revolver. A mumbling growl followed, and Pollock fired at the sound. There was a yelp, and something dark passed for a moment across the hazy blue of the doorway. 'A dog!' said Pollock, lying down again.

In the early dawn he awoke again with a peculiar sense of unrest. The vague pain in his bones had returned. For some time he lay watching the red ants that were swarming over the ceiling, and then, as the light grew brighter, he looked over the edge of his hammock and saw something dark on the floor. He gave such a violent start that the hammock overset and flung him out.

He found himself lying, perhaps, a yard away from the head of the Porroh man. It had been disinterred by the dog, and the nose was grievously battered. Ants and flies swarmed over it. By an odd coincidence, it was still upside down, and with the same diabolical expression in the inverted eyes.

Pollock sat paralysed, and stared at the horror for some time. Then he got up and walked round it – giving it a wide berth – and out of the shed. The clear light of the sunrise, the living stir of vegetation before the breath of the dying land breeze, and the empty grave with the marks of the dog's paws, lightened the weight upon his mind a little.

He told Perea of the business as though it was a jest – a jest to be told with white lips. 'You should not have frighten de dog,' said Perea, with poorly simulated hilarity.

The next two days, until the steamer came, were spent by Pollock in making a more effectual disposition of his possession. Overcoming his aversion to handling the thing, he went down to the river mouth and threw it into the sea water, but by some miracle it escaped the crocodiles, and was cast up by the tide on the mud a little way up the river, to be found by an intelligent Arab half-breed, and offered for sale to Pollock and Perea as a curiosity, just on the edge of night. The native hung about in the brief twilight, making lower and lower offers, and at last, getting scared in some way by the evident dread these white men had for the thing, went off, and, passing Pollock's shed, threw his burden in there for Pollock to discover in the morning.

At this Pollock got into a kind of frenzy. He would burn the thing. He went out straightaway into the dawn, and had constructed a big pyre of brushwood before the heat of the day. He was interrupted by the hooter of the little paddle steamer from Monrovia to Bathurst, which was coming through the gap in the bar. 'Thank Heaven!' said Pollock, with infinite piety, when the meaning of the sound dawned upon him. With trembling hands he lit his pile of wood hastily, threw the head upon it, and went away to pack his portmanteau and make his adieux to Perea.

That afternoon, with a sense of infinite relief, Pollock watched the flat swampy foreshore of Sulyma grow small in the distance. The gap in the long line of white surge became narrower and narrower. It seemed to be closing in and cutting him off from his trouble. The feeling of dread and worry began to slip from him bit by bit. At Sulyma belief in Porroh malignity and Porroh magic had been in the air, his sense of Porroh had been vast, pervading, threatening, dreadful. Now manifestly the domain of Porroh was only a little place, a little black band between the sea and the blue cloudy Mendi uplands.

'Goodbye, Porroh!' said Pollock. 'Goodbye – certainly not *au revoir*.'

The captain of the steamer came and leant over the rail beside him, and wished him good evening, and spat at the froth of the wake in token of friendly ease.

'I picked up a rummy curio on the beach this go,' said the captain. 'It's a thing I never saw done this side of Indy before.'

'What might that be?' said Pollock.

'Pickled 'ed,' said the captain.

'*What!*' said Pollock.

''Ed smoked. 'Ed of one of these Porroh chaps, all ornamented with knife cuts. Why? What's up? Nothing? I shouldn't have took you for a nervous chap. Green in the face. By gosh! you're a bad sailor. All right, eh? Lord, how funny you went! ... Well, this 'ed I was telling you of is a bit rum in a way. I've got it, along with some snakes, in a jar of spirit in my cabin what I keeps for such curios, and I'm hanged if it don't float upsy down. Hullo!'

Pollock had given an incoherent cry, and had his hands in his hair. He ran towards the paddle-boxes with a half-formed idea of jumping into the sea, and then he realized his position and turned back towards the captain.

'Here!' said the captain. 'Jack Philips, just keep him off me! Stand off! No nearer, mister! What's the matter with you? Are you mad?'

Pollock put his hand to his head. It was no good explaining. 'I believe I am pretty nearly mad at times,' he said. 'It's a pain I have here. Comes suddenly. You'll excuse me, I hope.'

He was white and in a perspiration. He saw suddenly very clearly all the danger he ran of having his sanity doubted. He forced himself to restore the captain's confidence, by answering his sympathetic inquiries, noting his suggestions, even trying a spoonful of neat brandy in his cheek, and, that matter settled, asking a number of questions about the captain's private trade in curiosities. The captain described the head in detail. All the while Pollock was struggling to keep under a preposterous persuasion that the ship was as transparent as glass, and that he could distinctly see the inverted face looking at him from the cabin beneath his feet.

Pollock had a worse time almost on the steamer than he had at Sulyma. All day he had to control himself in spite of his intense perception of the imminent presence of that horrible head that was overshadowing his mind. At night his old nightmare returned, until, with a violent effort, he would force himself awake, rigid with the horror of it, and with the ghost of a hoarse scream in his throat.

He left the actual head behind at Bathurst, where he changed ship for Teneriffe, but not his dreams nor the dull ache in his bones. At Teneriffe Pollock transferred to a Cape liner, but the head followed him. He gambled, he tried chess, he even read books, but he knew the danger of drink. Yet whenever a round black shadow, a round black object came into his range, there he looked for the head, and – saw it. He knew clearly enough that his imagination was growing traitor to him, and yet at times it seemed the ship he sailed in, his fellow passengers, the sailors, the wide sea, were all part of a filmy phantasmagoria that hung, scarcely veiling it, between him and a horrible real world. Then the Porroh man, thrusting his diabolical face through that curtain, was the one real and undeniable thing. At that he would get up and touch things, taste something, gnaw something, burn his hand with a match, or run a needle into himself.

So, struggling grimly and silently with his excited imagination, Pollock reached England. He landed at Southampton, and went on straight from Waterloo to his banker's in Cornhill in a cab. There he transacted some business with the manager in a private room, and all the while the head hung like an ornament under the black marble mantel and dripped upon the fender. He could hear the drops fall, and see the red on the fender.

'A pretty fern,' said the manager, following his eyes. 'But it makes the fender rusty.'

'Very,' said Pollock; 'a *very* pretty fern. And that reminds me. Can you recommend me a physician for mind troubles? I've got a little – what is it? – hallucination.'

The head laughed savagely, wildly. Pollock was surprised the manager did not notice it. But the manager only stared at his face.

With the address of a doctor, Pollock presently emerged in Cornhill. There was no cab in sight, and so he went on down to the western end of the street, and essayed the crossing opposite the Mansion House. The crossing is hardly easy even for the expert Londoner; cabs, vans, carriages, mail carts, omnibuses go by in one incessant stream; to anyone fresh from the malarious solitudes of Sierra Leone it is a boiling, maddening confusion. But when an inverted head suddenly comes bouncing, like an India-rubber ball, between your legs, leaving distinct smears of blood every time it touches the ground, you can scarcely hope to avoid an accident. Pollock lifted his feet convulsively to avoid it, and then kicked at the thing furiously. Then something hit him violently in the back, and a hot pain ran up his arm.

He had been hit by the pole of an omnibus, and three of the fingers of his left hand smashed by the hoof of one of the horses – the very fingers, as it happened, that he shot from the Porroh man. They pulled him out from between the horses' legs, and found the address of the physician in his crushed hand.

For a couple of days Pollock's sensations were full of the sweet, pungent smell of chloroform, of painful operations that caused him no pain, of lying still and being given food and drink. Then he had a slight fever, and was very thirsty, and his old nightmare came back. It was only when it returned that he noticed it had left him for a day.

'If my skull had been smashed instead of my fingers, it might have gone altogether,' said Pollock, staring thoughtfully at the dark cushion that had taken on for the time the shape of the head.

Pollock at the first opportunity told the physician of his mind trouble. He knew clearly that he must go mad unless something should intervene to save him. He explained that he had witnessed a decapitation in Dahomey, and was haunted by one of the heads. Naturally, he did not care to state the actual facts. The physician looked grave.

Presently he spoke hesitatingly. 'As a child, did you get very much religious training?'

'Very little,' said Pollock.

A shade passed over the physician's face. 'I don't know if you have heard of the miraculous cures – it may be, of course, they are not miraculous – at Lourdes.'

'Faith-healing will hardly suit me, I am afraid,' said Pollock, with his eye on the dark cushion.

The head distorted its scarred features in an abominable grimace. The physician went upon a new track. 'It's all imagination,' he said, speaking with sudden briskness. 'A fair case for faith-healing, anyhow. Your nervous system has run down, you're in that twilight state of health when the bogles come easiest. The strong impression was too much for you. I must make you up a little mixture that will strengthen your nervous system – especially your brain. And you must take exercise.'

'I'm no good for faith-healing,' said Pollock.

'And therefore we must restore tone. Go in search of stimulating air – Scotland, Norway, the Alps——'

'Jericho, if you like,' said Pollock, 'where Naaman went.'

However, so soon as his fingers would let him, Pollock made a gallant attempt to follow out the doctor's suggestion. It was now November. He tried football, but to Pollock the game consisted in kicking a furious inverted head about a field. He was no good at the game. He kicked blindly, with a kind of horror, and when they put him back into goal, and the ball came swooping down upon him, he suddenly yelled and got out of its way. The discreditable stories that had driven him from England to wander in the tropics shut him off from any but men's society, and now his increasingly strange behaviour made even his man friends avoid him. The thing was no longer a thing of the eye merely; it gibbered at him, spoke to him. A horrible fear came upon him that presently, when he took hold of the apparition, it would no longer become some mere article of furniture, but would *feel* like a real dissevered head. Alone, he would curse at the thing, defy it, entreat it; once or twice, in spite of his grim self-control, he addressed it in the presence of others. He felt the growing suspicion in the eyes of the people that watched him – his landlady, the servant, his man.

One day early in December his cousin Arnold – his next of kin – came to see him and draw him out, and watch his sunken yellow face with narrow eager eyes. And it seemed to Pollock that the hat his cousin carried in his hand was no hat at all, but a Gorgon head that glared at him upside down, and fought with its eyes against his reason. However, he was still resolute to see the matter out. He got a bicycle, and, riding over the frosty road from Wandsworth to Kingston, found the thing rolling along at his side, and leaving a dark trail behind it. He set his teeth and rode faster. Then suddenly, as he came down the hill towards Richmond Park, the apparition rolled in front of him and under his wheel, so quickly that he had no time for thought, and, turning quickly to avoid it, was flung violently against a heap of stones and broke his left wrist.

The end came on Christmas morning. All night he had been in a fever, the bandages encircling his wrist like a band of fire, his dreams more vivid and terrible than ever. In the cold, colourless, uncertain light that came before the sunrise, he sat up in his bed, and saw the head upon the bracket in the place of the bronze jar that had stood there overnight.

'I know that is a bronze jar,' he said, with a chill doubt at his heart. Presently the doubt was irresistible. He got out of bed slowly, shivering, and advanced to the jar with his hand raised. Surely he would see now his imagination had deceived him, recognize the distinctive sheen of bronze. At last, after an age of hesitation, his fingers came down on the patterned cheek of the head. He withdrew them spasmodically. The last stage was reached. His sense of touch had betrayed him.

Trembling, stumbling against the bed, kicking against his shoes with his bare feet, a dark confusion eddying round him, he groped his way to the dressing table, took his razor from the drawer, and sat down on the bed with this in his hand. In the looking glass he saw his own face, colourless, haggard, full of the ultimate bitterness of despair.

He beheld in swift succession the incidents in the brief tale of his experience. His wretched home, his still more wretched schooldays, the years of vicious life he had led since then, one act of selfish dishonour leading to another: it was all clear and pitiless now, all its squalid folly, in the cold light of the dawn. He came to the hut, to the fight with the Porroh man, to the retreat down the river to Sulyma, to the Mendi assassin and his red parcel, to his frantic endeavours to destroy the head, to the growth of his hallucination. It was a hallucination! He *knew* it was. A hallucination merely. For a moment he snatched at hope. He looked away from the glass, and on the bracket, the inverted head grinned and grimaced at him ... With the stiff fingers of his bandaged hand he felt at his neck for the throb of his arteries. The morning was very cold, the steel blade felt like ice.

Lukundoo

Edward Lucas White

'It stands to reason,' said Twombly, 'that a man must accept the evidence of his own eyes, and when his eyes and ears agree, there can be no doubt. He has to believe what he has both seen and heard.'

'Not always,' put in Singleton, softly.

Every man turned towards Singleton. Twombly was standing on the hearth-rug, his back to the grate, his legs spread out, with his habitual air of dominating the room. Singleton, as usual, was as much as possible effaced in a corner. But when Singleton spoke he said something. We faced him in that flatteringly spontaneity of expectant silence which invites utterance.

'I was thinking,' he said, after an interval, 'of something I both saw and heard in Africa.'

Now, if there was one thing we had found impossible it had been to elicit from Singleton anything definite about his African experiences. As with the Alpinist in the story, who could only tell that he went up and came down, the sum of Singleton's revelations had been that he went there and came away. His words now riveted our attention at once. Twombly faded from the hearth-rug, but not one of us could ever recall having seen him go. The room readjusted itself, focused on Singleton, and there was some hasty and furtive lighting of fresh cigars. Singleton lit one also, but it went out immediately, and he never relit it.

I

We were in the Great Forest, exploring for pigmies. Van Rieten had a theory that the dwarfs found by Stanley and others were a mere cross-breed between ordinary Negroes and the real pigmies. He hoped to discover a race of men three feet tall at most, or shorter. We found no traces of any such beings.

Natives were few, game scarce; food, except game, there was none; and the deepest, dankest, drippingest forest all about. We were the only novelty in the country, no native we met had even seen a white man before, most had never heard of white men. All of a sudden, late one afternoon, there came into our camp an Englishman, and pretty well used up he was, too. We had heard no rumour of him; he had not only heard of us but had made an amazing five-day march to reach us. His guide and two bearers were nearly as done up as he. Even though he was in tatters and had five days' beard on, you could see he was naturally dapper and neat and the sort of man to shave daily. He was small, but wiry. His face was the sort of British face from which emotion has been so carefully banished that a foreigner is apt to think the wearer of the face incapable of any sort of feeling; the kind of face which, if it has any expression at all, expresses principally the resolution to go through the world decorously, without intruding upon or annoying anyone.

His name was Etcham. He introduced himself modestly, and ate with us so deliberately that we should never have suspected if our bearers had not had it from his bearers that he had had but three meals in the five days, and those small. After we had lit up he told us why he had come.

'My chief is ve'y seedy,' he said between puffs. 'He is bound to go out if he keeps this way. I thought perhaps ...'

He spoke quietly in a soft, even tone, but I could see little beads of sweat oozing out on his upper lip under his stubby moustache, and there was a tingle of repressed emotion in his tone, a veiled eagerness in his eye, a palpatating inward solicitude in his demeanour that moved me at once. Van Rieten had no sentiment in him; if he was moved he did not show it. But he listened. I was surprised at that. He was just the man to refuse at once. But he listened to Etcham's halting, diffident hints. He even asked questions.

'Who is your chief?'

'Stone,' Etcham lisped.

That electrified both of us.

'Ralph Stone?' we ejaculated together.

Etcham nodded.

For some minutes Van Rieten and I were silent. Van Rieten had never seen him, but I had been a classmate of Stone's, and Van Rieten and I had discussed him over many a camp-fire. We had heard of him two years before, south of Luebo in the Balunda country, which had been ringing with his theatrical strife against a Balunda witch-doctor, ending in the sorcerer's complete discomfiture and the abasement of his tribe before Stone. They had even broken the fetish-man's whistle and given Stone the pieces. It had been like the triumph of Elijah over the prophets of Baal, only more real to the Balunda.

We had thought of Stone as far off, if still in Africa at all, and here he turned up ahead of us and probably forestalling our quest.

II

Etcham's naming of Stone brought back to us all his tantalizing story, his fascinating parents, their tragic death; the brilliance of his college days; the dazzle of his millions; the promise of his young manhood; his wide notoriety, so nearly real fame; his romantic elopement with the meteoric authoress whose sudden cascade of fiction had made her so great a name so young, whose beauty and charm were so much heralded: the frightful scandal of the breach-of-promise suit that followed; his bride's devotion through it all; their sudden quarrel after it was all over; their divorce; the too much advertised announcement of his approaching marriage to the plaintiff in the breach-of-promise suit; his precipitate remarriage to his divorced bride; their second quarrel and second divorce; his departure from his native land; his advent in the dark continent. The sense of all this rushed over me and I believed Van Rieten felt it, too, as he sat silent.

Then he asked:

'Where is Werner?'

'Dead,' said Etcham. 'He died before I joined Stone.'

'You were not with Stone above Luebo?'

'No,' said Etcham, 'I joined him at Stanley Falls.'

'Who is with him?' Van Rieten asked.

'Only his Zanzibar servants and the bearers,' Etcham replied.

'What sort of bearers?' Van Rieten demanded.

'Mang-Battu men,' Etcham responded simply.

Now that impressed both Van Rieten and myself greatly. It bore out Stone's reputation as a notable leader of men. For up to that time no one had been able to use Mang-Battu as bearers outside of their own country, or to hold them for long or difficult expeditions.

'Were you long among the Mang-Battu?' was Van Rieten's next question.

'Some weeks,' said Etcham. 'Stone was interested in them and made up a fair-sized vocabulary of their words and phrases. He had a theory that they are an offshoot of the Balunda and he found much confirmation in their customs.'

'What do you live on?' Van Rieten inquired.

'Game, mostly,' Etcham lisped.

'How long has Stone been laid up?' Van Rieten next asked.

'More than a month,' Etcham answered.

'And you have been hunting for the camp?' Van Rieten exclaimed.

Etcham's face, burnt and flayed as it was, showed a flush.

'I missed some easy shots,' he admitted ruefully. 'I've not felt ve'y fit myself.'

'What's the matter with your chief?' Van Rieten inquired.

'Something like carbuncles,' Etcham replied.

'He ought to get over a carbuncle or two,' Van Rieten declared.

'They are not carbuncles,' Etcham explained. 'Nor one or two. He has had dozens, sometimes five at once. If they had been carbuncles he would have been dead long ago. But in some ways they are not so bad, though in others they are worse.'

'How do you mean?' Van Rieten queried.

'Well,' Etcham hesitated, 'they do not seem to inflame so deep nor so wide as carbuncles, nor to be so painful, nor to cause so much fever. But then they seem to be part of a disease that affects his mind. He let me help him dress the first, but the others he has hidden most carefully, from me and from the men. He keeps to his tent when they puff up, and will not let me change the dressings or be with him at all.'

'Have you plenty of dressings?' Van Rieten asked.

'We have some,' said Etcham doubtfully. 'But he won't use them; he washes out the dressings and uses them over and over.'

'How is he treating the swellings?' Van Rieten inquired.

'He slices them off clear down to flesh level, with his razor.'

'What?' Van Rieten shouted.

Etcham made no answer but looked him steadily in the eyes.

'I beg pardon,' Van Rieten hastened to say. 'You startled me. They can't be carbuncles. He'd have been dead long ago.'

'I thought I had said they are not carbuncles,' Etcham lisped.

'But the man must be crazy!' Van Rieten exclaimed.

'Just so,' said Etcham. 'He is beyond my advice or control.'

'How many has he treated that way?' Van Rieten demanded.

'Two, to my knowledge,' Etcham said.

'Two?' Van Rieten queried.

Etcham flushed again.

'I saw him,' he confessed, 'through a crack in the hut. I felt impelled to keep watch on him, as if he was not responsible.'

'I should think not,' Van Rieten agreed. 'And you saw him do that twice?'

'I conjecture,' said Etcham, 'that he did the like with all the rest.'

'How many has he had?' Van Rieten asked.

'Dozens,' Etcham lisped.

'Does he eat?' Van Rieten inquired.

'Like a wolf,' said Etcham. 'More than any two bearers.'

'Can he walk?' Van Rieten asked.

'He crawls a bit, groaning,' said Etcham simply.

'Little fever, you say,' Van Rieten ruminated.

'Enough and too much,' Etcham declared.

'Has he been delirious?' Van Rieten asked.

'Only twice,' Etcham replied; 'once when the first swelling broke, and once later. He would not let anyone come near him then. But we could hear him talking, talking steadily and it scared the natives.'

'Was he talking their patter in delirium?' Van Rieten demanded.

'No,' said Etcham, 'but he was talking some similar lingo Hamed Burghash said he was talking Balunda. I know too little Balunda. I do not learn languages readily. Stone learned more Mang-Battu in a week than I could have learned in a year. But I seemed to hear words like Mang-Battu words. Anyhow the Mang-Battu bearers were scared.'

'Scared?' Van Rieten repeated, questioningly.

'So were the Zanzibar men, even Hamed Burghash, and so was I,' said Etcham, 'only for a different reason. He talked in two voices.'

'In two voices?' Van Rieten reflected.

'Yes,' said Etcham, more excitedly than he had yet spoken. 'In two voices, like a conversation. One was his own, one a small, thin bleaty voice like nothing I ever heard. I seemed to make out, among the sounds the deep voice made, something like Mang-Battu words I knew, as *nedru*, *metababa*, and *nedo*, their terms for "head", "shoulder", "thigh", and perhaps *kudra* and *nekere* ("speak" and "whistle"); and among the noises of the shrill voice *matomipa*, *angunzi* and *kamomami* ("kill", "death", and "hate"). Hamed Burghash said he also heard those words, He knew Mang-Battu far better than I.'

'What did the bearers say?' Van Rieten asked.

'They said, *"Lukundoo, Lukundoo!"* ' Etcham replied. 'I did not know that word; Hamed Burghash said it was Mang-Battu for "leopard".'

'It's Mang-Battu for "witchcraft",' said Van Rieten.

'I don't wonder they thought so,' said Etcham. 'It was enough to make one believe in sorcery to listen to those two voices.'

'One voice answering the other?' Van Rieten asked perfunctorily.

Etcham's face went grey under his tan.

'Sometimes both at once,' he answered huskily.

'Both at once!' Van Rieten ejaculated.

'It sounded that way to the men, too,' said Etcham. 'And that was not all.'

He stopped and looked helplessly at us for a moment.

'Could a man talk and whistle at the same time?' he asked.

'How do you mean?' Van Rieten queried.

'We could hear Stone talking away, his big, deep-chested baritone rumbling away, and through it all we could hear a high shrill whistle, the oddest, wheezy sound. You know, no matter how shrilly a grown man may whistle, the note has a different quality from the whistle of a boy or a woman or a little girl. They sound more treble, somehow. Well, if you can imagine the smallest girl who could whistle keeping it up tunelessly right along, that whistle was like that, only even more piercing, and it sounded right through Stone's bass tones.'

'And you didn't go to him?' Van Rieten cried.

'He is not given to threats,' Etcham disclaimed. 'But he had threatened, not volubly, nor like a sick man, but quietly and firmly, that if any man of us (he lumped me in with the men), came near him while he was in his trouble, that man should die. And it was not so much his words as his manner. It was like a monarch commanding respected privacy for a death-bed. One simply could not transgress.'

'I see,' said Van Rieten shortly.

'He's ve'y seedy,' Etcham repeated helplessly. 'I thought perhaps . . .'

His absorbing affection for Stone, his real love for him, shone out through his envelope of conventional training. Worship of Stone was plainly his master passion.

Like many competent men, Van Rieten had a streak of hard selfishness in him. It came to the surface then. He said we carried our lives in our hands from day to day just as genuinely as Stone; that he did not forget the ties of blood and calling between any two explorers, but that there was no sense in imperilling one party for a very problematical benefit to a man probably beyond any help; that it was enough of a task to hunt for one party; that if the two were united, providing food would be more than doubly difficult; that the risk of starvation was too great. Deflecting our march seven full days' journey (he complimented Etcham on his marching powers) might ruin our expedition entirely.

III

Van Rieten had logic on his side and he had a way with him. Etcham sat there apologetic and deferential, like a fourth-form schoolboy before a head master. Van Rieten wound up.

'I am after pigmies, at the risk of my life. After pigmies I go.'

'Perhaps, then, these will interest you,' said Etcham, very quietly.

He took two objects out of the sidepocket of his blouse, and handed them to Van Rieten. They were round, bigger than big plums, and smaller than small peaches, about the right size to enclose in an average hand. They were black, and at first I did not see what they were.

'Pigmies!' Van Rieten exclaimed. 'Pigmies, indeed! Why, they wouldn't be two feet high! Do you mean to claim that these are adult heads?'

'I claim nothing,' Etcham answered evenly. 'You can see for yourself.'

Van Rieten passed one of the heads to me. The sun was just setting and I examined it closely. A dried head it was, perfectly preserved, and the flesh as hard as Argentine jerked beef. A bit of a vertebra stuck out where the muscles of the vanished neck had shrivelled into folds. The puny chin was sharp on a projecting jaw, the minute teeth white and even between the retracted lips, the tiny nose was flat, the little forehead retreating, there were inconsiderable clumps of stunted wool on the Lilliputian cranium. There was nothing babyish, childish or youthful about the head, rather it was mature to senility.

'Where did these come from?' Van Rieten inquired.

'I do not know,' Etcham replied precisely. 'I found them among Stone's effects while rummaging for medicines or drugs or anything that could help me to help him. I do not know where he got them. But I'll swear he did not have them when we entered this district.'

'Are you sure?' Van Rieten queried, his eyes big and fixed on Etcham's.

'Ve'y sure,' lisped Etcham.

'But how could he have come by them without your knowledge?' Van Rieten demurred.

'Sometimes we were apart ten days at a time hunting,' said Etcham. 'Stone is not a talking man. He gave me no account of his doings and Hamed Burghash keeps a still tongue and a tight hold on the men.'

'You have examined these heads?' Van Rieten asked.

'Minutely,' said Etcham.

Van Rieten took out his notebook. He was a methodical chap. He tore out a leaf, folded it and divided it equally into three pieces. He gave one to me and one to Etcham.

'Just for a test of my impressions,' he said, 'I want each of us to write separately just what he is most reminded of by these heads. Then I want to compare the writings.'

I handed Etcham a pencil and he wrote. Then he handed the pencil back to me and I wrote.

'Read the three,' said Van Rieten, handing me his piece.

Van Rieten had written:

'An old Balunda witch-doctor.'

Etcham had written:

'An old Mang-Battu fetish-man.'

I had written:

'An old Katongo magician.'

'There!' Van Rieten exclaimed. 'Look at that! There is nothing Wagabi or Batwa or Wambuttu or Wabotu about these heads. Nor anything pigmy either.'

'I thought as much,' said Etcham.

'And you say he did not have them before?'

'To a certainty he did not,' Etcham asserted.

'It is worth following up,' said Van Rieten. 'I'll go with you. And first of all, I'll do my best to save Stone.'

He put out his hand and Etcham clasped it silently. He was grateful all over.

IV

Nothing but Etcham's fever of solicitude could have taken him in five days over the track. It took him eight days to retrace with full knowledge of it and our party to help. We could not have done it in seven, and Etcham urged us on, in a repressed fury of anxiety, no mere fever of duty to his chief, but a real ardour of devotion, a glow of personal adoration for Stone which blazed under his dry conventional exterior and showed in spite of him.

We found Stone well cared for. Etcham had seen to a good, high thorn *zareeba* round the camp, the huts were well built and thatched, and Stone's was as good as their resources would permit. Hamed Burghash was not named after two Seyyids for nothing. He had in him the making of a sultan. He had kept the Mang-Battu together, not a man had slipped off, and he had kept them in order. Also he was a deft nurse and a faithful servant.

The two other Zanzibaris had done some creditable hunting. Though all were hungry, the camp was far from starvation.

Stone was on a canvas cot and there was a sort of collapsible camp-stool-table, like a Turkish tabouret, by the cot. It had a water-bottle and some vials on it and Stone's watch, also his razor in its case.

Stone was clean and not emaciated, but he was far gone; not unconscious, but in a daze; past commanding or resisting anyone. He did not seem to see us enter or to know we were there. I should have recognized him anywhere. His boyish dash and grace had vanished utterly, of course. But his head was even more leonine; his hair was still abundant, yellow and wavy; the close, crisped blond beard he had grown during his illness did not alter him. He was big and big-chested yet. His eyes were dull and he mumbled and babbled mere meaningless syllables, not words.

Etcham helped Van Rieten to uncover him, and look him over. He was in good muscle for a man so long bedridden. There were no scars on him except about his knees, shoulders and chest. On each knee and above it he had a full score of roundish cicatrices, and a dozen or more on each shoulder, all in front. Two or three were open wounds, and four or five barely healed. He had no fresh swellings, except two, one on each side, on his pectoral muscles, the one on the left being higher up and farther out than the other. They did not look like boils or carbuncles, but as if something blunt and hard were being pushed up through the fairly healthy flesh and skin, not much inflamed.

'I should not lance those,' said Van Rieten, and Etcham assented.

They made Stone as comfortable as they could, and just before sunset we looked in at him again. He was lying on his back, and his chest showed big and massive yet, but he lay as if in a stupor. We left Etcham with him and went into the next hut, which Etcham had resigned to us. The jungle noises were no different there than anywhere else for months past, and I was soon fast asleep.

V

Sometime in the pitch dark I found myself awake and listening. I could hear two voices, one Stone's, the other sibilant and wheezy. I knew Stone's voice after all the years had passed since I heard it last. The other was like nothing I remembered. It had less volume than the wail of a new-born baby, yet there was an insistent carrying power to it, like the shrilling of an insect. As I listened I heard Van Rieten breathing near me in the dark, then he heard me and realized that I was listening, too. Like Etcham I knew little Balunda, but I could make out a word or two. The voices alternated with intervals of silence between.

Then suddenly both sounded at once and fast. Stone's baritone basso, full as if he were in perfect health, and that incredibly stridulous falsetto, both jabbering at once like the voices of two people quarrelling and trying to talk each other down.

'I can't stand this,' said Van Rieten. 'Let's have a look at him.'

He had one of those cylindrical electric night-candles. He fumbled about for it, touched the button and beckoned me to come with him. Outside of the hut he motioned me to stand still, and instinctively turned off the light, as if seeing made listening difficult.

Except for a faint glow from the embers of the bearers' fire we were in complete darkness, little starlight struggled through the trees, the river made but a faint murmuring. We could hear the two voices together and then suddenly the creaking voice changed into a razor-edged, slicing whistle, indescribably cutting, continuing right through Stone's grumbling torrent of croaking words.

'Good God!' exclaimed Van Rieten.

Abruptly he turned on the light.

We found Etcham utterly asleep, exhausted by his long anxiety and the exertions of his phenomenal march and relaxed completely now that the load was in a sense shifted from his shoulders to Van Rieten's. Even the light on his face did not wake him.

The whistle had ceased and the two voices now sounded together. Both came from Stone's cot, where the concentrated white ray showed him lying just as we had left him, except that he had tossed his arms above his head and had torn the coverings and bandages from his chest.

The swelling on his right breast had broken. Van Rieten aimed the centre line of the light at it and we saw it plainly. From his flesh, grown out of it, there protruded a head, such a head as the dried specimens Etcham had shown us, as if it were a miniature of the head of a Balunda fetish-man. It was black, shining black as the blackest African skin; it rolled the whites of its wicked, wee eyes and showed its microscopic teeth between lips repulsively negroid in their red fullness, even in so diminutive a face. It had crisp, fuzzy wool on its minikin skull, it turned malignantly from side to side and chittered incessantly in that inconceivable falsetto. Stone babbled brokenly against its patter.

Van Rieten turned from Stone and waked Etcham, with some difficulty. When he was awake and saw it all, Etcham stared and said not one word.

'You saw him slice off two swellings?' Van Rieten asked.

Etcham nodded, chokingly.

'Did he bleed much?' Van Rieten demanded.

'Very little,' Etcham replied.

'You hold his arms,' said Van Rieten to Etcham.

He took up Stone's razor and handed me the light. Stone showed no sign of seeing the light or of knowing we were there. But the little head mewled and screeched at us.

Van Rieten's hand was steady, and the sweep of the razor even and true. Stone bled amazingly little and Van Rieten dressed the wound as if it had been a bruise or scrape.

Stone had stopped talking the instant the excrescent head was severed. Van Rieten did all that could be done for Stone and then fairly grabbed the light from me. Snatching up a gun he scanned the ground by the cot and brought the butt down once and twice, viciously.

We went back to our hut, but I doubt if I slept.

VI

Next day, near noon, in broad daylight, we heard the two voices from Stone's hut. We found Etcham dropped asleep by his charge. The swelling on the left had broken, and just such another head was there miauling and spluttering. Etcham woke up and three of us stood there and glared. Stone interjected hoarse vocables into the tinkling gurgle of the portent's utterance.

Van Rieten stepped forward, took up Stone's razor and knelt down by the cot. The atomy of a head squealed a wheezy snarl at him.

Then suddenly Stone spoke English.

'Who are you with my razor?'

Van Rieten started back and stood up.

Stone's eyes were clear now and bright, they roved about the hut.

'The end,' he said, 'I recognize the end. I seem to see Etcham, as if in life. But Singleton! Ah, Singleton! Ghosts of my boyhood come to watch me pass! And you, strange spectre with the black beard and my razor! Aroint ye all!'

'I'm no ghost, Stone,' I managed to say. 'I'm alive. So are Etcham and Van Rieten. We are here to help you.'

'Van Rieten!' he exclaimed. 'My work passes on to a better man. Luck go with you, Van Rieten.'

Van Rieten went nearer to him.

'Just hold still a moment, old man,' he said soothingly. 'It will be only one twinge.'

'I've held still for many such twinges,' Stone answered quite distinctly. 'Let me be. Let me die in my own way. The hydra was nothing to do this. You can cut off ten, a hundred, a thousand heads, but the curse you cannot cut off, or take off. What's soaked into the bone won't come out of the flesh, any more than what's bred there. Don't hack me any more. Promise!'

His voice had all the old commanding tone of his boyhood and it swayed Van Rieten as it always had swayed everybody.

'I promise,' said Van Rieten.

Almost as he said the word Stone's eyes filmed again.

Then we three sat about Stone and watched that hideous, gibbering prodigy grow up out of Stone's flesh, till two horrid, spindling little black arms disengaged themselves. The infinitesimal nails were perfect to the barely perceptible moon at the quick, the pink spot on the palm was horridly natural. These arms gesticulated and the right plucked towards Stone's blond beard.

'I can't stand this,' Van Rieten exclaimed and took up the razor again.

Instantly Stone's eyes opened, hard and glittering.

'Van Rieten break his word?' he enunciated slowly. 'Never!'

'But we must help you,' Van Rieten gasped.

'I am past all help and all hurting,' said Stone. 'This is my hour. This curse is not put on me; it grew out of me, like this horror here. Even now I go.'

His eyes closed and we stood helpless, the adherent figure spouting shrill sentences.

In a moment Stone spoke again.

'You speak all tongues?' he asked quickly.

And the emergent minikin replied in sudden English:

'Yea, verily, all that you speak,' putting out its microscopic tongue, writhing its lips and wagging its head from side to side. We could see the thready ribs on its exiguous flanks heave as if the thing breathed.

'Has she forgiven me?' Stone asked in a muffled strangle.

'Not while the stars shine on Lake Pontachartrain will she forgive.'

And then Stone, all with one motion, wrenched himself over on his side. The next instant he was dead.

When Singleton's voice ceased the room was hushed for a space. We could hear each other breathing. Twombly, the tactless, broke the silence.

'I presume,' he said, 'you cut off the little minikin and brought it home in alcohol.'

Singleton turned on him a stern countenance.

'We buried Stone,' he said, 'unmutilated as he died.'

'But,' said the unconscionable Twombly, 'the whole thing is incredible.'

Singleton stiffened.

'I did not expect you to believe it,' he said; 'I began by saying that although I heard and saw it, when I look back on it I cannot credit it myself.'

The Troll

T. H. White

'My father,' said Mr Marx, 'used to say that an experience like the one I am about to relate was apt to shake one's interest in mundane matters. Naturally he did not expect to be believed, and he did not mind whether he was or not. He did not himself believe in the supernatural, but the thing happened, and he proposed to tell it as simply as possible. It was stupid of him to say that it shook his faith in mundane affairs, for it was just as mundane as anything else. Indeed the really frightening part about it was the horribly tangible atmosphere in which it took place. None of the outlines wavered in the least. The creature would have been less remarkable if it had been less natural. It seemed to overcome the usual laws without being immune to them.

'My father was a keen fisherman, and used to go to all sorts of places for his fish. On one occasion he made Abisko his Lapland base, a comfortable railway hotel, one hundred and fifty miles within the Arctic circle. He travelled the prodigious length of Sweden (I believe it is as far from the South of Sweden to the North, as it is from the South of Sweden to the South of Italy) in the electric railway, and arrived tired out. He went to bed early, sleeping almost immediately, although it was bright daylight outside; as it is in those parts through the night at that time of the year. Not the least shaking part of his experience was that it should all have happened under the sun.

'He went to bed early, and slept, and dreamt. I may as well make it clear at once, as clear as the outlines of that creature in the northern sun, that his story did not turn out to be a dream in the last paragraph. The division between sleeping and waking was abrupt, although the feeling of both was the same. They were both in the same sphere of horrible absurdity though in the former he was asleep and in the latter almost terribly awake. He tried to be asleep several times.

'My father always used to tell one of his dreams, because it somehow seemed of a piece with what was to follow. He believed that it was a consequence of the thing's presence in the next room. My father dreamed of blood.

'It was the vividness of the dreams that was impressive, their minute detail and horrible reality. The blood came through the keyhole of a locked door which communicated with the next room. I suppose the two rooms had originally been designed *ensuite*. It ran down the door panel with a viscous ripple, like the artificial one created in the conduit of Trumpingdon Street. But it was heavy, and smelt. The slow welling of it sopped the carpet and reached the bed. It was warm and sticky. My father woke up with the impression that it was all over his hands. He was rubbing his first two fingers together, trying to rid them of the greasy adhesion where the fingers joined.

'My father knew what he had got to do. Let me make it clear that he was now perfectly wide awake, but he knew what he had got to do. He got out of bed, under this irresistible knowledge, and looked through the keyhole into the next room.

'I suppose the best way to tell the story is simply to narrate it, without an effort to carry belief. The thing did not require belief. It was not a feeling of horror in one's bones, or a misty outline, or anything that needed to be given actuality by an act of faith. It was as solid as a wardrobe. You don't have to believe in wardrobes. They are there, with corners.

'What my father saw through the keyhole in the next room was a Troll. It was eminently solid, about eight feet high, and dressed in brightly ornamented skins. It had a blue face, with yellow eyes, and on its head there was a woolly sort of nightcap with a red bobble on top. The features were Mongolian. Its body was long and sturdy, like the trunk of a tree. Its legs were short and thick like the elephant's feet that used to be cut off for umbrella stands, and its arms were wasted: little rudimentary members like the forelegs of a kangaroo. Its head and neck were very thick and massive. On the whole, it looked like a grotesque doll.

'That was the horror of it. Imagine a perfectly normal golliwog (but without the association of a Christie minstrel) standing in the corner of a room, eight feet high. The creature was as ordinary as that, as tangible, as stuffed, and as ungainly at the joints: but it could move itself about.

'The Troll was eating a lady. Poor girl, she was tightly clutched to its breast by those rudimentary arms, with her head on a level with its mouth. She was dressed in a nightdress which had crumpled up under her armpits, so that she was a pitiful naked offering, like a classical picture of Andromeda. Mercifully, she appeared to have fainted.

'Just as my father applied his eye to the keyhole, the Troll opened its mouth and bit off her head. Then, holding the neck between the bright blue lips, he sucked the bare meat dry. She shrivelled, like a squeezed orange, and her heels kicked. The creature had a look of thoughtful ecstacy. When the girl seemed to have lost succulence as an orange she was lifted into the air. She vanished in two bites. The Troll remained leaning against the wall, munching patiently and casting its eyes about with a vague benevolence. Then it leant forward from the low hips, like a jack-knife folding in half, and opened its mouth to lick the blood up from the carpet. The mouth was incandescent inside, like a gas fire, and the blood evaporated before its tongue, like dust before a vacuum cleaner. It straightened itself, the arms dangling before it in patient uselessness, and fixed its eyes upon the keyhole.

'My father crawled back to bed, like a hunted fox after fifteen miles. At first it was because he was afraid that the creature had seen him through the hole, but afterwards it was because of his reason. A man can attribute many night-time appearances to the imagination, and can ultimately persuade himself that creatures of the dark did not exist. But this was an appearance in a sunlit room, with all the solidity of a wardrobe and unfortunately almost none of its possibility. He spent the first ten minutes making sure that he was awake, and the rest of the night trying to hope that he was asleep. It was either that, or else he was mad.

'It is not pleasant to doubt one's sanity. There are no satisfactory tests. One can pinch oneself to see if one is asleep, but there are no means of determining the other problem. He spent some time opening and shutting his eyes, but the room seemed normal and remained unaltered. He also soused his head in a basin of cold water, without result. Then he lay on his back, for hours, watching the mosquitoes on the ceiling.

'He was tired when he was called. A bright Scandinavian maid admitted the full sunlight for him and told him that it was a fine day. He spoke to her several times, and watched her carefully, but she seemed to have no doubts about his behaviour. Evidently, then, he was not badly mad; and by now he had been thinking about the matter for so many hours that it had begun to get obscure. The outlines were blurring again, and he determined that the whole thing must have been a dream or a temporary delusion, something temporary, anyway, and finished with; so that there was no good in thinking about it longer. He got up, dressed himself fairly cheerfully, and went down to breakfast.

'These hotels used to run extraordinary well. There was a hostess always handy in a little office off the hall, who was delighted to answer any questions, spoke every conceivable language, and generally made it her business to make the guests feel at home. The particular hostess at Abisko was a lovely creature into the bargain. My father used to speak to her a good deal. He had an idea that when you had a bath in Sweden one of the maids was sent to wash you. As a matter of fact this sometimes used to be the case, but it was always an old maid and highly trusted. You had to keep yourself underwater and this was supposed to confer a cloak of invisibility. If you popped your knee out she was shocked. My father had a dim sort of hope that the hostess would be sent to bath him

one day: and I daresay he would have shocked her a good deal.
However, this is beside the point. As he passed through the hall something prompted him to ask about the room next to his. Had anybody,
he enquired, taken number twenty-three?

'"But, yes," said the lady manager with a bright smile, "twenty-three
is taken by a doctor professor from Uppsala and his wife, such a
charming couple!"

'My father wondered what the charming couple had been doing,
whilst the Troll was eating the lady in the nightdress. However, he
decided to think no more about it. He pulled himself together, and went
in to breakfast. The professor was sitting in an opposite corner (the
manageress had kindly pointed him out), looking mild and shortsighted,
by himself. My father thought he would go out for a long climb on the
mountains, since exercise was evidently what his constitution needed.

'He had a lovely day. Lake Torne blazed a deep blue below him, for
all its thirty miles, and the melting snow made a lacework of filigree
round the tops of the surrounding mountain basin. He got away from
the stunted birch trees, and the mossy bogs with the reindeer in them,
and the mosquitoes, too. He forded something that might have been a
temporary tributary of the Abiskojokk, having to take off his trousers
to do so and tucking his shirt up round his neck. He wanted to shout,
bracing himself against the glorious tug of the snow water, with his legs
crossing each other involuntarily as they passed, and the boulders
turning under his feet. His body made a bow wave in the water, which
climbed and feathered on his stomach, on the upstream side. When he
was under the opposite bank a stone turned in earnest, and he went in.
He came up, shouting with laughter, and made a loud remark which
has since become a classic in my family, "Thank God," he said, "I rolled
up my sleeves." He wrung out everything as best he could, and dressed
again in the wet clothes, and set off for the shoulder of Niakatjavelk. He
was dry and warm again in half a mile. Less than a thousand feet took
him over the snow line, and there, crawling on hands and knees, he came
face to face with what seemed to be the summit of ambition. He met an
ermine. They were both on all fours, so that there was a sort of equality
about the encounter, especially as the ermine was higher up than he was.
They looked at each other for a fifth of a second, without saying
anything, and then the ermine vanished. He searched for it everywhere
in vain, for the snow was only patchy. My father sat down on a dry rock,
to eat his well-soaked luncheon of chocolate and rye bread.

'Life is such unutterable hell, solely because it is sometimes beautiful.
If we could only be miserable all the time, if there could be no such
things as love or beauty or faith or hope, if I could be absolutely certain
that my love would never be returned: how much more simple life would
be. One could plod through the Siberian salt mines of existence without

being bothered about happiness. Unfortunately the happiness is there. There is always the chance (about eight hundred and fifty to one) that another heart will come to mine. I can't help hoping, and keeping faith, and loving beauty. Quite frequently I am not so miserable as it would be wise to be. And there, for my poor father sitting on his boulder above the snow, was stark happiness beating at the gates.

'The boulder on which he was sitting had probably never been sat upon before. It was 150 miles within the Arctic circle, on a mountain 5,000 feet high, looking down on a blue lake. The lake was so long that he could have sworn it sloped away at the ends, proving to the naked eye that the sweet earth was round. The railway line and the half-dozen houses of Abisko were hidden in the trees. The sun was warm on the boulder, blue on the snow, and his body tingled smooth from the spate water. His mouth watered for the chocolate, just behind the tip of his tongue.

'And yet, when he had eaten the chocolate – perhaps it was heavy on his stomach – there was the memory of the Troll. My father fell suddenly into a black mood, and began to think about the supernatural. Lapland was beautiful in the summer, with the sun sweeping round the horizon day and night, and the small tree leaves twinkling. It was not the sort of place for wicked things. But what about the winter? A picture of the Arctic night came before him, with the silence and the snow. Then the legendary wolves and bears snuffled at the far encampments, and the nameless winter spirits moved on their darkling courses. Lapland had always been associated with sorcery, even by Shakespeare. It was at the outskirts of the world that the Old Things accumulated, like driftwood round the edges of the sea. If one wanted to find a wise women, one went to the rims of the Hebrides; on the coast of Brittany one sought the mass of St Secaire. And what an outskirt Lapland was! It was an outskirt not only of Europe, but of civilization. It had no boundaries. The Lapps went with the reindeer, and where the reindeer were was Lapland. Curiously indefinite region, suitable to the indefinite things. The Lapps were not Christians. What a fund of power they must have had behind them, a power against Christ. My father realized with a shock that he was living in the age of the reindeer, a period contiguous to the mammoth and the fossil.

'Well, this was not what he had come out to do. He dismissed the nightmares with an effort, got up from his boulder, and began the scramble back to his hotel. It was impossible that a professor from Abisko could become a Troll.

'As my father was going in to dinner that evening the manageress stopped him in the hall.

'"We have had a day so sad," she said. "The poor Dr Professor has disappeared his wife. She has been missing since last night. The Dr Professor is inconsolable."

'My father then knew for certain that he had lost his reason.

'He went blindly to dinner, without making any answer, and began to eat a thick sour-cream soup that was taken cold with pepper and sugar. The professor was still sitting in his corner, a sandy-headed man with thick spectacles and a desolate expression. He was looking at my father, and my father, with the soup spoon halfway to his mouth, looked at him. You know that eye-to-eye recognition, when two people look deeply into each other's pupils, and burrow to the soul? It usually comes before love. I mean the clear, deep, milk-eyed recognition expressed by the poet Donne. Their eyebeams twisted and did thread their eyes upon a double string. My father recognized that the Professor was a Troll, and the professor recognized my father's recognition. Both of them knew that the professor had eaten his wife.

'My father put down his soup spoon, and the Professor began to grow. The top of his head lifted and expanded, like a great loaf rising in an oven; his face went red and purple, and finally blue; the whole ungainly upperworks began to sway and topple towards the ceiling. My father looked about him. The other diners were eating unconcernedly. Nobody else could see it, and he was definitely mad at last. When he looked at the Troll again, the creature bowed. The enormous superstructure inclined itself towards him from the hips, and grinned seductively.

'My father got up from his table experimentally, and advanced towards the Troll, arranging his feet on the carpet with excessive care. He did not find it easy to walk, or to approach the monster, but it was a question of his reason. If he was mad, he was mad; and it was essential that he should come to grips with the thing, in order to make certain.

'He stood before it like a small boy, and held out his hand, saying, "Good evening."

'"Ho! Ho!" said the Troll, "little mannikin. And what shall I have for my supper tonight?"

'Then it held out its wizened furry paw and took my father by the hand.

'My father went straight out of the dining-room, walking on air. He found the manageress in the passage and held out his hand to her.

'"I'm afraid I have burnt my hand," he said. "Do you think you could tie it up?"

'The manageress said, "But it is a very bad burn. There are blisters all over the back. Of course, I will bind it up at once."

'He explained that he had burnt it on one of the spirit lamps at the sideboard. He could scarcely conceal his delight. One cannot burn oneself by being insane.

'"I saw you talking to the Dr Professor," said the manageress, as she was putting on the bandage. "He is a sympathetic gentleman, is he not?"

*

'The relief about his sanity soon gave place to other troubles. The Troll had eaten its wife and given him a blister, but it had also made an unpleasant remark about its supper that evening. It proposed to eat my father. Now very few people can have been in a position to decide what to do when a Troll earmarks them for its next meal. To begin with, although it was a tangible Troll in two ways, it had been invisible to the other diners. This put my father in a difficult position. He could not, for instance, ask for protection. He could scarcely go to the manageress and say, "Professor Skal is an odd kind of werewolf, ate his wife last night, and proposes to eat me this evening." He would have found himself in a looney-bin at once. Besides, he was too proud to do this, and still too confused. Whatever the proofs and blisters, he did not find it easy to believe in professors that turned into Trolls. He had lived in the normal world all his life, and at his age, it was difficult to start learning afresh. It would have been quite easy for a baby, who was still co-ordinating the world, to cope with the Troll situation: for my father, not. He kept trying to fit in somewhere, without disturbing the universe. He kept telling himself that it was nonsense: one did not get eaten by professors. It was like having a fever, and telling oneself that it was all right, really, only a delirium, only something that would pass.

'There was that feeling on the one side, the desperate assertion of all the truths that he had learned so far, the tussle to keep the world from drifting, the brave but intimidated refusal to give in or to make a fool of himself.

'On the other side there was stark terror. However much one struggled to be merely deluded, or hitched up momentarily in an odd pocket of space-time, there was panic. There was the urge to go away as quickly as possible, to flee the dreadful Troll. Unfortunately the last train had left Abisko, and there was nowhere else to go.

'My father was not able to distinguish these trends of thought. For him they were at the time intricately muddled together. He was in a whirl. A proud man, and an agnostic, he stuck to his muddled guns alone. He was terribly afraid of the Troll, but he could not afford to admit its existence. All his mental processes remained hung up, whilst he talked on the terrace, in a state of suspended animation, with an American tourist who had come to Abisko to photograph the midnight sun.

'The American told my father that the Abisko railway was the northernmost electric railway in the world, that twelve trains passed through it every day travelling between Uppsala and Narvik, that the population of Abo was 12,000 in 1862, and that Gustavus Adolphus ascended the throne of Sweden in 1611. He also gave some facts about Greta Garbo.

'My father told the American that a dead baby was required for the mass of St Secaire, that an elemental was a kind of mouth in space that sucked at you and tried to gulp you down, that homeopathic magic was practised by the aborigines of Australia, and that a Lapland woman was careful at her confinement to have no knots or loops about her person, lest these should make the delivery difficult.

'The American, who had been looking at my father in a strange way for some time, took offence at this and walked away; so that there was nothing for it but to go to bed.

'My father walked upstairs on will power alone. His faculties seemed to have shrunk and confused themselves. He had to help himself with the banister. He seemed to be navigating himself by wireless, from the spot about a foot above his forehead. The issues that were involved had ceased to have any meaning, but he went on doggedly up the stairs, moved forward by pride and contrariety. It was physical fear that alienated him from his body, the same fear that he had felt as a boy, walking down long corridors to be beaten. He walked firmly up the stairs.

'Oddly enough, he went to sleep at once. He had climbed all day and been awake all night and suffered emotional extremes. Like a condemned man, who was to be hanged in the morning, my father gave the whole business up and went to sleep.

'He was woken at midnight exactly. He heard the American on the terrace below his window, explaining excitedly that there had been a cloud on the last two nights at 11.58, thus making it impossible to photograph the midnight sun. He heard the camera click.

'There seemed to be sudden storm of hail and wind. It roared at his window-sill, and the window curtains lifted themselves taut, pointing horizontally into the room. The shriek and rattle of the tempest framed the window in a crescendo of growing sound, an increasing blizzard directed towards himself. A blue paw come over the sill.

'My father turned over and hid his head in the pillow. He could feel the domed head dawning at the window and the eyes fixing themselves upon the small of his back. He could feel the places physically, about four inches apart. They itched. Or else the rest of his body itched, except those places. He could feel the creature growing into the room, glowing like ice, and giving off a storm. His mosquito curtains rose in its afflatus, uncovering him, leaving him defenceless. He was in such an ecstasy of terror that he almost enjoyed it. He was like a bather plunging for the first time into freezing water and unable to articulate. He was trying to yell, but all he could do was to throw a series of hooting noises from his paralysed lungs. He became a part of the blizzard. The bedclothes were gone. He felt the Troll put out his hands.

'My father was an agnostic, but, like most idle men, he was not above having a bee in his bonnet. His favourite bee was the psychology of the

Catholic Church. He was ready to talk for hours about psycho-analysis and the confession. His greatest discovery had been the rosary.

'The rosary, my father used to say, was intended solely as a factual occupation which calmed the lower centres of the mind. The automatic telling of the beads liberated the higher centres to meditate upon the mysteries. They were a sedative, like knitting or counting sheep. There was no better cure for insomnia than a rosary. For several years he had given up deep breathing or regular counting. When he was sleepless he lay on his back and told his beads, and there was a small rosary in the pocket of his pyjama coat.

'The Troll put out its hands, to take him round the waist. He became completely paralysed, as if he had been winded. The Troll put its hand upon the beads.

'They met, the occult forces, in a clash above my father's heart. There was an explosion, he said, a quick creation of power. Positive and negative. A flash, a beam. Something like the splutter with which the antenna of a tram meets its overhead wires again, when it is being changed about.

'The Troll made a high squealing noice, like a crab being boiled, and began rapidly to dwindle in size. It dropped my father and turned about, and ran wailing, as if it had been terribly burnt, for the window. Its colour waned as its size decreased. It was one of those air-toys now, that expire with a piercing whistle. It scrambled over the window-sill, scarcely larger than a little child, and sagging visibly.

'My father leaped out of bed and followed it to the window. He saw it drop on the terrace like a toad, gather itself together, stumble off, staggering and whistling like a bat, down the valley of the Abiskolokk.

'My father fainted.

'In the morning the manageress said, "There has been such a terrible tragedy. The poor Dr Professor was found this morning in the lake. The story about his wife had certainly unhinged his mind."

'A subscription for a wreath was started by the American, to which my father subscribed five shillings; and the body was shipped off next morning, on one of the twelve trains that travel between Uppsala and Narvik every day.'

The Lips

Henry S. Whitehead

The *Saul Taverner*, blackbirder, Luke Martin, master, up from Cartagena, came to her anchor in the harbour of St Thomas, capital, and chief town of the Danish West Indies. A Martinique barkentine berthed to leeward of her, sent a fully manned boat ashore after the harbour-master with a request for permission to change anchorage. Luke Martin's shore boat was only a few lengths behind the French-man's. Martin shouted after the officer whom it landed:

'Tell Lollik I'll change places with ye, an' welcome! What ye carryin' – brandy? I'll take six cases off'n ye.'

The barkentine's mate, a French-Island mulatto, nodded over his shoulder, and noted down the order in a leather pocketbook without slackening his pace. It was no joyful experience to lie in a semi-enclosed harbour directly to leeward of a slaver, and haste was indicated despite propitiatory orders for brandy. 'Very well, Captain,' said the mate, stiffly.

Martin landed as the Martinique mate rounded a corner to the left and disappeared from view in the direction of the harbour-master's. Martin scowled after him, muttering to himself.

'Airs! Talkin' English – language of the islands; thinkin' in French, you an' your airs! An' yer gran'father came outta blackbird ship like's not! You an' your airs!'

Reaching the corner the mate had turned, Martin glanced after him momentarily, then turned to the right, mounting a slight rise. His business ashore took him to the fort. He intended to land his cargo, or a portion of it, that night. The colony was short of field hands. With the help of troops from Martinique, French troops, and Spaniards down from its nearer neighbour, Porto Rico, it had just put down a bloody uprising on its subsidiary island of St Jan. Many of the slaves had been killed in the joint armed reprisal of the year 1833.

Luke Martin got his permission to land his cargo, therefore, without difficulty, and being a Yankee bucko who let no grass grow under his feet, four bells in the afternoon watch saw the hatches off and the decks of the *Saul Taverner* swarming with manacled Blacks for the ceremony of washing-down.

Huddled together, blinking in the glaring sun of a July afternoon under parallel 18, north latitude, the mass of swart humanity were soaped, with handfuls of waste out of soft-soap buckets, scrubbed with brushes on the ends of short handles, and rinsed off with other buckets. Boatloads of Negroes surrounded the ship to see the washing-down, and these were kept at a distance by a swearing third mate told off for the purpose.

By seven bells the washing-down was completed, and before sundown a row of lighters, each guarded by a pair of Danish gendarmes with muskets and fixed bayonets, had ranged alongside for the taking off of the hundred and seventeen Blacks who were to be landed, most of whom would be sent to replenish the labourers on the plantations of St Jan off the other side of the island of St Thomas.

The disembarking process began just after dark, to the light of lanterns. Great care was exercised by all concerned lest any escape by plunging overboard. A tally-clerk from shore checked off the Blacks as they went over the side into the lighters, and these, as they became filled, were rowed to the landing-stage by other slaves, bending over six great sweeps in each of the stub-bowed, heavy wooden boats.

Among the huddled black bodies of the very last batch stood a woman, very tall and thin, with a new-born child, black as a coal, at her breasts. The woman stood a little aloof from the others, farther from the low rail of the *Saul Taverner*'s forward deck, crooning to her infant. Behind her approached Luke Martin, impatient of his unloading, and cut at her thin ankles with his rhinoceros leather whip. The woman did not wince. Instead she turned her head and muttered a few syllables in a low tone, in the Eboe dialect. Martin shoved her into the mass of Blacks, cursing roundly as he cut a second time at the spindling shins.

The woman turned, very quietly and softly, as he was passing behind her, let her head fall softly on Martin's shoulder and whispered into his ear. The motion was so delicate as to simulate a caress, but Martin's curse died in his throat. He howled in pain as the woman raised her head, and his whip clattered on the deck boarding while the hand which had held it went to the shoulder. The woman, deftly holding her infant, had moved in among the huddling Blacks, a dozen or more of whom intervened between her and Martin, who hopped on one foot and cursed, a vicious, continuous stream of foul epithets; then, still cursing, made his way in haste to his cabin after an antiseptic, any idea of revenge swallowed up in his superstitious dread of what might happen to him if he did not, forthwith, dress the ghastly wound just under his left ear, where the black woman had caused her firm, white and shining teeth to meet in the great muscle of his neck between shoulder and jaw.

When he emerged, ten minutes later, the wound now soaked in permanganate of potash, and roughly clotted with a clean cloth, the last lighter, under the impetus of its six sweeps, was halfway ashore, and the clerk of the government, from the fort, was awaiting him, with a bag of coin and a pair of gendarmes to guard it. He accompanied the government clerk below, where, the gendarmes at the cabin door, they figured and added and counted money for the next hour, a bottle of sound rum and a pair of glasses between them.

At two bells, under a shining moon, the *Saul Taverner*, taking advantage of the evening trade wind, was running for the harbour's mouth to stand away for Norfolk, Virginia, whence, empty, she would run up the coast for her home port of Boston, Massachusetts.

It was midnight, what with the care of his ship coming out of even the plain and safe harbour of St Thomas, before Martin the skipper, Culebra lighthouse off the port quarter, turned in. The wound in the top of his shoulder ached dully, and he sent for Matthew Pound, his first mate, to wash it out with more permanganate and dress it suitably. It was in an awkward place — curse the black slut! – for him to manage it for himself.

Pound went white and muttered under his breath at the ugly sight of it when Martin had removed his shirt, painfully, and eased off the cloth he had roughly laid over it, a cloth now stiff and clotted with the exuding blood drying on its inner surface, from the savage wound.

Thereafter, not liking the look on his mate's face, nor that whitening which the sight of the place in his neck had brought about, Martin dispensed with assistance, and dressed the wound himself.

He slept little that first night, but this was partly for thinking of the bargain he had driven with those short-handed Danes. They had been hard up for black meat to sweat on those hillside canefields over on St Jan. He could have disposed, easily, of his entire cargo, but that, unfortunately, was out of the question. He had, what with an exceptionally slow and hot voyage across the Caribbean from Cartagena, barely enough of his said cargo left to fulfil his engagement to deliver a certain number of head in Norfolk. But he would have been glad enough to rid his hold of them all — curse them! – and set his course straight for Boston. He was expecting to be married the day after his arrival. He was eager to get home, and even now the *Saul Taverner* was carrying as much sail as she could stand up under, heeling now to the unfailing trade winds of this latitude.

The wound ached and pained, none the less, and he found it well-nigh impossible to settle himself in a comparatively comfortable position on its account. He tossed and cursed far into the warm night. Towards morning he fell into a fitful doze.

The entire side of his neck and shoulder was one huge, searing ache when he awakened and pushed himself carefully upright with both hands. He could not bend his head nor, at first, move it from side to side. Dressing was a very painful process, but he managed it. He wanted to see what the bite looked like, but, as he never shaved during a voyage, there was no glass in his cabin. He bathed the sore place gingerly with bay rum, which hurt abominably and caused him to curse afresh. Dressed at last, he made his way up on deck, past the steward who was laying breakfast in his cabin. The steward, he thought, glanced at him curiously, but he could not be sure. No wonder. He had to walk sidewise, with the pain of his neck, like a crab. He ordered more sail, stuns'ls, and, these set and sheeted home, he returned to the cabin for breakfast.

Mid-afternoon saw him, despite the vessel's more than satisfactory speed and the progress of a long leg towards Boston and Lydia Farnham, in such a devilish temper that everyone on board the ship kept as far as possible out of his way. He took no night watches, these being divided among the three mates, and after his solitary supper, punctuated with numerous curses at a more than usually awkward steward, he went into his state-room, removed his shirt and singlet, and thoroughly rubbed the entire aching area with coconut oil. The pain now ran down his left arm to the elbow, and penetrated to all the cords of his neck, the muscles of which throbbed and burned atrociously.

The embrocation gave him a certain amount of relief. He remembered that the woman had muttered something. It was *not* Eboe, that jargon of *lingua franca* which served as a medium for the few remarks necessary between slavers and their human cattle. It was some outlandish coastal or tribal dialect. He had not caught it, sensed its meaning; though there had resided in those few syllables some germ of deadly meaning. He remembered, vaguely, the cadence of the syllables, even though their meaning had been unknown to him. Wearing, aching, depressed, he turned in, and this time, almost immediately, he fell asleep.

And in his sleep, those syllables were repeated to him, into his left ear, endlessly, over and over again, and in his sleep he knew their meaning; and when he awoke, a swaying beam of pouring moonlight coming through his porthole, at four bells after midnight, the cold sweat had made his pillow clammy wet and stood dankly in the hollows of his eyes and soaked his tangled beard.

Burning from head to foot, he rose and lit the candle in his binnacle-light, and cursed himself again for a fool for not acquiring a mirror through the day. Young Sumner, the third mate, shaved. One or two of the fo'castle hands, too. There would be mirrors on board. He must obtain one tomorrow. What was it the woman had said – those syllables? He shuddered. He could not remember. Why should he remember? Gibberish – nigger-talk! It was nothing. Merely the act of a bestial

Black. They were all alike. He should have taken the living hide off the wench. To bite him! Well, painful as it was, it should be well healed before he got back to Boston, and Lydia.

Laboriously, for he was very stiff and sore all along the left side, he climbed back into his bed, after blowing out the binnacle-light. That candlewick! It was very foul. He should have wet his thumb and finger and pinched it out. It was still smoking.

Then the syllables again, endlessly – over and over, and, now that he slept, and, somehow, knew that he slept and could not carry their meaning into the next waking state, *he knew what they meant*. Asleep, drowned in sleep, he tossed from side to side of his berth-bed, and the cold sweat ran in oily trickles down into his thick beard.

He awakened in the early light of morning in a state of horrified half-realization. He could not get up, it seemed. The ache now ran all through his body, which felt as though it had been beaten until flayed. One of the brandy bottles from the Martinique barkentine, opened the night of departure from St Thomas, was within reach. He got it, painfully, drew the cork with his teeth, holding the bottle in his right hand, and took a long, gasping drink of the neat spirit. He could feel it through him like liquid, golden fire. Ah! that was better. He raised the bottle again, set it back where it had been, half empty. He made a great effort to roll out of the berth, failed, sank back well-nigh helpless, his head humming and singing like a hive of angry bees.

He lay there, semi-stupefied now, vague and dreadful things working within his head, his mind, his body; things brewing, seething, there inside him, as though something had entered into him and was growing there where the focus of pain throbbed, in the great muscles of his neck on the left side.

There, an hour later, a timid steward found him, after repeated and unanswered knocks on the state-room door. The steward had at last ventured to open the door a mere peeping-slit, and then, softly closing it behind him, and white-faced, hastened to find Pound, the first mate.

Pound, after consultation with the second mate, Sumner, accompanied the steward to the state-room door, opening off the captain's cabin. Even there, hard bucko that he was, he hesitated. No one aboard the *Saul Taverner* approached Captain Luke Martin with a sense of ease or anything like self-assurance. Pound repeated the steward's door-opening, peeped within, and thereafter entered the cabin, shutting the door.

Martin lay on his right side, the bed-clothes pushed down to near his waist. He slept in his singlet, and the left side of his neck was uppermost. Pound looked long at the wound, his face like chalk, his hands and lips trembling. Then he softly departed, shutting the door behind him a second time, and went thoughtfully up on deck again. He sought out young Sumner and the two spoke together for several minutes. Then Sumner went below to his cabin, and, emerging on the deck, looked furtively all around him. Observing the coast clear, he drew from beneath his drill jacket something twice the size of his hand, and again glancing about to make sure he was not observed, dropped the article overboard. It flashed in the bright morning sun as it turned about in the air before the waters received it forever. It was his small cabin shaving-mirror.

At four bells in the forenoon, Pound again descended to the captain's cabin. This time Martin's voice, a weak voice, answered his discreet knock and at its invitation he entered the state-room. Martin now lay on his back, his left side away from the door.

'How are you feeling, sir?' asked Pound.

'Better,' murmured Martin; 'this damned thing!' He indicated the left side of his neck with a motion of his right thumb. 'I got some sleep this morning. Just woke up, just now. It's better – the worst of it over, I reckon.'

A pause fell between the men. There seemed nothing more to say. Finally, after several twitches and fidgeting, Pound mentioned several details about the ship, the surest way to enlist Martin's interest at any time. Martin replied, and Pound took his departure.

Martin had spoken the truth when he alleged he was better. He had awakened with a sense that the worst was over. The wound ached abominably still, but the unpleasantness was distinctly lessened. He got up, rather languidly, slowly pulled on his deck clothes, called for coffee through the state-room door.

Yet, when he emerged on his deck ten minutes later, his face was drawn and haggard, and there was a look in his eyes that kept the men silent. He looked over the ship professionally, the regular six bells morning inspection, but he was preoccupied and his usual intense interest in anything concerned with his ship was this day merely perfunctory. For, nearly constantly now that the savage pain was somewhat allayed and tending to grow less as the deck exercise cleared his mind and body of their poisons, those last syllables, the muttered syllables in his left ear when the Black woman's head had lain for an instant on his shoulder, those syllables which were not in Eboe, kept repeating themselves to him. It was as though they were constantly reiterated in his physical ear rather than merely mentally; vague syllables, with one word, 'l'kundu', standing out and pounding itself deeper and deeper into his consciousness.

'Hearin' things!' he muttered to himself as he descended to his cabin on the conclusion of the routine morning inspection a half-hour before noon. He did not go up on deck again for the noon observations. He remained, sitting very quietly there in his cabin, listening to what was being whispered over and over again in his left ear, the ear above the wound in his neck muscle.

It was highly unusual for this full-blooded bucko skipper to be quiet as his cabin steward roundly noted. The explanation was, however, very far from the steward's mind. He imagined that the wound had had a devastating effect upon the captain's nerves, and so far his intuition was a right one. But beyond that the steward's crude psychology did not penetrate. He would have been sceptical, amused, scornful, had anyone suggested to him the true reason for this unaccustomed silence and quietude on the part of his employer. Captain Luke Martin, for the first time in his heady and truculent career, was frightened.

He ate little for his midday dinner, and immediately afterward retired to his state-room. He came out again, almost at once, however, and mounted the cabin ladder to the after deck. The *Saul Taverner*, carrying a heavy load of canvas, was spanking along at a good twelve knots. Martin looked aloft, like a sound sailor-man, when he emerged on deck, but his preoccupied gaze came down and seemed to young Sumner, who touched his hat to him, to look inward. Martin was addressing him.

'I want the lend of your lookin'-glass,' said he in quiet tones.

Young Sumner started, felt the blood leave his face. This was what Pound had warned him about; why he had thrown his glass over the side.

'Sorry, sir. It ain't along with me this 'vyage, sir. I had it till we lay in St Thomas. But now it's gone. I couldn't shave this mornin', sir.' The young mate made an evidential gesture, rubbing a sun-burned hand across his day's growth of beard on a weak but not unhandsome face.

He expected a bull-like roar of annoyance from the captain. Instead Martin merely nodded absently, and walked forward. Sumner watched him interestedly until he reached the hatch leading to the crew's quarters below decks forward. Then:

'Cripes! He'll get one from Dave Sloan!' And young Sumner ran to find Pound and tell him that the captain would probably have a looking-glass within a minute. He was very curious to know the whys and wherefores of his senior mate's unusual request about his own looking-glass. He had obeyed, but he wanted to know; for here, indeed, was something very strange. Pound had merely told him the captain mustn't see that wound in his neck, which was high enough up so that without a glass he could not manage to look at it.

'What's it like, Mr Pound?' he ventured to inquire.

'It's wot you'd name kinder livid-like,' returned Pound, slowly. 'It's a kind of purplish. Looks like – nigger lips!'

Back in his state-room, Martin, after closing the door leading to the cabin, started to take off his shirt. He was half-way through this operation when he was summoned on deck. He hastily readjusted the shirt, almost shame-facedly, as though discovered in some shameful act, and mounted the ladder. Pound engaged him for twenty minutes, ship matters. He gave his decisions in the same half-hearted voice which was so new to those about him, and descended again.

The bit of mirror-glass which he had borrowed from Sloan in the fo'castle was gone from his washstand. He looked, painfully, all over the cabin for it, but it was not there. Ordinarily such a thing happening would have elicited a very tempest of raging curses. Now he sat down, almost helplessly, and stared about the state-room with unseeing eyes. But not with unheeding ears! The voice was speaking English now, no longer gibberish syllables grouped about the one clear word, '*l'kundu*'. The voice in his left ear was compelling, tense, repetitive. 'Over the side,' it was repeating to him, and again, and yet again, 'Over the side!'

He sat there a long time. Then, at last, perhaps, an hour later, his face, which there was no one by to see, now pinched, drawn and grey in the bold challenging afternoon light in the white-painted state-room, he rose, slowly, and with almost furtive motions began to pull off his shirt.

He got it off, laid it on his berth, drew off the light singlet which he wore under it, and slowly, tentatively, with his right hand, reached for the wound in his neck. As his hand approached it, he felt cold and weak. At last his hand, fingers groping, touched the sore and tender area of the wound, felt about, found the wound itself . . .

It was Pound who found him, two hours later, huddled in a heap on the cramped floor of the state-room, naked to the waist, unconscious.

It was Pound, hard old Pound, who laboriously propped the captain's great bulk – for he was a heavy-set man, standing six feet in height – into his chair, pulled the singlet and then the discarded shirt over his head and then poured brandy between his bluish lips. It required half an hour of the mate's rough restoratives, brandy, chafing of the hands, slapping the limp, huge wrists, before Captain Luke Martin's eyelids fluttered and the big man gradually came awake.

But Pound found the monosyllabic answers to his few, brief questions cryptic, inappropriate. It was as though Martin were answering someone else, some other voice.

'I will,' he said, wearily, and again, 'Yes, I will!'

It was then, looking him up and down in considerable puzzlement, that the mate saw the blood on the fingers of his right hand, picked up the great, heavy hand now lying limply on the arm of the state-room chair.

The three middle fingers had been bleeding for some time. The blood from them was now dry and clotted. Pound, picking up the hand, examining it in the light of the lowering afternoon sun, saw that these fingers had been savagely cut, or, it looked like, *sawed*. It was as though the saw-teeth that had ground and torn them had grated along their bones. It was a ghastly wound.

Pound, trembling from head to foot, fumbling about the medicine case, mixed a bowl of permanganate solution, soaked the unresisting hand, bound it up. He spoke to Martin several times, but Martin's eyes were looking at something far away, his ears deaf to his mate's words. Now and again he nodded his head acquiescently, and once more, before old Pound left him, sitting there limply, he muttered, 'Yes, yes! – I will, I will!'

Pound visited him again just before four bells in the early evening, supper time. He was still seated, looking, somehow, shrunken, apathetic.

'Supper, Captain?' inquired Pound tentatively. Martin did not raise his eyes. His lips moved, however, and Pound bent to catch what was being said.

'Yes, yes, yes,' said Martin. 'I will, I will – yes, I will!'

'It's laid in the cabin, sir,' ventured Pound, but he got no reply, and he slipped out, closing the door behind him.

'The captain's sick, Maguire,' said Pound to the little steward. 'You might as well take down the table and all that, and then go forward as soon as you're finished.'

'Ay ay, sir,' replied the wondering steward, and proceeded to unset the cabin table according to these orders. Pound saw him through with these duties, followed him out on deck, saw that he went forward as directed. Then he returned, softly.

He paused outside the state-room door, listened. There was someone talking there, someone besides the skipper, a thick voice, like one of the Negroes, but very faint; thick, guttural, but light; a voice like a young boy's or – a woman's. Pound, stupefied, listened, his ear now directly against the door. He could not catch, through that thickness, what was being said, but it was in form, by the repeated sounds, the captain's voice alternating with the light, guttural voice, clearly a conversation, like question and answer, question and answer. The ship had no boy. Of women there were a couple of dozen, but all of them were battened below, under hatches, Black women, down in the stinking manhold. Besides, the captain – there could not be a woman in there with him. No woman, no one at all, could have got in. The state-room had been occupied only by the captain when he had left it fifteen minutes before. He had not been out of sight of the closed door all that time. Yet – he listened the more intently, his mind now wholly intrigued by this strange riddle.

He caught the cadence of Martin's words, now, the same cadence, he knew instinctively, as that of the broken sentence he had been repeating to him in his half-dazed state while he was binding up those gashed fingers. Those fingers! He shuddered. The *Saul Taverner* was a hell-ship. None was better aware of that than he, who had largely contributed, through many voyages in her, to that sinister reputation she bore, but – this! This was something like real hell.

'Yes, yes – I will, I will, I will——' that was the swing, the tonal cadence of what Martin was saying at more or less regular intervals in there; then the guttural, light voice – the two going on alternately, one after the other, no pauses in that outlandish conversation.

Abruptly the conversation ceased. It was as though a sound-proof door had been pulled down over it. Pound straightened himself up, waited a minute, then knocked on the door.

The door was abruptly thrown open from inside, and Captain Luke Martin, his eyes, glassy, unseeing, stepped out, Pound giving way before him. The Captain paused in the middle of his cabin, looking about him, his eyes still bearing that 'unseeing' look. Then he made his way straight towards the companion ladder. He was going up on deck, it seemed. His clothes hung on him now, his shirt awry, his trousers crumpled and seamed where he had lain on the floor, sat, huddled up, in the small chair where Pound had placed him.

Pound followed him up the ladder.

Once on deck, he made his way straight to the port rail, and stood, looking, still as though 'unseeingly', out over the billowing waves. It was dark now; the sub-tropic dusk had lately fallen. The ship was quiet save for the noise of her sharp bows as they went to cut through the middle North Atlantic swell on her twelve-knot way to Virginia.

Suddenly old Pound sprang forward, grappled with Martin. The captain had started to climb the rail – suicide, that was it, then – those voices!

The thwarting of what seemed to be his purpose aroused Martin at last. Behind him lay a middle-aged man's lifetime of command, of following his own will in all things. He was not accustomed to being thwarted, to any resistance, which, aboard his own ship, always went down, died still-born, before his bull-like bellow, his truculent fists.

He grappled in turn with his mate, and a long, desperate, and withal a silent struggle began there on the deck, lighted only by the light from the captain's cabin below, the light of the great binnacle lamp of whale oil, through the skylights set above-decks for daytime illumination below.

In the course of that silent, deadly struggle, Pound seeking to drag the captain back from the vicinity of the rail, the captain laying about him with vicious blows, the man became rapidly dishevelled. Martin had been coatless, and a great swath of his white shirt came away in the clutching grip of Pound, baring his neck and left shoulder.

Pound slackened, let go, shrank and reeled away, covering his eyes lest they be blasted from their sockets by the horror which he had seen.

For there, where the shirt had been torn away and exposed the side of Martin's neck, stood a pair of blackish-purple, perfectly formed, blubbery lips; and as he gazed, appalled, horrified, the lips had opened in a wide yawn, exposing great, shining African teeth, from between which, before he could bury his face in his hands away from this horror, a long, pink tongue had protruded and licked the lips ...

And when old Pound, shaking now to his very marrow, cold with the horror of this dreadful portent there on the deck warm with the pulsing breath of the trade wind, had recovered himself sufficiently to look again towards the place where the master of the *Saul Taverner* had struggled with him there against the railing, that place stood empty and no trace of Luke Martin so much as ruffled the phosphorescent surface of the *Saul Taverner*'s creaming wake.

Mummy to the Rescue

Angus Wilson

Nurse Ramsay was an incongruous figure in her friend Marjorie's dainty little room. Her muscular, almost masculine, arms and legs seemed to emerge uneasily from the cosy chintz-covered chair, her broad, thick-fingered hands moved cumbrously among the Venetian glass swans and crocheted silk table mats. Tonight she seemed even more like an Amazon at rest. She was half asleep after a tiring and difficult day with her charge, yet the knowledge that she must get up from her hostess's cheerful fireside and make her way home along the deserted village street through torrents of rain and against a bitter gale forced her into painful, bad-tempered wakefulness. Her huge brow was puckered with lines of resentment, her lips set tight with envy of her friend's independence. It was easy enough to be dainty and sweet if you had a place of your own, but a nurse's position – neither servant nor companion – was a very different matter. She bit almost savagely into the chocolate biscuits, arranged so prettily by Marjorie in the little silver dish, and her glass of warm lemonade seemed only to add to the sourness of her mood.

'Of course, if they weren't so wealthy,' she said, 'they'd have to send her away, granddaughter or no granddaughter. She's got completely out of hand.'

'I suppose the old people like to have her with them,' said Marjorie in her jolly, refined voice. She licked the chocolate from her fingers, each in turn, holding them out in a babyish, captivating way of which, however, Nurse Ramsay was too cross to take any notice. 'But she *does* sound a holy terror. Poor old Joey,' for so she called Nurse Ramsay, 'you must have a time with her. They've spoilt her, that's the trouble.'

Nurse Ramsay drew her legs apart, and the heavy woollen skirt hitched above her knees, displaying the thick grey of her winter knickers, allowing a suspender to glint in the firelight.

'Spoilt,' she said in her deep voice with its Australian twang. 'I should think *so* if you *can* spoil a cracked pot. I've had many tiresome ones, but our dear Celia takes the biscuit. The tempers, the sulking, you wouldn't believe, and violent, too, sometimes; of course she doesn't know her own strength. So selfish with her toys – that's Mrs Hartley's fault. "Whatever she wants, Nurse," she told me, "we must give her, it's the least we can do." Well! I ask you – of course the old lady's getting a bit queer herself, that's the trouble, and the old gentleman's not much better. "You're asking for trouble," I told her, but you might as well talk to a stone wall. You should have heard the fuss the other day just because I couldn't find an old doll. "If other little girls bit and scratched when they lost their dolls," I said.'

Marjorie gave a little scream of laughter. Nurse Ramsay scowled; she was always suspicious of ridicule.

'What's so funny about that?' she asked.

'Oh nothing I s'pose,' said Marjorie, 'if you're used to it, but better you than me.'

'I should think so,' said Nurse Ramsay. 'Why, Doctor Lardner said to me only the other day, "Nobody but you would stand it, Nurse; you must have nerves of steel." I suppose I am unusually ...'

But Marjorie had closed her ears to a familiar story. She was busy wiping a chocolate stain from her pretty blue *crêpe de Chine* frock, liberally soaking her little lace-bordered hanky with spittle to perform the task. Really Joey was always full of moans nowadays.

It was so very dark in the little bed and if you turned one way you would fall out and if you turned the other it was wall and you were shut in. Celia held her doll very tightly to her. She was shaking all over with fright. Nanny had pushed and scratched so because she wanted Mummy in bed with her. Nanny always tried to stop her having Mummy, because she was jealous. But you had to be careful, you had to watch your time, because however much you bit, squelching and driving the teeth into the arm-flesh, cracking the bone, they could always tie you in, as they had done before, and then even Granny didn't help you. So she had pretended to Nanny that she was beaten, that she would do without Mummy. But Nanny did not know – Mummy was in bed. Celia pushed back the clothes and looked at the familiar blue wool by the light of the moonbeam from the window-shutter. 'It's all right when Mummy's with you, darling,' so long ago she had said that, before she went on the ship, leaving her with Granny. 'I shall be back with you before you can say Jack Robinson,' she had said, as Celia sat on the edge of the cabin trunk and wrapped her doll in the old blue cardigan. She did not come and she did not come and then she was there all the time in the blue cardigan and if she was with you it was all right. But you had to be very careful not to let them part you from Mummy's protection – they could do it by force, but only for a little because Granny wouldn't allow it; but the worst was when they tricked you into losing; Nanny had done that once and they had searched and searched, at least all of them except Nanny, and she pretended to, but all the time you could tell from her eyes that she was wishing they would never find. The look in Nanny's eyes had enraged Celia and she had scratched until the blood ran. That had meant a bad time following, with Granny angry and Grandad's voice loud and stern, and being held into bed and little white pills. No, it was important never to be separated – so Celia took Mummy and, very carefully passing the arms round her neck, she knotted them to the bedpost behind her. It was very difficult to do, but at last she was satisfied that Nanny could not separate them. Then she lay back and watched the yellow moonlight from the window. Yellow was the middle light, and as they drove behind Goddard in the car – Goddard who gave the barley-sugar – with Granny smelling of flowers, they would say yellow that was the middle light, and green we move, and red we must stop, and green we move, and yellow was the middle light, and red we stop ...

'It's simply a question of the money not being there,' said old Mr Hartley, and his voice was cracked and irritable. He didn't like the business any more than his wife, and yet her refusal to comprehend financial dealings – thirty-five years before he would have found it feminine, charming – was putting him into the role of advocate, of cruel realist. He had already succumbed to a glass of port in his agitation at the whole idea, and the thought of tommorow's gout was a further irritant.

'Well, you know best, dear, of course,' his wife answered in that calm, pacifying voice which had vexed him over so many years, 'but you've often said we ought to change our lawyers, that Mr Cartwright was a terrible old woman ...'

'Yes, yes, I know,' Mr Hartley broke in, 'Cartwright's an old fool, but he isn't responsible for taxation and this damned government. The truth is, my dear, we're living on very diminished capital and we just can't afford it.'

'Well, I do my best to economize,' said Mrs Hartley, 'but prices ...'

'I know, I know,' Mr Hartley broke in again, 'but it isn't a question of cheeseparing here and there. We've got to change our whole way of living. In the first place we've got to find somewhere cheaper and smaller to live.'

'Well, I don't know how you think we're all going to fit into a smaller house,' said his wife.

'That's just the point,' he replied, 'I don't.' He pulled his upper lip over the lower and stared into the fire, then he looked up at his wife as though he expected her to be waiting for him to say more. But she had no thought for his continuing, only a deep abhorrence and refusal of the proposal he had implied. She folded her embroidery and, getting up, she moved the pot of cyclamens from the little table by the window. 'You've been letting Nurse Ramsay get at you,' she said.

'Letting Nurse Ramsay get at me,' echoed the old man savagely, 'what nonsense you do talk, dear. Anyone would think I was a child who couldn't think for myself.'

'We're neither of us young, dear,' Mrs Hartley said drily, 'old people *are* a bit childish, you know.'

Such flashes of realism in the even dullness of his wife's thought only irritated Mr Hartley more.

'One thing is clear to me,' he said sharply, 'on this subject you'll never see sense. Celia gets worse and worse in her behaviour. Nurse Ramsay won't put up with it much longer and we'll never get another nurse nowadays.'

Mrs Hartley set out the patience cards on the little table. 'Celia's always very sweet with me,' she said. 'I don't see what Nurse has to grumble at.'

'My dear,' Mr Hartley said, and his tone was tender and soothing, 'be reasonable. It can't be very pleasant, you know – all those rages and the difficulty with feeding, and really she's less able to be clean in her habits than two years ago.'

The coarseness of the old man's allusion made Mrs Hartley's hand tremble. She said nothing, however, but 'red on black'. Her silence encouraged her husband.

'I want your help, Alice, over this, can't you see that? Don't force me to act alone. Come over with me and see this place at Dagmere; you're so much better at judging these things than I am.'

Mrs Hartley was silent for a few minutes, then, 'Very well,' she said, 'we'll drive over tomorrow.' But her daughter's voice was in her ears. 'I'm leaving her with you, Mother. I know she'll be in good hands.'

Celia was on the deck of the ship, the sun shone brightly, the gongs beat, the whistles blew and her pink hair ribbons were flying in the wind. All the stair rails were painted bright red, pillar-box red like blood, and that was Celia's favourite colour. Red meant we must stop, so Celia stopped. The gentleman in the postman's suit came up to her. 'Go on,' he said, 'don't stand there gaping like a sawney.' She wanted to tell him that it was red and that she couldn't go, but the whistles and the gongs made such a noise that he couldn't hear her. 'Go on,' he cried, and he clapped his hands over her head. Such a wind blew when he clapped his hands that her hair ribbons blew off. Celia began to cry. 'A nice thing if every little girl cried when her ribbons blew away,' said Nurse Ramsay. She hoped to make Celia run after them, although it was red and that meant we must stop. But there was Granny beckoning to her and there were the hair ribbons dancing in the sunshine a little way ahead – they were two little pink dolls. So Celia ran, although it was red. And now the side of the ship had gone and great waves came up to pull her down, green and grey. 'Mummy, Mummy,' she cried, but the waves were folding over her. Mummy would not come, and suddenly there was Mummy holding out her arms to save her – Mummy all in blue. Celia ran into her mother's arms and she sobbed on her mother's bosom; she would not be lonely now, now she was safe. But Celia's Mummy's arms folded right round her neck, tighter and tighter. 'Don't, Mummy, don't. You're hurting me,' Celia cried, and she looked up to see her mummy's eyes cruel and hard like Nurse Ramsay's. Celia began to scream and to fight, but her Mummy's hands closed more and more tightly around her neck, crushing and pulping.

Nurse Ramsay heard the screams as she came up the dark drive. The battery in her torch had given out and she was feeling her way beside the wet bushes. The screams penetrated slowly into her consciousness, for she was oppressed by the memory of that humiliating scene at the Flannel Hop when Ivy had made such a fool of her in front of Ronnie Armitage. 'Really, it's getting impossible,' she thought at first, 'you can't leave her alone for half an hour now without trouble.' Then suddenly something in the screams made her quicken her pace, and now she was running in panic, the branches of the rhododendrons and laurel bushes catching at her like long, spiky arms.

When she reached Celia's bedroom, it was already too late. No efforts of poor old Mr Hartley or even of Goddard could bring life back to those flushed, purple cheeks, that swollen black neck. Dr Lardner, who came shortly after, said that death was due as much to failure of the heart as to strangulation. 'She must have woken herself in struggling to free her neck from the woollen jacket,' he said, 'and the fright acted upon an already weakened heart.' It was easy to believe as one surveyed the body: the wreck of a great Britannia blonde, thirteen stone at least – she had put on weight ever since her twenty-fifth year – the round blue eyes might have fascinated had they not stared in childish idiocy, the masses of golden hair won praise had they not sprouted in tufts on the great pink cheeks, allying the poor lunatic to the animal world, marking her off from normal men and women.

Nurse Ramsay said the whole thing was a judgement. 'If they hadn't been so obstinate and had agreed to send her to a proper home she'd have been alive today,' she added. But Mrs Hartley, who was a religious woman, offered thanks to God that night that Death had come in time to prevent her being taken away. 'It's almost as though her mother had come to help her when she was in trouble,' she thought.

Moonlight Sonata

Alexander Woollcott

If this report were to be published in its own England, I would have to
cross my fingers in a little foreword explaining that all the characters
were fictitious – which stern requirement of the British libel law would
embarrass me slightly because none of the characters is fictitious, and
the story – told to Katharine Cornell by Clemence Dane and by
Katharine Cornell told to me – chronicles what, to the best of my
knowledge and belief, actually befell a young English physician whom
I shall call Alvan Barach, because that does not happen to be his name.
It is an account of a hitherto unreported adventure he had two years
ago when he went down into Kent to visit an old friend – let us call *him*
Ellery Cazalet – who spent most of his days on the links and most of his
nights wondering how he would ever pay the death duties on the
collapsing family manor-house to which he had indignantly fallen heir.
This house was a shabby little cousin to Compton Wynyates, with
roof-tiles of Tudor red making it cosy in the noonday sun, and a hoarse
bell which, from the clock tower, had been contemptuously scattering
the hours like coins ever since Henry VIII was a rosy stripling. Within,
Cazalet could afford only a doddering couple to fend for him, and the
once sumptuous gardens did much as they pleased under the care of a
single gardener. I think I must risk giving the gardener's real name, for
none I could invent would have so appropriate a flavour. It was John
Scripture, and he was assisted, from time to time, by an aged and lunatic
father who, in his lucid intervals, would be let out from his captivity
under the eaves of the lodge to potter amid the lewd topiarian
extravagance of the hedges.
The doctor was to come down when he could, with a promise of some
good golf, long nights of exquisite silence and a ghost or two thrown in
if his fancy ran that way. It was characteristic of his rather ponderous
humour that, in writing to fix a day, he addressed Cazalet at 'The
Creeps, Sevenoaks, Kent'. When he arrived, it was to find his host away
from home and not due back until all hours. Barach was to dine alone
with a reproachful setter for a companion, and not wait up. His bed-

room on the ground floor was beautifully panelled from footboard to ceiling, but some misguided housekeeper under the fourth George had fallen upon the lovely woodwork with a can of black varnish. The dowry brought by a Cazalet bride of the mauve decade had been invested in a few vintage bathrooms, and one of these had replaced a prayer closet that once opened into this bedroom. There was only a candle to read by, but the light of a full moon came waveringly through the wind-stirred vines that half curtained the mullioned windows.

In this museum, Barach dropped off to sleep. He did not know how long he had slept when he found himself awake again, and conscious that something was astir in the room. It took him a moment to place the movement, but at last, in a patch of moonlight, he made out a hunched figure that seemed to be sitting with bent, engrossed head in the chair by the door. It was the hand, or rather the whole arm, that was moving, tracing a recurrent if irregular course in the air. At first the gesture was teasingly half-familiar, and then Barach recognized it as the one a woman makes when embroidering. There would be a hesitation as if the needle were being thrust through some taut, resistant material, and then, each time, the long, swift, sure pull of the thread.

To the startled guest, this seemed the least menacing activity he had ever heard ascribed to a ghost, but just the same he had only one idea, and that was to get out of that room with all possible dispatch. His mind made a hasty reconnaissance. The door into the hall was out of the question, for madness lay that way. At least he would have to pass right by that weaving arm. Nor did he relish a blind plunge into the thorny shrubbery beneath his window, and a barefoot scamper across the frosty turf. Of course, there was the bathroom, but that was small comfort if he could not get out of it by another door. In a spasm of concentration, he remembered that he *had* seen another door. Just at the moment of this realization, he heard the comfortingly actual sound of a car coming up the drive, and guessed that it was his host returning. In one magnificent movement, he leaped to the floor, bounded into the bathroom, and bolted its door behind him. The floor of the room beyond was quilted with moonlight. Wading through that, he arrived breathless, but unmolested, in the corridor. Farther along he could see the lamp left burning in the entrance hall and hear the clatter of his host closing the front door.

As Barach came hurrying out of the darkness, to greet him, Cazalet boomed his delight at such affability, and famished by his long, cold ride, proposed an immediate raid on the larder. The doctor, already sheepish at his recent panic, said nothing about it, and was all for food at once. With lighted candles held high, the foraging party descended on the offices, and mine host was descanting on the merits of cold roast beef, Cheddar cheese, and milk as a light midnight snack, when he stumbled over a bundle on the floor. With a cheerful curse at the old goody of the kitchen who was always leaving something about, he bent to see what it was this time, and let out a whistle of surprise. Then, by two candles held low, he and the doctor saw something they will not forget while they live. It was the body of the cook. Just the body. The head was gone. On the floor alongside lay a bloody cleaver.

'Old Scripture, by God!' Cazalet cried out, and, in a flash, Barach guessed. Still clutching a candle in one hand, he dragged his companion back through the interminable house to the room from which he had fled, motioning him to be silent, tiptoeing the final steps. That precaution was wasted, for a regiment could not have disturbed the rapt contentment of the ceremony still in progress within. The old lunatic had not left his seat by the door. Between his knees he still held the head of the women he had killed. Scrupulously, happily, crooning at his work, he was plucking out the grey hairs one by one.

Acknowledgements

The Editor gratefully acknowledges permission to reprint copyright material to the following: The Estate of E. F. Benson and A. P. Watt Ltd. for Negotium Perambulans. *Sir Charles Birkin for* Text for Today. *Robert Bloch and the Scott Meredith Literary Agency, Inc., 845 Third Avenue, New York, N.Y. 10022, U.S.A. for* Return to the Sabbath. *The Author for* Hothouse; © *Sydney J. Bounds 1974. The Harold Matson Co. Inc. for* The October Game; *copyright* © *1948 by Weird Tales,* © *renewed 1975 by Ray Bradbury. The Author for* The Horror at Chilton Castle; *copyright 1963 by Joseph Payne Brennan; from 'Scream at Midnight'. Anthony Burgess for* An American Organ. *Candida Donadio & Associates Inc. for* Heartburn *by Hortense Calisher; copyright* © *1950, renewed 1978 by Hortense Calisher. Random House Inc. for* Miriam; *copyright 1945 and renewed 1973 by Conde Nast Publications Inc. Reprinted from 'Selected Writings of Truman Capote', by Truman Capote. The Author for* The Monster; © *R. Chetwynd-Hayes 1970. Hughes Massie Ltd. and Dodd, Mead & Co. Inc. for* The Last Séance, *from 'The Hound of Death', published by Wm. Collins,* © *Agatha Christie 1933; also from 'Double Sin and Other Stories', published by Dodd, Mead & Co. Inc.; copyright 1926 by Agatha Christie; copyright renewed 1956 by Agatha Christie; copyright* © *1961 by Christie Copyrights Trust. A. D. Peters & Co. Ltd. for* De Mortuis *by John Collier, from 'Fancies and Goodnights'. The Author for* Green Fingers; © *1968 by R. C. Cook. Murray Pollinger and Alfred A. Knopf Inc. for* The Landlady; *copyright* © *1959 by Roald Dahl; reprinted from 'Kiss Kiss' by Roald Dahl, published by Michael Joseph, Penguin Books Ltd. and Alfred A. Knopf Inc.; this story originally appeared in 'The New Yorker'.* Nursery Tea *is* © *Mary Danby 1978. The Author for* Activity Time; © *Monica Dickens 1981. Curtis Brown Ltd., London and New York, for* The Specialty of the House; *copyright* © *1948 by Stanley Ellin; copyright* © *renewed 1976 by Stanley Ellin. The Author for* If Thy Right Hand Offend Thee . . .; © *A. E. Ellis 1974. Elizabeth Fancett and M.B.A. Literary Agents Ltd. for* Someone in the Room. *Curtis Brown Ltd., London, and Random House Inc. for* A Rose for Emily; *copyright 1930 and renewed 1958 by William Faulkner; reprinted from 'Collected Stories of William Faulkner'. A. D. Peters & Co. Ltd., for* The Man Who Didn't Ask Why *by C. S. Forester. The Author for* Jane; © *Jane Gaskell 1968.* The Quiet Man *is* © *Terry Gisbourne 1974. Wm. Heinemann Ltd. and Diogenes Verlag AG, Zurich, for* The Snail-Watcher, *from Patricia Highsmith's story collection 'Eleven', first published in 1964 by Gamma and in 1970 by Wm. Heinemann Ltd. Copyright* © *1964 by Patricia Highsmith. Wm. Heinemann Ltd. for* Comrade Death, *from 'The Horrible Dummy' by Gerald Kersh. The Harold Matson Co. Inc. for* The Salem Horror *by Henry Kuttner; copyright* © *1937 by Weird Tales, Inc.,* © *renewed 1965 by Weird Tales, Inc. The Author and A. P. Watt Ltd. for* Cold Spell; © *David Langford 1980. A. M. Heath & Co. Ltd. and Arkham House Publishers, Inc., Sauk City, Wisconsin, for* The Hound *by H. P. Lovecraft. The Author for* The Thirteenth Kestrel; © *Roger Malisson 1976. The Harold Matson Co. Inc. for* No Such Thing as a Vampire *by Richard Matheson; originally published in 'Playboy'; copyright* © *1959 by HMH Publishing Co. Inc. Kirby McCauley Ltd. for* The House of Horror *by Seabury Quinn.*

Davis Publications, Inc. (present proprietors of 'Unknown Worlds') for The Refugee *by Jane Rice; first published in 'Unknown Worlds'; copyright 1943 by Street & Smith Publications, Inc.; copyright renewed by The Conde Nast Publications, Inc. Robert Silverberg and the Scott Meredith Literary Agency, Inc., 845 Third Avenue, New York, N.Y. 10022, U.S.A. for* Back from the Grave; © *Magnum Publications Inc. 1958. Frances Stephens and M.B.A. Literary Agents Ltd. for* Claws. *The E. J. Carnell Literary Agency for* It; © *1940 by Street & Smith Publications, Inc., renewed* © *1961 by Theodore Sturgeon. The Author for* See How They Run; © *1981 by Terry Tapp. The Author for* Pat-a-Cake, Pat-a-Cake; © *Bernard Taylor 1976. William F. Temple and the E. J. Carnell Literary Agency for* The Whispering Gallery; © *1953 by Ziff-Davis Publishing Co. The Author for* Now Showing at the Roxy; © *Harry E. Turner 1977. A. D. Peters & Co. Ltd. for* The Man Who Liked Dickens, *from 'Black Mischief' by Evelyn Waugh. The Author and the E. J. Carnell Literary Agency for* Buffy; © *Philip Welby 1978. The Estate of H. G. Wells and A. P. Watt Ltd. for* Pollock and the Porroh Man. *A. M. Heath & Co. Ltd. for* Lukundoo *by Edward Lucas White. David Higham Associates Ltd. and G. P. Putnam's Sons for* The Troll *from 'The Maharajah and Other Stories' by T. H. White, published by Macdonald and G. P. Putnam's Sons; copyright* © *1981 by Lloyds Bank Trust Company (Channel Islands) Ltd. Arkham House Publishers, Sauk City, Wisconsin 53583, U.S.A. for* The Lips *by Henry S. Whitehead. The Author, Martin Secker & Warburg Ltd. and Viking Penguin Inc. for* Mummy to the Rescue, *from 'Such Darling Dodos' and 'Death Dance',* © *1949, 1950, 1957 by Angus Wilson. Viking Penguin Inc. for* Moonlight Sonata, *from 'The Portable Woollcott',* © *1934 by Alexander Woollcott, renewed* © *1962 by Joseph P. Hennessey. Hallie Burnett for* The Cocoon *by John B. L. Goodwin.*

Every effort has been made to trace the owners of the copyright material in this book. In the case of any question arising as to the use of any such material, the Editor would be pleased to receive notification of this.